The
Lobsang Pun
Novels

The Lobsang Pun Novels

The Thunder Dragon Gate
and
Old Ugly-Face

Talbot Mundy

LEONAUR

The Lobsang Pun Novels
The Thunder Dragon Gate
and
Old Ugly-Face
by Talbot Mundy

FIRST EDITION

First published under the titles
The Thunder Dragon Gate
and
Old Ugly-Face

Leonaur is an imprint
of Oakpast Ltd

ISBN: 978-1-78282-186-1 (hardcover)
ISBN: 978-1-78282-187-8 (softcover)

http://www.leonaur.com

Publisher's Notes

Contents

The Thunder Dragon Gate

CHAPTER 1

It was one of those days when not even Cockneys like London. Spring had made a false start. Fog, wind, rain, sleet, and a prevalent stench of damp wool. Even the street noises sounded flat and discouraged. Big Ben was invisible through the fog from Trafalgar Square, and the lions around Nelson's monument with rain streaming from their granite flanks resembled mythical ocean monsters. Lights in the windows of Cockspur Street suggested warmth, and there was a good smell of hot bread and pastry exuding through the doors of tea shops, but that only made the streets feel more unpleasant.

Tom Grayne turned up his overcoat collar, stuck his hands in his pockets, and without particular malice cursed the umbrellas of passers-by.

No one noticed him much. He was fairly big, tolerably well dressed. He was obviously in the pink of condition; he walked with the gait of a man who knows where he is going, and why, and what he will do when he gets there—the unhurried, slow-looking but devouring stride of a man who has walked great distances.

A policeman with the water streaming from his black cape nodded to him.

"Oh, hello Smithers. Nice day for your job!"

"H-awful! But we 'as to get used to it."

"When do they close the Aliens Registration Office at Bow Street?"

"Five o'clock I *think*, but you've plenty of time. I didn't know you were a foreigner."

"American, born in London, Smithers. Dual citizenship. Two sets of very suspicious officials to convince I'm not a traitor to the human race."

Tom Grayne grinned, but as a matter of fact he savagely resented the indignity of having to report in person and register his address every month. He had a right to British citizenship if he should choose to claim it. He chose not. As he saw it, he had a right to be and to do what he pleased, and to go where he pleased, provided he didn't make a nuisance of himself. He detested bureaucracy, hated to ask favours, loathed having to explain himself, and liked people who didn't put on artificial lugs.

He wasn't unreasonable about anything else, so far as he knew, but by the time he turned out of the Strand toward Bow Street police station he was feeling hostile, and he was glad of it. He wanted to punch somebody. But there was nobody to punch except a few poor devils trudging through the rain, and a policeman leading along a prisoner. One does not punch policemen profitably, and besides, a policeman especially in London is what he pretends to be, so he doesn't stir antagonism, or shouldn't. But the smug stride of that particular one, and the melancholy resignation of his prisoner, who trudged beside him un-handcuffed, goaded Tom's already pugnacious disposition and aroused his sympathy at the same time. He felt an almost irresistible impulse to horn in and be a nuisance.

Even so, he might have gone about his own business, down in the basement, but there was something familiar about the prisoner's appearance that held his attention. He hesitated. He didn't recognise the prisoner. He had never seen him before; he was positive about that. But he felt the same sort of wordless and unreasoned impulse that makes a man choose something unusual for dinner. He followed through the main door to the desk, where an alert-looking sergeant stood ready to book the new arrival. Tom was just in time to overhear the charge. Then he knew instantly that his hunch had been right. Memory overflowed.

"Thö-pa-ga—of the Josays Sept of the Kyungpo—whatever that means—country of origin Tibet—home town Lhasa."

"How d'you spell it? Here, give me that warrant. Go on."

"Last known address—"

"Yes, all right, that's written here."

"Charged with noncompliance with the Aliens Registration Act, under section—"

"Yes, that's on the warrant."

"Arrested at eighty-eight Oxted Street."

"Say anything?"

"Said nothing."

"All right. Cell eighteen."

"Bail!" said Tom Grayne, suddenly, as if he were making the high bid at an auction.

"Who are you, sir?"

Before Tom could answer a man entered who looked much more Mongolian than the prisoner. The prisoner might have passed for a New Orleans quarter-breed at first glance. He was a good-looking fellow, with a sad face and an air of patient resignation. But this other man looked like a devil. His head was framed in the hood of a long, black, glistening waterproof. He had brilliant, sunken eyes, high cheek-bones and a skin like dirty parchment. He was several inches more than six feet tall, and fairly broad in proportion. More like a figure of death than a human being. He spoke rapidly to the prisoner, who stared sullenly but didn't answer. The desk-sergeant caught one word, thrice repeated:

"*Shang-shang?* Sounds like Chinese."

Tom unbuttoned his overcoat in an unconscious gesture. This was something he could lend a hand at. He interpreted:

"Tibetan. Something like a cross between a harpy and a nightmare, with eight legs."

"Is there one in the Zoo?" the sergeant asked.

"No, nor in *Nuttall's Dictionary.* A *shang-shang* is employed by magicians in Tibet to terrify people to death and then to hound them into hell after death."

"Never heard of that one," said the sergeant, "although we've some strange superstitions in London—more than you might suppose. We had some witches in here a week ago, arrested for alleged practises that 'ud make your hair stand on end if you weren't used to horrors—and bunkum."

Slowly, in Tibetan, through thin peculiarly mobile lips that seemed to enjoy the flavour of the words, and with his face thrust close to Tom Grayne's, the man who looked like death spoke:

"You-who-know-the-meaning-of-a-*shang-shang*—if-you-do-not-wish-to-add-experience-to-hearsay—let-alone-that-one-who-is-a-stranger-to-you!"

"Go to hell," Tom answered, in plain English. He added the equivalent in the Tibetan language.

"What's your name, you?" said the sergeant.

The tall Tibetan produced a soiled card from an inner pocket. The sergeant laid it on the desk and speared it with a pencil-point.

"*Doctor* Noropa, eh? What kind of doctor? Medicine? Law? Music? Philosophy? We'd a man in here the other day who called himself a doctor of blackmail. What do you want here? You a friend of the prisoner?"

Instead of answering, the tall man turned and walked out. The sergeant wrote on a slip of paper the name and address that were on the card and handed the paper to a man in uniform at a desk behind him.

"Check that. Have him followed. Step lively.—And now you, sir"— he stared penetratingly at Tom Grayne—"I think you mentioned bail. Are you a householder?"

"No. Is there any charge against the prisoner besides not having registered as an alien?"

"No, not at present. But that one's serious. He's liable to imprisonment and subsequent deportation. If you're not a householder—"

"Phone," said Tom Grayne. He went to the coin-in-the-slot machine, in the booth in the corner. The prisoner laid the contents of his pockets on the desk; he had been marched off to a cell before Tom was out of the booth.

"Sergeant, I have phoned to Professor Mayor at an address in Bloomsbury. He will be here with a solicitor's clerk as fast as a taxi can bring him."

"Professor Mayor, eh?" The sergeant's manner changed perceptibly. "Of Bloomsbury? Not Clarence Mayor? The Home Office Expert?"

"British Museum—specialist on Tibetan manuscripts and works of art."

"That's the man. The Home Office calls him in on special cases. Does he know the prisoner?"

"I think not. But he is as interested as I am."

"What makes you so interested, if I may ask?"

"Tibet is my subject."

"Ever been there?"

"Yes."

"Oh."

Tom Grayne went outside, and below to the basement. He reported no change of address. There was no one else in the office. The uniformed clerk behind the long counter was civil and inclined to make conversation:

"With all the hotels and boarding-houses there are in London, I can't help wondering why you stay at that address, sir. Not that it's any concern of mine. I'm merely curious."

"I don't mind telling you," said Tom Grayne. "It's inexpensive and I can live there as I please. I live hard, so as to keep fit. There are no luxuries in the country I hope to re visit before long, and the climate might easily kill a man who'd lived soft. I even practise not eating for days at a time."

"Some folk," said the clerk, "starve 'emselves just to annoy the police. We'd one man in the cells who wouldn't eat because, he said, he was a high-caste Hindu, but he turned out to be a Scotch bigamist."

Tom returned to the upstairs office and waited for Mayor, who came in presently wiping rain from gold-rimmed spectacles and followed by a stoop-shouldered lawyer's clerk in a bowler hat, who went straight to the desk.

"Silly fellow!" said Mayor, wiping his pinkish, boyish-looking old cheeks with a big silk handkerchief. "Befriending *shang-shang* victims? What next? Thö-pa-ga, you say his name is? Wasn't he at Oxford?"

"Yes. I thought you'd be interested."

"If I weren't, I shouldn't have left a comfortable fireside, tea, buttered toast and a book."

"Come and have supper at my place and we'll find out why this fellow was in hiding."

"Good heavens! Your place? You live in a fish-shed, don't you?"

"Not quite. I can make you comfortable. Good grub. I have a notion it might be dangerous to take him to your house."

"Dampness—fog—rats! Tom Grayne, I haven't your fortitude. However, perhaps it's wiser. Very well. I'll risk my health and my opinion of you."

The formalities of bailing out the prisoner took time. Mayor was at the desk for several minutes. After that, he went into the phone booth, talked for a long time and emerged chuckling as if he had played a good joke.

"Can you accommodate four, Tom? I've invited O'Mally."

"Who is O'Mally?"

"Horace Farquarson O'Mally of Harley Street, you ignoramus. Consulting physician to half the crowned heads and multimillionaires in the world."

"Okay. What's he good at?"

"He likes Chateau Yquem. You'll have to stop and get some at a

11

place I'll show you. He can smell a vintage from a mile off."

Thö-pa-ga was under bail by the time O'Mally arrived, very fashionably dressed. Top hat, spats, a monocle. He looked as tough as a prize-fighter, with Chesterfieldian manners.

"Came away in the middle of an operation, I suppose?" said Mayor. "Or did you leave another death-bed?"

"Who told you my patients ever die?" O'Mally answered, in a voice like a disciplined thunder-storm. "Is this the man?" He refixed his monocle, stared at Thö-pa-ga for about two electric seconds, and then faced Tom Grayne.

"Our host," said Mayor.

"I have heard of you," said O'Mally. "How do you do?" He shook hands.

"Don't you tell him how you are," said Mayor. "Let him find out. He will cut you open if you let him."

No one spoke to Thö-pa-ga; he stood looking orientally calm, incurious, melancholy. The solicitor's clerk snapped his little handbag shut and vanished into the rain.

"My car is waiting," said O'Mally.

Mayor laughed: "I once rode in a royal wheelbarrow. I knew a gardener at Windsor Castle when I was a small boy. I know how to behave. My feet are wet; will they ruin the carpet?"

O'Mally and Mayor raised their hats to the Law, or the desk, or the King or somebody—perhaps to the sergeant; he looked pleased. Tom Grayne thrust his arm through Thö-pa-ga's and followed, into a Rolls Royce limousine that bore an almost microscopical coat of arms on the door panel.

Chapter 2

All London was streaming homeward for the night. The limousine with its oddly assorted passengers sped along streets that were rivers of liquid fire, with the traffic incredibly borne on the surface. They stopped for several minutes at a wine shop favourably known to Mayor, whence Tom Grayne emerged with a brown paper parcel. Thence they headed for Kew and the river, where Tom gave intricate directions to the chauffeur, and at last they had to leave the limousine to thread their way on foot, in almost darkness, through pools of slush, beneath dripping eaves. O'Mally didn't seem to mind that his top hat was being ruined, but Mayor was plaintive; he had to be lent a hand along the slippery and rather rotten planking of a wharf. But at the end of the wharf was shelter.

Tom unlocked the door of what looked in the dark like a fish- or net-shed. But when he lighted a couple of oil lamps the place was cosy enough. There was a big stove; he had that going in a minute. There was everything a man of Tom Grayne's disposition needed, and nothing he didn't need. Bunks, cooking-pots, shelves of books, a sink, two tables, a few chairs, two big lockers.

"Umn! No woman, eh," O'Mally remarked.

"Good job, too," said Mayor. "Can you imagine the kind of woman Grayne would select?"

"He would choose an actress," said O'Mally. "Each of them would try to make the other famous and there'd be the usual divorce. Or am I in poor form this evening?"

"Someone died on you?" Mayor asked.

"This place," said Tom, "was rented by a retired sea captain, who fixed it up to suit himself. But someone thought he had money and murdered him. He died on that bunk with his throat cut, and I read about it in the paper—front-page illustration with an X to mark the spot, and so on—three-day mystery. I came to look and found the landlord sure he'd never get another tenant because people are afraid of ghosts. So I rented it cheap."

"And the ghosts?" asked Mayor.

Thö-pa-ga shuddered. Tom was already cooking supper. Coffee was on. A pot of stew was simmering and beginning to smell delicious. Tom laid the table. Mayor opened the paper package.

"I told you Chateau Yquem!"

"I liked the shape of those bottles better. It's Berncasteler Doktor '21. Help yourself."

O'Mally took the corkscrew from its nail on the wall and pulled a cork expertly. He shook down his clinical thermometer and inserted it in the neck of the bottle.

"Good enough," he remarked after a minute. "I am now in no hurry."

"No more patients?" Mayor asked. "Have they all found you out?"

"I am on vacation—first in nearly four years. I catch the eight o'clock boat train for Harwich tomorrow evening. Going to Moscow. A man of whom I'm jealous has cut off a dog's head and kept it alive for three days, during which it eats and reacts to sight and sound. That interests me. Where's a wine glass? These they?" He produced cut glasses from an old sea captain's wine chest. "Are they clean?"

"Boiled."

"What's that delicious smell?" asked Mayor.

"Lobster mulligan. Or do you mean the toasted barley? I eat barley. So, I think, will our friend."

Mayor was pulling off his boots and socks. Thö-pa-ga was doing nothing, saying nothing, seated on one of the bunks with the palms of his hands on the edge, as if he expected to have to jump up at a second's notice.

"May I have that dish-pan nearly full of hot water, and then some mustard," said Mayor. "Unlike O'Mally, I'm important. Serious things might happen if I were to catch a bad cold."

O'Mally filled a wine glass. "Yes," he said, "if you should die, and this mysterious gentleman from Tibet should take it into his head to disappear, they would confiscate the house you have pledged as security." He walked over to the Tibetan. "Drink this."

Thö-pa-ga shook his head.

"Abstainer? Never mind. It's medicine. Drink it"

"What do you suppose is wrong with him?" Tom Grayne asked, stirring the mulligan.

"I know," O'Mally answered. "It requires no thought whatever. Come along, young fellow—you understand English, don't you? Drink this."

The Tibetan hesitated, smiled wistfully and then suddenly obeyed. He swallowed the wine at a gulp. The wind howled under the eaves and he shuddered either at that or at the feel of the wine as it went down. O'Mally nodded.

"My professional advice would be: return as soon as possible to Tibet." He was watching Thö-pa-ga's eyes. "He will talk presently. He has been wanting to talk all the way from Bow Street. He has been thoroughly frightened, and he is suffering from—"

"Words of one syllable, please!" said Mayor. "I can use twenty-one-syllable Sanskrit words, but mine mean something." Mayor was sloshing his feet in the dish-pan and the steam from the hot mustard-and-water had dimmed his spectacles. He wiped them, to watch Thö-pa-ga.

"He is suffering from being too near sea level," said O'Mally. "If he really is from Tibet, he is used to a minimum altitude of twelve or fourteen thousand feet. It is as if he had taken to deep-sea diving without the proper physique and training. Barometric pressure for

14

prolonged periods, plus a constitutional lack of resistance to micro-organisms that don't exist at high altitudes, produce a mental and physical change. But those are a vicious circle; one produces the other. He will die if he doesn't return to Tibet."

"I would rather die," Thö-pa-ga said suddenly, in good English. The wind howled. They all shuddered.

"Damn our English climate!" Mayor exclaimed. "They say it's worse in Tibet, but I don't believe it!" It wasn't the wind that had made him shudder. He knew that.

Tom Grayne struck the stew-pot with an iron spoon:

"Yesterday's mulligan, warmed up—canned soup added—home-made barley bread baked by a Stornoway fisherman's widow, New Zealand butter, American cheese, celery and white wine. Come and get it."

They drew up chairs to the table. Thö-pa-ga elected to eat mulligan. Tom Grayne munched barley alone.

"Wise enough, if you vary your diet now and then. But it's hell to be wise," said O'Mally. "Are you in training?"

"Yes, for Tibet. The important thing is not to eat too often. Discipline your belly."

"Don't forget the sugar. When do you go to Tibet?"

There was no time to answer. There came a peremptory knock at the door. It sounded authoritative, like a police man's, only there was a suggestion of deliberate rhythm, as if it might be a prearranged signal. A weird howl of wind drove squalling rain against the side of the hut. Beneath, the river sucked and splashed amid wharf-piles. Thö-pa-ga froze motionless.

"Now I understand why I came," O'Mally remarked. He poured wine for Thö-pa-ga. "This is very interesting."

Tom Grayne went to the door and opened a peephole. He could see nothing; it was all dark outside.

"Who's there?" he demanded.

No answer. No sound outside except wind and splash.

"Perhaps your chauffeur?"

"No," said O'Mally, "I sent him home. Can you open the door without cooling the stew?"

Mayor pulled a blanket from the bunk behind him and wrapped it around his knees. Tom Grayne tried to open the door only a few inches, against the wind. A hand seized it—wrenched it suddenly. A man crashed into him, thrusting him backward on his heels. The door

15

slammed. It was Dr. Noropa, in his dripping black waterproof. He turned calmly and bolted the door.

"Give me some more of that excellent stew before he murders us," said Mayor.

O'Mally snorted: "Don't talk nonsense. Grayne can lick him. I can help, if necessary."

Thö-pa-ga neither moved nor seemed to breathe; he stared straight in front of him. He looked guilty of something and ready for death. There was silence for probably sixty seconds. Then, from the midst of a circle of rain from his dripping waterproof, the gaunt Noropa spoke:

"I come to tell you Thö-pa-ga is time-is-come. If you know what is *shang-shang*, you will let him alone. Thö-pa-ga must go home."

"Well, he should," said O'Mally. "But who are you?"

"I know who you are," Noropa answered. He looked at Mayor. "And I know who you are." Then, at last he met Tom Grayne's eyes. "You, who should know better, having been in Tibet, do you wish a *shang-shang* sending?"

"Yes. I never saw one. Send the thing by parcel post. Get out of here."

Noropa's death-like face betrayed no emotion. Tom Grayne slid the bolt and Noropa walked out, forcing the door open against the wind with such prodigious strength that he seemed hardly to have to exert himself.

The door slammed. Then suddenly Thö-pa-ga gulped wine and shook off silence. He seemed unconscious of O'Mally's professional critical gaze. His left hand rested on the table, but he seemed not even aware that O'Mally's fingers touched his wrist. He spoke, if to anyone at all, to Mayor:

"You, who are kind to a stranger, you don't know. Me they will not kill. Because me they need for purposes. But you they will make away with by magical means. That is to say, if you befriend me. It is therefore not seemly for me to have friends, because I get them into trouble."

"Oh, come now, come," said Mayor. "The police at Bow Street showed me your record. You're an Oxford graduate. You surely don't believe in magic."

"You mean, *you* don't," said O'Mally. "Early environment, early associations, ill health, worry, nostalgia, *and* persecution—don't overlook that—readily produce receptivity to hypnotic suggestion. Those are words of one syllable, more or less. They're all in the dictionary.

16

Have you caught cold?"

"No," said Mayor.

"That was magic. Before you were put into knickerbockers, your mother or your maiden aunt or your nurse told you a hot mustard foot-bath would prevent colds in the head. It won't, of course. But it did, didn't it? Don't interrupt him—go on talking, Thö-pa-ga. Who are you? Why are you in London?"

"I am of a sub-*sept* of the Josays Sept of the Kyungpo. It is a secret sub-*sept*, and my father, who was a nobleman, was Keeper of the Thunder Dragon Gate, of which you have never heard."

"Oh, yes, indeed we've heard of it," said Mayor. "Tom Grayne knows as well as you or I do, it's a figure of speech. It means a state of consciousness, through which the *Arhants* have to pass on the Road to Enlightenment. It is referred to in the New Testament as the Eye of a Needle."

"That," said Thö-pa-ga, "is what you may have read in books, or what you have deduced. But what I know is other wise, and so I warn you. When my father had died and my mother was made to go into a nunnery, I wished never to become the Keeper of the Thunder Dragon Gate, although they said I had inherited my father's spirit and his duty also. There was an Englishman who came to Lhasa, a very kind man who represented the Indian Government. I ran away and asked that Englishman to give me work to do. He begged my freedom from the Dalai Lama. There was money. It was simple. I was sent to Oxford for an education, and I have it. But before I reached Oxford, he who had done me that great kindness was already dead—they said, of poison. And at Oxford there began to be a very soon beginning of a *shang-shang* sending not at all a mystery to me."

The blinded window-pane above the back of Mayor's head smashed suddenly—three distinct crashes of splintering glass. The wine bottle broke into a dozen pieces. The mulligan stew-pot fell off the stove to the floor. O'Mally stared at his top hat, on a nail on the wall. There was a hole through it.

"This is London, England," O'Mally remarked. "Or am I dreaming?"

Tom Grayne took a flashlight from the locker, leaned his weight against the wind-blown door and walked out.

"They will not kill me," said Thö-pa-ga, "because they need me for a purpose. But they will kill you—each of you and everyone."

"Who are 'they'?" asked Mayor.

17

O'Mally reached for his top hat. "Exactly! Who are they? Does a *shang-shang* spit a soft-nose Webley bullet? Go on—don't interrupt him, Mayor—tell us. I wish now I weren't going to Russia."

CHAPTER 3

A police whistle—three shrill blasts. In rain and darkness there is no other sound like that. O'Mally straightened his tie. The whistle shrilled again. Tom Grayne wrenched the door open and came in, dripping.

"Cops!" he said abruptly.

He had hardly said it when the door thundered to a man's fist. He uncovered the peephole—peered through.

"Yes, it's the Law. Shall I let 'em in?"

In response to O'Mally's nod he leaned his weight against the door. A policeman's flashlight—foot—knee—shoulder—face beneath an oilcloth-covered helmet—an official voice:

"What's going on in here? There's a broken window—"

"Come in—for God's sake, come in and let's shut the door!"

Two policemen entered, oil-skinned, bulky, suspicious, cautious because they had no warrant.

"Anybody hurt? A fight? Any firearms in here?"

O'Mally answered: "No."

"May I have your names, please—*and* addresses."

O'Mally produced his card. He showed the flap of his wallet, then his new passport.

"Thank you, Sir 'Grace. And these others?"

"Dr. Mayor of the British Museum and the Home Office. Mr. Tom Grayne, American. Mr. Thö-pa-ga, from Tibet."

"Ah! How long has *he* been in here?"

O'Mally gave a telegraphically terse synopsis of what had happened. He described Noropa.

The policeman produced his note-book. "I was asked in—"

Tom interrupted him: "Yes, I invited you in. Take a seat at the table; you'll write easier."

He poured them coffee. One policeman stood, sipping noisily. He didn't like American coffee, but he was polite about it. The other sat, reading aloud what he wrote:

"Nine-eighteen p.m. A man was seen and heard to fire three shots with a revolver in the direction of this shed—occupied by—broken window—broken wine bottle, upset cook-pot—"

18

"*And* a top hat ruined," said O'Mally.

"—hole in a top hat. Does any of you gentlemen know how it happened, or why? Bearing in mind, please, that anything you say may be taken down and used in evidence against you."

Tom Grayne told the whole story. The policeman wrote down the details of Tom's passport.

"And now what next?" O'Mally asked. "You were tipped off by Bow Street to follow Noropa, and he followed my car. Am I right, constable?"

"I'm sure I don't know, sir. I'm what is known as acting on information received. I've no warrant, but I could get one. I heard three shots, saw one of them, and flashed my light on a tall man in a hooded black waterproof. I saw him throw his revolver into the river. There were other witnesses besides me. I believe it would be best for all concerned if his here Mister Thö-pa-ga (two dots, you said, over the 0) would come with me to the police station—I mean, if he'd come willing—and be locked up for the night, where he'd be safe and warm and comfortable, and we could make enquiries in the morning."

Thö-pa-ga reached for his overcoat.

"Damn!" remarked O'Mally. "We were just getting his story. Professor Mayor went bail for him. Ask the professor."

Mayor glanced at Thö-pa-ga. The Tibetan nodded; he had already buttoned his overcoat up to his ears.

"I don't understand my legal position," said Mayor. "You must do as you see fit, constable."

"He seems willing to come with me, sir."

"I'll go with the policeman and Thö-pa-ga," said Tom Grayne. "There's plenty more wine. You two make yourselves at home until I come back."

Mayor nodded.

"Very well," said O'Mally. "Are they pursuing Noropa?"

"Begging your pardon, sir," the constable answered, "the man wasn't identified. He slipped away into the shadows, but I daresay he won't go far before they catch him. If it should happen his name's Noropa he'd have more than a bit to explain. There's a watch being kept on this place; you'll be safe here until daylight. Or I could phone for your car, Sir 'Orace."

"No thanks."

"As you say, sir."

It was a long way to the police station. Tom Grayne trudged

through the storm in silence beside Thö-pa-ga, who kept stride with the policeman. There was no sense in trying to talk to Thö-pa-ga, who seemed more gloomy than ever—an unusual state of mind for a Tibetan; Tibetans usually laugh at anything. Tom felt baffled. He had already begun to count on this accidental meeting as just the very stroke of luck he had been hoping for for months. Thö-pa-ga might—anything is possible—might help him to re-enter Tibet. If not, he might have connections in Tibet who would honour an introduction. No plan yet, of course, but a strong hunch. Busted hunches are more disappointing than broken promises: one expects results from a hunch. This was the wrong kind of result.

At the police station, what with sending out a messenger to find a cigarette slot-machine, and then telling the long tale all over again for the benefit of the sergeant on night duty, nearly two hours went by. There was no sense in making a mystery for the police; the obvious thing to do was to keep them friendly.

So it was after midnight before Tom Grayne returned to the storm-swept hut where he had left his guests. He found O'Mally stoking the stove and arguing with Mayor.

"That is why," Mayor was saying, "I need your influence."

"At the Foreign Office? I have none—none whatever," O'Mally answered. "I'm consulted now and then by the Home Office, just as you are, in special cases. At the Foreign Office I'm an absolute non-entity."

"How about the India Office?"

"Worse and worse! An Indian Rajah, who got himself into political trouble, was one of my patients. I'm supposed to have advised him how to prove he didn't poison his aunt."

"Give him wine, Grayne! Make him drink it. O'Mally, I am not your patient, so you needn't lie to me. I happen to *know* you're on the Foreign Office list. That's why I invited you here. I repeat: if I should go to the Foreign Office, with a Home Office introduction, and tell that graciously insolent Sphinx Ambleby that Tom Grayne ought to go to Tibet, I should be courteously informed that no one is allowed to enter Tibet. Even as it is, Grayne is on the black book for having entered Tibet and remained there without permission. If you were asked what you think of him, what would you say?"

"I wouldn't tell him or you that," O'Mally answered.

"Say it, then, behind his back, to Ambleby." Mayor sipped wine. O'Mally clipped the end of a big cigar, with a platinum clipper—a personal gift from a crowned head. Mayor continued: "You are Ambleby's physician. He's a credit to you. Hundreds of people have wished him dead a thousand times over, but you've kept him alive. Oh, yes, I heard all about his being poisoned by a spy, and how you invented an antidote."

"I didn't."

"It was kept out of the papers, if that's what you mean. And I know, without being able to prove it, that you're off to Russia on a medical errand of your own, but with a secret errand, too, for Mr. Foreign-Office-Secret-Service Ambleby, who has a high opinion of your gift for bluff innocence and discreet observation."

"You are guessing," said O'Mally. "You are talking nonsense."

"If," said Mayor, "*you* should go to Ambleby, and tell him what I have just now told you; and tell him your real opinion of Tom Grayne, Ambleby would regard that as a very proper introduction. I tell you, he hasn't another man to send to Tibet; there simply isn't one available who has Tom Grayne's knowledge of the country, Tom's physique and Tom's ability to take care of himself. And I repeat: this case isn't simple. It isn't merely a Tibetan feud; nor is it just another psychopathic case for you to pause and analyze on your way to a peerage. It's—"

He hesitated. O'Mally grinned.

"Go on, man! Are you weakening? Say it!"

"I have said it already three times."

"Grayne know what you think it is?"

"Yes. He and I together deciphered a Japanese document that baffled me until Tom broke the code. If it were known Tom had seen it, I should never be trusted again. It was one of those documents that governments always denounce as forgeries when secret service agents find them in a dead man's wallet."

O'Mally looked sharply at Grayne: "What do *you* think it is?"

"I agree with Mayor."

"You agree with him because you wish to go to Tibet?"

"No, Sir Horace. I intend to return to Tibet with or without a Foreign Office permit. You may say so, if you want to."

O'Mally liked that. He uncorked another bottle of wine. He filled a glass for Grayne, who had hitherto not tasted it.

"Here's luck to you! So you agree with Mayor? Splendid! You believe, then, that this is a cog in the wheels of a Japanese scheme to get control of China?"

"Sure as you're alive," said Tom Grayne.

"I'm alive, my boy. I'm alive and interested."

"Then do your plain duty!" said Mayor. He was getting short-tempered. He laughed at himself. Then he yawned. "Strong wine—not used to it." Suddenly he clutched the table.

The wind was howling, but it wasn't wind that shook the door. O'Mally dropped his monocle—caught it in mid-air—pretended he did it on purpose. Grayne picked up a heavy broomstick.

"Sh-h-h!" said Mayor.

They all listened. One lamp flickered out, short of oil. The river sucked the wharf-piles. The wind howled. The shed creaked. The door thudded again, three times, as if someone kicked it.

"You're an en-n-t-tertaining host!" said Mayor. His teeth chattered.

Grayne went to the peephole, saw nothing and suddenly opened the door. The other lamp blew out. It was pitch dark, and a gale in the room.

"Duck!" yelled O'Mally. He upended the table, crashing everything to the floor. He and Mayor crouched behind the table. The door slammed. The stove belched smoke. Grayne had hold of someone. They were struggling, crashing among upset chairs and broken dishes.

"Hold him!" O'Mally shouted. "I'm coming!"

But he tripped over a table-leg and before he was up the door opened and slammed. A sudden blinding electric torch—darkness again.

"All right, sir, all right, I have him! Has he hurt you?"

"Police?" asked Mayor's voice. "Sure you've got him?"

"Yes, sir, he's out o' mischief for the present. Get up, you! Stand over there!"

The policeman held his flashlight steady until O'Mally relighted the lamp.

"Lucky I saw him! Sure you're not hurt, sir?"

Noropa, handcuffed, with his hands behind him, stood glaring with his back to the wall. One of Noropa's eyes was closing up; he was bending a bit forward, as if hit in the wind. Tom Grayne's coat was torn and there was blood on his lip. O'Mally took a stride toward Tom:

"Hurt?"

"No."

O'Mally examined the prisoner. The policeman stared at the mess

22

on the floor.

"Did he do all this?"

"No, he didn't," said O'Mally.

"Thought he couldn't have. I was close on his heels. How did all this 'appen?"

O'Mally laughed testily. "It was a part of my arrangements for going to Russia! I didn't wish to be shot. You say you followed him here?"

"Yes, sir. The constable on watch at the end of the alley saw him first, but I was on my way here with a message, so I killed two birds with one stone, as you might say. All I saw him do was kick the door. Maybe when they search him at the station—"

"What's the message?"

"Oh, yes. I took the liberty a while ago of phoning for your auto. Sir 'Grace. It's 'ere already, at the street corner, two 'undred yards away. We had to phone Scotland Yard about all this. They phoned back ten minutes later to say there's a gentleman from the Foreign Office—"

"Didn't I say so?" Mayor interrupted.

"He said, sir, you'd know his name without his giving it, and he'd be very much obliged if, on your way home, you'd drop in and see him."

"At his office?"

"No, at his rooms."

"Told you so," Mayor repeated.

Tom was staring at Noropa. "You're no Tibetan! You're not Chinese, either! Are you?"

Noropa said nothing. He glared with one eye; the other was already swollen shut.

"They may need my hat for evidence," remarked O'Mally. "Lend me one of yours, Grayne—yes, that cap will do nicely, thanks. Are you coming, Mayor? I can drop you at your house on my way to—"

"Victoria Street, Westminster!" said Mayor. "Yes, I know where you're going."

The policeman led his prisoner outside. O'Mally waited until the door had slammed shut behind them.

"Just one moment. You, Mayor. And you, Grayne. If either of you should mention my name, in connection with this night's work, or for any other reason, at the Foreign Office, it would be breach of confidence, an unfriendly gesture and a damned serious indiscretion. Have I made myself clear? Very well. Thank you, Grayne, for supper

23

and entertainment. Both were excellent. Goodnight. See you again some day, I hope."

"Goodnight, Tom," said Mayor. "How early can you be at my house in the morning?"

"Much too early for you. I'll be waiting for you down stairs."

Mayor winked twice behind his gold-rimmed spectacles. He jerked his respectable gray head toward O'Mally's back. Grayne let them out.

He had cleaned the place and was asleep on a bunk within ten minutes.

Chapter 4

It was like any other door in the long, dim, draughty corridor, except that a man in blue uniform stood outside and asked Tom Grayne's business. The Foreign Office is like all the rest of Whitehall; comfort hadn't been invented when they built it. On the other hand, tradition was already ancient; it grows older, but it never dies, in that kind of building. The muscular, military-looking man in blue tapped on the door as if a lady were asleep within, opened the door cautiously, tiptoed in, murmured, and came out smiling. A neatly dressed Japanese gentleman walked along the corridor from behind Tom Grayne and turned the corner at the far end.

"Go right in, sir. Mr. Ambleby expects you."

Tom Grayne circumnavigated a beautiful old Spanish leather screen, so arranged that whoever stepped into the room presented his face to the desk in profile in the light from a high window. There was a coal fire, in a hideously dignified Georgian fireplace. Over the fireplace was a three-quarter length mirror—new glass in an antique frame; it very clearly reflected whoever entered the room, but it did not reveal the desk to him who entered.

Against a background of books, in the dimness behind a big, antique desk, sat Arthur Tremaine Ambleby. An astonishing man, because he was so different from what one expected. He stood up as Tom Grayne entered and without a word, but with a very gracious gesture, offered him the chair beside the desk. That placed Tom in the light from the window.

Ambleby looked like a poet, or perhaps an editor of a very learned review. He looked capable of having written Locksley Hall, or he might have translated Homer into English elegiacs. Gray hair. Wise eyes. A clean-shaven, courteous, civilized face. A dark leather bow tie.

A leather waistcoat. An immaculately tailored jacket of a colour that couldn't be guessed exactly against the background of books in the dimness. A man of perhaps sixty, who looked fifty and conveyed, without the slightest trace of self-importance, the impression of knowing all the secrets in the world and thoroughly enjoying them.

"Professor Mayor told me to come and see you," said Tom.

Ambleby nodded. There was nothing on his desk. No notes. No papers. Nothing that suggested that the room might be the exact centre of an invisible spider-web of secrets that reached all over the world, into men's minds, hopes, ambitions, histories, forgetting nothing, overlooking not much. There were no files in the room. There was not even a door leading into another room where files perhaps might be.

"Yes," said Ambleby. "I spoke with Professor Mayor at three o'clock this morning and we discussed you. You have helped him, I believe, to decipher some curious documents in Tibetan and—er—and other languages."

Tom Grayne kept silence. He liked this man, right off the bat. He was just the kind of man he did like. Knew his stuff. Nobody's fool. But Tom was thoroughly on guard against him; he anticipated one of those simple, utterly innocent traps that are much harder not to fall into than the complicated sort. It appeared:

"You have an acquaintance in Harley Street?"

"No."

"Wasn't he with you last night?"

"Man who wears a monocle and spats? Oh, yes, I've met him. That's all. He doesn't know me. I don't know him."

"You have visited Tibet?"

"Yes. I intend to return."

"And you use an American passport?"

"Yes."

"How do you propose to do it? You understand that the terms of a treaty between the Tibetan and Indian Governments preclude our supplying you with anything in the nature of a permit?"

"Yes."

"We couldn't even give you unofficial recognition. Quite the contrary."

"Yes, I understand that."

"How then do you propose to enter Tibet?"

"That, sir, is my secret. Short of locking me up or shooting me, I'm fairly confident that nobody can prevent my getting in."

"I know how you got in, as you call it, last time."

"Yes, but I'm not an animal. I don't try the same trick twice running."

"What do you propose to do in Tibet?"

"Study the country. It's my subject."

"Some very interesting books have been written about Tibet," said Ambleby. "Which particular field will your book cover?"

Tom avoided that trap also. "I don't write books. The British Museum is crowded with information about Tibet that needs checking. Anything I learn for a fact I'll report to Mayor. He can do as he likes with it."

"Does he supply you with funds?"

"No, I have enough money of my own. I don't need much, the way I travel."

"You know a Tibetan named Thö-pa-ga?"

"Slightly. I know where he is. Professor Mayor withdrew bail at the request of the police, so Thö-pa-ga is either on his way from Kew or else already in a cell at Bow Street."

"Do you know a Tibetan named Noropa?"

"Yes. He isn't a Tibetan."

"You surprise me. What do you think he is?"

"I know. He's half-Jap, half-Chinese—I'd say a Chinese father, and that's unusual."

"He bears a bad reputation," said Ambleby. "Who is the person named John Sinclair, who was in the place where you live when the reporters called early this morning?"

"Oh—that's me. I invented that name. Old friend, phoned for by Tom Grayne to come and occupy the place in his absence.—Hadn't seen me recently—hadn't had time to talk over the phone—just hurried over—didn't know where I was, or when I'd be back."

"Well, Mr. Grayne, I am not in a position to do anything for you officially. You are well recommended. As far as I am concerned, there is no objection to your entering Tibet, *if you can do it*. But, of course, that has nothing to do with my office. I have been in communication with the Home Office, and with Scotland Yard. I know what took place yesterday. Would you object to telling me, in confidence, what you think it all means?"

"Thö-pa-ga," said Tom, "is wanted back in Tibet. Noropa has been sent to hound him back there. That's as clear as daylight. Probably Noropa pestered him with *shang-shang* magic, until he went into hiding. Then Noropa tipped him off to the police for not registering a change of address, and got him locked up, so he'd be deported."

"Yes, that seems clear. But why should Noropa fire three bullets through your window?"

"Simple. It costs money to return to Tibet, but if you're deported you travel free. Maybe, too, he wants to return on the same ship with Thö-pa-ga. He was careful to throw his pistol into the river. It would be pretty difficult, I imagine, to convict him of anything serious. And-"

"Yes? And?"

"If Noropa were deported by the British Government, that wouldn't compromise any foreign legation that otherwise might have to get him visas and supply the necessary funds, and all that."

Ambleby listened as if he were being told something that he didn't know. He looked vaguely, politely, not exactly incredulous but noncommittal. Tom Grayne knew he was being studied, parsed, analysed, doped out, criticized, considered—all behind a mask of courteously guarded interest.

One thing was already quite clear in Tom's mind: if he wanted Ambleby's help in any way, for any purpose, he had first to demonstrate his own value, and even so the help would not be openly done or acknowledged. Ambleby would tell him nothing more than he already knew.

"Hell!" Tom said suddenly. "Mayor gave me a hint who you are, so I'll talk horse. The Japs will have to starve and even cease to be a nation if they can't grab China. There's nothing else for them to do. Therefore, China it is. And China used to own Tibet. The new ruler of Tibet will be a young child in the hands of regents. That's to say when they've found the right child, and they haven't yet, though they pretended they had. But the Tashi Lama, is another story. He's the religious head of things. His influence, under a semi–political mask, still reaches all through China, along Buddhist channels. The Japs thoroughly understand the Buddhist psychology."

"Do you think they do?" asked Ambleby.

"Sure. Lots of Japs are Buddhists. They understand it, anyhow, a damned sight better than the Germans understood the rest of us in 1914. There's a secret *sept* in Lhasa called the Wishful-ones-who-stand-in-awe-before-the-Thunder-Dragon-Gate. It's one word. They are reputed to be black magicians. They're said to be (and I think it's true) the only Tibetan really secret *sept* who will admit Chinamen

27

into their ranks. Thö-pa-ga's father was the figurehead lama known as the Worshipfully-born-Keeper-of-the-Thunder-Dragon-Gate. That is also one word. Most lamas are forbidden to marry, but that particular lama is obliged to marry. He has to marry a woman selected for him by the men in the dark, who have the real power. They are known as the Worshipful-nameless-ones-in-the-dark-who-see-the-light-that-is-coming. That again is one word. The Keeper of the Thunder Dragon Gate is merely their mouthpiece, but he issues oracular messages, prophecies and commands, that filter through, in writing and by word of mouth to wherever Buddhism has any influence open or secret. The office of Keeper of the Thunder Dragon Gate descends from father to son, which is another thing unusual in Tibet. Every thirteenth one in succession is always named Thö-pa-ga. The name means 'Wonderful-to-hear.' And there's a tradition, thoroughly believed, that the ones named Thö-pa-ga are more important than the others: that their coming always coincides with great changes."

"Yes, I know all that," said Ambleby. It was a rather surprising admission from him.

Tom continued:

"Well then, what is there to stop the Japs from getting control of the Keeper of the Thunder Dragon Gate? If he's a *shang-shang* victim—that's to say if he has been thoroughly well *voodooed*—they can make him send out propaganda, by word of mouth and secret writing, that should favourably influence quite a lot of Chinese in the matter of Japanese designs on China."

"Do you think the Chinese might be influenced in that way?"

"Just as readily as we Americans were coaxed into the World War. Why not? Artfully managed propaganda can accomplish anything. But it has to be artful. The Japs understand that perfectly. That's why they prepared a throne in Manchukuo for the ex-Emperor of China. That's again why about thirty million Chinese have already emigrated into Manchukuo. The emperor isn't a Chinaman, he's a Manchu. They know it. He has no power. They know that. But he means something to the Chinese mind that can't be substituted. All the Japs have to do after that, is to provide a tolerable government, for which the Chinese give the puppet emperor the credit."

"So you think Thö-pa-ga is being hounded back to Tibet to become the mouthpiece of Japan?"

"Yes, to about a hundred million people—some of 'em in India, some in Ceylon and Burma—some in French Indo-China—many of 'em in Malaysia and the Dutch East Indies—but the great majority in China."

"But why, Mr. Grayne, should they go to all that trouble? For instance, supposing young Thö-pa-ga should have been shot dead in your dwelling last night, why couldn't they put a substitute in his place?"

"That's exactly what they will do—and they'll pick an obedient nitwit, someone they have thoroughly psychologised to do the job, if they can't get hold of the real man. But if you know the first thing about Tibet, you'll realize they'd prefer the right man. Those people believe their own medicine. A substituted Thö-pa-ga would undo their own belief in themselves and their magic. This man probably has well-known birthmarks. And besides, they'd have to murder him before they could put in a substitute. They'd have a job on their hands to bring the substitute in from abroad, because it's common knowledge in Lhasa that Thö-pa-ga was sent to England for an education. The Dalai Lama's regents, who hate the Tashi Lama like the devil, would be pretty sure to try to expose and denounce a substitute. The Japs wouldn't have any faith in a substitute, either."

Ambleby betrayed no other emotion than courteous interest.

"It does sometimes happen," he said, "that certain governments employ a strictly unofficial means toward an undeclared objective. I have, of course, no knowledge of Japanese methods. However, there is a medical report to the effect that Thö-pa-ga might die soon, if he were permitted to remain in England. In the circumstances, since there is a balance to the credit of the fund that was sent from Tibetan sources for his Oxford education, it might be quite the proper thing to send him home in charge of someone. Are you willing to undertake that? Could you leave, say, day after tomorrow, from Hendon?"

"Oh, yes."

Ambleby's next remark withdrew the corner of a veil from undercover statecraft:

"Dr. Noropa will be deported, I am told. In England there are legal difficulties, but in India he can be detained for enquiries, under an Order in Council that provides for such contingencies. You are unlikely to be troubled by Noropa.—Do you happen to know anyone in Delhi?" The question sounded quite casual.

"Oh, yes."

"For instance?"

"Oh, lots of people."

Ambleby smiled. "It wouldn't help you in the least," he said, "if you should mention me. But when you reach Delhi, if you should call on Mr. Norman Johnson, of the Bureau of Ethnology, and mention Professor Mayor, you might find Mr. Norman Johnson helpful. He would be interested to meet Thö-pa-ga. With his help, I imagine Thö-pa-ga will be able to reach Tibet."

"Okay."

"Could you leave your passport with me? I will have it visaed. I am informed that the police have saved your effects from being put out into the rain by your landlord."

"Oh?"

"Yes. It appears the wharf is unsafe. Where would you like your things sent?"

Tom smiled. All his private papers were locked in a bank vault.

"Robbin's Hotel," he said, "Golden Square."

"Very well, Mr. Grayne. Thö-pa-ga will meet you at the plane, at Hendon, day after tomorrow. Your ticket as far as Delhi and your passport shall be handed to you at the same time. Keep away, please, from Professor Mayor. No harm, I think, in phoning to him, provided you use discretion, but don't be seen at his house or in his company. I think that is all for the present. Should you ever return alive from— er—Delhi, drop in and see me."

"Thank you. Yes, I'll do that."

It was raining like the devil. Tom took a taxi. It was followed by another taxi to Robbin's Hotel, an old-fashioned place, recently redecorated, of the type that Americans dread but the English permit to survive. Tom went straight to the desk and signed the register. A very well-dressed Japanese followed him into the hotel, asked for mail, received it and stood reading it near the desk.

"Can I have my usual room? Any mail for me?" Tom asked.

"Yes, the same room. No, Mr. Grayne, no letters."

"Is Miss Burbage in? I will speak on the phone."

"Booth One, sir."

"Hello Elsa."

"Hello Tom. Did you read the morning paper?"

"No. Why should I?"

"You're on the front page."

"That's no reason. Get your facts from him as knows 'em! Listen: you'll need your cheque-book."

"Tom, are you in trouble?"

"Hell, no. Have you your passport? Indian tourist visa?"

"I have had it in my purse for six weeks."

"Cut along down to Cooks and buy yourself a reservation on the plane for Karachi, day after tomorrow. Better go to the bank first.— Yes, about that much—draw out plenty—fifty pounds more would be better. After you've made your reservation, meet me in the downstairs room at Doby's."

"All right, Tom."

He returned to the desk. The Jap was still there, writing something. "I'm expecting a couple of suitcases and a load of junk from Kew. Put the junk in the cellar—everything else into my room."

"Yes, sir. Did you see your name on the front page?"

"Sure. I spelt it for them."

They had spelt his name wrong, which was all to the good. He turned up his overcoat collar, thrust his fists into his pockets and walked out, striding like a man who meant to walk around the world. As he turned the corner he saw the Jap standing in the hotel door-way—saw him nod to a taxi-driver. The taxi drove away, slowly, and turned the same corner. It might mean nothing. But he was the same smart, well-dressed Japanese who had walked along the corridor in the Foreign Office.

Chapter 5

"Tom, I don't look excited. I swear I don't! Yes, I got the last seat there was. They had just sold the last-but-one. I have twelve hundred pounds in the bank. I have kept a small trunk packed ever since you warned me to be ready. And I'm so sick of Robbin's Hotel—no I'm not, I love it!—I will kick it goodbye, and come back a couple of years from now and love it all over again!"

"Kick your trunk goodbye," he answered. "Stick some doodads in a handbag. Buy all the rest of the stuff in India."

"Tom, this isn't true! It simply isn't."

"It won't be, if you don't listen carefully. The least slip, and it's all off. They'd cancel everything."

"I am all ears."

She wasn't. She had remarkably well-shaped ears, half hidden in a wind-blown bob of curly dark hair, under a Cossack *kaftan*. She was so small, and full of naturally ready laughter, that she looked almost Tom Grayne's opposite, except for a similar, equally hard to define but quite evident vigour of being. She might be twenty-two or twenty-three, but looked younger. She had small, strong, sun-browned hands. Her feet were tucked under her, in the big red leather arm-chair. Doby's downstairs fireplace was living up to its reputation; it was about the most comfortable fireside in London in rainy weather. There were a lot of luncheon tables, but no one ever came there much before twelve-thirty. The waiter had brought tea, taken his cue from the size of the tip, and left them alone. The tea was untouched.

"You take the airplane bus to Hendon," said Tom, "day after to-morrow. I take a taxi. There'll be a messenger with flowers for you and some fruit and chocolates, in the name of oh, any old name I think of when I order 'em. We're just nodding acquaintances, you and I. We get to know each other a bit on the journey, and after that, you use your wiles on Thö-pa-ga. Worm your way into his confidence."

"I've never been in a plane. I want to make enormous noises on a B-flat saxophone."

"You understand now, don't you, how all this happened? Or shall I repeat it?"

"No, no. I have understood you. I understand that Thö-pa-ga is being hounded back to Tibet, and that he doesn't guess what we're after, or know you except for last night's happenings, or trust you or trust anyone else."

"Thö-pa-ga," said Tom, "needs friends. He needs them badly. He needs someone to whom he can talk. He has a persecution complex, and I don't blame him, poor devil. He's a particularly sensitive type of oriental. He would instantly detect an unsympathetic motive. He suspects Mayor. He suspects me. He mustn't suspect you, and there's only one possible way to fix that. You must make up your mind to be his friend, no matter what he does or what happens to him. You must be absolutely on the level with him. Never tell me his secrets without his full permission. Gradually get him to trust me."

"And then what?"

"I told you: he needs friends, not enemies. We can't get what we're after on a basis of something for nothing. Thö-pa-ga comes first, or we'll be fooled badly. All of us will be."

"How about Uncle Clarence?"

"Not one word to him! Not a hint! Not a word to a soul except Emily Foster, and nothing to her except to repeat instructions, from a public phone booth, if you think it necessary—but don't go near her. She is simply to put an thing you send to her into another envelope and mail it to Professor Clarence Mayor. Your Uncle Clarence doesn't know our private code. It would be a mistake if he did. The idea is this: you know the code by heart—you're sure? Word perfect?"

"I can say it backwards. I can signal it faster than you can read it."

"Okay. If I should write from India to Professor Mayor in London, my letters would be read in transit, even if they should never reach him, which they very likely wouldn't. But if I send something to you, by mail or messenger, in code, and you decode it and mail it to Emily Foster—an innocent, middle-aged lady who lives at Dorking—and she re-mails it to your Uncle Clarence, he will safely receive an unsigned communication that can't easily be traced back."

"Then you and I won't be together in India?"

"Not noticeably, to begin with. Certainly not in the same hotel. You're a tourist, remember. You'll have to play that part carefully; tourists, as a rule, don't visit India in the hot season. Don't let on that you can read Tibetan, or that you know anything about Tibet. Don't even let Thö-pa-ga know that, if you can help it. But if you get caught knowing more than girls of your age usually know, you can admit that you've studied a bit at the British Museum and that you picked up odds and ends from Thö-pa-ga on the journey."

"I'll be careful."

"Better be. If you make even one bad break, the Indian Government, of course, would simply ask us to leave India. But the Tibetan gang would give us the works. Very likely poison."

"I don't see why I can't tell Uncle Clarence. Isn't he in on it?"

"No, you chucklehead! He doesn't even guess that the deaf-and-dumb loony, who files away the notes I send him, copies them and passes them along."

"Tom, *that* poor old thing?"

"He's a Polak, whose father was an interpreter at the U.S. consulate in Warsaw for twenty-five years. Draw your own conclusions, but keep them under your hat. The system is run on a basis of never letting one agent know another agent, or what the other agent is doing if it can be helped, and never letting anyone agent know more than necessary. Your Uncle Clarence is a useful man, in his particular line. They'd can him in a second if they guessed his deaf-and-dumb clerk is my go-between. If they thought Mayor guessed what you're up to, they'd never trust him again. It's an unforgivable offense to have a private iron in the fire, and an almost unthinkable thing for a girl like you to try to enter Tibet. If you should tell Mayor, he'd be furious. He'd warn Ambleby. That would be the end of me. They're only using me because there's no one else who fits the problem at the moment. If they guessed you are in my confidence, they'd have no use for me whatever. I'm only using them because it's the best chance in sight. They haven't okayed me yet. The man in Delhi may not like my guts. They're touchy, the Indian Government crew; they like the Foreign Office outfit about as much as I like being told what to believe. The India Office people, here in London, love me like a Bolshevik."

Elsa looked puzzled. Curled in the chair, she suggested a terrier, aching to be taken hunting, absolutely confident that any hunting, under Tom's direction, would be first rate. Some women, even today, have that excellent faith in a man. But it was not as simple as all that evidently.

"Then, if we get into Tibet—"

"*When* we get there," he corrected.

"All right, when! You will—you say we're merely making use of them—you will ditch all this and—"

"Don't believe that for a second," he answered. "Nothing for nothing in this world. Make your bargain, settle clearly in your own mind what the bargain is, then deliver the goods or bust. It isn't only the British Empire that is vitally interested in knowing who is planning what in China. I'm as interested in the Thunder Dragon Gate as they are. If I weren't, I'd find some other way of getting into Tibet. Pay as you go. Then you get what you're after. Speaking of which, you'd better go and buy yourself a letter of credit. Have it drawn on a bank in Delhi. If you've anything to say to me at the hotel, talk deaf-and-dumb and use the code. Don't phone my room if you can avoid it. Store your trunk. Twenty-eight pounds of luggage. Burn your boats. Hernando Cortez had nothing on you and me."

"I know it. Tom, do you guess how thoroughly I've burned my boats? They're ashes. If I don't make good, I'm done for."

"Scared?"

"No, Tom, are you? Please don't be. I won't let you down. I'm little to look at, but—d'you think I'm—"

He interrupted: "Don't talk piffle. You're game, all right. You're on the level. But some jobs are too tough for some people. Even now it's not too late to call it off. I'd trust you to hold your tongue."

"I have burned my boats!" she answered. "Tibet!"

Tom scowled. He hated to have to explain himself.

"You're full of enthusiasm," he said, "so you believe what you wish to believe. I'm reminding you for the last time—"

"Don't, Tom, you don't need to."

She might as well have tried to stop a steam-roller.

"You've no rating. None. I've no authority from anyone to tell you my secrets—let alone to try to get you into Tibet."

"Tom, I know all that. You're being generous beyond the dreams of—"

"Generous nothing. If you'll keep your head you can be useful. There isn't another girl on earth who has your special ability. But remember, I turned you down flat in the first instance, and I told you why."

"Yes, Tom."

"Certain people trust me because they know I don't get tangled up with any woman who might soften me or blurt out what I'm doing. I have trained you as well as I could in the little time we've had. But we're taking a whale of a long chance. Both of us. If it were known I married you to give you a certain amount of possible legal protection in case I'm bumped off, they'd rate me from then on as a sentimental-ist. In my profession that's the zero rating."

Elsa nodded. "They should rate you AAA One hundred plus."

"That's the point. They rate a fellow by results. You can't look to me for the slightest recognition of anything but your personal value to me as an assistant, strictly on your merits—and a secret assistant at that."

"I expect nothing else."

"Not now, you don't. But you don't know what's ahead. No mat-ter how tight the jam you're in, you've got to stick to the agreement. Your only value to me is your intelligence, obedience and pluck. I want nothing else from you. Your marriage certificate simply entitles you to the key to my strongbox if I'm bumped off. Your marriage is so secret, and so otherwise meaningless, that you mayn't even get a divorce without my permission—and I won't give permission until secrecy no longer matters."

"Yes," she said. "I agree. I understand perfectly."

"I'm trying to get you into Tibet simply and solely because I think you'll be useful."

"I will deserve it," she answered.

"Damn!" he said suddenly, *sotto voce*.

The Jap had come in. The same Jap. Because of the high chair-back Tom hadn't noticed him until he slipped into a chair in the corner by the row of pegs, on which they had hung their overcoats. The Jap ordered tea. When the waiter had brought it he sat sipping and studying something that he took from an envelope. He didn't stare noticeably.

"Get your coat," Tom signalled with the fingers of one hand. "What is he reading?"

Elsa went and powdered her nose before she lifted her coat from the peg. She used a rather large square mirror. She was less than six feet away from the Jap. There was not a lot of light in that corner of the room; the manipulation of the mirror was quite plausible.

"Airplane ticket," she announced, when she returned to the fireside.

"Where to?"

"Couldn't read it, but it looks like Karachi."

CHAPTER 6

Eiji Sarao, the Japanese merchant, made himself altogether too agreeable. He was very widely traveled. He could talk the colloquial peasant speech that passes muster along the Chino-Tibetan border, and he missed no opportunity, on the long flight from London to Karachi, to get in conversation with Tom, Elsa and Thö-pa-ga.

However, Thö-pa-ga was ill—not plane-sick but becoming feeble from some obscure ailment that was aggravated, if not produced by his mental depression. It had been very difficult indeed to talk to Thö-pa-ga. He was an aristocrat; he resented that peasant dialect, and besides, he had partly forgotten it, or said he had. Mr. Eiji Sarao had not learned much from Thö-pa-ga.

But he made it almost impossible for Tom and Elsa to exchange confidences. His bright little eyes watched them continually. He detected their use of finger signals. He tacitly assumed that they were travelling together. At every pause in the long journey, he tried to get them into a three-cornered conversation.

At Karachi he had no trouble at all with the immigration authorities. Tom, on the other hand, had to enter an office near the hangar and answer searching questions. His passport, visaed in red ink by the India Office, merely stated that he was accompanying Mr. Thö-pa-ga as far as Delhi. The immigration officer, a gray-moustached ex-soldier, referred to a little indexed memorandum-book.

"You have visited India before, Mr. Grayne. Weren't you invited to leave?"

"Yes. But do you recognise that visa?"

"That isn't the point. For what reason, two years ago, were you told to get out?"

"I wasn't. As you put it the first time, I was invited to leave. You can get the facts from your files, can't you? If you choose to disregard that visa, take the consequences. I have no idea what they'll be. For all I know, you may have authority to override the India Office. If so, do it and let's see what happens."

The officer smiled. He had very intelligent brown eyes. "What is the nature of your relationship with Mr. Eiji Sarao?" he asked after a moment.

"You mean that Jap who traveled on the same plane? None whatever. I don't know him. Never spoke to him or heard his name before he boarded the plane at Hendon."

"I am informed that you and he made frequent use of the deaf-and-dumb alphabet during the journey."

Tom laughed. "That airplane steward probably has one glass eye. Did he say he saw the Jap doing it?"

"Very well, to whom were you signalling?"

"To myself, for practise."

"Mm! Have you designs on Tibet this time?"

"Delhi."

"Nothing beyond Delhi? Are you willing to agree to do your business in Delhi, and to leave India within a reasonable time—say, three weeks?"

"No."

"Understand me, Mr. Grayne: I have no information that suggests you should be classed with what are commonly called undesirable aliens. But it might put the Indian Government to a very great deal of trouble and expense if you should attempt to repeat your former indiscretion. Tibet is a closed frontier. To bring you back from the border of Tibet would be a thoroughly unnecessary episode, that might have awkward diplomatic consequences, and is well to guard against."

"Okay. Guard against it."

"Will you give your promise, in writing?"

"You mean not to enter Tibet?"

"Not to try to enter Tibet. You could never do it again, I can assure you. But not to try to do it."

"If a promise is all you want," said Tom, "I'll make one. How's this: I promise faithfully, on my word of honour, to do everything humanly possible to get into Tibet as soon as I can."

The officer grinned.

37

"Well, you're frank about it! Any friends in Delhi?"

"Dozens."

"To whom do you intend to deliver Mr. Thö-pa-ga?"

"To the first good doctor I can find. The man's sick."

The officer scribbled a name and address on a slip of paper.

"Dr. Lewis has had a lot of experience with Tibetan cases. He was stationed for a long time at Darjeeling. Try him. Very well, Mr. Grayne, I shall have to report you as dangerous."

"Deadly!" Tom answered. "Obviously in league with a Japanese cotton-goods salesman to bring about a communist revolution led by shamans from Tibet!"

The officer stood up to shake hands. "I enjoyed your article on Tibetan magic in the *Asian Review*," he remarked.

"I didn't write it," said Tom.

"Isn't your *nom de plume* Bloomsbury?"

"No."

"Will you give my regards to Dr. Lewis?"

"Yes."

It had been almost on the tip of Tom Grayne's tongue to say that P.K. Bloomsbury was Dr. Clarence Mayor's *nom de plume*. Not that that mattered. Dozens of people knew it. But if Tom had confessed that *he* knew it, that might have had disastrous consequences. As he had drummed into Elsa's consciousness on every possible occasion, there is no knowing who has been told to discover, by means of apparently innocent questions, whether or not you can be trusted not to mention names or claim acquaintance with men on the inside.

And now, the Jap even invaded the same compartment on the train. He was very courteous. He offered aspirin to Thö-pa-ga, who seemed to suffer tortures from the heat and lolled back limply in a corner. Eiji Sarao knew all about Delhi hotels; he recommended one to Elsa—told her, too, of shops where she could buy whatever clothes she might need. Elsa, observing Tom's signal, accepted the Jap's advice about where to stay. Tom remarked he would probably stay with a friend; leading questions only led to more and more evasive answers.

When they reached Delhi at last, and the heat under the station roof almost made Thö-pa-ga collapse, the extremely friendly Mr. Eiji Sarao was rather evidently puzzled by the farewell between Tom and Elsa.

"Goodbye. Thanks for all your kindness."

"Kindness nothing. I enjoyed your company. Hope you'll enjoy

India. Perhaps we'll meet again someday, somewhere. Who knows? Goodbye."

Tom took a taxi with Thö-pa-ga to Dr. Lewis's office. That address had not been given him for nothing. No one—absolutely no one was going to take responsibility for his entering Tibet. They wanted him to do it, off his own bat, at his own risk. No one was going to tell him anything, of any importance, in so many plain words. If he hadn't enough intelligence to understand hints, then he was the wrong man for the job and the usual governmental agencies would easily stop him in the course of the usual day's work. If he hadn't wits enough, he would be stymied without being able to say that anyone had even as much as suggested to him that it might be possible to cross the Tibetan border.

That immigration officer wasn't the regular man; he hadn't even known where to look for the switch to regulate the force of the electric-fan in the office. But he had done his job pretty well. He had served warning to Tom to look out for the departmental mechanism that prevents the unwise, wishful wanderer from breaking bounds. He had warned him, too, against Eiji Sarao—as if that were necessary!

In the taxi, whirling through the crowded Delhi semi-modern streets that reeked of hot humanity and sprinkled pavement, he didn't have to bother about Thö-pa-ga. The man was almost comatose, although Tom was pretty sure he wasn't as ill as he looked; he was suffering from a sort of psychic blue funk. It was probably true, as he had declared suddenly in the shed that night, that he would rather die than return to Tibet. Perhaps Dr. Lewis could fix that. If not, a high elevation would do it. Meanwhile, Eiji Sarao? Noropa? The mysterious Noropa had had time to phone to half the Japanese in London in the interval between the Bow Street incident and his arrest that night at Kew.

Embassies and consulates don't openly employ a *shang-shang* expert. It would be an absolutely safe bet that no one, not even the secret service, or Scotland Yard, or Ambleby could prove any connection between "Doctor" Noropa and the Japanese Government. No doubt Eiji Sarao was an eminent man of affairs who represented a Tokyo cotton combine, as he said. But some third person, who knew Noropa, also might know Eiji Sarao. Or possibly Eiji Sarao knew Noropa. Eiji Sarao's visit to the Foreign Office might have been a mere coincidence; there was no reason why a distinguished foreign visitor to London shouldn't call there. But it hardly looked like a coincidence that Eiji Sarao booked a seat on that plane to Karachi. It was certainly not a coincidence that he had followed from Robbin's Hotel to Doby's downstairs lunch room. He had probably had a spy in the street—perhaps a taxi-driver.

It would be a fairly safe bet that a warning was already *en route,* in the innocent guise of a commercial telegram, to some confederate in Northern India to keep an eye on Tom Grayne *and* Elsa Burbage. Not so good.

Someone in Eiji Sarao's pay certainly would go through Elsa's belongings at the hotel. Japs excel at that game; in Japan they even open all the letters that the tourist school-marms send home to their sisters and their cousins and their aunts. They wouldn't learn much from Elsa's luggage.

Dr. Lewis's office turned out to be on the ground floor of a hospital courtyard. There was the usual crowd of patients and patients' relatives squatting on the shady side of the yard; the usual half-obsequious, half-insolent *chuprassi,* at the office door; the usual *Chi-chi* clerk, inclined to give him self airs; the usual delay, on bent-wood chairs beneath a whirling fan. A vague smell of iodoform. A portrait of King George on an otherwise blank wall. A "no smoking" sign. A painted glass window in a door marked "Private. No admittance." A spot of glass, from which the paint had been removed, about the size of a half-rupee, at about the height of a man's eye from the floor.

Tom was aware he was being stared at through the peep-hole for two or three minutes before the door opened and Dr. Lewis came out to greet him. He was in a white suit, white aproned, pulling off rubber gloves. A jolly-looking fellow. Sharp nose. One eyebrow higher than the other. Two or three scars on his face. Straight, unruly, almost carrot-coloured hair. Very likely fifty, perhaps older. Half his right-hand middle finger missing.

"Mr. Tom Grayne? How do you do? Come in. This the patient? Someone phoned me from Karachi to expect you. Bring him in and let's see what's wrong."

He motioned Tom to a chair beside a desk and led Thö-pa-ga to another chair beside a window. He got busy at once with a stethoscope.

There was a long counter at one end of the room, burdened with all sorts of bottles, phials, scales and retorts. On the desk was a microscope and a lot of implements. Something that smelt pretty rank was boiling in a covered container over an alcohol burner on a white-enameled table on wheels. There was nothing in the room worth particular attention except Lewis himself, the fact that he had indicated that particular chair beside the desk instead of either of two other chairs—and the radio message that lay on the desk, exactly where whoever should use that particular chair couldn't possibly help seeing it. Tom's eyes devoured it:

Dr. Morgan Lewis
Edith Cavell Memorial Hospital
Delhi, India
Await by air mail grain considered suitable for *shang-shang* experiment and also necessary Mongolian extract recommend both to your discreet attention
Best wishes and kind regards   Horace O'Mally"

The date tallied. Sir Horace O'Mally had despatched that from London before leaving for Russia—after his midnight interview with somebody in Westminster.

Thö-pa-ga had his shirt off. He was being systematically thumped. The doctor strode to the desk presently, touched a button and returned to the patient. He appeared to doubt one of the lungs. He resumed business with the stethoscope, until an orderly appeared—another *Chi-chi*, twice as dark as the Tibetan.

"Bath—bed—light diet—observation. Private room. And tell the head nurse I will be up there to study the case in half an hour."

"Card, sir?"

"I will sign that later."

"It's against the rule, sir, to—"

"Do as I tell you."

Thö-pa-ga, with his shirt unbuttoned, followed the orderly out of the room. Dr. Lewis came and smiled in front of Tom Grayne. He lit a cigarette and offered his case.

"The rules," he remarked, "are blessed in the breach, like etiquette. But breach 'em at the right time! That thing boiling in there is a gentleman's liver. He hadn't sense enough to break a rule. He was too polite. He ate what was put in front of him. We shall know soon what it was he died of, and perhaps who did it—although that's less likely. Your man will be dead pretty soon if you can't get him up to the Hills. I can probably put him in shape for the journey. I advise Darjeeling."

He picked up the radio message, as if he hadn't known it was there. He put it into a drawer.

41

"Do you happen to know my friend Horace O'Mally of Harley Street?"

"No," said Tom Grayne. "I have met him, once, casually, that's all."

"Didn't he leave on a visit to Moscow?"

"I don't know."

"Take that other chair, it's easier, and tell me something that you do know."

"Well," said Tom, "I know the road to Tibet."

"Good. Then you don't need my advice to be careful what you eat and drink. I'm going to give you some iron rations of my own invention, for emergency use, when you happen to doubt what's set in front of you."

"Damned kind of you."

"No. Merely thoughtful. Have your meals with me while you're in Delhi."

CHAPTER 7

"I Spent eleven years near the Tibetan border," said Lewis. He wasn't looking at Tom Grayne; he stuck his hands deep in his pants pockets, leaned against the desk, and talked familiarly, as if to an old acquaintance, as if there was no need to do any thawing whatever. Tom, however, knew that any overt attempt on his part to win Lewis's confidence would have the opposite effect. He maintained his reserve and let the doctor do the leading.

"Sikkim?" he suggested.

"Yes, and Bhutan."

"Good country. I bet you liked it."

"Yes. I made a lot of friends among the lamas. Knew a lot of sorcerers, too—*shamans*—all sorts of people. Tried to swap facts with 'em. Couldn't. I spent two-thirds of my pay on medicines and so on, to give to the *shamans*: cascara, quinine and stuff like that, that they passed along as elementary magic. In exchange they'd tell me pretty nearly any thing I knew already, but nothing more than that. Poisons? Couldn't get a word from them. Magic? They'd laugh and swear there was no such thing. If you added it up, I daresay I spent a third of my time trying to get what I supposed you'd call the low-down on a *shang-shang*. I used to write to O'Mally in London. He's well read. He's a very intelligent student of the vagaries of the human mind, is Sir Horace O'Mally. But his suggestions of lines of investigation led nowhere. Our letters on the *shang*-shang subject alone would make a

42

fat volume. In the end we both came to the same conclusion."

"That a *shang-shang* exists in the realm of illusion," Tom suggested.

"No. It lives and moves and has its being, but the legends about it are lies. That's why a *shang-shang* is so damned deadly. And I'm convinced that the Thugs, who used to terrorize India, were rather mild and inoffensive gentry compared to the *shang-shang* magicians. They're a very highly organised, intelligent and mysterious gang of terrorists, with no discoverable motive for their practises other than sheer malice and self-importance."

"Did you happen to hear of the Thunder Dragon Gate?" Tom asked him.

Lewis glanced at him sharply and looked away again. "Yes. I did. That's where *shang-shang* sendings are supposed to come from. I'm convinced it's an actual temple or shrine of some sort. But I don't know where it is."

"Thö-pa-ga is the hereditary Keeper of the Thunder Dragon Gate," said Tom Grayne.

Again Lewis looked straight at him. "Has he told you anything about it?"

"Nothing that I didn't know already."

Lewis nodded. "I might be able to make him talk. Care to come upstairs and see me try?"

"No," Tom answered. "He's suspicious of me as it is. I want his confidence. If you can help me indirectly to get that, I'll reciprocate, if, as and when possible."

Lewis nodded again. "Where are you staying in Delhi?"

"Don't know yet. Came straight here."

"Try Ingleby's Hotel. It's a new place."

"Okay, thanks, I'll do that. Any suggestions about Darjeeling?"

"Are you acquainted there? Do you happen to know the Ringding Gelong Monastery? The abbot's name is—damn, I'll forget my own name next—well, no matter, it's in my note-book."

"Mu-ni Gam-po," said Tom.

"Oh, you know him, do you? Well, you couldn't do better than take your man to that monastery. The high elevation, the familiar monastic atmosphere and old Mu-ni Gam-po's amused arbitrariness should do more to restore him to health than anything else I can think of. How did he react to air plane altitudes?"

"Splendid. At high altitudes he grew almost talkative."

43

"To you?"

"No. I didn't crowd him. I let him talk to anyone he pleased. I haven't asked him a question beyond is he feeling better, or how about a clean shirt or a stick of chewing-gum. I'm not trouble, I'm the lad who pulls him out of it and doesn't give a damn why."

"All right. Well, I'll go upstairs and see him. If you'll dine with me, I'll meet you at the Service Club at nine; I'll be there waiting for you."

"I haven't a dress suit."

"Very well, meet me at Logan's—know where that is?"

"Sure. I'll like the grub at Logan's better. Club grub dulls my intuition. It's all right when you've nothing important to do. Could I have a slip of paper?"

Tom wrote a short note, sealed it in a plain envelope and addressed it to himself at Ingleby's Hotel.

"Memo. Dine tonight at Logan's 9 p.m. Cancel other engagement by phone.

Memo. Buy some American chewing-gum."

He almost never made written memoranda. He didn't have to; he had trained his memory. But he gave the envelope and a coin to a filthy-looking Punjabi, who was loafing in front of the hospital. The man offered his services with rather noticeable persistence. He was possibly a spy. Anyhow, Tom hoped so. He told him to deliver the message at Ingleby's Hotel, and watched him for half a block, until he was quite sure he was being followed by a much better-dressed Punjabi Moslem. That settled it. Tom took a taxi in the opposite direction, made sure that he wasn't being followed by another taxi, and then drove to one of the new administration buildings, where he had some difficulty in finding the Ethnographic Office. When he found it at last, at the end of an upstairs passage, he was rather guardedly welcomed by Norman Johnson, a man in spectacles, bulky, morose and used to being treated with more deference than Tom betrayed.

"Professor Clarence Mayor of the British Museum suggested I should call on you."

"Oh, yes?" He didn't even invite Tom to be seated. The room was lined with evidently much-consulted books. The desk was piled with papers. There was an atmosphere, an emphatic suggestion of too much work to be done and too little time in which to do it. "What does Mayor want? I have a whole file of his letters. He always wants something that he could dig up for himself in the museum if he had the patience. What is it this time?"

"Nothing that he told me."

"Aren't you the man who entered Tibet?"

"I have been in Tibet."

"Well, I must say it surprises me that Mayor should send you to me. He knows perfectly well it's forbidden to do what you did. Does he think I'm going to help you to repeat the offense?"

"I don't know what he thinks, and I'm damned if I care," Tom answered.

"Haven't you any other introduction?"

"No."

"Know anyone at the Foreign Office?"

"No."

"Remaining long in Delhi?"

"No."

"Where are you going from here?"

"Darjeeling."

"I may perhaps meet you there. I should be there now, but there was too much work to be done here first."

"Mail or messages will reach me at the Hindu Kush Hotel in Darjeeling," said Tom.

"And in Delhi?"

"Ingleby's. I see you're busy. I'll be off."

"Good of you. Yes, I am busy. I will look forward to a conversation with you in Darjeeling."

So much for him. Tom chuckled as he walked out. He didn't expect to be kissed on both cheeks and told what to do. One very famous explorer, officially forbidden to enter Tibet, cooled his heels for months, continually applying for permission and continually rebuffed, until at last he waked up and discovered that a road had been made all clear for him. All he had to do was to pretend he had slipped across the Tibetan border without the Indian Government's knowledge. No competent secret service has any sympathy for stupidity; and no successful government does openly what is better done left-handed in the dark.

Tom drove to Ingleby's Hotel, registered and ordered his bag brought from the station. There was no self-addressed message. Good. Pretty stupid of someone. A really smart man would have opened it, read it, sealed it up again and sent it on its way. He took a shower in his room and went down to the broad veranda that faced the street and a row of good green trees. It was already late afternoon. About a dozen people were using the long chairs, drinking. They all stared and immediately lost interest. Tom took a chair at the far end. He ordered ginger-ale—hated the stuff, but you have to order something; it was too hot for tea. He sat still, frowning, doing nothing, mentally reviewing the day's conversations and wondering about Elsa. He was a bit worried about her. But his frown relaxed when a *box-wallah* spotted him and patiently worked his way along the veranda, offering cheap jewellery and similar rubbish for sale. Because he expected just that, Tom spotted the *legerdermain* with which the fellow added a small box of spearmint chewing-gum. As he drew near he placed it in full view on the top tray.

"Melikani tschooin-gum, *sahib? Bohut atcha*—new-fresh-jus' arrive by steamer—same as sell in New York, Paris, London—original package—good—cheap—guaranteed."

Tom bought his entire stock of the stuff. It didn't seem to have been tampered with. There was no evidence of the wrappers having been disturbed. A moment later he silently cursed himself and laid the box on the floor at his left hand. A very pleasant-looking missionary woman in the next chair on his right leaned toward him and spoke:

"If I had seen the chewing-gum, I would have bought some. Do you want it all? May I buy some from you?"

Well, he couldn't tell her he suspected it was poisoned. He couldn't let her go ahead and take a chance and chew the stuff.

"Sorry," he answered. "It's for a sick friend. Promised him." Pretty lame excuse, that. Better touch it up a bit. "I'm going for a stroll," he added. "If you like, I'll get some for you. Would you like a whole box?"

"No, no, please don't trouble. It was just a passing fancy. I haven't dared to eat any Indian sweets since I was poisoned in Darjeeling."

She met Tom's gaze steadily. Gray-eyed, gray-haired. Jolly-looking woman, with a good grim trouble-eating lip line. Good ears. Scarred knuckles. Carried her head right. Licked a whale of a lot of bad grief in her day. Damn her, why didn't she break ice? Suddenly she did it, quite naturally:

"Are you Mr. Tom Grayne? Someone we both know phoned a few minutes ago to say you're going to Darjeeling. So am I—tomorrow morning. Do you know Darjeeling? Perhaps I can be of some use to you there. I keep a school for Hill children."

She didn't mention Ethnological growling Johnson's name, so he'd be damned if he would. How could he check up?

46

"Do you know Mu-ni Gam-po?" he asked.

"We're great friends."

"Give him my kind regards."

"Would you care to meet him at my house?" she suggested.

Tom hesitated, although he didn't appear to. The unlikeliest people are on the inside. Equally unlikely people are among the mischief-makers and merely curious who imagine themselves on the inside.

"I'd enjoy meeting Mu-ni Gam-po anywhere," he answered.

"I am Nancy Strong," she said. "Does that mean anything?"

"Yes."

He wondered why he hadn't guessed it. But a man can't remember everything. He should, but he doesn't; a brain doesn't work that way. He had heard of her scores of times, from scores of people. Even her Christian enemies spoke of her with respectful appreciation. Tom remembered a district judge remarking that the more he hated her the more he liked her. Funny—he had imagined her as a totally different type of woman; he had avoided meeting her for that reason. Had forgotten her for the same reason.

"You will call on me?" she asked.

"Sorry I didn't long ago."

"I will look forward to it."

She got up, so of course Tom did, and she walked away with an air that made her look as likable as one of those rather impoverished county gentlefolk, who, all the world over, keep the good traditions going while the bad ones die. Tom went into the lobby and wrote a letter to Elsa, in code lest Eiji Sarao should see it:

Not for Mayor. Go as soon as you like to Darjeeling. Any good hotel will do. Soon after you get there call on Miss Nancy Strong, School for Hill Children. Tell her all you care to about Thö-pa-ga but show no interest in me. Everything progressing favourably. Better destroy this.

Tom.

He mailed it, stuffed his hands into his hip-pockets, and went for a stroll.

CHAPTER 8

Logan's is a queer place. Its proprietor is Greek and the cooking Chinese. It stands at a corner where a busy street becomes a tributary of the Chandni Chowk and never less than thirteen nations mix into a stream that readily becomes a turbulent vortex. Any wind of politics can whip that swarm into a tantrum. In time of riot it is one of the first points that the armoured lorries and machine-guns visit. European and American ladies have frequently been spat on at that corner by oriental gentlemen of prejudice and peculiar views.

Tom Grayne, at three minutes to nine, with his hands in his pockets, was more alert than he looked, but he was almost not alert enough. As he crossed the street toward Logan's a Ford roadster whipped around the corner, driven by a nondescript in a dirty turban. It missed him by less than an inch. As he turned his head to try to recognise the driver or take the car's number, a second Ford, coming the same way, actually touched him as it whirled by. He stepped backward against a burly Sikh, who cursed him savagely, inviting a blow, that would have led to a fight, that would have brought the police. Tom knew better than to get himself into police toils.

He grinned at the Sikh: "Run and tell them what you would have done if you'd dared!"

He walked into Logan's, where Dr. Lewis was already seated at a table. He sat down facing him and laid the box of chewing-gum on the table.

"Doped out yet what ailed that liver you were boiling?"

"Yes. A very rare poison, distilled from the roots of a small plant that grows in Sikkim. It takes twenty or thirty roots to yield a few drops of the stuff. It's sure death in a couple of days—attacks the liver—and seems to break it down in a way that I don't understand. I'm sending some of it to O'Mally. He won't make much of it steeped in alcohol—or I think not. But he'll enjoy the poison—three drops that would kill I don't know how many people."

Eiji Sarao entered. He nodded and smiled to Tom and took a table whence he could watch without turning his head. Tom spoke to Lewis:

"The two sticks of gum that are lying loose on top are new ones that I bought half an hour ago at Catesby and Simonds. Take one."

"Why? I hate the stuff."

Tom insisted. He took the other loose stick, broke off the paper, and chewed it. Lewis followed suit. Both chewed. They ordered dinner.

"After dinner, take the box," said Tom, "and have it analyzed." He explained why, and how he had come by the box. "Eiji Sarao," he added, "is having a whale of a good time watching us chew. Don't

48

look at him. He's grinning to himself like a Chinese idol—cocksure funeral-tomorrow kind of grin. Any news at your end?"

"Yes. Quite a bit. A man who said he had come recently from Giang-tze, showing what may have been forged credentials from the Tashi Lama of all improbable people, came to the hospital and demanded to see Thö-pa-ga."

"How did he know he was in there?"

"That's the point. I asked him. He was nonplussed for a second, but they're quick to cover up, are those Northerners; they're not like Indians. An Indian only thinks he's inscrutable; whereas a trained Tibetan, is. He told me Thö-pa-ga has been expected for a long time, so he was on the lookout for him. He said that a patient who was discharged this afternoon had run and told him. Lie, of course."

"Sure. Eiji Sarao told him, that's a safe bet. Did your visitor interview Thö-pa-ga?"

"No. Thought of letting him. Thought better of it. I said he's too ill. He isn't. Lungs are right enough. He'll get well at a high altitude, but he has been eating the wrong kind of food—such slush as this, for instance. Altitude and monastery grub will soon put him to rights. I didn't even tell Thö-pa-ga he'd had a visitor."

"Good."

"But he knew it."

"Uh-huh?"

"I was sent for in a hurry. He was sitting up in bed raving. Said he'd seen a *shang-shang*, so there must be someone come from Tibet."

"Anyone else see it?"

"Yes. The head nurse. Thö-pa-ga is in a small room with his bed by the open window. There's no fire-escape there, but the wall is easily negotiable by any active person. I could climb it myself. In fact, we all suspect that window has been used to deliver forbidden drugs to patients. There's a locked fly-proof screen, but the wire gauze was recently damaged by a violent patient who tried to commit suicide. It was repaired, but the repair was badly done—probably on purpose— and the fact wasn't brought to my attention. It is quite easy, from outside, to detach and pull outward a whole corner of the wire gauze. Thö-pa-ga had asked for shaving tackle and a mirror. The head nurse let him have them. It's usual, unless forbidden in special cases. She had let him have one of those nickel-framed magnifying mirrors that was left behind by a patient and never claimed. Safety razor. She had left him with the mirror against his knees, leaning back against a heap of pillows, with his back to the window, shaving him self.

"He started raving before she had reached the next room. She was back in the nick of time to see through the window what *she* said (and she may have been right) was a Tibetan devil-mask. But she said it was green, which hardly fits. She's a good, strong, level-headed woman, but she may have been too badly frightened to observe it accurately. Thö-pa-ga had seen it in the shaving mirror, magnified and probably distorted. First he said it was a *shang-shang*. Then he said it was his own soul looking at him! The nurse had to keep him from cutting his throat. He had the blade out of the safety razor. So she couldn't look out of the window; and, of course, by the time they'd sent for me the thing was gone. I raised particular hell, but no one who had any business in the yard below would admit having seen anything."

Tom watched Eiji Sarao get up and go. They nodded to each other.

"If I were the Indian Government," he said to Lewis, "I would run Mr. Eiji Sarao out of the country so fast that he'd burn the tracks."

"And the evidence, too!" Lewis answered. "Understand me, I'm entirely ignorant of what it's all about or what the government intends. I know nothing about you. Nothing. You called on me, mentioned the name of a mutual friend, and I'm living up to the Welsh reputation for hospitality."

"Quite so."

"So I'm going to introduce you, simply as an act of hospitable kindness, to a *rajah*. Have you eaten enough of this ullage? Like some dessert? More coffee? Let's go then. He's the Rajah of Naini Kol, which is a little bit of a principality tucked away in the Hills a couple of hundred miles from here."

"I think I've heard of him. Isn't he the scientist?"

"M-m-yes. He dabbles. He can afford it. His name is Dowlah, which it shouldn't be. He's a descendant on the female side of the famous Suraja-ud-Dowlah of Clive's day. Adopted or something. Anyhow, he hasn't inherited political ambition. He neglects his subjects, which is very fortunate for them; they're backward, but they're pretty decently ruled by a fat prime minister, who's too afraid of them to try any tyranny and too honest to steal; a damned rogue but a good bloke, if you understand me. He has his points. Dowlah has traveled a good deal, but he lives most of the time nowadays in Delhi. He is one of my private patients; I had to treat him for a nervous condition induced by too much effort to become a scientist without the necessary mental training."

"Strange hour to call on him, isn't it?"

"I'll tell you another peculiar thing. We're going to call on him without anyone knowing but you, he and I. I'm going to leave you alone with him. Come and see me in the morning at the hospital and I'll let you know what reaction I get from this chewing-gum."

They took a taxi to Lewis's club, where Lewis squandered nearly two hours talking to acquaintances while Tom, on a veranda chair, sat staring at the night. But at last Lewis borrowed a friend's auto, driven by an ex-*sepoy*. They were whirled after that through so many streets that Tom was hard put to it to keep his sense of direction. Obeying orders, the ex-*sepoy*, a *mahratta*, doubled and redoubled on the course until there was no longer the slightest question of their being followed. The car stopped at last in almost total darkness, beneath *neem* trees, on the western outskirts of the city.

Lewis dismissed the car. He and Tom walked to a high teak gate that opened in response to knocks and admitted them into a heavily scented garden. A fountain splashed. A path led to a front door, in a house that looked centuries old but recently modernized. An ancient, white-bearded attendant in a white smock emerged like a ghost from the shadows, greeted Lewis profoundly, and rang the bell.

CHAPTER 9

Rajah Dowlah of Naini Kol, to put it mildly, did not stand on ceremony. Someone had opened the front door by mechanical means; there wasn't a servant in sight as he came like a dancing master down the hall to greet his guests. The hall was severely furnished in the latest modern fashion—metal chairs—one astonishing oil painting—indirect light—imported travertine—a long strip of gloxinia-hued hand-woven carpet. There were two full-length mirrors, framed in chromium; the one at the end that faced the front door made the hall seem twice as long as it actually was, and you seemed to walk toward yourself.

The *rajah* was in a European dinner-jacket and canary-coloured silk turban. He didn't walk, he pranced. He didn't smile, he giggled. He didn't hold out his hand, he flourished it. He didn't shake hands, he shook himself, offering a hand to either guest and using theirs for leverage.

"Lewis, old thing, how are you? Who is your friend? Not a patient, I hope?"

He had very intelligent eyes. Beneath an air of triviality and gush he seemed to have the coldly concentrated, alert attention of a gambler, in a game where the stakes are big and the opponents not notorious for fair play.

"Don't talk nonsense, Lewis! No, no, I won't listen to you! You must have a drink and a smoke. You must stay at least until after I've shown you my latest!"

"Perpetual motion?" asked Lewis.

Dowlah giggled at Tom. "He's jealous! He's afraid they will make me an F.R.S.!—Lewis, you incredulous old Taffy, I have a *shang-shang*! Alive! In captivity! Come along and I'll show you."

"You're a damned liar," said Lewis. "I'll look."

The *rajah* led the way. The library, as he called it, was as full of scientific instruments as books. It was a big room, lined with travertine. There was another full-length chromium-framed mirror, its effect spoiled by a cabinet that stood against it, draped with a huge embroidered silk shawl. There were microscopes, cameras, retorts, but none of the dirt and disorder that usually accompany amateur nights into physics. There were also three big easy chairs, a table, decanters, siphons. The *rajah* offered whisky and cigars. Lewis accepted both, Tom neither; Tom had a way of declining, without excuse or apology, that left nothing to argue about. Then, suddenly:

"I can't wait, Lewis! I simply must show you!"

"Go ahead, Dowlah, you idiot. Show us!"

Dowlah led, on excited tiptoes, toward the glass cabinet that stood in front of the mirror. He jerked off the silk shawl and revealed a glass case, six feet long, four wide, standing on a heavy teak table.

"Hold your breath! Sssh-sh! Take a look! Take a look!"

On the floor of the glass case was a brute like a huge green spider with a body as big as a quart pot, spiked like a horned toad's. Its legs were two or three times as long as a spider-crab's and had projecting bristles. It was emerald green. It had a face like a shrunken devil-mask—a blind malignant face. Its real eyes were on top. They were opal coloured. Its mandibles moved continually, as if it were feeding itself on something that it couldn't see. There was a big, dead rat near one corner of the cage, caught in a network of web as thick as sewing silk, and sucked dry.

"Weighs seven pounds, six ounces and a half," said Dowlah. "Angry! Mad angry! She's from the Hills. The heat here maddens her. But isn't she a beauty! Lewis, my boy, that's a genuine *shang-shang*. She's a

52

young one. They say they grow to be twice her size. That's the beast you said doesn't exist! That's the killer-spider of the Himalayas that can thrive up near the snow line. That's the origin of half the Tibetan legends, and of nearly all the superstition, about murder by magic! Death? Hah! There's death for you, Lewis my boy! How'd you like that on a dark night! Devilish death! Painful! Worse than a *hamadryad*! If the tales are true, that creature's bite sets every nerve in its victim's body aflame with agony. But you can't scream. You can't move. You die speechless. Would you like to see her kill another rat now?"

"No," said Lewis. "How d'you know it's a *shang-shang* and how did you get it?"

Dowlah didn't answer the questions. "How would you like her loose in your bedroom?" he retorted. "That's her job! That's what the *shamans* catch 'em for! They're a thousand times as dangerous and difficult to catch as cobras or panthers. I'll show you. This brute can jump clear across the room, so keep out of its way! Out of *her* way! She's the female of the species. The male is small, dark red, non-poisonous. She invariably kills and eats him. However, I'll let her loose and show you what she's good for."

"No, you won't," said Lewis.

"Oh, yes. It's quite simple. If you don't get between her and where she's going, you'll be quite safe until after she gets there. I'll trap her all right. You watch. I'll show you how it's done. She has a one-track mind, like any other spider—always does the same thing in the same way. She's almost human in that respect. Stand over there by the wall."

It was a very long room. On another table, against the wall at the far end, there was a glass case similar to the one that contained the *shang-shang*, similarly covered with a silk drape. Its hinged top was raised and held open by a string suspended from a pulley on the wall; it could be opened and shut from half a room away. Dowlah took a small stick like a conductor's baton, tied a wad of cloth to the end, dipped the wad in something in a saucer—

"Warm meat extract. Blood is better. But when she's very angry warm meat extract does the trick."

He opened a small slide at one end of the glass case and proceeded to irritate the *shang-shang* with the rag on the end of the stick. The thing's ferocity was horrible. It flew at the stick. It bit the rag. Its leg movements were so swift and powerful that it seemed to fly. The interior of the six-foot-long case became a whirl of something vividly green that moved too swiftly for the eye to follow. Dowlah removed

53

the stick and closed the slide. The monstrous insect crouched itself over the slide and appeared to be trying to force it open.

"Now!" said Dowlah. "Watch this! *Arichnida ferox shang-shang Dowlah!* They will hardly be so jealous as to deny it the use of my name, will they? I'm its discoverer. I'm the first to have a captive *shang-shang* under observation."

He began to touch the floor, tables, furniture, even the books on the shelves, with the rag on the end of the stick. He laid a zigzag scent that led all over one half of the room, until he finally came to the open glass case, untied the rag and dropped it in. Then he removed the saucer of meat extract into the hall, closed the door again, locked it to prevent a servant from entering unannounced, switched off the two electric ceiling-fans, attached the end of a cord to a ring on the lid of the case, stood back ten feet away—pulled the cord—opened the lid.

Out came the *shang-shang*, swiftly, with a sidewise spider movement. It crouched on the glass on the top of the cabinet. Seen against the mirror, in three dimensions, it was nauseating—an emerald horror.

"God!" exclaimed Lewis.

Tom Grayne noticed a bottle of cyanide on a shelf in a case behind him. It might be better than no weapon in a pinch.

The Rajah giggled: "Tee-hee! Isn't she a lulu! Find her an adjective, Mr. Grayne—lulu is already antique—isn't she entitled to a new word? You're an American. You invent it!"

"Shut up! For God's sake, watch the brute!" Lewis said irritably. "Here, give me that window-pole. I warn you, I'm going to swat your *shang-shang* if it heads my way."

"Don't you worry. She won't. But I bet you couldn't hit her—not with that," said Dowlah.

Lewis reached down the brass-hooked pole from the ring on the ventilator window up high on the wall.

The *shang-shang* began to move again, crabwise, with its legs spread wide. It looked like three different things, all horrible: crab, spider, octopus. It moved like none of them—like all three of them—raising its body up and down. Suddenly it leaped to the floor, soundless—crouched there, swaying as if ready for a spring—then dashed in a sudden, absolutely silent zigzag course from point to point that had been touched by the rag on the end of the stick. Almost lightning speed, effortless.

From the time it started it seemed less than a second before Dowlah

54

let go the cord that shut the lid of the cage at the end of the room.

"Phew!" Lewis leaned on the window-pole and wiped his forehead. "The damned thing scared me. I admit it."

"Now you know," said Dowlah, "how the *shamans* kill a victim. First find a *shang-shang*. Where to find them is a secret that's been well kept. Next, catch a female. If you can do that without being killed, you're a magician! After that, contrive to touch your victim with something smelly that excites a *shang-shang's* anger. Blood! Human blood, if you have it. Make a trail back to your *shang-shang*. Let her go. And you've one more mysterious murder!"

"Can they catch 'em again?" asked Lewis.

"I don't know, but I doubt it. Mrs. Shang-shang, I imagine, makes tracks for the Hills. She likes high altitudes. Her natural food is mice, snakes, birds—and her unfortunate husband."

"Are you sure she's in that case?" asked Tom Grayne. He glanced again at the cyanide bottle.

"Yes, she's in there. I keep the sides of the case covered because she gets so angry if she can't hide behind something."

"You damned fool!" exclaimed Lewis. "She isn't in there! Look! That's her leg! She's between the case and the wall! By God, she's coming for us!"

Tom reached down the cyanide. Lewis held the window-pole like a spear.

"Pretty pussy!" remarked Dowlah. "Now we have to use our guessing apparatus—eh, what?"

Lewis exploded: "God damn! Where's your shotgun?"

"Don't kill her! Man alive, don't kill her! Let's be scientific!" Dowlah seized the silk shawl that had covered the nearer of the two glass cabinets.

The *shang-shang* moved. Another leg appeared above the cabinet. Tom set the cyanide bottle on a table and pulled down two drapes from the wall. He offered one to Lewis.

"Bull-ring tactics. If she bites that she'll waste her venom."

The *shang-shang* emerged. Its opal-coloured eyes looked rotten with cancered malice. They shone in the electric light like iridescent evil. Suddenly the creature darted up the wall, zigzagged across the ceiling like a silent green shadow, and vanished through the ventilator window. It was hinged along the bottom. It had opened downward when Lewis jerked away the window-pole.

"Sinners and drunkards in care of the Lord!" said Lewis. "Well, we have her!" He used the pole to slam the ventilator shut. "She can't get out of there."

"Oh, can't she? I could cry," said Dowlah. He let go fathoms of profanity in an unknown tongue. "I hadn't even photographed her! All I have now is a dead rat, from which to extract poison that the analysts will say is something else! Oh, why am I irreligious? Why haven't I a God to blame? Oh, damn! You jinxes! You brace of alien intruders! There's a shaft there that leads to another, larger one that sticks up through the roof."

"No screen on it?"

"No, double-damn my magnanimity! There was one of those cowls at the top, that spin and suck the air up. It needed repairs. I permitted a delay of three days because the man who had taken the thing to his workshop had a sick son. That was why I kept the ventilator shut. Lewis, you calamity! I know now why the Welsh worship goats and are weaned on onions!"

"Better send out an alarm," said Lewis. "If she gets out, she'll be killing someone."

"Oh, yes? Are you going to say you saw a *shang-shang*? Even now, you're known as Crazy Taffy. You'd be sent home and locked up."

"Remember your manners," said Lewis.

Dowlah threw himself into a chair and sat with his head between his hands. "Lewis, old thing, I would pay you, or anyone else, half a *lakh* of *rupees* to bring that *shang-shang* back again alive! I'd pay a whole *lakh* if I had it."

"You haven't half a *lakh*," said Lewis.

"Can't we climb the roof?" asked Tom Grayne. "If we had a good thick bag that it couldn't bit through—"

Dowlah interrupted. "Did you see my roof? It's as steep as a candle-extinguisher. It was built by a Swiss, to keep our lousy Hindu gods from sitting on it. No. I don't mind being silly, if there's any sense in it. But I don't chase a runaway *shang-shang*. She's gone, she's gone. Dammit, she's gone. She can hide—kill—scoot—she will make for the open country—then the Hills. Whoever sees her will believe his sins have found him out. Snakes will get the credit for any murdering she does. Lewis, you unlucky omen, have another drink, and go away, and leave me alone with my sorrow."

"I will leave you alone with Tom Grayne," Lewis answered. "Yes, I need a drink, please."

Dowlah studied Tom Grayne. He kept glancing at him so intently that he poured Lewis's tumbler nearly half-full of whisky. Then the soda ran over the top. He handed the drink to Lewis without looking at him.

"Yes," he said to Tom at last, "I'd like to talk with you. You're the only man in the room who wasn't frightened."

"Hell," Tom answered, "I was scared stiff."

CHAPTER 10

The *rajah* seemed to have collapsed for the time being. He sprawled in an armchair, absent-mindedly jerking at the trigger of an empty soda-water siphon. But he was studying Tom, and Tom knew it. There were going to be no preliminaries. There was a tacit assumption already that each man understood the other's importance. Each wanted the upper hand. There would be a battle of wits, and, like a dog fight, it would begin in the middle.

"I've a thought," said Tom Grayne.

"Drown it then in whisky. I can think of nothing but the loss of my pet. That isn't thought, it's emotion. All is lost save honour, which is not an asset."

"If we should open that ventilator," Tom continued, "the brute might return. She might try to kill you. We could catch her." He went and opened the ventilator. "Have you, for instance, a big butterfly-net on a fairly long pole?"

"She won't come back. She could bite through a muslin net. She's too quick to be caught. You couldn't hit her with a shotgun. Don't talk like a cuckoo."

Dowlah took a long drink. Then he got up and locked the decanter away.

"Out of sight, out of mind," he remarked. "Who is that girl who came with you to Delhi? I will save you the trouble of lying. Her name is Elsa Burbage. Who—what—why? You'd better tell me."

"Why should I talk to you about a girl who happened to be on the plane?" Tom answered. He hadn't expected that twist. He wasn't ready for it, but he betrayed no embarrassment.

"You and I," said Dowlah, "have to understand each other. As a doctor, Lewis is a regular, orthodox run-of-the-mill mediocrity. But are you such an ass as to suppose he brought you here to save a wench's reputation by being sentimentally evasive?"

"Lewis didn't tell you about Elsa Burbage. Who did?"

"What's she good at?" Dowlah asked him.

"Can you see the whites of my eyes?" Tom retorted. "You fire first. If we put that saucer full of meat extract up there near the ventilator, possibly the *shang-shang* might come down to get it. If she's hungry—"

"If she's hungry she will hunt for something she likes better than warm Bovril. What I hope," said Dowlah, "is that she will go and kill the *shaman* from whom my servant stole her. That would save me some emotions. My servant should have killed the *shaman*, but he didn't."

"So the *shaman's* gunning for you?"

"Yes, but not with a gun. I don't know why he brought the creature to Delhi. I do know that if he learns who stole her, my number is up. That is why I didn't send out an alarm. I don't want a Tibetan *shang-shang* tamer heaping blessings on me."

"There may be more than one *shang-shang* in Delhi," said Tom. "A man named Thö-pa-ga is rather credibly reported to have seen one through a bedroom window."

"Oh, that? Don't be silly. That would be a dummy on a pole. They want to scare Thö-pa-ga back to Tibet in a proper state of dismal-mindedness. Tibetans, even educated ones, believe a *shang-shang* not only can kill them but hound them in hell after death. There's a man in Delhi who has come for Thö-pa-ga. He owns the *shaman* who owned the *shang-shang*. He's an anonymous Number One, in hiding. He won't want you in the way and he doesn't love me—not if he's sane, he doesn't. You and I are equally in danger. But before I play with you I want to know more about you. Who is Elsa Burbage?"

"You tell me," Tom answered.

There was no longer the slightest trace of nonsense about Dowlah. His yellow turban suggested mustard-gas. His nose was an interrogation mark, his eyes insolent.

"Very well, I will tell you. Elsa Burbage is a girl who holds her tongue too damned well to be innocent. Why won't she talk about you?"

"Have you tried to make her do it?" Tom asked. He sounded, looked, was casual. There was no anger in his eyes, no particular interest. The battle was on.

Dowlah chuckled. "You seem as close as she is! Elsa Burbage can't be persuaded to talk even with her big toe in a nut cracker. She wouldn't even yell."

"If her feelings were any of my concern, you wouldn't dare to tell me that," said Tom. "Talk horse. Why am I here?"

No embarrassment. Not a trace of it. Tom's hands were at ease, unclenched. His voice was level, his eyes cold. Dowlah tried another angle:

"I propose to help you into Tibet, Mr. Tom Grayne. If I do that, what will you do for me in return?"

"Nothing. Why should you help me, if you could get along somehow else? I'm necessary, or I shouldn't be here."

Dowlah nodded. "Well, I'll tell you. I'm afraid of this Elsa Burbage. You appear trustworthy. You have been well recommended to me. But a girl—well, Eiji Sarao has warned me. He says he saw you two together in London. He says Thö-pa-ga has come more or less under her influence."

Tom betrayed no surprise whatever. He understood the system. He was not being tested to find out how much or how little he knew, but whether or not he would tell what he knew.

"Am I wasting time? Why am I here?" he repeated.

"Eiji Sarao told me you intend to find the Thunder Dragon Gate and to go in."

"Not he. Someone else told you that."

"Is it true?"

"Ask your informant. I don't tell my business without good reason."

"Eiji Sarao says you know Noropa."

"If you believe Eiji Sarao, why ask me about it?"

Dowlah grinned. "Why, do you suppose, do I enjoy the confidences of a Japanese cotton-mill representative?"

"Easy. You're the conman. Probably the Jap secret service people imagine you're their number one bet on the Indian board. Probably Eiji Sarao trusts you, to the extent that a Jap spy trusts anyone. He probably believes you're a secret enemy of the Indian Government."

"Not so bad," said Dowlah. "Now it's your turn. Who is Elsa Burbage?"

"If I knew, I wouldn't tell you."

"Very well then, answer this one. Thö-pa-ga needs very artful handling, if you hope to find the Thunder Dragon Gate. You will have to use Thö-pa-ga. There is no other possible way. Elsa Burbage is reported, by Eiji Sarao, who is a rather keen observer, to have Thö-pa-ga's confidence, more or less. Thö-pa-ga, he says, shows a tendency—nothing more than a tendency yet—to open up—almost to be in love

59

with her. If so, she might be useful. It 'ud be devilish risky to use an inexperienced girl, but we could kill her if she made a *faux pas*. Do you think she'd tune in?"

"How should I know?" Tom answered. "Why not ask her?"

"Very well, I will," said Dowlah.

He got up, and went out into the hall, leaving the door open. Tom caught a glimpse of him in the mirror behind the case that had contained the *shang-shang*. Saw him enter a door in the hall. Saw him govern his face as he came back.

"She appears unconscious at the moment," he said as he closed the door behind him. "I suppose we rather overdid the third degree."

"You're overdoing tommyrot!" Tom answered. "Bring her in."

Dowlah laughed. He returned to the hall. Tom waited calmly. If Elsa had made any bad breaks, she had made them. If she hadn't, she hadn't. Nothing to be gained by getting worked up. He would know, in a minute, how she came to be there.

But it was nearly five minutes before Dowlah returned.

Elsa had hold of his arm. Tom watched them in the mirror. She walked beside him as if they were old friends. She was laughing at some joke he had made. A bit pale—a trifle wild-eyed—just a trace excited—but well in control of herself. She looked very small beside the tall, lean Dowlah.

She walked at Dowlah's right. The fingers of her right hand moved like lightning—shorthand—almost too fast for Tom to read it. He was afraid Dowlah might notice it in the mirror; not that it mattered much, because Dowlah couldn't understand it, but he glanced at the mirror to make sure. He almost betrayed that he was startled. His blood ran cold. It wasn't so much that he saw Eiji Sarao's face peering through the partly open door, disturbing though that was; it might mean anything. But, peering over Eiji Sarao's shoulder from behind him, was Noropa—unmistakably Noropa—the six-foot eight-inch figure of death, who should be in an English prison. How the devil had Noropa reached Delhi?

Only one glimpse. The *rajah* turned to close the door, and Elsa's fingers kept on furnishing vital information. He had to watch them. She could see Tom in the mirror, but she pretended not to—made no sign of recognition. She was be having splendidly.

Dowlah pretended to be trying the lock. He turned suddenly, to try to catch them making signals, but he couldn't see Elsa's right hand. She finished signalling. Tom stood up:

60

"Well, Elsa Burbage! It hasn't taken you long to find your feet in Delhi! Pleased to meet you again."

"Good evening, Tom. I'm less surprised than you are. You're the kind of man, aren't you, who turns up in all sorts of unexpected places."

Dowlah looked amused. "Nothing unexpected about me," he remarked. "I'm the most conventional, correct and predictable man in the world. And I'm as easy to fool as the income-tax man."

CHAPTER 11

Rajah Dowlah resumed his mask of inconsequential inanity. He giggled as he pulled up an armchair for Elsa beneath the ceiling fan and arranged a huge cushion. But he was watching for signals. Tom was quite sure of that. Three times in less than sixty seconds he saw him glance at the mirror behind the empty *shang-shang* cage. Evidently Dowlah wanted to know too much and to tell too little before committing himself. It was time to unmask Dowlah's batteries. The weather in the passes leading toward Tibet wouldn't wait on Dowlah's moods.

Tom went and unlocked the door without a word. He strode into the hall. He heard Dowlah's voice behind him:

"Silly ass, he's jealous!"

Then Elsa's: "Kindly take your hands off!"

But almost any man can make a girl say "take your hands off!" It's particularly easy for an oriental to make a white woman say it. Tom didn't even glance backward.

He tried the door on the left. It was locked, although he could hear someone on the far side. The second door opened readily. He walked into a beautiful room—apricot-hued carpet, travertine walls, indirect lighting—three or four exquisite Chinese vases—modern chairs and chaise longue. Three men: Eiji Sarao, Noropa and another.

A bit of a puzzle, that third man. Tall—obese—a little round embroidered skullcap on a bald head—a full, shovel-shaped beard, dyed with *henna*—a fine white linen smock beneath a severely cut black frock-coat—long white pantaloons—Persian slippers. Vaguely he resembled a friar, only he lacked the fringe of hair and looked less insolent. He put on *pince-nez* to stare at Tom, but his gaze was mild, inoffensive, rather bovine.

Eiji Sarao's eyes glittered amid leathery wrinkles. If he was startled, he didn't show it. He smiled, stuck his hands in his dinner-jacket pockets and waited for Tom to speak first. Tom didn't speak—not yet. He went straight up to Noropa, swiftly, as if he meant to hit him. The tall Mongolian, looking more than ever like a figure of death, took a short step backwards. He threw his left hand forward, palm outward, as if to ward off an expected blow. Tom seized his wrist. There was a second's spasm of *jiu-jitsu*, but Tom had expected that. Noropa's arm curled in an agonied knot behind his back; he could obey, or, if it pleased him, lose the use of that arm for ever. He surrendered, speechless.

"So you know that?" said Eiji Sarao. He was still smiling; his hands were still in his side-pockets, with his thumbs outside. "Please tell me why you violate this person." He spoke as if he were asking the way or something.

"I will tell you in the library," Tom answered. "Last door on the right at the end of the hall. Now, please. I don't want to have to knock this man cold, but if I have to tackle you, I'll do it. Turn to the right, then last door on the right—go straight in."

The obese man in the *pince-nez* with the *henna*-tinted beard had got out of his chair. He looked now rather like a father-abbot about to bless some penitents.

"Who are you?" Tom asked him.

"I am the prime minister of Naini Kol."

"Oh. Pardon the disturbance. Come along if you care to. Suit yourself."

"I always do," he answered. Then he wiped his *pince-nez* on a white silk handkerchief and stood aside to signify that he preferred to walk last. That was all right with Tom; a fat prime minister wasn't likely to use a blackjack. Poison, yes, perhaps, but not an automatic. Besides, Dr. Lewis had been at pains to describe him; he was very likely all right.

Noropa said never a word. He was nearly a head taller than Tom, and Tom was six feet in his socks. He had the vaguely buttery-smoky smell of a Tibetan, but Tom was more than ever sure he wasn't one. He had on a more or less European black silk suit, brand new. There was a knife under his shirt, held in place by his belt; he had to hold his stomach tight against the belt to keep the knife from slipping. No Tibetan would have done that; a Tibetan by nature pouches a thing in his shirt as a kangaroo carries her young. He permitted himself to be marched along the hall toward the library. Eiji Sarao opened the library door. They all entered the room in a group, Eiji Sarao leading, in order to signal to the *rajah*, as Tom noticed in the mirror. The prime minister came last, closed the door, locked it, but made no signal.

All eyes were on Tom Grayne, so it was easy for Elsa to use the fingers of her left hand; they moved as rapidly as a concert pianist's and not even Eiji Sarao saw it. By the time his glittering brown eyes had moved to see what Tom was looking at, Tom already had Elsa's information. Tom pushed Noropa into a chair, removed his long knife, tossed it on the table and then let go his wrist. Noropa's lips moved, but he said nothing audible; he sat chafing his arm. Rajah Dowlah giggled. Eiji Sarao scowled at him; he looked suddenly bossy, like a Japanese official ordering a tourist not to photograph a barrack gate.

"Congratulations!" said Tom. "Good staff work! You must need Noropa pretty badly, though, to spirit him so quickly from a jail in London. Looks like a miracle."

Eiji Sarao smiled. He raised his shoulders in a deprecating gesture.

"I am sorrow for you," he said gently. "You are found out. You are American Government spy. It is better you go home."

Tom's voice was equally restrained, but less silky:

"Mr. Eiji Sarao, I want both your hands over your head— now— quickly! Up with them!"

"You'd better do it, Eiji!" said the *rajah*. "I don't want him killed in my house. Better humour him."

The Japanese didn't obey, but he took his hands out of his pockets, probably to protect himself. He was obviously puzzled. Tom's hands were into his pockets before he could turn to glare at Dowlah. One hip-pocket and the inside jacket-pocket. Quick work. Eiji Sarao sprang away and struck very smartly at Tom's forearm, but he just missed paralyzing the muscle he aimed at. The crack of his heel on Tom's instep didn't hurt much because Tom was ready for that—all Japanese know that dodge, and it's quite a trick to counter it.

Eiji Sarao's inside pocket tore. Tom had what he wanted. Eiji Sarao glared, straightening his jacket, ruffled, indignant, dignified, bewildered, savage, but still in command of his manners.

"I am no longer sorrow for you. It is your fault that you shall be liquidated."

That was a strange word for a Japanese to select. But what was more significant was Eiji Sarao's glare at Dowlah. He expected support, protection. He didn't get it. He was baffled. Tom, on the other hand, noticed that Dowlah was looking well pleased with the turn of events.

Tom examined his find. Three documents that Eiji Sarao had not had time or opportunity to stow safely away. One was his own memorandum about the dinner engagement with Lewis, and the chewing-gum. The second was the coded message he had mailed to Elsa. Stolen from the mail. Not so easy to do. It meant a thoroughly well-organised spy-system. Tom's fingers told Elsa its contents. The third was a cablegram in French, from Paris, signed "Jeanne Marcel," enclosed in an envelope with a Pondicherry postmark and addressed to Eiji Sarao in Delhi. That one he translated aloud into English: "Harley has wired from Moscow warning someone to tell Barley you are in charge of negotiations."

"Someone" might be Ambleby. "Harley" was undoubtedly Sir Horace O'Mally, who lived and performed his miracles of doctoring in Harley Street. "Barley," equally undoubtedly, was Tom Grayne. It was just the kind of message that gets by the censors without arousing suspicion.

"Swell network," said Tom. "Moscow to London—by way of Finland?—phoned to Paris—cabled to Pondicherry— innocent-looking envelope from Pondicherry to your hotel—and you a perfectly innocent piece-goods salesman! Clever. You Japs are up against it, aren't you, what with Russia watching you as well as Great Britain and the British Indian Government. To use your own phrase, I am sorrow for you. Care to come with me to Tibet?"

Eiji Sarao's expression changed. He looked maliciously amused.

"You," he answered, "you are going nowhere."

Tom retorted: "Well, it's pretty obvious that Dowlah is liaison man between Japan and certain Indian seditionists. Your dilemma is that Dowlah fears you'll double-cross him. Almost anyone could guess that in the dark. He feels he has gone a bit too far. He can't afford to be caught with the goods."

"Can anyone afford that?" the prime minister asked. He was sitting like a bishop in an arm-chair, next to Elsa; it appeared he liked them young, small, with a wind-blown bob. She did look good. Her frock was obviously bought that afternoon in Delhi, but it suited her. The old chap's taste in women evidently wasn't as eccentric as his figure.

"Take a seat, Mr. Sarao. You'll get tired standing," said Tom. He was watching Elsa's fingers. It didn't matter that the prime minister was also watching them; even if he could read that rapid shorthand code, it didn't matter. And if Eiji Sarao, as seemed possible, could read at any rate some of it, that didn't matter either, because his back was toward her. He sat down, dignified but as comfortless as a suspicious cat, on a chair near Noropa. Tom could look straight at him and, at the same time, watch Dowlah in the mirror. At the moment he didn't need any more information from Elsa, she had told him enough.

Dowlah's face was dramatic—amused, amazed, alert—a mask of semi-imbecility, a bit too transparent; beneath it was almost savage excitement. Tom resumed the offensive. Spur-of-the-moment guess-work. Hammer-blows of downright statement. He was like a man in the ring, slugging his opponent to compel him to reveal his weakness.

"Mr. Eiji Sarao, the Russian, British and Indian Governments all know what your game is. You're no mystery. The British Home Office allowed Noropa to leave England at his own expense. That's obvious. He took the plane to Paris, flew from there to Damascus, and made connections with a fast special plane that happened to be leaving for Karachi. That's equally obvious. Surely, even you must realize you're being watched. Do you, or does the Japanese Foreign Office want it known that Rajah Dowlah has been their secret agent for Lord knows how long?"

"As for me, rather than face that, I would bump myself off," said the prime minister. "They would send me to the Andamans. Have you ever seen the Andamans? Have you heard of them? Ugh!"

Tom hadn't expected support from him; he looked too bovine to be a conspirator. Eiji Sarao said nothing. Tom continued:

"You have made some bad breaks, Mr. Eiji Sarao. In the first place you behaved suspiciously in London. On the journey you were too damned inquisitive. Here, you walked straight into a couple of my traps. You tried to have me poisoned with chewing-gum. You tried to have me killed in the street. You robbed the mail. Why are you here tonight?"

No answer.

"All right. Hold your tongue and listen. Your grip on Rajah Dowlah is the old one, that all secret services use: if he doesn't obey orders, he'll be tipped off to his own government. That would be the end of Dowlah. Or so you think. But how about the end of your own rope? Your Foreign Office won't ask questions if you're not heard from for a while. Not official questions. Nothing through diplomatic channels. You're not going to be heard from. Would you care to come with me to Tibet?"

"Say more," said Eiji Sarao. His face was a mask.

"Someone has come to Delhi to take charge of Thö-pa-ga? Who is he?"

Eiji Sarao's expression changed. It became vacant. He shook his head. He didn't know. But he overplayed it; it was clear enough that he did know.

"Well, you've a minute or two to refresh your memory," said Tom. "This afternoon you very kindly showed Miss Burbage where to do her shopping. Why did you introduce her, in the back room of a clothing shop, to an alleged Chinese, allegedly from Turkestan, to whom, however, you spoke Japanese? And why did you explain to him what sympathy she feels for Thö-pa-ga, and how gratefully he reacts to it?"

"I didn't. You are guessing," said Eiji Sarao. "No one can have told you such a—"

He shut up suddenly. It possibly had occurred to him that Elsa might have signalled the information.

Tom glanced at Dowlah. With the corner of his eye he had detected signs that Dowlah wasn't as amused or confident as he wished to appear.

"Tell him what you think, Dowlah."

Dowlah rose nobly to the occasion. No man possibly could have looked more embarrassed, more silly, more incompetent to carry his end of a dilemma. He even pulled off his turban, ran his fingers through his black hair and wiped his forehead with a handkerchief.

"I am frightened!" he said, after several seconds. "Double-dammit and to hell with all this, do I pay a minister to sit still and fold hands on his belly? Curse you, Abdul Mirza, all this comes of listening to you! You talked me into it. Get me out of it! Hurry up now! Wake up! Tell him what I think —or what I ought to think—or, if you're worth your salary, what I will think!"

The prime minister rose out of his chair. He was a tall man. Standing, he carried his big belly with dignity. He stroked his *hennaed* beard with both hands, parting it in the middle. His mildly intelligent dark eyes, behind ridiculous *pince-nez*, looked at each face in turn but dwelt longest on Elsa's. His little gold-embroidered skullcap, slightly awry, suggested a caricature of the pill-box caps that British cavalrymen used to wear for the delight of French cartoonists.

"To discuss the modesty of my emolument, and to compare it with the nature of my services, seems inappropriate at this time," he began. "I think it also inappropriate to enter into details of an alleged—ah—foreign entanglement that, if it did in fact exist, would be—ah—deadlier to handle than a—ah—cobra. I am for simple solutions, though they may appear—ah—complicated."

"Cut all that!" said Dowlah. "Tell us."

"Fortunately Mr. Grayne wants something, which only we are willing to supply. I am informed that he wishes to go to Tibet for a secret purpose. Only we can help him. Then it follows that a basis exists, whereupon—"

"You may cut that, too," said Dowlah. "This isn't my birthday. You're not honeying the tax-payers. Talk sense."

"Sense is this," said the prime minister. "Neither Tibet nor Japan would welcome Mr. Grayne: Tibet simply from a habit of excluding visitors—Japan in order not to let the light of curiosity expose a beautiful intrigue."

"You blimp, you talk like an unpaid radio performer," Dowlah interrupted.

The prime minister wiped his *pince-nez*.

"It appears to me," he said, "that we should first assure ourselves of secrecy, and next decide who shall accompany Mr. Grayne. If Mr. Eiji Sarao, or Mr. Grayne, or this extremely beautiful young lady, should betray by the merest accident our motives, our intentions or our— ah—secret affiliations—that would be a catastrophe comparable to the fate of the Czar of Russia."

"Cut that, too!" said Dowlah. "You make me shudder. Do you understand him, Eiji? The fat fool means we're in a fix. I'm through. No more of this sort of game for me. I know the ropes; you'd ruin me by tipping me off to the British, if I gave you half a chance. But I won't. You and that fellow Noropa go with Tom Grayne to Tibet, where I hope you all get bitten by a *shang-shng!*"

Abdul Mirza sat down, drooped his eyelids and appeared to lapse into a dream. Tom resumed the offensive, for Eiji Sarao's benefit:

"Miss Burbage came here to dinner on Eiji Sarao's invitation, but at your suggestion, Dowlah. Why?"

Dowlah didn't hesitate a second. He exploded like a petulant weakling, found out and blurting the truth:

"Why? Damn you, because Eiji said she's with you. So she is! She and you are prisoners! You don't believe it? Show them, Abdul Mirza! Get up, you fat loafer! Go and show them!"

The prime minister hove himself out of the armchair with a sigh. He wiped his *pince-nez,* put his feet into his slippers, walked to the door, listened, unlocked it, opened it wide and stepped backward. Armed men!

There was no longer a light in the hall. But the light from the room shone on the faces of at least a dozen men—dark-skinned, turbaned, *cummerbunded*, bearded—six in the front row. There were faces behind them, and more heads in the shadow beyond.

"Prisoners!" said Dowlah. He strode to the door, pushing Abdul Mirza back toward the middle of the room. Without a word of explanation or warning he switched out the lights.

In pitch-black darkness Tom took one step sideways and five forward, reached Elsa's chair and groped for her hand. She could touch-read; there was no need for her to see his fingers.

"Well done. Just what I wanted to know."

"But on whose side is Dowlah?"

"His own, you cuckoo!"

There was a sudden cat-fight exclamation in the darkness from about the spot where Tom was standing when the lights went out.

"Keep your hair on!" Tom signalled. Those were ten tough seconds for a girl who was new to the game. He could feel Elsa as taut as a violin-string. Something fell to the floor. Dowlah turned the lights on.

Blood ran from Eiji Sarao's neck. Not much blood; the blow had missed his jugular. Noropa's knife lay on the floor. Noropa stood near Eiji and gaped like a ghost that saw a super-ghost and couldn't understand. Not even a Mongolian terrorist can see in total darkness. Noropa had stabbed the wrong man.

Dowlah laughed. The armed men hadn't moved in the doorway. There was an altogether new, dynamic note in Dowlah's voice:

"I thought you'd try that, Eiji! You fool, how dare you try to kill a man in my house?"

"I didn't!" said Eiji.

"Liar!" Dowlah answered. "*You* meant to use *jiu-jitsu!*"

Dowlah went to a nest of drawers on a shelf and pulled out medicated cotton—gauze—bandages—tossed them to Eiji Sarao. Then he turned fiercely on Abdul Mirza. It was clear enough now that Dowlah was covering almost hysterical nervousness under a cloak of insolence.

"You should be at Geneva, you should! When you've finished thinking up some resolutions, go and phone for Dr. Lewis! Care to lie down, Eiji? Very well then, they'll show you a bed."

He gestured like a conductor coaxing woodwind through a waning tumult of the brass. Four men armed with sabres marched in. Two of them hustled Noropa pretty roughly. The other two politely led out Eiji Sarao, supporting him between them.

Dowlah came near and stood grinning at Tom and Elsa. He had to grin for thirty seconds before he could speak with an air of being rather scornfully amused. He was only calm on the surface. There was an expression in his eyes that suggested almost terror. It was certainly not less than anxiety.

"Don't you wish," he said, "you had a private army! I'm allowed two hundred and twenty-four men, but I'm supposed to keep 'em all at Naini Kol. I'd get hell if it were known I have a few of 'em in Delhi. However, you don't do badly, you two. I'll have to work up such a system of signals as you use—it's a dandy. Damned if I can read it."

"Miss Burbage would like a drink. Can she have one?" Tom asked.

Dowlah turned away to unlock the liquor cabinet. Tom's fingers signalled:

"Admit nothing. Tell him nothing until he tells us."

CHAPTER 12

Dowlah pressed a button on the wall and spoke into a telephone that looked like a small brass ventilator:

"*Barraff!*"

Ice arrived on a dumb-waiter, along with siphons. He poured two drinks and glanced at Tom.

"You?"

"No thanks."

Dowlah drank deep, watching Elsa sip hers. "Got me to look away, didn't you! Well, you're a smart pair. I admit it. Both of you shall go to Tibet. I don't envy you. I wouldn't go there for a fortune. Frost-bite at eighteen thousand feet. Holy murder stalking you at every turn of the road. Tibetans are jolly people. I've seen 'em flog a girl as pretty as you, Elsa Burbage, and then leave her naked to die of cold in the night."

For about fifteen minutes he described the tortures that Tibetans and their neighbouring semi-Chinese cousins use on foreigners.

"Mr. Grayne has told me all about it," Elsa interrupted at last.

"Dowlah, you're wasting time," said Tom. "If you've a card up your sleeve, either play it or call the game. Make up your mind to do one or the other."

Dowlah giggled again. "I am not your nurse," he answered. "Think you're very clever, don't you! If you are, you'll have to prove it. Show your own hand."

"Very well," Tom answered. "If it's my lead, lock up Eiji Sarao and loose Noropa."

"Do you want him with you in Tibet?" Dowlah could ask a silly question with the earnest innocence of a really artful attorney.

"No, you ass. But I'm going to have your confidence, or else your enmity, right now."

Dowlah chuckled. He sat down on the arm of a chair and crossed his legs. The giggle had gone, like the moisture from the outside of a glass.

"Which do you prefer?" he asked.

"Frankly, I don't give a damn. I'd rather buck you than count on you and be let down. My guess is that you're in a corner. You don't act like a man who can please himself what he'll do next. What use are you to me?"

"What do you want?" asked Dowlah.

There was a knock at the door. Dowlah went and unlocked it. Abdul Mirza entered, a bit too meek looking and benevolent to be innocent of mischief. He wiped his *pince-nez,* to get a better look at Elsa.

"Dr. Lewis is here," he remarked. "He is stitching up Eiji Sarao. I have not told Dr. Lewis how it happened."

Dowlah seemed relieved to have someone to brow-beat.

"Sit down, you bag of platitudes! Listen to what this man wants."

Abdul Mirza looked over the top of his *pince-nez* at Tom.

"I think he will demand too much," he answered. "Such men usually do. What is it?"

"I want Eiji Sarao under lock and key. Turn Noropa loose to make his own mistakes. Eiji Sarao won't talk, and I don't think you'll find any information in his wallet—"

"Not a thing, not a thing," said Abdul Mirza. "Nothing but a correctly visaed passport and some money."

"—but to hold him *incommunicado* may throw the whole Japanese system out of gear between here and Tibet, for the time being."

Dowlah nodded. Abdul Mirza readjusted his *pince-nez*, belched, and addressed a remark to the ceiling:

"Naini Kol is not a resort for tourists. We had the runaway wife of a twenty-one gun *maharajah* there for two years, and no one knew it."

"No one would know it now, if you weren't such a clapper-tongued ass," said Dowlah. "Go on, Tom Grayne. What else?"

"Anyone could play it," said Tom. "It's one, two, three. Noropa is

70

a fanatic, with a certain narrow intelligence, who obeys orders from high up. He's a Number One man's *factotum*. Turned loose, he'll behave like a dog that you can count on absolutely to betray his owner by his effort to protect him. He has a one-track mind, and it's a bad track. That's why someone sent him to London to scare Thö-pa-ga back to Tibet. That's why the British Foreign Office let him fly to India; they turned him loose just to see what he'd do. I want him locked up, talked to, and helped to escape."

"Who's to talk to him?" asked Dowlah.

Tom glanced at Elsa. Dowlah's eyes studied her thought fully. He nodded.

"Noropa must be given to understand," said Tom, "that Eiji Sarao has a secret and tremendously important message that he absolutely must deliver to the personage who came from Tibet to take charge of Thö-pa-ga. Noropa wounded Eiji. How should he know the wound isn't serious?"

"The personage from Tibet isn't, so to speak, notorious for simple-minded incompetence or, let us call it complacency," Abdul Mirza remarked.

"Take it or leave it," Tom answered. "I have said what I want."

Someone knocked on the door.

Abdul Mirza seemed suddenly to wake up. He stared over the top of his *pince-nez*.

"Answer the door," commanded Dowlah. "If it's Dr. Lewis, let him in."

Lewis breezed in. He had the half-comical air of a physician who has competently dealt with a disaster that he foresaw—a sort of "well, boys, what next?" expression.

"Grayne, your chewing-gum kills rats," he said cheerfully. Then he looked hard at Dowlah. "I have just taken five stitches in the neck of that Gurkha."

"Quarrelsome people, Gurkhas," said Abdul Mirza.

"Yes, and reticent," said Lewis. "He didn't tell me his name, or how it happened. Pour me a drink, Dowlah. Nothing serious. The Gurkha will be all right in a day or two. What a striking resemblance they bear to the Japs. Oh, by the way, your *shang-shang* has been celebrating her escape. There are two snake-bite cases, one man, one woman, miles apart, both of 'em bitten in bed on a roof, both paralyzed and speechless—dying, of course—probably dead already. Thirty or forty people swear they have seen the devil and at least one mosque is full of Moslems praying to be

71

saved from it. A police officer saw the thing. He tried to shoot it. He described it as three times the size of a goat, and he's at the club now, getting drunk and rather tired of being laughed at."

"Dr. Lewis, Miss Burbage," said Dowlah.

Lewis ceased looking at her sideways. He stared.

"How d'you do. Are you the lady who befriended a Tibetan named Thö-pa-ga, on the plane from London? He keeps asking for you."

"How is he?"

"Oh, I think he's coming along all right. He should be fit to travel in a few days. If you've time, I wish you'd call and see him. New to India?"

"Yes. My first visit."

"Take care what you eat." Lewis glanced at Tom Grayne.

"Miss Burbage tells me she'll be going to Darjeeling," said Tom.

"Oh. That so? Uh-huh. Well, I'll tell you. Perhaps it would be better, after all, not to call on Thö-pa-ga. Drop me a line instead—to Dr. Morgan Lewis, Edith Cavell Hospital, and let me know when you're off. I'll try to get him off by the same train. I'm sure that any kindness you can show him will be a godsend to him. He's lonely. Not homesick. Quite the reverse. The poor devil doesn't want to go home."

"Glad to do whatever I can," said Elsa.

"Careful what you eat, remember!"

"Thank you for the warning."

"Heart all right? Can you stand high altitudes? Darjeeling, you know, is a great many thousand feet higher than Delhi. How's the blood-pressure? Care to have me test that?"

Tom's fingers moved.

"How awfully kind of you," said Elsa.

"Come into the other room," said Lewis. "It'll only take a minute or two."

Elsa uncurled her legs from the armchair and followed Lewis out into the hall.

"Damn his eyes," said Dowlah. "Taffy was a Welshman, Taffy was a thief, Taffy came to my house and stole a girl from under both our noses! He's a rotten doctor, but he's good at learning more than anybody tells him."

"Rot!" Tom answered. "Pretty decent of him."

"Oh, yes?" Dowlah stared in assumed amazement. "Are you such a cuckoo as all that? Do you think anyone but she and you will give a damn if either of you dies in Tibet?"

Tom didn't answer. He was as curious as Dowlah, at least as curious, to know what Lewis and Elsa were talking about. However, Elsa would tell him soon enough, whereas she wouldn't tell Dowlah. He had the edge on Dowlah.

Dowlah knew it; he finished his drink and poured himself another.

CHAPTER 13

Abdul Mirza's pudgy, but somehow competent-looking fingers were interlocked on his belly. He leaned back in the armchair, looked over the top of his *pince-nez*, coughed to call attention to himself and spoke:

"It is my duty to advise Your Highness. You are what is called a semi-independent ruler. You are now, however, semi- so-to-speak menaced by three antagonistic elements—Tibetan, Japanese, British—to say nothing of the Indian police, who are not students of extenuating circumstances. As Your Highness well knows, the police and the secret intelligence are mutually exclusive, and to each other incomprehensible necessities of state. To be foul of the police is not a signal for help from certain quarters that I need not name. Call that semi-independence, or if it suits you better, call it a dilemma—a predicament—a—"

"You are a sententious mule," Dowlah interrupted. "Cut the prologue."

But Abdul Mirza was not to be hurried. He was conceivably talking for Tom's benefit; else why lecture the *rajah* in Tom's presence? He continued:

"It is true that Your Highness possesses a certain gift for sub-diplomatic, I might say almost subterranean intrigue. But unless the Japanese have changed their character within the last hour or two, they will presently learn that you have double-crossed them. And unless they have changed their religion, they will know what to do about that. Will the British Government protect you? Or will it moralistically make a gesture to the Japanese by strafing you for having done what it knew you were doing and what it secretly but non-committally approved? Answer me that one. As for the Tibetans, there is no need to remind you that the Thunder Dragon Gate is not a source of abstract homiletics. Nobody knows much about it except that it is certainly a source of fanatical ferocity controlled by *Bön*-tutored Tibetan *shamans*, (the oldest extant spiritual tradition of Tibet), who will presently discover it was you who stole their *shang-shang*."

"I will tell them you did that," said Dowlah.

"Then I fervently hope that the indescribable felicity of being Your Highness's prime minister may descend upon more competent shoulders. As for me, I shall learn what eternity is—if it is."

Tom listened, but he was watching the open ventilator. One of the *shang-shang's* green legs kept appearing. Just the tip of it. A spidery web-spinning motion. No sign of a web. Dowlah seemed unaware of it. The prime minister's back was toward it. Perhaps Dowlah had lied about the cowl on the roof being missing. Maybe he knew the monster couldn't possibly escape. Perhaps he knew how to recapture it uninjured. There were some phials of chloroform and cans of ether on the shelf where the cyanide stood; he might intend to try those. The possession of a living *shang-shang* would be worth almost any risk, to a man of Dowlah's temperament.

But didn't it mean that there must be more than one *shang-shang* in Delhi? Otherwise, what about the people who, according to Lewis's account, had been bitten to death? What about the police officer who had seen a *shang-shang* and had tried to shoot it?

Abdul Mirza went on talking like a rather sleepy lecturer to a class of theological students:

"There are reasons beyond reason's comprehension. It is sometimes wise to act unreasonably, simply because all the reasonable actions will be used or foreseen by one's opponent. There isn't any reasonable reason for employing Miss Elsa Burbage. Therefore—"

"*You* didn't think of that," said Dowlah.

Abdul Mirza bowed. "I thank Your Highness for the compliment. You and Mr. Grayne thought of that. I have only called attention to the fact that the thought is irrational and therefore at the moment— ah—"

He perked up suddenly, glanced at Tom and then looked straight at Dowlah. In a surprisingly sharp voice he added:

"Can't you recognise Nemesis? Cover your tracks!"

Dowlah walked out of the room. Tom took the pole and closed the ventilator. Abdul Mirza nodded approval:

"As it happens, quite unnecessary, Mr. Tom Grayne. No one could overhear us through that ventilator."

He polished his *pince-nez* furiously. Tom waited. He noticed he hadn't slammed the ventilator tight enough. The brass latch hadn't caught in the socket.

"Young man, you remind me of a bomb with the fuse ignited. I have seen one. It looked as patiently potent as you. It was dealt with by removing the fuse."

Tom said nothing.

"You are an American citizen?"

"Yes."

"It is known that the United States State Department is very interested in the efforts being made by Japan to get control of China."

"Yes," said Tom. "I've read a lot about that in the daily papers."

"If I thought you were an agent of the United States' secret service, I would trust you more than I could other wise," said Abdul Mirza. His manner more than vaguely suggested a father-confessor explaining the essential difference between cardinal and venial sin. He placed his finger-tips together and continued:

"Not that American secret agents are so specially competent or reliable, but because I should then understand your—ah—real motive. It is men's motives that—ah—govern probable behaviour in—ah—circumstances that demand discretion. There are no witnesses. Tell me."

Tom laughed. "Hell. I know nothing about that. But do you suppose a secret agent would admit he was one? My goal is the Thunder Dragon Gate. I couldn't find it last time. If my efforts this time have any particular value to your intelligence department, hitch your trailer to my tow-bar. Okay with me. I've no secrets."

"But you have a mistress?"

"Me? No. Can't afford it. I have nothing to offer the kind of woman who could interest me. Besides, women have a way of becoming too important. A man can't have his cake and eat it. Liquor, tobacco and women are off the menu."

"Why, then, did Miss Elsa Burbage, tactfully and with charming discretion, but nevertheless plainly admit, this evening at dinner, that her relationship with you is of a special nature?"

"She didn't," Tom answered. "You guessed it—*after* dinner."

"You are very clever with your signals to each other."

Silence from Tom. The ventilator fell forward on its chain, wide open. Four of the *shang-shang's* legs, and then part of its hideous, blind face appeared. It couldn't possibly see, because its eyes were on top of its back. It might be listening, smelling, or using some extra sense that humans can't imagine.

"An intelligent, competent, daring young lady is your Miss Elsa Burbage!" Abdul Mirza was watching Tom's face, but Tom's expression

75

didn't make him glance up at the ventilator. He continued speaking, quite unconscious of the green monster that moved its mandibles beneath a snout like a Tibetan devil's.

"A personage from Tibet, who has been reported to me to be eager to talk with Eiji Sarao, is here in Delhi. It is probable that the personage was concealed, and listened, perhaps even saw Miss Burbage in the back room of a shop to which she was escorted by Eiji Sarao this afternoon."

"He can't have learned much," Tom answered. "He is probably the Number One man from whom Noropa gets his orders."

"Correct. And let us hope that he did not learn too much. He expects Eiji Sarao to tell him more."

The *shang-shang* retreated until only the tip of one leg was visible. Abdul Mirza continued:

"For the moment we have Eiji Sarao—ah—fortunately in disposed. Dr. Lewis gave him a—ah—sedative. Noropa, in another room, has been permitted to believe that Eiji Sarao is dying. Noropa is not afraid of us. He cares nothing for Eiji Sarao. He understands our predicament. He knows it would be inconvenient for us to hand him over to the police. Because such people as Noropa have been trained from early infancy to more than Jesuitical obedience, they dread, beyond anything that you and I can imagine, the anger of their master—the anger of him whom they obey. Do you follow me?"

"Sure. Tell me something I don't know."

"Very well then, Mr. Tom Grayne, your success or failure now depends on our convincing the Number One personage that Miss Elsa Burbage means nothing to you, but that she is indispensable to Thö-pa-ga, who otherwise will rather die than go to Tibet and become the so-called Keeper of the Thunder Dragon Gate." Abdul Mirza looked over the top of his *pince-nez*. "She is not your mistress? Not your wife? Sweetheart?"

"I already told you," Tom answered. "No, she isn't."

"That," Abdul Mirza remarked, "is what I mean by removing the fuse from the bomb."

Tom kept the corner of one eye on the *shang-shang*.

Abdul Mirza insisted: "You assure me she is not your property in any way? Is she free to behave as she pleases?"

"Hell, yes."

"Thö-pa-ga, when he returns to Tibet, will find a woman waiting for him," said Abdul Mirza. "She has been well trained, by *Bön* magi-

76

cians, who are very expert. She is of a tribe whose women have been accustomed for many centuries to discipline a number of husbands. Polyandry. The reverse of polygamy. Dual moral code reversed and votes for men unthinkable. The inferiority of the male so well established that the women beat their husbands. The women are the sorcerers and priestesses. This one is to control Thö-pa-ga. The magicians control her. Japan proposes to control them."

"Yes? Well?"

"Eiji Sarao, when the effect of the—ah—sedative wears off, may suspect that the Japanese secret service has—ah—overestimated the—ah—affection of Rajah Dowlah. But—Dr. Lewis has ordered Eiji Sarao kept quiet. We can provide for him, I assure you, a more than monastic retreat. It will—ah—as we will explain to him—preserve him from the—ah—undiplomatic attentions of the police who will wish to know more about some poisoned chewing-gum. Having made an unprovoked attack upon a guest in Rajah Dowlah's house, he is, moreover, in no position to make any protest that would cause police investigation."

Tom nodded. "Sure thing. He'd be canned by his own people, right off the bat."

"Very well then, Mr. Tom Grayne, someone has made the bright suggestion that if Miss Burbage should—from—ah—sheer young feminine excitement—compromise herself a bit with Thö-pa-ga, something might come of it."

"For instance?"

"She might be believed, if she should carry a secret message from Eiji Sarao."

"To whom?"

"To the Number One man."

"Better fetch her in and ask her."

"She has gone already."

"Alone?"

"No. Noropa took her."

Tom didn't have to restrain his voice or control his eyes. The *shang-shang* gave him all the excuse he needed for using words like punches:

"Don't move suddenly! You hear me? Get out of your chair quietly and pussy-foot for the door! The *shang-shang's* coming down the wall!"

"Oh, *Allah!*"

"I said, move slowly!"

The prime minister's slippers were off. He held his breath and tiptoed barefoot, with his hands high, like a man balancing himself along a wall. Tom picked up one of the slippers. He hurled it and hit the *shang-shang* at the same moment that Abdul Mirza jumped out of the room and slammed the door behind him. The slipper fell to the floor.

The *shang-shang* spread out like a huge green crab, shot down the wall—pounced on the slipper—bit it—worried it— carried it— dropped it and fled to the end of the room. It made no sound. Midway up the end wall it spread itself again and crouched, dancing a little, like a livid green octopus, staring with huge opal eyes. Its mandibles moved continually. It was head downward, if that sickening blind mask was its head.

Tom reached for the window-pole. He put the hook into the slipper and drew it toward him. It had been torn by the *shang-shang's* jaws. There was slimy liquid on it. There was just one chance that the brute had spilled all her poison—might want to creep away like a teased snake, and hide, and brew more. Pretty slim chance, that. But he had to do something. The monster was watching him. It wouldn't stay long where it was. No use trying to hit it with a bottle or with Noropa's knife; its eyes were on top; it could see a missile coming. Safer to try to catch the damned thing.

He went and opened the glass cage, the one by the mirror. Keeping an eye on the *shang-shang*, he covered the cage with the shawl to make it look like a nice dark hiding-place. The cord that passed through a pulley to hold the lid open was a long one. Taking care to keep the poison off his fingers he tied the free end of the cord to the slipper. It was a fool's chance, but it might work. Probably the *shang-shang* hadn't any brains to speak of. Probably, as Dowlah had said, it always did the same thing in the same way. Question was, what would it do? Which same thing? Perhaps its habit was to spring at people. It could jump like a flash of green light, without apparent effort. No use waiting for it to do that.

Tom threw the slipper on the end of the cord as far as it would reach. It fell about five feet away from the wall, directly underneath the *shang-shang*. The brute didn't move. Probably hadn't seen the slipper coming. Eyes on top, like a spider's that can't see a marauding wasp until it's close enough for a fight to the death. The worst part of the brute was its silence—that and its moving mandibles that seemed to be stuffing invisible food into its blind face. It pulsed on the tips of its long legs as if pruning itself for a spring off the wall.

Tom drew the slipper along the floor, slowly, in short jerks. Still the *shang-shang* didn't move. He put the slipper into the cage and untied it, taking care to leave a scent up the side of the cage. Then he picked up the other slipper. Someone tried the doorknob. Dowlah's voice:

"Grayne, are you in there? Are you all right?"

"Yes. Dammit, keep out!"

Tom turned the key in the door and hurled the slipper. It hit the wall hard, about two feet higher up than the *shang-shang*. The monster saw that one—saw it coming—wasn't there when it hit—dodged, as quick as light, toward the corner. Even so, it reached the floor before the slipper did. It climbed the table, crawled along it. Suddenly it seemed to go mad. It danced on the table-top. It knocked over an electric lamp. Then it got under the table and hung head-downward.

That was a chance. Heavy drapes, then chloroform. Tom reached for a drape. As if the *shang-shang* knew what he intended, it crept out on the far side of the table, four legs on top, four underneath, mandible-end upward—angry. Tom picked up a book and threw that. The brute saw it coming and leaped to the floor, exactly on the trail of the slipper. It had followed the trail and was into the cage in less than the time between two heartbeats. It savaged the slipper instantly. The lid thudded shut. Tom went and shot the brass bolts home. Then he arranged the covering shawl neatly, shoved one hand in his pocket and went and opened the door.

Dowlah stared at him: "The *shang-shang*?"

"In the cage. Where's Elsa?"

"Elsa Burbage? What do you care?" Dowlah answered. "For the *shang-shang*, I congratulate you in the name of Science, my immortal mistress." He went and peeped into the cage. "You pretty, precious pussy! Tweet-tweet!"

CHAPTER 14

Dowlah went and picked up the lamp that the *shang-shang* had knocked over. He rearranged a number of other objects, lit a cigarette and smiled reflectively.

"You are a wonderful fellow," he remarked. "I believe I'd trust you if I held a pledge from you of some sort."

"No witnesses," said Tom. "It's getting late. Talk turkey."

Dowlah took a mock-poetic pose.

"Science!" he remarked. "My immortal mistress Science! My only love! My muse! She takes nothing for granted—searches all things; questions all things. Each of us is a potential danger to all the others. One little blunder, and whoopsy-daisy!—all sorts of plain and fancy combustibles—two or three million volts of malice—a short circuit—whoopee! Whoever caused the short circuit would burn, and bad luck to him! But then what? When the moralists discover what their governments are doing, governments have to go to war to prove how virtuous they are. Tell me now: what have you discovered so far?"

"That you're afraid," Tom answered.

Dowlah giggled, like a woman being tempted to betray her something less than irreproachable virtue.

"Do be seated, Grayne. Standing, you give me an inferiority complex. That's better. Have you ever considered the appalling fact, that of a thousand volunteers for secret sub-diplomacy, very rarely one is found fit for the work?"

"No," Tom answered. "Sub-diplomats don't come applying to me for a job."

"Of any thousand," said Dowlah, "twenty-five may be fit for policemen; fit for regular routine duty subject to the rules. One or two if competently handled may be fit for rather ticklish situations; such men as Eiji Sarao, for in stance—not really clever. Seldom one, and never more than one, in any thousand who begin by being spies, is fit to be trusted to understand what he's doing. How long have you been in the secret service?"

"Never was," said Tom. "My subject's Tibet."

"Would you care to come with me to Tibet?"

"If I thought you were really going there," said Tom, "I'd think that over."

"Well, if I were really going, I might make you an offer. You speak Tibetan?"

"Fat chance I should have in Tibet, if I couldn't."

"What strange things men study!" Dowlah remarked. "Except for my scientific researches, which I am frequently assured are puerile and undisciplined, I have studied very little. I was sent to the usual school for princes' sons. We were taught the three princely virtues: mediocrity, hypocrisy and cricket. I was good at the first two. Common sense was an extra, but nobody took that. Tibetan was not in the curriculum."

He glanced at the *shang-shang* cage, got up and crossed the room to change the angle of an electric-fan, so that it would blow on the cage and cool the monster inside it. When he sat down again he glanced at the shelves of books, as if wondering what to say next.

"Well, goodnight," said Tom. "I see we're getting nowhere. I'll go to the hotel and turn in."

Dowlah betrayed an almost imperceptible flutter of annoyance.

"No, don't go yet. I expect an interesting visitor."

"At this hour?"

"Time means nothing to him. Did you ever hear of the Most Reverend and Holy Lobsang Pun?"

Tom almost betrayed excitement. "No," he answered.

"He is the Tashi Lama's confidential representative."

Dowlah was watching Tom's face, but apparently he detected nothing to suggest that Tom was more than politely interested.

"Lobsang Pun," he continued, "is probably in Delhi to persuade our government to help the Tashi Lama to return to Tibet. Since the Dalai Lama died in Lhasa there's been a slowly developing chance for the Tashi Lama to return and seize control."

Dowlah appeared to be talking to kill time. He looked as if he were thinking of something else while he made conversation.

"Strange system of government, isn't it," he continued. "But it couldn't be worse than ours, so perhaps it's better. Dalai Lama in Lhasa, in charge of civil affairs. Tashi Lama, at Tashi-lunpo, in charge of spiritual law and order. Theoretically equals. Both of 'em moralists. Actually as chummy as a couple of bobcats in a cage with one bird between 'em."

"That's the fault of their subordinates," said Tom. "As a general rule, it isn't the men at the top who make trouble. It's the men who want to be on top."

Dowlah nodded. "Yes," he said, "the man who wants to see his master cock of all the dunghills is a menace. And what a way to choose a successor when one of 'em dies! I daresay it's as good as our way, if you don't mind poison as a political argument. It's logical enough to have the Tashi Lama superintend the selection of a dead Dalai Lama's successor—and the Dalai Lama, in turn, do the same thing when a Tashi Lama dies. But what actually happens? A committee gets itself appointed to go hunting, at public expense, all over Tibet, for a child who was born at the hour of the late lamented ruler's death. Eventually they find one with certain birth-marks. Those and his horoscope are supposed to prove he's a reincarnation of the deceased. That's as good as any plebiscite. Perhaps it's better. But again, what happens? A Council of Regents gets itself appointed to educate the child, and to govern in the child's name, until his eighteenth year.

"So, if they poison him before he's eighteen, that gives 'em another eighteen years of power. And, of course, the followers of the surviving Lama scheme like devils to control the Board of Regents. Lobsang Pun would like that job. You know, they haven't chosen the child yet. They said they had. The political gang in Lhasa tried to rush proceedings before the Tashi Lama could return from exile. But he started from Peking the moment he heard the news. He made a prodigious forced march to the Tibetan border. Some say he used a Chinese airplane. Some say camels. Anyhow, there he is, on the eastern border of Tibet. They won't let him enter Tibet, but without him they can't legally select a new Dalai Lama. Stalemate, unless Lobsang Pun can move a hidden piece or two."

"Do you know him well?" Tom asked.

Dowlah avoided the question. "Lobsang Pun," he said, "is a picturesque prelate with a string of astonishing titles half a yard long. He has a reputation for severity. No vices. He imposes floggings on sinners who use tobacco, and on ladies who are scandalously indiscreet. He has traveled—widely. And he has been through the Tibetan self-denial mill—frightful austerities—said to have lived somewhere near Mt. Everest, at an altitude of seventeen thousand feet or so, immured in a cave, naked in all weathers and fed on five grains of parched barley a day—for two years—until he was sent for by the Tashi Lama. Some say he did it to convince the Tashi Lama of his iron will. Those fellows believe in more than theory. They like their secret diplomatic agents to be practically tested first, before they trust them. Even so, they sometimes pick a wrong 'un. Lobsang Pun is as right as a *shang-shang*, if you get my meaning. When he comes, don't talk Tibetan."

Tom's eyes smiled. Dowlah noticed it.

"Lobsang Pun knows English none too perfectly. Stick to English and perhaps he'll slip up."

"All right."

"Have a drink on that," said Dowlah.

"No thanks."

They were silent for several minutes before a knock at the door announced the visitor. Abdul Mirza bowed him alone into the room, said nothing, retired and closed the door. Dowlah got up and stood with his back to the *shang-shang* cage. Tom stood, smiling. All three bowed simultaneously. The Most Reverend and Holy Lama Lobsang Pun murmured his blessing.

He was even more astonishing than when Tom last saw him. He had been fat then, but he had grown fatter. If he was recently from Tibet, it was amazing that he shouldn't have lost weight on the exhausting journey. A big drum belly bulged above his girdle. An unruly thatch of black hair. A black *toga*. Black robe. A jade rosary, each bead carved to resemble a human skull. A nose like an owl's beak, protruding between cheeks that looked as if he were puffing them out on purpose. High cheek-bones. Twinkling, deep-sunk, humorous, malicious black eyes. Pretty nearly six feet of him.

He didn't appear to suffer from the heat. If it was true that he had once lived immured in a cave near Mt. Everest (and it might be true), then perhaps, too, he had partly learned the hermits' mysterious art of enduring extremes of temperature. He had certainly recovered from the effects of the alleged diet of five grains of barley a day.

He had a grand voice. He and Dowlah, going through the ritual of polite question and answer about each other's health, sounded like priest and acolyte intoning a litany. Not a phrase was omitted, to the last, almost physically embracing:

"Your Highness's happiness?"

And Dowlah's: "That is crowned and rendered deathless by Your Eminence's visit."

During the entire ritual Lobsang Pun was watching Tom's face in the mirror behind Dowlah. He chose a chair from which he could continue that espionage. But he pretended not to recognise Tom until the Rajah formally introduced him. Tom winked.

Instantly, the *lama's* features broke into an ivory-leathery torment of grinning wrinkles. He opened a mouth from which half the teeth were missing and roared with laughter that shook his big belly. He seized Tom's hands and shook them as if they were prayer pumps.

"Tum-Glain! Tum-Glain! Oo-ha-ha-hah!—Player efficacious! 'Leven hunderd monks all playing that the snow not overtaking you! I ordering it. Oo-ha-ha-hah!"

Tom returned the laugh. It was a thoroughly Tibetan joke.

"Your Eminence's confidence in prayer almost persuades me to become a Tantric Buddhist! You expelled me, as I don't doubt you remember, just a few days ahead of the winter blizzards. At the time I thought you cruel—even homicidal, but I see I was mistaken."

"Oo-ha-ha-ha-hah!"

83

The Most Reverend and Holy Lobsang Pun hadn't had such a laugh since the news of the late lamented Dalai Lama's death. Even so, there was a hint of gales of laughter in reserve. He might be saving those for the day when the Tashi Lama should return across the border and become the ruler of Tibet without any rival at all.

He let go Tom's hands at last and leaned back in the chair, studying him intently, lowering his eyebrows, pouting judicious lips.

Dowlah watched both of them, visibly puzzled. He appeared slightly nervous. He interrupted the tense silence:

"Somebody has told His Eminence that you, Tom Grayne, were Thö-pa-ga's protector in London. That your influence in certain quarters preserved Thö-pa-ga from prison. That at great self-sacrifice you brought him to India, neglecting your own interests. And that here in Delhi you lodged him in a safe place where his enemies couldn't get at him. Is that an exaggeration?"

"It is," Tom answered. "His Eminence is a man of vast experience. He'll believe we're lying to him if we yes each other."

"Oo-ha-ha-ha-hah! Thö-pa-ga having many enemies," said Lobsang Pun. "You his friend, you Tum-Glain?"

"I don't think he trusts me."

Suddenly again the *lama* burst into roars of laughter.

"Player efficacious. Oh, yes! Ah-ha-ha!"

He nodded to Dowlah. Enough. The interview was at an end. He was used to terminating interviews. He scrooged himself up from the armchair, became solemn, flicked like lightning about twenty or thirty beads of his rosary, bestowed his blessing and began to stride toward the door—long strides, taken slowly, to permit the proper courteous expressions of regret that he should take away the splendour of his presence.

Dowlah followed him into the hall, shutting the library door with a slam that flatly told Tom to remain in the room. There was quite a bit of noise in the hall, but through the thick door it was impossible to guess what caused it. It might be the commotion of departing guests. All was quiet when Dowlah returned after fifteen or twenty minutes. He looked excited.

"That's the Number One man," he remarked. "That's the fellow who showed the Japanese what they can do in Tibet. Money couldn't buy him. But a chance to make his nominal master, the Tashi Lama, sole ruler of Tibet would justify him, in his own opinion, for setting all the nations of the world at one another's throats. He would know how to go about it, too, the old devil. I like him, and I wish he liked me. Grayne, you surprised me. You lied with artistic calm. I didn't guess you knew him. You behaved a lot better than I'd have done. By God, if he had ever kicked me out to perish in the snow, and had the impudence to pray for me on top of that, I'd have shown some resentment. However, it's too late to discuss that. I won't detain you any longer."

He paused. He gave Tom a chance to question him. He went and poured himself another drink. He needed one, to judge by the way he swallowed it. Tom stood waiting, silent.

"Damn you," Dowlah said at last, "you're tough. Why don't you ask about Elsa Burbage?"

Tom laughed: "You're responsible. She's your guest."

"I perceive you're a sensible man," said Dowlah. "Nowadays it's no one's business what a young woman is doing at 4 a.m."

"As late as that, is it?"

"Yes. Lewis doesn't usually turn up at the hospital much before nine in the morning. But the doctor who should be on duty was taken ill, so Lewis is on the job. You'll find a taxi at the front gate."

"Okay. Goodnight."

"Don't tell Lewis anything. Let him tell you."

Dowlah poured himself another drink.

A dark-skinned, bearded servant, whom Tom hadn't seen before, accompanied him to the front gate. There was a decrepit taxi waiting there. Its driver was a Sikh, three good sheets to the wind and sleepy. He didn't know how to find the hospital. So it was nearly 5 a.m. when Tom walked into Lewis's office and found him irritably adjusting an electric light for the microscope on his desk. Lewis looked tired out and bad tempered. On the desk was Elsa's small white hand kerchief embroidered with a blue goose on the wing—one of a dozen that Tom had bought for her in London from a man who had no legs and did that kind of thing for a living. There was no possibility of it not being her handkerchief. Lewis slipped it into a drawer, after he was sure Tom had seen it.

"Is she here in the hospital?" Tom asked.

"No, she isn't."

"Let me see that."

Lewis took it out of the drawer and laid it on the desk, blue goose upward. Tom took it, sniffed it, eyed it, stuffed it into his pocket.

"Meaning?" Lewis asked him.

"Nothing. How is Thö-pa-ga?"

"Gone," said Lewis. "Damn your chewing-gum. It kills rats. But it isn't a metallic poison, and it doesn't show colour. It may take me two or three days to analyse it."

"Uh-huh? Gone since when?"

"Half an hour ago."

"With your permission?"

"Didn't need it," said Lewis. "No law against his going. I was operating—emergency accident case. Elsa Burbage came in a closed carriage and took him away. I was told about it through the slide in the door of the operating room. I couldn't leave what I was doing—bad case of haemorrhage."

"Gone where?"

"God knows. Haven't you any notion where she'd head for?"

The phone rang. Lewis answered it with a smile of contemptuous reserve.

"No," he said over the phone. "No. There isn't a snake in the world that makes an incision an inch long or an inch deep. No. Snake venom doesn't ever do that to the victim's liver."

He hung up. He caught Tom studying the handkerchief again. In the corner below the blue goose was a small square marked with lipstick. It meant that Elsa was all right and that she knew what to do next.

But beneath that, done in eyebrow pencil was a broad-arrow mark, so small that it only covered about ten threads. That meant:

Beware of—

In the opposite corner, also done with eyebrow pencil, was a row of short upright lines in groups, with lipstick dots between to separate them.

||||·|||||||||||||||||·|||||||||||||||||||||||||||·||||||
|||||·|·|||||||||

He counted them, using the light from Lewis's microscope:

4.15.23.12.1.8.
D. O. W. L. A. H.

He nodded to Lewis. "Thanks," he said. "I get you."

CHAPTER 15

There was a railway timetable on Lewis's desk. Lewis drew attention to it by picking it up and tossing it down again. That looked like a pretty straight hint.

"That blasted *shang-shang*," he remarked, "has left a trail all over Delhi. Some of my *confrères* are deducing, from the shape of its bite, that a new sort of human Jack the Ripper is at large."

"Maybe there's a pack of 'em loose and lighting for home," Tom suggested.

Lewis seemed to wish to know nothing about it. He shook his head.

"If it weren't for an efficient censorship," he said, "there'd be a thousand of them in the morning paper, plus a score of Tibetans escaped from the observation ward! I shall have to report this poisoned chewing-gum to the police. If you're in Delhi, they'll interrogate you."

Tom smiled. Lewis didn't. He looked worried.

"Goodbye," said Tom.

"Goodbye. Take care of yourself."

"Thanks for your hospitality."

Lewis merely stared. Tom held out his hand. Lewis shook it. Tom walked out.

He refused the first and second taxi that offered themselves, got into the third one, drove around a bit to make sure he wasn't being followed and then went to the hotel. The door porter was asleep. So was the clerk behind the desk. He was only seen by a nondescript sweeper, who was at no pains to pretend not to notice him and therefore probably wasn't a spy.

He bathed and packed the little zipper suitcase that contained all his belongings. It had been searched in his absence; even his socks had been unfolded and refolded differently. The stitching of the case had been unpicked at one corner and something—probably a sliver of split bamboo—had been inserted between the lining and the leather. However, that might not mean much. It might have been done to find out whether he was the sort of idiot who carries codes or any other important information in a zipper suitcase. Or one of Eiji Sarao's agents might have done it. If so, he hadn't learned much.

Tom awoke the desk clerk, paid his bill and left no forwarding address. He carried his own bag to a taxi, pitched it in and told the man to drive around the corner and wait for him there. Then he walked in the opposite direction around the block. All sorts of people up at daybreak on all sorts of business. A strong smell of streets being cleaned and watered. Nobody seemed interested in his movements. He drove to the station, fairly sure he hadn't been observed or followed.

Typical Indian railway-station crowd. Usual din. Usual smelly droves of natives who had slept on the platform all night for fear of losing the morning train, or perhaps to save money. Notice board. No need to ask questions. Express train at 8 a.m. making connections for Darjeeling. Ticket. Reservation—lucky he was early—good seat and no trouble at all—didn't even have to bribe the reservation clerk. Corner table in the restaurant, with a full view of door and windows. Strong tea and boiled eggs—the best pick-me-up in the world after a sleepless night. Into a corner seat, in a front-end compartment, with a good view of the entire length of the platform, half an hour before starting time. A bit heavy-eyed now, but alert. No Elsa. No one who looked even remotely like her.

She should be headed for Darjeeling. This was the first train she could have caught. True, Eiji Sarao had stolen the letter that instructed her to do that. But Tom had signalled the message to her in Dowlah's library when he recovered the letter from Eiji Sarao's pockets. Eiji Sarao might already have had it copied, but it wasn't likely that anyone could break that code, without almost incredible luck, short of a couple of weeks of hard work. The code was based on an almost unknown Tibetan poem. Names of people and places would be particularly baffling for a code-breaker, however expert, because each syllable referred to a different syllable in a different Tibetan word.

So it was at least a million to one that no one had under stood the message in time to prevent Elsa from taking Thö-pa-ga to Darjeeling. According to Lewis, Elsa had taken Thö-pa-ga away in a carriage. Whose carriage? Five minutes to go. No sign of Elsa.

Four minutes before starting time came Nancy Strong, in a plain print frock, walking down the platform like a teacher on her way to school, making no fuss, followed by a string of porters who also made no fuss because they knew they would get exactly what was coming to them, neither more nor less. Nancy Strong got into a compartment midway down the train.

Two minutes to go. The train already crowded, and no one yet but Nancy Strong whom Tom even knew by sight. Then suddenly, in a hurry, Abdul Mirza, in a turban and gray alpaca frock-coat. Six servants, all running and making a fuss. Ten or twelve porters. Two long strings of jasmine buds looped over Abdul Mirza's shoulders. One servant with a whole basket full of books and magazines. The end of

Abdul Mirza's turban unavailingly employed to hide part of his face. No platform farewells—into the train like a shot, midway between Nancy Strong's and Tom's compartment, and more than sixty seconds to spare. Why the hurry? About two compartments-full of turbaned secretaries—people of that type anyhow—scrambled into the train after him in such a hysterical hurry that Tom couldn't even count them. They were either six or seven, all in one another's way.

Three last-minute passengers—running—porters ahead and following. Conductor's whistle. Engine whistle. And away—out into fierce white sunshine. No Thö-pa-ga. No Elsa.

Swell train. All the fancy novelties—cool air—ice water— glare-proof glass—a better dining-car than any pre-war king ever had—lots too many men to ask if you needed anything. White man's burden hell, it was a white man's shocking waste of other people's money, grudgingly, not too politely shared with the duskier gentry who were taxed to pay for the extravagance.

That wouldn't do. Thinking that kind of tripe is what keeps a fellow from minding his own business. No risk of being murdered on the train in daylight. Tom leaned back and was fast asleep in less than two minutes.

It was several hours before he awoke and strolled along the corridor. The door of Abdul Mirza's compartment was closed and the curtains down. Further down the train Nancy Strong sat by the open door of a compartment that contained three other people. One was an Indian lady who couldn't endure life very well with her feet on the floor. Nancy Strong had made room for her to get her feet up and looked as if she wished she hadn't. She nodded to Tom, got up and followed him into the corridor.

"What are you looking peaked about, Mr. Grayne?"

"Am I?"

"How is your sick friend?"

"Which one?"

"The other. Not the one who wanted chewing-gum."

"I don't know."

A train corridor is a perfectly safe place for confidences. Two in conversation can look both ways. They can't be overheard above the noise of the train, unless they have screech-owl tourists' voices. Nancy Strong—graying, forty-five or fifty years old, humorous, was inviting confidence. Her experienced, sensible eyes conveyed that information without a word said. But Tom's eyes were as intelligible as hers. She understood—laughed:

"What a job your mother must have had! Excuse me, won't you. My business in life is getting suspicious youngsters to tell me their troubles."

"Do I look suspicious?"

"No, of course not. And you're not exactly a youngster. But you wouldn't tell me anything I don't know, would you?"

"Probably I don't know anything you don't know," Tom answered.

"Now, now. I didn't mean to insult you. Our mutual acquaintance spoke of you, over the phone, with such terse approval that I'm more than curious."

"So am I," said Tom. "I listen like a hole in the ground."

"My informant said something about a girl."

Tom froze.

Matter-of-factly, Nancy Strong applied the necessary heat to thaw him.

"India is a wonderful country for a girl who isn't cursed with too good looks, or too much money, or too many brains. She can find a satisfactory husband in almost any place she visits, if she is properly introduced. But without the proper introduction, India is almost the worst country to come to. And for a girl who hasn't introductions, but who has more than normal intelligence, it's the most dangerous country on earth."

"Why do you say that?"

"Because I know it. A really bright girl's curiosity will lead her into danger that she hasn't the experience to deal with. At the same time, it will keep her away from the good, kind, stupid people who don't ever know that such dangers exist, because their lives are too humdrum."

"Your life humdrum?" Tom asked.

"I am neither good, kind nor stupid," she answered. "If I were good, those little devils of Hill children wouldn't like me. If I were kind, the Almighty would give me a villa at Nice, with nothing more cruel to do than cut the flowers in the garden. And if I were stupid, I shouldn't be talking to you."

"I'm all alone, up forward," said Tom.

"Very well."

They went and sat facing each other in Tom's compartment, silent for about five minutes, just as if they were old friends, with the wheels beneath them thumping a monotonous refrain that suggested, as train wheels always do suggest, that life rolls onward as a river, torn by the rocks that it leaves behind, and healed by distance. Tom spoke first:

"So they've passed the ball to you, have they?"

"No," she said. "I think it's your ball. But I can tell you what no one else will. I am unofficial. Nothing whatever that I say has the slightest authority. I'm a gossip. If you should quote me, you would be quoting a garrulous, middle-aged spinster who was a victim of her own romantic imagination."

"Shoot," said Tom. "I get you."

"Don't shoot me, if I say a few things that you won't like."

"Say what you please," he answered. "I'll listen. I won't quote you. I won't ask questions. But I won't answer 'em either, unless I see fit."

She nodded. "Yes, I think we understand each other. Well, by way of gossip, I learned of your bringing Thö-pa-ga to India. Curiously enough, my advice was asked about it. I suggested Mu-ni Gam-po in Darjeeling. My advice was asked because it happens that Thö-pa-ga was lodged in my house in Darjeeling for several weeks, some years ago, when he was on his way to Oxford for an English education. Would you believe I have lived in Tibet?"

Tom stared. "Tell what you care to," he said. "I won't ask."

"And you won't quote me?"

"All right. No. I promise."

He was studying her skin. Any woman nowadays can buy almost any complexion except the kind you have to go and fight for on frozen and dust-laden *plateaux*, sixteen thousand feet or so above sea level. He had noticed it when he first met her. Funny he hadn't recognised it. Reasonable, though. In all history there haven't been half a dozen white women in Tibet.

"Thö-pa-ga," she said, "was a rather precocious boy suffering from a severe case of persecution complex. Has he recovered from it?"

"Not to speak of. He's as superstitious as a Kokonor yak-herd. But they gave him a B.A. degree at Oxford."

"He was very suspicious of me," said Nancy Strong. "To ease his homesickness I had made the mistake of talking only Tibetan to him. The poor young persecuted runaway—for that is what he actually was—associated me, because I was a woman speaking Tibetan, with a woman they were going to make him marry if they could ever force him to return. At the end of four weeks, when at last I understood that, I began to disillusion him about me. But by the time I had found the one femininely friendly angle from which he could be reached,

91

the money had come and he had to resume his journey toward Europe."

She paused, but Tom made no comment. So she shot a question at him:

"Have you brought Miss Burbage with you to exploit that femininely friendly angle?"

Tom wasn't to be caught off-guard as easily as that. He answered matter of factly:

"So far as I know, they met for the first time on the plane from London to Karachi. Thö-pa-ga appears to like her."

"Does she like him?"

"Honest to God, I don't know," he answered.

"But she loves you?"

"What makes you ask that?"

"Never mind why I ask. Tell me."

"How should I know? Why should she? Elsa Burbage is a girl with unusual gifts, who has had a very unusual education and opportunities. So far as I know, she is not in love with anyone."

"But you love her?"

"Never been in love in my life," Tom answered. "Don't know what it feels like."

"Well, of course, you realize, don't you, that such a person as you are, can't bring an unusual girl to India without arousing comment."

"I had hoped to escape that," said Tom.

Nancy Strong smiled. "Mr. Grayne, one of the funniest things in life is the occasional disingenuousness of otherwise hard-headed, intelligent men! Did you really think she wouldn't be checked back to the day of her birth? How much money do you suppose the Indian Government spends in a month on cables, just for a *leetle* more information than is written on the face of a passport? Even I, a mere gossip, know this much: Elsa Burbage is a niece of Dr. Clarence Mayor of the British Museum, where she has had the run of the oriental department. Her father, Colonel of a Fusilier regiment, was killed in action in 1917. Her mother, an ex-actress of considerable reputation in her day, died in 1929, of heart-failure following an attempt to climb the Matterhorn. Elsa Burbage has an inherited income of eight hundred pounds a year; an honour degree from London University; a junior teacher's certificate for oriental languages and oriental art; a good seat in a saddle; a little house in Dorking rented to a friend; dark hair; very beautiful eyes; a slightly pert nose; a ready laugh; a quiet conversational voice; and she sings high soprano. I have never seen her, and never heard of her until yesterday. Now what?"

"You tell me," Tom answered.

"I intend to tell you."

"Let me order tea first. Fruit—crackers—jam? I'll have some with you."

He rang the service bell. He needed an interruption. So far as he knew, he hadn't betrayed what he felt. But he was feeling rather as if someone had suddenly punched him in the wind.

He gave the order to the waiter.

"So they know all that, do they?" he asked when the waiter had gone.

"They know a lot more than that," said Nancy Strong.

CHAPTER 16

"I am going to Dutch aunt you," Nancy Strong resumed when the waiter had removed the tea things.

"Very well. I'll play Dutch nephew."

"You're a man in a million, Mr. Grayne, or you wouldn't be secretly approved by certain people who can't afford to make mistakes."

Tom smiled. "That's the formula. Praise 'em and then swat 'em! I can take it."

"But there isn't a known exception, is there, to the rule that geniuses all have blind arcs, which cause them to behave like lunatics, or savages, or children? A genius is never stupid in his own field. But there is always a zone where his genius, with its natural self-confidence, invades what is to him a no-man's land. For instance, a poet will try farming. That is an extreme instance. Virgil and Horace did it. Horace's farm was stocked chiefly with wine and women. Virgil tells us, in beautiful language, how the bees get honey from carrion. They were both good poets. Bad farmers. Aren't you trying to make a steel tool out of honey?"

Tom rested his jaw on a fist whose sinews resembled moulded bronze. He didn't answer. He wasn't going to until he knew the answer.

Nancy Strong continued: "No one but a genius would ever have thought of employing a twenty-three-year-old girl as a secret accomplice on such an expedition as yours. It bears the genius-stamp of unexpectedness. Elsa Burbage must be a very competent girl, or you would never have considered her. She may be old enough. I was twen-

93

ty-four when I went to Tibet. If I could stand the conditions, probably she can. I lived there, secretly—and it's still a rather close secret—as the mistress of a Tibetan nobleman. His wealth has supported my school in Darjeeling for the past twenty-one years."

That was a staggerer. And yet, come to think of it, it wasn't. Nancy Strong had obviously said yes to experience. Her eyes said it. She had made the yes good. She had side-stepped nothing that could be tackled, and licked, and turned to account.

"Is he still living?" Tom asked, searching memory of people he had known in Tibet. She might be giving him an important clue.

She ignored the question.

"So I know what I'm talking about, Mr. Grayne, when I say that Elsa Burbage isn't in safe hands."

"How d'you mean—safe?"

"I mean you."

"She's in no kind of danger from me," Tom answered.

"That, Mr. Grayne, is what I daresay you believe. Iron-man though you probably are, if you were secretly in love with her, you couldn't possibly keep your secret in the face of what she will almost certainly experience. That is why I asked whether you are in love with each other. Would you care to know why I left Tibet?"

"If you choose to tell. I won't quote you."

"Because my nobleman, who was in love with me, couldn't endure the indignities from which even he couldn't protect me. There were Chinese *ambans* in Tibet in my day. Their malice was almost incredibly ingenious."

Tom wanted to ask her whether she loved her nobleman. She knew he wanted to. She paused long enough to let him ask. But he could see in her eyes the iron answer ready. No sense in inviting a snub.

She continued: "It is quite agreeable to you to be made use of by men who treat you as they would a weapon. They try you out, then use you, and you ask nothing better. You don't expect to be rescued if you get into trouble. Your value is that you're competent and silent. Their value to you is that they can let you do what you couldn't without their leave and, at least to some extent, without their secret help. They wouldn't turn you loose if they thought you might get into trouble for sentimental reasons. They wouldn't risk using that kind of weapon. But is she a weapon such as you are?"

"Intelligence branch becoming sentimental?" Tom asked.

"No. Don't be silly. And don't try to make me think you're not feel-

94

ing a twinge of guilt. I am watching your eyes. Are you her friend?"

"I like her first rate."

"Somebody told me that a hospital nurse has reported that Thö-pa-ga talks, even in his sleep, of Elsa Burbage. That may be a slight exaggeration. But it seems to be a fact that she has his confidence. I gathered there must be a very good reason for wanting Thö-pa-ga to confide in someone.

I have been asked to find out whether Elsa Burbage has in her the necessary steel to make it possible for her to go through with what perhaps may happen."

"Then you know where she is?"

"No, I don't."

Tom scowled. But he detected the ghost of an observant smile, so he straightened out the frown. Nancy Strong continued:

"The men with whom you are dealing wouldn't send one of their own daughters on such an errand as you're letting Elsa Burbage undertake. In a way they resemble surgeons. Their sentiment ends where the operation begins. They trust nobody—not even one another. They can't. They mustn't. They must find out, but they must never be found out. They send a man or a woman into danger or worse as ruthlessly, and with as little compunction as a general who sends a platoon by night to a position from which he knows they can't return alive. There are all sorts of problems. They can use all kinds of women, from a Mata Hari to an Edith Cavell, each in her own field.",

Tom smiled reproachfully. "I said I'd listen. But—well, never mind, we've lots of time. Go ahead."

"Yes," she said, "I know you know all that. But you haven't thought what it probably means for Elsa Burbage. A woman, Mr. Grayne, who doesn't adventure off the beaten path is entitled to and usually gets conventionally humane and sometimes chivalrous treatment, even nowadays. But the minute she consciously oversteps the line, she has forfeited her feminine rights and privileges. She is no more entitled then to chivalrous consideration than, for instance, you are. No part of her is any longer sacred. She becomes a weapon. And a weapon that breaks, misfires, becomes rusty, or useless for any other reason, is simply thrown away."

"What do you propose to do about it?" Tom asked.

"Nothing. I was asked to study and report, not to interfere or advise. But I was also asked to get in touch with you."

"And to report on me, too?"

"Are you angry?"

"If I were, I wouldn't let you know it."

"Will you play fair?"

"Now what?"

"I have told you an intimate personal secret. Don't you think it would be fair play to do me a very personal favour in return?"

"Say what you mean."

"Send Elsa Burbage home to England!"

"Uh-huh. So, if you okay her, she may go to Tibet, but you don't want the responsibility? Is that the idea?"

"You said you wouldn't ask questions. Send her home, Mr. Grayne."

"What makes you think she'd obey me? Do you think I would have any use for a girl who would scram because someone had told me that someone else said she was soft?"

"Very well. Will you try to persuade her to go home?"

"Because you told me your secret? Are the cases parallel?"

"If you know India, and the Hills, and Tibet, then you know I'm right. If you don't know what I mean, then you had no right to bring a young girl to India."

Tom conceded a point. "Well, you did lay your bet on the board, I admit. Okay, I will put it up to her. But I don't guarantee the result."

"Thank you. I believe you will keep your promise." Suddenly she laughed. "But it's a good example of why the individuals of whom we were speaking mustn't trust each other. I had absolutely no right to exact that promise. It's entirely personal between you and me."

"I know better than that," Tom answered. "You're obeying orders and shielding the man who told you what to do. That's proper. Tell you what. Move your things into my compartment and have it all to yourself. You'll be more comfortable without someone's feet in your lap. I'll find a shake-down somewhere else on the train."

She nodded—understood him to mean he wasn't angry.

"Isn't there plenty of room for us both in here?"

"Yes, I suppose there is."

Tom went in search of a porter to bring her belongings from the other compartment. He took his time about it. He put his own bag on the corner seat that Miss Strong had vacated, with a belligerent abruptness that amounted to an ultimatum. The seat was henceforth his. He wasn't at all sure he wanted much more of Nancy Strong's conversation. She wasn't likely to tell him anything important, and it might prove too easy to tell her too much.

Chapter 17

Tom tried to peer into Abdul Mirza's compartment, but the blinds were drawn. So were the blinds of the other compartment, in which the staff of secretaries, or whatever they were, were as silent as dead men. He loafed about for a while in the corridor, but the compartment doors didn't open, so after half an hour or so he returned and sat down again opposite Nancy Strong.

"Done Dutch aunting?" he hinted.

"No. I am just getting into my stride. It's very good of you to listen. Do you know a little church in Bristol named St. John's? A stone church, where the Clifton Road crosses the street that leads to the Suspension Bridge?"

Tom stared hard. Her eyes were laughing at him. It was a palpable hit, and he couldn't hide it.

"Why didn't you pull this out of the bag to begin with?" he retorted.

"It was at the bottom of the bag. And besides, I'm a woman. Please believe it is a sheer coincidence that I happen to know that church. I went there to attend my sister's wedding, during the last year of the World War."

"Well? What of it?"

"It's your turn," she answered. "Tell me."

"So they know that, do they?"

"Oh, yes. But they would like to know more. Why did you marry Elsa Burbage?"

"Dammit, why shouldn't I marry her?"

"You seem to think you shouldn't have. Isn't she—"

Tom interrupted. He spoke quietly, without emphasis, and yet every other word was like a hammer-blow. It was as if he were laying his thoughts on an anvil and cracking them up for his own analysis.

"I will tell you this much, Elsa Burbage is a little bit of a Cossacky-looking, well-bred smiler. She has as much pluck as intelligence. As much intelligence as good looks. Too good looking, as a matter of fact, but too intelligent to be spoiled by fools who'd like to paw her over. She's on the level. Knows her stuff. I taught her most of it, but she learned a lot in the British Museum. She can read Tibetan as well as I can, and I'm rated an expert. I have a big strong-box in a bank vault chock-a-block with real stuff that I've not had time to study, let alone

97

to translate. Elsa is to have all that, if I get bumped off. And there's other stuff in there, that shouldn't be seen for a generation. Elsa would know what to destroy and what to keep and what to publish. As I said, she's on the level. She'd do the right thing. She couldn't be tempted to do the wrong thing."

"But she married you. Was that the wrong thing?"

"The worst break I ever made. A sentimental mistake. They're the worst kind. I could have consulted a lawyer and made a will leaving the contents of the strong-box to her."

"But perhaps you were afraid she might marry someone else?" said Nancy Strong. "You know the proverb: *a mistress keeps a secret for a week, a wife as long as she loves you, a friend forever, but other men's wives never leave off telling it.*"

"No," Tom answered. "I don't own her. We agreed she can have a divorce, at my expense, on demand, at any time, provided she doesn't swap horses in midstream. If she should fall in love, she'd have to wait until she could get a divorce, in Mexico or somewhere, without getting my name into public print. It was to be a strictly secret marriage, for strictly business purposes."

"Now that the secret is out, she may have a divorce?"

"Yes. Why not? She'd better do it. D'you know why I've been trusted, quite a bit, by certain people?"

"I believe I can guess," Nancy Strong answered. She was just plump enough to be unable to suppress a slight ripple of mirth. "You are probably known as a man who can't be taken in or hoodwinked by any woman. Were you hood winked by Elsa Burbage?"

"No, I wasn't. I've told you what she is. I'll back my judgment against yours or anyone's. In fact, that's what I did do. She was wild to come to India, and to help me to enter Tibet. She had worked so hard, and schooled herself, and saved her money, and kept physically fit, and so set her teeth into the job of making herself useful to me, that I yessed her. I shouldn't have. But I did. I even said I'd try to get her into Tibet. She deserves it. She's ace-high to any deuce of an adventuress I ever met."

"But that isn't why you married her?"

"Yes, that's one reason. If I should get bumped off, she might stand a better chance as my legal widow than if people should find out she'd merely tagged me along. I've seen several women get a hell of a cold deal because they couldn't show a marriage certificate. And they were damned good women; I'm not talking about kept women or Shanghai passage-beggars."

"You admit you made a bad break."

"Only time in my life I was sentimental."

Nancy Strong a bit too visibly suppressed an Old Faithful geyser of amusement. She used her handkerchief. It did sound a bit like a sneeze. But she controlled her voice perfectly:

"Hadn't you better ask her to go away and divorce you? Didn't you say, in Mexico?"

"I'll have to think that over."

Tom went out and paced the corridor. He had something else to think about. Dowlah. Abdul Mirza. Noropa. For fifteen or twenty minutes he kept an eye on the doors of two closed compartments. However, no luck yet. So he returned and sat down again.

"Verdict?" Nancy Strong asked.

"Guilty. I shouldn't have done it. It was probably vanity. I guess a psychoanalyst would say I craved a she-disciple, to make me feel like a guru. Elsa will stick to her guns, mind you. Why shouldn't she? But the marriage has ruined the team. If I order her home, she can claim privilege. If I should offer any mushy reasons for avoiding danger, she can quote our bargain. We agreed, she's entitled to take all chances, at her own risk, same as I am."

Nancy Strong opened her bag and snapped it shut, but she made no other sign of having reached a climax. Her voice was normal:

"Would you like me to suggest in the proper quarter that she should be sent home? That would not involve you. She would never know who advised, or who ordered it. She need never know that you and I discussed her."

"Go to hell," Tom answered. "Before I'd do her any dirt like that, I'd brain you with a monkey-wrench and throw the wrench into the works. If you or they want her run out of India, say it to me. I'll pull my freight and hers, too. I know how to get to Tibet without double-crossing a good kid."

Nancy Strong rippled all over with laughter.

"Very creditable, Mr. Grayne! One of these days, when you do fall in love with a girl, I wonder what lengths you won't go to for her sake. She will be able to count on you when her back is turned, won't she! Very well, I promise I won't suggest any official move of that sort."

"Care for some dinner?"

She laughed again. "You have a grand way of denying anger. Yes, I would like dinner. Do you trust me to keep my promise?"

"If they order her deported, I will know at whose door to deliver the bouquet," he answered.

"And if they don't—no flowers, Mr. Grayne, by request."

"Understood and agreed. Let's go eat."

No sign of Abdul Mirza, nor of any of his companions, except that a waiter was removing soiled dishes from the prime minister's compartment, but he had closed the door behind him before Tom could get a glimpse. However, it wasn't that compartment that interested him as much as the other. Prime ministers, as a rule, don't do their own dirty work; they look the other way while someone does it who can be repudiated after the event. The other compartment door was shut, blinds drawn, and not a sound within.

However, he had better luck after dinner. A silk-clad secretary sort of person came out of Abdul Mirza's compartment and entered the other one just as Tom entered the corridor on his way from the dining-car. Nancy Strong, behind him, was left imagining what she pleased. Tom passed the door in time to get one swift glimpse before it slammed shut. He had seen what he wanted.

"Do you sleep well on a train?" he asked when he and Nancy Strong had sat down again facing each other.

"Yes. I usually turn in early and sleep till daylight."

"Okay. I won't disturb you. I may find someone to talk to. Might talk all night."

"Talk to me, if that's your trouble."

But the spell was broken. Conversation lagged. It was barely ten o'clock when Tom strolled down the corridor and claimed the lower berth on which he had left his bag. He sprawled with the bag under his elbows, so that he could see under the blind into the corridor. It was midnight, or later, before he moved from that position. Then he opened the door, making hardly a sound, and tiptoed out.

He was almost too late. By the time he reached the car ahead there was someone standing by the door of the compartment in which Nancy Strong lay asleep. A very tall, bare-headed man in a dark suit. He had opened the door and was trying to peer into the dark interior. His back was toward Tom. The corridor lights were turned low. There were deep shadows.

Train thief? Hardly likely on a modern express train.

There is a whole caste of professional thieves whose only means of livelihood is robbing Indian trains and their passengers. So almost anything was possible. But the man looked familiar.

Tom crowded himself against the curve at the end of the corridor. The man appeared to be listening. He opened the door a trifle wider. Apparently the slight squeak of the hinges awoke Nancy Strong or perhaps she hadn't been asleep. She switched on the light. The man scooted away, along the corridor toward the car ahead. Tom didn't follow; a train corridor is a mean place for a fight, especially with someone who probably carries a knife, or worse. Instead, he went and told Nancy Strong to lock the door on the inside.

"I've found a man to talk to. Goodnight. See you in the morning."

He went and turned in—slept like a top. He didn't wake until the train neared Siliguri.

CHAPTER 18

"Siliguri! Change for Darjeeling!"

Pulses begin to beat faster at Siliguri. There the two-foot gauge Himalayan Mountain Railway awaits the transcontinental mails. Six hundred feet above sea level, six thousand feet below Darjeeling, and piping hot from the snipe and rice swamps of Bengal, Siliguri is the threshold of another world. The plains cease. The mountains begin. The early morning excites imagination—sends it leaping from forest to forest, across the intervening tea gardens, toward the grandest view on earth, where the Himalayan ranges rise against the northern sky.

Tom pitched his bag to a Lepcha porter on the platform and followed it. He was the first passenger to leave the train. There were all sorts of people on the platform, all in motion—Lepchas, Gurkhas, Tibetans, Bengalis—tea-planters in Terai hats—British and Indian soldiers—police—gazelle-eyed women—beggars and thieves and princes' sons. Tom told his porter to go and wait for him "perhaps a long time" in the shade near the auto-parking place.

He knew the station well. A score of strides and he was hidden in the almost dark room where the emergency oil-lanterns stand in a row on a shelf. There was only one small dirty window, rather high up; he had to stand on a box and clear a peephole through the dust. He saw Abdul Mirza and his companions, and presently Nancy Strong go hurrying after their baggage toward the narrow gauge train. But no Noropa—not yet. He was almost beginning to lose hope that Noropa had seen him enter the lamp room, when he caught sight of a man coming along the platform from the rear end of the train.

Sure thing! Unmistakably Noropa, in an ill-fitting, hurriedly-made bazaar suit and a Lepcha turban, looking like a schoolteacher. He was wearing spectacles, probably plain glass. He was stooping a little to make his great height less noticeable. No bag, no porter. He threaded his way through the dwindling crowd as if he had business at the far end of the platform.

There was a momentary tumult of excitement, just in front of the window, where some Indian passengers were being met by noisy friends and relatives. Someone's caged monkey got loose and a dog gave chase. Shrieks, shouts, roars of laughter. Noropa was very clever, the way he snatched the opportunity to step sideways and make for the lamp-room door. He didn't dash in. He stopped and stooped to tie his shoe-lace, so as to look back and make sure he was unobserved. Then he entered quite quietly.

But he didn't shut the door swiftly enough. He drew his weapon just a fraction of a second too soon; the light shone on it before the door shut and Tom recognised the kind of weapon he had to deal with. That was half the battle, but the other half wasn't so simple. He didn't want a corpse on his hands, nor even a badly injured man. He didn't want a police investigation. He would never be forgiven if he set police investigators on the *qui vive*.

There wasn't a word spoken. Hardly a sound. Noropa's weapon broke against the stone wall. Tom's fist thudded on the point of No-ropa's chin—dropped him like a steer in a shambles. He lay still. It was a pippin of a punch on the jaw; he was likely to lie there for several minutes.

Tom examined the weapon—eighteen inches of bright tool steel as thin as a bodkin, set into a heavy brass-bound wooden hilt. Hilt and blade both hollow. A strong spring and about an ounce of poison in the hilt that would have gone squirting through the blade into any wound it made. No smell that Tom recognised. Probably a quite rare poison. It was oozing out through the broken blade—thick, sticky stuff like molasses. He stuck the blade into a crack in the wall to let it bleed, so to speak, without leaving a menace for some lamp-trimmer's naked foot.

Noropa stirred, opened his eyes and blinked. Tom stooped over him, lifted him by the shoulders—the man was as heavy as lead—and set him sitting against the wall. The door opened suddenly. Sunlight fell full on Noropa's death-mask face. The station-master—Anglo-Indian, natty, alert, helmeted, smartly uniformed in white—stood staring. All three men had presence of mind. The station-master took a step backward to glance left and right for the railway police. Noropa sat still, pretending to be much less conscious than he was. Tom spoke to the station-master:

"Could you get me some ice water? I think he was looking for the lavatory. I saw him go in here and fall down, so I followed to see what was the matter."

"Why did you shut the door?" asked the station-master. He was suspicious, but Tom's easy assurance impressed him, and there was no obvious sign of a struggle. Noropa's chin on his chest concealed the mark of the blow.

"Was it shut? I didn't notice. I guess I kicked it when I tried to lift him."

"Who is he?"

"How should I know?"

"By his turban he's a Lepcha," said the station-master.

"Yes. He's on his way to Darjeeling. He told me that on the train," Tom answered.

"Well, he has missed the Mountain train. It's pulling out now. Has he a ticket?"

"How should I know? I've no right to look in his pockets. Tell you what," said Tom, "I'm going up by road, so I'll give him a lift. If he isn't better by the time we reach the hotel I'll take him to a doctor. Will you help me get him out of here?"

"I'll call a couple of porters. Have you engaged a car? I'll see if I can get one for you."

When the station-master turned his back Tom shook his fist under Noropa's nose for silence. It was hardly necessary. Noropa had heard, understood. He even smiled assent to Tom's lie about what had happened. Tom took the knife from the crack in the wall, wrapped it in a rag that he snatched from the lamp-shelf and thrust it into Noropa's jacket-pocket, forcing it down between the jacket and the cheap Italian half-lining. He picked up the broken half of the blade and put that into Noropa's side-pocket. Noropa understood that also: if the police should show up and become curious, they would find that deadly weapon on the person of its owner.

The station-master returned with two porters.

"There's only one auto left," he said. "It's a ramshackle old thing, but you'll have to take it if you don't want to wait for a couple of hours. He looks better already, doesn't he. Some of them, if they're not used to it, get train-sick. But I'd take him to a hospital, if I were you, and let 'em find out what's wrong. Come on, you, these porters will help you out o'here."

Chapter 19

It was an ancient Sunbeam. Its spare tyre was down to the canvas; the four tyres in use were only slightly better. The springs of the worn cushions were concealed by a folded stable blanket. The Bengali Moslem driver knew no English.

The engine sounded like a machine-gun getting hot and about ready to jam; it was a question which would give out first, engine or tires. But Tom couldn't afford to let it go at that. With a grin at the driver he raised the hood, pretending to give a half-turn to the screws on a couple of oil cups. What he actually did was to open the newly fitted brass water plug just enough to establish a steady drip, good for ten or twelve miles at a guess, supposing the radiator was full to start with. It probably was full; there was a water faucet near by and the water cost nothing.

Then away, on the rear seat beside Noropa, with a rattle like a tinker's cart and the canvas top nodding like a processional canopy. Rubber tooter, blowing like the devil to make the Siliguri bullock-carts get out of the way. Dead slow, choking dusty, until they turned toward the mountain and began the long, comparatively easy, beautifully engineered ascent.

Tom recovered the weapon then. His left fist, knotted like a club, commanded the situation; his right hand searched Noropa's pockets competently, considering that picking pockets wasn't his normal occupation. All he found was the poisoned dagger in two parts, several hundred *rupees* in paper money, a few small coins and a white gold wristwatch with a broken strap. It was all right, it wasn't Elsa's watch, though it did look like it for a moment. No return ticket. One Tibetan coin among the small change wasn't anything to arouse comment. But the ten-*rupee* notes were brand new.

"All a traveller needs nowadays is money, isn't it," said Tom. "Here you are—take it. When a man like you goes to a bank with a cheque they give him all the dirty money in the till. Who gave you nice clean banknotes?"

No answer, but Noropa seemed surprised to get his money back. He stowed it away carefully, eyeing Tom sideways, Tom pretending to watch the road.

"Ah! Thought so! Drop it, or I'll break your wrist!"

No punch necessary that time. A small knife hidden in a pocket in Noropa's shirt had fallen crosswise and hadn't come out handily. It fell to the floor of the car as his big-boned forearm creaked in Tom's doubled grip. Tom put his foot on the knife.

"Any more weapons? Kick your shoes off."

He felt Noropa all over, tapping lightly, because it is easy to overlook quite bulky objects if the searcher uses too much pressure. It was all right, the man was completely disarmed now. For at least an hour or two he wouldn't feel exactly tempted to use that right forearm. He was rubbing it with the other hand. There was pain in his eyes. They weren't pleasant eyes to look at. Framed in the blue-rimmed plain glass spectacles they looked like the eyes of a man on the rack, so full of hate that no pain could conquer him.

"I've conquered tougher guys than you," Tom remarked in a matter-of-fact voice. "None of you terrorists can ever stomach your own stuff. Somewhere between here and Darjeeling you're going to break. Do you know what that means?"

No answer.

"You can have it as rough as you choose. I'm not squeamish."

No answer.

"Where is Miss Elsa Burbage?"

"Not knowing."

"Where is Thö-pa-ga?"

"Not knowing."

"Where is the Holy Lama Lobsang Pun?"

Silence.

"So you're afraid of Lobsang Pun. What could he do to you?"

"You-who-know-what-*shang-shang*-is—you-bloody-fool-you-break-my-arm—you-get-a-*shang-shang*-sending."

"Trot out your *shang-shang*. Who killed Eiji Sarao?"

Got him! The meaning of his sudden stare was unmistakable. Someone—very likely Abdul Mirza, but perhaps Dowlah, had told Noropa that Eiji Sarao was dead of that wound in the neck. Tom felt fairly confident that Eiji Sarao was really being secretly conveyed to Naini Kol. But Noropa believed him dead. That was clear. A lucky shot, that. Now for another, a thousand to one shot, that wouldn't do any harm if it didn't come off:

"Lobsang Pun was angry that you killed Eiji Sarao. You come after me, to kill me, to make Lobsang Pun forgive you for having killed Eiji."

Silence. Had the shot missed? Then suddenly:

"You-bloody-fool-you—*shang-shang*-sending-killing-you-like-Eiji!"

That was a stumper.

"Are you so crazy that you kid yourself you're a *shang-shang*?"

No answer. Tom, his imagination leaping from guess to guess, plugged home another disturbing question without a query mark:

"Rajah Dowlah told you Lobsang Pun demanded that you kill me, because the Japanese demanded it, because I'm bad for the plan to make use of Thö-pa-ga."

Got him again! Noropa shook his head in dissent too vehemently. His eyes glazed with the smoky oriental sullenness that guards the truth that has been touched but still perhaps only guessed at, not discovered.

"You're an awful boob," said Tom, "if you believed that yarn. You haven't a Chinaman's chance to curry favour with Lobsang Pun. He's through with you. If you had killed me, he'd have had you hanged by the British. Or, if they wouldn't do it, he'd have had you fed to *shang-shangs*."

Noropa shuddered. The mention of Lobsang Pun's name seemed to make him as nervous as a *chela* who hears his *guru* being blasphemed.

"As for Dowlah," said Tom, "if you trust him, you're a worse fool even than I thought you. Dowlah believes in neither god nor devil. He'd betray anyone, if he thought he couldn't be found out, just for the sake of feeling clever. What did Dowlah tell you about me?"

No answer.

"Dowlah told you they've decided they don't need me but they can use Miss Elsa Burbage."

Noropa's intelligence laired in a cavernous mystery of superstition. To him, every breath a man breathed—every word a man said, had a dark metaphysical cause; it served some devil's purpose, or it could not be. Sulky, sullen, he was frightened by the accuracy of Tom's guesswork. It seemed to him supernatural. It had far more effect on him than the punch on the jaw and the agonied arm. Tom continued:

"So Dowlah gave you a weapon and money, but he didn't tell Abdul Mirza. You traveled with Abdul Mirza's staff, but they can swear they knew nothing about it."

No answer.

They had crossed the wandering narrow-gauge railway track a

dozen times, when the rotten old rattletrap car at last did even better than Tom hoped. Half-way through a mile-wide belt of deodars, between two tea estates, the radiator boiled and a rear tyre blew like a gun going off. The Bengali driver, in a rising off-key yell of misery, named three men, probably mechanics. He invited *Allah* (blessed be His Prophet) to impregnate them and all their progeny forever with deathless worms and inward-growing boils that should destroy their rest and make sleep a torment. Having attended to that, he got down to attend to the tyre. Tom eyed Noropa:

"Put your shoes on and get out."

The set-up was perfect. A dark wilderness of trees. A convenient hollow out of earshot from the road. Probably at least an hour's work for the Bengali, patching that rotten tyre and then finding out what was wrong with the engine. Even if he should think of tightening the water plug, he had nothing in which to fetch water; he would have to go in search of a vessel of some sort. There was plenty of time, and no risk whatever of interruption.

Noropa tried to escape. Tom's toe hooked his instep as he ducked around a big tree. He fell headlong and got up be cause he was kicked up. There isn't any fun in kicking even murderers who use poisoned daggers, but there was no sense in half-doing the job. Noropa walked backward after that. He didn't dare to shout for help, nor did he dare take his eyes off Tom; a fellow whose team had depended on him, not so many years ago, for an occasional drop-goal from the seventy-five yard line, has a remarkably accurate aim and a toe that can hurt. Noropa fell, naturally, several times. He was kicked up again. He picked up a rock. It was kicked out of his hand before he could raise his hand to throw it. By the time they reached the bottom of the hollow he was possessed by an inferiority complex that even his malice hadn't heat enough to burn off. Tom did nothing to reduce it:

"You miserable mongrel. Why d'you call yourself Tibetan? You couldn't fool a Tibetan. You're Chinese-Jap. Chinks and Japs are not allowed in Inner Tibet."

Silence. It amounted to sulky assent. No Tibetan would have swallowed that insult without protest. Tom's guesses were beginning to have the feel of accuracy. It was like working out a mathematical equation with a number of unknowns. Get one right and the others logically follow.

"I'd give a dollar to know your early history, you useless pye-dog."

Not a word at random. The word "useless" specially chosen. "Pye-dog" was pretty scurrilous, but it was better than its American equivalent, at the moment.

"You've had an education of sorts. You're a Christian convert. You were kicked out of your church."

A hit! Mystery men hate to be stripped of their veils. They prefer physical torture; vanity helps them to endure that. Noropa stood still enough, but his mind almost visibly shrank. It found no shelter.

"You're a killer. You probably murdered a Christian priest somewhere in China. Not for money. You'd be too superstitious. The first thing they teach you black magicians is you mustn't kill for money. Did you want to take holy orders? Did a father-confessor say no? Told you you weren't fit for the priesthood? That it?"

Silence.

"Tell me when I'm mistaken, won't you! Turned down. Revenge. Was it you?—or wasn't it?—who tipped off the Chinese to scough a mission? But a taste of religion had shown you a way to become important. Couldn't get by as a Christian. Tried another line, eh? Fell in with a *shaman?* You've the symptoms. One of those wandering wizards who sell poisons and love-potions? Taught you that your ugly mug was fine for scaring women, kids, sick folk, and superstitious peasants. Hell, you even tried to scare me with it, in London."

The eyes, now, of a cornered animal that daren't fight and can't run. The eyes of a gangster, not only cut off from, but deserted by his gang. Defiance dead. Nothing left but a lonely, self-pitying gloom that a man, however tough he may be, can't keep out of his. eyes when he knows the gang has disowned him. There is the same look in the eyes of an animal that has been driven from the herd.

"Who taught you Tantric Buddhism?" Tom demanded. "Did you learn it in Peking, hanging around the legations, doing odds and ends of spy work, while you looked for a religion that you could get your teeth into? Lots of exiled Tibetans in Peking."

He was taking long chances. You can't expect a bull's-eye every guess, not even when the guessing is comparatively easy. But he was watching Noropa's eyes; there wasn't a hint of a gleam of triumph to suggest that he was guessing badly. There wasn't even a look of momentary relief.

"And then the Tashi Lama—Panchen Lama, you'd call him—fled from Shigatse in Tibet to escape from the political gang in Lhasa. Wanted to go to Urga in Mongolia. But the Chinese Government was afraid the Russians might get control of him, so they forced him to go to Peking, where they gave him an apartment in the imperial palace. The Jap legation had sense enough to see his value in a second. You haven't brains enough to have thought of that. But by that time you'd made yourself pretty useful to the undercover agents of the Japanese legation. Hadn't you? And of course, they threatened you. That's routine. Obey, or be betrayed to the Chinese and repudiated—then left to your fate. The prospect of the tortures in a Chinese dungeon didn't tempt you, but a chance to get your teeth into a good mysterious religion did. One way or another you wormed your way into the Tashi— that's to say the Panchen Lama's establishment in Peking, as a spy for the Japanese. Guard? Or were you posing as a humble supplicant for religious teaching? Or both? Answer: is that how you came to meet Lobsang Pun?"

No answer. A glare of sullen obstinacy, instantly met by a resounding crack on the jaw from Tom's fist.

"You heard me. Answer."

"Yes."

"Thought so. Who told you about the Thunder Dragon Gate and Thö-pa-ga?"

Silence. Noropa was rubbing his jaw. His lips were trembling. His fingers twitched. Insolence had begun to yield to self-pity. To keep him from rebuilding his mental resistance, Tom went at him swiftly from another angle:

"All sorts of undercover dirty work goes on, doesn't it, that the Tashi—I mean Panchen Lama doesn't know about. His Holiness is a gentle, benevolent man of peace. Some of his followers aren't. They're more ambitious for him than he is for himself. They don't tell him all that goes on, do they?"

Noropa looked puzzled. Suddenly Tom shot a statement at him, and a question:

"The Most Reverend and Holy Lobsang Pun was with the Panchen Lama for a while in Peking. Was it he who told you about Thö-pa-ga. Did Lobsang Pun tell you about the Thunder Dragon Gate?"

Silence.

"Bound you to secrecy, did he? Shall I repeat the oath for you?"

"No!" It was almost a shout.

Tom laughed. He did repeat the oath, in Tibetan:

This supplicant, in deep humility applying for a revelation from

the earthly custodian of wisdom and continual blessings—
standing in awe before the blessed sacraments and in the holy
presence of innumerable saints, solemnly avowing secrecy, will-
ingly accepts the penalty of being *shang-shang*-hunted through
hell forever, without rest or other mercy, if violating this secret
at any time for any reason.

"May you die of it!" said Noropa.

Tom laughed again. He continued:

"Lobsang Pun was intriguing for Japanese help to enable the
Panchen Lama to return to Tibet and kick out the political gang in
Lhasa. He wasn't expecting anything for nothing, either. Didn't the
Japanese recommend you to Lobsang Pun as a suitable man to be sent
to England to make Thö-pa-ga return to Tibet? Answer!"

Noropa mumbled. The combination of being kicked and hit and
stripped of mystery had left him almost without a will of his own.

"You—you-knowing-so-well-all-that-why-you-asking-me?" he
stuttered.

"Who sent you to the Thunder Dragon Gate for training before
sending you to London? Lobsang Pun?"

No answer.

"Lobsang Pun would never send you into Inner Tibet. You know as
well as I do, it's sure death for a lama to do that without definite orders
from Lhasa. If he did it, they'd drown him. And Lobsang Pun couldn't
get orders from Lhasa. How could he? He's the Tashi—Panchen Lama's man. But you crave to go to Inner Tibet. You would like to link
up with *Bön* magicians. I know your yearning. There are plenty like
you with that complaint, but you have it badly. Therefore you attached
yourself to Lobsang Pun. And him you fear and obey. There never was
a terrorist who didn't have to have a secret him-who-is-to-be-obeyed.
That's all that keeps you from dying of fear. Lobsang Pun is your"—
he used a Tibetan word—"undeniable-one-whose-unspoken-wish-
is-sooner-to-be-obeyed-than-the-spoken-commands-of-any-other-
person. Lobsang Pun is my friend."

That was a staggerer. Noropa took off his spectacles, wiped his face
with his sleeve and muttered. He was cursing Tom and summoning
dark forces. Failed by the powers of darkness, there would be nothing
left on which to base resistance. Tom went at him again:

"You half-magicians all believe your own stuff, until you find
it won't work. You can't even keep a secret." He took a dangerous

chance now. "The Thunder Dragon Gate is near the border between Tibet and Nepal, near Mount Everest, where the Most Reverend and Holy Lama Lobsang Pun is supposed to have spent two years immured in a cave."

Pure deduction, based on a retentive memory of hints and chance remarks. If it missed it would restore Noropa's self-confidence. But there wasn't a glimmering hint of superior knowledge in Noropa's eyes. On the contrary, a look of utter desperation had crept into them. Tom followed up:

"You weren't accepted as a disciple by Lobsang Pun. You're not his *chela*. You're a stool-pigeon. Such a man as Lobsang Pun could see through you in half a second. But he helped you to become a novice in the Thunder Dragon Gate, because he could do that without betraying his own oath. Later, he sent you to England, because you can speak English. Your job was to compel Thö-pa-ga to return. You weren't ordered to return from England. Who the hell wants a stinker like you when you've done your business? When you followed Thö-pa-ga to India, you found that Lobsang Pun was very angry with you for having dared to get in touch with the Japanese secret agents in London and Paris. Who were you that you should dare to step out?"

Noropa's face was a picture. The last layer of all of his skin of mystery was being torn off. Tom went on flaying mercilessly:

"Eiji Sarao paid your fare to India. Lobsang Pun was particularly angry with you for knowing Eiji Sarao. Now you're afraid that Lobsang Pun will slam the door on you forever. Why shouldn't he?"

Pause—a rather long one. Then:

"I am the only man in the world who can influence Lobsang Pun to overlook your misbehaviour."

Not a flutter, but a kind of false dawn in Noropa's eyes. It vanished. No hurry. Two or three more mental wallops, and almost any spark of hope would look attractive.

"Lobsang Pun believes you killed Eiji Sarao because you had been rebuked for knowing Eiji Sarao and for accepting his money."

First miss! But it accomplished more than a hit. Noropa leaped with relief at a chance to prove that Tom didn't know everything.

"Damn-fool-Eiji-waking-up-and-going-library-looking-for-Dowlah-not-there-opening-cage-and-*shang-shang*-bit-him."

"Where's the *shang-shang*?"

"Library-door-open-escaping-into-hall-and-out-through-open-window-goodbye."

111

Tom didn't dare to laugh. Noropa had no sense of humour. He couldn't be moved by imagination of Dowlah's mourning for his lost pet and the efforts of sceptics to explain away the *shang-shang's* killings.

"What d'you think Lobsang Pun will do to you when he learns you took money from Rajah Dowlah to kill me? I am Lobsang Pun's friend."

Silence.

"What will Dowlah do when he learns you failed?"

More silence.

"What will Lobsang Pun do when he learns you told me where the Thunder Dragon Gate is?"

"Ah-h-h! Not me! Not telling! Never!"

"No? Try to make Lobsang Pun believe you didn't tell me! Try to make the guardians of the Thunder Dragon Gate believe you didn't tell me!"

" You-who-so-well-knowing-Lobsang-Pun-you-say-you-talking-him-for-me-yes-why-you-say-that?"

Quietly: "Where is Miss Elsa Burbage?"

"Not knowing."

Tom's foot moved. Noropa flinched—spoke suddenly:

"Girl-and-Thö-pa-ga-in-auto-to-Darjeeling."

"Where is the Holy Lama Lobsang Pun?"

"In-auto-to-Darjeeling."

"Same auto?"

"Maybe 'nother auto. Not knowing."

"Coming to Darjeeling, is he? Do you want me to protect you?"

"You-you-saying-you-his-friend-you-doing-that?"

"If you obey me. You're a coward. You're a mongrel. But I'll give you a chance."

Noropa's answering gesture was one of almost weird humility. Like a de-fanged cobra, he would need time to grow new fangs and brew new venom.

"But if you miss your chance, don't look to me for pity. Walk ahead. To the car. And get in."

Noropa didn't like walking ahead. He couldn't walk fast, he had been kicked too painfully. To reach the road was about all he could manage. The Bengali had decided to take a chance with the spare tire; the blown one was beyond his skill to repair. He had carried water in a borrowed kerosene tin, but he hadn't thought of tightening the water plug. Tom attended to that.

Chapter 20

Darjeeling enjoys a climate. It endures the weather. All the way up the magnificent drive from Siliguri Tom leaned back on the comfortless cushions and let his lungs fill with pine scent borne on the snow-sweetened breezes from the Roof of the World. He sat cornerwise, to keep an eye on Noropa, but he only spoke to him once in a while, with long pauses, always speaking suddenly, to give the man no time to invent lies.

"Can you catch a *shang-shang?*"

"No, no!"

"You useless duffer!"

"Not-yet-learning-how-to-do-it. That-is-secret-only-known-to-some-few-persons-specially-chosen."

"Uh-huh. Do they ever get bitten?"

"No, no. Same-as-serpent-charmers-never-bitten-knowing-proper-magic."

"Is a *shang-shang* solitary?"

"Oh, yes." Noropa shuddered. "She-*shang-shang*-slaying-any-other-coming-near-it."

"Who said so?"

"I seeing."

"When?"

"Two-three time."

Sudden rain put an end to the conversation. Not the climate, weather. Black clouds, shot with lightning, rolled above the mountain. Purple gloom. Chill air. A stupendous deluge that in two or three seconds made an overflowing bathtub of the canvas top. Noropa, speaking vehemently, named the devils who had done it. Being rotten, the canvas burst and let fall about a hundred pounds of water into Tom's and Noropa's laps. The spare tire chose that moment for a blow-out. The driver announced he was out of petrol. With the air of resignation of a captain who has done his utmost and now proposes to sink with the ship, he bowed his head over the wheel and nasally praised *Allah.*

Tom paid him and left him. A walk in the rain would do Noropa good; it would supple him up where the kicks had left him stiff and painful. It was only three or four miles to their destination. Noropa could carry the bag. That, too, would do him good. It would serve to increase his consciousness of defeat. Noropa made a fuss about it. He pretended the elevation made him breathless, that the rain chilled him and that the sheer weight of the downpour broke his strength. But he didn't like being laughed at, and he liked still less the prospect of being kicked. So he shouldered the bag and walked ahead, as commanded.

To reach the Ringding Gelong Monastery, you avoid the township. You follow the wonderful road that skirts the cliff, where landslides once fell in the rain upon snoozing villages and buried them and all the intervening forest beneath hundreds of acres of wet earth. Four miles along that road, above an aromatic ocean of deodars, and you round a corner and see the monastery rather suddenly, a bit below you. It faces the Himalayas, with Darjeeling above, at its back. From its roof you can see Tibet. In fine weather the horizon-long Himalayas seem only a few miles distant.

The rain over Darjeeling, being due to the weather, not the climate, cleared as suddenly as it had come. The sun light burst forth and shone upon gleaming rocks and roaring torrents. It was almost impossible to hear anything above the raging of rain-fed waterfalls. Tom paused to stare at the northern sky line. He loved that view. He watched a dark patch, about the size of a postage stamp, moving across the surface of the distant snow—a storm in the Hills—a killer. His ears were full of the cascade music. He didn't hear a car overtake him—wasn't, in fact, aware of it until it passed and stopped beside Noropa, who was waiting patiently. An Indian policeman got out of the car and ordered Noropa to the front seat beside the driver. Noropa obeyed without saying a word, as if he believed Tom had done this by superior magic. What else could it be? Tom hadn't phoned—wired—sent a message ahead.

A police officer on the rear seat called to Tom:

"Is that your bag he's carrying?"

Tom went up and took the bag in silence. The officer stood up to remove his waterproof.

"You're wet through," he remarked. "How far are you going?"

"I'll be all right. Not far. Is he under arrest?"

"Detention. Suspected of being an unregistered alien—held for investigation." The officer looked straight into Tom's eyes. He wasn't smiling, but his eyes looked merry. "*Incommunicado*," he added. "The station-master phoned from Siliguri. You're expected, so we kept a dekko lifting. Followed you along to a quiet place. Is his name Noropa?"

"That's what he says his name is. Who expects me?"

"Someone at the Ringding Gelong Monastery."

114

"Okay."

The officer studied the beaten-dog glare in Noropa's eyes:

"Did you have any trouble with this man?"

"None whatever. Take care of him, please. I guess I'll need him."

Hugging Noropa's poisoned dagger beneath his jacket, and carrying his own bag, Tom trudged away toward the monastery, humming to himself.

CHAPTER 21

The Ringding Gelong Monastery is a rather large one, built in the Tibetan style, with a great main building like a keep and a number of courtyards. It dates from the days when Darjeeling was within the political boundary ruled by the Maharajah of Sikkim. There were no railways in those days. So there are stables, in the first courtyard, for a great number of transport animals. Almost the first thing Tom noticed, as he did his greetings under the arch over the main entrance, was that the stables in the first courtyard were crowded with Tibetan ponies. There were more than forty obvious camp-followers squatting in groups in the yard, smelly fellows with their sheepskin jackets rolled up beside them. Loads by the dozen, roped and ready.

"Tum-Glain! Tum-Glain!" The sloe-eyed monk on duty at the gate was all smiles. He took Tom's bag and passed it to another monk.

Tom was expected; they made that evident. They asked all the proper questions about his health and well-being, and they blessed him with countless blessings. But beyond that, they said nothing at all.

He was led across two courtyards, in one of which some devil-dancers were practising. Their steps looked very comical without masks and costumes. They were being narrowly watched by twenty Tibetans who were seated with their backs against the wall, beneath a long wooden gallery that served as corridor for the cells and dormitories on the upper story. One was an obvious *shaman* of the type who wander all over Tibet, Turkestan and Mongolia, working fake magical cures, selling poison and telling fortunes. The men who sat near him looked like herdsmen.

But one man sat apart. A *Bön* priest, six paces away from a sturdy-looking novice. They two were hooded mystery men—magicians— real practitioners of the black arts that survived the conversion of Tibet to Buddhism. There was no mistaking them. They were what Noropa craved to be. Insolent eyes. Lips that wouldn't care to tell the truth if they were offered for it all the plunder in the world.

Until they noticed Tom's arrival all the others were as rapt as children at a picture-show, dividing their attention between the devil-dancers and the monks on the opposite roof who were extracting one another's beards with tweezers. But they two sat in meditation in the attitude that only *Bön* magicians can assume. It is acquired by years of self-torture, and it looks like a caricature of the posture of Buddhist saints.

They had strange-looking luggage. It was certainly not Tibetan—or, at any rate, the baskets weren't. Those might have come from the Salween country in Upper Burma, where there is cane of which to make such things and a more or less Chinese idea of what cane can be fashioned to do. Shaped like flat loaves, to be slung on poles and borne by women, or to be mounted one on each side of a horse. The two biggest were round, like snake-charmers' baskets, only much bigger—cart-wheel diameter—with slightly domed lids, and neatly covered with waterproofed cloth. Nothing Tibetan about that.

All the same, all those men were recently from Tibet. They bore all the signs of having come a long way, by forced marches. Except for the *Bön* magician and his novice, who sat motionless, they were all munching the last of their Tibetan cheese. On top of one basket was a hunk of yak-meat that stank like the devil; they had partly covered it with a scrap of cloth and the cloth was black with flies. All except the *Bön* magicians stared at Tom with the silent curiosity of nomads.

Tom turned aside to speak to them. The *Bön* priest ignored him as if he didn't exist. So did the novice. He asked the others, in Tibetan, whose servants they were. They got up and stood between him and the big baskets.

The monk came running and almost dragged Tom away. He led him up the well-remembered stone steps to the gallery. The *Bön* priest moved. Followed by his novice he went to the middle of the courtyard and got in the way of the dancers, in order to watch Tom as he walked the entire length of the gallery and turned down a passage toward where Abbot Mu-ni Gam-po's chamber faced the winds from the Roof of the World.

Through a heavy teak door into the antechamber. That was nothing more than a wide, dim, masonry passage with a very small window and stone benches against the walls for the attendant monks. There were four monks. The most solemn of the four—he had ears that resembled the lugs on a cast-iron cooking-pot—entered the inner room and came out bowing. He dismissed Tom's guide with scant ceremony. The guide was evidently not a suitable person to enter that sanctum on a Thursday forenoon. Tom entered alone. The thick door thudded at his back.

A weird light, from two arched windows wide apart in masonry walls many feet thick. Heavy roof beams in the gloom above the shafts of sunshine. An image of Chenrezi, against one wall, flanked by beautiful paintings of the Buddha. Two prayer wheels on a heavy table that was almost invisible in mid-room because of the difficult light. A prayer drum, in an iron frame on the floor, rigged up with a treadle and the free-wheel mechanism from a bicycle. Old Mu-ni Gam-po was notorious as an innovator, and a humorist to boot. The prayer drum had been given a good treadling, perhaps by the monk who had announced Tom; it went on spinning for two or three minutes; two or three hundred repetitions of the thousands of prayers written on little scraps of paper in the drum.

There were two men in the room, but the light was so baffling that he could only recognise one of them. Old Abbot Mu-ni Gam-po hadn't changed in the least. He stepped down from his dais between the windows, black-robed and benevolent, all smiles and blessings.

"Tum-Glain! Tum-Glain!"

He was very stoop-shouldered from reading and writing all day long in a light that would have destroyed most men's eyesight. As thin as a wraith, all wrinkles. Big ears with long lobes. Big, good-humoured eyes and a firm mouth. Skin the colour of old parchment. Full of chuckles that shook his frail body. A deep voice:

"Tum-Glain! Tum-Glain!" Then in sonorous Tibetan: "O Nobly Born, a hundred thousand times a hundred thousand welcomes!"

Two or three minutes (and Tom out of practise) of galloping Tibetan syllables, chained together into words a yard long that spilled themselves into sentences like sunlit water burbling over gravel. Then old Mu-ni Gam-po took Tom's hand and led him toward the farther window. In the shadow to one side of it the other man sat on a throne like the Abbot's, only smaller, of raised masonry spread with a woollen rug woven in Lhasa and blessed in Tashi-lunpo. Mu-ni Gam-po patted Tom between the shoulders as he introduced him to the son of sunlight, incarnation of Kun-fu-tse and blessed with millions of blessings—Norman Johnson!

"How d'you do," he said gruffly, staring as if Tom hadn't any business to be there.

Tom laughed. He went and treadled the prayer drum until it spun like an electric fan.

"That's how," he answered. "I'm raring to go."

"Oh, yes?" said Johnson.

His manner and appearance were the same as they had been in Delhi. There was the same sullen glower in his eyes, the same hectoring note in his voice, the same heft to his shoulders, even in repose, as if he were thrusting his way through a crowd.

"Don't you ever sit down?" he demanded.

Tom went and sat on the deep window embrasure between him and Mu-ni Gam-po. There was nowhere else to sit, except the table or the floor. Mu-ni Gam-po struck a gong, commanded, and presently a monk brought in a chair. He set it facing the light. Tom moved it out of the wedge-shaped zone of sunlight and sat down where he could watch both men's faces as conveniently as they could watch his.

Johnson glared at Tom as if he were some sort of strange animal under scrutiny. However, Tom didn't mind being stared at.

"You interrupted a conversation," said Johnson, after at least a minute's silence. "The Reverend Abbot was giving me his views of the situation in Tibet. His Reverence, as I dare say you know, is a Yellow-hat Lama. His religious convictions impose upon him a consistently pacifistic attitude. The present state of anarchy in Tibet deeply grieves him. His constant prayers have inspired him, so he tells me, to keep this monastery open to all-comers, of whatever faction. Thus he keeps himself well informed of what is happening beyond the border. He would like to return to Tibet, to die in peace at Tashi-lunpo."

He talked like a lecturer to a class of students of anatomy—as if there were a corpse in front of him and the students must listen whether they liked or not.

"However," he continued, "should His Reverence return to Tibet, he might be murdered without having accomplished anything."

He paused. He appeared to expect comment. Tom glanced at the Abbot:

"What would happen to this monastery, if His Reverence should go away? No fat brethren as long as he's here! No unchaste ones who aren't whipped and given 'solitary.' None who dares to miss a midnight service! I've attended those services—cold—draughty—full ceremonial—no cuts. But he makes 'em like it."

Mu-ni Gam-po beamed. Johnson shot a sudden question at Tom.

"Do you know what happened to the Dalai Lama?"

118

"Sure. They poisoned him."

"Who did?"

"Some of his own political gang in Lhasa."

"Why?"

"He was too pro-British, for one thing. Too sincere. Wouldn't stand for sending *Bön* monks to try to poison the exiled Tashi Lama. He was for letting the Tashi Lama return to Tibet."

"How long were you in Tibet?"

"Two years."

"You knew the Dalai Lama, of course? I mean, you met him?"

"Well," said Tom, "they poisoned him. You can't ask him that, can you."

"I am trying to discover where your prejudices lie, Mr. Grayne."

"They don't lie," said Tom. "It's the truth, I haven't any. I'm here to listen."

"I have been told you propose to return to Tibet."

No answer.

"It is no business of mine," said Johnson. "My department is a purely decorative one. I assemble dry facts and write reports that no one reads. I understand you carry an American passport."

"Yes. I have it with me."

"Do you know that there are laws and treaties specifically forbidding foreigners of almost every nationality from entering Tibet?"

"Yes," said Tom, "I understand that."

"The Indian Government has solemnly pledged itself not to permit British subjects to cross the Tibetan border."

Tom sat silent. Mu-ni Gam-po appeared to have gone into meditation. Johnson resumed:

"An Englishwoman, who marries an American, becomes an American citizen, doesn't she, Mr. Grayne?"

Tom laughed. "Damned if I know. The laws are funny. She'd be eligible, under certain conditions. Go on. You're telling me."

"No American," said Johnson, "can be classified as British. That might not hold in Tibet, where I imagine they don't know the difference. But we are under no treaty obligations to guard the Tibetan frontier against American citizens. We are equally under no obligation to protect Americans in Tibet."

"Hell. D'you mean you wouldn't send the British fleet to Lhasa, over them thar hills?"

Johnson rose abruptly. "I must go. I have an appointment. Will you see me to the stair-head?"

"Come back, Tum-Glain. Come quick back," said Mu-ni Gam-po.

Johnson shook hands with the Abbot and then lingered in the anteroom to talk with one of the attendant monks. Tom went ahead and waited midway along the gallery, where he watched the devil-dancers until Johnson overtook him.

"Are you hurt?" asked Johnson. "You carry your left arm pretty close to your side."

"No," said Tom. "I'm all right."

Johnson shed his brusqueness: "Quite a scholar, the old Abbot. He is worried about some books in the British Museum. He wants them sent to him, to be returned to Tibet, on the ground that they're sacred and were stolen in the first instance. The request seems reasonable. I have put him in touch with Dr. Mayor. You know Mayor, I believe."

"Yes," said Tom, "I know him." He wasn't going to get garrulous just because a brusque ethnologist had suddenly turned civil.

"Funny," said Johnson. "Old Mu-ni Gam-po wouldn't write to Mayor for fear his correspondence might be opened by the censor. We've a pretty drastic censorship in force, on account of the Indian Nationalist troubles and one thing and another. But that needn't have bothered him. I suppose he's touchy. I had to apply for authority to give him my personal word of honour that his letters won't be opened in transit." He stared at Tom. "Of course," he added, "we never censor anything that comes from Tibet addressed to Mu-ni Gam-po himself. If we did, he'd soon know it. He might retaliate by ceasing to keep us informed, and that'ud be awkward. Those rogues down below us, for instance, have undoubtedly brought him secret news. If it's important he'll drop us a hint. Do you know anyone in Dorking?"

"I did," Tom answered. He looked as suddenly casual as a hunter who sees his quarry with the side of his eye.

Johnson smiled. "Dangerous place, Dorking. Lots of traffic accidents. Police there are very officious."

Tom reciprocated promptly. He could hardly have asked for a plainer hint.

"Thank you. Speaking of police," he said, "some of your men might recognise this." He produced Noropa's dagger from under his left arm. "Careful! It's poisoned."

"Found that, did you? May I have it?"

"Yes," said Tom. "If you can't find its original owner, label it a

120

souvenir from—" he began to spell it, pausing on the second letter—
"D—o—"

"Dorking! Yes, yes. I must show this to Abdul Mirza. He arrived this morning to discuss the mysterious death of a Japanese merchant. Abdul Mirza knows someone who is rather an authority on unusual weapons and rare poisons. You know Abdul Mirza?"

"Good guy."

"Very. To all intents and purposes he governs Naini Kol. I must get him to ask his scientific friend about this thing—dagger would you call it?—before the—ah—scientific friend goes into retirement. Abdul Mirza tells me you know Lobsang Pun."

"Know him? The old hellion booted me out of Tibet. Damn his eyes, he waited until it was almost a cinch I'd be caught by winter in the passes."

"So you're enemies, eh?"

"I like him first rate," Tom answered. "The man's a gentleman. He wouldn't stoop to dirty murder. But he'd laugh like hell if you or I should run into something we couldn't buck. Then he'd pray for our souls, to a bunch of saints who know what humour is. He's a high altitude, high church humorist."

"He's a dangerous man," said Johnson. "If old Lobsang Pun could have persuaded the Japanese to do the fighting for him, the Tashi Lama would be spiritual ruler of Asia, with all the temporal power that Lobsang Pun could filch for him. But the Japanese, as I understand it, turned him down. Both sides wanted too much, I imagine. Such men as Lobsang Pun make bitter enemies. If he should happen to be murdered while he's under our protection, there'd be hell to pay. But who knows which his enemies are?" He changed the subject abruptly:

"I hope the police didn't give you a scare this morning, Mr. Grayne. The station-master phoned them from Siliguri, so something had to be done in the way of eyewash."

"Scaring me wouldn't matter," said Tom. "I'm used to it. But third degree would—"

"Tut-tut, man, we never use it. In special cases, to prevent anything of that sort, it's the rule for an officer to keep a prisoner under continuous observation. That Noropa person is a mean customer. It was just as well to lock him up until we could discuss him with you. We don't want an American citizen murdered in India. Your State Department could be very unpleasant about it."

"Oh, they wouldn't bother about me," said Tom. "I may need No-

121

ropa."

"You may have him—delivered, if you like, in cellophane. Simply press the button."

"If they should tell him he was being let go as a personal favour to me, he'd come and find me. He's feeling friendly at the moment."

"Very well. But he'd better be shadowed, or he might double back. We don't want him in Delhi."

"Thank you for the tip about how to get my mail through."

"Not at all. You may count on that. You'll reciprocate, of course?"

"You bet."

"Anything addressed to me in Delhi, in any kind of envelope marked Secret, reaches me unopened. Thunder Dragon Gate! Where is it? What is it? Why is it? Facts, if you please, Mr. Grayne. And don't get bumped off. It isn't you I'm thinking of."

"Sure. I get you."

"Well then, good luck."

"Thanks, and same to you."

Johnson turned away abruptly and strode along the gallery toward the stone stairs. Tom turned the other way, toward the Abbot's chamber. Neither man glanced backward. Tom was humming to himself. His stride was vigorous—springy—the stride of a man who smells the wind and sees the long trail open.

CHAPTER 22

Tom lost no time about eliminating Dorking from his line of communication. Abbot Mu-ni Gam-po was delighted to have him draft a letter in English to Professor Mayor. The abbot copied the letter, in beautiful handwriting, taking nearly an hour to do it. He enclosed with it, in the same sealed envelop, one in Tom's handwriting that Mayor's deaf-and-dumb filing clerk would know what to do with.

Carefully written with one of Mu-ni Gam-po's fine pens, it covered two sheets of closely written paper. The fine pen-point went through the paper here and there. Mayor would read the letter and toss it to the deaf-and-dumb Pole to be filed away. The Pole would transcribe the pen-pricked letters only. They would then read:

Eiji Sarao dead. Jap system may be out of gear for time being. Indian Government Number One using me and in return guarantees my mail by this route secret. Leaving for Tibet. Pronto.

122

The Polish filing clerk would add to that message the words "No. 88 to No. 1" and would mail it, in a plain envelope, to an address in the west of London. It would reach Washington sooner or later.

The next thing was to get Mu-ni Gam-po to act as secret post-master and to protect all letters with his big Tibetan seal. That had to be done tactfully. Very reverend abbots, even more than other people, mustn't let the right hand know the good or evil that the left is doing. It says so, definitely, in nearly all the sacred scriptures, of all nations.

So there was patiently copious conversation, cordial, evasive of the issue, guarded. The abbot continually questioned Tom about European politics. Tom knew not much more about those than he had read in the papers. In fact, the abbot knew more than he did. Tom kept re-turning to the subject of the Tibetan books in the British Museum, little by little increasing the stress on the fact that he was intimately friendly with Professor Mayor. The abbot wished to be told about President Roosevelt.

They had drunk not less than twenty cups of tea apiece, and it was growing dark; they had discussed the probable action of the League of Nations in regard to Italy and Ethiopia, the behaviour of Japan in Manchukuo, and the state of religion in Russia; Tom had had to strug-gle to explain the New Deal in the United States (it was the first time he had ever seriously tried to understand it!) before Mu-ni Gam-po gently and persuasively suggested that, if Tom should write now and then to Professor Mayor, and if he, the humble Abbot Mu-ni Gam-po should forward the letters, perhaps Professor Mayor might be thereby reminded to employ a little of his illustrious influence to procure the return of the stolen sacred books. That settled that. They understood each other without having swapped any naive confidences. Not even Tom would be able to swear that the abbot knew what was going on.

Then solemn ceremony in the monastery chapel, Tom looking down from the gloom of the heavily beamed gallery. A lamp-lit altar, spread with the Eight Happy Symbols and large incense pots. A great stone image of Chenrezi, twenty-five feet high, between smaller im-ages of Padma Sambhava and Atisa. The entire dimness hung with painted banners. Rows on rows of half-seen monks all bowed in the flickering shadows cast by scores of tiny oil lamps. At intervals they laid their foreheads on the floor in adoration. Gongs, horns, a tinkling silver bell. A murmur, a drone that swelled into a chant and died away, to be awakened again by Mu-ni Gam-po's golden voice. In his robes, in the lamp-lit dimness, the old abbot looked like a wooden carving come to life; his acolytes and ministering monks, patient though they were, in comparison resembled lively worldlings in a hurry to be through with ceremony and receive their blessing. There was no sign of the *Bön* magician's party, though they might have been beneath the gallery, where Tom couldn't have seen them.

After that, the evening meal in the dim refectory. The old abbot ate supper alone; not even for Tum-Glain would he set aside that rule. Tom filed into the refectory behind the hooded monks, all two by two, and took his seat near the door. Prayer, blessing, silence, save for the sound of munching and the noise of spoons and platters. Tea, cheese, barley bread. Good grub. Tom was used to it. He had long ago learned how to chew the lightly cooked grain so that, like the monks, he needed not enough of it to bloat him, though he ate enough to leave the table feeling fit for a forced march.

Again, not a sign of the *Bön* magician's party. Perhaps, as rank heretics and blasphemers, they were being fed in the outer courtyard along with the stablemen and horsemen.

Prayer, quite a lot of that. Blessing, a bit quick and perfunctory. Then up the stone stair to the guest cell, along a passage leading from the gallery between two long dormitories, fifty yards from the Abbot's chamber at the other corner of the building. Good clean quarters, though a trifle draughty from the small, square, unglazed windows that faced the Himalayas. Plain stone walls and floor. A truckle bed. A chair. A little table. A lamp in a niche in the wall. A strip of matting. A teak door two inches thick, without a lock but with a peephole for the dutiful-observant-brother-going-rounds-approving-silent-meditation-and-no-visiting each-other-in-the-night.

The sound of a bell about every fifteen minutes. Dutiful-observant-brother's eye, and then his big mouth at the peephole and his knuckles on the teak:

Blessed-night-of-celebration-of-wonder-working-incarnation-of-the-precious-Lord-Avalokitesvara-whose-mission-is-to-liberate-humanity-from-the-Eight-Great-Perils-humbly-make-your-meditation-before-midnight-service.

Thud-thud again on the teak and the slap on stone of dutiful-observant-brother's retreating sandals. *Thud-thud* on another door, and another, and another. A monk might sleep if he could.

Then the weather again, not the climate. Darjeeling actually boasts of a hundred inches of rain in June. But it wasn't June. It was merely getting ready for June, six weeks ahead. The rain came down in swishing torrents that cascaded to the courtyard flags until night was all one tumult of crashing and gurgling water.

Damp walls, as cold as the devil. Meditation indicated. Tom, in two shirts and his sleeved leather waistcoat, was meditating where to buy the necessary garments for the venture into Tibet, when he heard a clatter in the inner courtyard that sounded more like stones being thrown from the roof than falling rain. A twenty-foot *radong*, (ritual trumpet shaped bell), blared like a fog horn. Shouts. Hoof-beats—couldn't be anything else: the walls re-echoed them until they sounded like a regiment of horse arriving.

Tom made his way to the gallery by torchlight reflected off the wet walls of the courtyard. A fabulous scene. Some of the light was electric—one of Mu-ni Gam-po's innovations, very good for discovering monks up to mischief in holes and corners. Economical, too: penalty-of-work-in-meditation-time-on-monastery-woodpile-paying-cost-of-batteries-for-torches.

Seen through the rain from above, the electric torches and the spluttering pine-knots weirdly suggested a wet night in Trafalgar Square. There were things that suggested Landseer's lions, dripping wet. In place of Nelson's Column in the midst, there was a man on horseback.

Couldn't possibly mistake that man—even from above, in pouring rain, near midnight—even under that pointed black hood, on a steaming horse, beneath a small black canopy on long poles held by four men, that kept him liberally splashed with water from its tasselled fringe whenever the horse moved or the bearers fell out of step. He was riding forward across the courtyard toward the gallery, dead slow.

The things that looked at first like Landseer's lions revealed themselves after a moment or two as enormous, shapeless loads covered by black tarpaulins. Six or eight men—a confusion of legs—staggered beneath each.

There were monks on the run, all hooded, with their robes up and the torchlight gleaming on wet bare thighs and calves. Greetings. A great howdydo of obeisance. A big yellow umbrella that wouldn't come open was being made ready by monks who struggled against gusty squalls at the foot of the gallery stairs. Even the Lord Abbot of a Ringding Gelong Monastery must be summoned from his bed, or meditation as the case may be, to do the honours for such a prelate as

125

the Most Reverend and Holy Lobsang Pun.

It was he all right. He bulked on the back of the horse like a black balloon, but he sat the saddle like an experienced horseman. The thrice-blessed horse was a little bit gone in the knees and looked inclined to kneel and pray beneath the staggering weight. But the total effect was magnificent.

Tom stared. Lobsang Pun on the march meant climax. It meant that one of Asia's dynamic geniuses had decided to forge an event or two, instead of waiting for Time and Destiny to do it.

Mu-ni Gam-po passed, followed by his four attendants, hurrying along the gallery. They took no notice of Tom. They had passed him a minute ago; he was leaning, head and shoulders in the rain, with his elbows on the rail, when he felt a touch on his shoulder. He didn't turn. Probably one of the monks had been sent to tell him to keep out of sight. He stole the last second to stare at the scene.

"So you're Tum-Glain, are you! I asked for Mr. Tom Grayne and they corrected my pronunciation!"

"Elsa! Well, thank the Lord! Where's Thö-pa-ga?"

"At Nancy Strong's."

"How is he?"

"Moony. But he's better. He began to get better as soon as we started to climb from Siliguri."

"Moony? About you?"

"Yes. And he's afraid to go to Tibet. He's like a man awaiting execution. Nancy Strong offered to keep him as a teacher in her school, but he says—you know his funny phrases—spiritual things might happen. What he means is, he's afraid of *shang-shang* sendings. He's afraid they would wish them on Nancy Strong."

"She lend you the waterproof? It's nearly big enough for Lobsang Pun! Who brought you here?"

"I came. I didn't need to be brought. I held Lobsang Pun's horse's tail. He didn't mind. Nancy Strong says you will send me back to England. Tom—please!"

"How did you come from Delhi?"

"Someone's carriage to the Edith Cavell Hospital, I don't know whose. Then—"

"Why did you go to the hospital?"

"Dr. Lewis asked me to, at Dowlah's house, when he was testing my blood-pressure. He didn't test it seriously. What he wanted to do was to talk. I didn't see him at the hospital. He was operating, or so

126

the head night-nurse said. They brought Thö-pa-ga down—he was hysterical, he was so glad to see me—and the carriage took us about twenty minutes' drive through dark streets to a place where a big closed Daimler car was waiting. Someone had brought my bag from the hotel and paid the bill, the receipt was on top of the bag, tucked under the strap. We were off in a minute. It was a perfectly wonderful drive, and—"

"Before that happened, did Dowlah send you with a message to Lobsang Pun?"

"No. Abdul Mirza's servant did. He begged me not to mention Dowlah, so I didn't. He asked me to go with Noropa, in a closed carriage, and say that Eiji Sarao was dying and must speak to Lobsang Pun before it was too late. The house we went to seemed to be heavily guarded. We drove through so many streets in the dark that I haven't the slightest idea where it was. The walls were hung with Tibetan pictures. Lobsang Pun turned out to be the man to whom Eiji Sarao had introduced me through a panel in the wall of a shop in the Chandni Chowk that afternoon. Tom, it was fun. I loved it. All intriguey. Lobsang Pun—enormous—like a great gorilla in a black robe—in a rather dark room, all lined with carved wood. Of course I knew Eiji Sarao wasn't really dying. I lied to a most reverend and holy prelate! Wasn't that awful? He could speak pretty good English, and he asked me lots of questions about Thö-pa-ga."

"Did he speak to Noropa?"

"Yes. He cursed him. He called someone and ordered Noropa driven from the house. They treated Noropa pretty roughly. I felt sorry for him, though on the way in the carriage he had done his best to scare me. He kept looking into my eyes. He kept repeating one sentence: 'Telling Lobsang Pun Noropa brought you! Telling Lobsang Pun Noropa brought you!' I think he tried to hypnotise me, but perhaps he's mad. Anyhow, I didn't say Noropa had brought me. The last I saw of Noropa was when he was thrown out of that house into a dark street. Lobsang Pun came with me in the carriage, back to Dowlah's house, and another carriage followed us, full of, I think, Tibetans. They all had weapons, and excepting Lobsang Pun they all acted scared. Lobsang Pun seemed just the opposite of scared. He treated me like a favourite niece or something. He held my hand all the way in the carriage and kept patting it and laughing."

"So you were in Dowlah's house when Lobsang Pun was in there?"

127

"No, I wasn't. Abdul Mirza met me at the front door and took me back to the carriage. He leaned through the window and said 'Be clever, sweet maid, and let who will be good. Open your eyes and shut your mouth, be kind to Thö-pa-ga, and you shall see where King George will send you!' He told the coachman where to drive, and the next thing I was at the hospital, where I knew what to do."

"You did well," said Tom. "Did Dowlah proposition you at any time?"

"Oh, yes. All through dinner. He was rather good at it. He has an original line. I couldn't consult you of course, so I pretended to be awfully thrilled but rather scared."

"Why didn't you come here first?" Tom asked. "Why did you go to Nancy Strong's house?"

"Shouldn't I have? Thö-pa-ga wanted to go there. Dr. Lewis had advised it, though he said I should probably find you here. It was awfully late, but Nancy Strong seemed to expect us. She had food ready, and two bedrooms prepared. She expected me to stay the night. But Tom, her account of her conversation with you in the train—I couldn't stay still until I had asked you about it. She said—"

"How did you meet Lobsang Pun again?"

"He came to Nancy Strong's house on horseback. I've no idea where he came from. He may have overtaken us in another auto during the night. Or he may have come by plane. I simply don't know. He demanded to see Thö-pa-ga, who was already in bed, so Nancy Strong took him to Thö-pa-ga's bedroom, and I don't know what happened. I should say he was alone with Thö-pa-ga for at least half an hour. Nancy Strong told me Lobsang Pun was coming here to see Mu-ni Gam-po. She said she was glad he was leaving her house, because his enemies are after him and there might be serious trouble. So I borrowed her waterproof, and I didn't ask Lobsang Pun's leave or anything. I just held on to his horse's tail, because it was dark and I could hardly force my way against the rain. I'm wet, but here I am. And now, Tom, tell me."

He met her eyes and spoke bluntly:

"I have promised to do my best to persuade you to return to England."

Elsa waited several seconds before she answered. Her face, in the reflected torchlight, was a picture of alarm—wide-eyed. She didn't flinch, but her voice changed:

"Tom, do you think that's honourable?"

Tom's voice had changed, too: "I can't go back on a promise."

A pause—bleak, grim, gusty—eyes to eyes in semi-darkness.

"How about your promise to me?"

Thunder and lightning cannonaded for sixty seconds before he could answer:

"That was conditional."

He writhed. He knew he couldn't keep her from detecting it. He knew the keenness of her enthusiasm, the sharpness of her disappointment. He could guess how she felt by how he himself felt. That was why he had set his jaw and raised his voice to make it harshly penetrate the noise of splashing and of voices echoed off the courtyard walls. Even in his own ears it sounded cruel.

Lobsang Pun and Mu-ni Gam-po, followed by a dozen monks, were coming up the stone stairway. He took Elsa's arm and almost hustled her into the dark passage that led toward his cell. There he faced her again. It wasn't easier, even so, where he could hardly see her eyes.

"Conditional on the marriage being secret," he said. "It isn't. They know it."

"Yes," she answered. "Nancy Strong didn't say so, but I knew she knew it, from the way she spoke about your conversation on the train." She laid her hands on his forearms. "Tom—do you believe I told?"

"No. I know you didn't."

"Did you tell?"

"No. But I've admitted it. They've checked back. Simply routine, that. Punch a button nowadays, and you can find out anything, about anybody. The gaff's blown, Elsa."

"Tom, are you being fair? Have I failed you? Is there any reason, that we didn't discuss before we left England, why you should order me home now?"

"No, by God," he answered. "Damn the woman. I told her flat I wouldn't order you home."

"Then I won't go."

"Fine," said Tom. "That settles that. Tell her I kept my promise."

She laughed, suddenly, gaily. "Tom, you're—Please forgive me. I was scared. I was afraid I hadn't made good. I should have know you wouldn't use a trick to get rid of me. She didn't say so, but she made me think you had asked her to have me sent home."

"Hold on to yourself," he answered. "Scares have hardly begun. Eiji Sarao is dead—of a *shang-shang* bite. They've canned Dowlah—caught

129

him double-crossing every one, I don't doubt. They have okayed you, unless Nancy Strong should report unfavourably and I don't think she will. They've given me my head and all the privilege I could ask. I have Noropa by the short hair. I've a line on where the Thunder Dragon Gate is. Now we go to the mat with Lobsang Pun. The old bird's a top-notcher, so there won't be any easy show-down. He's the Tashi Lama's political chief of staff. He's the Tibetan Number One. When Number One steps out, there's trouble. If his enemies are out to get him, that's my answer to all the prayers I've prayed since I was your size. You'd better stay and see the midnight ceremony. Are you too wet? Are you tired? Wait, I'll get a blanket for you. If we're in the gallery before the show begins there'll be no questions asked."

CHAPTER 23

The dark gallery ran the entire length of one side of the chapel. It was so high up under the roof that Tom could touch the rafters. No lamps up there, but there was plenty to look at if one could only see it. Wood carving. Pictures. His little pocket flashlight hardly served to show the details of a Tantric Hell depicted on a panel on the rear wall. A sound, while he and Elsa were looking at that, drew his attention to the fact that they were not alone in the gallery. He left her in the dark and went to investigate.

The *Bön* magician, his novice, the *shaman* and four more of the party he had seen in the courtyard, were grouped together at the far end, in the darkest corner. They had had to move the benches to make room for their two big baskets covered with black waterproofing. They stirred like evil birds disturbed by the pin-ray light. The *shaman* spoke, in Tibetan. He said nothing polite. Tom didn't answer. There was nothing to be gained by trying to make conversation. He groped his way back to Elsa and they went to the opposite end of the gallery overlooking the high altar. The benches were too low for anyone seated to see over the rail to the floor below, so they leaned on the breast-high rail.

There were little lights on the altar, and two big lamps at the opposite end, but all the middle of the chapel was in darkness until two monks entered, one with an electric torch to show the other where to use his taper on a long pole. They lighted all the little oil-lamps in the niches in the walls, and in the iron lanterns hanging from the beams, until the chapel was aswim with smoky light that spread rich shadows flickering amid coloured banners and upon the calm features

130

of Chenrezi above the high altar. But it was almost as dark as before, up there in the gallery.

After a while the gallery door squeaked open and thudded shut. Footsteps. Stealthy. No slap of sandals. Tom used his flashlight. It wasn't bigger than a cigarette-case; it made a circle of light about two feet in diameter.

In the midst of that appeared Noropa's death-mask face—Noropa's eyes, like a cat's. He was smiling—the first smile Tom had seen on that humourless face—wan, hideous, a bit pitiful, unpleasant. He came forward, making very little noise for such a tall, strong, awkward specimen. He thrust his face close to Tom's, stuttered and then spoke with more than his usual breathless speed, as if a thousand syllables could form only one word:

"My-not-knowing-you-such-very-Number-One-man-they-letting-me-go-saying-you-demanding.   Now-my-understanding-youplotecting-my-obeying."

The man was trembling with excitement, or relief, or anxiety—or perhaps with all three. He could speak English better than that when he was in a normal condition.

"What did the police do to you?" Tom asked.

"Nothing-only-telling-me-your-being-Number-One-Amelikan. My-being-glad-plotection-and-obeying-Number-One."

"Go and find out what's in those baskets. Come back and tell me."

Tom drew Elsa close to him. She snuggled and he felt for given for suggesting she should go home. He laid his hand on her neck to feel if she was shivering with cold. She wasn't. He found her hand and used their private code:

"Giving Noropa his chance. That man in the far corner is a black magician—*Bön*—perhaps a hot wire."

"Do you trust Noropa?"

"Too friendly all of a sudden."

Monks began filing in, two by two, until the floor below resembled a dark carpet of bowed heads. At the far end, facing the altar, a raised stone platform was left clear. The wall behind it was hung with pictures of Tibetan saints. Old Mu-ni Gam-po, followed by acolytes and ministrants, entered to the sound of a gong and weird wind-music that accompanied a chant. He took his seat on the high-backed throne-chair beside the altar. Motionless, in heavy vestments, he looked like a carving in old wood and ivory. One monk, seated beside a flat drum, which he tapped with a strangely irregular beat, intoned a hymn. Most of the words went lost amid the rafters. But it wasn't a regular Buddhist hymn. It sounded more like a ballad describing miraculous feats by the followers of the holy saint Avalokitesvara, against the sinful minions of the Eight Great Perils. Decidedly not pacifistic poetry. Mu-ni Gam-po looked ill at ease. The monks kept glancing at each other.

Silence, as if something had gone wrong. It lasted two or three minutes. The noise of rain and wind from the courtyard suggested a storm at sea. There was a sudden booming blare of *radongs*—twenty-foot long trumpets. All the monks' faces turned toward a door beneath the gallery. There was thudding and commotion, but Tom and Elsa couldn't lean over far enough to see what caused it. The devil-dancers appeared—sixteen of them, two abreast, in grotesque devil-masks and full costume.

Tom signalled to Elsa: "Something fishy. Devil-dancing is done outdoors. Looks to me like trouble brewing. Tibetan monks are scrappers when they're roused."

"Would they fight in here?" she answered.

"Fight anywhere, like hornets. Rouse 'em, that's all."

The monks had to make way for the devil-dancers, who forced quite a wide passage down the midst of the chapel, dancing a curious, stealthy step, in a formation that opened and closed like scissor-blades. The same step constantly repeated. Behind them came a heavy *palanquin*, borne on poles by eight monks. It was a closed, old-fashioned thing, held together by big wooden pegs inserted into tongues protruding through slots in the woodwork. Its shape looked almost Chinese. But the dragon, on the panel that could be seen from the gallery, wasn't Chinese. It was a crudely painted monster with a devil's face and eight legs, belching a crimson fury of flame through a long snout that was almost like a trumpet.

Elsa signalled Tom: "The monks look scared."

"Hold on to yourself," he answered. "Don't talk. Watch. Keep close to me."

She crowded herself against him, so that he shouldn't have to look for her. He put his arm around her.

Behind the *palanquin*—at a noticeable distance behind it— walked Lobsang Pun. He was preceded by one attendant bearing a bronze *dorje* on a cushion—a thing shaped like a thunder-bolt. It meant that he represented the Tashi Lama. He was dressed in the full robes of a Yellow-hat *lamaistic* hierarch, including cone-shaped hood. He looked

132

enormous. He took long strides, slowly, that made his robes sway, so he looked arrogant.

He paused, exactly in the middle of the chapel and faced the high altar, until his eight attendant monks had formed into a group behind him. Then, with convincing reverence, he bowed before the image of Chenrezi. Nothing could have been more decorous, meek, dignified. He appeared unconscious of the disturbance behind him. One of his attendants slapped a monk belonging to the monastery who hadn't backed out of the way fast enough. There was quite a scuffle. Lobsang Pun marched forward toward the high altar, followed by only seven attendants; the eighth was being carried out, apparently stunned by a blow on the head. He bowed to Mu-ni Gam-po and then seated himself on a throne like the abbot's, on the other side of the altar, with his attendants grouped on his left hand.

Elsa whispered: "Do you notice the abbot's face?"

Tom signalled: "Shut up! Watch!"

The *palanquin* was carried to the dais at the far end of the chapel. The bearers' clothing was slightly different from that of Mu-ni Gam-po's congregation. They might perhaps be Lobsang Pun's men. As they raised the *palanquin* to the dais one of them slipped on the stone. He fell and was soundly kicked in the ribs by one of Mu-ni Gam-po's monks. He seized the monk's leg in both hands and bit it. He was kicked in the face. The *palanquin* almost toppled over, but a monk with a sharp stick came and restored order, prodding as if he were driving animals to market. He was a very efficient person, competent to prod the right man at the proper moment. The *palanquin* was lifted to the dais and planted there facing the altar with its poles removed. The devil-dancers, on the floor to right and left of it, swayed and gestured. They appeared not to be illustrating any midnight adoration theme.

Abbot Mu-ni Gam-po looked like a man in the seat of torture. His face was a picture of impotent indignation. He raised his right hand. One of his acolytes struck a gong. There was a subdued blare of horns. There began the regular midnight ritual, more than vaguely resembling High Mass droned by long-used, rather listless voices. But Lobsang Pun's voice was as clear as a bell. He led the chanting. By the vigour of his reverence he recreated a sensation of mystical midnight devotion. The ritual grew real.

"Arbitrary old devil," Tom signalled to Elsa. "Champion churchman. Hellion. Humorist. I bet his plan is to commit Mu-ni Gam-po to something the old chap disapproves. But I think there's trouble brewing."

Noropa groped his way back stealthily. He appeared excited. He came to Tom's left side and whispered.

"Their-saying-baskets-containing-relics-for-blessing-by-Holy-Lobsang-Pun-when-this-service-finishing."

Tom signalled to Elsa:

"Beats me how that *Bön* magician got in here unchallenged. He wears a Japanese dagger. I saw the hilt. Think he must have told Mu-ni Gam-po he is Lobsang Pun's *protégé*. Perhaps has a forged document. I bet he's laying for Lobsang Pun. You're going to see some magic. Fold that blanket so that you can spread it wide in a second, then wrap it back on your shoulders."

Noropa whispered again. He thought Tom hadn't heard; he seemed more excited than ever. The second hymn ceased. It was time for the homily. Mu-ni Gam-po should have delivered that, but Lobsang Pun seemed to be stealing the show. One of his attendants brought him a sacred book and laid it opened on his lap.

There fell a silence so intense that there seemed to be no wall to deaden the splashing of rain. Lobsang Pun leaned forward in the teacher's attitude, one elbow on his knee, and read a long text from very ancient scripture. Mu-ni Gam-po perceptibly shuddered. The very last word of the text, pronounced slowly, distinctly, with an even stress on each syllable, was like three distinct words of command:

"The name of him whose spoken word in Thunder Dragon Gate shall move men's minds and stir their hearts, so that these things shall come to pass, shall be like unto the Holy Spirit that directs his sayings: THÖ-PA-GA! (wonderful-to-hear.)"

He paused. At the far end of the chapel someone opened the *palanquin*. The leaves of the double door banged sharply against the sides. Every head in the chapel faced suddenly in that direction. Within the *palanquin*, motionless, looking like a dead man except that his eyelids moved, sat Thö-pa-ga. The devil-dancers had not ceased swaying. Their monotonous motion emphasized Thö-pa-ga's stillness. Two monks directed flashlights at Thö-pa-ga's face. His eyes shone like dark jewels.

Mu-ni Gam-po stood up. Tom gripped Elsa's hand to signal to her. There was all the electric suspense that precedes sudden bloodshed. A sensation of resented sacrilege, increased and heated by Lobsang Pun's air of triumph.

134

Lobsang Pun hove himself up from his throne-chair. Before Mu-ni Gam-po could forestall him by dismissing the monks to their cells as he seemed to intend, Lobsang Pun stole the thunder. His magnificent voice rang through the chapel. In the name of His Holiness the Tashi Lama he proclaimed Thö-pa-ga the Keeper of the Thunder Dragon Gate, the Mouthpiece and the Voice of Prophecy, the Sender-forth—

Even he had to cease. Even his beaked, belligerent, triumphant face froze. Not a doubt of it: he wasn't pretending. He was struck dumb. Horror. Amazement. All eyes followed his.

A gasp of fear struck like a gust of wind and died away into ghastly silence. Three hundred prayer wheels were snatched from girdles and set whirling. Three hundred monks backed away in a wave toward the wall that faced the gallery. The rear ranks kicked and struck at those in front to save themselves from being crushed.

A *shang-shang* was on the chapel wall, midway between Thö-pa-ga and the far end of the gallery. It was motionless, except that its mandibles moved. Elsa's hand clutched Tom's.

He signalled: "Opportunity!"

The brute was hugely bigger than the one that had escaped from Dowlah's house. Its livid green body was about three feet long. The spread of its hairy legs was not less than ten feet, perhaps twelve. In the basket it must have curled them in under itself. Crab, spider, octopus, all three, and devil features added. Its eyes were horrors of the size of tea-plates, motionless, without irises. They looked like opalescent sores. Its snout was a foot long; the moving mandibles beneath it seemed to be wiping one another in preparation for a meal.

About a hundred monks threw themselves prostrate on the chapel floor. Old Abbot Mu-ni Gam-po was the first to break silence. He began to chant a *mantram*. His voice broke, but two hundred monks took up the *mantram*. In a moment the roof was booming to the chant. It appeared to annoy the *shang-shang*. It moved like a spider up and down the wall, then suddenly, almost too swiftly for eye to follow, it shot sideways, and became still again directly over Thö-pa-ga's head. Thö-pa-ga didn't move; he was like a man in a trance. Some fool blew a *radong*. Two monks turned their flashlights on the monster.

The flashlights seemed to drive the brute crazy. It began to scamper all over the walls, making no sound whatever. It passed along the wooden front of the gallery with the tips of its upper legs over the rail. Tom jerked Elsa away, but the brute had passed before they could step backward. Noropa fled into the gloom, upsetting benches. The *shang-*

shang leaped to the floor of the chapel. It made two or three short starts in different directions and then scooted toward the high altar, climbed that and continued upward over the great image of Chenrezi to the gloom of the wall above. There it became motionless again, visible only by its eyes that reflected the chapel lights like pale danger signals, one above the other.

Lobsang Pun stood his ground. So did Mu-ni Gam-po, but he changed the *mantram*; Lobsang Pun stuck to the first one, and about half the monks did the same, so that for at least a minute there was a babel of voices, and two tunes. Noropa came sneaking back and Tom seized his wrist. Lobsang Pun was looking up at the gallery. Tom began to drag Noropa toward the far end of the gallery.

"Stay where you are!" he commanded. But Elsa followed. Tom didn't know it, because Noropa began to resist and to try to break away. Tom hit him hard enough to slow him up:

"You fool, here's your chance!"

But Noropa became panicky. He struggled. He wouldn't be dragged, he was useless. Tom knocked him out of the way and hurried forward. Elsa overtook him.

"Damn you," he said. "Obey orders!"

But she wouldn't obey. There wasn't time to argue. He couldn't treat her like Noropa.

The *Bön* magician was coming toward him, followed by his novice and the *shaman*. They seemed in a hurry, but they hesitated. Behind them, the other four men were carrying the big black baskets, one basket empty with the lid half-open. The *Bön* magician had his hands inside his black robe, getting something ready in the line of sharp-edged, very likely poisoned magic. Tom hesitated, too. He glanced back at Elsa:

"Damn you, run! There's a *shang-shang* in that other basket! I'm going to turn it loose. Get the hell out of here!"

"No," she answered. "Go ahead. I've a blanket in case you need it."

Tom had learned combative magic on football fields. The magician cannoned backward into his novice. The novice crashed into the *shaman*. They both fell. Tom leaped them and bucked the basket-bearers. The empty basket and the man who carried it went reeling away over upset benches. The three who held the other basket dropped it, to put up a fight. There were ends of benches in the way that tripped them. One of them stopped a hay-maker that cracked on his jaw like the blow of a meat-axe. There was an awful din below the gallery, but no time to guess what caused it. Tom heard Elsa's voice:

"They're taking Thö-pa-ga away !"

No time to look. He hove up the big black basket and balanced it on the gallery rail. It stank foul. He tore off the waterproof cover and it stank worse. There was an iron hasp and a big iron padlock—no key. He wrenched the hasp until it tore loose from the cane into which it was threaded and wired. Then he opened the lid and hove the basket over, to the floor below. It spilled a *shang-shang*. The awful brute crept out and spread itself on top of the basket. It was even larger than the other, but it looked sick—or perhaps it was stiff from close confinement.

"Tom! Help!"

Elsa's stifled scream, from down in the dark on the gallery floor. Flashlight. The *shaman* and the *Bön* magician's novice were trying to gag her with her own blanket. Two of the basket-porters stood in Tom's way. They were as easy as ninepins. But he stumbled over the legs of an upset bench and didn't kick the *shaman* hard enough. The *shaman*, *Bön* magician, novice and all the rest of them fled from the gallery, slamming the door. Noropa nowhere to be seen, perhaps hiding among upset benches.

"Hurt?"

"No, not much."

"Good girl. They'd have pulled that off, if you'd obeyed me."

They returned to the rail. Sudden silence had fallen again. A monk's foot rutching on the chapel floor was an explosion of noise. Four monks, running into the gallery with flashlights, made a prodigious din as they stumbled over upset benches. Elsa's fingers signalled on the back of Tom's hand:

"The devil-dancers were trying to drag Thö-pa-ga away."

No sign of them now. Thö-pa-ga sat quite still. All the monks were crowded back against the far wall, but the devil-dancers weren't there any longer. They might have fled under the gallery, out of sight. One *shang-shang* was still on the wall above the high altar. The other was on the floor in mid-chapel. It pulsed up and down on the tips of its wide-spread legs as if flexing them. The monks in the gallery turned their flashlights on the monsters. Tom signalled Elsa:

"Unless Noropa lied, they'll fight. They're cannibals. That's why they're rare."

The brute on the wall dropped to the altar and poised it self, hanging over so that its eyes, on top of its body, looked straight at the other brute. The one on the floor began to pulse up and down more violently. Stuff that looked like froth bubbled on the end of its snout. Suddenly it launched itself toward the high altar. The other fled up the wall. The big one gave chase. Lobsang Pun's voice broke upon the breath less silence, booming scripture:

"Blessings create blessings in an endless cycle. Evil creates evil until evil-doers perish. For the devils shall destroy them selves and one another, and their dupes shall perish with them."

The *shang-shangs* vanished, up amid the shadows of the roof beams. The flashlights discovered them. One dropped to the floor—a fifty-foot drop on to stone that made hardly a sound. The other followed, flourishing its legs in mid-air. It missed its pounce by a yard. The first one fled to the altar, leaped it and crouched with its body resting on Chenrezi's head. The other followed, not so fast now, stalking, crab-wise, with a kind of see-saw movement. It stood still on the altar plat-form between the abbot and Lobsang Pun. Slowly it approached the altar, climbing it crab-wise, in short, almost imperceptible movements. When it reached Chenrezi's feet the other pounced on it. The chapel seethed with its congregation's gasp of horror.

The brutes fought in Chenrezi's lap and all over the altar, knocking altar vessels to the floor with a crash that broke the spell that had held the monks motionless. Some of them ran and hustled Mu-ni Gam-po away from the altar platform. The competent fellow with the sharp stick ran and tried to belabour the brutes. He was joined by taper-on-a-pole. They prodded, whacked, and hit nothing except the altar and Chenrezi's statue, for several minutes. But they were gallant fellows. They stuck to it. The *shang-shangs* fought like wolverines, dragon-flies, octopuses, tearing, leaping, gnawing off each other's legs. They were as quick as lightning. The only sound they made was of rending flesh. They were tearing each other to pieces in a lather of vile froth. One had torn the other's eyes out before the brave man with the stick hit one of them at last. He skewered the blind one. Then he beat the other. It had only three legs left. It dragged itself toward him. Lobsang Pun picked up a heavy charcoal brazier and crushed the brute. Then he laughed—his big laugh from the depths of his huge belly:

"Oo-ha-ha-ha-ha-hah!"

The monks swarmed around the altar. Tom seized Elsa's wrist. He didn't signal, he spoke:

"Come and talk to Thö-pa-ga. It's trespass, but I guess he needs us."

No sign of Noropa. They hurried out of the gallery and down the stone stairs. That brought them into the courtyard. They had to run in the rain around a stone building and its long buttresses to the chapel entrance. Double door. Dark vestibule. Another double door— it swung open against them.

Tom caught a glimpse, against the light within the chapel, of grinning devil-masks and of Thö-pa-ga between the *Bön* magician and the *shaman*, coming on the run toward him. Something struck him on the head. He lost consciousness.

Chapter 24

Tom didn't remain long unconscious. He was alone in the vestibule, in almost total darkness. There was a lot of noise in the chapel. He could feel his scalp was bleeding, but not too badly. He had evidently been hit on the top of the head with a cudgel. He felt dazed. When he stood up it took him a minute or two before he could steady himself. Then he went out into the rain and doused his head under a gush of water from a drainpipe off the gallery roof. After a minute of that he was wet to the skin, and sore-headed, but in full possession of his senses.

As fast as he could run he crossed two courtyards to the monastery gate. The monk on gatehouse duty came out of meditation rather resentfully, spinning his prayer wheel.

Yes. A number of people, including the *Bön* magician and some devil-dancers and others, had passed out through the gate about fifteen minutes ago, and good riddance to them. The *Bön* magician had produced a document that bore Lobsang Pun's signature. Forgery? Nonsense! Who would dare to forge Lobsang Pun's blessed name? In all there were probably thirty people, but he wasn't sure, he hadn't counted. There had been others waiting for them outside, he didn't know how many. To the Powers of Darkness with such rogues. He had locked the gate behind them and returned to his prayers.

No, he hadn't noticed Elsa, nor anyone who looked like a European woman. No, he hadn't seen Thö-pa-ga; didn't know what he looked like; didn't wish to know. Yes, they had all seemed to be in a great hurry, but in no greater hurry than he had been to see the last of them. He didn't know what had come over Mu-ni Gam-po of late, that he should admit such people to the monastery. Those devil-dancers, for instance: not like good Darjeeling devil-dancers. Dissolute, bold, ill-mannered fellows, recently from Tibet, where they must have been corrupted by political and religious quarrels.

The rain ceased. No, the monk wouldn't open the gate for Tom—not unless he had an order from the abbot. It would have to be in writing. Yes Lobsang Pun's written order would be all right, because Lobsang Pun was a high dignitary, even higher than the abbot. No, if Tom should try to climb the wall, he would summon the watch, who were armed with cudgels. The gate would be opened again at sunrise, and no sooner. Then respectable people could walk out with the holy abbot's blessing, and might the blessing go with them wherever they should set foot.

Tom returned to the inner courtyard. All the monks had poured out of the chapel. Mu-ni Gam-po looked deathly sick; he was being supported by his four attendants. Tom wasn't allowed to approach him. A monk thrust a spluttering torch so close to Tom's face that it singed his eyebrows. He said the holy abbot might be dying. If so, he mustn't be interrupted; otherwise his spirit might be hounded away by *shang-shangs* and prevented from reincarnating at an early moment. None but holy men who knew how to deal with *shang-shangs* should come anywhere near him; but if he didn't die Tom might speak with him tomorrow. Several other monks were of the same mind. It was no use trying to approach the abbot.

Faggots. At least a hundred monks were bringing them. They were building a big pyre in the centre of the courtyard, spreading it evenly, waist high. Others were carrying a big black sheet out of the chapel, holding it by the four corners. They were surrounded by monks with twirling prayer wheels, all chanting a *mantram*. Other monks were blowing horns. On the sheet lay the bright green remains of the two *shang-shangs*, looking smaller than when they were alive, because most of their long legs had been bitten off while they fought and they had been swept into a heap.

Behind the black sheet marched Lobsang Pun, exorcising. He was closely followed by his personal attendants, all singing at the top of their lungs and whirling prayer wheels. With his *dorje* in his right hand Lobsang Pun described magical signs in the air. He had a great reputation as an exorcist. He looked the part. The torchlight crimsoned his big, beaked face. His swaying gait lent something even more than dignity. He looked victorious, triumphant. He, not Mu-ni Gam-po, had quoted the scriptural text that set the *shang-shangs* to slaying each other—evil destroying evil! He believed that. There wasn't a scrap of insincerity about him. His was faith militant, triumphant.

They laid the *shang-shangs*, desecrated black curtain and all, on the pyre. The wood was dry. A dozen torches plunged into the faggots. The flames leaped, crimsoning the surrounding walls. The wet courtyard paving resembled a lake of liquid fire, on which shadowy, two-dimensional monks stood twirling prayer wheels, throwing shadows in their turn that made flickering waves of wet light. The monks pitched their chant against the roar and crackle of the flames.

Tom watched Lobsang Pun until he turned away from the scene, but that wasn't until Mu-ni Gam-po's four attendants had half-carried the old man up the gallery stairs. It appeared that Lobsang Pun didn't exactly crave the abbot's company or conversation just then. He showed no sympathy for the abbot—none whatever—no concern about him. He walked down a narrow passage off the courtyard. Tom followed. A door was slammed in his face. He thrust and kicked it open before there was time to shoot the bolt. He was inside before anyone could prevent him.

A four-square stone-walled room. Lobsang Pun. Seven monks. One sturdy wooden bed. A heavy table. Benches. An imported oil lantern. Six or eight candles and a little oil lamp in a niche in the wall. Some heaps of corded luggage. All seven monks had Mauser pistols; each man's loaded pistol lay in its holster on the table, with belt attached. When Tom entered they buckled on their pistols in a hurry, beneath their robes.

Not a word. Tom and Lobsang Pun stared at each other. With his right thumb, like a London policeman directing traffic, Tom indicated the seven monks, one by one, then the door. Lobsang Pun nodded. He, too, gestured. The monks filed out. Tom shot the bolt in the door behind the last one.

"Tum-Glain! Tum-Glain!"

"Your Eminence?"

Silence again. Lobsang Pun spoke in a challenging tone in Tibetan:

"Your wanting what?"

Tom answered in Tibetan. He didn't dare to be misunderstood. He knew more Tibetan than Lobsang Pun knew English. But he hadn't time nor mood to adorn his language with the phrases, of humility and reverence, that ought to have preceded and loaded every sentence. The structure of his phrases was as nearly English as the Tibetan speech would permit. It was crude, but it didn't make Lobsang Pun

141

laugh.

"Write your permit for me to travel where I please in Tibet."

Lobsang Pun looked startled, as if by an idea. Oriental diplomat, he temporized, to gain time to think:

"Tum-Glain, who am I that I should write that?"

Tom retorted bluntly: "I didn't ask who you are. I know. I am saying: write that permit or take the consequences. I will use it and take the consequences."

"Tum-Glain—"

"Do you want to be arrested by the British authorities on the charge that your agent, bearing your instructions, over your signature, threw *shang-shangs* into a monastery chapel and then carried off Thö-pa-ga and Miss Elsa Burbage?"

The arbitrary absolutist Lobsang Pun made no attempt to appear indifferent. He was visibly shocked:

"Tum-Glain, that is untrue!"

"Prove it! That *Bön* magician showed the monk at the gate a document with your signature. Probably that same document passed him across the border into British territory with his baggage unexamined. He used it to get admission to this monastery. Forgery perhaps, but prove it!"

"Tum-Glain, I am on my way to Tibet. I will swiftly overtake and punish."

"Overtake? You?" Tom's fist thumped the table. "I want five or six of your best men. Ten horses. Provisions. That permit. After that, if you can overtake me you're a wizard! Here's the table. Pen. Ink. Paper. Sand. A chair. Sit down and write!"

"But Tum-Glain, they can not have gone far—not yet. My seven monks—"

Tom snorted: "Oh, yes, Mauser pistols. Pursuit. A fight on British territory! Dacoity! Sikkim military police! Your Eminence, if the police, here in Darjeeling, get a hint of what has happened, every road will be blocked by telephone within half an hour. Then what? Do you wish to stay here and face an enquiry?"

"You shall not go to the police!" said Lobsang Pun. His eyes blazed indignation.

Tom laughed. "Very well then, write that permit, and the order for horses, provisions and five men."

"Tell your thinking, Tum-Glain."

"I will tell you your own thoughts!" Tom answered. "That *Bön* magician, who carries a forged authority from you—or isn't it forged?—was wearing a Japanese dagger in his girdle. You came to India to get the British to support the Tashi Lama. Don't say you didn't. I know you did. You'd been intriguing with the Japanese, but they wanted too much in return for their help, so you turned pro-British without warning the Japs. But the British weren't any too enthusiastic. They didn't want you in Delhi—you and your Tibetan intrigues, so you were diplomatically hung up. You only heard of Thö-pa-ga's return from England after he reached Delhi. Eiji Sarao told you about it. You hadn't expected Thö-pa-ga so soon. You weren't quite ready. But the opposition was."

"Your not understanding what you're talking, Tum-Glain."

"Oh, no? Listen to this, then. The Japanese saw through your turn-about-face, so they lined up promptly with the Lhasa gang who murdered the Dalai Lama. That *Bön* magician belongs to the Lhasa outfit. They, you, Russia and Japan all want control of the Thunder Dragon Gate. You want it for His Holiness the Tashi Lama's benefit, and for him only, in order to make him the ruler of Tibet. They want it in order to keep the Tashi Lama out of Tibet. Russia wants it to use against Japan. The Japanese want it for propaganda purposes, to further their aims in China and Inner Mongolia. Now then: if the Lhasa politicians get the Thunder Dragon Gate, and if the Japanese control them, what chance has the Tashi Lama?"

Silence. Lobsang Pun's expression was a mixture of out raged dignity, suspicion, embarrassment, alertness and lurking humour. The humour was in ambush, behind cunning eyes. But he liked Tom. He couldn't disguise that he liked him. A brow-beater himself, he respected a man who stood up to him and dared to bully him with questions that carried no question-mark. Tom kept hard at him:

"You know well you'd be discredited forever if there's a police investigation."

"No police, Tum-Glain."

"Very well then, listen. Suppose they kill Thö-pa-ga. Suppose he dies on the journey. How would that suit you? Would they admit he's dead? Not likely! He'd be out of the way. They'd bury him, or throw his body to the dogs, and put another in his place—they'd pick a devil—and they'd say he was the real man just returned from abroad. The very first thing that their devil would do would be to denounce the Tashi Lama from the Thunder Dragon Gate. After that, he'd begin prophesying that the long-awaited, all-redeeming Maitreya, who is to unite Asia under one benign government, is the Emperor of Japan! Am I right?"

No answer.

"What will they do to Elsa Burbage, if Thö-pa-ga dies on the journey? Do you want the credit for that—you and your *Bön* magician, who, you *say* forged your name to a document!"

A plea at last. Not guilty! Accomplished diplomatic liar Lobsang Pun might be, but his eyes told the truth. Black, oriental, malicious, reserved, fierce, intelligent eyes, they were. But they weren't lying now. Whatever his intentions might have been, concerning Elsa, he hadn't been a party of her abduction. He perceived its implications.

"Tum-Glain, they didn't—"

"They did. They have carried her off to keep Thö-pa-ga from dying of terror and depression. That dog Noropa suggested it to them. If Thö-pa-ga dies, they'll kill her. Then what?"

Lobsang Pun displayed a philosophic doubt on that score.

"Tum-Glain, now your talking foolishness. Why their killing a young woman? Nancy Strong, true, not stolen, but having lived long in Tibet, not dead yet."

"Uh-huh? Write that permit!"

"She being your woman?"

"You've sixty seconds to take that pen in your hand."

The diplomat's canniness came to the surface:

"Tum-Glain, your not wanting police, eh? Why not?"

"Very well, I'll tell you. More than two years ago, when you turned me out of Tibet, I was hunting for the Thunder Dragon Gate. I am hunting for it now, and so is Elsa Burbage. Stop either of us—stop us if you dare! Time's up. Write. Here you are." He dragged the heavy chair to the table. "Sit down. Write."

Lobsang Pun sat and took the pen in hand, but he still hesitated:

"Tum-Glain, no good. My representing Blessed Holiness Panchen Rinpoche, Tashi Lama. His being exiled beyond border of Tibet—"

"Don't I know that? Do you think I'll show your permit to the soldiers or officials from Lhasa? Sign your name as representative plenipotentiary, and set your seal to it. There isn't a tax-ridden layman in all Tibet, nor a decent monk, who doesn't love His Holiness the Tashi Lama and want him home again at Tashi-lunpo. Write it. I'll take the consequences."

Lobsang Pun demurred. "Tum-Glain, my writing evidence, my aiding your entering Tibet, contrary to law? Signing my sentence of death!"

"I'm American. There is no law against my entering Tibet. Against all other foreigners, yes. An American, no."

"They not understanding that."

"Does Your Eminence understand that every minute is of consequence? I'll take care your enemies don't get hold of the permit to use against you. Rather than that, I'll eat it."

Lobsang Pun wrote. But he paused again before he signed.

"Tum-Glain, your never returning alive!"

"No? You went in, didn't you? Here you are. Are you dead?"

"Tum-Glain, my not going in there. Never. More than two years, many years ago, not daring, staying outside."

"You sent Noropa in."

"No. His not going in, also."

"Too bad. Well, Your Eminence, signature please. Now the seal. Thank you."

Tom sanded the document and stowed it away in an inner pocket. Then he opened the door.

By word of mouth, to one of his seven attendant monks, Lobsang Pun gave the order for horses, provisions and five men.

CHAPTER 25

"His Holy Eminence commands you to give me that pistol," said Tom.

All seven monks looked stonily indignant. Lobsang Pun had commanded nothing of the sort. But he didn't deny it. Tom unbuckled a Mauser, belt and all, from the waist of the monk who had been told to see about horses, provisions and men. He strapped it on under his own shirt. Lobsang Pun roared:

"Oo-ha-ha-ha-hah! Tum-Glain!"

Then he did an astonishing thing. He ordered all the other monks to unload their pistols and to give Tom the ammunition.

"Your going quick, you, Tum-Glain, better not letting my catching you! Oo-ha-ha-hah!"

Unexpectedly he offered to shake hands. He wouldn't let go. He belly-roared his blessings until Tom almost tore himself loose. The monks couldn't get out of his way fast enough.

He ran up the gallery steps, fetched his bag from the guest cell and demanded to see Mu-ni Gam-po. If the abbot really was dying of shock, it might be possible to invent a new line of communication

145

even on the spur of that moment. But the monks told him to wait. They were not in the least impressed by his impatience. Fuming at delay, he watched the monks in the courtyard shovelling the fire, burying the *shang-shangs'* ashes beneath a huge cone of glowing crimson embers. They were taking no chances on the brutes returning to life!

But there was something else going on. Twice, two messengers ran past him along the gallery, going and coming. They crossed the fire-lit courtyard and vanished in the direction of the main gate. A monk came and said the abbot would see Tom presently, but he must wait a little longer.

Ten more minutes passed, and then came Abdul Mirza up the stairs, all alone, wrapped head and shoulders in a shawl. Tom didn't recognise him until they were face to face.

"You?"

"You?"

"Do you know what has happened here?" Tom asked.

"I know nothing. I am looking for Noropa."

"You won't find him. How did you get by the main gate?"

"Oh, I made a noise like a prayer wheel. What are you doing here with your bag in your hand?"

"Waiting for word with the abbot. What had you to do with Dowlah sending Noropa to stab me with a poisoned dagger? Noropa traveled with your party."

"Yes, Noropa begged to be allowed to travel under my protection. He said he was coming here to beg facilities to return to Tibet."

"What is Dowlah doing?"

Abdul Mirza made a wry face. "He has vanished. Are you on your way to Tibet? Can I help you with equipment?"

"Thanks, I guess that's all attended to."

"Have you money?"

"Yes. Indian *rupees.*"

"Then why wait? It is my private opinion, Mr. Grayne, that Rajah Dowlah also is on his way to Tibet. I have no proof, but I believe he knows where the Thunder Dragon Gate is. I am not in his confidence. I never have been. It has always been a game between him and me, as to which could outwit the other. It was my duty to prevent him from making serious mistakes, but he has made at least one too many. Your arrival on the scene, I think, precipitated crowning indiscretion. He was always ambitious, always jealous. Even as a boy he was possessed by irrepressible curiosity. Contempt for other people's intelligence is his worst fault. I believe his plans have been secretly laid for a long time. He believes the Thunder Dragon Gate will give him fame and power. He, and twenty men, have vanished."

Tom saw what looked like light on the situation.

"Listen," he said, "a *Bön* magician, devil-dancers and some others, less than an hour ago, raised hell here with a couple of *shang-shangs* at the midnight service. They have carried off Thö-pa-ga and Elsa Burbage. D'you think Dowlah had a hand in that?"

Abdul Mirza stared into Tom's eyes. His own were far-sighted from advancing age, and he couldn't get out his *pince-nez* quickly from under the shawl.

"You say they carried them off? And you wait here? No, I don't think Dowlah had a hand in that. He can't have, or I think not. How could he? He will take advantage of it, if he learns it has happened. He is very partial to European women. Intelligent ones. Young ones. Good looking. Unconventional. Have you warned the police?"

"Of course I haven't."

"There are very efficient police in Sikkim," said Abdul Mirza.

"Yes, a damned sight too efficient. At a word they'd be under way in less than fifteen minutes."

"Are you afraid the abductors would murder Miss Burbage, if pursued by the police? I think that unlikely."

"That isn't the point," Tom answered. "You should know that."

"My young friend, then what is the point?"

"If a *Bön* magician and his party can cross the passes at this time of year, and reach the Thunder Dragon Gate, I can follow. If they can get in, I can."

"And Miss Elsa Burbage? Mr. Grayne, the police—I am afraid. If it should be said I knew, but that I did nothing, did not tell the police—"

"All right, you don't know. You haven't spoken to me. You haven't seen me. Can't wait any longer on the abbot. Goodbye."

Tom went hurrying to the stables. The monk stood swinging a lantern. There were several men in line—some packed loads—two tents—a string of ten shaggy Tibetan ponies. He could see at a glance that one pony was lame; the other nine were probably not much better, and the men worse—malingerers, thieves, weaklings. The monk, no doubt, was out for vengeance for the requisitioned Mauser pistol.

Tom examined the loads first, rejected one tent as unnecessary and demanded another load of tea, sugar and canned milk. Then an extra

147

load of cheese, and another of ground barley. He rejected a bale of rotten dried apricots. They stank. He found another bale of them that didn't stink. He demanded more blankets. By a high-handed display of impatience and money he bought, at an outrageous price from a sleepy Tibetan, a sheepskin coat and hat. They reeked of *ghee*, (clarified butter), and yak-dung smoke, but they were in good condition. Then he went into the stable and requisitioned the ten ponies that were haltered in a line in the dark at the farther end.

That started a fine rebellion. The monk went nearly frantic. Those were the special personal ponies reserved for the use of the Holy and Reverend Lobsang Pun!

"Yes," said Tom. "I guessed that."

He didn't actually have to fight, but he did have to go in and lead out the ponies. Such a row was raised about them that he found out who the best men were, because the monk appealed to them and ignored the others. So Tom picked five of those. He promised each of them a bonus of fifty *rupees*, over and above regular pay.

"*Bhod!* Now!"

So be the trail lay northward, men and beasts were willing. Saddling up took next to no time. Such delay as there was, saved valuable minutes. Abdul Mirza caused it. He came, wrapped in his shawl, like a prowling Haroun al Raschid of Baghdad. He had an order to open the main gate, which Tom did not have. True, he might have managed with Lobsang Pun's seal and signature, but Abdul Mirza's signed pass from the abbot was better.

"Tom Grayne, I have salved my conscience, such as it is. You appear to have none, so may peace ride with you. We have been too stupid, some of us statesmen. Others have been too clever for their own good. Between those extremes, the middle, and perhaps the only wise course, is madness. Go ahead and be mad, and may *Allah* guide you."

"How's the abbot?"

"Shocked. Recovering. But almost overwhelmed with spiritual dread. He feels a consciousness of sin that held open the door to the *shang-shang* sending. The poor old fellow thoroughly believes that burning *shang-shangs'* corpses is merely a gesture that soothes ignorant monks but can't allay the spiritual menace. You saw those monsters fight?"

"Yes."

"What Dowlah missed! How that sight would have thrilled him!"

"Did you speak of me to the abbot?"

"Yes. He sends his blessing. He will pray to a thousand saints to protect you, wherever you go. I don't know what he meant, but he mentioned some sacred books. He begs you kindly not to forget to write about them."

"Did you speak of Elsa Burbage?"

"Why inflict on him more anxiety? No. Nor of Noropa. I prevaricated, Mr. Grayne, about Noropa. I didn't come here to enquire about him. Mu-ni Gam-po is occasionally very well informed. I hoped that perhaps he had heard something of Dowlah's plans—some rumour—or perhaps some detail about provisions and porters waiting for him between here and Tibet."

"Well?"

"He knows nothing."

"What's your particular worry about Dowlah?"

"Twenty-one years my prince! Tom Grayne, it needs more than twenty-one hours to destroy an aging man's love for the boy he tried to build into a man. I always knew he was a rogue. May *Allah*, blessed be His Prophet, show me mercy—I have never been able to love sincerely persons who were so righteous that butter wouldn't melt in their mouths!"

Abdul Mirza glanced into the stable and took a horse-blanket down from a hook on the wall. He removed his own beautiful Kashmir shawl and wrapped the smelly blanket over his head and shoulders.

"It will be cold in the passes. Should you overtake her, she may need this."

"I will say it's a present from you."

"And will you do me a favour?"

"If it's possible. What?"

"Dowlah's bankers in Delhi were served, this midnight, by phone and special messenger, with an order forbidding them to cash Dowlah's drafts or to forward money to him through their agents or by any other means. They will not dare to disobey that order. If you should find Dowlah, will you give him this package?"

"What is it?"

"Ten thousand *rupees*. All I have."

"I knew you were a good egg," Tom answered. "Yes, I'll do that. If he kills me, he'll take it anyhow. Go ahead, will you, and get 'em to open the gate. I'm ready. Let's go."

CHAPTER 26

The Tibetans hadn't seen the *shang-shang* battle, but they had heard about it. Storm or no storm, they were in a momentary mood to go as far away as possible, at top speed. Abdul Mirza had his carriage waiting outside the monastery gate. He was staying at the Hindu Kush Hotel. He promised to wake the clerk, get Tom's mail, should there be any, and send it by messenger to Nancy Strong's house.

Rain, thunder, lightning. Deserted, dark streets. Even the police were under cover. A light in Nancy Strong's living-room. All the rest of her house dark. No one at the gate. A fork of lightning revealed a rather bare compound with a lean-to children's play-shed that served to shelter the men and ponies.

Tom had a deuce of a time to get the front door opened. Rain and thunder out-dinned his thumping on the panel, and there was no bell. However, a servant opened at last, dried him off a bit and showed him into the living-room. Nancy Strong, in a quilted dressing-gown, was hugging the fire, reading and making notes. She looked middle-aged and untidy with her gray hair down over her shoulders, but she didn't seem embarrassed. She looked over the top of horn-rimmed reading-glasses and shot a question at Tom before he had time to speak:

"Did you persuade her?"

"No."

"Did you try?"

"Yes. Nothing doing. I want her bag, please."

"Your Elsa Burbage is exactly the kind of girl I feared she might be. You are using a thoroughbred, Tom Grayne, to do a mule's job."

"Too late to discuss that," he answered.

"Thö-pa-ga? Lobsang Pun?"

"Ask Johnson. He probably knows by now. Perhaps he'll tell you. Tell him I said nothing. Or you might ask Abdul Mirza. He's more talkative."

Nancy Strong went for Elsa's bag. Apparently it had to be repacked; she was a long time bringing it. Tom paced the room, staring at framed Tibetan photographs. There was one of Lobsang Pun, many years younger, in a silver frame on the piano. A portrait of the late Dalai Lama. Several Tibetan landscapes in water-colour, a bit schoolmarmy in conception and execution, but not too bad—probably Nancy Strong's work. Several photos of Nancy Strong, young and rather good look-ing, in Tibetan costume, two on horseback and one on camelback.

Tom's ears were alert. He heard a pounding on the front door and opened it to Abdul Mirza's messenger. A telegram. Nothing else.

Harley believes Teivos salesman either on the way or perhaps already making bid for contract. Cavell.

Marching orders! Gate into Tibet open and its custodians not looking! Sir Horace O'Mally of Harley Street, physician extraordinary to kings and millionaires, had evidently learned a lot more in Moscow than how to cut off a dog's head and keep it alive. The word "Teivos" couldn't be anything else than "Soviet" reversed. "Soviet salesman" must mean "Russian secret agent," on his way to the Thunder Dragon Gate or there already. "Cavell" was certainly Dr. Morgan Lewis of the Edith Cavell Hospital.

If the telegram meant anything whatever, it meant: "Ride like the devil and get there ahead of them all!"

The United States, Great Britain, Russia, Japan, the Tibetan Council of Regents in Lhasa, and the agents of the Tashi Lama, were all in the running! Dowlah, Lobsang Pun, the *Bön* magician, and how many others?

Nancy Strong brought two bags, Elsa's and another filled with such luxuries as raisins, chocolate, soap, face cream and a small first-aid kit.

"I have nothing small enough for her, so I have put in needles, thread, scissors. She will have to make her own warm clothing, of any material she can get. Oh, you iron men! Is she out in this storm? Have you plenty of money? Have you a Mauser pistol? Tibetans believe a Mauser has some sort of magical superiority over all other weapons. They won't face Mausers. Have you ammunition? You won't be able to get any in Tibet. Have you wind-proof clothing?"

Tom almost tore himself away. He didn't even wave his hand as she stood in the open doorway with the yellow light behind her. He was afraid she might summon him back for some last-minute argument.

He had no difficulty in getting the Tibetans and ponies to face the storm again. The Tibetans laughed. They said it would cease before daylight, and it did. There were washed-out roads and some dangerous bridges, but nothing to delay a small, self-sufficient, experienced party. The going might have held up dude explorers, or a heavily laden caravan. But the ponies' loads were reasonably light. There was nothing to be bought but corn, in small quantities, to enable the ponies to keep up the gruelling pace; so they didn't have to linger anywhere and answer questions. The principal problem for three days was to remove leeches from the ponies' legs and bellies every time they crossed one of the almost countless streams in the tropical valley bottoms.

Up from the steaming jungle, up above the tree line, above the clouds. Down again into the tropical heat. Up again, over the freezing sky line, sleeping, all huddled together for warmth, in one tent. No privacy, but no chance for conspiracy. The seeds of mutiny are laid in whispers in the night, but the Tibetans couldn't whisper in the night without Tom's overhearing.

His hardiness puzzled them. He did more than his share of the work. He could load two ponies while anyone of them was loading one. He ate the same coarse food, consumed the same greasy salted tea and seemed to have an even greater craving than their own to reach the Roof of the World and its windy desolation.

He asked no questions along the road. There were fifty trails through Sikkim that the *Bön* magician's party might have taken, but they all had to converge to one point. There the *Bön* magician might be held up by the police or border officials, but more likely he would get by with Lobsang Pun's forged signature. The Sikkim military police might spot Elsa, but more probably not, if she were swaddled up in blankets. The road into Tibet was open to let Thö-pa-ga go home and unlock a secret.

Once over the seventeen thousand-foot Sepo La, there were two roads. One of them toward Lhasa. A main road, absolutely certain to be guarded by Tibetan troops. If the *Bön* magician intended to take that road, then it was of the utmost importance to head him off. But if his objective was the Thunder Dragon Gate, and if the Thunder Dragon Gate was somewhere near the northern slope of Everest, he would take that other road, westward, skirting Nepal. Somewhere along that rarely traveled western road was a Yellow-hat monastery. It would be Lobsang Pun's only possible base for supplies. As the Tashi Lama's representative the old prelate was to all intents and purposes an outlaw in Tibet. If his objective, also, was the Thunder Dragon Gate, that monastery, whose monks were very likely faithful to the exiled Tashi Lama, would be his first goal. There was nowhere else where he could have left provisions safe from bandits and Tibetan troops.

Tom talked it over with the headman, who wasn't much impressed by the need for haste. The more he thought about the *Bön* magician, the less he liked the prospect of over taking him.

"Tum-Glain, I saw it happen. I saw those devil-dancers pull their costumes off, in darkness, in the stable courtyard, pack them hurriedly and, shouldering their own loads, follow the *Bön's* party out through the gate, on foot.

152

"That," he insisted, "means they had animals waiting for them, hidden somewhere, ready. They behaved like men who have a plan well laid. That they dared to offend the Holy Lobsang Pun is proof enough that they are bad rogues. Such men are cunning. They use magic. They can make themselves invisible. They wouldn't take a straight road through Sikkim. That black devil knows where he can get supplies from people in out-of-the-way places who won't betray which way he went for fear he might send them a sending. I say, they are far behind us."

Tom watched for signs of Elsa. There were countless *chortens*, cairns, trees beside the road to which pious travellers had tied strips of rags to flutter ceaseless prayers in the wind. But there was no rag that might have been torn from Elsa's dress. In the lead, on the sturdiest pony, mile after mile, day after day, Tom searched with tireless eyes for anything whatever that she might have put to use as an intelligible signal.

The Tibetans laughed, not at him, but at the notion that a prayer streamer might be a message to anyone in this world.

"Those are to bring blessings upon us. *Om mane padme hum!*, (The most important mantra in Buddhism.) They repeat it again and again."

"Watch, I tell you! Unless they tied her hand and foot, she will leave her mark somewhere. It isn't likely they would ill treat her. That would have a bad effect on Thö-pa-ga, and it is him they think of."

"For Thö-pa-ga, so I have heard, they have another woman waiting," said the headman. "Is this one your woman? If so, she should give them the slip."

"She will stand by Thö-pa-ga," Tom answered.

"Oh, is she his woman?"

"Keep your eyes open for some sign of her."

But they saw no sign until the ten wearying ponies had toiled up the long gradual ascent of the Sepo La. Near the cairn at the summit, that marks the boundary between Sikkim and Tibet, was the first snow—a mere acre or two in the lee of a ledge, out of reach of the bitter westerly wind. The Tibetans made haste to off-load. The ponies rolled in the snow on the edge of a fifty-foot precipice, while Tom hunted for signs of the *Bön's* party having bivouacked thereabouts. There were plenty of traces of traders' caravans. There were skeletons of yaks and ponies, scattered apart and cracked up by wolves. But nothing recent. There was nothing attached to the boundary cairn, or hidden near it.

But in a hollow a considerable distance off the road he found embers and a lot of horse-dung that was not many hours old. A party that had carried wood up to that elevation, and that could afford to waste embers and not to burn the horse-dung, must have plenty of ponies and be travelling in great haste. He examined the ground carefully, kicked over a stone and picked up one of Elsa's blue goose handkerchiefs.

It was very likely her last one. The headman laughed like a child at the embroidered blue goose.

"Such a prayer flag should bring happiness! Better leave it where you found it, Tum-Glain."

No lipstick marks. Probably she hadn't any lipstick. But, wrapped in the handkerchief, there was a small strip of bark off a piece of firewood. On the inside it showed thumb nail marks. First, a broad-arrow mark. Danger. Then a series of groups of nail marks, as easy to read as a telegram if one knew the code:

"Thöpe well. *Böns* fear pursuit. Look out for ambush. Turning westward."

Nothing about herself. No complaint. Nothing to indicate whether she was being well or ill treated.

"Leave it where you found it, Tum-Glain. Interfering with happy prayers brings miserable curses. We have trouble enough."

It was high noon. Men and ponies wished to bivouac in the shelter of that hollow, and the ponies had earned it. But Tom fed the ponies and refused to pitch camp. There would be a full moon. Night, with the moon on the snow would be nearly as bright as day, and for many miles there would be an easy, gradual descent to a level of about fifteen thousand feet.

"Forward!"

"Tum-Glain, we are too few. The *Bön* magician is a devil with plenty of servants, who will kill us if we overtake them. They might see us from a long way off and use magic against us. Better keep far behind them until we are overtaken by the Holy Blessed Lobsang Pun Rinpoche."

"Did he order you to obey me?"

"Yes."

"Then obey."

By nightfall they had reached the fork where the rough but clearly marked track toward Lhasa winds around to the right of an unclimbable peak. The other road, westward toward the maze of mountains

154

that hide Nepal, is little used and usually difficult to find. But it was easy now. There was a maze of hoof-prints in the snow. Even before moonrise it was easy to tell that the track had been ploughed up too recently for the blown snow to hide it again.

There was no avoiding a halt to rest men and animals. The Tibetans boiled tea in the lee of a rock, and while he waited for moonrise Tom checked up on his previous guess work. It was dangerous to ask questions, because if the headman should start lying to him there would be no end to it. He had to pretend he knew the main facts and needed only to know minor details.

"Soon we shall run out of food for the ponies. How far is it to the monastery where the Holy Lobsang Pun has stored his supplies?"

"Three days. Four days."

"At my speed?"

"Perhaps two days, if the ponies can endure it. This is a bad road. It leads upward and upward. Once it was a main road toward Nepal, but the pass into Nepal is so steep and high that it has been abandoned these many years, and now only a few monks use this road—they and bandits—and some pilgrims."

"What pilgrims?"

"I have never heard what pilgrims, nor whither they go, nor why."

The beginning of lies and evasions. Tom pretended to lose interest. It was enough for the moment that he knew he was right about that monastery. Moonlight touched the far-off peaks and made them serenely beautiful. The loveliest view in the world. It filled the Tibetans with mystic fears. They spoke of spirits, and of snow-men, and of devils. Not even they knew which of those peaks was Everest, although they claimed to know what monstrous phantoms lived on which mountain. There were a score of moonlit summits, perhaps a hundred miles away, or less, all indescribably white against moonlit sky. On some of them no human being had ever set foot. Somewhere in among them was a valley, unmapped; unphotographed even from the air; unvisited even by Sven Hedin, (Swedish explorer), or by the Mt. Everest expeditions; sacred; dreaded secret.

Tom questioned the headman: "Year after year, pilgrims by the hundred visit a secret valley down yonder. How is it that the secret is so well kept?"

"Tum-Glain, who would speak of such a valley?"

"How, then, do they find the valley?"

"How should I know?"

"Some of them," said Tom, "come hundreds of miles, measuring the way by lying prone on the earth after each step."

"Why shouldn't they?" said the headman. "But what should I know about it?"

The headman turned questioner: "Tum-Glain, are you thinking of daring to fight that *Bön* magician? All that darkness between here and there is full of devils that will aid him but oppose us."

"Where he leads," Tom answered, "we can follow."

"Not so, Tum-Glain. I know the way to the first monastery, which is easy enough to find. But he knows caverns, hermitages, secret valleys, where he may have hidden what he needs for the journey. He can go faster than we. And he will kill that woman, just to spite you, if you press him hard. Those *Böns* are devils."

"Keep your eyes open for signs of her. If she possibly can do it, she will leave a mark to show us where to follow."

"But the snow, Tum-Glain, is continually driven by the gales that never cease hereabouts. It will cover any marks she might make, even if she makes any. I think she will be suffering from the cold. Unless you follow fast, you may find her dead or dying. But if you follow too fast, you will have to fight the *Bön* magician. He might kill her, rather than let you have her before she has served his purpose, whatever that may be. I say, wait here, feeding the ponies as little as possible, until the Blessed Lobsang Pun Rinpoche overtakes us. He will use some magic on the *Bön* that will bring him bad luck, so that perhaps he will let the girl go."

"You're warm and well fed, among friends, in your own land. You talk like a lucky fool," Tom answered.

He redistributed the ponies' loads, doing most of the work himself, pressed forward, until midnight, camped, and was away again at daybreak, wearing out men and ponies without getting as much as a sight of the *Bön* magician's party.

Most of the following day the wind blew with hurricane force, ice-cold from the peaks around Everest. But he disregarded the Tibetans' protests and bucked the wind, with as few halts as possible. The blown snow had covered all tracks, but the magician's ponies could be no better than his; the magician's strength no greater than his own. No sign, all day, of Elsa, who was probably too numbed by cold and altitude to think of anything but how to keep life in her body.

But late that afternoon the wind died down to a normal gale. Soon after that, where the track emerged from a grim defile on to a bit of a plateau where the snow lay sheltered from the wind, there were signs of two considerable parties having met and milled around on the snow before they all went westward. There was horse-dung, still unfrozen.

"Bandits!" pronounced the headman. "See, they came this way, captured them with no trouble at all, and carried them off along the way they came, no doubt to some secret cavern. All Tibet is full of bandits since the Blessed Holiness Tashi Lama Rinpoche was driven into exile. His Blessed Holiness took religion with him, and evil people are no longer afraid to do wrong."

Tom decided to rest men and animals, but he only waited until moonlight silvered the distant summits. Then he was off in the lead, on foot, leaving men and ponies to follow. The track wound amid dismal piles of raw rock sketched by star light against faintly luminous snow, along a ledge around a precipice. It was almost too dark to see the edge, and the altitude was telling on him. It made his head swim. His heart pounded like a trip-hammer. He felt his way with one hand on the face of the cliff, his fingers numb with cold in spite of a big sheepskin glove. But the men obeyed. He could hear them coming. They made a lot of noise, stumbling over loose rock. If they could stand it, he could.

Then the moon rose. The rough track opened out on to a few square miles of hummocky plateau, patched with snow and wind-blown rock. It was hedged in by a wilderness of snow-clad peaks. In the distance, perched like a swallow's nest on an almost unclimbable crag, perhaps seventeen thousand feet above sea level, the monastery walls were etched gray by the light of the moon. The winding track was a series of dark shadows and pale white snow. To the right of the track, two hundred yards ahead, or less, sat a man with his back to a rock.

The man didn't move, although he appeared to at first. It was his unfastened yak-skin coat that fluttered in the wind. He was dead. He couldn't possibly be alive, and sit still, facing the wind, with his coat open, in that temperature. Fifty yards or so beyond him, against another rock, also with his coat unfastened, sat another man. Between the two there was a shadowy track in the snow, as if the man farther away had dragged himself to the place where he sat, and had died there. It looked as if they had killed each other.

Tom went up and examined the first man. He was the *Bön* magi-

157

cian. He sat bareheaded, with his head tilted back against the rock, so that he was staring at the sky with his mouth wide open and a bullet hole in his forehead, about an inch above the right eye. He was stone-cold, but his watch was still going. He hadn't been touched by birds or animals. Apparently he hadn't been looted, not even of his Japanese dagger.

Tom examined him more closely. There was nothing in the pockets of his long sleeves, nor in the looseness of the *bokkus* above his belt, where a Tibetan normally carries his odds and ends and even his provisions. The Japanese dagger was tight in its sheath. He had no firearms, pistol holster, ammunition belt. No money. And no document bearing Lobsang Pun's signature. Nothing in writing whatever. He had been thoroughly looted by someone to whom a silver watch and an expensive dagger were of no interest.

The other man was the *Bön* magician's novice, with a bullet hole beneath his left eye. He hadn't dragged himself along the snow. He had been shot, standing, where he now sat propped carefully against a rock. The tracks in the snow had been made by someone walking from one dead body to the other and back again. He had a Japanese, or it might be Korean knife in a sheath at his waist, a heavy jade charm at his neck, and a Japanese silk shirt underneath a heavy woollen sweater made in Massachusetts. There was nothing in his pockets.

Barring bullet holes and the blood on their faces, there was no evidence of a fight. They appeared to have left the road at points more than fifty paces apart, to have walked about fifty yards along parallel courses almost due northward, to have turned when they reached those rocks, and to have been shot at rather close range. Then someone had walked back and forth, more than once, from one to the other.

"Bandits!" remarked the headman, when he came up with the leg-weary ponies. "I said so."

"Would a bandit leave behind a silver watch, jade charm, daggers, good clothing, boots?"

"Tum-Glain, someone may have warned the bandits of Your Excellency's coming, so that they fled in haste."

Tom went and examined the ponies. They were dog-tired. But by dividing up the loads it might be possible to reach the monastery. He did the work with numbed hands, and then led the way, leaving the five Tibetans to follow on foot, arguing about the proper distribution of the *Böns'* belongings.

Moonlight gleamed on the two bodies, sitting, naked now, staring at the sky. The Tibetans had been careful to leave them in the proper attitude of death. There would be wolves soon, and then, in the morning, vultures.

CHAPTER 27

Midnight amid the frozen filth at the foot of the cliff on which the monastery perched. Utterly foundered ponies. A path led steeply upward, in and out of moonlight, like a monstrous, fantastic stairway in a dream. The loaded ponies couldn't possibly negotiate that. Notched against the moon two or three hundred feet in the air, there was a dark projection with something hanging to it. That was the monastery elevator, operated by a hand winch—a big basket made fast to a hide rope that passed over a roller at the end of a beam. It was sure to descend presently. The monks had seen Tom's party crossing the snow in moonlight and had sounded several long blasts on their *radongs*.

Tom was feeding the ponies with scraps of stale barley bread, with his back toward the steep stone ramp at the foot of the ascending path, when someone touched his elbow. He turned suddenly and stared into the face of a woman.

It was a clean face, which is rare in Tibet. Her features were Chinese. Astonishingly good looking in that weird light. Age difficult to guess—perhaps twenty-seven, or even thirty. The moonlight filled her eyes with sparks of pale green swimming in golden brown. She was wearing, over the customary woollen clothing of a Tibetan lady, an American man's coonskin overcoat of very fine quality. She was breathing hard.

She had evidently come down that monstrous stairway. An active, healthy, daring, intolerant-looking woman, with an odour of expensive perfume.

"I am Su-li Wing," she remarked, as if the name explained everything. "Who are you?"

She spoke in a rather Chinesey voice, with a synthetic accent.

"Staying in the monastery?" Tom asked.

She laughed: "Men only! They won't admit me. If you are seen talking to me, they won't admit you."

"Anything particular to talk about?"

She laughed again. "Very well, Mr. Mind-your-own-business-with-ten-tired-ponies, do you know a man named Rajah Dowlah?"

"Why do you ask?"

"Shortly before sunset he shot two monks. Perhaps you saw their bodies. He seized and carried off an English girl, and a Tibetan named Thö-pa-ga. Do you happen to know who they are?"

"How do you know he did it?"

"I saw him do it. If you're Tom Grayne I am glad to meet you. I will tell you."

"Yes, I'm Tom Grayne."

"I was Dowlah's friend. I was waiting for him in Nepal. He met me at Khatmandu and we crossed the forbidden Khambu-shar-kang Pass. It was a dreadful journey. The idea was to get into Tibet ahead of Lobsang Pun—and ahead of you, too, if you should still be alive. Dowlah seemed to think you were probably dead. We turned in this direction to requisition some of Lobsang Pun's supplies, that Dowlah guessed were in this monastery. Scouts went ahead of us. They brought back word so we all rode forward, past this monastery, and held up a party who turned out to be Thö-pa-ga in charge of a *Bön* magician, with an English girl whose name is Elsa Something-or-other, a mongrel named Noropa, a lot of devil-dancers and some others. There were about thirty of them; about forty of us. There wasn't a fight. They were exhausted after a hard march. Noropa shouted to them to surrender and the devil-dancers all obeyed him. Dowlah's men are nearly all from Naini Kol, and well armed. The *Bön* magician had a pistol, but they took it away from him."

Tom began off-loading the ponies. They were too tired to roll. The five Tibetans piled the loads against the wind and took shelter behind them. The ponies herded themselves in a melancholy group behind a flying buttress of gray rock.

"Are you listening?" asked Su-li Wing. "If you know Dowlah as well as he says he knows you, perhaps you can guess what it meant to him to capture Thö-pa-ga. He had expected to have to set an ambush, further westward, and to fight Lobsang Pun's party."

"I suppose it meant nothing to you?" Tom suggested.

"Oh, no. Nothing! I am the woman, who was to replace the woman, who has been waiting for several years for Thö-pa-ga. Dowlah said Elsa Something-or-other is worth a dozen of me. He left me flat, here, in the night, without luggage or servants."

Tom stepped more into the moonlight. She followed him. That way he could see her face better.

"How is Elsa Burbage?" he demanded. "Did she seem all right? Did you speak to her? What did she say?"

160

"Very little to me. She was all wrapped up in smelly sheep skin, so I can hardly say I saw her. She was very angry with Dowlah because he and Noropa shot the *Bön* magician and his novice. Dowlah ordered them to go and stand where he could speak to them separately, each out of the other's hearing. Then he and Noropa walked up and blew their brains out. Dowlah flew into a rage with me after that because I told him he was a fool to start murdering people. He would have shot me, if he had dared, but Thö-pa-ga and Elsa Burbage defied him. That was the only reason why he didn't shoot me. I was surprised at Thö-pa-ga. Dowlah had said he was a spiritless booby. He isn't. He took that girl's part and he swore like an English lord."

"You seem to think you know who I am."

"Oh, yes. Who else could you be? Dowlah told me. All the way over that awful pass from Khatmandu, whenever we had any conversation, he kept laughing about Tom Grayne, the American spy. He said you were dead, but I think he doubted it. He seemed surprised when one of the *Bön* magician's men claimed to have killed you with a club when they carried off Thö-pa-ga in Darjeeling. Dowlah told that to Elsa Burbage."

"Did she believe it?"

"I don't know. She didn't say."

"So Dowlah found his way through Nepal, did he? That took some doing. You say you're his friend?"

"I said, I *was* his friend."

"What are you now?"

"Well, I came all the way from Peking to Lhasa, lived more than a year in Tibet and traveled from Lhasa to Khatmandu, at my own expense, on the strength of Dowlah's promises. I kept him very well informed of what is happening in Tibet. I organised most of his secret line of communication. And I know he took to himself the credit for all the work that I did. He left me without money or food or servants, as he expressed it, to entertain the monks. I suppose I think of Dowlah what Elsa Burbage thinks of you, if she has any sense. Is it true she was your girl friend? Dowlah said you sold her to Thö-pa-ga. He laughed about it. She'll belong to Dowlah soon, unless you do in Dowlah. Or do you count on her to seduce Dowlah and betray him to you?"

"Before Peking, where were you?" Tom asked.

"Do you think I'm a can of sardines?" she retorted. "You ask questions like a—"

"Moscow?"

161

"Since you've guessed it, yes."

"Lenin Institute, for special training? Former member of the Kuomintang? Now Revolutionary Instrument Number So-and-so?"

"Supposing that's true, then what?"

"Did you play with Dowlah with the notion of getting to India under his protection and stirring up sedition among the Indian women?"

"You're smart, aren't you! Get me close enough to Dowlah to kill him, and I'll tell you anything you want to know."

Tom laughed. "Tell me why you and he quarrelled. If I believe that, perhaps I'll believe the rest of it. Look out! Stand clear. Here comes the hotel elevator! You say the monks won't give you shelter?"

"No. No women. And I made a mistake. I shouldn't have mentioned the Thunder Dragon Gate. I did it to impress them. But it worked the wrong way. Now they say I'm *shang-shang*-ridden. They know more than you'd think. They have mysterious ways of sending and receiving messages. They don't know who Dowlah is, but they knew his name—knew he was coming. They expect Lobsang Pun, and they had sent a messenger along the road eastward to warn all travellers against Dowlah. The *Bön* captured the messenger, but he escaped when Dowlah shot the two magicians. Have you anything to eat?"

CHAPTER 28

It could hardly be called a basket. It was a crate built of tamarisk boughs, lashed with raw-hide. It swung in the wind at the end of its rope and made a sort of parachute landing, about a hundred feet to one side of its beam. Two monks let themselves out, no worse for the adventure—smiling, gentle-looking fellows, spinning prayer wheels at sight of Su-li Wing, courteous to Tom, and even reverential when he showed them Lobsang Pun's seal in the moonlight. One by one they pressed the seal against their foreheads.

After that, they invited Tom to enter the basket and be hauled up. But he wanted food for the ponies, nothing else. He had his own tent. He reproached them for refusing shelter to Su-li Wing. They whirled their prayer wheels in self-defence, and appealed to Tom's own Tibetan followers for corroboration that it wasn't customary, or even lawful to admit women. Above all, not that woman. There and then mutiny started.

The headman announced he was going no further. He and his

men would wait for the Holy Lobsang Pun, whose servants they were. He demanded to be paid off, and to receive the promised bonus. Taking his cue from the monks, he declared Su-li Wing was a witch who would bring to pass terrible disaster. When the Holy Lobsang Pun Rinpoche should come and exorcise the evil that otherwise would certainly result from the *Bön* magician's death, then it might be sensible to dare new dangers. He climbed into the basket. Tom hauled him out.

"One of the others may go up, along with the monks, and bring down plenty of feed for the ponies. After that, you may all go to the devil. Ask Lobsang Pun for your bonus and see what you get!"

So one man went up, he and the monks singing together in the cage that swung in the biting wind and bumped the cliff. The ascent took fifteen minutes. At the summit they had to catch a mooring rope and be hauled in to a dock that was out of sight from below. Meanwhile, the headman tried to change Tom's mind. He couldn't. So he changed his own. He would go anywhere with Tum-Glain, now, at once, or at any other time. But it would be better to have nothing to do with that woman.

"If these holy monks, who are good people, won't give her shelter, she must be very evil."

"Pitch the tent. Prepare tea," Tom ordered.

He spread his own blankets, on a doubled yak-hide on the snow, for Su-li Wing. She turned in, well fed by the Tibetans, and fell asleep almost at once. When the basket came down with several loads of grain, and he had fed the ponies, Tom turned in, between her and the headman. The Tibetans put a prayer streamer and a turquoise charm between her and him. They chanted several *mantrams* before falling asleep.

When the first daylight stole into the tent, Tom lay still watching Su-li Wing searching his bag. She found Abdul Mirza's package, weighed—felt—considered it. Presently her hand came feeling inside Tom's jacket for his Mauser pistol. She stifled a scream when he gripped her wrist and held on until she let go of the Mauser and he was sure she hadn't a knife in her other hand.

"Dowlah took mine," she remarked matter of factly. "You are not such an oaf as Dowlah said you are. You sleep like a weasel, with one eye open."

The Tibetans boiled tea again, over horse-dung fuel. The monks sent down a meal of hot barley porridge, with the abbot's compliments. Tom went to examine the ponies. He fed them before he returned to the tent.

"Su-li Wing, how tired were Dowlah's ponies?" he demanded.

"Nearly as tired as yours. He left food for them, and his tents, in charge of two men at this end of the high pass that leads to Nepal. That's where he's camped with your girl friend. But what do you think you can do to Dowlah? You and five men with one pistol between you! If you want my help, buy it."

"Su-li Wing you are going to talk."

"Oh, am I? Suppose I wait for Lobsang Pun. These monks expect him. What if I wait and talk to him?"

Tom reached inside her coonskin coat. She had cached some dry bread, cheese and two cans of condensed milk. He placed them out of reach.

"Wait for Lobsang Pun if you like. You'll be hungry."

"You'd let me starve?"

"Sure, why not?"

"Buy me. Tom Grayne, I need money. Dowlah took mine. I know more about Tibet than you'd ever dream. And I need five thousand *rupees*."

"What for?"

"It costs money to return to Peking."

"Not five thousand *rupees*, it doesn't."

"Well, can I live in Peking on nothing? Tom Grayne, what I know is worth a high price. You could sell it two or three times over, if you're clever."

"Perhaps you've been too clever," Tom answered. "Moscow wouldn't leave you short of funds if you'd played straight. Dowlah took your money? He'd do it. But I bet you hadn't any. You hadn't paid your servants, or they'd have stood by you, not Dowlah. Talk, Su-li Wing, or I'll leave you flat."

"Will you give me a break, if I tell?"

"Depends on what you tell. You'd better come clean."

"Tom Grayne, there's a Russian named Pavlov, who is so jealous of me that he can't see straight. He ditched me and reported me to Moscow."

"Bela Pavlov? The half-Hungarian who shot the Chinese magistrate in Urga three years ago? Was it he who polished up your English? I was at school with that bird. He and I learned Tibetan from a Chinese herbalist in Cleveland. Where is he?"

"That is part of the information that I will sell, for a fair price."

"Try to sell it to Lobsang Pun. I've heard he has 'em whipped if they won't answer questions. Compared to that old humorist, I'm easy. I will stake you to some journey money, on conditions. Lobsang Pun would stake you to the fresh air and a flogging, with his blessing to follow. Why did you quarrel with Dowlah? Tell it like a telegram. I don't want any dope on communism, or why girls leave home."

"Are you so wise you know truth when you hear it?" she retorted.

"Well, I'll try you. Did you know that Dowlah is unmarried—that he has no *ranee*?"

"I never gave a damn about it, one way or the other."

"I told Dowlah in a message that I sent to him by way of Nepal, that he could make me Ranee of Naini Kol or I would betray to the Indian Government his link-up with Moscow. In that way, I could have restored my standing with the Comintern. I could do a lot with the Indian women. Dowlah answered he would do it. That was why I went to Khatmandu to meet him."

"Why didn't Dowlah kill you somewhere in the passes?" Tom asked. "Who'd have blamed him?"

"He thought he needed me," she said, "until he captured Elsa Burbage. After that, he'd have liked to kill me, but she made such a fuss about his killing the *Bön* magicians that he thought twice. He's sweet on her. He doesn't want to quarrel with her. He supposed I would die of hunger, anyhow, or perhaps be eaten by wolves. He knew the monks wouldn't shelter me. Like a fool, I told him that every monk between here and Lhasa believes it was I who killed Tara-eke. I didn't. Pavlov did that. But they blame me, because Pavlov said I did it. The monks don't mind her being killed. Her very name makes them shudder. But whoever kills a devil is supposed to be entered into by that devil's spirit. That makes you safe from assault. They're afraid to do anything to you—that includes giving you food and shelter."

"Who was Tara-eke?"

"The woman they were keeping for Thö-pa-ga, to make him mentally complacent. Pavlov shot her. Then the Böns of Djaring-dzong—some of them have been to Moscow—tried to put me in her place. The abbot wouldn't let them. So they tried to kill him."

"Who tried?"

"The Thunder Dragon Gate people. Pavlov said that was my fault, because I wouldn't go in and face it."

"Face what?"

"It. In the Thunder Dragon Gate. You wouldn't believe if I told. Let's say, I don't know. Perhaps Dowlah will make your Elsa Burbage face it."

"How did you keep in touch with Dowlah, while he was in Delhi, and you in Tibet?"

"Oh, I went to see him in Delhi. I was ordered to do that. I traveled as a pilgrim across Nepal. On the return journey I arranged the line of communication. They teach you in Moscow how to do that, and it's always easier to do in a forbidden country than an open one, because the people of a closed country feel mysterious and like to have dangerous secrets. After that Dowlah came and met me once in Khatmandu, and then again this time."

"How many Japanese at Djaring-dzong?"

"Oh, fourteen or fifteen, under a man named Chou Wang, whose real name is Naosuki. They pretend they're Chinese Buddhists and very pious, but the monks know better. It was Chou Wang, as he calls himself, who persuaded the Thunder Dragon Gate people to send a *shang-shang* party into India, to scare Lobsang Pun and to get hold of Thö-pa-ga, because it was known that Lobsang Pun had sent Noropa to London to compel Thö-pa-ga to return home. They couldn't do much without Thö-pa-ga. They couldn't put a substitute in his place as long as he was alive, because he might show up some day. And they didn't dare to murder him in England or in India, because the story might reach Tibet—and besides, the Japanese connection with it might have leaked out. The English are very fussy about murder, unless they do it them selves with machine-guns. But they can kill anybody in the Thunder Dragon Gate, and no one the wiser. The Japanese have a substitute ready for Thö-pa-ga if he should prove intractable."

Tom was keeping an eye on the ponies. He was giving them all the time they needed to munch barley and recover their spirit. They were hardy little bad-tempered brutes. One of them was already kicking at the others. It was already warm in the direct rays of the sun, although it was zero cold in the shade of the tent. It was nearly time to saddle up. Tom glanced at the five Tibetans, talking together in low tones.

"And Dowlah?" he asked. "Are he and Pavlov buddies? I mean, are they riding the same horse?"

"No," she answered. "Dowlah was afraid of Pavlov. He had never met him, but he knew his reputation. Dowlah wouldn't move until I sent him word that Pavlov had fled to Sinkiang. The monks drove Pavlov away not long after he shot Tara-eke."

Tom stared at her a moment.

"You shot Tara-eke," he said suddenly. "You blamed Pavlov for it and he bolted. Is that his coat you're wearing?"

"No."

"Uh-huh? Pavlov," said Tom, "is no easy mark. You must be pretty hot stuff if you put one over on him. Pavlov got him self booted out of the United States for sedition, racketeering and living off the earnings of prostitutes. He went to Russia and became an agent of the Comintern. Trusted agents of the Comintern aren't sentimentalists. But they don't leave women subordinates without funds, in such a country as Tibet, merely because they're jealous. Jealous of you? I know Pavlov. He's a hard, mean, cynical killer, without a compunction in his kit. He's too sure of himself to know what jealousy feels like. You could lie about that for a year, and I wouldn't believe you. Did he try to kill you before he bolted? Quick now! Come clean!"

"Yes," she answered. "What made Dowlah think you're stupid?"

"If he thinks I'm dead, that's even better."

Tom caught the headman's eye and signed to him to begin loading the ponies. The Tibetans began pulling down and rolling up the tent and roping loads. Since daybreak they had been sitting on the upturned saddles, to warm them a bit for the ponies' backs. If a Tibetan thinks of a pony's back, without being ordered to do it, he has something else than mere benevolence in mind. Tom quietly cocked the Mauser underneath his jacket, but he continued talking:

"Dowlah counted on capturing Thö-pa-ga?"

"Yes. But he expected to have to waylay Lobsang Pun. That is why he brought so many men. He expected Lobsang Pun would get possession of Thö-pa-ga in Darjeeling. It was very difficult to bring so many men across Nepal. Forbidden country, even to Dowlah. Terrible roads. The Gurkhas as suspicious as snakes. If it hadn't been for my preparations, he could never have done it. They all had to wrap their weapons inside their loads and pose as pilgrims. Even so, we were pursued, pretty nearly to the top of the Kambu-shar-kang. Dowlah's men almost mutinied. They can't stand the cold and the high altitudes. Dowlah planned to lay an ambush for Lobsang Pun, somewhere near this monastery, but I think he doubted his men. That was why he was so delighted when things turned out as they did."

Tom whipped out his pistol. He didn't say anything. He didn't need to. The five Tibetans reined in. They had mounted the five best ponies and were trying to steal away. Warm saddles had been only one precaution; they were leading a pony loaded with nearly all the remaining food. They dismounted and stuck out their tongues, each man thrusting his right ear forward with his hand, in sign of humiliation. Tom gestured with the all-commanding Mauser and they returned to work, loading the other ponies. Then he beckoned the headman.

"What is the usual punishment for that offense?"

"A flogging. But Your Excellency doesn't do usual things. And of what use would flogged men be?"

"You are the headman."

"Yes, Your Honour."

"Therefore, it was your fault. Shall I send you with a letter to the Holy Lobsang Pun, inviting him to administer justice?"

"Better anything than His Blessed Holiness's anger!" said the headman. "Let me beat these others, and then next time they won't listen to me if I tell them to desert Your Excellency."

"It is you who shall be punished. Since you are too wise to take back a letter to His Holiness Lobsang Pun, you shall have a chance to restore yourself in my favour, and earn merit, by other means."

"What is it?"

"I will tell you at the right time."

Tom examined the loads and the ponies' girths. He hoisted Su-li Wing onto a pony with scant ceremony, and gave her a double blanket for her legs. He commanded the Tibetans to walk beside their mounts. He led the way on foot, striding too fast for the loaded ponies, westward, toward Mt. Everest, that gleamed in the sun in the midst of the frozen tumult of peaks that rear themselves against the sky between Nepal and Tibet.

CHAPTER 29

"Tum-Glain," said the headman, "who shall protect us from all the devils of these parts? This is evil country. There are snow-men, who come like the wind from the mountain-tops."

"Have you ever seen one?"

"No. But I have heard of them. They bite off the tip of a man's nose and toes and fingers. They leave the rest of his body undestroyed, and frozen. A man can't get another body until this one is utterly decomposed. And the gods won't defend us against them unless we have some blessed person with us who knows how to pray, and whose prayers are acceptable because of merit earned in former lives. You and I lack merit. Otherwise, you wouldn't be a foreigner and I wouldn't be compelled to obey you."

"Acquire merit by obedience," Tom answered; and that gave the headman enough to think about to keep him quiet for a couple of hours.

It was easier to think than to talk, with the bitter wind blowing a gale from the eternal ice and snow of the tremendous peaks that blocked the horizon. With the monastery out of sight behind them, they were now completely surrounded by mountains, whose devils, said the headman, created the wind, so that there was no protection from it. Westerly, it seemed to come from every direction. It followed ravines and glaciers, dividing into howling blasts that fought with one another as they struck the open spaces at different angles and whirl-winded the snow in great clouds from wherever it clung.

It wasn't easy even to think. Cold and altitude combined to pro-duce the deadly lethargy that had to be fought against minute by minute, stride by stride. Frequent halts were necessary.

"Let us ride, Tum-Glain!" advised the headman. "The beasts are stronger than we are."

But it was better to preserve the riding ponies' strength against emergency. Dowlah might have a number of comparatively fresh mounts. The main thing was to get in touch with Elsa: let her know she was closely followed.

During one halt, Su-li Wing, with her back to the wind, made an-other attempt to persuade Tom. She was as sentimental as the blizzard; as persuasive as the butt-end of a Marxian realist's club.

"Why don't you pitch the tent and be sensible? Are you so crazy about your girl friend that you forget Dowlah has weapons? She is all right. She has all my luggage. There is even perfume in one of the bags. Dowlah's tents are luxurious, and the cots have air mattresses. She is clean and comfortable, and being made love to by Dowlah. No woman is in trouble while she is being made love to—not as long as it lasts. If Dowlah should shoot you, you won't have a chance even to be second fiddle."

At the next halt she was even more contentious. Wind, snow-glare and the ultra-violet rays were irritating her beyond endurance.

"Are those her bags among the loads? Give them to me, then, in exchange for mine that Dowlah stole from me to give to her. I need face cream. I need snow spectacles. Dowlah took mine. Are you such a brute that you don't care how badly I suffer? God! I wouldn't choose to be your girl!"

169

Tom gave her the stump of a stearine candle from the tent lantern.

"Warm that under your arm-pit. Smear it on under your eyes. Keep your face covered. You don't have to look charming. It would be wasted on me."

It was about a mile after that when Tom caught sight of two men crouching in the shelter of a frozen snowdrift that formed a bridge between two rocks. They were alive, those two. They appeared to be armed.

"Bandits!" announced the headman.

"Dowlah's scouts!" said Su-li Wing. "Just beyond that spur of raw rock is the ravine where the track begins that leads upward to the pass into Nepal. That's where he pitched camp. Oh, you damned fool! Turn back before it's too late! Listen. Is it the Thunder Dragon Gate you're after? Turn back, and I will show you the other way in! It's longer, and more difficult. But we will have the wind behind us at least part of the way, and if we travel fast we may get there ahead of him. Do that, and I'll show you how to defeat him and let other people kill him."

"Shut up!" Tom commanded. He turned to the headman.

"Go forward alone. Tell those two men to come here to me."

"They may kill me."

"To earn merit, after behaving treacherously, a man, should be willing to run some risk."

"Well, that is true. But if they kill me, it will be your *karma*. I will try it. Tum-Glain, if they shoot me, you must ask the Holy Lobsang Pun Rinpoche to pray for me—many prayers. After all, I am his servant. I don't want to go to hell. It takes a long time to get out of hell, and then one has to be gin at the bottom with all sorts of miserable incarnations—worms and rats and such-like."

He mounted and rode forward slowly. Both men came toward him. They were not Tibetans. As they came nearer they appeared to be turbaned Indians, in good wind-proof clothing. One had a rifle wrapped in greased cloth; the other a repeating pistol in a holster. They walked awkwardly over the snow, stumbling, as if their feet were frozen.

They evidently had no speech in common with Tom's headman. After two or three minutes of futile gesturing they took hold of his saddle, one on either side, and submitted to be half-towed to where Tom waited for them. Bearded. Brown-eyed. Military looking. They saluted respectfully. After the man with the repeating pistol had beaten the frozen snow out of his beard and had smoothed it a bit, he handed

Tom a scrap of folded tin-foil from a cigarette tin.

Tom turned his back to the wind, removed his gloves and unfolded the tin foil within the shelter of his opened over coat. Inside it was a piece of thin white paper, also from a cigarette tin. It was almost covered with pin-pricks. He smeared the back of the paper with soot from the top of the candle-lantern. It was easy to read then:

"Thöpe is being splendid. Dowlah says you dead. I don't believe but fear you may be too late. Tom, I think Dowlah is desperate. His men are mutinous. I will carry on to give you every possible chance. Man who takes this offered help me escape but Thundergate not far now and you may be near. So will stick it out. Good luck. Elsa."

Tom turned to the man with the rifle and spoke in Hindustanee: "What has happened?"

"*Sahib*, Rajah Dowlah brought us *sepoys* of Naini Kol, by way of Khatmandu in Nepal, across the Roof of the World. We came by forced marches, not knowing why, but because we were his men and he ordered it." He stared at Su-li Wing. "In Khatmandu, this woman waited for us. And as long as she was with us all went well, although the Gurkhas of Nepal made trouble. But she showed us how to escape from the Gurkhas. In the high pass we nearly perished. After we had pitched camp at the foot of the pass, Rajah Dowlah led us along this way, past a monastery. He commanded us to attack a party of Tibetans, who rode toward us. But there was no fighting. They surrendered. He, and a man named Noropa whom we had seen in Delhi, slew two leaders of the party, and from one of the dead leaders he took a writing—I know not what, but it pleased him greatly. There were many Tibetans, and among them an English lady, who gave me that message when I crawled to the tent before daybreak, whispering to her that we *sepoys* of Naini Kol are honourable men, who perceive that we are being forced to become brigands, to which we now refuse consent before it shall be too late."

"How is she?" Tom demanded.

"*Sahib*, she is a very brave young woman, full of mockery of Rajah Dowlah. When he entered her tent she threw hot tea at him. There is a Tibetan named Thö-pa-ga among the prisoners. They protect each other, they two, and they share the same tent. He was in there when I crept to the tent for speech with her. I said: we *sepoys* of Naini Kol would protect her. I told her the truth, that we had agreed among us to go no farther with Rajah Dowlah, but to see what could be done about reaching India by some other route. She spoke to me of Tum-

Glain, and I remembered having seen Your Honour through the door of His Highness's library, one night in Delhi. She begged me, if by any means I could, to deliver a message to Your Honour. So I promised, and she pricked it with a pin by candlelight. When morning came we refused to march. There was a bad scene. His Highness rode away westward, with the lady and with all the Tibetans we had captured."

"Had you all your weapons?"

"No. Nor much food, *sahib*. Rajah Dowlah had sent that man Noropa in the night to steal as many rifles from us as he could. He stole nine, one by one I suppose, while their owners slept. We were very weary. Rajah Dowlah had said we need not post a sentry. Knowing we were disaffected, before daylight he had armed those Tibetans with the rifles that Noropa stole from us."

"Did you try to protect Miss Burbage?"

"Yes. We called to her. We bade her turn back, and we slapped our rifles. She saw, *sahib*. She heard. She understood. She waved her hand and said nothing, smiling. But at me she looked with meaning, as much as to say I should not forget my promise. Had she appealed to us, we would have acted otherwise. But it seemed to us all that she knew what she was doing."

"Did Dowlah take all the ponies?"

"No, he left the lame ones."

"How many are you?"

"Twenty men, *sahib*, with one pistol and eleven rifles."

"Weren't you forty, all told?"

"We from Naini Kol are twenty men. There were also twenty porters—Sherpas from Nepal. They all deserted by way of the pass, at daybreak. We feared to follow, not being mountaineers. Sherpas are like monkeys on a mountain, and they love snow."

"Who is in command of you?"

"I am, *sahib*."

"Have you any money?"

"No."

"Enough provisions to reach India?"

"Perhaps. How far is it? By which road? *Sahib*, did we do wrong to permit the English lady to ride away? We are true men, we *sepoys*. We deserted our prince because our *izzat*, was offended by the murders we saw him do. We are afraid, but we are not cowards. If the *sahib* will take command of us, we will obey."

"I find no fault," Tom answered. "That is, if you are telling the truth."

"If I have lied by as much as a word, may *Allah* do so to me, and worse!"

Tom went to his bag and broke open Abdul Mirza's package. He counted out fifteen hundred *rupees*. He gave a thousand *rupees* to the man from Naini Kol.

"I can't accept your offer. You and your men must march to India by way of the Sepo La. Start immediately. Wire from the first telegraph-station in Sikkim to Abdul Mirza, in care of Miss Nancy Strong of Darjeeling. I will write her address for you. She will know where he is. You will report to Abdul Mirza, at whatever place he directs, and you will tell him that I gave you money for your journey, so that you needn't beg or pillage. If, on your way you should encounter a Tibetan priest-nobleman named Lobsang Pun, with a large following, you may tell him your story and say that Tum-Glain urges him to come with all possible speed. Thereafter, until you meet His Excellency Abdul Mirza face to face, you hold your tongue, lest trouble come of it. Silence. Do you understand that?"

"*Atcha, sahib.* But how shall we find this what is it? this Sepo La?"

"This lady—Su-li Wing—will show you. Ask her no questions, and you will not need to lie when you say, like an honest soldier, that you know nothing against her. When you reach India, but no sooner, give her this, for herself."

Tom handed him five hundred *rupees*. Then he turned to Su-li Wing:

"There you are. I said I'd stake you to some journey money. You've an escort thrown in."

"Do you mean you're running me out of Tibet?" she demanded.

"Yes. Without prejudice. Tell your own story. About the worst they can do is to deport you from India and pay your fare."

"Do you call that giving me a break? Marching orders and five hundred miserable *rupees*? My luggage, that your girl friend has stolen, is worth at least five thousand *rupees*! I hope Dowlah rapes her, and then kills her! Give me her luggage. It's worth at least *something*."

Tom turned again to the man from Naini Kol.

"Did Rajah Dowlah carry off this lady's luggage?"

"No, *sahib*. There are several loads of it. His Highness offered it to the English lady, but she refused. She wouldn't even permit the porters to carry it into the tent we pitched for her."

"Snooty little bitch!" said Su-li Wing.

173

Dowlah's campsite, at the foot of the almost unnegotiable pass into Nepal, looked stricken, dismal, hopeless. The men from Naini Kol lined up and faced the wind. They were ashamed of being mutineers. They said so. They were equally ashamed of feeling beaten by the cold, the unaccustomed food and the altitude. They were angry with their *subadar*, for having agreed to return to India. They said that vehemently. They felt guilty of having let Elsa Burbage ride away with Dowlah. Muffled to their ears, and with their loads already packed on half-starved and exhausted ponies, they demanded, with chattering teeth, to be given a chance to restore their *izzat*—their soldierly honour.

"That's a brave offer," said Tom. "I respect you for it. But I can't accept. I'm not a British official, I'm American. You men are in foreign territory without permission or authority from anyone. As I see it, you obeyed your *rajah's* orders until you had reason to believe he was acting criminally. After that, you refused to obey. Well and good. But if the Tibetan soldiers from Kalimpong should catch you, you'd be massacred. That might cause bad international trouble. I am here as a foreigner at my own risk. I have no authority. But I have given your *subadar* a letter to Abdul Mirza, and I don't think you will be in disgrace when you get back, if you hold your tongues."

Su-li Wing tried harder than the men from Naini Kol to change Tom's mind.

"Look here," she said, "Tom Grayne, I'm for sale. You buy—yes?"

"No, I've told you."

"Don't you be a damned fool," she insisted. "If you follow Dowlah, he will kill your girl friend, sooner than let you get her. I know him. Once a man of Dowlah's type be comes a killer, he goes on killing. I have seen scores of men, in China and in Russia, who burned their bridges after intriguing themselves into a desperate situation because they thought themselves more clever than anyone else. They all took to murder. First they killed one person, then another, and then several. After that, they were like wolves that kill sheep, because to kill sheep is so easy."

"You're a killer yourself," Tom answered.

"You can't prove it! But you can buy me. I will stay bought. Give me the breaks, and I will show you how to get what you want in Tibet. I will show you how to get ahead of Dowlah. I haven't told you all I know. We professional spies should be as members of one brotherhood."

"Goodbye" said Tom. "Good luck to you. Short rations as far as Sikkim, Su-li Wing. After that you'll be able to eat your fill. If you take my advice, you'll talk small when you get to India."

He offered to shake hands. She refused. He returned with a genial grin the salute of the men from Naini Kol, then rode away at the head of his Tibetans. He was uncertain why they followed without protest. But after a mile or two the headman explained:

"Tum-Glain, in some other incarnation you must have done something to entitle you to wisdom in this one. In another life you ought to be entitled to some mercy, for your mercy to us now. We feared that for a punishment you might dismiss us and take some of those Indians instead. Then the soldiers from Kalimpong would have killed us, should they catch them, as is likely, because that woman is a bad-luck bringer."

"You think, then, that the Tibetan authorities may send out a patrol from Kalimpong?"

"Why not?"

"Along this road?"

"No. The soldiers are afraid of the evil spirits hereabouts, so their officers wouldn't be able to lead them along this road. But they will block the road. Why shouldn't they?"

"Do you think the Tibetan troops will oppose the Holy Lobsang Pun Rinpoche?"

"A million blessings on His Sacredness, they might! There is no knowing how wicked or how stupid soldiers can be. But His Blessed Holiness would make a magic, I think, and get by them unseen. If he wishes to come this way, he will do it."

Tom made the most of the Tibetans' changed mood. He accomplished marvels of marching, changing the loads frequently from one pony to another. But Dowlah's speed was next thing to a miracle. Two days and two nights at his heels, but not a sight of him. Tom's mood was merciless to man and beast, himself included, but instead of causing mutiny it stirred the Tibetans' superstition in his favour. Whenever he called a halt, to let them boil their slimy salted tea, in some cave or lee of a rock, or beside black and white water that welled amid treeless wastes of moraine and snow, their remarks revealed less curiosity than guarded approval. It was the same when they huddled together at night, in the tent.

"Tum-Glain, tell us how is it that you, a foreigner, who hadn't the advantage of being born in this blessed beautiful land, nevertheless are so good to be with? You speak our speech so that it sounds comical, although we understand you, and you understand us. Which is it? Were you one of us in a former life? Were you reborn into some miserable foreign country for your former sins? Or are you a foreigner, too good for your own wretched country, being made ready, because of merit, to be reborn, at the proper time, in this blessed land? If so, better die soon, sooner to be reborn!"

One more day, speed dwindling, and then food for the famished ponies! A load of barley on the snow, beside a dead horse. Ravens had arrived, but no vultures. The horse's carcass was hardly cold. The Tibetans apologized for cutting off meat for themselves. They admitted they were robbing birds and wolves. It wasn't decent food. Nevertheless, it wasn't so indecent as if they themselves had killed the animal. Hungry men mayn't be choosers. They were pious about it. They said their prayers for the soul of the sinner that had been incarnated in the horse because of sins in former lives. They wished him a better incarnation next time. They ate the meat raw, ravenously, throwing stones at the ravens because they are birds of very bad omen for the liberated soul whose dead carcass they insult with their beaks. They shouted aloud for the vultures to come and drive the ravens away.

Tom studied the trail, protecting his eyes from the wind with his gloved hand. It would be dark in less than two hours. The dead horse lay exactly at the summit of a narrow pass between high mountains that were part of the jumble of summits that hide Everest from almost every direction. From where he stood, a crag-flanked, bouldered gorge led downward, so nearly straight between the flanks of mountains that he could see the black-purple shadow of a valley, perhaps twenty miles away, five thousand feet below him. Darker seams in that shadow might even be tamarisk scrub. It looked like comfortable country, as one reckons comfort in Tibet. Fuel. Less wind. Altitude where breathing would be no effort, where three or four hours' deep sleep would really rest man and beast.

But the ponies couldn't possibly do twenty more miles. It might take them another day to reach that valley. They needed eight hours' rest, and another meal, before attempting the boulder-strewn descent. It would be a sheer impossibility in darkness. It would be many hours before the moon would rise over the peaks, and then not long before it would pass behind other peaks, so there would be no night march in any event. He looked for a good place to bivouac, wishing he had field-glasses.

Presently, on the right-hand side of the descending trail, about four or five miles away, and two hundred feet above it, he saw what looked, in the sunset shadow, like the mouth of a cave. If he could have only afforded the time, it would be a good place to await the morning sun. A good place any how. It seemed accessible. There would be room in there for the ponies, and no need to pitch the tent. He pointed it out to the Tibetans and led the way.

For a while he lost sight of it, because the track led down ward, a thousand feet in half a mile, between broken cliffs where the loaded ponies had to be manhandled over the slippery rock. Then he saw it again, through a saw-tooth gap—halted—beckoned the headman:

"Can you see anyone in that cave?"

"Bandits! Let us turn back!"

"How many can you see?"

"One."

"I also. Man or woman?"

"I can't tell. It is someone sitting by a fire of sticks, not a dung-fire. That means horses, or else porters, and that means danger for us. There are no prayer flags hereabouts. This is a country where the holy *lamas* haven't driven away the devils. So whoever is here is a *dugpa*, who obeys devils, or else they obey him, which would be even worse. Let us turn back quickly, while there is time."

Tom led forward, doing two men's share of the exhausting work of holding up ponies over rock worn smooth by ice and wind. Here and there a hoof-mark was discernible. In one place, on a pocket of frozen snow, there were at least twenty hoof-marks. But no sign of Elsa.

At last the ponies stood heaving, with trembling legs, while he studied the mouth of an ascending, winding track that led through a break in the rock wall on the right hand, toward the cave on the mountain-side. From where he stood he couldn't see the cave, but it was a well-worn causeway that led to it. Some of it was artificial, laid with flat stones set edgewise. There were traces of yak-dung in the crevices, left by the men who had gathered the stuff for fuel. There was quite a lot of yak-dung farther down the trail toward the dark valley, and some of that was recent.

The Tibetans refused to go a step farther. They declared they would wait for the moon and then turn back, unless someone should come from that cave, meanwhile, and kill them all. They were panic-stubborn.

177

"Tum-Glain, if we die at *dugpas'* hands, without a holy *lama* to protect us, devils will pursue our souls through outer darkness. No, not
another footstep forward! Go on alone, if you are as brave as all that."

Tom glanced at the pony that carried the load that held the money-
bag. That pony—it was his own, the strongest—might perhaps have
had enough strength to retreat uphill. Tom laughed at the headman.

"What would you do with money in the next world?"

Then he filled his lungs and shouted:

"Hullo-hullo-hullo! *Koi hai! Koi hai!*"

The shout went clamouring from crag to crag. It seemed endless.
It was like a thousand hollow voices of the devils of the night, that
came hurrying out of the valley. The Tibetans laid their foreheads on
the rock between flattened hands. The headman moaned the sacred
"Om mane padme hum!" The others, a word behind him, moaned it
louder, until they caught up with him, all chanting faster and faster. It
sounded like "Three Blind Mice."

Tom cocked the Mauser and waited, gripping the butt with his
ungloved hand inside his overcoat. He was dog-tired. He leaned in the
icy shadow of a huge boulder in the middle of the track, flexing his
muscles to keep them from growing numb.

It seemed ten minutes, but the shadow wasn't ten minutes deeper,
before footsteps clamoured on the causeway. Echoes magnified them
into a prodigious noise that resembled the clatter of small stones falling from the higher ledges. Who ever was coming made no secret of it.
But Tom stayed in the dark where he was, making sure of his footing.
He made sure of his grip on the Mauser. The Tibetans ceased chanting
and lay as still as dead men.

It seemed ten more minutes before a man came and stood in the
gap, in the last of the reflected sunset, staring. He was wearing snow-
spectacles, with his head in a hood, above wind-proof, fur-lined clothing. He stared at the Tibetans—at the ponies—pulled off his spectacles
to peer into the deepening shadows—

Tom spoke, quite quietly:

"Dowlah, put your hands up! Put them high over your head!"

"Oh, it's you, is it? I thought—I mean, I hoped they had buried
you in Darjeeling."

"I won't repeat the warning."

Dowlah put his hands up. "Curse you, are you an immortal? Where's
that Chinese woman? You must have passed her."

"Keep your hands up!"

Tom told the headman to go and search him. Comforted by the Mauser, the headman obeyed.

Dowlah had no weapon.

CHAPTER 31

"You see, I had to sleep," said Dowlah. "Hee-hee! I've had a good sleep. You haven't had. What are you going to do about that Mauser? Shoot me, or strike a bargain?"

They sat facing each other, across a wood-fire near the mouth of the cave, their faces glowing but their backs protected with heavy sheepskin from the icy wind. No moon yet. Pitch dark. The Tibetans had refused to enter the cave. They said it belonged to *dugpas*; it was occupied by home less souls, too wicked to have bodies. They were afraid, too, of Dowlah. But Tom had prevailed on them to lead the foundered ponies, and to climb with the loads, to a wide ledge below and beyond the cave. There they had pitched the tent and had a fire of their own, amid leaping shadows.

The cave contained plenty of fuel, tied in yak-load bundles. Tom had cooked tea and a meal for himself and Dowlah. No lantern. Fire-light was sufficient.

Tom was sleepy. Dowlah knew it. Tom had shaved recently and his tired face looked at least civilized, but Dowlah's tangle of black whiskers was a scandalous mess, through which his eyes gleamed with fire-lit malice. The dilettante, amateur scientist's pose had vanished, but he hadn't lost his giggle. If he was feeling beaten or afraid, he didn't show it.

Tom forced the issue. "My Tibetans," he said, "are out of gas. Four flats to a man. They won't go another yard forward. In the morning I'm going to take the two best ponies and go on alone."

"To your death," said Dowlah.

"You may go with my Tibetans," Tom answered. "Over take your own men. They're a bit ashamed of having let you make a monkey of yourself. They'll take you safe back to India. The British will probably let you go and live in Monte Carlo on a pension, like the other rotten *rajahs*, who aren't worth hanging. They're not bad sorts, the British. True, you're a bloody murderer, and they'll soon know it. You're a double-triple-crosser, and they already know that. But they've plenty of sense. They're not likely to make a public scandal, if you accept banishment and hold your tongue."

"My dear man, what an imbecile you are," said Dowlah. "You're a poor spy and a worse psychologist. Do you mistake me for a man who will accept humiliation? Are you going to use that Mauser?"

"I don't have to," Tom answered. "I need sleep. I'm going to fix you first. What has happened?"

"Produce a drink and I'll tell you."

"I don't use liquor. There's plenty of tea. Help yourself. I won't ask any question twice. How did Elsa put one over on you?"

Dowlah grinned. "You strong, silent, tough, abstemious, big blundering brutes never fail to fall for little women, do you! You may as well be disillusioned now as later. I will tell you the truth about your sweet-innocent Elsa Burbage. Smart little devil! I told her you're dead, as I supposed you were. A man said he had killed you. She didn't care a damn. Not a damn, Mr. Lowly Lothario Grayne. Mr. Mute Mephistopheles Grayne and your miniature Marguerite! She began to play her own hand from that minute."

He paused, watching Tom's eyes in the firelight. His own eyes were contemptuous, but cunningly alert. He continued:

"I confess she put one over on me, as you call it. She saw me get rid of Su-li Wing, and I don't doubt that gave her this idea. Clever little hypocrite! Butter wouldn't melt in her mouth. Pretended to be sorry for Su-li Wing. Needed clothing like the devil, but wouldn't even look at the other woman's luggage. Su-li Wing fooled Pavlov, but she hadn't guts enough to kill him, and she hadn't brains enough to fool me. All Su-li Wing ever wanted was Thö-pa-ga. He is all that anybody needs, to get control of the Thunder Dragon Gate. Elsa Burbage has him by the heartstrings."

He paused again, but Tom's eyes told him nothing. He continued:

"It was one of those crises, Grayne, that occur in the midst of all well-laid intrigues. The unpredictable. My men had become a liability—a dangerous nuisance. Carefully-chosen men, nevertheless mutinous. So I armed some of the *Böns* with their weapons and told them to go home. They're sure to fall foul of Tibetan troops from Kalimpong or some where, and be wiped out. Serve them right, the ingrates!"

Tom put some wood on the fire.

"Of course," said Dowlah, "I realized at once, in Delhi, that Elsa Burbage was merely using you for her own ends. She hadn't been in my house twenty minutes before she was measuring me with her eyes for a—"

Tom interrupted: "Cut that, Dowlah, if you need your front

180

teeth."

Dowlah chuckled. "Grayne, accept your natural role of victim of a pretty little woman's cunning! She is quite capable of taking care of herself. The *Bön* magician's men—more than half of them devil-dancers—regard Thö-pa-ga as the incarnation of a god. She is the god's handmaiden. His daffadowndilly. His joy. Thanks to her companionship—and whatever else—Thö-pa-ga has recovered his spirits. They share the same tent."

"To protect her from you?" Tom suggested.

"Oh, I hadn't a chance. Not a chance. Don't be jealous. The *Böns* gave her credit for preserving Thö-pa-ga's life, so she very soon had the *Böns* eating out of her hand. Even that treacherous dog Noropa grovels to her. It was he who gave her one of my men's pistols. She had the impudence to threaten me with it. Tee-hee! Imagine being held up, at my age, by a ninety-pound girl with a Mauser! I don't believe she knows how to pull the trigger."

"She can hit an egg with a service repeater at thirty feet five times out of six," said Tom.

"Oh, can she? Well, the *Böns* were a bit difficult. You see, I had shot their leaders. I had to do that. It wouldn't have been safe to get rid of my own men while those two rascals were alive. Without leaders, and with Thö-pa-ga and Elsa Burbage on my side, the *Böns* should have been easy to manage, but I underestimated her spunk and cunning. I expected she would regard me as a rescuer. Instead, she jockeyed me into the position of having to look to her for protection. She can talk Tibetan, confound her! I can't. I had to depend on her influence with Thö-pa-ga to keep the *Böns* from killing me. I had to pipe down, as they say in the navy. The only tactical error that she made was preserving my life. I can't imagine why she did it."

"How did you travel so fast?" Tom asked him.

"Oh, the *Böns* had caches of provisions and fresh remounts. Good ponies. We rode like the devil. One brute burst his heart at the top of a hill."

"That's how I found you."

"Lucky blunderer! Grayne, you were riding to certain death."

"Talk sense," said Tom. "Your number's up, Dowlah. You know it."

"Grayne, if you had half the intuition of a dog, you would know without being told, that I have burned my bridges. No retreat possible. And I'm not the man to be beaten by a situation like this. There's Noropa, a half-boiled mystic who believes the gods will love him if

181

he swaps horses often enough. By flattering him and telling him a few facts more or less embellished, I contrived to undermine egregious Elsa's position. She will find she has no secrets, but lots of opposition when she gets to Djaring-dzong. Because of promises that I made to Noropa, he is quite sure to bring or send a rescue-party. According to my calculation, they should be here by noon tomorrow."

"Does Noropa trust you? Or you him?"

"No. But he has seen my credentials."

"The forged letter that you stole from the man you murdered?"

"Who says it's forged? Who's to prove it, you infatuated ass? It's from the Tashi Lama himself."

"Bunk."

"Hah! I haven't it on me. It's well hidden. If you should shoot me, you couldn't find it. If I had known of its existence a year ago I would have got hold of it in time to avoid all this mess. I have known for more than a year that I would have to bolt sooner or later. Abdul Mirza, damn him, betrayed me a day too soon. But no matter. I got away, through Nepal. That route fooled them."

"You rewarded Su-li Wing for it, didn't you!"

"Blackmailing bitch!" Dowlah spat into the fire. "When we reached this place, I did lose a trick, I admit. There was another gang of *Bön* monks waiting for us, down below there on the trail, with a herd of yaks. Murderous-looking swine. They put most of our loads on the yaks and sent the ponies along unloaded, downhill. Some of them wanted to kill me. Elsa prompted Thö-pa-ga, and he objected. Someone challenged his identity, so they stripped him naked behind a screen of blankets, to look for his birthmarks. He has 'em. They bowed down and worshipped. He'll be a wonder, under proper control. He had to do a lot of talking to protect me, but he did it. Elsa Burbage asked me to go up to this cave, where I'd be safe while Thö-pa-ga orated. I had no suspicion of what the little sorceress intended. I got some of the Tibetans to carry up a few of my personal loads and light a fire. I made tea, and I opened a bottle of prunes. I declare she had doped them. I remember noticing that the cap wasn't screwed on the bottle tightly. When I awoke, it was morning. I had been disarmed. There was no one in sight."

Tom eyed him with curiosity. "You sceptics," he said, "are always credulous. Where would Elsa get dope?"

"Damned if I know. Perhaps you gave it to her for Thö-pa-ga. Would a Tibetan have written in the ashes, with a stick or his fingers, in English: 'Now it's your turn to be left flat. How do you like it?' Waspy little devil! She'll be singing to another tune though, before those Tibetans have finished, unless you accept my offer."

"You haven't made any offer," said Tom. "You weren't doped. You were drunk. On the way up here I saw the broken whisky bottle where you threw it. Frazzled nerves, and your last bottle of Scotch. One slug might make you pye-eyed at this altitude. You drank a whole bottle and fell asleep. Are the fumes still in your head? Or are you going to listen to sense?"

"The point is: have you any sense?" Dowlah retorted. "Are you vain enough to think I have been talking for your entertainment? Do you flatter yourself that I enjoy your company? Or that I have the slightest intention of accepting favours from you? I wish you in hell."

Tom grinned. "Same to you. I'll bet on my wish. You'll starve here, betting on Noropa, until Lobsang Pun turns up, and he'll send you to hell with bells on. You haven't food, tent, money, horse or weapon. What's your offer?"

"I know where the Thunder Dragon Gate is."

"So do I! Down in the valley. Less than a day's march. I've had that doped out since day before yesterday. This must be the valley that explains the fifty-mile discrepancies on all the maps."

"But I know how to get in!"

"Says you, Dowlah."

"And I know what to do when I get there."

"I know what to do with you, unless you come clean, Dowlah. I'm not going to let a crook like you keep me awake much longer. Speak up."

"Very well. I will tell you enough to satisfy you that I know a great deal more."

Dowlah stared at the night. There was a wistful melancholy in his eyes, as if he were bidding silent farewell to a treasured secret. He leaned forward as if he couldn't force himself to say it aloud; he must whisper it. Suddenly he scraped up embers with his naked hands and pitched them at Tom's face. As quick as a snake he made a grab for the Mauser—and took the consequences.

"Cry out when you've had enough," said Tom.

Ready for anything, he had dodged most of the embers, a bit singed, nothing serious. He took Dowlah by the neck and rubbed his face in the hot ashes.

"If you want to be killed, try one more trick!"

He kicked the fire together, holding Dowlah by the neck to examine his face by the light.

"Help yourself to cooking grease from that can. Smear on plenty."

Dowlah spat ashes. He snarled: "I won't forgive that."

Tom gave him tea to wash the ashes from his mouth.

"Dowlah, you're a busted flush and a rotter. But I'll give you a break if you act sensibly. You've taken crazy chances. It's a cinch you've a card up your sleeve, or think you have. You count on someone in the Thunder Dragon Gate. Who is he?"

Dowlah tied a handkerchief over a scorched eyelid. It made him look like a coloured-supplement pirate. Tom fetched a bundle of wood and began feeding the fire.

"Sixty seconds," he remarked. "I'll count 'em. One—two—"

Dowlah interrupted: "You do show an occasional spark of intelligence. Yes. You have guessed it."

"Do I count? My limit's sixty."

"I have the goods on Naosuki. Do you know who he is?"

Tom laughed outright. "Must be good goods! Naosuki is the man who faked the Soviet Army mobilization plans that were sold to Germany. He sent the genuine ones to Japan. All the insiders were laughing about it. Goods on Naosuki, have you? Just now he goes by the name of Chou Wang. I've never met him, but that's the ninth or tenth name that I've heard of him using. He's the toughest and trickiest secret mischief-maker that Japan ever turned loose. He's the man who played the fiddle for the recent dance in Sinkiang that cost China a province. Before that, in China, he was too smart even for Borodin. Dowlah, are you still so full of whisky that you really believe you can blackmail Chou Wang? What's to stop him from having you bumped off? He'd no more hesitate to do that than to kill a bed-bug."

Dowlah snorted disgust. "What is the use of talking to a fool like you!"

"It's your only chance," Tom answered. "Tell me the truth and make me believe it. I promised old Abdul Mirza to give you a break if you'd give me half an excuse."

"Oh. What did Abdul Mirza tell you?"

"Plenty. Do I start counting? All right. One—two—"

"I was in trouble some years ago," said Dowlah. "Never mind what. Abdul Mirza suggested to me that the best way to regain prestige with the Indian Government would be to distinguish myself as a secret agent. Damn his eyes, they had already made him ruler of my state,

184

to all intents and purposes. I was deeply in debt. Even my house in Delhi belongs to a swine of a money-lender. He even holds a bill of sale on the furniture. Instead of increasing my income, Abdul Mirza cut it to the bone, to relieve taxation. He is one of those humbugging democrats who wants to be loved by multitudes. However, I have a natural gift for this game. I did pretty well. But no better than rather well, until I got in touch with Naosuki. Yes, he is Chou Wang at the moment. I did him lots of favours. You know how it is. You've sold your country's secrets scores of times, I don't doubt."

"I never knew 'em," said Tom. "Our State Department keeps the secrets, along with the gold, in a locked tin box."

"Don't be a sententious hypocrite!" Dowlah retorted. "There isn't an international spy in the world who doesn't make a business of selling anything he knows to whoever will pay. How much! That's the only question. I could never get enough money, but what I craved was intellectual excitement. Chou Wang was the man to provide that. I excited him, and he me. All of us have our Elsa Burbages on the job. Few of them are quite as smart as yours; but very few of us are such blundering boobies as you. Through a woman in Singapore, who found a fool of your type in a responsible position, I obtained for Naosuki photostatic copies of some plans of the new British naval base. They're in Japan now. He has very likely sold copies of them to several nations. In exchange, he supplied me with details of some of the Japanese defences of Formosa. Very opportune. I turned those over to the British Secret Intelligence in the nick of time to allay their suspicions of me."

"What's the idea of bragging to me that you're a worse crook than I thought you?" Tom asked.

He stirred the fire. Dowlah's uncovered eye glittered with contemptuous malice. He lighted a cigarette before he answered:

"Tom Grayne, unless you can develop enough sense to agree with me, you will be dead, or worse, by tomorrow night. Have you ever been tortured? If you kill me now, I shall have ceased to care who knows my secrets. When they kill you, you will cease to remember them. Is that clear? You ass, you said you wish to be convinced. I am convincing you. In simple phrases. Adapted to your mulish intellect. For my own purpose. To persuade you that I mean what I say in all seriousness, and that I know what I'm talking about."

"Go ahead," said Tom. "I'll listen."

"What I did not turn over to the British Secret Intelligence was

Naosuki's private code and some plans of the fortifications of Kobe that reveal his finger-prints under the microscope. He sent those to me in exchange for certain details of the new American anti-aircraft guns."

Tom grinned. "How did you get those?"

Dowlah grinned back. "If you want that information, buy it! I will sell it to you. Naosuki is afraid of nothing on earth except myself and the Japanese Secret Intelligence. The Japanese are a strange people, as I daresay you know. Naosuki is an unmitigated blackguard, who would rather die, of any kind of torture, than be shown up as a traitor to his own country. Traitor he is. So you see, I have him. Have you enough intelligence to understand that?"

"If he should kill you, how could you betray him?" Tom retorted. "Left the evidence in India, I suppose, to be sent to Japan, in case you and he quarrel? Dowlah, you're not so bright. How can you communicate with India? Seems to me, Dowlah, that you've lost your senses along with your number. Too much liquor? All you nervous numbers seem to go by that route."

Dowlah leaned forward and tapped Tom's knee.

"Naosuki knows that unless my secret agent in India should hear from me, at frequent intervals, my agent will convey that evidence to Tokyo and give it to the Japanese Government."

"Hell! Hasn't Naosuki any agents? Do you kid yourself that his man can't shadow your man, and kill him?"

"No, Mr. Tom Grayne, I never kid myself, as you poetically phrase it. I have stolen a march on Naosuki. My messenger is already on the way to Tokyo. He may be there already. Naosuki's number is up, but he doesn't suspect it. By wireless, and secret lines of communication by way of India, it will take the Japanese two or three weeks to reach Chou Wang and kill him, or make him kill himself, or make his subordinates kill him. But they'll do it. They never fail to kill their traitors. By that time, thanks to Naosuki, you and I will have possession of the Thunder Dragon Gate and Thö-pa-ga. I hate to do it, but I'm going to have to okay you with Naosuki, in exchange for the protection of your Mauser until we connect with him. That is my offer."

Tom stirred the fire and added fuel. "What do you propose to do with the Thunder Dragon Gate?" he asked.

"Even you may appreciate that when you get there. Ditch Elsa. Have her, if she's alive. I don't care what you do with her. But if you've any sense at all you will give her to Thö-pa-ga and let her make a fool of him. Thö-pa-ga is the whole problem. There is nothing more to it than

Thö-pa-ga. I will put one thought into your thick head and let it try to find lodgement. Suppose you should return to America and offer your opulent government a continuous, day after day, week after week, authoritative, psychologically skilful anti-Japanese propaganda to reach the whole of Asia, but especially China, how much would they pay?"

"Oh. I'm the salesman, am I?"

"And no sales resistance!" said Dowlah. "You know there's a world war coming. If Mussolini doesn't start it, someone else will. All Europe, India, Africa. Japan's opportunity to gobble China! Bang goes America's trade, along with all the capital invested in China. America's alternatives are guns or propaganda. The Thunder Dragon Gate is worth at least a billion to any government. And think of the chance for us to make a splash in the world—ten times the splash that Lenin made!"

"Yes, I'm thinking of that," said Tom. "I draw a modest salary, for taking chances now and then to stop that kind of splash before it happens."

"You? You think you can stop it?"

"I don't know yet. I'm going to keep a promise I made to Abdul Mirza. He gave me money for you, but I gave some of it to your destitute men and to Su-li Wing. I'm giving you what's left."

"How much?"

"Eight thousand five hundred *rupees*."

"Keep it! I daresay that's as much as you earn in a couple of years. In exchange for it, lend me a pony and escort me either as far as the Djaring-dzong Monastery, or until Noropa's messengers meet us on the way. After that, you may go to the devil."

"Here's your money," said Tom. "I'm going to the tent now, to sleep with the Tibetans. Don't try to hire 'em to murder me. I might get rough. Offer them a fair price in the morning and perhaps they'll take you with them."

"Where to?"

"Damned if I care, Dowlah. Goodnight."

Chapter 32

Dowlah, a mere fire-lit shadow at daybreak, called from the mouth of the cave.

"To your death, you idiot!"

The Tibetan headman remonstrated:

"Tum-Glain, turn back with us. We dare not go with you down into that valley. Nobly Born, it is from down yonder that come the *shang-shangs*. It is bad luck even to speak of the place. But we like you. We wish to save you from terrible things. Perhaps Your Honour hasn't heard that *shang-shangs* kill a man in this world, and then hound him in the next, so that he can't reincarnate. Down yonder they give dead men's bodies to the *shang-shangs* instead of feeding them to the dogs and vultures as is decent. Give that man Dowlah a pony. You wait here. Let it happen to him. Perhaps then—"

Tom interrupted. "Do as I said in the night. Delay him. Later, if he wants a pony, let him have one and follow me, if he wishes. As for you, I have praised you in that letter that I have given you for Lobsang Pun. The sooner you deliver it, the sooner you will receive his commendation and his blessing."

"But if His Holiness Lobsang Pun Rinpoche should not be coming this way, then what?"

"His Holiness is too shrewd not to come," Tom answered. "The point is that he should come quickly."

Dowlah shouted again from the mouth of the cave.

"Grayne, I want to talk to you. Come up here for a few minutes."

Tom continued talking to the headman:

"Don't rob him. Money or valuables taken from a killer, such as he is, are very evil and produce nothing but bad luck. Hold him here until the sun warms the morning a bit. Then let him have a pony and go his own way. You go yours. Is there another road than this that the Holy Lobsang Pun might follow?"

"Oh, yes, there is a shorter way than this one. It turns off this side of that monastery where they let down the basket. It saves a great distance, and it rejoins this road not far from where the dead horse lay. But it is a sacred road, and only holy people dare to use it. That is why the *Böns* didn't use it. Even those rogues wouldn't have dared to bring foreigners by that route."

"But you are the Holy Lobsang Pun's servants, so you may go and meet him along that road? Do that. If you meet him, bid him make haste."

"Nobly Born, Dowlah may follow and kill you! Better let us take him with us."

Tom laughed. He answered with a Tibetan proverb: "The dog that follows in order to steal, by his bark betrays the men who come to slay."

He shook hands with all the Tibetans and started on his way with the two best ponies, lightly loaded. No tent. The loads were principally food, Elsa's bags and his own.

In the distance, from above, the sharp descent had looked almost straight. It actually wound like the narrow track of a snake between fifty-foot cliffs that had once contained a glacier. It was choked with smooth boulders, and in many places so steep and difficult that he had to lend the ponies his strength to save them from crashing headlong.

At the end of ten miles he had descended something like four thousand feet. There he rested on a sloping acre of moraine that provided the first clear view of the valley into which the trail led. Down below there, spring had already greened scant herbage on the banks of aquamarine-coloured streams.

The serene splendour produced an almost hypnotic sensation of unreality. Much warmer, and the air much easier to breathe. Ponies sweating. No sign of the Monastery of Djaring-dzong. It probably faced southward, around a corner to the right, where there was a vague haze. Not smoke. It looked more like steam from hot springs, hardly moving on a breath of wind. The westerly gale, that blows all day long on Everest, seemed not to touch that valley.

Tom hadn't long to rest. He had twice caught sight of Dowlah, miles behind, once riding, and once scrambling be side his miserable pony down a fifty-foot glissade. The Tibetans must have been impatient to get started up the steep grade and got rid of him sooner than Tom anticipated.

Uphill from the valley were coming three men, who might be the rescue-party that Dowlah had said he expected. Because of turns and intervening crags and boulders, they had been invisible until they were quite near. They were riding yaks, brutes that can climb like goats. One man had a bow and arrows; the others had heavy, old-fashioned, long-barrelled guns with two-legged metal supports on which to rest the weapon when in use.

The man with the bow and arrows seemed to be the leader. He vaulted off his yak, stuck out his tongue at Tom respectfully, placed his hand behind his ear and walked straight forward with a letter in his hand.

"Nobly Born, are you Rajah Dowlah?"

Rajah Dowlah's name was on the outside of the sealed parchment envelope. It had been written with a brush dipped in Chinese ink. The handwriting was unmistakably Elsa's. Tom almost snatched the letter from the Tibetan's hand, broke the wax seal and tugged it from the parchment envelope. It was in code, difficult to read because of the brush strokes. He lay on a rock in the sun to work it out with the aid of a pencil. The Tibetans began transferring his loads to the yaks.

Dear Tom,

I *know* you're not dead, although Noropa and the others all say you are. There is a man here who says he killed you in Darjeeling, but I saw the blow, so I don't believe him. I know you're coming. I know it. I will stick this out to the very end, to give you all the possible chances. I couldn't think of any other way than this to get a message to you, but if Dowlah gets it he can't read it, so no matter. Dowlah is expected by a man named Chou Wang, who is a devil. This is a dreadful place. There have been murders and a kind of civil war is going on.

The abbot, who is a Yellow-hat and a friend of Mu-ni Gampo, is Chou Wang's prisoner. Chou Wang has some people here who look to me like Japanese. They are well armed. But they are in fear of their lives from a faction of Red-hats and *Böns* who occupy the other half of the monastery and are supposed to obey a man named Pavlov. There seems to be no Pavlov, but I think he is a man who was murdered or else escaped after either he or Su-li Wing shot the woman who was being kept here for Thö-pa-ga. So says Noropa, who, however, seldom tells the same tale twice running and is obsequious one minute, insolent the next.

Chou Wang hates my influence over Thö-pa-ga, who is being a brick and is respected by all except Chou Wang, who bullies him. He bullies everybody. He scoffs at the idea of substituting me for the Tibetan woman who was shot, but Thöpe and I are playing that hand for lack of a better. Chou Wang had Noropa flogged severely for not having killed Dowlah, whom Chou Wang fears, I don't know why. Now Noropa is spying on Thöpe and me, toadying to Chou Wang, but I think he would like to kill Chou Wang, whom he certainly hates. But he would kill me if Chou Wang ordered it, as Thö-pa-ga believes he intends. Chou Wang interrogated me so menacingly about Dowlah that I had to pretend to weaken to avoid violence. He even threatened torture. Thinking me weak, he became careless, so I caught on that he would like to trap Dowlah, who he fears is too cunning to come within reach.

I doped out that they both pretend friendship for each other but are actually enemies and from something that Chou Wang said about Su-li Wing, it appears that she obeyed Chou Wang's orders to betray Dowlah to the Indian Government. Chou Wang accused me of being Dowlah's accomplice. Then I thought of pretending to write to Dowlah asking him to come and take me away. Chou Wang jumped at that. He thinks I am very simple and scared out of my wits. But I insisted Thöpe must see the letter before it goes. Thöpe shall show it to Chou Wang. I am writing two letters, and when Chou Wang has read the one to Dowlah Thöpe will destroy it and substitute this. Perhaps Chou Wang will kill me, when he thinks I have done what he wants. But we may be able to defeat Chou Wang by my pretending to be Thöpe's wife or mistress.

It appears these monks won't stand for murdering Thöpe's woman. But it's awkward. Thöpe takes it seriously. He insists you are dead and that you came to him in a dream and said so. He wants me to be another Nancy Strong and live with him in Tibet, and I daren't be too stand-offish or he might blow up. Thöpe has my pistol safely hidden and not even Chou Wang dares to touch Thöpe or search him. Some of these monks seem decent although madly superstitious, and I think I could persuade them to send me safely away. But that wouldn't be right, because I think Thöpe can get me inside the Thunder Dragon Gate, and that may make it possible for me to smuggle you in, though I don't yet know how. Tom, I can't imagine you dead.

I know you're not dead. I know it. I can't imagine you doing any thing but win through. I know you will. I'm counting on it. I'm positive you're not far away. You shall not fail through any cowardice of mine. I have described you, not Dowlah, to the messengers, though Dowlah's name is on the envelop. So, if you get this, you will know I am almost at the end of my tether but counting on you. Tom, if you should come too late, this is goodbye and God bless you.   Elsa.

Tom shoved the letter into his pocket. The Tibetan messenger led one of the yaks toward him, blindfolded, because if a yak should see the act of mounting he would presently use his horns to get rid of his rider.

"Nobly Born, a good beast, who will carry you in comfort."
Suddenly he saw Tom's eyes. He stepped backward.

"Have I done wrong? Have I spoken offense?"

Tom vaulted on to the yak from behind.

"How far to the monastery?"

"Nobly Born, being downhill, it should take two-thirds of the time from daybreak until now. Your Honour's eyes are angry. How have I given offense?"

"You haven't. Walk beside me and let us talk as we go."

CHAPTER 33

Dowlah was either an expert or immensely reckless horse man. He wasn't more than two miles behind when Tom saw him crossing the sloping moraine where he had read Elsa's letter. As he vanished again in the bed of the winding track, the snub-nosed, gently mannered Tibetan asked:

"Does Your Honour know who that is who follows?"

"Have you heard of Tum-Glain?" Tom answered.

"No."

"Are you a monk?"

"Yes, of the Josays Sept, that used to keep the Thunder Dragon Gate, until these changes came to pass. Some of us began to wear lay clothing as a protest. Later, they forced us all to do that, and made us labour at the mean tasks. We, who used to receive the pilgrims and instruct them, are now *rhagbyas*, reckoned of no account. They even make us handle dead men's bodies. They have taken away even our prayer wheels."

Tom quoted the Tibetan proverb:

"*Night follows the day, but day follows the night.*"

"Nobly Born, this is a long night! Ever since the Holy Panchen Lama Rinpoche was driven away into exile from Tashi-lunpo by the blasphemers in Lhasa who control the army, there has been nothing like the old order. Foreigners came here—two factions—both claiming—we say falsely—high authority from Lhasa. But who has true authority in all Tibet since the Holy Dalai Lama Rinpoche died? Who knows? They have found none yet to replace him. No Tashi Lama! No Dalai Lama! No Thö-pa-ga! In all sacred Tibet, no voice of true authority that all may trust! No longer are the pilgrims sent away from here to the ends of the earth with blessed messages of peace and wisdom from the lips of the Thö-pa-ga."

"Hasn't Thö-pa-ga returned? I heard he had."

"Nobly Born, yes—with a woman, of whom we know nothing

192

except that Thö-pa-ga loves her. Why should he love a foreign woman? Is it the sign of the end of all things?"

"Where is the woman?"

"I don't know. She was in the monastery. But I think now she is with Thö-pa-ga within the Thunder Dragon Gate. They say it. In the old days, none would have dared to take her in there. But our abbot admitted those black devils of *Böns* to the monastery, because the Holy Panchen Lama Rinpoche said that there is no such thing as evil men, but only evil that corrupts men by illusion. Prayer and meditation might have conquered their evil. But there was too much evil, and they too fond of it. It was they and their cursed magicians who brought the *shang*-shangs hither, and put them within the Thunder Dragon Gate, so that no one else dared to enter. The *shang-shang* doesn't harm them, because their souls are black."

"*Shang-shang*? One or many?"

"One now. At first there were many. The dreadful monsters destroy one another unless prevented. Who is to prevent? The females kill the males, and it is said that the *shamans* can't find any more males on the mountain-ledges. There were five left, and one little male that was harmless and very afraid. Four of them the *shamans* took to India, in baskets, I don't know why. Some said it was to terrify His Holy Eminence Lobsang Pun. Others, that it was to greet Thö-pa-ga, who was known to be coming. Perhaps it was for both those reasons. But they left the great one within the Thunder Dragon Gate, with the one male—the very little one. She slew it. Nobly Born, she is enormous and old. She is the mother of all those others."

"Whom do the *Böns* obey?" Tom asked. His eyes were as alert as his ears. He could still not see the monastery. Half a mile ahead, a thousand feet lower, the track divided left and right. The left-hand fork led upward, past a number of caves; but it seemed to lead downward again in the distance and to curve to the right to rejoin the other. Half-way along the right-hand track, he caught sight of a number of men on foot. It was only a quick glimpse, through a gap. He wasn't sure how many.

The monk answered: "They obey Chou Wang, as I do also, since I must. Chou Wang ordered me to bring that letter to Your Honour."

"Who are the men coming uphill toward us?"

"Nobly Born, I don't know."

"Which of the roads below should we take?"

"The one to the right is easier."

"Let us take the left one swiftly. They behave like men who wish not to be seen."

The monk made no objection. That, in a Tibetan, was remarkable. All three monks went to great pains to keep out of sight, from above or below, until the loaded yaks and unloaded ponies began to scramble up the steep left-hand fork behind a fanged screen of enormous boulders.

"You are afraid of those fellows?"

"Nobly Born, we Josays never know nowadays what to expect. They shoot us one at a time, for no reason at all except that we are faithful and say our prayers. If we are seen speaking together they shoot us."

"Who do?"

"Chou Wang and his followers, who declare they are Chinese, although we doubt it. They seem to us like foreigners from some other country. Perhaps devils. They throw our shot bodies, while they are still warm, to the *shang-shang*. Does Your Honour know that *shang-shangs* are the images in this world of the monsters that pursue the dead through all eternity? Who shall be saved from *shang-shangs* in the other world, whose body has been mauled by them in this present life?"

"Why haven't you run away?"

"We are the faithful. We await the coming of the Holy Panchen Lama Rinpoche, or of his delegate the Holy Lobsang Pun, to restore the old order. Lobsang Pun sent word. He promised it shall not be long now. Should he come here and find no faithful?"

"How many are you?"

"Nine-and-forty. We were eighty."

"Why do you trust me with these confidences?"

"Why not? We faithful await a messenger from Lobsang Pun Rinpoche, who isn't likely to send anyone we know, lest the messenger should be recognised by the *Böns* and slain. I have never before heard the name Rajah Dowlah. How should I know Your Honour's business? You speak and you look like one who has authority. You might be the messenger, to say His Holiness is coming. If not, no matter. What harm could you do?"

Tom pulled out his permit with Lobsang Pun's seal and signature. He unfolded it and held it in front of the monk's eyes.

The monk stared. He almost went mad. He jumped, danced, slapped his thighs, thrust forward his forehead for Tom to touch it with the seal. He held it pressed against his forehead as long as Tom would let him. The other two came scrambling over rocks to see what the excitement was about, saw the seal and signature, and began chanting. All three laid their foreheads on the ground until Tom ordered them to get up.

"My name isn't Dowlah. I am Tum-Glain. Here, you see it written. That man who rides the road below us is Dowlah. They who are coming toward him on foot are probably some of the *Böns* who brought Thö-pa-ga. They have been sent secretly by a man named Noropa, who may be with them. Have you faithful any weapons?"

"Only such as these things, and no powder! We are men of peace, not killers, such as *Böns* are."

"Would you fight, if I would lead you?"

"No, Nobly Born. We aspire to merit, on the Middle Way."

"Would you kill a *shang-shang*?"

"We are not killers of anything."

"What if I should do it?"

"We would bless you!"

"You three, with the yaks and ponies, go as fast as you can to the monastery. Get your forty-nine together, if you can, and tell them I'm the man who saved the Holy Lobsang Pun from two of the *shang-shangs* that the *Böns* took to India! Tell them I'm coming to kill the big one! Wait now—wait a minute! Secretly if possible, get word to that woman who came with Thö-pa-ga. Say to her you have spoken with Tum-Glain. In proof of it, give her this."

He opened Elsa's bag, groped at random and found a little red vanity-case. The monk hid it in the voluminous *bokkus* above his belt.

"There is magic in that bag. Good white magic, blessed by His Holiness Lobsang Pun. Take care that she gets it, and no one else sees it. Tell her Tum-Glain is close at hand and very pleased with her. Repeat that."

"Tum-Glain is close at hand and very pleased with her."

"Right. If you faithful want to acquire great merit, and to receive the thousand-fold-fruitful-blessing of the Holy-Panchen-Lama-Rinpoche-Representative Lobsang Pun—in person, mind you, he shall bless you in person, touching you with his right hand—then obey that woman! Do whatever she tells you! For every act of obedience with which you obey her, I will demand, for each of you faithful, one thousand blessings from Lobsang Pun Rinpoche! Now hurry!"

Tom set the example. He was out of the monks' sight in thirty seconds, keeping his head and shoulders low as he clambered diagonally, zigzag, downward, toward the point where he estimated Dowlah would meet the men coming uphill. He scrambled, slid, fell, clambered and arrived in time to look down from a ledge and see Dowlah talking to Noropa. There were seven others. They turned and led the way down hill, Noropa leading, Dowlah bringing up the rear. Tom scrambled along the ledge. He shouted:

"Dowlah!"

Almost too late. A machine-gun from behind some rocks on Tom's left ripped out half a belt that mowed down all the Tibetans and Dowlah's pony. Noropa was the first to be hit. Dowlah crawled out from under his pony, took cover, and climbed until Tom could take him by both hands and haul him to the ledge.

"Got your Mauser?" he asked, panting. There was blood on his knees from the climb.

"Lie still."

Six men climbed down from the machine-gun nest into the narrow road-bed to examine their victims. They were dressed in padded khaki uniforms without insignia, and woolen puttees—short, stocky-looking fellows, as active as cats. Tom crawled along the ledge, making too much noise over loose rock. There was a tumbled heap of boulders between him and the spot he had marked down as the machine-gun nest. Holding his breath, and with the Mauser ready, he peered over—eyes to eyes, breath to breath with a Japanese who was looking to see what made the noise. The Mauser's muzzle touched the Jap's nose.

"Shoot, you idiot!"

But it was Tom's left fist that sent the Jap sprawling head-over-heels into the hollow, where a Japanese machine-gun lay in place on its tripod in a gap between boulders. Tom jumped on to him. He wasn't hurt much. He had a knife, but no pistol. He shouted, once, but a kick in the ribs stopped him and the shout didn't seem to be heard by the men below. Dowlah scrambled down into the hollow and went straight for the machine-gun. Tom objected—with the Mauser.

"Come here, Dowlah. Stand there. Keep still."

Instead of admitting that he knew Japanese, Tom tried the Japanese with Tibetan, getting no more response than an ambiguous grin. He tried English. The grin changed to a defensive, tight-lipped alertness. So he continued in English, speaking slowly:

"You are one of Naosuki's men. Don't lie about it. I know. He calls himself Chou Wang. This man is Rajah Dowlah, to whom Naosuki

196

sold the plans of the fortifications of Kobe. The evidence against Nao-suki is already in the hands of the Japanese Foreign Office. Naosuki is a traitor to his emperor."

"Who are you?"

"A traveler. Perhaps you have heard of Eiji Sarao? Knowing I was on my way to join an expedition, Eiji Sarao asked me to find you people, and to say that as many of you as are found in Naosuki's outfit will be handed over to your own government. Unless you, too, are traitors to your emperor, you will separate yourselves from Naosuki."

"Why he—Eiji Sarao not make that in writing?"

"Eiji Sarao is dead," Tom answered. "That was his dying message. Get down there and tell those others!"

"Why should they believe?"

"Dowlah," said Tom, "go down there with him, establish your identity, and tell them."

"What do you take me for?" asked Dowlah.

"I won't tell you again, I'll kick you down there."

"Why didn't you let them shoot me in the first instance? Is this your bucolic idea of a joke?"

"One—two—"

Dowlah obeyed. Because his knees hurt him he let the Japanese help him down the face of the steep ledge. Tom covered him with the machine-gun. It was in good order and perfectly placed; it could sweep the road below in either direction. There was a small box of ammunition. Two loaded Japanese military rifles lay on a blanket behind a boulder. Below, Noropa's body lay, more hideous in death than when alive. Dowlah talked like a machine-gun, too fast, very nervous and too emphatic.

Tom couldn't hear what he said. He lowered his voice—lowered it again. He appeared to be bargaining like a huckster, and the Japs, clustered around him, seemed in doubt what to do. At last he climbed back, swearing savagely at the pain in his knees.

"They want us to come and confront Naosuki."

"Do you dare?" Tom asked him.

"No. He'd shoot me on sight. Those men admit they were acting on Naosuki's orders to blow me to hell."

"Will you go if I go with you?"

"No, you madman! I might have convinced Naosuki he's mistaken in mistrusting me if you hadn't told that fellow what I've done. You blew my last chance, and your own, too, when you did that, damn you!"

"Okay, I'll go alone," Tom answered.

"You are absolutely mad," said Dowlah. "*Pogal!, (idiot),* You have *la rage*—hydrophobia!"

Tom unloaded both the Japanese rifles. He smashed one rifle against a rock. He used the other as a club to break the lock of the machine-gun. Then he smashed that rifle, too.

"Play your own game, Dowlah."

"Curse you. You might at least have let me have one of those weapons."

"Taking no chances on you, Dowlah."

"Chances? But you go with those men?"

"Sure thing. Got to get into the monastery."

CHAPTER 34

There were outcrops of onyx. A two-mile march into a valley that roared with the hurrying water of scores of streams. Stone bridges, well built. The monastery came suddenly into view around the thousand-foot high corner of a cliff that curved like the handle and blade of a sickle. There were splits in the face of the cliff; rough trails marked by *chortens*, vanished into them.

The monastery was almost snow-white; the diagonal shadow across its face, bright blue. It was backed by snow-clad mountains that looked like huge waves breaking in dazzling foam. On the roof were the usual *chortens*, bells and Buddhistic symbols. There was almost no wind, so the bells were silent. From behind the main building there arose a cloud of dense white steam to a great height before it mushroomed and spread, shutting off part of the view of the mountains. A high wall enclosed the monastery—main building, two long wings, and what looked like a small town of jumbled roofs. Heads peered over the wall; until they moved they looked like big black birds.

Tom walked behind the Japanese. There had been an argument about that. They all had repeaters, but he had his Mauser, so they yielded the point, grinning, as much as to say they could manage him comfortably when they should be out of Dowlah's range. They had no idea Tom had broken the machine-gun.

Striding along behind them, he was careful to look as little as possible like a prisoner. They didn't know he understood Japanese, so they talked. They seemed to be puzzled, anxious, discontented.

He noticed a prodigiously long radio aerial strung high above the monastery roof. That was the only modern touch; it looked new; the copper wire hadn't turned green.

The very military-looking man in command of the escort seemed rather afraid of his men. He was almost diffident toward them. They kept whispering to one another without turning their heads, the way prisoners and monks do where there is a rule of silence. Twice he told them they had not acted nobly in refusing to try to recapture the machine-gun and rifles. They laughed, and one of them retorted that he hadn't led with any noticeable valour. Discipline seemed to have become undermined by resentment or disillusion.

The trails debouching on the monastery from the fissures in the face of the cliff looked well worn. Tales of pilgrims from the ends of Asia, secretly wending their way to the Thunder Dragon Gate for words from the lips of "Wonderful-to-hear," seemed credible. There were caves, too, in plenty that might be, or might formerly have been occupied by solitary hermits. It might be true that His Holy Magnificence Lobsang Pun had once occupied one of those. There isn't any limit to religious eccentricity in Tibet. Humility earned in a cave at thirty below zero is exchangeable for arbitrary vigour.

Outside the monastery main gate there was a huge heap of refuse and stable manure. It was being carried away in baskets by men in the rags of religious clothing. They appeared to be starving. One of them, bent under his stenching load, didn't get out of the way soon enough. He was knocked down, and kicked as he lay, by the man in command of the escort, who seemed relieved by encountering someone on whom he dared to vent malice.

Tom helped the monk to his feet. The Japanese had marched a dozen paces before they realized what he was doing. They didn't hear what he said in Tibetan:

"The Holy Lobsang Pun Rinpoche is coming! Run swiftly and tell your brothers!"

The Japanese, cockier now they were close to the wall, surrounded Tom. They tried to make him march in their midst. Their leader, having kicked a man and feeling consequently overbearing, laid a hand on him with the usual Japanese assurance that no foreigner knows anything about *jiu-jitsu*. He began to use pressure and his other hand reached for Tom's Mauser. So he landed on the manure heap, heels-over-head, on his face, with a mouth full of filth. Tom drew the Mauser.

"Shoot it out if you like! There are others coming. Kill me, and see

199

what you get!"

The man who knew English interpreted. Two or three of them got in the way to prevent shooting and one of them went to his officer's rescue, brushing him off and talking to him. Tom caught the name Naosuki.

The great gate opened. They marched in, Tom last. There were forty or fifty monks within the wall, in groups that seemed unfriendly to one another. At least two groups. Perhaps three. They had a sort of jail-yard atmosphere. Instead of laughing at the sight of a foreigner, as would be normal in Tibet, they scowled; instead of whirling prayer wheels, they talked in surly undertones, group by group. Some had cudgels.

At irregular intervals there was an unplaceable sound like muted thunder. It seemed to come from every direction. It was like an earthquake noise, without any perceptible earth tremor. Weird.

Tom's escort turned sharp to the right, marched along the face of the right wing of the monastery and turned left into a long courtyard that separated the wing from a maze of stores and stables. There were several big *chortens*, and a building that looked like a mausoleum, with a flight of stone steps leading to a door near the top of the wall.

At the far end of the yard was an enormous prayer wheel, built of heavy lumber. It was at least fifty feet high, about twelve feet broad, big enough to contain millions of prayers written on scraps of paper. It had been recently mended with iron straps. It was kept in motion by a waterfall that plunged out of the cliff above it, turned the wheel and spilled into a sluice, along which it vanished into a hole in the ground. The officer went and washed his face at the sluice, rinsing his mouth and grimacing savagely.

Near the wheel a couple of obvious Japanese, dressed as Tibetans, stood guard with rifles over a small, newly built stone shed, into which a raw-hide belt disappeared. The great wheel had been hitched to a dynamo; its hum was quite distinct above the *thump-thump-thump* of the wheel and the splash of water.

The man who knew English grinned at Tom. He seemed tolerably unresentful of the punch he had had in the jaw. He touched his own chest. His eyes nearly disappeared amid wrinkles as he grinned with the pride of showmanship:

"Dynamo—come in pieces—long way—killing many horses—camels! Me, mechanic!"

"*Banzai!*" Tom answered, purposely mispronouncing the word,

200

and the Japanese laughed.

Through a thick door in the wall on the left hand they entered a long, dark, draughty passage. Near the door there were some monks on mats, engaged in silent meditation. One of them stood up and bowed to the Japanese with surprising humility, although he didn't stick his tongue out. They took no notice of him. Behind their backs he pressed a scrap of paper into Tom's hand. Then he squatted again on his mat and appeared to resume his meditation where it left off.

Tom unfolded the scrap of paper. Where a shaft of sun light filtered through a narrow slot high in the wall he stopped and pretended to blow his nose. Every man of the escort faced about suspiciously, but he managed to read the note without their seeing it.

> Your message received. Oh, Tom! Thundergate entrance is through chapel. Beware of *shang-shang*. Sudden rumour that Lobsang Pun is coming has created new situation. They believe he must be bringing a foreign army. Thöpe and abbot busy propaganding you are special sending to prepare way for Lobsang. Chou Wang, deadly desperate, has locked me in room behind his office, but this monk is pro-abbot. He will deliver this to you and get me out of here. He promises.   Elsa.

Tom crunched the paper in his left fist and followed the Japs. There were two stands of piled rifles with fixed bayonets, near a door at the end of the long passage. Opposite the door was another, open, through which came cigarette smoke and the talk and laughter of the guard. One sentry lounged near the rifles. He knocked on the closed door. A bell rang. He opened the door. The escort stood aside for Tom. Two of them, the commander and the man who knew English, followed him into the room, where they stood at attention to right and left of the door.

Stone walls. Pictures of heaven and hell. Against one wall a large radio-receiving set, not yet quite fully assembled, with all its parts exposed to view. One window, glazed with oiled paper. A charcoal brazier. A tea urn. An immense table. Some Chinese cigarettes. A rather small man seated at the table, facing the door, in a heavy wooden chair heaped with cushions. An automatic pistol on the table within reach of his right hand. In front of him, near the ink-pot, a big bronze *dorje*, emblem of authority. Beside him, at his right, a kneeling monk was rummaging in one of Elsa's bags and laying her belongings one by one on the table. Tom's bag was also on the floor, as yet unopened. A high, carved screen behind the man in the chair suggested that there might be a door there leading into another room.

Tom walked straight up to the table and spoke first, standing with his back to the window within reach of the kneeling monk.

"Are you Chou Wang-Naosuki?"

The man at the table touched the automatic. After one sharp glance at Tom he nodded to the officer, who at once began speaking very rapidly in Japanese, reporting what had happened. He spoke so fast that Tom could hardly follow what he said, but that gave him plenty of time to study the man in front of him.

Small, but mentally and physically powerful. His eyes and moustache were cat-like. Not a trace of humour. Prodigious shoulders for his size, lumpy with muscle and rather stooped. He was wearing a magnificent embroidered Tibetan lama's cloak over a red Russian blouse. He looked incapable of any emotion other than sulky delight in enforcing his will. Brown, absolutely merciless eyes of the colour of English ale, which revealed nothing except that mercy wasn't in them.

"Why was this man not disarmed?" he demanded angrily.

Before the officer could answer he met Tom's eyes and said sharply, in English:

"Lay your weapon on the desk."

Tom went one step nearer to the kneeling monk.

"You damned rat, Naosuki!"

Naosuki pushed his chair back, stood up suddenly and snatched his automatic off the desk. Tom kicked the kneeling monk and sent him sprawling against Naosuki's legs, upsetting his balance and spoiling his aim. His bullet pierced the paper window, followed by another. Tom's fist hit him hard on the nose. With his other hand he snatched Naosuki's automatic, hurled it through the window, splitting the oiled paper from top to bottom, letting in a flood of cold, bright day light.

It all happened too quickly for the other two men in the room to do anything about it. By the time they had drawn their weapons, Naosuki was writhing in Tom's arms, barking his own shins against the table edge in his efforts to kick Tom's, and crying out to his men not to shoot. They might have shot Tom, but they would much more probably have killed Naosuki.

The noise brought the guard on the run. They nearly broke the door down in their hurry. The *Bön* monk, on the floor under the table, tried to get his teeth into Tom's leg, but all he bit was the top of a

202

boot. Tom had Naosuki helpless in an agonizing hold. He shook him the way a terrier shakes a rat, hefted him and pitched him across the table into the midst of the guard. Their rifles broke his fall. He slid to the floor unharmed, off sloping butts and bayonets and got up fuming like a madman, making horrible faces. He seemed on the verge of an epileptic fit. Tom's feat of strength so astonished the guard that they stood still gaping at him.

He kicked the monk in the face to make him let go. Then he sat down in Naosuki's chair, a split second ahead of a bullet that splintered the screen. He produced his Mauser, but didn't answer the shot. And at last he spoke Japanese, using the jargon that passes muster along harbour-fronts, pungent, plain. He hadn't time to remember grammar and flowers of speech:

"I have been sent to tell you fools to clear out before you're caught in that man Naosuki's company. Have the others told you that he betrayed your Emperor's secrets to Rajah Dowlah?"

Plainly, the guard had been talking it over. Plainly, they had long suspected Naosuki. Plainly, if they could only feel justified, they were ready to turn on him.

"Naosuki is a thief, a murderer, a forger, a liar and a traitor to his emperor," said Tom. "What are you honest men going to do about it?"

Naosuki tried to snatch an automatic from a man's belt, but its owner wouldn't let him have it.

"The game is up," said Tom. "Your expedition has failed. Naosuki betrayed you by betraying his emperor. Save your emperor's face and what is left of your own honour by going away swiftly, leaving no disgraceful tracks. You may take a pack-train from the monastery stables and get out of Tibet by the way you came. You may do what you please with Naosuki."

"Who says it?" asked one of the guard.

"I say it, and who I am is none of your business. Naosuki has been counting on the support of Tibetan troops from Lhasa and Kalimpong. It isn't coming. There isn't a soldier, officer or man, in Tibet who would dare to invade this sacred valley to support foreigners, or for any other reason than to rid the place of foreigners. There's a force on the march, how ever, that doesn't consist of Tibetan soldiers. You will be cornered here like rats, unless you pull out quickly. If you're caught, you'll be sent to Japan by way of India, with a letter to say you are Naosuki's accomplices. The proof of Naosuki's treason to his emperor is in Japan now."

They all stared at Naosuki. Tom continued:

"Naosuki sent you out to shoot the man who knows the truth about him—Dowlah. By saving Dowlah, I have saved you all from being parties to Naosuki's guilt. Now I will save you from something else."

He stood up, pulled aside the screen and let it fall to the floor with a crash. There was a locked door, with a key in the lock. He went on talking:

"Living or dead, do you wish to be known or remembered as savages? Have you been parties to the rape or torture of a defenceless woman? You see her bags. Naosuki was dishonourably pilfering from them. You see her clothing on the table. Where is she?"

He turned the huge key in the ancient lock and flung the door wide open. It revealed a bare room—empty. The key fell to the floor. He picked it up and stuck it in the lock on the inside of the door, carelessly, as if he wasn't thinking what he was doing.

"Where is she? What has Naosuki done to her?"

Naosuki was speechless, making grimaces as inhuman as a tragic actor's on a Japanese print.

"You were told you were heroes," said Tom. "You were told you were being sent to do an honourable duty for Japan, to make it easy for Japan to conquer Asia. You have been lied to and misled by a traitor who sold his emperor's secrets. Where is that woman?"

Without the slightest suggestion of hurry, he entered the inner room and shut the door behind him. The ancient lock, as he turned the key, made hardly any noise. It was a very thick door; through it he could barely hear the murmur of angry argument.

There was another door, unlocked, with the key on the outside. On the stone floor near it was the broken lip-stick with which Elsa had scrawled on the panel:

Chapel. Hurry. Elsa.

He hurried, with methodical decision, making better speed than if he had run wildly. There was a maze of doors and corridors, stone stairways leading to the upper floor and downward to the kitchens and into echoing cellars. There were passages within walls that were twelve feet thick. At almost every corner there was a dark hole where a monk might sit and meditate or lurk in ambush.

But there was no one in sight, only sounds of men running—the boom of a great bell—a roar of voices from a long way off, like a sea-roar—and the weird, intermittent, irregular muffled thunder-sound that shook nothing but seemed to come from all directions. Then, suddenly, the unmistakable *staccato* rattle of rifle-fire—no guessing whence it came, along echoing passages.

Out into a courtyard, and the sound of rifle firing louder. A long cloister to a courtyard behind the monastery. Steam—lots of it. On the far side of the courtyard a big chapel, door wide open and a riot roar coming through it. Tom entered quietly.

No sign of Elsa or of Thö-pa-ga, but a monk with bull lungs, standing on a platform, was holding up Elsa's frock. It was the frock she bought in Delhi. He was tearing it into strips, like prayer streamers, and distributing them at random to whoever could get near enough. At the end of the chapel, on the altar platform, an old man in a yellow robe, who couldn't be anyone else than the abbot, surrounded by a dozen monks who were protecting him, held a carved box above his head. It probably contained sacred relics. The monks surrounding him were all shouting at once, and one of them was pounding an enormous gong as if his life depended on it.

There were not less than a dozen dead or dying or severely wounded monks underfoot, amid pools of blood. In mid-chapel about thirty monks were fighting thirty or forty half-starved wretches in rags, who were led by the bow-and-arrow yak-man who had told Tom he wouldn't fight in any circumstances. He wasn't using bow and arrows. He and his two comrades, for some reason better fed than the scarecrows they led, were hard at it with cudgels. Religious frenzy had burst the restraint of doctrine. The meek had inherited righteous indignation. The skulls of the proud were cracking.

It was easy to distinguish the proud. They were *Böns*, with their backs to the wall—the long wall, with a dais in the middle and a gallery above that. They were the well-fed ones.

Beneath the gallery, behind the dais, was a studded door, deeply carved and painted red. On either side of it were hideous tantric images of devils devouring men who yearned upward in agony toward the carved head and shoulders of Gautama Buddha, smiling from an arched recess, illuminated by coloured glass lamps in the dimness above the door and below the gallery.

Apparently no one had any firearms, but there were missiles flying in all directions, chiefly prayer wheels and brass lamps. Nearly all the paper windows were broken. The *Böns* seemed to outnumber all the

205

others, but to have used up all the missiles within their reach. They were chanting, to invoke their magic and to fortify their courage. The man who was tearing Elsa's dress into strips appeared not to be a *Bön*. It was hard to guess what he was. He seemed to be preaching a war of his own. It was he who first caught sight of Tom. He went into a frenzy, pointing at him, bellowing, slobbering. Impossible to tell what he was shouting about—demanding summary execution or offering welcome.

Tom went for him. As he crossed the floor, scrumming his way through the brawl, a bow-and-arrow man let drive at him from the gloom under the gallery. The arrow buried itself in a monk's back. Someone slew the bowman with a bronze candlestick. Another bow-man, from the doorway by which Tom had entered, took a shot at the abbot. He hit him. The abbot fell. There was a roar of rage. Someone struck down that bowman from behind. A man entered, cowled like a monk, but black-whiskered like no monk in all Tibet. He had a rusty sword, but when he tried to use it someone snatched it from him, and in a second there were ten monks fighting for it, all in a scrimmage, rolling over one another on the floor.

The new arrival followed Tom. He reached him just as Tom reached the man who was tearing into little pieces the last shreds of Elsa's dress.

"Where's your Mauser, you fool?"

Dowlah! He and Tom became the centre of a maelstrom of yelling monks. Dowlah shouted in Tom's ear:

"Japs shot the stable-men—took all the best horses—they're on the run with all the loot they could pack!"

"Who's coming?"

"Damned if I know! Someone. They'd an outpost in a cave up on the mountain. I saw the flash of his helio. Look out! Who's that? Where's your Mauser?"

Chou Wang-Naosuki! Dressed in his yellow *lamaistic* robe. Silent in the doorway. Stoop-shouldered. Head forward. Scowling. In his right hand an automatic.

Tom couldn't draw the Mauser. The monks were pressing him too closely. Dowlah tried to snatch the weapon. Failing, he ducked. Chou Wang-Naosuki drew down his eyebrows, raised his right hand, took deliberate aim at Tom, fired, missed him and killed the bull-lunged fellow who had torn up Elsa's dress.

Panic. Imprecations—yells of terror—anger. Everyone except the

Böns who had their backs to the door scattered in search of cover. They struggled to hide behind one another. Naosuki calmly entered the chapel. Dowlah almost screamed at Tom:

"Shoot him, you damned idiot!"

"Any dog can kill," Tom answered.

He did draw the Mauser. He whipped it out, thrusting Dowlah aside. The shove forced Dowlah backward, off-balance. A monk tripped him. He fell. Naosuki laughed suddenly—once. It was like a big dog's sullen bark. He tossed his weapon to the floor at Tom's feet. Dowlah pounced on it— leaped to his feet—aimed—drew the trigger. Empty! Naosuki had used his last shell. He sneered and walked toward the door under the gallery. The *Böns* made way for him. One of them opened the big red door. He entered, not looking backward.

Tom went through the midst of the *Böns* with such explosive ferocity that he reached the door before the brass bar fell in place. He charged through, Dowlah behind him, into darkness.

"Elsa!"

No answer.

"Elsa!"

CHAPTER 35

Nothing but an echo in the darkness. Silence. Then muffled thunder. That sound, and the accompanying warmth, explained itself and the steam that could be seen from far off. Masses of boiling water down below somewhere—one of earth's cauldrons, obedient to some incalculable rhythm. Tom groped for his pocket flashlight. He and Dowlah were in a tunnel whose walls were coated with a black shiny film of glassy basalt. There were niches in the wall on both sides; there were pottery lamps on some of them, but no lamp burning. Tom shouted again:

"Elsa!"

Echo. Underground thunder. Silence. Then someone's footsteps. Naosuki's? Somewhere ahead, at an unguessable distance, there appeared a patch of dim light about the size of a man's hand. Tom strode forward, Dowlah lagging. It turned out to be reflected light, at a turn of the tunnel—dim daylight. It increased. The tunnel made several turns, grew narrower, then wider and opened suddenly into a daylit space so full of steam that it was all whirling whiteness and noise.

"Grand place for a miracle!" said Dowlah. "Look out for *shang-shangs*. Can you use a Mauser?"

Tom answered irritably: "Shut up!"

Dowlah shoved his elbow. "There's Naosuki! Go on—shoot! You can't miss!"

"Damn you, pipe down, or I'll kill you!"

Dowlah giggled: "Write him a courteous letter! Why not? Your name should be Woodrow!"

Naosuki, silhouetted against whirling white steam, stood framed in the mouth of the tunnel, staring down into the place where the steam came from. Tom hurried toward him. Naosuki glanced backward along the tunnel, turned left and vanished.

Dowlah clutched Tom's arm. "Look out!" he said. "I warn you! He'll be waiting for us around the corner. Give me the pistol. You go forward, and when he jumps out at you, I'll shoot him!"

Tom shook him off. He hurried to the spot where Naosuki had stood. It was the lip of a crater, slippery with some kind of glassy lava. Left and right a wet path vanished into steam. The sudden, muted thunder of water boiling underground was almost deafening. There was a surge of invisible water that fell back on itself. Steam belched upward. And then silence.

"Elsa!" Tom shouted. "Elsa!"

No answer. He took the left-hand path and followed Naosuki, blinded by the white steam, keeping his hand on the sheer face of the encircling rock wall. The smooth, wet path sloped outward toward the crater. Dowlah slipped and grabbed him, almost dragging him over the edge, but the wall was covered with carvings of monsters; Tom's fingers caught a devil by the open mouth and hung on. After that he made Dowlah keep five or six paces behind.

It was all noise—muffled, deadened, ominous. There was a vague smell of sulphurous gas. Scraps of sky appeared, brilliant blue, and here and there, through gaps in the whirling steam, there were glimpses of wet cliffs hundreds of feet high.

The path widened. It became fifty feet wide. There were stone altars, of onyx, very ancient, in a curved row near the edge of the crater. Grooves on the tops of the altars led to holes through which blood could run off.

"Human sacrifice!" said Dowlah. "Tee-hee! Kill 'em beautifully! Chuck 'em in and boil 'em, for a meal for devils in the next world! Holy! Holy! Holy! That's the door to the *Bön*-po hell, that crater! They've boiled your Elsa, I bet you!" He giggled, stepping backward out of range of Tom's fist. But he needn't have troubled. He had lost, if he ever had it, any power over Tom's impulses.

The carved cliff closed in again toward the crater's edge, but it sloped backward, letting in more light than on the far side.

"There he is!" said Dowlah. "Shoot him! Damn you, shoot him! I say, shoot him!"

A hundred feet up, a half-arch of glistening wet rock, shaped like a pheasant's spur, curved outward from the cliff and was almost lost to sight in steam above the crater. Hewn steps in the rock face zigzagged upward toward it. On the farthest tip, looking like a ghost in the steam, stood Naosuki, motionless. In his *lama's* robe he looked like a high priest. Tom called to him:

"Naosuki! Do you know where Elsa Burbage is? Your life for hers!"

No answer. Naosuki took no notice whatever. Suddenly he cried aloud in Japanese and leaped, feet foremost and together, with his robe wrapped tight around him and his right hand raised. He vanished into steam. The muted thunder rose and greeted him. The invisible boiling surge up-hove and laved a smooth wall, falling back upon itself.

"*Banzai!*" said Tom, and that time he pronounced it properly. He turned on Dowlah. "That's more than you've the guts to do!"

Dowlah sat down on an onyx altar, with his head between his hands.

"All I need is a drink," he remarked. Then, suddenly recovering his self-control, savagely: "You blockhead! Do you realize there's nothing now between you and me and what we're after?"

There came a cry through the craterous thunder. It sounded far off. Tom shouted:

"Elsa! Elsa!"

He began running. He followed the path until it curved under the projecting half-arch. Beyond that it turned left again along a wider ledge. Around that corner there was a door, once painted red, but nearly all the paint had scaled off. It was heavily reinforced with iron. Four feet from the bottom was an iron grille, about ten inches square. It had a huge iron padlock, not very ancient, not very rusty, slick with recent greasing.

"Elsa!" he shouted.

"Tom? Oh, thank God!"

"Coming!"

He resumed his unhurried mood. He examined the lock, rubbing his thumb along the surface. It bore the legend: *Honorable East India*

Company. 1845.

"Tom, we're in here with a *shang-shang*! Thöpe has fainted. It's dark."

"Half a minute!"

He put a shot into the padlock. Then another. He found a rock then and hammered. The padlock broke. The door swung open and Elsa nearly fell into his arms. She was wearing Tibetan clothes, too big for her, with turquoise jewels.

"Get Thöpe, Tom."

"Okay. Watch Dowlah."

He groped in darkness, found a leg and dragged out the Tibetan, left him lying, stepped inside again and shut the door. Then he spoke through the grille:

"Elsa—come on—tell me."

She answered quietly, with her face as close as his to the grille: "Tom, please come out of there."

"Good girl now. Hang on to yourself. Tell me."

"Tom, there's a passage for thirty feet. Beyond that there's a cavern with a great pit at the far end. If you look for a long time by the light of the grille, you can see the *shang-shang's* eyes on the rear wall."

"Okay. I can see them. It's the last of the brutes. No hurry. If it comes toward me I couldn't miss it. How did you get in here?"

"There was a fight in the chapel. About Thöpe—and me. The *Böns* said, if Thöpe is genuine he can manage the *shang-shang*. They tore my clothes off and gave me these, and brought us here and left us."

"Where's your revolver?"

"Noropa stole it."

"Okay. Noropa's dead. Dowlah's unarmed, but watch him."

"Where is he?"

"Damned if I know. Stay where you are, and yell like hell if he starts anything."

Tom switched on his little pencil of light and went slowly forward into stenching darkness. To right and left were about a dozen cells hewn in the rock, with doors made of poles set two inches apart. Most of the doors stood ajar. Away ahead in the darkness the *shang-shang's* eyes glowed pale opal, as big as soup plates, almost exactly one above the other. All the rest of the brute was invisible. The eyes didn't move, didn't blink. They looked unreal, almost like holes in the rock through which a wan light entered.

At the end of thirty or forty feet the passage widened into a broad

210

cavern and the pin-light picked up the edge of a gap in the floor at the farther end. It extended the full width of the floor and as far as the rear wall. Mutterings came out of it, but no steam. Near the edge of the gap was a naked human corpse, dried up, like a mummy.

With the Mauser in his right hand and the light in his left, Tom leaned against the corner where the passage opened into the cavern. He tried to trace the outlines of the monster, but it was so huge that the pin-light couldn't follow its spidery legs into the darkness. Its body was as big as a barrel, vivid green, and foul with what looked like crimson fungus. Its mandibles moved. It was beginning to blubber with foam at the snout. The light annoyed it. It moved.

Tom fired—two shots, one at each eye. The second shot was probably a miss. The *shang-shang* curled up like a swatted spider and vanished, writhing, down into the chasm.

Tom went and looked, but the pin-light couldn't fathom the utter darkness. He could hear water, but couldn't see it. He pushed the human corpse into the chasm and turned away, striding resolutely, not too fast, lest horror should make him lose his self-control.

Dowlah was nowhere in sight when he opened the door. Thö-pa-ga was standing beside Elsa, looking mournful, but twice the man he was when Tom last saw him. In spite of having fainted, there were signs of iron in him, and of self-control. He had more actual control than Tom had at the moment. He was dressed in gorgeous yellow silk, with an embroidered crimson toga. He held out his hand. In his peculiar, stately English he said:

"Mr. Grayne, I thanking you so much for all this."

"Thöpe has been a perfect brick," said Elsa.

They were all embarrassed. Tom was watching Elsa sideways. She said nothing.

"I, who ran away from destiny, am disciplined," said Thö-pa-ga.

Tom didn't know what to say.

"Where's Dowlah?" he demanded.

Suddenly he turned to Elsa and took hold of her and kissed her. He kissed her a long time. She was quite still in his arms, but he could feel her heart thumping as fast as his own.

"Tom," she said at last, "you don't owe me anything. It's dear of you, and generous, but—"

He interrupted: "I lied to you like hell. I half knew I was lying. You're a damned good gallant little woman and I loved you from the day we first met. But neither do you owe me anything. Go and get

211

your divorce."

She chuckled, with her arms on his shoulders.

"Tom, I lied much worse than you did! I believe you meant it, or at least you believed you meant it. I didn't! Not once, for a single minute. I've been all yours, any time you'd have me, from then until now! But have I played fair?"

He almost crushed her.

"Thöpe, old fellow—"

Thö-pa-ga smiled wanly. "Oh," he said, "I take the Middle Way, I think, from now on. I am no good in the world."

"Rot!" Tom answered. "Buck up! But for you, this place would be a *shang-shang*-ridden nest of lousy propaganda! Thanks to you there are no more *shang-shangs*. Take the credit for it! Take hold! Clean up! Run the show and root hard for the Tashi Lama. He's a good man. Work to get him back to Tashi-lunpo. Do a man's job. Help to keep all foreign devils out of Tibet!"

Elsa interrupted: "Tom, is it as over as all that? Is it true about Lobsang Pun? Is he here yet?"

"Let's go see. Where's Dowlah?"

No sign of Dowlah. They returned around the crater amid steam and muted thunder and then groped their way along the tunnel to the great red door. It was locked. There was a roar of voices in the chapel, frantic gong-beats, and a new noise—the triumphant blare of conches and long *radongs*.

Thö-pa-ga protested: "Wait here! That man Dowlah—"

"Ride yourself!" Tom interrupted. "Now's your big chance. If they opened for Dowlah, they'll open for us. If Dowlah hasn't found some liquor he has shot his last bolt. Stand back."

He fired three shots at the door and reloaded his Mauser. A monk opened the door. Thö-pa-ga stepped through, then he, then Elsa. The sunlight through the smashed windows was dazzling. The place was a wreck. Monks' dead bodies lay in pools of blood, in a litter of fallen banners, pictures and broken lamps. No sign of Dowlah. The monks were marching around and around the chapel to a blare of trumpets and thunder of drums. They swarmed around Thö-pa-ga.

"Your chance!" Tom shouted at him.

The monks bore Thö-pa-ga away toward the altar. He stood there smiling. There fell a hush, breathless. No other sound than the groan of a wounded monk and the flutter of torn window paper. Then Thö-pa-ga's voice, ringing clear:

"*Om mane padme hum!* Blessed be the Word that goes forth! There are no more *shang-shangs!* The Thunder Dragon Gate no longer speaks for Evil. Clean up! Clean up!"

Tom hurried Elsa out of the chapel. In the yard, between the chapel and the monastery wall, stood twenty bearded skeletons in sheepskins, beside scarecrow ponies. Dowlah's men! On the monastery steps stood Dowlah, staring at them, and they stared at him. They didn't see Tom and Elsa; even Dowlah didn't. They weren't speaking. They were simply staring at Dowlah in resentful silence, and he at them. Dowlah turned his back and walked into the monastery. Tom went up and spoke in Hindustanee to the *subadar.*

"What are you doing here?"

"*Sahib,* that Holiness Lobsang Pun is a *bahadur* of the old school! Aye, a *burra* wallah general *bahadur!* There is the spirit in him. On our way we met him, near that monastery. Lo, he swept us up and rolled us westward! We have marched like men in a dream. He had a hundred monks behind him, and more than two hundred ponies and yaks. That monastery belched provisions for him—aye, and more monks. And he knew where those devils of *Böns* had *cached* their *ghee* and barley meal. Nay, nay, we haven't starved, nor have our ponies. He marched us thin! He is a magic-maker! That Lobsang Pun Bahadur could conquer the world! If he sleeps, then he sleeps on horseback, and it needs relays of horses in half-hour spells to stagger at such speed beneath His Honour's weight!"

"And the woman—Su-li Wing?"

"She came, too. She has no more heart for India than we have, with our shame upon us. But we saw no shame in being led by Lobsang Pun Bahadur. Bold he is, and arrogant, and godly. He could make a dead man march to the world's end! Lo, behold us, *sahib,* we are all here, not a man is missing."

"And now what?"

"God knows, *sahib.*"

Tom and Elsa went into the monastery. They had to step over the legs of monks who sprawled, dead weary, in the corridors. They had loads, but no weapons. More than half of them were asleep on any kind of mat or blanket they had been able to find. Some of them lay like dead men, snoring on the flagstones.

At the end of a passage there was a crowd of monks outside an open door, through which came Lobsang Pun's voice, reprimanding, roaring orders. Unmistakably his voice, ringing with energy. In the midst of the monks lay Dowlah, stone dead, in a pool of blood. There was a knife in his back.

Not a monk had laid a hand on Su-li Wing. She was standing near the door, still wearing her coonskin overcoat. She seemed to have shrivelled inside it. She looked utterly worn out, and years older. But when she saw Tom and Elsa she laughed—metallic—nasal—high pitched—cruel.

"You wouldn't give me a break," she said, "but there's your Dowlah! He saw me. He knew I did it."

She stood aside to let Tom and Elsa enter the room. The abbot's dead body lay in state on a table with lighted candles, surrounded by kneeling monks. Lobsang Pun was in a great chair by a table loaded with the monastery records. Monks were on the run with more records. He had some *Böns* up in front of him, with their hands tied. He was pronouncing sentences, pursing his lips to taste the flavour of godliness and then opening them wide to roar:

"Mercy to man and beast. It isn't merciful to let men die in sin. That foul stuff leaves, the way it entered, through the body. Two hours' flogging!"

The minute he saw Tom and Elsa he roared with laughter. They went up and bowed.

"*Shang-shang?*" he demanded.

"Your Eminence, the last one is dead," Tom answered.

"Chou Wang-Naosuki?"

"Dead, too. Thö-pa-ga is safe in the chapel."

"Yes, I knowing it."

"I have the honour to present my wife, Your Eminence."

"Oo-ha-ha-ha-hah! Tum-Glain, what your doing in Tibet? Get out! Go home!"

Tom laughed. He liked Lobsang Pun. He struck his right hand on his pocket.

"Your Reverend and Holy Eminence," he said, "has surely not forgotten that permit to travel wherever I please in Tibet."

"What your wanting?"

"Ponies. Provisions. An outfit. Men—I might take Dowlah's, if Your Eminence can't spare a few. I will follow the trail of the Japs. I want a messenger tomorrow morning, to carry my mail to Mu-ni Gam-po in Darjeeling."

Lobsang Pun stared at Elsa. His big beak of a nose twitched and his eyes almost disappeared into a maze of wrinkles. He smiled at her.

He chuckled.

"You?" he demanded.

"Tom says I have won my spurs, Your Eminence. I am his wife. I will go where he goes."

"Tum-Glain! Oo-ha-ha-ha-hah! What about that Chinese woman?"

"Send her packing," Tom answered. "Send her to India."

Lobsang Pun objected. "Better mercifully two hours' flogging. Beat the sin out. Save her a million years in hell."

Tom grinned: "Your Eminence's magnanimity is famous. But I beg you, as a personal favour to me, not to waste it on that woman. Please let her go."

Lobsang Pun looked scandalized. His eyes glared autocratic indignation.

"What your wanting, Tum-Glain? Two women? One not enough for you? Your being too sinful. My letting Su-li Wing go, unadmonished by two hours' whipping, if Thö-pa-ga requesting. Otherwise, my blessing her with suitable rebuke."

"Very well," Tom answered, "I will plead with Thö-pa-ga. By the way, Your Eminence, the money in Rajah Dowlah's pocket belongs to Abdul Mirza, who's a good old honest fellow with a lean purse. May he have it?"

"Yes, my sending to him."

"And I think you'll find a letter, bearing your signature—"

"Forged!"

"That he took from the *Bön* magician—"

"Oo-ha-ha! I have it! See? I have it.—Now you, Tum-Glain, now your knowing Thunder Dragon Gate, your going to the moon next? Tum-Glain! Elsa! Oo-hah-ha-ha-ha-hah!"

Old Ugly-Face

DEDICATION

To Collier Young—Lest Distance Dim Good Fellowship

Our hearts know better than to envy men,
Still less their women, who by tongue and pen
With soulless ideology declare: "What dies
Is all we live for. Violence and lies,
Our high aims justify. The ends we seek
Are things, more things. The poor and weak,
Unnourished in the headlong race to pay
New debts to evil while we toil and pray
To politics for wealth—do they not, day by day
Receive, of our good charity, their bread?
Are we not wonderful?"

We are. We are. And yet ...
There was a Voice that more than hinted how
By means more manly than we practice now
A wide world's consciousness can lose its dread
Of drifting toward endless death:—instead
New visioned, may create a world at last
Worth loving for its future, not its past.

INTRODUCTION

'Tis not too late to seek a newer world.—Alfred, Lord Tennyson:
Ulysses

Set in Tibet, the story concerns a group of men and women who
are vitally involved in an exciting situation in that forbidden land of
towering mountain peaks and age-old secrets. The Dalai Lama had
died, and the choice of a successor to the most influential position

in Tibet is a matter of utmost concern to the agents of various foreign governments and to Tom Grayne, unofficially representing the United States, Andrew Gunning, his free-lance friend, and Elsa Burbage, in Tibet under unusual circumstances. Above all, the future of Tibet lies in the hands of the Most Reverend Lobsang Pun, known as Old Ugly-Face, a wrinkled, stout Tibetan prelate of uncertain age, a genuine mystic whose mission in life is to preserve the seeds of sanity in a world gone mad. Grayne and Gunning are both in love with Elsa, and out of this conflict between life-long friends arises a drama of absorbing interest—a drama intensified by international intrigue, treachery, unbelievable courage in the face of the greatest adversity, and the prodigious efforts of Old Ugly-Face to win control of the newly appointed Dalai Lama.

PART ONE
CHAPTER 1

Things seemed vague that evening. Darjeeling felt as if it were somewhere over and beyond its own sensational horizon. The damp stone monastery walls had lost reality, as if thought were the substance and thing its shadow. Andrew Gunning strode along the white-walled passage, beneath flickering brass lamps, between pictures of Buddhist saints. The thin, worn carpet on the stone flags muted his heavy foot-fall into rhythmic thuds that pulsed like heartbeats, regular, and strong, but strangely detached, unreal. An outdoor man, sturdily built, he looked as if his passion were as strong as his muscles and equally under control. He looked obstinate, cautious, capable of proud and perhaps patient but swiftly vigorous anger. As a first impression that was accurate enough and no injustice done. But he was not a man who readily revealed himself to strangers. He could keep his thoughts to himself. Second and later impressions of him always left observers a bit puzzled.

He knocked on the ancient cedar door at the dark end of the passage and waited listening, exactly, and in the same mood as he would have listened for an animal's cry in the forest, or for the telltale murmur of changing wind in the distance. Good ears, well shaped, not too tightly packed against a studious-looking head. A thatch of untidy tawny hair, inherited from some Viking ancestor who raided Britain before the Normans landed and who doubtless found Roman-Northumbrian wenches an agreeable change from the shrews of the Baltic night. American born. Unclannish. Habitually slightly parted

218

lips. Well-bred narrow nostrils. Easy shoulders; a neck so strong that it looked careless. Sensible eyes. A plain man, therefore dangerous. Only simple people could predict what Andrew Gunning might do. Complicated people seldom understood what he had done or was doing at the moment.

Because the monastery was built centuries ago, in the days when Darjeeling was a fortress city of war-torn Sikkim, the deodar-cedar door was a foot thick. He had to knock twice. And because the rain splashed musically through an open window, and the monastery mood discouraged shouting, he was answered at last by the sound of a small bronze bell. An historic bell. Its temperate G would have gone lost in the thunder of camps or the hum of affairs. For fifty years, five hundred years ago, it had invited silence while a Wise Saint meditated on the mystery of man: whence, whither, why. A most excellent bell.

Andrew opened the door into a plain arrangement of ideas; the comfort of ideas in right relation to each other. A white-walled room, so nearly square that its size made no impression; it was good to be in, and that was enough. Two windows, one facing eternal snow, the Himalayas, the Roof of the World, Tibet; but that window was closed for the night by a shutter of cedar and curtained with woven wool from somewhere north of Tang La Ra. The other window, ten by two and iron-barred against the curiosity of innocence (the Tantric Buddhist monks are innocent, and consequently naughty), opened on the rain-splashed inner courtyard. There were glimpses through it of wet-bronze legged monks about their communal duties, with their skirts tucked into their girdles. Some of them were singing; merry-minded fellows, curiously indifferent to rain and icy wind, but venially sinfully inquisitive about the female occupant of Cell Eleven. They were only preserved from the cardinal sin of impudence by the all-seeing eye of Brother Overseer Lan-shi Ling who looked down on their labors from the covered gallery, reminding them, when necessary, that though the eye and the ear may sin, it is the soul which pays. O brothers, look ye neither to the right nor left. The path leads upward!

Elsa lay curled on a Scots plaid steamer rug that had been stained by travel. It was spread over big flat cushions stuffed with the swans-down that lies like wind-blown blossom on the shore of Lake Manasarowar—sacred wild swans and a sacred lake. The cushions were piled on a throne built of blocks of holy basalt from a mountain whose name no Tibetan will utter (lest the ever-watchful *dugpas* should overhear and find and desecrate the mountain's holiness). That throne on which

Elsa sprawled was really a guest bed reserved for visiting Lord Abbots who occasionally come, with secret news, and solemn meekness, but implacably critical zeal, to bestow their blessing on the monastery or to refuse approval, as the case may be. Hearts had been broken in that room, from that throne; personal destinies had crumbled in the calm impersonal fire of visiting Lord Abbots' views of what is sinful and what isn't. Centuries old though the monastery is, Elsa Burbage was the first woman ever to have crossed the threshold of the inner courtyard. She was well aware of that. At the moment it was almost the only excuse for self-confidence that she could use as a shield against despair. The eleventh chamber on the north side had been hers for a number of weeks. It was she who had named it Cell Eleven for luck and brevity. Its real name, all one word in Tibetan, is Countless-thou-sands—of—times—blessed—place—of—meditation—piously—re-served—for— wisdom-loving-holy-lamas-from-blessed-mountains-conferring-sanctity-and-merit-by-their-benevolent-presence. That, of course, is a far better name than Cell Eleven, but it takes too long to say.

Elsa smiled at Andrew Gunning, but she didn't speak for a few moments. She and he had no need to toss words at each other. Kindness can be as irritating as pity. So can courtesy. Such formalities as un-friendly or suspicious people have to impose on themselves and each other had gone downwind months ago, blown by the bitter winds of Tibet and by the more subtle but even less merciful forces of human extremity. There remained a comradeship that speech could easily blaspheme but could neither enlarge nor explain.

Andrew sat down on a stone ledge near the open window. The ledge was covered with snow leopard skin, a comfortless upholstery; but Tibetans don't care for physical comfort, don't even know what it is; and snow leopard skin is a very valuable, so they say, provision against sly earth currents that intrude into a meditator's thought and undo virtue, as the termites undo buildings in the dark. Andrew leaned his back against the whitewashed wall, and he didn't say anything ei-ther. He just looked at Elsa, schooling himself not to feel sorry for her because he loathed the spiritual snobbery that drools that sort of insolence.

The glow from a charcoal brazier coloured Elsa's pale face and made her eyes, beneath the dark hair, look much bigger than they actually were; it made them gleam with unnatural light that suggested visions and dreams, like a cat's eyes when it stares at the hearth. The effect of unreality was increased by the leap of candlelight and by the Tibetan paintings on silk that loomed amid a mystery of shadows on the white walls. It was Andrew who spoke first:

"Not so long ago, just for looking like that, they'd have burned you for a witch."

"Burning sounds dreadful, but it must be soon over," she answered. "Do you suppose it's worse than feeling useless and disillusioned?"

He scowled suddenly and smiled slowly: "It's the first time I've heard you use words like that."

"I never felt quite like this before. Not quite like it."

Andrew Cunning's method was to kill out pity and to mask what sympathy he felt beneath brusqueness: "Feel like cracking?" he asked.

"It seems to have happened. I want to say what I mean. But I can't. It's as if I had been an insect all along without knowing it."

Andrew looked as cautious, alert and careful as if he were still— hunting some animal of whose ways he was ignorant. He had a presentiment. He was going to be asked what he couldn't answer, and told what he didn't want to know. So he said what he did know:

"Life is a fight. The more sensitive you are, the worse it hurts. But you can't cure man or horse with hard names. You have to think straight and know what you're fighting about."

"Andrew, I did it. I've done it. I lost. I said insect because insects wear their skeletons outside and their personalities inside. They're armour-plated. But when they crack—"

"Then they grow a new shell or they die."

"It isn't so easy to just die and be done with it. Andrew, I've reached a jumping-off place, but there's nowhere to jump to. I'm not complaining. I'm telling you because there's no one else to tell. Even song doesn't sound good any more. Tomorrow isn't. There's only a string of dried yesterdays."

He showed his teeth in a friendly belligerent grin: "So it's Andrew. You call me Andy when you think I'm stupid. Drew, when we're talking on even terms. Andrew, when you need help. But it won't work. I'm feeling the way you do, as near as a man can feel the way a woman does. I was in the chapel just now. Same ritual. Same monks, solemnity, beauty and all the rest of it. It felt as flat as canned stuff."

"Then you do understand what I mean."

"No. When you use a word like insect to explain your feelings— damned if I understand."

"Drew, your inconsistencies hide something so strong that I'm almost afraid of it sometimes. I am now."

"No call for you to be scared of me. Inconsistencies? What do you mean?"

"You know what I mean. I've heard you use real bad language—Tibetan and English—that would make a Billingsgate fish-porter's hair curl."

"Maybe. But that was for tactical reasons, to get a pack-train moving or something of that sort. And besides, I'm not a woman."

She laughed. "Drew, did anyone ever accuse you of being effeminate! Please, Andrew! What I meant is, that if you'll raise that iron visor of yours and really listen, it would be such a comfort. But if that's selfish, and you'd rather—"

"Talk away. I'm interested."

"I want to talk to the real you."

"Go ahead. Shoot. But don't talk down to me. I hate that."

"Down to you?"

"Yes. Don't use language aimed at cracking my mental resistance. I'm in a sympathetic mood, if that means anything. I'd like to understand. Words like insect don't apply. You're not a louse."

"Andrew, you've been so generous to me that—"

"That line heads in nowhere, either. I did what you'd have done if things had been the other way around. So let's call that past history and carry on."

"—so generous, and so unselfish, that I haven't dared, I don't think I've even wanted, to impose on you any more. Besides, I understand perfectly that just physical things like forced marches and danger, and even metaphysical things like ditching your whole year's plans because a friend is in trouble—"

"I didn't have any plans, so I didn't ditch 'em. I was letting Tom Grayne do the head work."

"—means no more to you than a change of the wind, or a change of diet. You actually like it. I know that. I know too—I understand perfectly—that you enjoyed that dreadful ordeal in the blizzard—"

"You and I shared that. What else could I have done than what I did? Don't let's talk about it."

"You did impossible things. You brought me alive out of death. But that doesn't give me the right to ask you to do something even more difficult."

He smiled reminiscently. There isn't anything more difficult, in terms of ordinary human experience, than to act man-midwife to a girl whose first baby is born in a blizzard that blows the tent away at sixteen thousand feet above sea level. If he had been a doctor—but he wasn't. Elsa and child survived, and he was secretly so proud of that test of his own resourcefulness that he couldn't speak of it. He even disciplined the smile into a kind of up-wind stare.

"Andrew, don't laugh at me, please. I want to talk to the man who pulled me through that."

"You've the right to," he answered. "You came through, colours flying. Shoot the works."

But Elsa found it hard to begin. She was afraid of seeming unwilling to face the future. But she did fear the future. And she was afraid to raise Andrew Gunning's visor. She had seen him in action, in emergency, in crisis. She had seen him tempted, bewildered, baffled, half starved and almost overwhelmed by exhaustion; but always, in anger, in defeat, mistaken effort, success, nothing less than a man. She knew almost none of his motives, not even his real reason for joining Tom Grayne in Tibet. She knew almost none of his secrets. She was afraid to guess at them for fear her guess might prove true. So she was silent for at least five minutes, afraid of what Andrew Gunning might think of her, if she should go on talking. The silence was as loaded with thought as the leaping shadows were full of hue from the charcoal and flickering candlelight. Elsa made two or three attempts to begin, but Andrew gave her no encouragement. The words died on her lips.

A bell on the monastery roof reminded the monks to do something or other. It drew attention to the silence. Gusty wind flickered the candles. Andrew got up and put more charcoal on the brazier, resumed his seat on the snow leopard skin and waited. It was he who spoke first:

"Begin, why don't you? What's the trouble?"

"I told you. You objected to the word insect. My shell is broken. I'm afraid. That's the trouble."

"I'm scared, too," he answered. "Everybody gets scared once in so often. But would you trade places with any other girl?"

"Andrew, I'd love to! But I don't believe it would be fair to trade places."

Andrew rose to the occasion guardedly: "See here, Elsa; you haven't got to live in Brooklyn, or Blackheath, or Chicago, or Tooting Beck. You don't have to go to cocktail parties and pink teas, or listen to radio yawp—or argue about dialectics with intellectual asses who think envy is inspiration and that Karl Marx is Jesus. You're not leading a second-hand life. You don't have to care a damn what mugwumps think. You needn't say yes to the axe-grinders. What more do you want? Everybody gets afraid at some time or other."

"Andrew, I want to talk about things that one doesn't discuss."

"Well," he said, "I knew that. Why don't you begin?"

"Are you sure you don't mind?"

"Of course I mind. I hate it. You're going to try to drag out your secret thoughts and smear them on the wall for me to look at. You'll come closer to doing it than most people could. I suppose it's the end of friendship. You'll never forgive me for knowing what you've never told Tom."

"How do you know I've never told Tom?"

Andrew grinned. He pulled out his clasp knife and a hunk of hundred-year-old cedar from his hip pocket, shifted his position away from the flickering candle toward the steady glow of the charcoal brazier and resumed the whittling of a head of Chenrezi where he had left off the day before. Elsa watched him with emotions that ranged from baffled anger to despair. They were all one emotion, but they felt like wild dogs tearing at her: stark torture. However, there was no one but Andrew Gunning who could understand what she wanted to tell, what she must tell, even at the risk of friendship.

"Won't you leave off carving that thing, Andrew?"

"No. You'll find it easier if I look at this instead of you. Besides, it helps me to think. Go ahead. Talk." He went on carving, turning the thing in his hands to study the planes in the glow from the brazier, puckering his eyes, remembering the statue of Chenrezi in the monastery chapel.

"Drew, I'm a failure. I'm not even a tragic failure. Merely a flop—no dignity."

He sharpened the point of his knife on a pocket hone and resumed the carving of the Lord Chenrezi's smile.

"Andrew, please listen. I've come to the end of everything, at twenty-three. No more destiny. Nothing. I took my future in my own hands, and everything I had, and all I knew and was and could become. And I took all chances and—and—offered it up."

"You had a perfect right to," he answered. "Everybody has to do that when he's fed up with cant and rant and humbug and gets a glimpse of something worth going after. You're no exception."

"But it didn't work out, Andrew. It was like Cain's sacrifice. It wasn't acceptable."

224

"Okay. Kill Abel. That's the historic retort. It won't get you far. But try it. It's one degree better than killing your own faith."

"I don't mind about me. And I've no faith left."

"You mean no humour, don't you? That's just second-hand talk. Have you been reading Swinburne again? About weariest rivers winding somewhere safe to sea? He was drunk when he wrote it."

"Oh well. Yes. I do mind—having let Tom down—having put you to all this inconvenience. I can still feel. Yes. I still have faith in some people. But not in me any longer. Instead of being the help I thought I'd be, and that Tom thought I'd be, I'm worse than a total loss. I'm a liability. Yes, you're right, I do mind about me."

Andrew glanced at her. She was dry-eyed. No sign of hysteria. She had drawn the steamer rug over her knees and was staring at the glowing brazier. She didn't even look quite hopeless. She was hoping for a new view, and she hoped he had it.

"I've talked defeat," he said, "plenty of times."

"You? You, Andrew! To other people?"

"No. To myself. That's worse. But it never was true. I never really meant it. See here, Elsa; merely looking at one angle, you're not a run-of-the-mill, college-educated product. You've got ideas."

"I wish I hadn't. Ideas only give you a headache and make you dangerous to other people."

"You're not stuck in a social rut. You don't feel bound by the latest fashion in ideology or—"

"I wish I did! I wish I liked that kind of thing! I wish I could make myself be herd-minded and believe what other people believe, and do what they do, and like it. I wish I were a Fascist or a Communist—something genuinely coarse and gross and stupid! Andrew, with all my heart I wish it!"

"If you feel that way, why consult me?" he retorted, looking obstinate. He turned the head of Chenrezi upside down and whittled savagely at the rough base. "I think you're well off."

"You mean in having no future?"

"Carve your own future." He hacked at Chenrezi.

"I'll have to. But it will be as lifeless as what you're doing now with your knife and a piece of wood:"

"Piffle! This isn't lifeless. I've a genius for this kind of thing. What's more, I do good live thinking while I'm working at it. But my talent can't hold a candle to yours. For instance, you're the only woman in the world who can translate ancient Tibetan intelligently. What's wrong with that? You've plenty of it to do. Here you are, safe as a saint in a—"

"Yes, yes, I've counted my blessings and added plenty *per cent!* Andrew, please! Don't talk as if you're trying to sell me a plot in a cemetery! I don't have to be told that I might as well be in the British Museum. I've been working all day long at translation. I'd go mad if I didn't."

"Having luck with it?"

"Yes. The more wretched I feel, the easier it comes. The only real labour is writing it out—can't write fast enough."

"You mean it's like automatic writing? I know a man in New York who wrote a darned good novel that way."

"No. It isn't a bit like that. I look at the Tibetan writing and all at once it means something in English. I don't know how to explain it. It's like reading music notes at sight and being able to transpose them into a different key without thinking about it. Of course, it isn't really like that, but—why don't you let me talk of what I want to talk about!"

Andrew held up Chenrezi's head and studied the curve of a nostril. "It doesn't seem to me you have much kick coming," he answered. "There's any number of real people who would almost sell their souls for the gift that you came by without even having to work for it."

She laughed. "If you think I didn't work for it, you guess again, Andrew! Tibetan wasn't a gift, as you call it. I earned that honestly, and love it. It's the other part that I hate. It's a curse. As a child it got me into so much trouble that I left home when I was sixteen. I almost didn't have any friends. It brought me nothing but grief, and mistrust, and misery, until I met Tom in the British Museum Library. After that, it began to be wonderful, because Tom—"

"Yes. Tom told me about it."

"Andrew, let me tell it. You've only heard Tom's version. He told the truth, but not all the truth. He can't possibly have told my side of it, because he never knew it. I don't believe he even guessed it."

"Tom's a pretty shrewd guesser. "

"I know. But how could Tom possibly guess what even I didn't know, about me, until—until I had torn it right out of myself, and forced myself to look at it? Tom isn't clairvoyant. Sometimes I think you are. But Tom isn't. So he can't possibly have told you all about me."

Andrew shut his clasp knife. "All right," he said. "You tell it. I'll listen. If I don't believe you, I'll say so."

"Andrew, if you don't believe me, then that will be the end of friendship. Because I'm going to be merciless—I mean to me. It may be the last time that you and I will ever talk together intimately. I don't want to pry into your secrets. I do want to tell mine."

Andrew studied his carving of Chenrezi's head for half a minute. Then he put it into his pocket and stared at Elsa. The rain splashed in the courtyard. The guttering candlelight half hid her amid trembling shadows. A slight, small girl of twenty-three, in a black tailored shirt. Dreamy intelligent eyes. Something like a feminine version of Michelangelo's David.

"Go ahead," said Andrew. "Sling your pebble at Goliath, but try not to hit me. If there's anything I hate it's being told what I'd sooner not know. I'm a hell of a good hater."

"I suppose you'll hate me. Will you please try not to. I'm going to risk it, but—"

"If you won't let well enough alone, go to it. I won't interrupt."

But interruption came. It seemed timed to the second, as if someone's daimon didn't want a veil drawn aside. It was simple scheduled monastery routine, but it felt like a hint from destiny.

CHAPTER 2

The interruption was a thudding on the thick door. It sounded far off, almost alarming. But when Elsa touched the bronze bell it turned out to be only two wrinkled old Tibetan monks. One was the abbot's physician. The other brought tea in a brass urn—buttered tea stewed and salted, that isn't so awful once you're used to it. The smiling old doctor professed not to know why there were three cups. It was not his business. He had brought medicine for Elsa. He poured it from a silver vial into a spoon of rhinoceros horn, opened his own mouth by way of suggestion, pushed the spoon halfway down Elsa's throat and turned it until she gagged and swallowed the horrible stuff. He watched her cough, crossing his fingers, murmuring sacred words to ward off devils. Then he murmured a blessing, stowed the utterly unsanitary spoon into an inner pocket, corked the vial, smiled at Andrew Gunning with a shrewd, almost monkey-like glance of his deeply set dark eyes and walked out, whirling his prayer wheel, followed by the monk with the brass tray. When the door thudded shut Andrew seized the opportunity to change the subject:

"So you're still on the sick list?"

"No, I'm quite well. But Abbot Mu-ni Gam-po insists that I'm still full of devils that need driving out. He says it was devils that killed my baby. So he sends his doctor three times a day. If I should refuse to swallow that nasty stuff, I don't know what would happen."

"You'd be a fool to refuse. Old Mu-ni Gam-po knows his magic. Some of our modern doctors get the same results by a different method. There's not much choice between a stupid M.D. and an ignorant magician. Either will kill you. And the good magician or the good M.D. will cure you, if your soul wants to stay in your body."

"Souls can be cruel to bodies," she answered. "Mine is cruel. It insists on staying in me. Andrew, you pour the tea, will you? I can't reach it without getting up."

He filled two cups, then went and peered through the window bars before resuming his seat.

"No eavesdroppers," he said. "Not at the moment."

"Did you think there might be?"

"Yes. There's at least one monk who reports to Bulah Singh. You know what that means. C.I.D. Confidential—indiscreet—dirty. Bulah Singh reads your mail before you get it—if you get it. However, I hope you've changed your mind about talking. It's always better to say nothing."

"You make it difficult, Andrew. I believe you're hiding something."

"Well," he answered, "I guess that's true. But it needn't stop you from telling me the worst, if you feel you've got to. Go on. You're heartsick and scared. You think you can cure it by offering me to the gods, if there are any gods."

"Not you, Andrew. But if I lose your friendship—"

Same thing! But go to it. What's all this that Tom Grayne doesn't know?"

"Andrew, I met Tom for the first time in the British Museum Library. I was studying Tibetan because I like it, and so few other people study it, and because it's difficult, and because Professor Mayor, who happens to be my uncle, is in charge of the Tibetan section. I didn't know then that Professor Mayor had anything to do with the secret service. But later he asked me to help Tom decipher some difficult letters that were written in a kind of shorthand. I have a talent for that kind of thing. It isn't brain work; it's a kind of clairvoyance. One thing led to another. Tom found me useful. I didn't know then that Tom was in the pay of the American State Department."

228

"He wasn't," said Andrew. "He never has been, and he isn't. The American State Department isn't crazy. It hasn't any money to spend on people like Tom and me. On top of that, it wouldn't choose to be caught with the goods. I'm unpaid. Tom gets bare expenses and a pittance from a member of the United States Senate who likes to know what he's talking about. If Tom's information should happen to reach the State Department, that's nobody's business."

"Andrew, let me tell it, please."

"Okay. But tell it right. You went off on the wrong foot. You met Tom. You and he got married. Then what?"

"Tom wasn't in love with me."

"Yes he was."

"And I wasn't in love with Tom."

"Yes you were."

"Andrew, you're observant and kind and sometimes wonderfully intuitive, but this is something that you haven't understood. Onlookers never do understand that kind of thing. You weren't even an onlooker, not in the beginning. You had never even heard of me, and you only knew Tom by hearsay, until you met us in Tibet. And by that time, things were different. In the beginning Tom was in love with his job and with nothing else in the world. He was heartwhole, and ruthless—scrupulously faithful."

"Tom has gray iron scruples, but no morals," said Andrew. "Tom's sentimental bigot."

"Tom is the most intensely moral man I ever met."

"I guess we're at odds about definitions. We may mean the same thing. Go ahead."

"Tom found me useful. I had enough money to pay my own expenses. I'm healthy, and active, and I'm so small that I don't tire a horse the way some people do. I don't care a bit about luxuries, and I can keep my temper and hold my tongue. So Tom offered to take me to India."

"Yes," said Andrew. "I know all about that. There was a homesick Tibetan in London named Tho-pa-ga. Tom wanted to take Tho-pa-ga to Tibet, and he wanted you along to supply the feminine touch. Tom told me all about it. You did such a good job that when the Tibetans kidnapped Tho-pa-ga to make him Keeper of the Thunder Dragon Gate, they kidnapped you along with him to keep up his spirits. Tom went in pursuit, and the Lama Lobsang Pun saved the lot of you in the nick of time. Tho-pa-ga turned out to be a miserable flop, all pious melancholy and no backbone. In love with you, wasn't he?"

"Tho-pa-ga," said Elsa, "was just an overgrown and overeducated moon-calf who needed a nurse."

Andrew nodded. "Tom made a bloomer that time. Tho-pa-ga was a ruinous man to bet on. Bound to let you down. In England he was homesick for Tibet. As soon as he reached Tibet, he was homesick for England. Tom was a fool to waste time on him. Tho-pa-ga's religion was such a mixture of magic and sentimentality, all glued into a rotten mess by a kind of superstitious fatalism, that he couldn't possibly have been a success in a key position. No one respected him. The only friends he made were political Tibetan monks who spotted him for an easy mark. So of course he was poisoned. Anybody could have foretold that. And the business of preventing Tibet from being saved from herself by the Japs and Russians had to begin all over again. That was why I was sent from Shanghai to find you and Tom."

"Andrew, if you really don't want to hear my side of it, why not simply refuse to listen, instead of trying to get me to talk about something else? Just say so. Just go out and leave me alone. Then there'll be no one left except Abbot Mu-ni Gam-po. But—"

"You been talking to him?"

"Yes. He cast my horoscope, from five or six different aspects."

"Did he show you the result?"

"Yes. But I can't read a horoscope. Looking at it gave me a sensation of danger and fear and abject fatalism that I knew I shouldn't have. But Mu-ni Gam-po wouldn't explain it, beyond saying something about Uranus and Neptune in the twelfth house, with afflicted Venus, and Sun rising in Aries. I don't know what that means. He wouldn't let me tell him what I'm trying to tell you."

Andrew laughed dryly: "Mu-ni Gam-po is wiser than I am! Go ahead. Tell me about the afflicted Venus. Crucify her!"

"I've done it, Andrew, but I didn't think it was that at the time. Tom married me secretly in England, in a spirit of scrupulous fair play. I was so in love with the idea of not being a grub any longer—of getting away from England and all that smug mediocrity, and credulous scepticism, and stupid, stuffy pretence of being something that you're not—I was so excited by the thought of travelling in India and being really useful— that I would have done whatever Tom asked me to do. It was his idea, our getting married."

Andrew grinned—glanced at her.

"It was Tom's idea! I never dreamed of it until he suggested it. He had a double motive."

"Yes. Tom's ambidextrous. He lets his left hand know what his right hand's doing. But lets nobody else know."

"Tom wanted to protect me, in case anything should happen to him. He also wanted me to have the right to open his strongbox in the bank vault. Those were his motives."

"Let's leave that lay. Tom and you got married secretly. And you weren't in love with each other. Then what?"

"I fell in love with Tom. This is the part that isn't easy to tell."

"Remember! I haven't asked you to tell it."

"No, Andrew. But I must tell someone. Mu-ni Gam-po won't listen.

"I guess he knows it without being told. He's wise. The more he knows, the less he says. But why not try Nancy Strong at the Mission School? Nancy is a hard-bitten old soldier with a heart like Mary Magdalene's and the guts of a grenadier. She'd even have a good cry with you, if that's how you feel. Then she'd tell you something worse out of her own experience, and you'd have a good laugh and feel better."

"She's a woman, Andrew. No woman could understand. She'd only see my side of it; and I can see that too well already. I want you to listen because you'll see Tom's side of it."

"Didn't Tom see his side of it?"

"Of course he did. But, Andrew, did you ever try to get Tom to complain, or to blame anyone else for what happened to him, or to cry over spilt milk, or to lock a door after the horse has bolted—or to do any of those wishy-washy things that ordinary people do? Tom is—"

"You're right there. Tom isn't ordinary. He's ornery, if you know what that means. Nancy Strong should have married him."

That changed Elsa's mood for a moment. She couldn't help laughing. Nancy Strong was old enough to be Tom Grayne's mother. Not even Tom Grayne would have a chance against her in a tussle of wills. Even government fears Nancy.

"It will come easier now you're laughing," said Andrew. "Tell the funny part first. Go ahead."

"It's no joke, Andrew. It's all disillusionment and anticlimax. Even being kidnapped and carried off, and being cold and hungry in the mountains and in danger of being killed—and not knowing what had happened to Tom, but just hoping he would turn up—and then seeing him suddenly—and all the fighting at the Thunder Dragon Gate—every least tiny bit of it was wonderful and clean and good. It was life. It felt like being blown on a big wind, and something new every minute. After Tom had helped Lobsang Pun to seize control of the monastery, it was even fun when that old despot turned us out to go and shift for ourselves. Lobsang Pun washed his hands of us. And Tom took the trail of the Japanese secret agents, taking me with him because there was nothing else he could do about it. Those were hard times, but they were utterly wonderful. We crossed the border of Sinkiang; and we were in touch with the exiled Tashi Lama twice before they poisoned him."

"They'll poison Tom one of these days," said Andrew. "He'll find out just one thing too many. Then he'll begin to wonder what disagreed with him."

"I did all the cooking," said Elsa.

"That's nothing. They poison the meat before it's killed. If you don't eat meat, they poison the salt and tea and sugar. They put poison in the dust that blows into your cup. Tibetans are real nice people, but they don't like you to know more than's good for their peace of mind. That's what Tibetans are after—peace of mind."

"I wish I had some! Andrew, listen to me. I betrayed Tom. Not he me. I betrayed him."

"Tell it if you must. But don't say I asked for it. I'll believe it or not, as I see fit."

"Ours was an absolutely hard and fast agreement. We hadn't pretended to be in love with each other. I was to be Tom's assistant, and to obey orders. Tom made the stipulation, and I agreed to it instantly, that there was to be no love-making and no man and wife stuff. Ours was simply a temporary arrangement for business purposes. Either of us was to be free to divorce the other as soon as there was no longer any reason for being married."

Andrew put all the malice he could into a slowly broadening grin. "I've heard of lots of folks," he said, "who believed they were stronger than sex. I've even fallen for that presumption once or twice myself. You're not the first—not by a long way. It's disillusioning, but human. I've never spoken to Tom about women. And of course everybody knows he's an iron-willed man. But I'd have betted all I've got. I'd have laid odds."

"Laid what odds?"

"Tom Grayne and you—or any other eligible woman—"

232

"What do you mean by eligible woman?"

"I mean any woman worth going overboard for. Tom and she, alone together, week after week, month after month, sharing the same tough time, growing more and more into each other's confidence—hell, I don't care what the previous agreement might be. She'd fall for Tom. She'd have to."

"Well, Andrew, you're wrong. Tom fell for me. I did it—five nights after we camped in that cave where you found us."

"That means a couple of months before I got there."

"Yes. You stopped it."

"Me? What had I to do with it? It was none of my business."

"No. But your arrival brought Tom to his senses. And me, too. Me especially. What I want you to understand is—"

"Sure, you've said that. I'm not mentally deaf."

"Before you came, Tom was depressed by a sense of failure. Everything seemed to have gone wrong. Our Tibetans were behaving badly. Some deserted. Others brought in false reports and were getting insolent. Tom and I weren't hitting it off the way we had done, because my clairvoyance wasn't as clear as usual. It was all about Europe instead of Tibet. What I did see about Tibet, Tom didn't believe. When spies came in and talked to him I couldn't get any clear picture of what they were thinking about. That made Tom irritable. It seemed to me we were drifting apart, and that Tom was sorry he had brought me with him. I made up my mind to change that by putting things on a more human basis."

"There's nothing new about that," Andrew remarked. "That's old stuff. Everybody does it."

"Does what?"

"Camouflages natural behaviour under a lot of phony excuses."

"Andrew, please don't try to tell me I couldn't have helped it. I know better. I don't want to be pitied. I want advice. I knew what Tom needed, or I thought I did. He was lonely and worried and more nearly afraid than I've ever seen him. So that night, after the Tibetans had gone into the other cave, I crept into Tom's bed and made him believe it was I who needed him. I seduced him."

"And is that what Tom doesn't know?"

"Of course Tom doesn't know it. He thinks I was just a weak woman who yielded to his natural physical yearning for a mate. At times like that things happen. It's super-physical and super-mental. The physical act is irresistible. But it never entered Tom's head that it

233

wasn't his fault."

"And of course it never entered your head," said Andrew, "that every time a Tibetan woman has made overtures to Tom he has compared her with you and sent a mental SOS in your direction that you responded to without knowing it."

"I did know it. My eyes were wide open. I knew Tom would lose his job if he were ever suspected of woman weakness. He's like a priest in that respect. He's trusted because—"

"Oh boloney!" Andrew interrupted. "That's just Tom's alibi. He kids himself. He made that up. He's scrupulous and sentimental about his job. The job comes first. It suits him to believe that getting tangled with a woman—any woman—would destroy his efficiency. So he invented that hokum about Spartan celibacy. He has read a lot of tripe, too, about sublimation of sex."

"Why do you say tripe? Andrew, there are hundreds of thousands of people who have no sex life, and don't want it, and are better off without it—priests, monks, nuns—there was Newton, who invented calculus—and my uncle, Professor Mayor—and the Lama Lobsang Pun—and there's Mu-ni Gam-po and all the monks in this monastery— and all the saints since history began—"

"Tom Grayne is no saint," said Andrew. "He's strong. He has energy and an iron will. He's on the level in the sense that he would stay bought if anyone could buy him, but nobody can. That's a number one rating. But he's no genuine ascetic. He trains himself to live hard and to abstain from tobacco and drink and women for the same reason that a professional athlete does. It pays dividends—not cash, but something he likes far better. That isn't asceticism. If Tom thought that the opposite of chastity would improve his intelligence he'd turn whore-master, scrupulously, without the slightest moral twinge. He might hate it. But he'd do it."

"Don't you believe I corrupted him?"

Andrew laughed. His eyes narrowed. His grin widened. He clasped his hands and laid his elbows on his thighs and looked at Elsa with amusement that hid neither from him nor from her the fact that anger lay near the surface now, banked up, growing strong under restraint. Suddenly it broke loose. He stood up.

"Elsa, don't be a damned fool. You corrupted Tom about as much as champagne could corrupt carbolic acid. The way a bird corrupts quicklime—or a rose corrupts the northeast wind."

"You're talking as if Tom were your enemy. Don't you like him?"

"You bet I like him. But he doesn't fool me. Neither do you."

"I don't want to fool you. I betrayed Tom."

"Now you've said it, are you going to cover up? Or will you answer questions?"

"I want to tell you the truth, Andrew, so that you will answer my questions."

"Okay. Answer this one first. Did Tom ever say he loved you?"

"Yes. But don't you know the difference between loving and being in love?"

Andrew sat down again. "When did it happen? I mean, when did Tom say it?"

"It happened—I mean Tom said it at the Thunder Dragon Gate, before Lobsang Pun sent us away."

"And what did you say?"

"I don't remember what I said. I was utterly happy. I didn't care where we went nor what we did—until I suddenly remembered the bargain. I knew Tom would remember it too. So I spoke of it first, because I didn't want to embarrass him by speaking of it when it might be almost too late."

"What did Tom say?"

"He was relieved. I knew he would be. And he was."

"Yeah, I don't doubt it. All Tibet to wander around in. No immediate impulse, and plenty of time. About three quarters of Tom's method is to start things moving and then wait and see."

"Please, Andrew! It's so difficult to tell, and I do so want you to believe me."

"I know what you want me to believe."

Andrew enjoyed the luxury at last of letting violence flow up the veins of his neck and along his forearms. There was just a hint of hardening muscle beneath the candle shadow on his cheek. Unknown to himself he looked ready to kill what he hated. Elsa noticed it.

"Andrew, you hate me for being the problem I am, and I don't blame you one bit. But be generous. Try to understand me. And then give me good advice, don't Pollyanna me. I want you to help me to face the music."

"What are you trying to be? A she-dictator staging an election? I vote the way I'm told to, and eat crow if you're wrong? Is that it?"

"No, Andrew. But the facts are plain and I want you to know them before you give me advice. I seduced Tom. I swore I wouldn't, but I did. As a result I became pregnant, in a cave, in Tibet, nearly a thousand miles away from any possible help. No woman has a right to do that to a man. If you hadn't turned up, Tom would have been in a much worse dilemma than he is in now. And it's bad enough now. Perhaps I ought to have just let myself die. I could have done that, because I was very close to death several times. It would have saved trouble for everybody."

"Stay in your own bracket and don't try to talk like a beaten drab," said Andrew. "You can't play coward well enough to convince yourself, let alone me."

"It isn't easy to play coward—one can only think about it, with people like Tom and you doing things," she retorted. "Who else in the world but you would have said yes without a second's hesitation when Tom asked you to take me to Darjeeling—nearly a thousand miles, and winter coming on—and not your business!"

"Any man would have done it."

"You think too highly of men! The point is that you did it, Andrew. And my baby was born in the snow. And you fought the blizzard and death and made miracles and stood by like a great big angry angel, and did what couldn't be done, and saved the baby and me, and brought both of us alive to Darjeeling. It wasn't your fault that the baby died—here, in the monastery."

"Nor your fault either. That was bad luck."

"It was Tom's baby."

"Seems to me it was your baby."

"It was Tom's one possible excuse to forgive me for what I'd done to him. And the baby is dead. Now what? Tell me, Andrew. What now?"

"You're overrating Tom's cussedness," he answered. "Tom isn't as hard as all that."

"Andrew, if the baby had lived there would have been no mystery about what to do. Tom's baby and mine. Quite simple. I'd have been the mother of Tom's baby. But now what am I? Nothing but a liability—a millstone fastened secretly to Tom's neck—a danger to him. A handicap—a nuisance—an expense—an obstacle."

Andrew grinned savagely. "Who filled the butchers' shops with big green flies?" he quoted. "Sure. You haven't any rights whatever."

"Listen, Andrew, please. I know what my legal rights are. I can go to Mexico or somewhere like that and divorce Tom, just as secretly as we got married. That was part of our agreement. But I want you to tell me Tom's side of it. Tom is all alone in Tibet and I can't consult him.

236

I can't even get a message to him. I've tried telepathy again and again. Sometimes I can see him clairvoyantly. But I get no response. Tom isn't clairvoyant—at any rate, not consciously he isn't."

"Tom has Grade A hunches," said Andrew. "What does he think those are?"

"There you go again, trying to get me off the subject! It isn't Tom's hunches that trouble me. It's Tom's sense of duty. Tom feels he has a duty to me. I know he does. Andrew, put yourself in Tom's place, and then tell me—"

"Can't be done. Besides, I wouldn't be in Tom's place for a million."

"What shall I do, that won't make Tom feel cheap or guilty, and that won't make him feel he should throw up his job and—"

She stopped speaking suddenly. Andrew was on his feet again. Anger burst through reticence. His face, in the glow from the brazier, was almost exactly as she remembered it in the blizzard-blown campfire light when the tent was torn loose in the gale and her baby was being born.

"God damn it!" he said suddenly. "Can't you fight back!"

"You mean fight Tom?"

"I mean fight that God-damned lousy theoretical suggestion stuff that makes you blame yourself for every situation that you don't like! The sun rises—praise the Lord!—God's in his heaven and all's well with the world. But when night comes—that's your fault! Bad weather—that's absolute, infallible, incontrovertible proof that you're a sinner! Damn that superstition about sin in the Garden of Eden!"

"Andrew, I'm not superstitious! I'm not! I am not!"

"Aren't you?'And the Lord God said unto the serpent, Because thou hast done this: upon thy belly shall thou go, and dust shall thou eat all the days of thy life.' Do you believe that or don't you?"

"I asked you to tell me what Tom really thinks."

"How the hell do I know what he thinks! Damn his eyes, I'm telling you what I think! You and he are not theories, or any bilge like that. You're not a legend. You're human beings. If you love each other—"

"Andrew, I can't come between Tom and his duty."

"Duty my eye! Don't you rate? Haven't you a soul to call your own? Is it less than his? Haven't you faith in your own vision? It was good enough, wasn't it, to pull up stakes and cash your savings and pitch your future into Tom's kit and go wandering where nine hard-gutted hellions out of ten wouldn't dream of daring to go! And now you talk about being licked by a lousy suggestion that you're a traitress! God! Sure. Yes. I'll tell you the answer—"

He paused because Elsa was no longer looking at him. Her attention had become fixed on something else. A quiet cough made him turn suddenly. The old Abbot Mu-ni Gam-po had entered unheard. He stood in shadow, black-robed, frail-looking, blinking through a parchment maze of wrinkles that were probably a smile, probably kindly, but beyond any doubt whatever were a mask revealing nothing that he did not wish to reveal. He spoke in English:

"May I listen to the wonderful answer? But may I first have tea, if there is any tea left in the urn? Let us all drink. Anger and tea so seldom mingle. Wisdom sometimes fills the nest from which the bird of anger flew."

CHAPTER 3

Andrew recovered reticence, and alertness with it. The arresting fact was that the Lord Abbot Mu-ni Gam-po had entered the room, contrary to custom, unannounced, unaccompanied. Andrew concentrated full attention on the fact. He watched the abbot help himself to tea and drink it noisily, Tibetan fashion. The old man wasn't likely to say what he meant; one had to spot hints, and they wouldn't be too plain. Elsa watched Andrew, wondering whether he got the same impression she did. There was emergency in the air. The swaying shadows felt loaded with secret crisis. It was like a dream, in which unrelated things happen. A gong boomed at the far end of the corridor, muted by silence and by the thick door and the splashing of rain through the open window. Mu-ni Gam-po moved his prayer wheel with a hardly perceptible wrist motion, twirling perhaps a hundred benedictions. Then he blinked at Andrew and spoke in Tibetan:

"Angry answer being now arrested on the lips of emotion, opportunity to gather knowledge before leaping blindly may be indicated."

"We were talking about duty and sin," said Andrew. He felt he had to say something.

"There is danger in another's duty—also duty in another's danger," the abbot remarked. "Sin is the result of conceit; it has no other basis. To discuss it is to argue about nothing, with vain words, in a void created by imagination."

The Lord Abbot sat down on the seat that Andrew had vacated. He motioned to Andrew to take the teak chair on the far side of the brazier between himself and Elsa. The old man looked almost Chinese, roguish and yet unworldly; humourous but serious nevertheless; humble, gentle, and yet full of dignity. After a minute's silence he spoke again in Tibetan, in a voice creaky with age but curiously vibrant with the unselfconscious habit of authority.

"Self-revelation, self-expression, seldom is attainable by such beginners as ourselves. It is invariably wise through meditation to permit reflection to reveal reality. We thus perceive ourselves in one another. Wisdom lives in silence."

Fact number two had presented itself. The Very Reverend Lord Abbot Mu-ni Gam-po was suggesting in his own elaborate way that a time for not talking too much was at hand and that the reasons within reasons for discretion would reveal themselves, if one only would have patience. And even patience was not strained too much. The gong boomed again at the far end of the corridor. A moment later the thick door opened. A monk moved in, barefooted, silent. He stood flicking his beads. The Lord Abbot nodded. The monk opened the door wider. Footsteps on carpeted stone came echoing forward. The atmosphere, the feel of things changed subtly. The dream sensation vanished. Something more like actuality replaced it. Dr. Morgan Lewis walked in and the monk closed the door, standing with his back to it. For a moment the flicking of the monk's beads was the only sound in the room, very distinctly heard against the splashing of rain in the outer night as Dr. Morgan Lewis glanced from one face to the other.

"Kind of you to let me come," he remarked, bowing to Mu-ni Gam-po and then to Elsa. Then he strode forward and shook hands with Andrew Gunning, carefully because a finger joint was missing from his right hand. Andrew had a reputation for sometimes forgetting his strength. One eyebrow perpetually higher than the other gave Lewis a quizzical look that was increased by untidy graying red hair, carefully clipped and groomed but always being ruffled by his restless fingers. He was a man of fifty with scars on his face and a wry, sceptical smile. But of what he was sceptical didn't appear.

"Well, what's the news?" he asked suddenly.

No one answered. Mu-ni Gam-po produced horn-rimmed spectacles with large lenses which he polished carefully before putting them on.

"I seem to have interrupted you at prayers," said Lewis. "Let me join in—I've brought the smell of hell with me—from Delhi. I snaffled a week's leave. Just got here—at least, that's the story. Must I operate to start the conversation flowing? How are you, Elsa?"

"Thank you, Dr. Lewis, I'm incredibly well."

Lewis stuck a monocle into his right eye. He was wearing a care-less-looking tweed suit, but by a strange kind of circumstantial magic the scrap of glass in his eye suggested military uniform and official secrets. It made him look dapper, smart, almost impudent. He walked toward Elsa.

"Good girl. Been obeying orders. Sleep. Rest. Plain food. But take a tip from me and don't get well too quickly."

He sat down beside Elsa, on the edge of the basalt throne, where he could watch Andrew Gunning beyond the brazier and be watched by Mu-ni Gam-po. His right hand drummed a signal on his knee in full view of the horn-rimmed spectacles. The Lord Abbot asked in English:

"Not too quickly? Does my patient need other treatment?"

"Well, I'll tell you," said Lewis. "As you know, I happened to be in Darjeeling soon after she arrived from Tibet a couple of months ago. I took the opportunity at that time to—"

Elsa interrupted. "Doctor, you came all the way from Bombay, by airplane, just to make sure I was getting proper treatment. That's true, isn't it? Please don't try to make generosity seem like an accident!"

Lewis glanced at her swiftly, then at Mu-ni Gam-po. He grinned wryly. "I admit that the government paid for the plane. It's less than once in a thousand years that a girl of your age suddenly arrives from Tibet and knows how to hold her tongue. Besides, you sent for me."

"Dr. Lewis, I didn't!"

Lewis adjusted his monocle. He glanced at Mu-ni Gam-po, and at Andrew Gunning, then stared at Elsa. "Young lady, we're among friends. Strictly between ourselves, I got your telepathic message. It was my first convincing evidence of clairvoyance. I said: convincing evidence. Tell the truth now, you asked me to come!"

"But I didn't! You were the only doctor I knew in all India. And I was ill and unhappy. They told me my baby was dying. So I remembered you, and thought about you, and—"

"And I saw and heard you," said Lewis. "Clear case of telepathy—but I'd be drummed from the medical ranks if I dared say so in public. The baby was dead before I got here. They'd call that proof that I'm a liar. But we pulled you through your trouble.—Tell me: what impression do you get now?"

Elsa hesitated: "You don't mean things in Europe? Hitler? Mussolini?"

"God forbid!" said Lewis. "What do you see here—now?"

"I've a strong impression that you're warning me of danger."

"Well, now. That's damned interesting."

"Did I guess right?"

"It wasn't guesswork. You saw it. Let's put it this way, talking in words of one syllable because I wish to be understood. One man's meat is another's poison. Facts are nothing but symbols of a metaphysic that we don't understand. Science, medicine included, is a scandalously overrated system for misinterpreting ascertained facts. And as a medical man it's my duty to say that Mu-ni Gam-po's medicine is an unscientific mixture of herbs that aren't in the pharmacopoeia and its use would be illegal in any civilized country."

"I don't want to be rude," Elsa answered, "but Mu-ni Gam-po's medicine made me feel well, and yours didn't."

Lewis laughed. He caught the Lord Abbot's eye, and the Lord Abbot smiled. Lewis shook his fist at the Lord Abbot. "Charlatan!" he said. "Quack! Heretic! Johnson used to let you dose him, and now where's Johnson? Gone! Gone home to England, where he'll die, one of these days, just as surely as my name's Morgan Lewis."

Andrew Gunning almost upset the brazier. "Johnson? Of the Ethnographic Survey? Gone? You mean he's left India?"

"Yes," said Lewis. "Irish promotion. Sent home in a hurry to advise the India Office and be made a baronet and be snubbed to death. I'll send flowers—perhaps cabbages. I didn't like him, but he was a very first-class man."

Andrew looked worried. "Who has taken Johnson's place?" he demanded.

"For the time being," said Lewis, "there's an abhorrent vacuum in process of being naturally filled with rumours. Bulah Singh is playing *locum tenens*, acting-Satan so to speak, but not as likely as he thinks he is to inherit the throne of hell. He lacks the incorruptible integrity. Bulah Singh might try to snatch some credit for himself by getting after unorthodox practitioners of medicine. You see, if Bulah Singh could tamper with Mu-ni Gam-po's medicine and create a scandal, he might sell his own brand of brimstone and treacle. I advise you to change doctors, young woman. Do you get what I mean?"

"No." Elsa stared at him, worried. "You're talking nonsense just to test my ability to read thought. But it doesn't work. I don't know what you mean."

"I'll try again," said Lewis. "Bulah Singh is rather competent but can't be trusted to deny himself the luxury of malice. He's a great man for detail—studies such curiosities as smoke against snow on the sky line and the contents of the loads of ponies getting ready to go northward. He thinks tactics and strategy are the same thing."

"Thanks," said Andrew.

Lewis readjusted the monocle, stared at Andrew and continued. "Bulah Singh is a rather cat-like fellow. I should say his weak point is that he might watch a mouse hole too long. He might even watch two or three mouse holes. If the mouse used something other than a hole in a wall, Bulah Singh's patience might make him look more like a stone Sphinx than an active cat.—By the way, do you find the view good from the monastery roof?"

"Grand view," said Andrew, "except when it's hidden by clouds; and that's most of the time."

"I am told," said Lewis, "that lots of people are watching for signs of the coming of spring. You've no news, I suppose, from Tibet?"

"It's got whiskers," said Andrew. "Came by the long route. Runner to Sinkiang. Radio to Shanghai, spatchcocked into Chinese bulletins intended for a Jap who has a Chinese mistress in Macao. Steamer to Hongkong. Third-class passenger to Pondicherry. Last lap secret."

Lewis grinned: "I could tell you the secret!"

"When in doubt, don't," said Andrew. "What do you want to know? I'll tell you."

"You say it's old news? Even if it's ugly news, I can face it." Lewis stressed three of the words with more than necessary emphasis. Then he felt Elsa's pulse with a professionally absent-minded air of having nothing else to do.

Andrew grinned. "That's a good cue. Right. Old Ugly-face is said to be a fugitive from Lhasa. He's reported to have lost his fight to control the young Dalai Lama and has had to go into hiding."

"Chapter one," said Lewis. "Chapter two, I suppose, gives more details."

"Sort of regular subscriber, aren't you? Yes, there's more of it, seeing it's you. Ram-pa Yap-shi, the Lord Abbot of Shig-po-ling, is top dog at the moment. He got away from Lhasa with the young Dalai Lama and all the cash in the treasury. He has fortified himself at Shig-po-ling, and has offered a big reward for the capture of Ugly-face dead or alive."

"That checks perfectly," said Lewis. "What else?"

"Not much else. Have you heard of Ambrose St. Malo?"

"Who is he?"

"I asked because I thought perhaps you know," said Andrew. "I've been warned to watch out for him."

"Ambrose St. Malo, eh? Where is he?"

"Somewhere in Tibet."

"That's vague."

"So is he vague."

"Bad egg?"

"Rotten. I'm told he stinks."

Lewis stood up. "Well," he said, "don't catch a chill on the monastery roof. And as for you, young lady, take my advice and change medicine. Mu-ni Gam-po's mysterious stuff isn't good for you any longer. You've had enough of it—more than enough. Try a change."

"But where should I go?"

"Try Nancy Strong. Even Bulah Singh wouldn't dare to fossick in Nancy Strong's medicine chest. Well, so long. See you again soon. Thanks for the information."

He bowed before Mu-ni Gam-po to let the old abbot touch the crown of his head with a special blessing. Andrew Gunning noted that they whispered to each other. Lewis walked out and the monk shut the door. Elsa spoke in a horrified whisper:

"Andrew! Why did you do it! Why did you tell him!"

The Lord Abbot Mu-ni Gam-po got up and bestowed a murmured blessing. The attendant monk opened the door, followed the Lord Abbot out and left the door slightly ajar. Andrew closed it tight and listened for a moment.

"Andrew, why did you tell Dr. Lewis—?"

CHAPTER 4

Andrew's face glowed red as he poked at the coals in the brazier with bronze tongs. He carefully placed lumps of charcoal in the burned-out spaces and then stood away from the fumes.

"Snow!" said Elsa. "Blizzards!—Rain!—Wind!—I can see them." There was a change in her voice. "Sometimes it's easy to tell what you're thinking about, Andrew. Only sometimes. Not often."

He turned and faced her. "Yes. It's too early. But that was the last call. Now or never."

"Marching orders?"

"Yes. You heard him. Morgan Lewis was warning me to get going if I don't want to be stopped by Bulah Singh."

"But, Andrew, why did you tell Dr. Lewis what you did, about Lobsang Pun and the Abbot of Shig-po-ling! Those are Tom's secrets. Tom warned you to tell no one except—"

"Except Johnson. But you heard that too. Johnson has gone—home to England. If Morgan Lewis hasn't taken Johnson's place, as head of the Tibetan section of the secret intelligence, I miss my guess badly. But Bulah Singh doesn't know yet—or I guess not—I think that's what Lewis meant."

"But Dr. Lewis is in charge of a hospital—"

"Johnson was in charge of the Ethnographic Survey. There weren't fifty people in the world who knew what Johnson's real job was. Probably not more than ten people know about Lewis—yet."

"But shouldn't you have known for sure before you—"

"Nothing for nothing in this world, Elsa. Pay as you go. Grabbing at something for nothing is the sure sign of a man who can't be trusted. Lewis told me his news, so I told him mine, although he knew it before I told him. He even knew about Ambrose St. Malo. The secret intelligence trick is to check one report against the other. One rumour, or even one fact means nothing; but if three, four, five, six rumours all check, that's different."

"But, Andrew, should you have told how you get your news?"

"Why not? Lewis wanted to know where Tom is. So I gave him a chance to put two and two together."

"But why tell him where Tom is?"

"Because he offered to help me to reach Tom."

"But, Andrew, he didn't. I heard everything he said."

"Elsa, sometimes you're so naive that it's hard to remember how smart you can be when you're in the mood. If Lewis doesn't mean to help me to get into Tibet, why in thunder do you think he'd tip me off that Bulah Singh is on the watch to prevent me?"

"But if Dr. Morgan Lewis has become the head of the secret intelligence, surely he can give orders to Bulah Singh, can't he? He can tell Bulah Singh to look the other way, while you—"

"Don't be ridiculous. If Morgan Lewis should make that mistake, Bulah Singh would obey the letter of the orders, but he'd watch more alertly than ever. From then on, he'd have an insider's nuisance value. Nine-tenths of the secret intelligence trick is to keep your subordinates mystified. Bulah Singh has orders to prevent anyone from getting into Tibet. Those are standing, routine orders. But I'll get through.

And Bulah Singh will be reprimanded; if he's ready for the trash can he'll be transferred and left wondering who did it to him. But he'll know why. Bulah Singh should have let old Mu-ni Gam-po alone. I'll bet that's where he slipped up. Mu-ni Gam-po is a philosopher who thinks in terms of centuries and has a sense of humour. Bulah Singh is a modern wise-guy who thinks he knows all the answers. Calls himself a sceptic. Actually he's a superstitious fool."

"Bulah Singh superstitious?"

"Sure. That's why he's so eager to prove he isn't."

"I think you're being overconfident, Andrew. Bulah Singh has the reputation of being anything but a fool."

Andrew governed his voice down to the note that flatly indicated patience. "You who can read thoughts! Can't you read between words? Lewis told us, as plainly as he dared, that Bulah Singh has been trying to get Mu-ni Gam-po into trouble for letting me use the monastery roof to watch for smoke signals telling when the pass is open into Tibet. That's why I call Bulah Singh a fool."

"But, Andrew, isn't it true that you—"

"Sure! And Bulah Singh fell for it—hard! Fell, too, for the ponies in the monastery stable."

"Well, they're your ponies. I think you're—"

Andrew stopped her with a gesture. "Listen: my ponies have been getting fat all winter, nearly a hundred miles from here. The loads are ten miles away from the ponies. The men are ten miles away from the loads."

"But, Andrew, it was only three days ago that I saw a big heap of loads with your name on them, piled up in two empty stalls in the stables in this monastery!"

Andrew grinned: "I don't know whether Mu-ni Gam-po knows my name is on them. Those are monastery loads—routine supplies for Tibet. Bulah Singh's spy will be watching those loads, and watching for my smoke signals too, long after I'm over the border, unless I miss my guess about Morgan Lewis."

"But if you're not really watching for smoke signals, how will you know when the snow has melted enough to make it possible to get through?"

"That was Bompo Tsering's job. He's done it. He brought word last night that there's only one bad place left, and that's negotiable."

"Where is Bompo Tsering?"

"He was ten miles away from the ponies, being watched by one of Bulah Singh's undercover men, who has lost most of his pay to Bompo Tsering at a game that they play with a board and sheeps' knuckle-bones. Just now Bompo Tsering is buying odds and ends and fretting to get away tonight instead of tomorrow."

"Tomorrow? You might have told me, Andrew. I never guessed you'd be going so soon. When Dr. Lewis spoke of my staying with Nancy Strong, I had a presentiment. But—" She left off speaking, staring at the brazier.

Andrew didn't answer. He paced the floor, clenching a wrist behind his back and stepping accurately on the cracks between the flagstones. After a minute or two he stood facing the narrow window and watched the rain in the courtyard, wondering what the devil to say to Elsa. Worse than that, he was wondering what the devil to say to Tom Grayne when he should reach him, nearly a thousand miles away, up over the Roof of the World. Elsa interrupted his train of thought:

"Andrew, if Dr. Morgan Lewis has become the head of the secret intelligence, and if Mu-ni Gam-po knows it, or even suspects it, why should Dr. Lewis have talked in riddles? Why couldn't he say things plainly?"

Andrew turned his back to the window. He answered almost absent-mindedly, because he was still trying to think what to say to her: "The monk who admitted Morgan Lewis and remained in the room is a spy who reports to Bulah Singh. That's why."

"Oh."

"See here, Elsa."

"Yes, Andrew. What is it?"

"What we were talking about just now."

"You mean about your going away tomorrow? I'd rather not talk about it."

"No. Before that."

"You mean before Mu-ni Gam-po and Dr. Lewis came in?"

"Yes. Have you written a letter for me to take to Tom Grayne?"

"Of course I have. I tore up a dozen attempts. But I got it finished two days ago. It's wrapped in oiled silk. Shall I give it to you now?"

"No. What did you write to him?"

"More than twenty pages, Andrew, both sides of the paper."

"If you don't care to tell me what you wrote, okay, it's none of my God-damned business. That suits me. I'll deliver the letter and say nothing."

"Andrew, you may read the letter if you want to."

246

"I don't want to."

Elsa uncurled herself, rearranged the cushions and sat nearly up-right. Her eyes looked hunted. "Nearly half the letter," she said, "is about the baby. After that I told Tom what I have told you. I told Tom he is free. I told him he needn't worry about me any more. His papers will be quite safe in the bank vault in London, and I'll leave the key with Professor Mayor. I told him how sorry I am to have caused him so much distress, and that he mustn't blame himself because it was absolutely all of it my fault. And—"

Andrew strode toward her: "That's what I'd have betted you'd done!" He sat down on the edge of the basalt throne exactly where Lewis had sat, glaring, and scowling so that his eyes were hardly visible beneath the lowered eyebrows. Then he suddenly controlled himself, pulled out the head of Chenrezi, resumed carving it and didn't speak until he knew his voice was steady. It almost seemed as if he was speaking to the carved face of Chenrezi:

"Elsa, I'm going to talk to you as a friend if it's the last time."

"That's what I asked you to do."

"You're not playing it straight."

"What do you mean, Andrew? I'm dishonest?"

"Why ask for advice, and insist on telling me the lowdown, when you'd shot your bolt already? Do you call that playing it straight? If you've done it, you've done it. So why ask me? Do you want to be told you're a Virgin Mary suffering for the sins of the world? All right, I'll—"

"You are too cruel, Andrew. I suppose I asked for it, but you might at least—"

"Pull my punches? I won't. I hate cruelty. But what do you call what you're doing? Go ahead, give it a name!"

"You said you'd tell me the answer!"

"Yes, but I didn't know then that you'd written to Tom and told him, from a thousand miles away, where he gets off. I only guessed it. Guesses don't cut ice."

Elsa stared at him wide-eyed. He waited for her to speak. She couldn't. She was almost afraid of him. Her parted lips and bewildered eyes might have checked him if he hadn't been carving that piece of wood. He continued, without looking at her.

"Tom never lied to you, did he?"

"No, never."

"Do you love each other?"

247

"I would never have conceived his baby if I didn't love him."

"But you don't love him now? Or are you letting Lovelace do your thinking: 'I could not love thee, dear, so much, lov'd I not honour more'—and all that piffle?"

"Andrew, what do you want me to do? I'm thought out. I don't know what to think. If you're going away, you might at least—"

"Do your thinking for you? Not I! And I won't yes you either. But see here. I'll use your phrase. You offered yourself—"

"Yes, like millions of other women, to an ideal—to an idea!"

"Boloney! You offered yourself to Tom Grayne. Tom accepted. If you've told me the truth, you've no right to run out on him. It's unfinished business."

Elsa broke down at last, sobbing quietly, trying to hide the sound from Andrew, counting on the flickering shadows and the male's natural gift for not noticing things. If he should guess she was crying he might suspect her of trying to arouse pity. He knew she was crying. But he knew her too well to entertain any such suspicion as that. Pretending not to notice, he told her bluntly, almost brutally, what she wanted to tell him:

"You're disillusioned. You feel helpless. You can't help Tom by staying here: you're too closely watched by Bulah Singh. You can't claim you're married, because that might get Tom in trouble. No one here knows who was your child's father; half of Darjeeling suspects me. You've roughed it long enough with Tom, on the Roof of the World, to know you'd die of constipated bitterness in the pink-tea world you came from. You'd hate like hell to go back to that. Your bit of an income would keep you off the dole. It 'ud pay bus fares and a library subscription. You could go to the cinema once or twice a week. You might even stand outside Buckingham Palace and watch the King go by. And you might get a job teaching school—but there'd be an inspector from the Board of Education to make sure you didn't teach the kids that there's any other standard of value than money, or any other viewpoint than a mugwump's."

"Yes, Andrew. Yes. Yes. Is that the answer?"

"I'm going soon. When I'm gone, you'll be alone."

"Lonely as a ghost!"

"Mu-ni Gam-po is sympathetic, but he mistrusts women. And Nancy Strong is a woman, so you don't trust her. You don't get along with women."

"Andrew, that isn't true."

"Yes, it is."

"You know nothing about it. You've never seen me with other women. How could you possibly know?"

"I'm telling you. You listen. What pulled you through bearing a child in a blizzard at sixteen thousand feet above sea level wasn't so much your guts as what you used 'em for. Don't forget. I was in on that episode."

"How could I ever forget?"

"You just wouldn't be licked because you were fighting back at the whole damned traditional curse that was laid on women when some Levite, who had returned from Babylon to Jerusalem under Ezra, re-wrote the Book of Genesis. You were fighting the Apostle Paul and the whole army of phony feminists. Do you want to tell me you can stand the company of women who yowl for sex equality and bet their sex against the field like any two-tailed penny in a crooked two-up joint? They nearly all do it. The political ones are the worst."

"But there are other kinds of women, Andrew."

"Yes, and you're one of the others. You're clairvoyant. You can see—"

"Andrew, I hate it! Don't pretend that's any good! It's a curse! It isn't even reliable. I can't use it when I want to, when it's needed, when it might help other people. It comes and goes, almost always at the wrong time. It makes me a stranger. People think it's uncanny. They pester me to tell their fortunes—especially other people's fortunes—and when I refuse they think I'm keeping back something too evil to tell. But if I do tell what I see, because I forget not to, they think I'm a witch in league with Satan—Oh, go away, Andrew! Go away! Leave me alone! I'm very, very grateful for all you've done. But there's nothing more you can do. I'm sorry I inflicted all this on you. It wasn't fair."

"Nothing's fair," he answered. "Nobody is. We're all liabilities, some of us doing our best, which isn't much. This world is the only hell we'll ever know. We've got to take it and make the best of it, because we can't leave it. It isn't a case of devil take the hindmost. The devil gets the front men first as the general rule, and gets all of us sooner or later."

"You believe in the devil?"

"Sure I do. You and I and all the rest of us are all one devil."

"I have never heard you even mention God, except when you're angry. Do you believe in God?"

249

"I don't believe in anything that I believe in," he answered. "Anything that we believe in is pretty sure to be wrong. But I know there's God. That's different. What you know can't hurt you. What do you know?"

"Oh, I've left off caring! No! There's no God! No Christ! Nothing! Go away, Andrew. I'll pack up and go to Nancy Strong's house. Mu-ni Gam-po will send my things after me. Please come and say goodbye before you leave for Tibet, and—" She sat suddenly bolt upright, possessed by a new idea. "Andrew! If I burn that letter—that I wrote for you to give to Tom—will you—will you tell him instead?"

"No. I won't. That was a hell of a letter to write to a man." He got to his feet. "Where is it?"

Elsa hesitated. Suddenly she got up and went to the writing table where her English translation of Tibetan folios lay piled in a heap. She took the letter from a leather folder. It was wrapped in oilskin and heavily sealed. She stood holding it between the fingers of both hands, looking thoroughbred—slim, mettlesome, beginning to be very angry. Andrew stood still, watching.

"You're proud, aren't you, Andrew? You're too proud to have a hand in what looks to you like cowardice. Your pride is cruel. You're hard. But I can be as hard as you are. So very well: I will burn the letter. Then you shall tell me the answer."

"Now you're talking," said Andrew.

"No, I'm not. I'm burning my bridges, once more, for the last time."

Andrew stepped aside and watched her lay the letter on the hot coal in the brazier. The burning silk stank; so did the sealing wax; it made her gasp, but even that didn't conceal from Andrew the fact that her expression changed while she watched the letter turn to ashes .At last she met his eyes, across the brazier.

"Andrew—just now you were thinking about the snow in the passes toward Tibet and what the spring storms will be like. I saw your mental picture—all the long trail—all of it—all in a moment."

"That's nothing," he answered. "Lots of people could do that. What else?"

"You weren't alone on the trail."

"Of course I wasn't. Don't be silly. There'll be Bompo Tsering and the rest of the Tibetan gang. There'll be ponies, and—"

"There was someone else—shadowy—someone who didn't belong, and yet did belong. It's hard to explain. It's as if the others, and

250

the ponies, and the loads, and the trail are all fixed in our mind and quite clear, including even the men's characters and the ponies' temperaments. But the other person was vague, as if you weren't sure, or didn't like the idea, or—"

"Who was it?" he demanded.

"Andrew! I've no right to ask this. It isn't fair. It isn't even reasonable. Will you let me go with you to Tibet?"

"Okay."

"Andrew, are you—"

"I said yes. The hell of it is, it means three extra ponies and maybe a couple of extra yaks to carry fodder for the ponies, and an extra tent, and your rations. It'll be harder to get away, and there'll be trouble about staying where they don't like women—and—"

"Oh, I know. It's impossible! Andrew, I shouldn't have asked. I know I shouldn't have."

"You can't play it straight anyhow else, if you can stand the journey. Can you stand it?"

"Andrew, I can stand anything! I'm as strong as a horse. Really I am. I'm all over it—quite well again. Andrew, honestly if I didn't know I could make it I wouldn't—"

"Okay. It'll be tough going."

"Don't I know it! But I did it before when I was heavy with child. It should be easier this time. But what will Tom say?"

"That's Tom's business."

"Tom told me to stay in Darjeeling."

"Yeah. I heard him. But he asked me to do the best I can for you. I said I would. So that's that. I'll go and see about those extra ponies before Bulah Singh gets wise to us."

"One minute, Andrew! Please wait! How about Dr. Morgan Lewis? What will he say?"

"We'll find that out soon enough. He won't be so easy as Bulah Singh. Can't fool Lewis. But he's on the level. I'm betting he's the new Number One in Johnson's place. If I'm right, we're in luck."

"Andrew, you're the kindest and most astonishing man in the world. What can I say that—"

"Say nothing. Just do as you're told and you'll be all right."

"Very well, Andrew. I know it's no use thanking you for anything. From now on I'm taking orders. You give them. Am I to go to Nancy Strong's house?"

"Sure. Lewis tipped us off about that."

251

"Very well. But Nancy will ask questions, and she'll know what kind of questions to ask."

"Answer her questions. Make sure no one overhears you, that's all. I'll see Mu-ni Gam-po on my way out and get him to sleight-of-hand you out of here by the back way, so that Bulah Singh won't know about it. He'll know Morgan Lewis has been here. So we'd better keep the curtains drawn and send out a rumour you've had a relapse. I'll attend to all that. How long will it take you to pack your things?"

"Fifteen–twenty minutes."

"Go to it. Keep under cover at Nancy Strong's until you hear from me again. I'll send saddlebags to Nancy's, and you'll have to get her to buy any extras you'll need. Leave your manuscripts with Mu-ni Gampo. Nancy Strong will take care of anything else you have to leave behind. Will you trust me to buy you a travelling kit?"

"Andrew, is there anything you can't be trusted to do?"

His expression made her wish she hadn't said it. He always shook off flattery, and even genuine praise and gratitude, as if the thought of it hurt him.

"Give me one of your boots," he answered. "I'll take that with me for, the right size."

Elsa produced a felt boot from a chest. Andrew wrapped it in a woollen shawl and tucked it under his arm.

"All right. Then I'll get going and attend to things. I'm glad you're coming."

"You're glad I'm coming? Andrew, please don't think you have to say that kind of thing. I'm—"

"You go to Nancy Strong's and be ready to start at a moment's notice, any hour, day or night. No letters, remember. No telegrams. No goodbyes for Bulah Singh to listen in on."

"Trust me. I wouldn't dream of it."

"There's nothing else, is there?"

"Yes, just one other thing. Andrew, I know you don't like sentimental scenes, so I won't make one. And besides, I'm so grateful to you that I couldn't say it anyhow. But—but—"

"Oh, that's all right. You keep your head and hold your tongue and you'll be all right. See you later."

Andrew walked out, leaving her standing beside the brazier, staring after him, wondering. The door slammed. The coals in the brazier sank. A bell summoned the monks to chapel. Silence became a dimension of dim-hued existence. With the faculty that she hated, of visualizing

252

absent people so clearly that they seemed more real than when they were actually present, she saw Andrew Gunning now, exactly as he had stood a few moments ago beside the brazier talking to her. But, as in a dream when time and space coalesce without confusion, she could simultaneously see him by the window, and on the edge of the basalt throne, carving Chenrezi's head, fencing verbally with Morgan Lewis, scowling at some of her own remarks. And there was Bulah Singh, the Sikh Chief of Police, gazing at her. Simultaneously there was Tom Grayne, hundreds of miles to the northward, solitary, in a cave, in Tibet. And she knew Tom was thinking of her. He was angry—unhappy—uncertain and—so it seemed to her vision—ashamed.

She dragged out a battered suitcase and began packing.

CHAPTER 5

At the end of the rain-swept courtyard Andrew mounted the stairs and tried to interview Mu-ni Gam-po. But at the corner of the long gallery, where the passage turned off to the abbot's apartment, he was told by a smiling monk that blessed meditation must not be disturbed. That was a plain diplomatic evasion. He could hear voices. Whoever was meditating in the abbot's apartment was doing it noisily with at least three voices.

Andrew paced the wooden gallery. His footsteps echoed across the courtyard. He was consequently watched by monks, whose gift for grapevine gossip was as well developed as if they had been prisoners in a penitentiary. He was a scandal, the butt of guesswork. The usual bells rang. The routine two-by-two and to-and-fro processions of monks through the courtyard arch continued—mysterious goings and comings, whose mystery was how humans could endure such routine.

It left off raining. A few stars appeared. The moon broke through hurrying clouds and was reflected like a stream of pure gold on the dark wet courtyard paving-stones. Lonely. Beautiful. Unreal. Andrew fought for a grip on reality—an enormously difficult thing to do in a crisis, in which the only certainty was that nothing was certain. Facts were dead things, meaning whatever one chose to make them mean. Ideas were playing havoc with the facts. Somewhere between fact and idea lay reason. But even reason was a mess of contradictions. The reason why he had simply, naturally, intuitively recognized the rightness of taking Elsa back to Tom Grayne was smothered and contradicted by plausible, logical matter of fact.

"Intuition is right. Logic is wrong—or there'd never be anything new. Yes there would, though. There's a logic of intuition."

So thought Andrew, with the part of him that did think. Part of his mind was musing on the trail toward Tibet—wind-swept passes twenty thousand feet above sea level—chasms and crags and the merciless rivers that shout like fighting devils between cliffs where eagles build their nests beneath a turquoise sky. He hated Tibet—loved it because he hated it, hatred and love being one. No need to think. He could half close his eyes and remember, just as clearly as one sees the Himalayan panorama from the Singalila Ridge. He knew all the known difficulties, and knew there were thousands more that he couldn't imagine. He could see what he did know, all in one picture: Tibet; Elsa; Tom Grayne. Those were facts that must interpret themselves—or be interpreted by the light of an idea that hadn't yet dawned on reason.

Andrew himself was a fact; a self-contradictory, curious fact— pitiless, generous, sceptical, credulous, all in one. A lover of conflict. A hater of quarrels. A poet, who had never written one line of poetry nor sung one song of his own making, yet who knew he was a poet. Paradoxical lover of lofty views that made him veil his thought with blunt, ungracious words. That much he knew of himself and could laugh at—at least smile at. He could see himself as a remarkably comical fellow, to be handled with alert discretion because there was a streak in him that he knew no more about than other people did and that caused him to surprise himself. He wasn't thinking about that; but he saw it, mentally, while he tried to concentrate on what to say to Mu-ni Gam-po.

The mental picture and conflict were interrupted suddenly by voices in the door of Mu-ni Gam-po's antechamber. He was instantly alert, but he continued pacing the gallery until he reached the head of the stairs. There he turned in no hurry and retraced his footsteps; becoming angry, not because he recognized the men coming toward him but because he had been too stupid not to expect them. Morgan Lewis, side by side with the Chief of Police Bulah Singh, in step together, laughing, joking—strangely military— looking figures in the cloistered dimness, though they were not in uniform. There was only one electric light, in an enamelled frame, on a beam of the gallery roof. All three came to a halt under it, sharply limned against the shadows, facing one another. Morgan Lewis produced his monocle, screwed it into his eye—a symptom—a gleaming symbol of urbane artfulness. Bulah Singh merely nodded, staring at the bundle under Andrew's arm that concealed Elsa's boot.

"This saves no end of looking for you," said Lewis. "Not on your way to see Mu-ni Gam-po, are you?"

"Sure. Is he in?"

"Yes. But don't waste time trying to see him. He's busy. Bulah Singh has brought some matters to his attention that will occupy him for several hours. You know Bulah Singh, don't you?"

"Sure." Andrew smiled because the lamplight shone full in his face and the Sikh was watching him intently.

"You should know each other better," said Lewis. "Both of you are good talkers. Why not get together sometime? Oh, by the way, Gunning, I asked Mu-ni Gam-po about that translation. He said he'd attend to it. So if that's what you wanted to see him about you needn't trouble."

The Sikh watched Andrew's face but Lewis distracted attention by dropping his monocle—caught it in the palm of his hand—tossed it two or three times, and replaced it in his eye.

"One of these days you'll be shot for doing that," the Sikh remarked. "Someone will mistake it for a signal and he'll plug you in the gizzard."

"I must cure myself of habits," Lewis answered. "The good habits are the worst ones."

"Are you walking my way?" Andrew asked, addressing both men. "I think I'll go to the hotel and maybe turn in."

"We're important people. We've a car," said Lewis. "We'll give you a lift. It's Bulah Singh's car but—"

"Perfectly delighted," said the Chief of Police, sounding as if he meant it. "Let's go. As a matter of fact, if Mr. Gunning can spare the time, I'd like a chat with him."

It was a command, not an invitation. There was malice in the Sikh's dark eyes. Andrew ignored that.

"Come and have a drink at the hotel," he suggested.

"Yes. I'm thirsty."

They walked together to the stair-head, Andrew on the outside, watching Lewis for a signal. Lewis made none. They tramped down the stone steps side by side, jumped one by one across the puddle at the foot of the stairs, drew abreast again and awoke the monastery echoes as they marched in step toward the archway that divided outer and inner courtyards. Not a word. Not a hint. Not a sign. Not even the monocle now; it had returned to Lewis's vest pocket. Andrew broke the silence:

255

"Lewis, you'll join us of course for a drink?"

"No. Not this time. I've a case to look up—very interesting case. Called in for consultation. So I think I'll drop you two at the hotel and send the car back for Bulah Singh—that's to say, if Bulah Singh will permit."

"Why, certainly." The Sikh appeared off guard and anxious to please. "Just tell the driver where to take you."

No one spoke again until they had tramped through the long dark archway and halfway across the outer courtyard. Then Bulah Singh spoke in a casual tone of voice that didn't quite conceal a tart sub-flavour:

"Lots of ponies in the monastery stables. Your loads are stowed here, aren't they, Gunning?"

"It saves renting a godown," Andrew answered. "I took the precaution of having the loads marked with my name, to prevent misunderstanding."

The Sikh was about to say something but Morgan Lewis interrupted: "By the way, if you're in no hurry, Bulah Singh, I'd like to keep your car until the consultation's over. Is that putting too much strain on your good nature?"

"Keep it as long as you please," said the Sikh. "Gunning will have to endure my company until you bring the car back, that's all."

Andrew suspected guile, but he did not glance at Morgan Lewis, lest Bulah Singh should also draw conclusions. The Sikh seemed unconscious of possible ulterior motive beneath Lewis's innocent air.

"Gunning and I should find plenty to talk about," he remarked. "I look forward to it." He very evidently did look forward to it.

Andrew got into the waiting car, in the narrow street outside the monastery front gate, aware of a new admiration for Morgan Lewis. "Translation" obviously meant that Elsa would be spirited away to Nancy Strong's house out of Bulah Singh's reach—she—Elijah in a chariot of petrol. And Lewis had cleverly jockeyed the Chief of Police into a corner, to be entertained and encouraged to talk while Lewis used unseen wires—perhaps telephone wires. Lewis was trusting him—perhaps trying him out. One false move, one ill-considered remark, and Bulah Singh might close the passes in spite of anything Lewis could do. Lewis probably had no executive authority, whereas the Sikh did have. Then worse would happen. Tom Grayne would be left without support or supplies, helpless, useless, more than nine hundred miles away over the Roof of the World.

It was abundantly clear to Andrew that the government was willing he should recross the forbidden frontier into Tibet—but that the Sikh wasn't in on the deal—not yet, at any rate—and there was conflict beneath the surface.

CHAPTER 6

Bulah Singh despised all amateurs. He was himself a professional in every sense of the word. He had taken courses in criminology in Germany and France; had written, for important quarterlies, a number of praiseworthy papers on the history and development of crime in India. He believed he had peered beneath the mask of consciousness and understood the underlying automatic metaphysical mechanics of human behaviour. He had dabbled in Karl Marx, Freud, Adler, Watson and Cesare Lombroso. He regarded himself as an atheist, but he had studied many religions diligently because of their obvious bearing on the problem of what people believe and are likely to do. Intellectually vain, he was equally vain of his appearance, careful to look as little like a policeman as possible. He didn't even look like a Sikh. He never wore a uniform if he could help it, bought his soft felt hats in Vienna and his clothes in London. A powerful, lean, clean-shaven, rather dark-skinned man with magnificent teeth and dark brown eyes that sometimes suggested gentleness and humour. It was his mouth, when he wasn't consciously controlling it, that betrayed him; it revealed cruelty, deliberately studied, intellectually built into the structure of his thought.

He sat down in a long armchair in the room next to Andrew's bedroom and was at pains to pretend to observe his surroundings. In a secret file at police headquarters there was a list of every single object in the room. In the same file were copies of all Andrew's recent correspondence, together with a not quite accurate account of his activities since the day he was born. Andrew guessed as much; he had detected finger marks on rifled documents; and besides, he was quite familiar with the means by which police in all the countries of the world inform themselves and one another. He held the whiskey bottle poised over a tumbler and raised one eyebrow.

"Up to the pretty," said Bulah Singh. "Not too much soda. No ice."

Andrew tossed Elsa's boot through the bedroom door and sat down facing him, after making sure that there was no one lurking in the corridor. That trick worked. The Sikh fell for it—boasted:

"Don't be nervous. One of my men is at the head of the stairs to make sure we're not interrupted. I planned this conversation."

"Very thoughtful of you."

"I have had to think about you." Bulah Singh lighted a cigarette, blew the smoke through his nose, crossed his knees and selected the English method of disarming frankness. "You have me puzzled."

"Sometimes I'm a puzzle to myself," said Andrew.

Bulah Singh stuck to the brusque British method. "Come now. No metaphysics. I'm a practical man. So are you. Let's lay cards on the table, faces upward."

Andrew's smile was as disarming as the Sikh's assumed frankness: "Okay. Suits me. You first."

Bulah Singh's eyes betrayed a flash of resentment. He was used to being feared and diffidently treated. He forgot for a tenth of a second to govern the line of his mouth. He led the ace of trumps:

"The frontier into Tibet is closed," he remarked, adding after a second's pause: "tight as a drum."

Andrew followed suit with a little one: "I've heard it's your business to see that no one gets through."

"Yes. Not even a native Tibetan can return home without my leave. When the passes are open—that won't be long now—there'll be quite an exodus. There are two ways to get permits. The wise ones will come to my office. The unwise ones will regret their lack of discretion."

Andrew offered no comment. He lighted his pipe.

"It's my impression," said Bulah Singh after a moment's silence, "that it's your immediate ambition to rejoin Tom Grayne in Tibet."

"I've thought of doing it," said Andrew. "But do you appreciate what a journey it would be by way of China, with China being raped by the Japanese? It would take at least six months—perhaps longer. It would cost like hell, too."

"Ah. But how about returning by the way you came?"

Andrew's smile widened: "Are you suggesting that I'm fool enough to try to escape your vigilance?"

"Tom Grayne was one of Johnson's pets," said Bulah Singh, tasting his whiskey. "That's how Tom Grayne got through." He watched Andrew's face narrowly, under lowered eyelids, over the top of the glass, then set the glass down slowly on the small brass-topped table beside the chair and continued: "Johnson is no longer with us. His worst fault was that he couldn't train a successor. The job is vacant. There are several candidates."

"Are you one of them?"

The Sikh avoided the question. "You are no tenderfoot," he remarked. "I think that is the correct word. You know as well as I do that reciprocity and mutual concessions are the secret of all bargains."

Andrew agreed: "Sure. Nothing for nothing."

Bulah Singh sipped whiskey without looking at him. No need to look; he had his victim interested. All that remained was to jiggle the bait: "Suppose I tell what I know," he suggested. "Then you tell what you know. Something might come of it."

"Swell."

"You are clever, Andrew Gunning, or I wouldn't waste time talking to you. Beneath that air of almost brutal directness you're as smart as a fox. But even foxes make mistakes. I happen to know that Tom Grayne is somewhere near Shig-po-ling, short of provisions. You want to take provisions to him. I have had to speak to the Abbot Mu-ni Gam-po about those loads of yours. If they should be moved from the monastery stable without my permission it would be awkward for Mu-ni Gam-po."

Andrew looked serious: "Glad you mentioned it. The old abbot has been kind to Elsa Burbage. Kind to me, too. I'd hate to make trouble for him."

Bulah Singh nodded: "Mu-ni Gam-po can't afford any more mistakes. He has been playing with fire for too many years. His method is shopworn— amateurish. His political sagacity is sticky with religion. It belongs to a dead era that has been decomposing since the World War and was buried at last when Johnson of the Ethnographic Survey left for England. Johnson was a typical B.S.I.—bigot, stupid, incorruptible. A reactionary."

"I never met him," said Andrew.

"So I understand. Johnson was trained, if you care to call it training, in the days when Whitehall's grip on India was strong. He was an amateur, with all the faults that go with it. Too many irons in the fire. No concentration. You're aware, I suppose, that the B.S.I. controls the Foreign Office? Actually it secretly rules the British Empire. It's even independently financed, from Persian oil wells. Well—there's a strong undercurrent in favour of changing all that, at least as concerns India. A professional—Indian by birth—responsible to Delhi, not Whitehall— do you get me?"

"Sure," said Andrew, gravely courteous. "Changes are going on

259

everywhere. Who'd heard of Stalin, Hitler, Mussolini, twenty, years ago? I guess it's simply a matter of the right man, at the right moment, with the right information and the right idea."

Bulah Singh blew a smoke ring and pushed his finger through it, indicating bull's-eye, first shot, and time to be careful. "I could use some information about Tibet," he remarked.

Andrew accepted the opening: "Yes, whoever could swing Tibet would be powerful. He could upset any political calculations. But are you young enough? And have you the backing in India?"

"I have detractors. I have enemies," said Bulah Singh. "Envy, jealousy, malice, are inseparable from politics. Very few people can be impersonal when it comes to making political appointments. As for impartiality, that consists in understanding neither side of a problem. Some very influential people, who call themselves impartial, and perhaps believe it, are opposed to the principle of putting an Indian into a key position, no matter what his qualifications. Their prejudices masquerade as principles. But I'm a realist. Hard facts are what interest me."

"What facts do you want to know?" Andrew asked.

"Well—for instance—" he blew smoke through his nose— "who pays you?"

"No one. I've a private income. I'm a free lance."

Bulah Singh's eyes hardened: "Ummnn. If I believed that, it might possibly simplify matters. But the fact is, you're an agent of the United States Department of State, or else of the treasury, or the army or navy, or possibly even the postal department. Who sent you from Shanghai to Shig-po-ling?"

"The same man who pays Tom Grayne," Andrew answered.

Bulah Singh sipped at his drink thoughtfully. "I know who pays Tom Grayne," he said after a moment.

"Swell. Then we needn't discuss it."

"You are unpaid? That is very interesting, if true. Have you any idea why the American Government should be interested in what's going on in Tibet? As a private citizen, unpaid, I suppose you feel free to discuss that?"

"Well," said Andrew, "since you ask me, it's my guess that the American Government doesn't give a good God-damn what's happening in Tibet. You'll have to take that or leave it. I believe it's the truth."

The Sikh sneered. "It is one hundred *per cent* true that you can't cross the border into Tibet—without my leave. You'd better talk."

"Well," said Andrew, "if my opinion's any use to you, I'd say that our army and navy are Watching Japan. Why shouldn't they? If they know what Japan's commitments and intentions are they can bear 'em in mind. If the Japs win, the Far East cat jumps one way. If the Chinese win, it jumps the other way. Forewarned is forearmed."

"Forewarned is what you are now," said Bulah Singh. If you want special favours—"

"I don't," said Andrew.

"If you don't want special inconvenience, and even special arrest, under special regulations, devised for the special purpose of preventing unauthorized or seditious acts—I advise you to tell me plainly why Tom Grayne is interested in the infant Dalai Lama, and what his and your interest amounts to."

"That's a long story," said Andrew. "You know, of course, how they go about getting a new Dalai Lama?"

Bulah Singh betrayed a flash of impatience. But he appeared to decide that Andrew wasn't quite ripe yet for plucking. "Yes," he said after a moment, "I have made a study of that. Such superstitions are more revealing than even Frazer points out in his Golden Bough. Have you read that?"

"Some of it," said Andrew. "I read two or three volumes and got bored."

"A study of Frazer explains why Hitler is inventing a new religion for the Germans; and why he attacks Christianity."

"What's your point?" asked Andrew. "What are you driving at?"

Bulah Singh's eyes were excited, but he talked on patiently: "The Tibetan superstition, that a dead Dalai Lama reincarnates almost instantly into the body of a newborn child, would be comical if it weren't actually, when it's well analyzed, the same old myth that's at the root of all religion. Of course in practice it sets up, a vicious circle because of the human craving for power. Poison is the obvious corollary; any criminologist could foretell that. The men behind the scenes poison a Dalai Lama and set up a Council of Regents, who then claim supernatural guidance and in due course they discover a child into whose body the poisoned victim is supposed to have reincarnated. They take the child away from his mother and control him until just before he comes of age. Then again they poison him, and begin all over. That makes it very nice for the Council of Regents."

"You seem to know as much about it as I do," said Andrew. "Why don't you come to the point? I won't betray your confidences."

The Sikh stared. He was startled: "Pardon me," he said. "Let's understand each other. It is your confidences that won't be betrayed—provided they're of value to me."

Andrew laughed. "The difficulty is, I know no more than you do. However, here's the low-down, for what it's worth. If you know it already, say so, and I'll stop talking. The Council of Regents in Lhasa, with one exception, are political crooks with phony religious credentials. For centuries it has been the first principle of the Tibetan political game to play off the Dalai Lama against the Panchen Lama, and make rivals of them, instead of co-rulers as they're supposed to be. But now there's neither Dalai nor Panchen Lama. A few years ago, you remember, they chased the Panchen Lama into exile in China, because he was too incorrigibly honest. After that, they poisoned the best Dalai Lama that Tibet ever had. That gave the ball to the political gang. So they staged the usual circus, scoured the countryside and discovered a newborn child whom they identified as the Dalai Lama's successor. The Panchen Lama imposed his official *veto*. But the Regents treated that as a joke because they had chased him out of Tibet and he couldn't come back. He died in exile quite recently. So the new infant Dalai Lama's divine right to the throne of Tibet stands unchallenged. He has a propaganda value."

"He has more than that," said the Sikh,

"Call it poker, if you prefer the word." Andrew was warming up. "The point is that China, Japan and Russia realise his potential value. They are employing some of the cleverest secret agents in the world, and almost unlimited money, to gain political control of Tibet. Tibet is not the obvious key, but it's the real key to the control of Asia. And the key to Tibet is the infant Dalai Lama. Have I made that clear?"

"Yes. That's a good precis. But there's nothing secret about it," said Bulah Singh. "It even appeared in the American newspapers. I have the clippings. What else do you know?"

"Probably no more than you know," said Andrew. "The self-appointed Council of Regents in Lhasa have been bribed alternately by Russian, Japanese and Chinese agents, and supplied with weapons and so on. They've been fed so much bull and boloney and lying propaganda that they're three parts crazy. They'd rather cut each other's throats than come in out of the wet. They all thought themselves Machiavellis, but now they feel more like hayseeds in a gyp-joint. There was only one member of the Council who ever rated as a real number one man. No doubt you've heard of him. They gave him the works. Damned near killed him. Chased him out of Lhasa. He's in hiding."

Bulah Singh's eyes narrowed. He interrupted. Which one do you refer to?"

"I don't know him personally. Never met him," said Andrew. "Tom Grayne knows him well."

"Ah." The Sikh's eyes glittered. "Then Elsa Burbage also knows him?"

Andrew noticed the tactical change of attack. He sensed the sudden lunge of directed thought, like a rapier under his guard.

"Dr. Lewis could tell you," he answered. He knew it wasn't a clever answer, but it gave him a second in which to think and recover.

The Sikh followed up: "I am asking you, not Lewis."

"Yes. I heard you."

"Is the man you mean the Ringding Gelong Lama Lobsang Pun?"

"If you know him, why ask me?" Andrew retorted.

The Sikh nodded dark then demanded suddenly: "Where is the infant Dalai Lama? Do you know?"

"You may have later news than mine," said Andrew, "but what happened is this: the Abbot of Shig-po-ling is no more a genuine abbot than you or I, but he's one of the Regents—his right name is Ram-pa Yap-shi. He carried off the infant Dalai Lama to the fortified monastery at Shig-po-ling, where he is dickering with Russian and Japanese agents. Perhaps with Chinese agents too. Presumably he'll sell out to the highest bidder."

The Sikh nodded: "That isn't news, but it's true. Physical possession of the infant Dalai Lama would be a bargain at any price," he remarked. "How old is he?"

"He must be about five years old by now."

"Still young enough. The Jesuits were right about catching them young. Mussolini is following suit. So are Stalin and Hitler—training infants. So is Nancy Strong, God damn her! Teach the child, the man obeys. Sow now and reap the Future. The child is father to the man. Educated by Japan, the Dalai Lama would be Japanese. Educated by a Russian expert, he would become more Russian than Stalin himself. What is Tom Grayne doing?"

Andrew grinned genially: "If I knew, I'd tell you."

"You do know. You have means of communication with Tom Grayne in Tibet."

Andrew stiffened. "If he and I corresponded by mail, you'd have no need to ask questions, would you?"

The Sikh also stiffened. He had finished feinting. He commenced actual assault. Its violence was hypnotic: "You correspond by way of Sinkiang, Hongkong and Macao. Smart work, but not secret from me. You have another, much more secret means. Cooperate, in that, with me—or take the consequences."

"I don't think I get you." said Andrew.

"No? I will drop you a hint."

"Go to it."

"Did you ever hear that during the World War the German High Seas Fleet put to sea, not long before the Battle of Jutland, simply and solely to find out whether it was true, as they suspected, that the British Admiralty had occult means of reading the German secret signals?"

"No, I never heard of that. I don't believe it," said Andrew.

"Don't you! Then read what Admiral Bacon says about it in his life of Lord Fisher. I can lend you the book."

"I don't care if it's in fifty books. I don't believe it," said Andrew.

Bulah Singh smiled importantly: "Von Tirpitz and Ludendorff did believe it. Why? Because they themselves were also trying to use occult means, in competition with the British secret intelligence."

"How do you know that?"

"I knew Ludendorff—after the war. But before the war, I was one of the secret observers appointed to watch the staff of the German crown prince when he came to India. Do you know why the crown prince was obliged to leave India so suddenly?"

"I was in short pants in those days," said Andrew. "I was learning all about Santa Claus and George Washington and the Cherry Tree, and how the doctor brings newborn babies in a handbag."

"Members of the crown prince's staff," said Bulah Sing, "were discovered attempting to establish a telepathic link with Indian seditionists for propaganda purposes in time of war. It was I who caught them at it. The crown prince was given his walking orders, and the Germans never did get beyond the experimental stage."

"That kind of thing is darned easy to say," Andrew remarked. "I should say it's less easy to prove."

'Impossible to prove!" The Sikh's eyes glowered like an angry dog's. "That is its value! Its virtue! Its importance. That is why you get away with it! That is why you and I can't deal on ordinary terms. There

264

must be guarantees. How do you wish to return to Tibet?"

"No orders yet," said Andrew eyeing him hard. "I've been wondering whether some of my correspondence has been held up."

The Sikh accepted the challenge: "Oh, I'll be quite frank about that. Your mail goes through the usual channels. The one you received from the United States last Tuesday was in code. I read it. It was signed 'Hofstedder.' It said something about taking a walk that suggested a possible double meaning. That's why I asked where you're hoping to go."

"I have the letter in my pocket," Andrew answered.

"Well, see here, Gunning. Let's suppose that the dice should be loaded a bit in your favour. Let's suppose you should slip over the border discreetly without any risk of being caught. Would you reciprocate?"

"How? In what way?"

"In any way I stipulate."

Andrew grinned: "That's a tall order. You'd better explain."

Bulah Singh stood up. He lighted another cigarette. He half closed his eyes. He came closer to Andrew, standing over him, looking down at him. His mouth didn't look like a man's any longer; it suggested a gash made by a surgeon's knife. He held his voice down to a flat monotone.

"I've got you by the short hair, Andrew Gunning. There's no India Office visa on your passport. There's the little matter of Elsa Burbage to be explained. And there are those loads at the monastery. Taking a walk is exactly you are going to do—in either of two directions. Agree with me, and over the Roof of the World with you. Otherwise, take the first boat from Calcutta or Bombay. Which is it?"

The knuckles of Andrew's fingers that clutched the chair-arm turned white under the pressure of self-control. The professional Bulah Singh should have noticed it, but he seemed not to. Andrew knew that Morgan Lewis had purposely left him alone with the Sikh. He couldn't risk anger. He glanced at his watch, at the door, at the window; made a rather amateurish effort to look furtive, realised that the Sikh saw through that, changed it to a sceptical grin that was far more effective, and said: "Sit down. Help yourself to a drink. Let's talk things over."

CHAPTER 7

Elsa's bazaar-bought raincoat made a pool around her feet on the floor of Nancy Strong's hallway. The turbaned servant who hung up the raincoat and knelt to wipe her wet shoes clucked solicitous comment. He was used to all kinds of people—even well-bred, gently mannered people in inexpensive clothes, who came without warning in the rain, at unconscionable hours. But why no galoshes? Why were her shoes not wetter than they were? If she hadn't walked, how had she got there? The effort of suppressing the urge to ask questions so occupied his mind that he forgot his manners and left her standing in the hall while he switched on the light in the living-room and frugally added pine knots to the blazing fire.

The hall was lined on both sides with books in shelves about shoulder-high; on the wall above those were plainly framed photographs of ex-pupils of Nancy's school. Tibet, Nepal and every province of India were represented. On top of the shelves were statuettes, done in clay by the pupils and baked in the school kiln. Some of them were very revealing portraits of Nancy Strong as seen through the eyes of attentive, inquisitive Indian youth. No two alike—even remotely alike—and yet all unmistakably Nancy Strong in one mood or another.

Elsa felt relieved that Nancy wasn't there to receive her. She needed time, after a wild ride through the rain with Dr. Lewis in Bulah Singh's car, to subdue emotions that made her heart beat quickly and her head feel almost like someone else's, full of unfamiliar thought that she recognized nevertheless as her own. She admired Nancy Strong, but she was conscious of being on guard against her. She even liked her. But she didn't quite trust her. Not quite. There was something about Nancy that always made her feel shy and reserved. Perhaps it was the school-teacher quality. It was a superficial manner, because Nancy had no unpleasant mannerisms. It was more likely a habit of thought, concealed but evident to Elsa's sensitive perception. Her perception was much too sensitive. Elsa knew it. She was always much too careful, and perhaps afraid, of meeting other people's minds in unmasked conflict. Each time she had met Nancy hitherto she hid always felt vaguely antagonistic, almost sulkily disposed to cover up her own thought and talk superficially, which she could do very well when she wanted to. Sometimes Nancy even made her feel like a small animal that creeps into its hole and watches, listens, wonders what next?

So when the servant ushered her into the vast living room she made an effort of will to be natural, at ease, and confident of welcome. It didn't quite work. But she achieved some success. The servant seemed to notice it. He smiled at her as he fussed around rearranging ashtrays, watching her furtively, waiting for her to sit down before going to summon his employer. She chose a chair near the door. But the moment he left the room she got up again and looked about her, as it were feeling for Nancy's atmosphere in order to meet her on even ground.

There was surely no other room in the world quite like that one. In the middle of the long wall opposite the door was a huge stone fireplace. In a horseshoe around that, within an oblong barricade of bookshelves, were large old-fashioned, overstuffed armchairs, each with a footstool and a small end-table beside it. The fire shone hospitably through an opening between the bookshelves, which were placed back to back, so that books faced both ways, inward toward the fireplace and outward toward the room. Outside that homelike, snug enclosure the room resembled almost a museum, except for touches of humour and a sensation of being lived in. The carpet was from Samarkand, too good to tread on. The curtains were from Lhasa, Bukhara and Peking. The walls were hung with Tibetan sacred paintings and some of Nancy Strong's own, less sacred but strongly unsentimental watercolours, of which the most noticeable was a portrait of the late Dalai Lama. There were devil-masks, Tibetan weapons, bronze bells, dories, silk embroidery and weird musical instruments. At one end of the room was a black grand piano that threw everything else out of balance. Its top was a maze of framed photographs. Elsa went up and studied them, growing mentally more confused and uncertain of Nancy's point of view as she looked, and remembered chance remarks, and guessed, and tried to imagine Nancy Strong in such strangely assorted company.

Three were of viceroys. There was Lord Kitchener in commander in chief's uniform. The ex-*Kaiser*, alongside Admiral of the Fleet Lord Fisher and the weirdly bearded Von Tirpitz. General Lord Allenby. An archbishop, a cardinal, two bishops. King George and Queen Mary. Senator Borah. General Smuts. Sun Yat-Sen. Gandhi. President Wilson and Theodore Roosevelt side by side. Mary Pickford, Will Rogers. The Grand Mufti of Jerusalem. Sven Hedin. General Younghusband. And no less than eleven Indian ruling princes. All autographed, and many of them bearing written record of affection.

But the most remarkable object in the room stood alone, on a small teak table, exactly midway between the door and the fireplace. One had to walk around it to reach the opening in the oblong screen of bookshelves. It was a much enlarged head and shoulder portrait of the Ringding Gelong Lama Lobsang Pun, known in Tibetan and English, and to friend and enemy alike, as Old Ugly-face. The portrait started floods of memories pouring into Elsa's mind, although it had been obviously taken long before she met him, in the days when he was reasonably thin and coming to be recognized in Far East diplomatic circles as the new enigma.

There was a magnificent cat on the hearth, with its back to the fire in feline recognition of the fact that the rain had only temporarily ceased. He would turn his face to the fire again when the rain resumed. Meanwhile, he studied Elsa with Sphinx-like detachment. His face looked something like Lobsang Pun's in the silver-framed photograph. It was only a vague resemblance, but there it was. You could look at either of them and catch yourself thinking about the other—wondering how many birds the cat had killed—how many secrets Old Ugly-face knew.

Elsa went and sat down by the fire. She made friendly overtures to the cat. But the cat took no notice, any more than Lobsang Pun would have done. So she leaned back and stared at the fire, thinking about Lobsang Pun, as she last saw him, at the Thunder Dragon Gate in Tibet. But she began to see Bulah Singh's face, growing larger and larger amid the burning pine knots. That was no good. It didn't frighten her, but it made her feel vaguely guilty of forgetting something that she should remember—secretly guilty of liking a man whom really she intensely disliked. To throw off that sensation and get her mind on something else she turned sideways in the armchair to glance at the rows of books, pulling out a few at random from the nearest shelf behind her. Aristotle, Lord Derby's Homer, Plato, Science and Health by Mary Baker Eddy. She returned them and tried again, kneeling on the chair to read the titles: the *Upanishads*, Freud, St. Paul's *Epistles to the Corinthians* in Greek, Fitzgerald's *Rubaiyat*, the Psalms in English, the second volume of Karl Marx's *Das Kapital* in German. The Tibetan *Book of the Dead*, Tennyson, Browning, the Bhagavad-Gita, a whole set of Dickens, the *Intimate Papers of Colonel House*, a set of Shakespeare, Hitler's *Mein Kampf* in German, the Bible, the *Koran*—

Elsa heard the door open. She jumped out of the chair, hurriedly straightened her skirt and went and stood in the opening between the bookcases, silhouetted with her back to the firelight, feeling rather like a bewildered child and not at all sure she was welcome.

CHAPTER 8

Something happened to the room when Nancy Strong entered and closed the door behind her, glancing around swiftly before she looked at Elsa. She even brought the grand piano into harmony with all the rest of it. Gray-haired, gray-eyed, gallantly old-fashioned, even dowdy. She wore one of those dependable brown wool frocks that department stores can be trusted to ship to customers of twenty-five years' standing. Woollen stockings. Tidy ankles. Scarred knuckles. Hands like a horseman's. Her face had no room left on it for ugliness, there was so much character. She was beautiful from having faced trouble and stood up to it and beaten it, times without number. A stormy-weather woman, matter-of-fact in her greeting of Elsa:

"Why did you get up? Sit down again. How did you get here?"

She took a chair beside Elsa facing the fire. The cat leaped into her lap.

"Dr. Morgan Lewis brought me, in a car belonging to the chief of police."

"Is the man mad? Did he let Bulah Singh's chauffeur know where you are?"

"Oh no. He sent the Indian chauffeur away on an errand and drove the car himself. He set me down before we reached the front gate, so as not to be seen."

"Take off your shoes and dry your feet at the fire: Does Mu-ni Gam-po know you've left the monastery?"

"Yes, I feel sure he knows. He sent his doctor and two other monks to lead me through a tunnel I've never seen before to a building quite a long way off, and out through a door in a wall to where Dr. Lewis was waiting with the car."

"And your luggage?"

"The monks will bring it. It was being wrapped in burlap, to look like bundles of rags for the carpet makers, when I came away."

"No need to worry about that then. It will be in the godown before midnight. Well, I suppose this means that Andrew Gunning has his marching orders."

Elsa nodded, too excited to answer. There was no need to say that she was going with Andrew. The news exuded from her. Nancy Strong shook her head so vehemently that a couple of hairpins fell out and she had to rearrange her gray mane. She spoke with a hairpin in her teeth:

"That man Morgan Lewis is worse than Johnson. Much worse. There's no limit to Lewis's masculine romanticism. The weaker sex

269

should set us women an example of restraint. But they don't. They know we're realists. They egg us on to do the things they can't do. Lewis is dangerous. It's too bad that we can't get along without dangerous men."

Elsa rallied to the challenge of injustice: "Dr. Lewis isn't responsible for my going back to Tibet. He thinks I'm going to stay here with you."

Nancy Strong's face flickered with the humour that had made her famous as a teacher beyond praise. "Do you think he believes you could teach my orphans to make carpets?" she asked. "Lewis is a Welsh romanticist whose ancestors were Druids. He would rather turn the corners than come straight to the point. He thinks ten minutes' notice is too much."

Elsa protested, a bit hotly: "Shouldn't I have come? I understood that you knew all about it. Dr. Lewis asked me to come here because Bulah Singh has been spying on Mu-ni Gam-po. I'm not sure, but I think Mu-ni Gam-po asked Dr. Lewis to smuggle me out of the monastery."

"My dear, you are more than welcome. If you hadn't come here, I would have felt sorry. Stay as long as you please. But you must stay indoors because Morgan Lewis has spread a rumour that you've had a relapse. I've already heard it over the phone from two infallible gossips. You're supposed to be in bed, in the dark, at the monastery, behind curtained windows, suffering from fever due to overwork translating Tibetan folios. You may even be dead by tomorrow, if Morgan Lewis is in good form and tongues wag fast enough."

"But if Bulah Singh should discover the truth, what then?" Elsa asked, suddenly frightened by the thought.

Nancy Strong noticed it: "Don't feel afraid of Bulah Singh, my dear. He is a mere policeman who would love to be a story-book devil. He would skin truth for its hide and tallow, if he knew how."

"Isn't he chief of police?"

"Yes."

"Can't he interfere with Andrew, if he finds out?"

"Perhaps. He is said to have some talent for police work. But he suffers from intellectual indigestion. And he is as superstitious as an old-fashioned witch-finder. Has he bothered you at all?"

"Yes and no. He was very polite. He called on me at the monastery, several times. Brought flowers."

"Tell me."

"I disliked him, first go off. Later, when Andrew told me that he reads my mail before I get it, I disliked him thoroughly. But I couldn't avoid seeing him when he called. And he made himself so extremely civil that it was quite difficult to refuse to do what he asked."

"What was it?"

"Well, he knows I speak fluent Tibetan. And he said he has a Tibetan prisoner in the jail who won't answer questions. He wanted me to hide behind a screen at police headquarters while that prisoner is being questioned and to use what he calls my subconsciousness to read the prisoner's thought while he is being questioned. He wanted me to do it without telling anyone else—especially Andrew or Mu-ni Gam-po."

Nancy Strong chuckled. "I told you, didn't I, that Bulah Singh is superstitious."

"He calls himself a psychologist," said Elsa.

"Bluff! He's an ambitious coward who believes that blackmail is a science and that double-crossing is a fine art. Did he offer you any compensation for your trouble?"

"He hinted that as chief of police he could probably smother—I think that was the word he used—the inquiries that were being made in certain quarters about my being a guest at the monastery and about my right to remain in India."

"Ah! I suspected as much! There are too many like him—far too many, always trying to trade on people's weakness. The key is that use of the word subconsciousness. Minus-minds. It's only plus-minds that aren't afraid of superconsciousness. Minus-minded people like Bulah Singh call everything they can't understand, subconsciousness. That makes them feel superior and scientific. Down in the recesses of his dark mind Bulah Singh believes in black magic, but he doesn't dare to admit that, even to himself. He wants to pile the faggots and watch you burn in your own flame. I want to talk to you about that."

Elsa protested, frowning. "Oh, Nancy Strong, I wish you wouldn't. Do let's talk about something else. There are so many things I want to—"

"Child, sit still and listen. I don't in the least mind your coming here at ten minutes' notice. In fact I'm very glad to have you. But you will either listen to me, or else go to your room. And I warn you: if you do go to your room you will miss the only chance I shall have to save you from making a fool of yourself. Which shall it be?"

She stroked the cat until it purred like a tea kettle. Elsa sighed:

271

"Very well. But I've had so much of it. And I do so hate it. Nancy, I'm returning to Tibet—secretly! Can't we talk about that? I have Andrew's full permission to answer any questions you ask."

"How did you get out of doing what Bulah Singh wanted? What excuse did you give?"

"You insist! Oh, very well. I told Bulah Singh what I have just told you: that I hate and detest clairvoyance. I told him it's bad enough not being able to help seeing things that you'd rather not see; but that to go ahead and do it deliberately, just for the hell of it, would be like doing something unclean."

"What did Bulah Singh say to that?"

"He laughed. He looked cruel. He called me superstitious, and he hinted that I'm a hypocrite. He said he was surprised that a girl who had come through my experience should be afraid to make use of a natural gift."

Nancy Strong reached for a cigarette and pushed the carved silver box across the side-table toward Elsa: "Reach for the matches, will you? I don't want to disturb the cat."

They smoked in silence for a minute or two. Elsa got up, poked the fire, put on a lump of wood and sat down again.

"You were a brave little fool in the first place," said Nancy Strong, staring at the end of her cigarette. "I did my level best—my fighting, interfering, irritating female damnedest to prevent you from going to Tibet with Tom Grayne. When I was secretly consulted, I went all the way to Delhi and back at my own expense to tell Johnson to stop you from going. And I tried to talk Tom Grayne out of it, during a whole afternoon on a train. I knew all about your secret marriage to Tom Grayne, and about your agreement to keep it on a business basis. You two ignorant children held out longer than I thought you would. There's a note in my diary that I made at the time. I'll look it up presently. I think I allowed Nature three months less than Nature actually needed. I didn't allow enough for your ingenuousness or for Tom Grayne's obstinacy."

"It was not Nature. And it wasn't Tom's fault. It was me," Elsa insisted. "I did it. I seduced Tom."

Nancy Strong swept that aside with a gesture. "*N'importe.* Never mind for the moment whose fault, if fault it was. *Il y a toujours un qui aime et l'autre qui se laisse aimer.* But the stuff that I packed into your first-aid kit? Where was that when that weakling let you lure him into sin?"

"I forgot it. I mean, I never thought of it."

"Elsa, my dear, it is no use your lying to me. You did think of it. You thought I was a nasty-minded female. Tell the truth now: didn't you throw it away?"

"Well, I didn't want Tom to know I had stuff like that with me. What could he possibly have thought if he'd found it? And besides, I didn't want an excuse or a temptation or a——"

Nancy Strong interrupted: "The trouble with you, my dear, is that you've got sex, and love, and religion, and loyalty all mixed up together with superstition and bravery in one bottle. Shake the bottle, and out pops human nature, cork and all. Added to that, you're clairvoyant and can't understand why other people don't see what you see."

Elsa curled up in the big chair, growing angry but doing her best to conceal it. "Oh well, I'm not natural. I know I'm not. I'm a freak."

"We're all freaks," Nancy answered. "Every last one of us. I'll tell you about me one of these days when I'm feeling reminiscent. But tell me about Tom Grayne. Does he expect you back in Tibet?"

"No, he doesn't. He told me to stay in Darjeeling."

"But you're going back to him?"

"Yes. I asked Andrew's advice, this evening."

Nancy stroked the cat the wrong way. The cat sought solitude, at full speed around the bookcase and under the grand piano. "Goon," said Nancy. "Tell me about it."

"But there's nothing to tell. Andrew told me to do my own thinking. I couldn't get him to say what he thought I should do. But when I asked him to take me back to Tibet, he agreed instantly and said it was the only possible answer if I wanted to play it straight."

"Play what straight?"

"He meant I should keep my bargain with Tom. He called it unfinished business. He made me feel like a thing without any will of my own— like something invented by Tom and Andrew."

"You mean you'd rather not go?"

"I'd rather go than do anything else on earth that I can think of. But I tried to tell you what it felt like when Andrew agreed to let me go with him. I can't really tell it because there aren't the right words. After my baby died, I did nothing but think for days and days and weeks. Even when I got well enough to work at Tibetan translation, one part of me was thinking, wondering what to do—what I should do—what was the right thing to do—"

"It didn't occur to you at any time to return to Tom?"

"Yes, of course it did, thousands of times. Hundreds and hundreds of times I saw him, clairvoyantly, just as clearly as I see you now—more clearly, because it's different. And I know Tom was thinking of me. But how could I get back to him—more than nine hundred miles—across that terrible country, without money or a permit to cross the border?"

"Terrible country? Then you don't like Tibet?"

"I love it—perhaps because it is terrible. Perhaps it sounds incredible to you, Nancy: but I loved every minute even of that agony when my baby was born in the snow. Go ahead: call me a romantic liar if you want to. But I tell you it's the unadorned truth."

"I never had that experience," said Nancy. "Now I'm too old, so I'll take your word for it. You make me wonder what I've missed: Did you quarrel with Tom?"

"No, of course I didn't. Tom doesn't quarrel with people. I do. But even I can't quarrel with a man who just gets thoughtful and says nothing."

"Umm. Did Tom and Andrew quarrel?"

"No indeed. Andrew was with us in Tibet for several months and there was never a cross word between them. We three were very happy together in that cave in the mountains. There was lots of hardship, and it was dangerous, but we all three loved it."

"So it amounts to this: that Andrew Gunning did what he did to oblige Tom Grayne?"

"Oh, if that's what you're driving at, I can give you a very quick answer. I believe Andrew hates me. I can't see why he shouldn't. I forced him to upset all his plans to return for supplies by way of Chwanben. I caused him unimaginable trouble. No one who hadn't seen it could imagine what Andrew had to do to get me safely to Darjeeling. Mind you, he had to deliver my baby in a blizzard. And he isn't a doctor! And even after we got here, and I was safe in the monastery, I couldn't help making things far more difficult for him than they would have been if he had come alone. People even think it was his baby. I'm not quite sure that Mu-ni Gam-po doesn't think so. I know Bulah Singh suspects it."

Nancy Strong tossed her cigarette into the fire and lighted another one. "The night is young," she remarked. "Long live the night. Go ahead. Tell me more."

"Tell you what?"

"About Andrew Gunning."

"I know very little about Andrew, except that he came from Columbus, Ohio, by way of Shanghai. He isn't a silent man, and he's well educated, but he doesn't talk about himself. I think he's the kindest man I've ever seen or heard of, but he resents being thanked, it makes him brusque and rude. And he's as cruel as all Tibet if he thinks you're being unjust or trying to sidestep responsibility. What do you know about him? He speaks very highly of you."

"Yes, they all do that," said Nancy. "Even Bulah Singh does. It's a habit, like driving on the right side of the street. You see I know enough to hang most of 'em. So they reward me for discretion by praising my chief fault."

"Nancy, why do such people as you, who have really accomplished something, always speak of themselves contemptuously? This school of yours is famous. So are you. And you know it."

"Never trust reputations, my dear. The difference between precept and practice is what makes men flatter me behind my back. They hope to God I won't tell what I know."

"Well, tell me what you know about Andrew Gunning."

"May I tell him what I know about you?"

"Yes, if you want to." Nancy Strong chuckled: "Smart girl. A disarming answer. However, I won't tell you about Andrew."

"He has told you his story?"

"They all do it. That's what makes life so interesting. I'm a sort of she- priest. An auntie-confessor. They all tell me sooner or later whose wives or husbands they're in love with, or tired of, or afraid of, and why."

"Why did Andrew leave home?"

"Why should I tell you? Can't you ask him?"

"I did. Of course I did. How could one help being interested in anyone who's as kind as Andrew has been to me. I played fair by telling all about me. But when I asked about him, he just dried up and I knew he was angry, although he tried not to show it."

"When did you ask him?"

"In Tibet, on the way here, before my baby was born. For days and days after that he broke the trail as if he were fighting a battle. He was furious. He made me think of one of those Vikings in the Scandinavian Sagas who fought because fighting was their religion. He seemed to me to be fighting invisible things:"

Nancy Strong probed cautiously: "That second-sight of yours. Did that tell you nothing?"

Elsa shuddered. "It's too much like dreams. It's worse: it's like peeping through keyholes, only more disreputable, because you don't risk being caught at it."

"Ah. But what did it tell you about Andrew Gunning?"

"Not much. Because I so hate it I nearly always shut my mind against it and try to think about something else. Don't ask me."

"But I do ask."

"I believe you can read my thought. Oh, very well, if you insist. Something dreadful happened in America that Andrew can't bear to think about. He can't go back home. Or he won't. I'm not sure which."

"But you're not afraid to go with him to Tibet?"

"What do you mean? Why should I be afraid?"

Nancy Strong, with her chin resting on a clenched fist and her elbow on the chair-arm, studied Elsa for about sixty seconds. Then she asked suddenly: "Has anybody ever told you how naive you are in some ways and how shrewd when one least expects it of you?"

"Yes. Andrew said it."

"When?"

"This evening."

"Well," said Nancy, "there's one point on which Andrew and I are agreed."

"Oh. Don't you like Andrew?"

Nancy Strong chuckled: "My dear, it is I who am setting the trap for you, not you for me. I have cross-examined too many hundred children—some of them were famous men, and some were Tibetan orphans, and some were scoundrels—to let anyone turn the tables on me. I won't tell you what I think about Andrew Gunning. But I'm going to say what I think about you.—Now, would you like some tea before we begin?"

"No, thanks."

"I won't offer you whiskey, because I want your undivided attention and no back alleys open for your thought to slide away into and hide. I'm going to make you face yourself."

"Nancy, I believe that fundamentally you're cruel."

"No. I despise cruelty. If you would rather go to bed, now, and—"

"And be despised as a coward! No, Nancy, you may go ahead. But it feels in advance like having to face an operation without anaesthetic."

The cat, whose face resembled Lobsang Pun's, returned and sprang

276

into Nancy's lap, purring like a kettle.

CHAPTER 9

There was no sound but the splashing of rain through the open window. Andrew leaned back in his chair and watched Bulah Singh with an expression that puzzled the chief of police, who was accustomed to reading fear or treachery or insolence, or all three, on the face of a victim. He intended to victimize Andrew. Andrew knew it. But both men were puzzled. Neither tried to make a secret of it. It was better tactics not to. For a few moments the Sikh walked around the room like a wrestler pondering which hold to try next. He even flexed his shoulders.

"See here," he said suddenly, "I'll be frank with you."

"Yes. We agreed we'd do that."

"I've made inquiries about you in Columbus and Cincinnati."

"Fifty, fifty," said Andrew. "I've the lowdown on you, from unimpeachable sources."

Bulah Singh looked stung. His voice went a quarter-note higher, sour-sharp: "My information is that you left home in embarrassing circumstances."

Andrew chose silence.

"You were employed in a law office, in Cincinnati. Is that right?"

"Yes. I got fed up with criminal law."

"So I have been given to believe. Shall we go into details?"

"Not if you want to continue the conversation," said Andrew. "There are things I don't talk about. That's one of them. Shall I put it more plainly? I mean—"

"Oh no. Sit still. I understand you very well. I wish you to understand me."

"Maybe I'm too dumb to understand you," Andrew suggested. "And you're using marked cards. But go ahead. Try me."

"Being a secret agent you will have no difficulty in grasping my meaning exactly. I'm an older man than you. I've had more experience. But we both know how many beans make five."

"I'm not in your class," Andrew answered. "But if you'll quit walking about like a caged animal I'll try to get what you're driving at. Sit down and drink your whiskey."

Bulah Singh resumed his seat and lighted a cigarette. He looked exasperated, but he evidently needed something too badly to risk taking offense. Andrew offered him no help whatever; he just sat still and waited until Bulah Singh resumed:

"You know as well as I do that from the bottom, all the way up to the top, every policeman and every intelligence officer has his own grapevine, his own informants, who report to him, and, who receive a certain amount of protection—or shall we call it immunity from interference—in exchange for secret information, *et cetera*. Make a note of that word et cetera."

"Yes," said Andrew. "It's a word like a conjurer's hat. Go ahead."

"All governments conduct their secret intelligence service on the same principle," said Bulah Singh. "The value of the number one man depends on his access to exclusive secret information. On that depends his ability to get things done without revealing his own hidden hand. There isn't a police or a secret service system in the world that isn't run on that basis."

"Well, you should know about that," said Andrew. "I guess you've made a study of it."

"An intensive study. A lifetime study. But there are other important points. One must be in a position to reward an efficient agent. And one must have such a hold over that agent that he can't run out, or dare to misinform, or double-cross, or disobey. You get me?"

Andrew nodded. "Sure. Club in one hand, cash in the other."

The Sikh promptly corrected him: "A club certainly, yes. But information that has to be paid for in currency seldom is worth what it costs. Besides, you don't need money. I know the amount of your bank balance. The point is that you wish to return to Tibet. And though you deny it, I know you are an agent of the American Government."

"I do deny that," Andrew answered. "Want to bet about it?"

The Sikh stiffened. "Perhaps you also deny a special interest in the lady who calls herself Elsa Burbage?"

"No. You're getting hot now. I'm concerned about her."

"I, also," said Bulah Singh. "If it should be made possible for you to enter Tibet—this is confidential, of course, strictly between ourselves—Elsa Burbage would remain here. Do you get my meaning?"

"No. Put it in plain words."

"You know, don't you, that Germans, and Russians, and Italians who wish to travel abroad—or who are sent abroad on diplomatic, or on business errands, are obliged to leave behind as hostage to guarantee good faith, some friend, or member of their family—parents perhaps—or a mistress, whose personal welfare is—well, you understand me, don't you?"

"Use plain speech. Say it."

"As I reminded you once before, there is no India Office visa on your passport. You can be run out of the country. So can Elsa Burbage, for having entered Tibet without official permission."

"You're out of your depth there," said Andrew. "Elsa's passport does bear an India Office visa. She can't be deported."

"Yes she can. I happen to know that she is Mrs. Tom Grayne, secretly married. So it's a false name on her passport. And there's a law against adultery in India. The little question of social morality enters in— nothing important in your eyes or mine—but—ah—a very convenient excuse for dealing drastically with the indiscreet. Adultery, being a public scandal, comes within the scope of police authority. A married woman, travelling in suspicious circumstances, alone with a man who is not her husband; and who is lodged, together with her unregistered baby, in a Buddhist monastery of all improbable places— and whose baby dies conveniently in spite of expert medical attention—comes well within reach of the law. Now—do we understand each other?"

Andrew answered coolly: "I don't think you understand me or Elsa Burbage."

Bulah Singh showed his wonderful teeth in a smile that was meant to intimidate. It almost did. For unless Dr. Morgan Lewis should know how to prevent it, Bulah Singh might make sordid accusations stick; and sheer malice might make him attempt it if Andrew should refuse to have dealings with him. It seemed as if Bulah Singh could read the thought behind Andrew's eyes:

"There is nothing more perilous, and therefore foolish," he remarked, "than to say no, to a secret proposal, when it is made in good faith by such a person as me. I am not a mere policeman. I am one who foresees coming events. The time for you to have said no was when we began our conversation. Now is the time to say yes."

Andrew subdued the impulse to use fists and feet and pitch the Sikh into the corridor. The Sikh spotted that. He loved to see a proud man forced to subdue anger. His own dark eyes brightened with amusement.

"What's the proposal?" Andrew demanded.

"You have heard of the Ringding Gelong Lama Lobsang Pun?"

"Sure. We were speaking of him just now."

"You have heard also of Ambrose St. Malo?"

"Yes. What about him?"

"Ambrose St. Malo," said Bulah Singh, "is an incorrigible scoundrel with genius for audacity. He is less scrupulous than a sacred ape. He accepts anyone's money. At present I believe he is being paid by Japan. But perhaps by Russia. He has crossed Tibet from Sinkiang, and to my actual knowledge he is looking for the Lama Lobsang Pun, who is in hiding. Ambrose St. Malo's purpose is to make sure of Lobsang Pun in order to capture the infant Dalai Lama and spirit him away into Sinkiang to sell him to Russia or Japan, I don't know which, and it makes no difference which."

"And where do you come into the picture?" Andrew demanded.

"It is my opportunity. Yours, too. Do what I tell you, and you may name your own reward."

"You must take me for a damned fool," said Andrew. "You couldn't buy a *coolie* with that kind of talk."

The Sikh ignored the comment and went straight to the point. "The infant Dalai Lama is the best bet in all Asia. Do you realise that? Whoever controls him, controls the subtle undercurrents that are the real, as distinguished from the superficial, political forces. Whoever brings the infant Dalai Lama to India, for protection—now do you get my meaning?"

"Yeah—but why can't you say it? There are no witnesses. You want Johnson's job. That's the idea, isn't it? You think you'll have a good chance to get it if I'll do the difficult dirty work, kidnap the baby Lama, bring him here and chuck him into your lap, to prove what a statesman you are. I won't do it."

"I don't want Johnson's job. And you can't afford to refuse my offer or my terms," said Bulah Singh. Andrew grinned obstinately: "I'll see your hand. What have you got?"

"I have you and Elsa Burbage."

"And a damned small kit of scruples, I imagine."

"If you go to Tibet on my terms, Elsa Burbage will be well taken care of at this end."

"By You?"

"Yes."

"Have you spoken about it to her?"

"Yes and no," said the Sikh. "I haven't mentioned your returning to Tibet. Even the best women are dangerous, intuitive creatures. They jump to conclusions and behave unpredictably. She is more than intuitive. She is clairvoyant. I wish to talk to you about that."

"Well, what of it?"

"Do you happen to have read a book called Man, the Unknown by Dr. Alexis Carrel?"

"Yes, I have the book in this room. One of your undercover men left fingerprints on two or three of the pages when he went through my effects. I wish you'd tell those filthy buzzards of yours to wash their hands before they come trespassing."

The Sikh smiled. "We were speaking of clairvoyance. Dr. Carrel is, I believe, the first really eminent western scientist who has dared to make the downright statement that clairvoyance is a scientific fact. He isn't one of those stuffy fools who confuse it with spiritualism and mediumship. He admits it's a demonstrated truth that clairvoyants can perceive the past, the present, and the future at one and the same time."

"I'd give a dollar to know what you're driving at," said Andrew. "Why don't you come to the point?"

"The point is this: clairvoyance is the means by which news is transmitted throughout Asia—especially India. There is nothing fantastic about that. It always has been so, and Indians have always known it. There are fully accredited instances of news having been transmitted from end to end of India faster than the telegraph could do it. Even Lord Roberts mentioned it in his biography. I speak as a realist—as a dealer in accurately ascertained, checked and correlated facts. It has been possible in numbers of instances to make an accurate time check and to prove beyond possible doubt that an occurrence, such as an earthquake or a death by accident or murder, and the receipt of the news hundreds of miles away, were simultaneous. So much for perception of the present: time and space, as commonly defined, have no existence for the clairvoyant. It is not known how the thing works. But we know that it does. I know that it does. So do you. So do hundreds of other people, of whom some are scientists, some are crazy with religion, and some are so mad that they have to be locked up."

Andrew sat still, studying Bulah Singh's ice-cold fury of concentration. The Sikh was long past the stage of excitement. He was letting flow the stored-up flood of conviction, which made him feel superior to Andrew, whom he suspected of moral cowardice. He wasn't afraid to manipulate mental dynamite. Andrew was afraid and would have to be forced. Contempt of Andrew as a mere prospective tool of his own higher intelligence blinded him to the fact that Andrew's contempt was as hot and living as his own was cold and cruel.

"You seem sold on that stuff," said Andrew.

"Sold? Are you—"

"You appear to believe."

"Believe? I know. I know more. I speak as a professional criminologist. Exact facts and statistics are my meat, tools, weapons. You may dismiss doubt when I tell you I know scores of instances of clairvoyant reading of the past. To my certain knowledge criminals have used it, and crime has been detected by the same means. The evidence has been obtained that convicted the prisoners. Do you believe it?"

"Belief is easy," said Andrew. "The trouble with me is that I never believe what I believe, if you get my meaning."

"You're a sceptic, are you? Well, that's in your favour. But listen to this. I speak plainly. I know eighteen instances—I have a record of them, fully documented and attested—of exactly accurate clairvoyant reading of the future. The predicted events came to pass exactly as clairvoyantly foreseen, in every detail. Now then. Do you see what I'm driving at?"

"No," said Andrew. To have said yes might have stopped the Sikh's self-revelation. Not improbably Morgan Lewis might—

The Sikh detected the thought. He stood up suddenly and stared down at Andrew: "Understand, Andrew Gunning! I don't permit my private conversation to be used as gossip. I know how to deal with offenders. Dr. Morgan Lewis is a *dilettante*—an amateur. He is inquisitive about telepathy. He may ask questions about me. If you value your life—I said life— did you hear me?—don't answer his questions."

Andrew grinned into that opening easily, smoothly: "I'd a notion you hadn't got me right, Bulah Singh. I make no one-sided bargains—not if I know it. There's only one way you and I can hit it off. Show cards. Make a square proposition. If you've something to sell, trot it out and let's look at it."

Forced again on the defensive the Sikh changed his tactics: "I can have you arrested."

"Sure you can. But what for? And can you make it stick?"

"Spying. I have copies of your correspondence."

"I know that," said Andrew. "Have you noticed I'm worried about it?"

"I have a list of all your hide-outs between here and that cave near Shig-po-ling where Tom Grayne is waiting for you."

Andrew laughed: "Hell, you're not offering to sell me that, are you?"

"I am not selling. I am telling you."

"Can't you tell it sitting down?"

Bulah Singh remained standing. His mouth was a symbol of ruthless and now reckless greed. Not money greed, but greed for power. He began taking chances now:

"I have what you Americans call the goods on Mu-ni Gam-po. I can use you as a means to ruin him, use him as a means to ruin you. I can throw your friend Tom Grayne to the wolves by arresting you and seizing the supplies you want to take to him. And I can make things very unpleasant for Elsa Burbage."

"But you haven't done it," said Andrew. "Why not?"

"Because I wish you to go to Tibet. I will arrange your escape across the border. Someone else, whom I have in mind, shall be blamed for it. I have it all thought out. You and Tom Grayne, with or without the co-operation of Lobsang Pun and Ambrose St. Malo, shall bring the infant Dalai Lama to India, and—"

"And what?"

"This is important."

"Why don't you come to the point? Are you scared to say it?"

"Elsa Burbage will be the hostage for the fulfilment of your bargain with me."

"You've said that already."

"I have been unable to persuade her to use clairvoyance in connection with inquiries I am making."

"Yeah. She said you asked her to listen in on a third degree or something like it. Turned you down, eh? You'll get nowhere along that line. She detests clairvoyance."

The Sikh pointed a finger at Andrew's face and stared along it as if he were sighting a gun: "You will change Elsa Burbage's mind about that. You will point out to her that your safety, and Tom Grayne's safety, and the success of our plan, and her own immunity from—call it persecution if you want to—depend on her cooperation with me."

"What kind of cooperation?"

"She will put her clairvoyance and her telepathic faculty at my disposal during the entire period of your absence in Tibet."

"What for?"

"For my purposes. She will report to me, exactly, in full detail, every clairvoyant or telepathic vision she receives. And she will obey me in the matter of sending messages at my dictation."

"And if she refuses?"

"So much the worse for her and for you and Tom Grayne."

"So that's it, eh?"

"Yes. And your answer is yes! Or take the consequences! Secrecy, of course, is essential. I warn you, I have made all arrangements to stop your mouth, and hers, too, forever, if one word of this should leak out."

An auto horn tooted in the street below the window. Andrew felt relieved. The Sikh looked savage. He thrust out his lower jaw and spoke slowly, in a level voice:

"Here comes Morgan Lewis now, with my car. Drop one hint to him of what I've said to you and—well—take the consequences."

CHAPTER 10

There was plenty of firelight from the hearth. Nancy Strong got up and switched off the electric light. The leaping shadows made the room seem smaller and more cosy. In the dimness Nancy Strong looked younger and less rugged but even more outwardly calm and inwardly alert. She sat down facing Elsa, studied her for a minute or two, then suddenly:

"Elsa, my dear, *the meek shall inherit the earth.* They always do. But who wants it? The pigs want it. But who else?"

"Pigs?"

"Yes. Poets create their own world. Pigs can't. The pig in every one of us destroys what the poet creates."

"What are you talking about?"

"You and the earth. Pigs and poets. Poet—you and pig—you. The earth is a synonym for what the Communists and Fascists and economists sell their souls and other people's bodies for. That's what you're trying to do."

"Communist? Fascist? Pig? Poet? Me? I don't want the earth. I don't own a yard of it. I don't understand you."

"You will presently. You must get into your head first that meekness and humility are opposites. You're meek. You've got to change."

"How?" asked Elsa.

"By turning it inside-out and becoming humble."

"Show me."

"Humble as Jesus."

Elsa rebelled instantly. All she needed was something to set her teeth into. "I don't like Jesus. Fed up with him. Don't believe in him."

"You mean you don't want to be crucified."

Elsa turned that over in her mind for several seconds. Then she said: "Nobody wants to be crucified."

"At the moment you're headed straight for it," said Nancy. "Why do you wish to return to Tibet?"

"Because it feels like the right thing to do, and I can think of nothing else to do."

"Does it feel like running away? Or like going forward?"

Elsa pondered that for a moment, then answered: "It feels like a fight."

"Against what? Kicking against what St. Paul called the pricks?"

"Damn St. Paul! I like him even less than Jesus. I'm not the least afraid of Tibet. I can endure anything—anything except the feeling that life's meaningless and I'm useless. Perhaps it's me that I'm fighting. I don't know. But why should my baby have died? All that agony for nothing—not that the agony mattered one bit, if only something worth while had come of it. Waste! Faith, hope, charity—all wasted!"

"Whose charity?"

"Andrew Cunning's."

"I don't believe it!" said Nancy. "If I thought Andrew Gunning really guilty of charity I would forbid him the door."

"You? You of all people?"

Nancy Strong chuckled: "Yes, I'm a rich hater—a poor pitier. I detest and despise strong hypocrites. There's some excuse for the weak ones. Andrew Gunning is strong. But I think he isn't guilty. Do you know any Greek?"

"Yes. Some. Forgotten most of it. Why?"

"*Agape* is the word that St. Paul used in Thirteenth Corinthians. It doesn't mean charity. That was a lazy mistranslation of a word that needs thinking about. Charity is sheer insolence. It always begins as an imposition on the meek, and it's all that the meek deserve. At first they like it. They experience the kind of gratitude that means a craving for more. They suck it dry, like ticks on a sick cow. It works both ways. It enlarges the insolence. And it makes the recipients greedy—pig—meek until it becomes old-fashioned slavery and destroys itself, dies of its own corruption, like smallpox and degeneracy and any other disgusting thing you can think of—eats itself up."

"Nancy, I supposed you were a charitable woman."

"God forbid!"

"Isn't this school a charity?"

"Over my dead body! '*Ayarn*', in the sense that St. Paul used the word, means milk of human kindness."

285

"What's the difference?"

"All the difference between plus and minus, good and evil, truth and untruth. Charity is sometimes a line of least resistance, sometimes a form of social blackmail, sometimes superstition, but never better than a substitute for kindness."

"Aren't you splitting hairs?" Elsa suggested.

"I've never split a hair, nor lied to a child like you, nor told the truth to a fool if I could possibly help it."

"You're in a strange mood, Nancy. Have I upset you by coming here?"

"No. Quite the contrary. Put some more wood on the fire."

Elsa heaped on wood and prodded with the poker until the sparks flew upward. She stared at the fire. Nancy Strong waited until she sat down. Then:

"What did you see?"

"Nothing."

"Don't lie. Time's too precious, Elsa. We have only tonight. Save the lies for the hypocrites. Tell me."

"It didn't mean anything."

"Never mind what it meant or didn't mean. If I tell you correctly what you saw, will you admit it?"

"Try me. I'm not good at being naked-minded. If I told it, it would sound like nonsense."

"You saw a cavern—Tom Grayne—Andrew Gunning— yourself—two strangers—and Lobsang Pun, facing one another around some loads on the cavern floor."

"Yes. I saw that. But how do you know?"

"What did you hear?"

Elsa stared, hesitating, tense, almost frightened.

Nancy followed up: "Shall I tell you what you heard?"

"If you think you know."

"Lobsang Pun was saying that the sun belongs to everybody; so whoever buys its light is a fool, and whoever sells it is a scoundrel."

"Yes, he was saying that. Nancy! Have you the same affliction I have?"

"I used to be meek about it, too," Nancy answered.

"But how could you see my picture? It was just a daydream like the ones I get when I'm translating Tibetan."

"That wasn't a daydream.—What language was Lobsang Pun using?"

"None that I recall. I expect it was thought-language. It was real, and at the same time unreal."

"You saw colour, form, substance, movement."

"Yes."

"Did you smell anything?"

"Smoke." Elsa glanced at the fire.

"Child, don't fool yourself. Don't run away from it. Deodar knots don't smell like yak-dung."

"Nancy, were you playing tricks? Are you a hypnotist? Were you making me see and hear and smell things?" "No. I don't hypnotize people. That's wicked. Can you see what I'm seeing now?"

"I don't want to."

"Let yourself look—to oblige me:"

"I can't see anything."

"'Where there is no vision, the people perish'! Look again. What do you see?"

"Nancy, please don't insist. I hate it. Tell me how not to see things. Then I'll bless you forever."

"That," said Nancy Strong, "is what I mean by meekness. It's a *nom de guerre* for the subtlest and deadliest sort of conceit."

"I didn't know I had any vanity left. I thought it was all gone, along with my baby and everything else."

"Conceit and vanity are opposites," said Nancy Strong. "We can't get along without vanity. That's consciousness of what we are and can do. Conceit is pretending to be something we're not, or else pretending to be not what we are."

"You seem to be a bigot about definitions."

"I despise them. But you need prodding with something sharp to make you vain and humble. Turn your meekness inside-out!"

"Is that what you teach children?"

"Yes, child. It is what experience has taught me."

Elsa sighed. "Well, let me tell you my side of it, Nancy. I won't whine, but I feel like confidences. If you can see things the way I do—"

"I know what you're going to say."

"Will you let me say it?"

"Yes. Telling it may help you. Go ahead."

"I've been clairvoyant ever since I can remember."

"Most people are, if they only knew it," said Nancy.

"When I was quite young I was whipped for telling lies, because I

287

said I could hear voices, like the Bible people and like Joan of Arc. I did hear voices. But I wasn't believed. So I learned to cover up. There were governesses and people like that who spied continually and tried to make me feel guilty. But there were sometimes months when I wasn't clairvoyant at all, and oh, how good those times were! But the times between kept getting shorter. So I was known as a problem child. That isn't anything to be vain about. It's something to try to forget."

"What sort of child do you think I was?" Nancy asked.

"Oh—did you get punished? Well, you'll understand at least some of it."

"I will make you understand, too, or else die in my tracks," said Nancy. "Go on, tell me."

Elsa shrugged her shoulders. "Doctors. Psychologists. Schoolteachers. Inquisition, and no end to it. Even the vicar, talking about the Witch of Endor and the devils that Jesus cast out of people. And I knew what every one of them was going to say before he said it. They were all stupid. Some of them were cruel. And some weren't even trying to be honest."

"Neither were you," said Nancy Strong.

"I was! I was honest at first. I was even happy about it and felt important. But I learned to tell lies later on to protect myself, if that's what you mean. Once I was in danger of being certified insane because I said the house was going to be broken into by thieves, who would poison the dog and steal the silver. Luckily the thieves did it. That saved me. But I was heartbroken about the dog. After that I was sent to boarding school. And there I was accused of cheating because I sometimes knew the answers without having to work them out."

Nancy Strong chuckled: "How did you try to explain it away?"

"How could I explain? Sometimes I was perfectly normal, as they called it, for weeks at a time. Then I was called stupid and sullen. And when they really did begin to be convinced that I could see and hear things clairvoyantly it was worse than ever. I was a freak. People tried to make use of me, and despised me at the same time. Some people called me a medium. I was accused of all sorts of things—vile things. Boys of my own age seemed to think I was a pervert. I was simply pestered by them—and by girls, too. And the decent boys weren't interested in anything but could I tell their fortunes? When I got older I couldn't even keep a teacher's job. No, Nancy, it's a curse, and it's no use your telling me anything else. With the exception of my uncle, Professor Mayor, and Tom, I haven't had one single even half-pleasant experience in connection with it. Most of them were disgusting, and some were cruel."

"Tell me about your husband," said Nancy. "What was Tom's reaction to your clairvoyance?"

"Tom calls it second-sight. It annoys him because it isn't dependable."

"Good!" said Nancy.

"What do you mean, good? It was tragic. It came between us. He began to get used to my knowing what he was thinking about before he said it. He began to expect that and to count on it. So when it didn't work he didn't believe me, and when it did work he doubted. He thought I was being temperamental, or perhaps critical of him. He began not to trust me so much. Do you call that good?"

"What I meant was that we're getting somewhere. Tell me about Andrew Gunning."

"There is nothing to tell. That is, nothing more than you know. Andrew keeps his thoughts to himself, and he knows how to mask them as a general rule. He carves little wooden images that he gives to people who appreciate them, and—"

Nancy Strong glanced at the mantelpiece, where smiled a six-inch wooden statuette of the Lord Buddha. It vaguely suggested a portrait of Nancy herself.

"Oh, is that one of Andrew's? So it is—I remember when he did it. Well, he does that kind of thing; and reads books; and gets furiously angry when he's thanked for being unselfish and kinder than anyone ever dreamed a man could be. That's almost all I know about Andrew, except that he saved my life when my baby was born, and I sometimes wish he hadn't. I believe he hates me, but he's too generous to—"

Nancy interrupted: "What is your vision of Andrew? Quick! Out with it! Don't pretty it up!"

"A man in the snow, leaning against the wind, leading— leading—"

"Does he ever talk to you about clairvoyance?"

"Hardly ever. He's too considerate. He knows I don't like it."

"Does he ever ask you to see things for him?"

"Never. He never asks anyone to do anything for him. He gives orders, when those are necessary. But he never asks favours. Even when we had to stay at Tibetan monasteries, he always found some way of making the monks feel that it was we who did them the favour. It was the same in the villages we passed through."

"We're getting somewhere again," said Nancy Strong. "Now—are you ready to listen to me?"

"Yes. This time I'll try not to interrupt. I only wanted you to understand before you begin. But please don't ask me to see and hear things. I won't do it. I will go back, and keep my bargain with Tom, but I won't do it for anyone else."

The telephone rang. Nancy Strong went into another room to answer it, behind two closed doors. She was gone a long time. Elsa sat curled in the armchair, staring at the fire, seeing—seeing—past, present and future, all mixed up in one connected movement that obeyed no laws of time and space, but was intelligible. Dr. Morgan Lewis wasn't in the picture at first. But it concerned him. He was there. And when she thought of him she saw him, clairvoyantly, monocle and all, smiling, excited, talking to someone whom she couldn't see. But she knew whom he was talking about.

Chapter 11

Dr. Morgan Lewis knocked twice. He gave Andrew and the Chief of Police plenty of time to assume such poses as they pleased before he walked in. He even turned his back toward them as he closed the door. As he stood wiping his monocle on his handkerchief he looked disarmingly unmelodramatic, mild, harmless—possibly even slightly bored by professional duties.

"It's raining like the devil," he remarked. He adjusted his monocle. "Thanks for the use of the car, Bulah Singh. It's outside. I told the driver to wait for you."

Bulah Singh wasn't deceived. Darkly alert, he vaguely overplayed casualness. "You've been quick," he observed. "Wasn't the consultation serious?"

"The man's dead," Lewis answered. "Poison. You'll get a report."

"Oh? Murder?"

Lewis nodded: "You'll say suicide."

"What do you say?" the Sikh asked.

Lewis stared at him: "Between us three and the four, walls—murder, yes. But who's to prove it?"

"Autopsy, I suppose?"

"Yes, first thing tomorrow. You know the man. He was in jail not long ago. A Japanese."

Andrew did a better job of masking alertness than the Sikh did; he left off scraping out his pipe and looked mildly interested, whereas

290

Bulah Singh's air of indifference was overdone:

"Not the tea-buyer—let me see, what was his name?"

"Koki Konoe," said Lewis, a bit dryly, a bit abruptly.

"A spy," said the Chief of Police. "I remember. He was detained for investigation. We couldn't prove anything."

"It will be even harder to prove," said Lewis, "that someone killed him by making him take his own life."

The Sikh raised his eyebrows: "Suggestion? You don't mean to say—"

"Yes," said Lewis. "But whose?" He was staring hard at the Sikh, who was at pains to look sceptical and slightly scornfully amused.

"Koki Konoe was a pretty good suggester himself," Bulah Singh answered. "If you should ask me, I would call him a first-class hypnotist. But—"

Lewis corrected him: "Third class. Not too good at that, or he wouldn't have lost the duel."

"Duel?"

"Yes, duel. Between duffers. The real experts are rare and not so easy to detect." He turned toward Andrew. "What did you know about Koki Konoe?"

The Sikh lighted a cigarette, watching Andrew.

"Nothing," said Andrew. He was watching the Sikh. The Sikh smiled.

"Didn't you meet him—talk with him?" asked Lewis. "Someone told me you did."

"Oh, yes, I met him."

"Tell us what happened."

"Nothing," said Andrew. "He was here in the hotel, one afternoon. I picked up an English newspaper from a chair in the lobby. He got in conversation by asking for the paper as soon as I'd be through with it."

"What did he talk about?"

"Nothing much. He talked like a man with a bad hangover. I got the impression that he was trying hard to cling to a fading intelligence."

"Very shrewd guess on your part," said Lewis. "What did he talk about?"

"It's a pretty good rule, isn't it, not to tell what people talk about, until you know why you're asked," said Andrew.

"Yes, that's safe," said Lewis, "sometimes."

The Sikh smiled and corrected him: "Always." He made a gesture with his cigarette. He and Lewis stared at each other. Andrew watched both of them. The Sikh's eyes met Andrew's. Lewis dropped his monocle into the palm of his hand and slipped it into his vest pocket.

"Well," said Bulah Singh, "it's getting late. I'll be off. Corpse at the mortuary?"

"Yes—probably there by now. Both doctors refused to sign the death certificate, and I concurred, so they phoned the police."

"I'll look into it," said Bulah Singh.

"You'll find it interesting," said Lewis. "Thanks again for the use of your car."

"Don't mention it. See you tomorrow. So long."

The Sikh walked out. Lewis almost ran across the room: "The phone's in your bedroom?" He closed the bedroom door behind him and was in there several minutes. When he came back he sat down facing Andrew. He was smiling as if well pleased by the phone conversation. He declined Andrew's gestured invitation to help himself to whiskey.

"Now, young man, out with it!"

"Out with what?"

"There are no witnesses. It's between you and me and—"

Andrew interrupted: "No, no. Easy on that stuff. You'll have to employ your regular spies if you want—"

"Gunning, I want confidential information. And I also propose to help you. Don't regard it as a business bargain. Think of me as your doctor. You know the rule: always tell your doctor and your lawyer everything."

Andrew shook his head: "Work in a criminal law office taught me such contempt for squawkers and anonymous informers that I'm leery of becoming one." He grinned genially. "Besides, it was an accepted fact in our office that you can always find a doctor to swear to anything, one side or the other, depending on who pays him."

Lewis raised his eyebrows: "Do you feel more at ease, now that you've fired that barrel? Fire the other one about 'choose your specialist, choose your disease,' and get that off your conscience. Then we'll talk."

Andrew grinned again: "You get what I'm driving at, don't you? I've nothing to sell."

"I wouldn't buy, if you had. I'm inviting your confidence," said Lewis.

"How about yours?" Andrew retorted. "Talking to you is one thing. Squawking to a bureau is another."

"Very well, let's make it personal," said Lewis. "This is between you and me and we'll keep it that way. I knew the Japanese was dead before I left you with Bulah Singh. I hoped Bulah Singh would talk."

"He did."

"I want to know what he said."

"Is it understood and agreed that I'm not squawking for protection, or any rot like that?"

"Understood."

"And I won't be made a party to any local intrigue?"

"Yes. That's a promise. Now then, what did he say?"

"Well, just before you came in, he said he's all set to kill me if I repeat to anyone what we talked about."

"Did he mention names?"

"In that connection yours was the only name that he did mention."

"Thanks," said Lewis. "I suppose the rest of it concerned you and Tibet and Tom Grayne."

"Most of it did. He offered to ease me across the frontier—on terms."

"Wants you, I suppose, to bring the infant Dalai Lama to Darjeeling?"

"Right—first shot. You seem to know your stuff! How did you figure that out?"

Lewis laughed. "It took more shots than a hundred to bring down that bird! Bulah Singh has inflated ambitions. He is a student of ambitions. He knows almost by heart the case histories of at least ten men who have attained power by Machiavellian means—Lenin, Trotsky, Stalin, Mussolini, Hitler, Mustapha Kemal, several South American dictators. Those men all started from scratch, so why shouldn't he? I wish you could see his library. What escapes Bulah Singh is the fact that there are ten thousand failures for one success in that field. He overlooks such elements as luck, time, place and competition. He realised, quite a number of years ago, that an Indian police officer, who plays to the gallery, presently lands in the discard. So he studied clandestine methods of becoming influential. He has been burrowing so hard underground and so far afield that Japan got news of it. Japan sent Koki Konoe to Darjeeling to uncover Bulah Singh's game while pretending to buy tea. Tell me about Koki Konoe. What happened between him and you, here in the hotel?"

"Darned little happened, because I spotted him as a hot wire first go off," said Andrew. "He planted a copy of the London Times in a chair in the lobby. I took the bait deliberately. When we got in conversation he drew my attention to a piece on an inside page about the medical use of hypnotism. On the next page there was a silly season letter from a retired colonel who said he'd seen the rope trick done in India, and photographed it, and found nothing on the plate. Said that was proof of mass-hypnotism."

"So it was," said Lewis. "But go ahead. What happened between you and Koki Konoe?"

"Well, after a bit of talk Koki Konoe gave me his card, with a Darjeeling address in pencil. He remarked he was lonely and needed someone to talk with. He kept the conversation going on the subject of hypnotism, until at last I showed some interest just to find out what his game was. He invited me to come and see him—said he'd show me how it's done. Said he'd teach me some *jujitsu*, too, if I was interested."

"You didn't accept the invitation?"

"No. I was good and wise to him by that time. *Jujitsu* might be up my street, but not hypnotism. I've seen 'em work it in Shanghai, in combination."

"*Jujitsu*," Lewis interrupted, "is a form of philosophy as well as being a system of physical combat."

"You bet it is. Say, those bozos can give you a physical-mental workout and put you to sleep and make you tell your whole past history plus anything else that you happen to know. They can even make you write it down and sign it."

"If you're ignorant, or afraid, or if your will is stronger than your judgment, they can do that without putting you to sleep," said Lewis. "Hypnotism was misnamed due to a misunderstanding of its nature. Hypnos means sleep. But hypnotism isn't a form of sleep. Sleep is a by-product— sometimes. Did you feel any pressure from Koki Konoe?"

"Oh, sure. Something like the impulse that a high-pressure salesman stirs up. Professional gamblers are good at the same thing. So are soma kinds of women. They make you sell yourself. But I know that trick. And he wasn't more than half powered anyhow. So I bought him a drink and walked out on him. Dead, is he? Have you a guess who killed him?"

"Mine may be as good as anybody's guess," said Lewis. "Koki Konoe was sent from Japan to check up among other things on Bulah Singh's negotiations with Ambrose St. Malo."

"So I guessed right? You do know St. Malo?"

"St. Malo and Bulah Singh—have been in correspondence for a long time."

"St. Malo is in Tibet," said Andrew.

"Yes. But they corresponded until recently by way of China, making use of third-class passengers on liners, some of it by word of mouth, some in writing, and some by underlining words in books and magazines."

"Gosh! St. Malo must have long lines out. That game costs money."

"Lots of it. He is spending Japanese and Russian money. But he will sell out of course to the highest bidder in sight at any critical moment."

"For God's sake, what could Bulah Singh bid? He can't get hold of money, can he?"

"No, no. Bulah Singh has no money. He is a student of psychology who thinks he knows more than he does. But he knows some of the rudiments. He understands, for instance, that such a man as St. Malo, who is a crooked gambler going after big bait, can always be taken with small bait if he's stampeded and tempted at the right time. Probably you are the small bait—you and Tom Grayne. I think St. Malo has been told you're coming and counts on using you in Tibet; and that Bulah Singh depends on you to force St. Malo's hand. But we'll get to that later. Let's stick to Koki Konoe for the moment. We knew all about him from our agent in Japan. We had him arrested. Our Indian jails are very well conducted nowadays. Even a chief of police can't interview a prisoner alone, except at the prisoner's own request."

"In that case there's no witness?"

"Theoretically none, within hearing. Both of them counted on that. But there's such a thing as a hole in a wall."

"Dictaphones, too, I suppose."

"Those things are expensive and sometimes inconvenient," said Lewis. "Koki Konoe made the request, so Bulah Singh visited him in the jail. Neither understood the other's language. They had to talk English. We have a full stenographic report of their conversation. Koki Konoe warned Bulah Singh that if he didn't let Tibet alone and drop his intrigue with St. Malo, he'd be liquidated."

"Murdered?"

"He didn't say. He left the suggestion to do its own work. On the surface it probably meant that the Jap secret service would betray Bulah Singh to us. That would be the commonplace procedure. But there was an unspoken threat of murder."

"If you know all this, why don't you arrest Bulah Singh?"

"For several reasons. The least of them is that we lack proof of where Koki Konoe got the poison that—"

Andrew interrupted: "Don't those fellows usually roll their own? I mean, don't they carry it, just in case? I've heard that all the Japs do it"

"Yes, some do, when the job's specially dangerous. But it's usually cyanide. And this wasn't a particularly dangerous job on the face of it. Besides, he was searched thoroughly at the time of arrest. No poison on him."

"What stuff killed him?"

"One of five Tibetan poisons that aren't in the pharmacopoeia. Two are sudden death, quicker than cyanide. One contracts all the muscles and kills in an hour by strangulation. One makes 'em blind and they die painfully in about a week from inflammation of the inner molecular layer followed by an obscure but sudden action on the brain. The fifth kills more slowly— about thirty days as a rule—by direct action on the cerebral cortex. The victim goes mad—reverses things—tells his secrets and makes secrets of trivialities. That was the stuff that killed him. That's why I was sent for."

"You got here after he was dead?"

"Between you and me, no. Secretly I have been here two days."

"Trying to track poison? There are lots of Tibetans in Darjeeling," said Andrew. "Koki Konoe could have bought the stuff."

"But why should he?"

"Scared."

"Of what?"

"Perhaps of Bulah Singh."

"Exactly. But how did Bulah Singh frighten a terrorist expert?"

Andrew laughed sourly: "Any man who knows the first thing about *jujitsu* should be able to answer that one. Shakespeare called it hoisting 'em with their own petard. The Jap's stuff got used against him. Look at it this way: Bulah Singh threatened me just now with death, if I do any talking. It happens I wasn't scared, so his stuff didn't work, although he convinced me he meant it. Koki Konoe, on the other hand, was scared stiff. Bulah Singh probably took advantage of that and stampeded him into—"

"Rudimentary, but as far as it goes, right," said Lewis. "Almost as much nonsense is talked about hypnotism, by responsible men who should know better, as about clairvoyance and telepathy. The common charlatans and malignant agitators know more about hypnotism than almost any of the so-called authorities even pretend to know. I could name the exceptions on the fingers of one hand. Science is afraid of it, although it has been successfully used in severe mental cases, and even to produce surgical anaesthesia. But repeated attempts to use it, especially in France, have led to scandal and recrimination. Hypnotism, like clairvoyance and telepathy, is an almost unexplored field that reputable men mistrust because of the inevitable reaction on themselves. But they're coming around nowadays to a cautious admission that Mesmer may after all have been on the right track with his theory of some kind of magnetic fluid passing from one person to another."

"What do you think about it?"

"I'm going to tell you," said Lewis, "between these four walls. I've a reason for telling. You mustn't quote me."

"Okay."

"You know the old proverb that *a little knowledge is a dangerous thing.* Very well. Bulah Singh is a dangerous hypnotist because he has a little knowledge. He's a conceited amateur, who considers himself a professional expert. The same was true of Koki Konoe, who was trained by the Japanese secret service. All secret services use it to some extent. The Japs use it a lot, at great personal risk because of their morbid tendency to suicide. The thing is a boomerang. The malicious use of hypnotism—as any experienced metaphysician knows—is always—not sometimes, but always associated with the idea of death. Koki Konoe and Bulah Singh used it against each other, with all possible malice. Most of us use it unconsciously, without much malice and without concentration, in much the same way that we use our other unconscious faculties."

"D'you mean, for instance, that I use it?" Andrew retorted. "See here, barring getting what I pay for in the way of plain obedience from men who hire me the use of their time, I'm almost fanatical about leaving other folks to do their own thinking."

"That's why I find it worth while talking to you," Lewis answered. "If you'll listen, I think you'll learn something you can use to good advantage. The secret of hypnotism—and it still is an unfathomed secret— resides in the ether, which fills all physical space and permeates all physical matter."

"Aristotle's ether? I thought that was an exploded theory."

"It was. But it no longer is," said Lewis. "We're returning to it. The existence of the ether has been mathematically and photographically proved—quite recently, by two young American scientists. We exist in the ether as fish exist in water. The whole physical, phenomenal universe exists in it. We don't know what its properties are. We think, hate, love, crave, envy—without knowing what we're doing with waves of imperceptible but prodigious etheric energy that the act of thinking causes more or less to concentrate and so to speak change direction. Does that mean anything to you? Perhaps thought—not brain, you understand, but thought—is something like a prism."

"You mean hypnosis is a force conveyed by or through the ether?"

"Perhaps. It's a dark subject. I have studied it, here in India, in the very home of hypnotism, for more than twenty-five years, and I confess that I don't know. But I do know it's the most powerful and dangerous force in the world, and that it's deliberately and constantly being used by people who no more know what it is than a dog knows what geometry is. Hitler, Mussolini, Goebbels, all use it. It'll boomerang them sooner or later. One of its camouflage names is suggestion. Other names are the evil eye, black magic, malicious animal magnetism, voodoo. It has dozens of names and pseudonyms. Propaganda is one of its milder uses. So-called self-hypnosis is one of its common results. It's the secret of all slavery of every kind whatever; of all subjection of one to another. It's the underlying cause of war, and of nearly all disease, poverty, misery, and injustice. Every effort to control or modify it is a vector that merely shifts the velocity."

"Bit of an alarmist, aren't you?" said Andrew.

"Not in the least," Lewis answered. "But I'm not an ostrich. Burying one's head in the sand of statistical facts is no more a protection against hypnotism—mass and personal—than it is against day and night."

"But you figure you know the answer?" Andrew didn't try to look anything but sceptical. He was wearing his obstinate grin, with his eyebrows lowered. "What is it? If you know, why not tell?"

"The answer," said Lewis, "is spiritual. It has been well told quite a number of times."

"You mean religion? Whose religion?"

"Any religion," said Lewis, "that isn't ecclesiastical and consequently based on mob-psychology. I'm not denouncing the regular repetition of words and songs. Those serve their purpose. They're about as useful as a bedside manner during diagnosis."

"Well then, what do you mean?"

"I mean the kind of education that Nancy Strong's pupils get."

Andrew whistled softly. He thought a moment. "Nancy," he said, "could pull the bung out of a barrel of Sphinxes and make 'm all tell what they forgot ten thousand years ago. What's more, they'd like doing it. But—isn't she one of your hot wires?"

Lewis ignored the question. "She is the only genuine Christian I know," he remarked. "I don't doubt there are lots of others, but I haven't met them."

"I would never have guessed you're a religious man," said Andrew.

"I'm a realist," said Lewis. "I don't believe in ignoring facts because they're metaphysical, or in letting the material tail wag the spiritual dog. I investigate facts to discover the truth about them."

"That's what Bulah Singh claims he does."

"But I simultaneously believe in the teachings of Jesus Christ," said Lewis. "Bulah Singh doesn't."

"Why should he?" said Andrew. "I'd hate to admit I agree with Bulah Singh about anything worth mentioning, but—"

Lewis suddenly changed the subject: "Hasn't Bulah Singh designs on Elsa Burbage?"

"He sure has," said Andrew. "He wants her here in Darjeeling. That was one of his conditions. But what has Jesus to do with it?"

"Did he say why he wants her here?"

"Yes. As a hostage for my behaviour in Tibet."

"Nothing else?"

"Yes. Clairvoyance. Telepathy."

Lewis laughed dryly. "I thought so. That's why I sent her to Nancy Strong. If Bulah Singh had a chance, he'd hypnotise her."

"He'll not get the chance. You needn't worry on that score," said Andrew. "But if he had her alone, do you think he could do it? Elsa's in a strange mood at the moment. She's good stuff. She's more intelligent than—"

Lewis laughed again. "Gunning, my boy, the more intelligent they are, and the stronger-willed they are, the easier they are, unless they know the answer. Bulah Singh made Koki Konoe kill himself."

"It beats me how he did it, or how you know he did it."

"The easiest victims," said Lewis, "are the intuitive, inspirational people. If they're unsuspicious and good-natured, so much the worse, because then they are more sensitive to impulse. It induces in them extremes of uncritical and unbalanced altruism. It produces our familiar friend the wishfulfilment complex. It drives some of them mad. The next easiest are the criminals who themselves dabble in hypnotism. It isn't difficult to understand how their stuff gets turned against them."

"Tell it. I'll try to follow you," said Andrew.

Lewis thought for a moment. "Perhaps a guess might help. Did Bulah Singh suggest to you that he knows something discreditable about your past in the United States?"

Andrew looked startled. "Yes, he did."

"Did he try to work up fear on that account?"

"Yes. But it didn't come off."

"Did he suggest by any chance that he could make a scandal about you and Elsa Burbage?"

"Yes. Damn him."

"And perhaps that he could starve Tom Grayne in Tibet by obstructing you?"

"Yes. He said that too. But how do you know?"

"After that, he made his proposal?"

"Yes."

"Well, now let's consider Koki Konoe. He was the criminal-hypnotist type. Bulah Singh, who knows his job as a policeman tolerably well, learned that Koki Konoe had a Hindu mistress. She stole, and delivered to the proper person, very embarrassing proof that Koki Konoe was lining his own pocket at Japan's expense. Buying tea—rigging the figures. So Bulah Singh introduced the fear element into Koki Konoe's thought by dropping a hint about what he knew about that Hindu mistress and the financial trickery. Fear of humiliation is stronger than fear of death, in the Japanese consciousness."

"Yeah—but where did the poison come in?"

"Bulah Singh gave that to Koki Konoe, for the alleged purpose of poisoning the Hindu mistress. Do you see the subtlety of that? Having planted the fear-suggestion, he excited the fear by pretending to supply a death-dealing remedy. But he simultaneously sent the Hindu mistress into hiding. Koki Konoe couldn't find her and so felt sure she had betrayed him. In that way Bulah Singh again increased the fear element. Koki Konoe, remember, had hinted, in jail, that Bulah Singh, might be murdered unless he did as he was told. So the idea of death, as a possible outcome of the conflict, was in Koki Konoe's mind in the beginning, even before Bulah Singh pretended to help him to murder the faithless woman. One good scare after that was enough. The death idea became a boomerang. Bulah Singh told Koki Konoe that the woman actually had betrayed him, and had then died of poison. Koki Konoe would be accused of having murdered her. All lies. But the suggestion, played up by a hypnotist, worked. Koki Konoe swallowed the poison."

"You seem darned cocksure about it," said Andrew. "How do you know all this?"

"Think it over," said Lewis. "How did I know that Elsa Burbage was ill in Darjeeling?"

"So you're clairvoyant?"

"Sometimes," said Lewis. "The difficulty is to prove what I intuitively know."

"Is Bulah Singh clairvoyant?"

"Not he. Perhaps he once was. But not nowadays. My discoveries, rudimentary though they are, have led me to believe that hypnotism and clairvoyance are almost mutually exclusive. Tentatively I define clairvoyance as release from hypnosis. The contrary appears to be equally true: hypnosis blanks out clairvoyance, so that a hypnotist loses his own vision. If I'm right about that, it would account for the phenomenal rise to power, and equally phenomenal fall of any number of people—especially of the criminal type. However, a hypnotist, shut off from clairvoyance—that is to say from vision—by his own thought process, nevertheless can hypnotise an unsuspecting clairvoyant. By that means he can learn what he couldn't possibly clairvoyantly see for himself. It is very frequently done. It is one of the means by which such astonishing confessions are extorted in Russia. Bulah Singh has been privately experimenting along that line for a number of years."

"Good God, why don't you chain that guy up?" said Andrew. "Chuck him in the clink and—"

Lewis laughed. "Gunning, my boy, you know enough criminal law to answer that one."

"Yes, I guess you can't convict a man of hypnotism. Courts would laugh at you."

"Experienced judges wouldn't laugh," said Lewis. "Especially here in India. They know better. But they'd have to demand legal evidence, which would be impossible to produce. Did Bulah Singh frighten you at all? Did he set up any interior worry?"

"Not in the least."

"Are you sure he didn't?"

"Yes."

"That's good." Lewis checked a flicker that would have become a smile if he had let it. "And now a personal matter. Would you care to tell me in confidence what occurred that induced you to leave the United States?"

"No. I never discuss that."

"Very well. But will you answer this? What is the state of affairs between you and Elsa Burbage?"

"She's Tom Grayne's wife."

"You're a moralist, aren't you?"

"Some. I don't go around bragging about it."

"It would shock you to be made the butt of a humiliating scandal about another man's wife?"

"I'd be troubled on her account."

"To avoid that—I mean, to save her from embarrassment—and especially if she should urge you—could you steer quite a different course than the one you have in mind at the moment?"

"Guess so. I could change plans at a moment's notice, if—but what are you driving at?"

"Didn't Bulah Singh suggest a drastic change in your Tibetan plan?"

"Yes."

"Didn't he hint at what might happen if you refuse?"

"He sure did—he even used the word persecution."

"And suggested that he knows about you something that you'd rather not discuss?"

Andrew nodded. Lewis adjusted his monocle. "You begin to understand his method?" He was silent for a moment. Then suddenly: "There are a number of reasons why we don't, at the moment, choose to remove Bulah Singh."

"Giving him more rope to hang himself?"

"We have our eye on him," said Lewis. "I frightened him purposely just now by talking about Koki Konoe."

"Well, I guess you know your business. But why scare him? Won't he cover his tracks?"

"No. They are covered. He will try to uncover mine," said Lewis. "And he may perhaps hasten his arrangements—may step things up a bit. I believe you will find Bulah Singh at Nancy Strong's house."

"But it's after midnight."

"That's nothing. Nancy's a night owl."

"Say—d'you suppose Bulah Singh knows Elsa isn't at the monastery?"

"Certainly he knows," said Lewis. "He is watching me like a cat. Why do you suppose I went to all that trouble to lay a smoke-screen, if not to make him think he is outwitting me?"

"I wish we had left Elsa in the monastery," said Andrew. "She was safe there."

"Bulah Singh couldn't have got at her there," Lewis answered. "I want her got at! I phoned Nancy just now to expect him. I feel sure that's where he went."

"You don't say." Andrew got up, hesitated from politeness, and then hinted bluntly: "Where are you staying tonight?"

Lewis laughed: "Here in your bedroom. May I? There are two beds. I may turn in. I'm a bit tired."

"You'll find all you need in the bureau drawer," said Andrew. "Help yourself. It's a long walk to Nancy's and no taxi at this time of night. I'll get going."

"I advise you to take that boot with you. It might cause complications if you leave it"

Andrew picked up Elsa's boot and tucked it under his arm.

"Careful!" said Lewis. "No breach of confidences! And above all, no explosions!"

"Okay."

"You don't look like a dove or a serpent, Gunning, my boy. But try to be as harmless as the one and as wise as the other."

Andrew laughed: "What d'you take me for? A zoo?"

"Emulate one of its inmates! Be observant but inarticulate. Coo, hiss, roar—but don't interpret the noises."

"Okay. So long."

"So long. Goodnight. I'll lock the door," said Lewis.

CHAPTER 12

Nancy Strong returned into the room, took the large photograph of Lobsang Pun in its silver frame from the small square table and set it on one of the armchairs in full firelight, facing Elsa. It was an age-less face, almost incredibly wrinkled, apparently not dark-skinned, but weathered. Beneath a *lama's* peaked hood, roguish Chinese-looking wise eyes gazed straight forward, seeming to see everything but to

303

tell nothing. The nose suggested an eagle's beak. The eyes combined a bird's bright far-sightedness and a cat's experienced incredulity; they were unconquerable eyes, interested, amused, unafraid. The portrait stirred memories that poured as daydreams into Elsa's thought. Nancy Strong interrupted:

"You recognise him?"

Elsa came out of reverie: "Of course. Who could forget him? But why Lobsang Pun so suddenly? Don't you want me to know that Dr. Lewis phoned you about me?"

"Tell me what you think about Lobsang Pun."

"You don't want to talk about Dr. Lewis? Oh, very well. But, Nancy, what difference can it make what I think about—"

"Tell me what you think about Lobsang Pun. Look straight at his portrait and tell me. I want to know."

Elsa stared at the portrait. "I don't understand him. I never did. He's an enigma. Tom likes him better than I do. He struck me as a tremendously powerful personality, but scornful and—"

"Scornful of what?"

"I don't know. Scornful and decidedly cruel."

"Was he cruel to you?"

"Yes. He was kind on several occasions, and almost courteous in his own high-handed way, but he could be as brusque as a gust of wind. He said astonishing things in broken English. He made me feel I was being laughed at. But I couldn't help liking him, most of the time. Yes. I like him."

"Did he laugh at, or with you?"

"I don't know. He laughed. He seemed to me cruel, and as ruthless as he is ugly to look at. He seemed to have no feeling of obligation or gratitude. After Tom had helped him to seize the Thunder Dragon Gate—and mind you, Tom took tremendous chances—he turned Tom and me out to shift for ourselves. Gave us no help whatever, beyond replenishing our supplies and exchanging some fresh ponies for our exhausted ones. I should say Lobsang Pun is a hugely intelligent and very dangerous man, who doesn't care twopence whose toes get trodden on when he—"

Nancy Strong interrupted: "Elsa, my dear, for nine years I was that man's *chela*."

"You? You, Nancy, a *chela*? You mean Lobsang Pun is a—then you are—"

"He is my teacher. I lived with him for nine years on terms of the

304

closest possible spiritual intimacy. I have wandered with him all over Tibet, and into China. I was with him in Peking, Tokyo and Seoul. This school was his doing. He ordered it."

"You mean it's Lobsang Pun's school?"

"No, no. Nothing like that. It's my school. As you remarked, he is ruthless. But I don't think you know what ruthless means. Scornful, but you don't know what of. He despises the conceit of fools who think their brains are the boundaries of wisdom, and that what their brains can't define can't possibly be true. I told him one day in Lhasa that I believed I could teach children what he had been teaching me. He said: go the Darjeeling and do it. It seemed impossible. I hadn't a *rupee*. But he told me to get out and go to Darjeeling and use my vision, instead of being afraid of myself, like a devil looking at its own reflection in a dirty mirror. He was ruthless. He wouldn't listen to my pleading for advice and help. He drove me away. It would take too long to tell you how I reached Darjeeling. But when I got here there was money in the bank, waiting for me."

"Whose money?"

"The money belonging to me and the children who were to come to my school and be waked up. Coin of the realm—good legal currency. Fools refuse to realise that one of the dimensions of every real idea is affluence. I was a fool, and afraid. But he wasn't. The money came quite naturally through business channels. All I had to do was sign a legal document. But it wouldn't have come; that money would have gone to someone else; it would never have entered my consciousness if I had disobeyed because of what I used to believe before I met Lobsang Pun."

"It sounds like a miracle, the way you tell it," said Elsa. "I used to believe in miracles. I've read Mrs. Eddy's books and some of Madame Blavatsky's. I believed in the loaves and fishes, and Elijah and the ravens—and even Lazarus, and the Resurrection. Honestly I did. I thought it was a miracle when Tom met me in the British Museum and offered me the chance to come to India. It seemed to be an answer to prayer. But now I don't believe, and I don't pray any more. I wish I did. Credulous people are better off."

"So you prefer conceit to credulity? God won't come into your trap, so you don't believe in God. Is that it?"

"Nancy, please explain what you mean. I don't feel conceited. Not meek either. I feel resentful, and bitter, and wish I didn't."

"You're in danger of becoming a convinced and self-convicted fool, imprisoned in fear."

"Nancy, I don't feel afraid. Really I don't. I'm willing to face anything except—"

"Except the key of the prison. And the open door. And life—faith—hope—courage!"

"Nancy, I have got courage. I'm just disillusioned, that's all. Life looks hideous."

"Would you call Lobsang Pun beautiful?"

Elsa laughed: "He's almost comically ugly. He must be almost the ugliest man in the world. Even his Tibetan servants used to refer to him as Old Ugly-face."

"Lobsang Pun's face is as ugly as the surface of life," Nancy Strong answered. "But look beneath the surface. I learned from that man all the faith that's in me and all that I know about beauty, truth, kindness, affluence and nowness, as dimensions of ideas."

"Dimensions? Of ideas?"

"Yes. Every genuine idea that ever was, or is, or will be, has all those dimensions, along with lots of others."

"But, Nancy, how can you talk such nonsense? How can an idea have dimensions? You can't conceive of a long or a short idea."

"Of course not. True dimensions are not boundaries or limitations. Space and time are like a frame that we look through. An idea hasn't time and space. It has completeness. That includes beauty, kindness, nowness. There's no distance in connection with it. Where did you get your ignorance? Whose particular wool is pulled over your eyes? Who taught you?"

"Oh, numbers of people have tried to. I've read tons of books—some of them are here on these shelves—Plato, Nietzsche, Kant, Schopenhauer—Spengler—Karl Marx—"

"But not the Twenty-third Psalm."

"Indeed, I know it by heart."

"What is the first line?"

"'*The Lord is my shepherd, I shall not want.*'"

"Good. Stop there. That's the whole secret. It's the one important thing to know and remember. All other knowledge is merely relative to that."

"But it isn't true, Nancy. I know it isn't. I've proved it's a lie. I used to believe it. I tried to prove it. I took everything I had—hope, faith, enthusiasm, trust in God, whoever or whatever He is, and offered them up—oh, how ungrudgingly. I hadn't a single mental reservation. I was simply enthusiastic and eager to live. Life felt suddenly like flowers in a garden in spring. I threw pride overboard, and money, and a career, and the good opinion of the few friends I had. I said: the Lord will provide. And now look at me. I haven't even my baby. And I haven't Tom Grayne's confidence. I'm married to him. I seduced him. He isn't really my husband."

"But you're going back to him?"

"Yes. Thanks to Andrew. Gunning's generosity. I like Tom. I admire him. I love him. But he doesn't love me. He never will. I'm a liability and he's too manly to admit it. So I'm returning to Tibet to set Tom free. After that I don't care what happens."

"No? But as I understand it you agreed, before you married, that either might divorce the other if—"

"Yes. It wasn't supposed to be a real marriage. It was an alliance."

"Do you remember what Talleyrand said about that?"

"No. Wasn't he Napoleon's Judas? I've been Tom Grayne's Judas."

"He was Napoleon's confidential minister. He said: 'Every alliance is a horse and rider.'"

"That sounds like one of those generalizations. But perhaps it's true. At any rate, I'm like an old man of the sea on Tom's shoulders, and he knows it, and I know it, and—"

"Isn't it a long way to go, just to tell Tom Grayne what he knows already?"

"A long way. Yes. But it's better than running away."

"And yet you're running from something nearer."

"What do you mean? I'm not running. I'm facing the fact."

"Something nearer than breathing, closer than hands and feet."

"You mean Tennyson's God? I don't believe in God. I did. But I don't now."

"I mean your vision."

"I haven't any. You mean clairvoyance? That's a disease!"

"Elsa, it is the substance of things hoped for. It is the evidence of things not seen by—"

"Nancy, it's naked hell! You ought to know, if you have the same affliction. I can't imagine how you endure it and keep your faith in—"

"Will you let me tell you?"

"Yes, if you won't be cruel about it. Don't tell me to count my blessings. I have a curse that outweighs all of them, and—"

"Listen, child. I am going to cell you in the fewest possible words, what Lobsang Pun took nine years to teach me."

307

"Before he kicked you out of Lhasa without a penny to find your way across Tibet! I call that evidence of cruelty."

"Before he kindly and unsentimentally forced me to do what he knew I could do, and what I wouldn't have done otherwise. No calf ever wants to be weaned."

"Are you going to kick me out? Very well, I'll go the minute you say so."

"I can prevent you from going to Tibet, Elsa. And unless you wake up, I will prevent you. Tibet is no land for a meek mouse. You must be willing to be what you are."

"What do you mean? What do you think I am?"

"Tell me what you yourself think you are."

"I don't know. I have given up trying to know. I feel like a discouraged female in a bad temper. But what's a female? Nothing! Protoplasm and sensation, stuck together with magnetism, and nobody knows what that is, except that it's said to be a form of motion—but motion what of?"

"You are an evidence of evolution."

"Evolution of what?"

"Evolution of consciousness. My dear, you're a proof of St. Paul's statement: 'for now we see through a glass darkly, but then face to face.' You're one degree of evolution ahead of most people. Your glass isn't quite so dark."

"If this is evolution, I'm headed the wrong way!"

"Listen, my dear. You can't prevent it, any more than the crops can prevent the weather. But you can make hell for yourself if you resist; because evolution breaks the moulds of consciousness as the roots of growing trees break rocks. Evolution is a spiritual, irresistible growth— upward and outward from the illusion of solid four-dimensional limited matter."

"Four dimensional?"

"Yes. Time is a dimension of matter. Length, breadth, depth and time. Or, more simply, space-time."

"Evolution upward toward what? Disillusionment? I'm there now."

"Growth toward reality, where the illusion of matter fades, true dimensions enter consciousness, and the secret place of the Most High yields its secret. Child, even now you can see through stone walls and across a thousand miles of mountains to where Tom Grayne is."

"Yes, but I can't make him see me, so it's only torture. I even know

308

what he's thinking about. But I can't warn him. I can see danger, but I can't make him see it. I can't even tell him our baby is dead. Don't, Nancy! Don't! You're seeing, and you're making me see! Please don't!"

"There are rules to be learned. No one can use even a hammer and a saw without knowing the rules. We can't even walk without first learning how to do it, or play the piano without learning the notes."

"Some people can. They do it naturally, without thinking. I can, and I never took a music lesson."

"You obey the rules intuitively. That doesn't make them not-rules. Rule Number One of Evolution, which is the Law of Life, is 'The Lord is my shepherd, I shall not want.'"

"Is that what you teach children! But Nancy, it isn't true! I know it isn't! It's a lie! I want my baby, for instance, and my husband's confidence, and faith that life's worth living, and—"

"Listen to the second rule. It's in the Ninety-first Psalm: '*He that dwelleth in the secret place of the Most High . . .*' You know the rest of it, don't you?"

"Of course. I know it by heart."

"What does your heart tell you?"

"Nothing. A heart is just a physical organ. What I used to believe has turned out so totally false that—Nancy, can you look around at the world, and then believe such piffle? War, cruelty, poverty, sickness, lying propaganda, pain, death—dead babies—not mine only— babies bombed to death in—"

"Listen to the third rule: '*And though I have the gift of prophecy, and understand all mysteries, and all knowledge; and though I have all faith, so that I could remove mountains, and have not the milk of human kindness, I am nothing.*'"

"Oh yes. Thirteenth Corinthians. I had to say it at school and then put sixpence in the poor box. Kindness? I don't even know what it means. I don't know much knowledge; and I've no faith left, although I did have some once; but I don't believe I ever did know what human kindness really means. I thought I was being kind to Tom. The fact is, I was cruel."

"My dear, if you will be kinder to yourself you will learn what skittles facts are."

"Oh, you mean mind over matter? Don't you believe in facts? Isn't it a fact that you and I are here, talking to each other? Isn't your school a fact? Wasn't my baby a fact? Mind can't change that, can it?"

"Try giving mind a chance."

"What do you mean?"

"Accept the fact of spiritual evolution. Recognize it. Trust your clairvoyant vision, and then look at the other facts."

"I can't trust it. I daren't. It's like dreams."

"Master it. Govern it."

"I can't. It runs away with me. It leads me into all kinds of—"

"Stop!"

Nancy Strong glanced at the clock on the mantelpiece. It was a quarter to twelve. She stood up and took a step toward Elsa. The firelight shone on their faces. They were half-reliefs, unreal, bright-eyed, against wavering shadow from which the cat's eyes watched them.

"We've had enough of that hysteria, young woman. Ally yourself one way or the other. Every alliance is a horse and a rider. Ride or be ridden. Tell me what you think your soul is."

"I haven't one:"

"Quite right. Now we're getting somewhere."

"I used to believe the old superstition that I have a soul to be saved from hell. It's a lie."

"Yes, it's a lie. You are your soul. How could you have what you are?"

"What do you mean?"

"You're not a body that has a soul. You are your soul. Soul! You have a body and brain that are no more you than that dress which your body is wearing. Wake up."

"I'm wide awake. At any rate, my brain tells me I am."

"Listen, Elsa. Your brain is no more you than this portrait is Lobsang Pun. Even the most bigoted and stupid second-rate scientists know nowadays that brains can't think. Brains are like radio sets, to be controlled and used and tuned in. They're too often tuned in to the sort of nonsense you've been talking tonight. Your mind is no more in your brain than Lobsang Pun is in his photograph."

"If my brain doesn't think, what does?"

"You do. And you will either believe what your senses tell you, in a glass darkly, or what you see face to face, with your clairvoyant vision. Your brain sees illusion, because it's part of the illusion, and you tune it in to the illusion. It can see reality if you'll let it. Clairvoyance is soul—vision—it's you—the real you—waking— one degree of evolution closer to reality, seeing things more nearly as they really are."

"But, Nancy, it's unendurable. It isn't—"

310

"Learn to control it. Others will do that for you, if you don't."

"How can others control it, if I can't?"

"They will control you without your knowing they're doing it, unless you remember the rules. And if they can't control you they will treat you the way they treated Jesus and Joan of Arc and countless others."

"Didn't Jesus know the rules?"

"Yes. Joan of Arc had soul-vision, but without understanding the rules. She won battles and saved France. But she had wielded the sword. She had accepted the reality of hatred, cruelty and death. You know what happened to her."

"You're not trying to encourage me with her fate, are you?"

"Jesus, on the other hand, had vision and knew all the rules. He rejected the sword, repudiated the brain-mind illusion of matter-substance, and—"

"Yes, and got crucified."

"But arose from the dead."

"You believe that? You don't believe that, do you?"

"I know it. That's different from believing. Whoever believes can disbelieve. I know."

"I wish I even believed."

"Jesus broke once and for all the solid hypnotic illusion of matter-consciousness, and said: 'I go my way.' It's a long way, Elsa. But it's the way of evolution. And they'll Joan of Arc you on the way, unless you remember the rules."

"That sounds cheerful!"

"'Who is not with me, is against me.' Trust the one or the other. The reality or the illusion. But don't try both, or you'll find yourself giving to Caesar the things that are God's and trying to buy God with Caesar's counterfeit credit."

"Nancy, there's no fanatic in me. Really there isn't. You sound as if you're inviting me to be a martyr."

"Yes. But not a fanatic. Martyr means living witness, not dead witness. A witness sees, knows, and gives evidence of the truth and nothing but the truth. A fanatic believes, but doesn't know; so he's afraid. Fear destroys the fanatic's sense of humour and makes him hysterical. A fanatic desires proof of what he believes but can't prove. He tries to create the proofs usually by doing violence to others. But a witness is proof of what he knows. He is it. He is the knowledge itself. He is the secret truth and its evidence."

311

"Why secret?"

"Because the self-styled realists can't see it. Their conceit won't let them see it. If they even believed it blindly they would take your truth and try to use it to strengthen materiality. The power-cravers, the money-hungry, the self-important—the opportunists—will use you, and then lose you, the way the French lost Joan of Arc. They'll canonize you when it's too late."

"Then you want me to see, and say nothing?"

"I am not inviting you to cast pearls before swine. Which side will you be witness for? You or your senses? Spirit or matter? Dark logic or bright intuition?"

Elsa quoted, laughing: "'*Almost thou persuadest me to—*'"

"My appeal is to you. Not the pig, but the poet. The real you. But if it helps you to use logic, use it," said Nancy. "Do you realise that you can't drop a grain of sand into the sea without eventually moving every drop of water in all the oceans in the world?"

"Yes, I read that years ago in the Atlantic Monthly. It seems almost incredible. But I suppose it's true."

"It is mathematically and physically true and demonstrable. But even the sea, as our senses perceive it, is only phenomenal—a part of the illusion of thought. You—you yourself with a grain of sand can move every drop of all those billions of tons of water. How much more then will one thought, violently flung, disturb the whole mass of illusion in which we think we live and move and have our being!"

"Good heavens—then shouldn't we think?"

"Yes. But think. Don't parrot other people's fears at second-hand. See—know—trust your vision—and remember Rule One."

"But not talk about it? Not tell anyone?"

"Not unless you want to be Joan-of-Arc'd by the thought manipulators, propagandists and the devils who use others' vision for their own ends."

"But you're telling it"

"I am talking to you, not to your material illusion. This is a communion, not a battle of brains. 'Where two or three are gathered together in my name ...'"

"I always wondered what that meant."

"Arguing with the crowd increases and enrages the illusion that already blinds them. It makes it easier for hypnotists to control them. That is the sole reason for secrecy. The truth enrages the liars. But one by one, two by two, sometimes three by three, we can find our way out from the illusion of desire, into reality. That makes it easier for all the others to follow."

"Mustn't we desire anything?"

"No. Desire presupposes that we have not. Desire is the exact opposite of real consciousness. Desire for the illusion of material means to the spiritual end made me hesitate to come here and start this school. But I gave up desiring. I obeyed, and came, and found what was needed. It was waiting for me. Desire, hatred, malice are the essence of illusion. They're its substance—what it's made of. They produce war, cruelty, poverty—and in the end disillusion—and then new beginnings. But why exhaust the horrors of illusion before—"

"Mayn't we own anything?"

"You'll find you can't help owning things. But don't let things own you. Never regard things as more than shadows of ideas."

The clock struck twelve. "Midnight," said Nancy Strong. "Middle of nothing. But we can't ignore time as long as we're imprisoned in it. Time waits for no man, and space confines us. But time and space are illusions. You and I can prove it."

The front door bell rang—sudden and loud. The servant's footsteps hurried along the hallway. Nancy Strong sat down.

"Remember," she said, "we can prove nothing, and be nothing, without the milk of human kindness. Even faith is worth nothing without it, and hope is a fool."

"How can you tell it from charity?"

"By its humour. That's the milk of it. Charity has absolutely no humour. True kindness is humour, plus vision and courage."

"Nancy, you don't seem particularly humorous this evening."

"Child, if I had laughed, you might have feared I was laughing at you instead of with you. Who is our visitor? Look."

"You mean go out and—"

"Look. It might be one of three people. Who is it?"

"Bulah Singh" said Elsa. "I can see him on the doorstep. What shall I do? I'm supposed to be ill at the monastery! Can't I escape to my room before he comes in here?"

"Run away if you wish," said Nancy Strong. "But why not face him? He is only a fact. And he has no sense of humour."

CHAPTER 13

Bulah Singh looked at his best as he entered Nancy Strong's big living room. The servant who ushered him in switched on the light, but at a sign from Nancy he switched it off again. The Sikh stood framed in the light from the hall, handsome, important, a shade mysterious. But when the servant closed the door at his back and he walked forward, then the firelight that shone on his eyes showed also the shape of his mouth. His stride was vaguely feline.

"I surprise you?" he suggested.

"No," said Nancy. "But didn't Miss Burbage's movements surprise you? I expected you would come here. Please put some wood on the fire before you sit down."

The Sikh complied. He didn't like doing it. Instead of making him feel at ease it cost him some of the tactical aggressiveness that he had studiously built up. He was aware that, behind his back, Nancy and Elsa were comparing notes—eyes meeting silently and uniting their mental resistance against him. He was at pains to look judicial and self-assured when he sat down, facing Elsa. But it didn't quite work. They formed a triangle, with firelight on their faces, high chair-backs behind them, and beyond that darkness. The cat lay on the hearthrug studying the occasional exploding spits of rain that fell down the chimney. Bulah Singh leaned forward and stroked the cat's head.

"A wet night," he remarked.

"Are you cold?" Nancy Strong asked him. "Would you care for a drink?"

"No, thanks. I came on important business. May I speak with Miss Burbage alone?"

"Why alone?" asked Elsa, wondering at herself. It was her own voice, but it didn't sound like hers.

The Sikh looked hard at her. "Because that may be to your advantage," he answered.

"Official business?" Nancy Strong suggested.

"Not yet. I would like to keep this part of it off the record. I am depending on you to be as discreet as I have known you to be on previous occasions."

"You don't want me to listen? Very well," said Nancy. "Shall I leave you alone together?"

"Nancy, I wish you wouldn't," said Elsa. "I've no secrets from you. I'd much rather you'd stay."

Nancy Strong smiled at the Sikh: "But Bulah Singh" she said, "wouldn't trust an old gossip like me. He knows all—tells nothing. He is like Akhnaton." That was the cat's name.

Bulah Singh was in the wrong mood. He didn't like the remark. "I

314

know some secrets," he retorted darkly. "It is my professional occupation to know what is going on. I was told that Miss Burbage was ill at the monastery. She appears to be quite well. Is it a secret why she was brought here by a back route—why the monks have put her luggage in your godown?"

"I advised it," said Nancy. "Has her luggage come? Good."

"If you had consulted me I would have provided transportation, openly and aboveboard," said Bulah Singh. "It is a good thing she is out of the monastery. That place is a nest of intrigue."

"Mu-ni Gam-po," Nancy answered, "has been my friend more years than I care to count. So I suppose that's a dig at me?"

The Sikh smiled ambushed insolence: "I know more than you suspect. Do you forget my offer to exchange confidences? You rejected it. You preferred to force me, instead, to use other means of finding out what it is my duty to know. Even you can't keep all the secrets."

"Flatterer!" said Nancy.

"May I speak to Miss Burbage, alone?"

"What do you want to talk about?" Elsa demanded. She felt rather contemptuous, strangely enough; but perhaps that was a reaction from Nancy Strong's attitude.

The Sikh looked hard at her: "About Andrew Gunning."

"Oh?"

"Yes."

Elsa felt her heart skip two beats. But when she spoke to Nancy her voice was quite normal: "Is there another room we can go into?"

"No, dear, stay where you are. I will go to my office and wait there. I have a letter to write."

"But you'll be cold."

"No, there's an oil stove. I will leave the office door ajar, so just call out to me when you've finished talking."

The Sikh stood until Nancy Strong left the room and the door shut with a thud and the click of a brass latch. Then, still standing:

"Miss Burbage, you are in a false position," he said abruptly. "You make a mistake when you try to keep your movements secret from me. It can't be done. Why are you here?"

He sat down, bolt upright, his face growing gradually more determined, more menacing, as he watched Elsa's. She was curled up in the armchair with her feet under her, because she had taken off her shoes to dry them at the fire and she didn't choose that the Sikh should see the hole in the toe of her stocking. She looked puzzled. Bulah Singh wanted her well frightened. She realised that. But he also wanted to present himself as a magnanimous official who could excuse and protect if properly respected. She understood that, too. She wasn't being clairvoyant in the usual way. The thought behind the Sikh's words was revealing itself as colour. It was muddy colour, dull red, steel-blue, and gray-green, one appearing through the other and never still for a moment. So she knew he was thinking of several alternatives and hesitating what to say. But she couldn't tell what it was all about, and she felt no alarm.

"I was invited here," she answered.

"Tell me," he said abruptly, "what do you know about Andrew Gunning's past in the United States?"

Elsa frowned, startled, but not frightened, though she felt she should be. There was calculated menace in the Sikh's carefully chosen tone of voice, and in the way his tongue played on his teeth above the outthrust lower lip. She felt that the attack was aimed at herself, not Andrew. Some of Nancy Strong's phrases began flooding her mind. They made no sense, and she didn't believe them, but there they were: proof of evolution—spiritual process—the Lord is my shepherd—milk of human kindness—wake up!

"I mean his history before you met him," said Bulah Singh. "I know enough about your present relationship."

That should have stung, but it didn't. It should have angered her. It didn't. She felt no impulse to answer. The Sikh repeated the question:

"What do you know about Andrew Gunning's past in the United States? He must have told you. Tell me. It is important."

That instant she saw a vision of Andrew. It was a composite memory-portrait. It included Andrew in a snowstorm, heating water on a yak-dung fire, in the lee of a rock, ready for an unborn baby—Andrew carving portraits of Chenrezi—Andrew and Dr. Lewis and Mu-ni Gam-po— but no Andrew at that moment. She had no idea where he was or what he might be doing.

"He has told me very little about America," she answered. "I know he went to college, and played football, and got a degree, and afterwards studied law. He isn't old enough, is he, to have done much more than that?"

"Did he never tell you about a criminal indictment?"

"No."

"For homicide?"

"No."

"Oh well, if you're not in his confidence," said Bulah Singh, "I'd better let things take their course. It might have been possible to save him."

Now she did feel afraid. "Save him? From what? Bulah Singh, what do you mean?"

"Use your clairvoyance!"

"What are you talking about? What has happened? Is Andrew in trouble?"

"Keep calm. He is in serious trouble. Your clairvoyance might help him. It might."

"Is Andrew hurt? Has something happened to him? Quick! Tell me!"

"Will you help him?"

"Of course I'll help him! What is it? Tell me!"

"Make a definite promise."

"If Andrew needs my help I will do anything I possibly can— anything."

"You promise?"

"That is a promise. Bulah Singh, unless you tell me at once what has happened I will ask Miss Strong to phone Dr. Lewis and—"

Bulah Singh interrupted: "Dr. Lewis has been investigating Andrew Gunning, and you too—as I daresay you will realise—if you cast your thought back over recent events."

"Dr.—Morgan—Lewis has—why, he's Tom Grayne's friend—he's my friend—he—"

"In the secret intelligence service there is no such thing as friendship," said Bulah Singh. "Dr. Morgan Lewis was your secret enemy, and Gunning's."

"Was? You said was?"

"Yes. I have serious news. Lewis knew all about Gunning's past in the United States. He found out every detail of his illegal preparations to return to Tibet. Perhaps you know how he found out. Lewis has dabbled for years in telepathy."

Elsa felt herself grow cold with self-accusing fear.

The Sikh continued: "Lewis learned from Mu-ni Gam-po that Gunning intends to find the Lama Lobsang Pun and help him to reach Tom Grayne. That is true, isn't it?"

"I don't know. I won't answer. What has happened to Andrew?"

"I came to ask you to help him. Lewis was a conceited man. He was jealous of me. He called on Gunning this evening and accused him of having bribed me to be deaf and blind to his arrangements to cross the border into Tibet."

"Has Andrew been arrested?"

"Not yet."

"What did happen? Where is Andrew now?"

"Listen carefully." The Sikh's mouth betrayed greedy triumph. His eyes stared at Elsa's. They didn't move. His eyelids didn't blink. He spoke slowly: "Lewis and Gunning quarreled. Lewis now lies dead in Gunning's room at the hotel."

Elsa came uncurled, bolt upright. The cat fled into the darkness.

"Dr. Lewis! Dead? Where is Andrew?"

"On his way to Tibet."

"You mean he's running away?"

"He can be overtaken, of course. But—"

"But what? Bulah Singh, are you lying? Are you trying to make me believe that Andrew killed Dr. Lewis?"

"Use your clairvoyance."

"I am trying to use it! I see nothing!"

"I left them alone together, in Gunning's room at the hotel. I had hardly reached my office at police headquarters when the news came by telephone."

"From whom?"

"From my man on the spot. Gunning had been seen leaving the hotel. I detailed an inspector and several men to trace Gunning's movements. He has vanished."

Elsa relaxed suddenly: "Bulah Singh, I don't believe one word of it! How could Andrew possibly get away? He had no horse—no motorcar."

The Sikh interrupted: "Gunning is a man of foresight and resource. He had anticipated this. He made his preparations in advance. Weren't you expecting him here?"

"No."

"You are up late."

"Talking, that's all." Then suddenly, staring at the Sikh's eyes: "Bulah Singh, are you lying about Andrew and Dr. Lewis?"

"Use your clairvoyance. Use it! Look!"

"I see the colour of your thought! I can't interpret that! I can't see Andrew. When my friends are in danger, I sometimes know it—sometimes—but—"

"Gunning is in no danger," said Bulah Singh, "if you do your

318

part."

"My part? My part? What do you mean?" Nancy Strong's words poured into her mind—no sense to them, but a kind of rhythm like running water: shall not want—dimensions of ideas—human kindness—Lord is my shepherd, I—

"Gunning's fate is in your hands," said Bulah Singh. His eyes didn't move. They were fixed on hers steadily. "Obey me, and he shall escape to Tibet."

"Obey you? What do you mean?"

"You know what I mean."

"I don't know. Tell me! Don't talk riddles."

"You do know. Look into my eyes. Now—obey me—and save Andrew Gunning."

"Obey you? How? Do what?"

"Use your clairvoyance."

"You mean now?"

"Continually. There is no other way to save Gunning from capture, indictment, conviction and death by hanging. Obey me, and he shall get clear away. I am your friend. Your only friend in India. Obey me and save Andrew Gunning."

Elsa was seeing visions, staring wide-eyed into the darkness beyond Bulah Singh. She saw Tom Grayne, in the cavern she knew so well, near Shig-po-ling, nine hundred miles away—Tom Grayne in danger; but she could only sense, she could not see the danger—Tom Grayne, waiting— waiting for the spring and for Andrew with men and supplies. She was hardly conscious of Bulah Singh's voice, speaking slowly in firm monotone:

"It was your fault that Gunning came to Darjeeling—your fault that Lewis found out all his plans—your fault—your fault. And now only you can save him—by obeying me, your friend—always—obeying me—always."

The front door bell rang. The Sikh began to speak more quickly: "Here come the plainclothes policemen to get clues to pursue Gunning. Only I can send them in a wrong direction. You must obey me. Promise to obey me. Say it!"

The bell rang again. The servant hurried along the hallway and undid the clattering chain on the front door.

"You are afraid," said Bulah Singh. "You are afraid for Andrew Gunning. But you know you need not fear, if you obey me. Answer: you will obey me."

319

The front door opened and the wind blustered in, carrying voices along the hallway.

"Answer," Bulah Singh commanded.

Elsa came out of reverie suddenly, looking straight at him. She smiled: "Yes, I'll answer. If it's as bad as you say it is, Bulah Singh, I will take Miss Strong's advice and—"

The door opened suddenly. Andrew Gunning strode into the room. The Sikh swore under his breath. Elsa stifled what was almost a scream.

CHAPTER 14

Elsa and Bulah Singh jumped to their feet and spoke simultaneously.

"Andrew!"

"You idiot!" The Sikh strode forward.

Andrew switched on the light: " 'Evening," he said. "What's the bright idea?" He appeared to expect the Sikh to attack him. He stood still, with a fighting smile and lowered eyebrows. The Sikh went close to him and spoke low-voiced:

"Go now, you fool—or you're next. You were warned."

"Yes," said Andrew. "On my way here one of my own men warned me to clear out. Is this your doing? Who shot Morgan Lewis?"

"On your way!" said the Sikh. "Someone shall overtake you with a message. Get going!"

"Andrew!" Elsa had crossed the room in stocking feet. She stood beside Bulah Singh. "Andrew, you're accused of—"

"I know."

Bulah Singh spoke with studied calmness: "If you don't want to hang, get going. Lewis lies dead in your room at the hotel, shot with your automatic."

Andrew answered stubbornly: "My automatic was turned in long ago for registration at police headquarters."

Bulah Singh sneered: "You have the receipt for it?"

"No," said Andrew. "One of your spies stole that when he searched my rooms. You framed this."

"It's a clear case," the Sikh answered. "You haven't a chance. If you wait, they will hang you as sure as time is your enemy! Go! Hurry! I will hold up pursuit while you cross the frontier."

"Nothing doing," said Andrew. "Arrest me, if you want to. I'll stay and find out who did kill Lewis. They'll need my evidence."

Elsa started to speak. Bulah Singh stepped sideways between her and Andrew and turned his back to her. He spoke with concentrated fury: "You'll not live to give evidence. Your only chance is to do what I told you to do, in Tibet. I'll keep in touch. You can't play tricks with me. Get going, or hang!"

Elsa stepped beside Andrew and faced the Sikh. He scowled, speaking to her with his jaw thrust forward: "They will convict Mu-ni Gam-po and you as accomplices. That means prison. Tom Grayne will be left flat in Tibet, for St. Malo to deal with and—"

Elsa touched Andrew's arm: "Andrew—"

"Elsa, you keep out of this. I'll—"

"Please, Andrew. Bulah Singh knows you didn't kill Dr. Lewis. I know he knows it. But if you stay here to face this out, they'll bring up all kinds of things against you. It may take months. Tom is waiting at Shig-po-ling, and—"

Andrew stared at her, amazed. Bulah Singh swore in Punjabi and then snarled in English: "Unless he goes, he'll hang. I guarantee that: If he goes, he's safe. So are you. I guarantee that also." He glared at Andrew: "But get going—damn you, get a move on!"

Andrew grinned obstinately. Elsa continued as if the Sikh hadn't spoken: "I will be all right here, Andrew. I'm not a bit afraid. The great thing is not to leave Tom in the lurch, isn't it?" She looked straight into Bulah Singh's eyes, keeping her hand on Andrew's forearm so that he bit back the hot speech he had ready. Between those two big men she looked like a pale child, wide-eyed with bedtime sleepiness. But they waited for her to speak—the Sikh suspicious—Andrew puzzled, half expecting her to begin telling visions. What she said to the Sikh surprised both of them.

"Hadn't you better go?" she suggested. "Leave me to persuade Andrew?"

The Sikh's face revealed instant triumph. He nodded. "Yes. Persuade him as you love him. I must go—to delay the pursuit. Goodbye, Gunning. You can save her. She can save you. I can protect both of you. Don't waste time!"

He glanced around as if he meditated going out through a window.

Andrew's lip curled: "You left your raincoat in the hall."

The Sikh nodded. He walked to the door, opened it, turned suddenly to stare at Andrew and said: "You will find your road clear if you go swiftly. I will keep in continual touch. Play my game—and you will find her safe when you return. But don't come back empty-handed."

He closed the door quietly and let himself out through the front door.

As it slammed the phone rang. It continued ringing until at the far end of the hall Nancy Strong shut the door of her office. Andrew and Elsa faced each other in silence, Andrew breathing through his nose, too furious to trust himself to speak. Elsa was afraid to speak for fear she might touch off the angry energy that she knew might cause him to act without thinking.

"It's a God-damned shame," he said suddenly, grinding his teeth. "Morgan Lewis was a good guy. Foxy. Too mysterious. But on the level. I wonder who shot him with my gun."

"We have only Bulah Singh's word for it," said Elsa.

"His word's worth nothing," Andrew agreed, "but Bompo Tsering met me with the whole story out here by the gate in the dark. He wanted me to run. It's less than an hour since Lewis warned me that Bulah Singh has designs on you. See here—" he hesitated, staring at her—"why did you take Bulah Singh's side of it? Why did you say you'd persuade me?"

"To get rid of him. To get him out of the way, so that we could decide what to do."

"Elsa, you haven't a chance on earth to persuade me to play that man's game. He's a devil. He's clever. But I've a hunch I can prove he killed Lewis. It may be hard to prove. He may have hypnotized some—just a moment—look me in the eyes—what was he doing in here?— Did he hypnotise you?"

"He tried."

"Are you sure he didn't?"

"Quite sure."

"Lewis told me you'd be easy for him if he caught you off guard."

"Ah, but I had been talking to Nancy Strong before Bulah Singh came."

"About hypnotism?"

"No. About pigs and poets. Don't ask now, Andrew, it would take too long to tell. Just think. Try to get your mind quiet. Don't be stampeded."

"Stampeded nothing."

"Was my boot in your room at the hotel?"

"Yes. Fortunately Lewis noticed it. So I brought it along—gave it to Bompo Tsering."

"Do you trust Bompo Tsering?"

"Yes. He might be outwitted. He scares easy. But he wouldn't betray me for luck or money. He said he had the story from a man at the hotel. He'd gone there to find me. So he ran and overtook me. Yes, I trust Bompo Tsering."

"So do I trust him. Did he say everything's ready?"

"Yes. He wanted me to bolt without coming here. He believes I did kill Lewis."

"Well, Andrew, I do think you'd better go. I don't think you're in danger. Can you get along without the things you had at the hotel?"

"Sure. I planned to leave all that stuff. Everything I need is up close to the border, ready for the take-off."

"Then go, Andrew. And God bless you. Please tell Tom what I asked you to tell him."

"No. Nothing doing. I'll send Bompo Tsering. He's a good headman. He'll make it. He'll get through somehow. I'll stay and face the music."

"Andrew—"

"What?"

She hesitated. They could hear the clock tick on the mantelpiece. "Will you trust me this one last time?"

"What do you mean?"

"Bulah Singh told me that Dr. Lewis is dead."

"I guess all Darjeeling knows it by now."

"But he isn't dead! Andrew, he isn't."

"Are you seeing things?"

"Yes! So you're not in danger. But if you don't go you will be, because Bulah Singh—"

He interrupted, speaking gently: "You've been under too much strain lately. That damned Sikh has got you frightened and all mixed up in your mind. But see here—"

"Andrew—Dr. Lewis is not dead. He isn't even hurt. And he's on your side."

"No one could sell me that he wasn't friendly," Andrew answered.

"So you go now—and trust Dr. Lewis."

"Swell idea! I suppose I'm to tell Tom Grayne I left you to the mercies of a dead doctor and a Sikh hypnotist? Take a good look with that vision of yours and see if you can see me doing it"

"Andrew, you must go. I know it will be all right if you do. But if you don't—things are known about you—I mean, things in the United States. I know none of the details but Bulah Singh does, and—"

Nancy Strong knocked on the door and came into the room. She glanced down the passage before closing the door. She looked grimly amused; but in the aura of her humour was a hint of a broom that sweeps clean.

"Elsa!—in your stocking feet—you should know better. These stone floors chill you right through the carpet. Go and warm your feet at the fire."

She switched off the light, took Elsa's hand and led her to the fireplace. Andrew followed.

"Put some wood on, Andrew."

He obeyed, stared, sat down facing them. There was silence for a moment while the fire leaped into a bright blaze. Then Nancy Strong breathed one of her sighs that smiled at the perplexity of things.

"You know the news?" asked Andrew.

"Yes. Oh, how much easier this world would be to live in if there weren't any men. Well, Elsa, I warned you that Morgan Lewis is dangerous."

Elsa, staring at the fire, said: "Bulah Singh is the danger,"

"Did he frighten you? Look at me!"

"Yes. But—"

"Look straight at me!"

"Yes. I was frightened—not at first, but after a minute or two. I had begun to feel there was no escape from him. Then suddenly I remembered what you had been saying—"

"I see you are all right," said Nancy Strong.

"Some of your phrases kept running through my mind, in back of my thought, like a refrain—like a tune that you can't forget—"

"And then you left off being meek! What do you think I was doing in my office?"

"You said you would write a letter."

"Here it is. Keep it. Child, much the easiest way to send good thinking straight to the one in need, is to write it down on paper, with a picture of the person in your mind. That forces you to concentrate. What did I write? Read it."

Elsa unfolded the paper, read it and glanced up at Nancy: "May I?"

Nancy nodded. Elsa handed the letter to Andrew. He held it to the firelight, frowning, puzzled, and glanced at both of them.

"That is strong magic," said Nancy. "Stronger than all the *mantras* and Yogic exercises from here to hell-and-gone, if you'll pardon my emphasis. We all know the magic. The thing is to use it."

Andrew folded Nancy's letter, stuffed it into his pocket and coughed to call attention to the fact that there was a crisis to deal with. Nancy looked at him sharply.

"It takes a lot of the milk of human kindness," she said, "to get some people out of the messes that their ignorant generosity gets them into. Did you ever see a ghost?"

"No, and I never wanted to," Andrew answered. "I need advice, badly. I'm going to be accused of shooting Dr. Morgan Lewis."

"That man is a menace," said Nancy. "Do ghosts use telephones?"

"I don't get you. Maybe I'm a bit—"

"Morgan Lewis is a menace to himself and to half Darjeeling at this very moment," said Nancy. "He is riding a motorcycle, in the dark, in the rain, without a headlight."

Elsa wriggled with delight. "Andrew, I told you!"

Andrew stared at Nancy Strong: "You mean Lewis isn't dead? How do you know?"

"He was talking to me a few minutes ago," said Nancy. "But of course—a motorcycle, at his time of life—and belonging at that to a Lepcha pharmacist's assistant—probably no brakes—and rotten tires—yes, he may be dead by this time—"

"He isn't!" said Elsa. "He's coming! I know it! I can feel it! He is bringing good news!"

"It will be bad news for someone," Nancy answered. "Unless that impudent Bulah Singh has sense enough to—"

"Listen!" said Elsa.

The machine-gun sputter of a decrepit motorcycle, hard-ridden, slowed up the drive and coughed to a standstill.

Elsa nodded triumphantly: "Dr. Lewis!"

"This has me beat," said Andrew. "The place feels like a mad-house."

"The whole world is a madhouse," said Nancy Strong. "You shot Morgan Lewis. Here comes his ghost. Perhaps his ghost is a little bit sane. We'll soon know."

The bell rang. The barefooted servant upset a chair in the hall in his hurry to reach the front door.

"I'm a failure," said Nancy. "I have had that servant for fifteen years. But I can't train him not to fear ghosts. Someone told him Lewis is dead. I told him Lewis is coming. So a dead man's here! And now listen to him."

Chapter 15

The door opened. The turbaned servant, white-eyed with superstition, staring at Lewis, switched on the light. Lewis waited for the servant to close the door behind him, then switched the light off. Andrew stood up. Lewis strode through the firelit gap between the screen of bookcases straight toward Elsa and stood beside the armchair, looking down at her, with the firelight gleaming on his monocle.

"Did you get my message?" he demanded.

"I knew you weren't hurt. I knew you were coming. Is that what you mean?"

"Did she? Can anyone prove it?"

"Yes," said Andrew.

"Yes," said Nancy Strong.

"Good girl!" said Lewis. "That settles it. You may return to Tibet with Andrew Gunning."

"Dr. Lewis, you're an angel," said Elsa. But everyone knew she resented his manner.

"It's the devil who lets people do as they please," Lewis answered. He nodded to her, recognizing unspoken comments. "Yes," he added, "you've been where I never had a chance to go. But all the same, I'm the purveyor of dispensations." He stared at Andrew: "You should be on your way now, and in hiding, before daylight."

Andrew squared his shoulders: "That suits me—seeing it's you, not Bulah Singh." He took the poker and prodded the fire.

"Gently!" Nancy warned him. "Gently! That poker once belonged to Lord Tennyson. Don't break it."

"Are the shutters tight?" Lewis asked.

"No," said Nancy, "not particularly. The repair-man didn't come."

Lewis chose the chair in the corner between bookcase and hearth.

"What more," he remarked, "could a man with a pistol ask for than shutters that can be opened from outside!"

"In twenty years, bullets have ruined three of my best books," Nancy remarked. "Weaklings have been bullet-minded ever since the World War. But an average of one in six or seven years isn't very exciting, is it?"

"Who got shot in my room at the hotel?" Andrew asked.

"No one," said Lewis. "But the top of your head is above the bookcase now, so sit down."

Andrew chose the chair in the corner facing Lewis. "Then the whole story's a fake?"

"My word, no. I was shot at, if there's such a thing as evidence. Gunning, you are circumstantially guilty of attempted murder with an unregistered Luger automatic known to belong to you. The bullet went into the bedroom wall. The Luger was tossed into a bureau drawer by whoever used it. You are now making tracks for the sky line. Now! You are on your way—now. You haven't spoken to me. I'm a ghost. If necessary you will lie about that, blackly and without equivocation, taking all the consequences."

"Okay. But I can't read thought. Do we get the lowdown?"

"Yes—from high Olympus." Lewis turned toward Elsa: "Tell what happened," he said quietly, taking her wrist.

"But, Dr. Lewis, I don't know what happened."

"Not yet, perhaps. But you haven't looked. Look now. What took place in Andrew Gunning's room at the hotel?"

"I don't know."

"If you hadn't touched her she might have been able to read it," said Nancy Strong. "It won't work that way, Morgan. You have made her self-conscious. You will have to tell your own story."

Andrew blundered to the rescue: "Besides, she hates that stuff," he objected. "Elsa; don't you let him rag you." He grinned pugnaciously at Lewis. "She's been run ragged by Bulah Singh, on top of her own worries. You let her alone."

Nancy Strong spoke with authority, as if Lewis were a small boy: "Morgan, Andrew is right. Don't be cruel. Tell all of us what you told me just now over the telephone. I want to hear it again."

"Since I'm in on this," said Andrew, "you might begin where we left off, in my room at the hotel. You warned me that Bulah Singh might trace Elsa here. So he did. I heard you lock my room door when I came away. After that, what?"

"I unlocked it again," said Lewis.

"So you knew what was going to happen? It was all in the bag?"

Lewis laughed: "That's a beautiful phrase. No, nothing's in the bag—yet; not even Bulah Singh, although he's so scared we can bet on his making another mistake."

"He seemed so cocksure here in this room, that he had me well fooled for a couple of minutes," said Andrew.

"Several of us may be in the bag, as you call it, unless you fool him by staying fooled," Lewis answered. "The same man who wants you to get going toward Tibet prevented these shutters from being repaired. Nearly all hypnotists are self-hypnotised into absurdly overestimating their own craftiness. Bulah Singh is no exception. He feels he is playing a sort of occult chess against inferior opponents. He is too busy scorning his opponents' ignorance to notice his own mistakes. He feels like an invisible influence, because hypnotism can't be fingerprinted, or photographed or boiled in a tube for analysis. He is so cocksure of the secrecy of what he's doing—and of the superiority of his own intelligence—that he did an almost incredibly stupid thing. He employed a down-at-heel Eurasian, suffering from catatonia—ordered him to shoot me with your pistol."

"What's catatonia?" asked Andrew.

"It's a form of schizophrenia. That's the up-to-date name for dementia praecox. The man also has more or less dormant syphilis, suppressed some years ago by quack treatment. He will die of it one of these days, unless they hang him. He has been hypnotized to the point where he's simply a diseased mass of anti-social illusions. Didn't you notice the man on your way out of your bedroom?"

"No," said Andrew.

"He was there, in the corridor, waiting. Perhaps he stepped into the lavatory to avoid you."

"Come to think of it," said Andrew, "Bulah Singh did mention, after you'd left us alone together in my room, that he'd posted a man at the stair-head to prevent anyone from listening in to our conversation."

"That was the man. Nathaniel Braganza Lemon. Not too bad-looking, but narrow between the eyes and a long, pointed chin. Degraded Virgo, in case you know what that means. Illegitimate son of an infantry corporal who was hanged for murdering the lad's Goanese-Japanese-Irish mother. Bad heredity. Bad environment. No character there to begin with. Plenty of hell rubbed into him as he grew up in the red-light district of Lahore and elsewhere. Persecution complex—envy, hatred, malice, greed—how he kept clear of the gallows I don't know. We've his prison and hospital record."

"And you knew he was laying for you?" Andrew asked.

"Yes. Fortunately! I know quite a lot about Lemon. Had him under observation for a while, in hospital, in Delhi. He was a nuisance. Had to discipline him. Wasn't mad enough to be locked up, nor sane enough to appreciate generous treatment at public expense. I turned

328

him out finally. Bulah Singh ran across him by chance on a visit to Delhi and brought him here for use as an informer—not a policeman, you understand—a mere spy, paid hardly enough from the secret fund to keep body and soul together. So it was actually Lemon who first drew my attention to Bulah Singh. I learned that Bulah Singh was using him for hypnotic experiments. That brought Bulah Singh automatically into my special orbit."

"Why?" asked Elsa, as if Lewis were the point at issue, not Lemon or Bulah Singh. The one word sounded almost like an ultimatum.

"Trust a woman to ask that question!"

"Won't you answer it, Dr. Lewis?"

"Yes." He smiled. "It isn't safe not to answer. You might start thought-reading and find out too much! The answer is: we keep track of counterfeiters. Hypnotism, unrestrained by moral discipline, and unsupervised by science, is counterfeit ambition. That is my phrase. Don't you quote it or they'll call you crazy. Ninety *per cent* of hypnotists become so intellectually vain and amoral that they think they can get away with anything, murder included."

"Ninety-nine *per cent* of them," said Nancy Strong.

"You and I don't agree there," said Lewis. "Anyhow, one thing leading to another, we discovered that Bulah Singh was hypnotizing various criminal types and making very interesting experiments. He was also using mediums and clairvoyants. By the use of suggestion he caused criminals to commit petty crimes, of the kind for which they were temperamentally suited. Then he would hypnotise a medium or a clairvoyant and command him to detect the crime. He soon discovered that the mediums were useless; and good clairvoyants are much harder to find. I knew what he was doing, but it was practically impossible to get legal evidence."

Elsa interrupted again: "Why?"

"Because a criminal hypnotist, speaking directly to the unconscious mind of the victim, commands the victim to act but to forget who ordered him to act, and also to forget the act itself."

"It's that trick of forgetting," said Nancy Strong, "that makes the whole wide world so easy to corrupt. We even forget what prime ministers and presidents said last week."

"We watched Bulah Singly" said Lewis, "on the general principle that the deliberate use of secret power over other people always— always, mind you—arouses appetite for more. It becomes insatiable. In that respect it's worse than drink or drugs. The greater the ap-

329

petite for power, the less the respect for truth. It's a self-stimulating vice, especially deadly when rooted in experience of actual authority and aggravated by intellectual conceit. That's the reason why so-called statesmen are such liars. It wasn't long before we uncovered Bulah Singh's little game."

"Why didn't you break him right then?" Andrew objected.

"For the same reason that we didn't deport Tom Grayne, and you too," Lewis answered. "Given time and opportunity Bulah Singh will break himself— beyond the slightest shadow of doubt he'll do that. But meanwhile, if he's carefully watched, we can learn even more from him than from you and Tom Grayne."

Elsa moved suddenly, startled: "Dr. Lewis! Do you mean you think Tom will—will break, as you call it?"

"Oh, yes. You're laboratory mice, that's all. Probably all three of you will meet your end in Tibet. The job is too big. You haven't a chance. But that's your lookout. We're none of us immortal."

"Oh, yes, we are," said Nancy Strong. "We all are."

Lewis smiled at her: "Immortal? In spite of us medical men?"

"Go on telling about Bulah Singly" said Nancy.

Lewis nodded. "Yes. If the immortal Nancy gets a word in sideways, there'll be—"

Nancy interrupted: "Time, Morgan, time! Tell your story."

Lewis laughed. "Very well.—Bulah Singh hypnotized Lemon. He gave him Gunning's Luger. He posted him in the hotel corridor and ordered him to shoot me if he could catch me alone in Gunning's room. Circumstantial evidence would point to Gunning, who would then have to obey Bulah Singh in all particulars or else hang for murder."

"Holy smoke, that Sikh took a long chance!" said Andrew.

"Longer than you guess," said Lewis. "Hypnotism is a boomerang."

"And, seems to me, you took an even longer chance."

"Oh no. Rudimentary hypnotism is as unintelligent as money. I was prepared for Lemon. When he opened the door and stuck his head through I hit him on the back of the neck with a piece of rubber hose."

"Swell. But he had a Luger! You don't call that taking a chance?"

"Oh no. I'm an anatomist; I know just where to hit. The rest, of course, was quite simple. I fired a shot with the Luger, to make things all nice and plausible, lifted Lemon on to your bed, tied him hand and

330

foot, tossed the Luger into an open bureau drawer, and phoned for the hotel manager. Hotel managers are valuable people if you take care to win their confidence. I operated on Mr. Nazareth, years ago, for an obscure spinal complaint. He very luckily recovered and has been absurdly grateful to me ever since for not having killed him. So we're excellent friends. Nazareth locked the door and refused to open it for anyone less than the chief of police. Messengers were sent to hunt up the chief of police. I cleared out, by the back way, while Nazareth spread all the necessary rumours. That's all. Except that you are on your way to Tibet."

Andrew laughed. "I'd give something to see Bulah Singh's face when he finds Lemon hog-tied on my bed."

"No chance of that," said Lewis. "Bulah Singh might have suicided Lemon with the Luger—perhaps with the butt end. Hypnotists whose little tricks don't work become hysterical. So I turned in an ambulance call."

"But you said the door was locked," Elsa objected. "If Mr. Nazareth wouldn't let them open the door—"

Lewis smiled: "Never say no to the fire brigade, the inspector of drains, or the ambulance man. Lemon is in hospital, safe, under observation."

"Any chance of getting Lemon to talk?" asked Andrew.

"I doubt it," said Lewis. "At any rate, not for a long time. He didn't see me—doesn't know who hit him—had been ordered to forget—I think he'll say nothing of any importance."

"Take the rap for attempted robbery or some charge like that?"

"He will probably entertain himself with secret mental pictures of me, being killed by him, in all sorts of peculiar ways. After that he will lapse into sex-dreams."

"And will Bulah Singh get off scot-free?" asked Elsa.

"Well, my dear girl, what can he be charged with at the moment? If Andrew Gunning clears out, as he is about to do, who can accuse Bulah Singh of doing what?"

Nancy Strong chuckled: "Andrew might stay," she suggested. "Put some wood on Andrew."

Andrew chose cedar knots thoughtfully, placing them carefully, thinking, thinking.

"Andrew Gunning goes before daylight," said Lewis, "while the going is good. Bulah Singh shall be informed of it." He glanced at Andrew: "I suppose he knows your route?"

331

"Boasted he did. I guess he knows some of it."

"Good. He will go his limit to make sure the route is kept wide open for you."

"And do I go with Andrew—now?" Elsa asked. "All right, I'm ready!"

Lewis stared at her. He looked almost shocked. "Of course not! Nancy Strong will turn you over to Mu-ni Gam-po's men. They will smuggle you through on their way northward. But we must always save face for the police; so Mu-ni Gam-po's loads, that are in the monastery stable with Gunning's name on them, will be sent in the wrong direction to give the police an excuse for a false hunt. Bulah Singh shall be correctly informed that Gunning bolted and left you behind. Is that clear?"

"Morgan!" said Nancy Strong. "You are too fond of being clever. What you actually are, is a romantic fifty-year-old schoolboy. What is to prevent Bulah Singh from killing Elsa to stop her from talking?"

"That's your job," said Lewis.

"Nonsense! How could I protect her? You had better have Bulah Singh pounced on now. Think! You have plenty of evidence to—"

Lewis interrupted: "No! No! All women think intuition is legal evidence and evidence is proof. Cases aren't cured by suppressing symptoms. No. If necessary, but not otherwise, I will try to get Bulah Singh suspended from duty for having let Gunning escape across the frontier. But I don't want to do even that. Bulah Singh may make some very informing mistake if we give him time. He's afraid. A frightened hypnotist is a dangerous fool who is trying to ride two wild horses. Their names are Physics and Metaphysics. That man is absolutely sure to come a cropper."

Suddenly Andrew got out of his chair, passed quietly through the gap between the bookcases and stood listening.

"Shutter?" asked Lewis.

"Yes. Quiet, please, everybody." Andrew walked to the corner window, about ten feet beyond where Lewis sat with his back to the bookcase. The closed shutter moved. The window opened about two inches. A hand appeared in the opening. Andrew grabbed at the hand but missed it.

"Who is it?" he demanded.

A voice answered in a hoarse whisper: "That you, Gunnigun?"

"Oh. You? Okay. Watch the house. Watch the windows. Wait for me. I won't be long now."

332

The shutter closed. Andrew closed the window.

"Your man?" asked Lewis.

"Yes. Bompo Tsering."

Elsa jumped up: "Oh, Andrew, let me speak to him, please! Tell him to wait a second." She hurried between the bookcases and then hesitated, in full firelight, beside the table on which Nancy Strong had set Lobsang Pun's portrait.

Suddenly, at the opposite end of the room, beyond the grand piano, another shutter opened, and then a window. Someone fired, straight at Elsa. The bullet smashed into the silver-framed portrait, knocking it to the floor with a clatter of breaking glass. Elsa stifled a scream as Andrew almost knocked her down, shoving her through the opening between the bookcases. He shoved so hard that she almost stumbled into the fire. Andrew ran down room toward the window. Someone outside slammed the shutter before he was halfway. The strangest part was that Nancy Strong didn't move in her armchair. She sat silent with her eyes shut.

"Did you see who it was?" asked Lewis.

"No," said Andrew. "Stay where you are, Lewis. Don't show yourself. The shot may have been meant for you."

"Nonsense!" Lewis answered. "No one could mistake you for me, even in firelight." His voice had the flat note of nervousness under control.

Nancy Strong spoke at last: "Andrew, come back here behind the bookcase."

Elsa seconded: "Andrew! Come back! He might try it again!"

"Just a moment." Andrew stooped for the picture, examined it, shook off some loose glass and then strode into the firelight. "Are you superstitious?" he asked. He showed the picture to Nancy Strong. There was a bullet hole exactly through the middle of Lobsang Pun's forehead.

"Yes," said Lewis, "she is superstitious. All women are."

"I am not," said Nancy. "Morgan, it is you who are superstitious. I am a realist. I was thinking of Lobsang Pun. He was thinking of me."

Elsa went closer to Nancy to look at her face and at the broken photograph. "What do you mean?" she asked. "You were—"

"The question," said Lewis, "is who fired that shot at Elsa?"

"Or at me," said Andrew. "The bullet passed straight between us."

"You men!" said Nancy. "Do you never use your intuition at the right time? Elsa, what do you see? Quickly—don't think about it!—

333

answer the question!"

Elsa stared for about half a second—stared into vacancy. Then she answered: "Bulah Singh, shooting at you!"

"That," said Nancy, "is clairvoyance."

"But it seems all wrong," Elsa objected. "You weren't even in sight from the window. Someone tried to shoot either Andrew or me."

"Trust your vision," said Nancy. "Facts are skittles. Look for the truth. Of what use would you be to Bulah Singh, as long as I'm in the way to stop him from interfering with you?"

Lewis confirmed that: "They were in full firelight. Bulah Singh wouldn't shoot either of the two people whom he hopes to use for his own ends."

Nancy spoke with assurance: "Someone who didn't know me by sight, and who had not been told there might be two women in the room, had orders to watch through the window and shoot me. He mistook Elsa for me. Someone else intervened and made him miss."

No one spoke for at least thirty seconds. Morgan Lewis's monocle was like a scandalized question mark. Elsa watched Andrew's face. At last Andrew said:

"Bompo Tsering can't have interfered to spoil the aim. He hadn't time to get around to that side of the house."

"I was thinking," said Nancy, "of Lobsang Pun. He was thinking of me. The bullet hit Lobsang Pun's photograph."

"Lobsang Pun is in Tibet, several hundred miles away," said Andrew.

Lewis laughed: "Nancy, you still deny that you're superstitious?".

"It was a coincidence," Nancy retorted, "like when one of your surgical cases gets well."

After that there was silence except for the blustering wind in the chimney and the spitting of raindrops on the fire.

CHAPTER 16

Andrew went to find Bompo Tsering, letting himself out through the front door. The frightened Lepcha servant chained the door behind him and then came into the room to ask Nancy Strong for orders. He peered at her around the corner of the bookcase. Nancy passed him the silver-framed photograph.

"Put that back on the table, please, Tashgyl. Then sweep up the broken glass. Careful! Don't cut yourself."

"Yes, Miss."

"After that pick up the window glass."

"Yes, Miss."

"And tomorrow morning, first thing, tell Jambool to come and put a new pane in the window."

"Yes, Miss."

"Are you too frightened to remember your manners? You shouldn't stare like that at Dr. Lewis."

"No, Miss."

"Very well, don't stare at him. Go and sweep up the glass."

But the Lepcha servant stood, in the opening between the bookcases, staring at Lewis. He seemed unable to move. Lewis got out of his armchair and walked toward him. The servant backed away, but Lewis caught the hand that held the broken photograph of Lobsang Pun and checked his retreat.

"Look at me—straight in the eyes," said Lewis.

The servant stared, numb with terror. His flat, good-natured face, beneath a voluminous turban, expressed no understanding at all—nothing but frightened emotion. It was like the face of a man awakened suddenly from deep sleep amid strange surroundings. Lewis kept hold of his wrist:

"Answer me! Did Bulah Singh *sahib*, the Chief of Police, ever promise you protection?"

"Yes, *sahib*."

"Said he likes you Lepcha people, and knows what a good, honest servant you are?"

"Yes, *sahib*."

"And how loyal you are to your employer, Miss Strong?"

"Yes, *sahib*."

"Then he asked you questions?"

"Yes, *sahib*."

"Lots of questions?"

"Yes, *sahib*."

"About your employer?"

"Yes, *sahib*."

"You have a brother in prison?"

"Yes, *sahib*."

"Did he suggest that he might persuade Miss Strong to befriend your brother?"

"Yes, *sahib*."

"Your brother has a wife?"

"Yes, *sahib*."

"Did Bulah Singh promise to protect your brother's wife until his release from prison?"

"Yes, *sahib*."

"But was your brother's wife unfaithful? Did she become the mistress of the Japanese Koki Konoe?"

"No, no, *sahib*. She not being the mistress. He being her master. She going with him, becoming his woman."

"Where is she now?"

"My not knowing."

"Did Bulah Singh suggest that you do know where she is?"

"Yes, *sahib*. But my not knowing. No! Not knowing!"

"Did Bulah Singh tell you I'm dead?"

"Yes, *sahib*."

"When?"

"Just now, *sahib*, not long ago, when my opening door, letting him in."

"Did he say that your brother's wife perhaps did the killing; and that if you want to keep out of trouble you'd better come and see him at the police *kana?*"

"Yes, *sahib*."

Lewis released his wrist: "Do what you were told to do."

The servant obeyed. He set the photograph back on the table. Then he knelt and began picking up broken glass. Lewis touched him on the shoulder. He took no notice, went on picking up pieces of glass, which he laid on the palm of his left hand. Lewis returned to the fireside:

"Confusion," he said. "Disassociation of cause and effect. Not that it matters, at the moment; but there's your hole in the wall, Nancy. There's the leak. That fellow has been so practiced on that when he's scared he obeys without thinking. Obedience provides the escape from a feeling of guilt."

"After fifteen years!" said Nancy. "And they call me a teacher! Morgan, can you do anything for him? You must! He has been a good servant."

"Opiates?" asked Lewis.

"No. I think not. In fact I'm sure not."

"Doesn't take opium pills? *Bhang?* Marijuana?"

"No. I know he doesn't."

"Liquor?"

336

"No."

"There are other secret vices," said Lewis, "that are equally destructive of discrimination. What does he do with his spare time?"

"I don't know."

"Well, I think I do know. I will go into his case history later." Lewis turned and faced Elsa. "Now, young lady. Do you see what might happen to you, unless you use your God-given faculties?"

Elsa resented it. She sat upright, protecting herself with a shield of indignation that was nevertheless (and she knew it) as full of holes as a net, from having resisted Nancy Strong's assault. She was conscious, too, of gratitude to Lewis for having come when her baby died. And she knew he still could stop her from returning to Tibet. There was no sense in antagonizing Lewis. But resentment felt like self-defence. She answered tartly:

"Am I accused now of secret vices?"

"Secret sloth," he retorted. "Dr. Lewis, aren't you overdoing—"

"No. I am diagnosing sloth—inertia, disguised as meekness. It's a form of self-indulgence."

"You, too? Nancy accused me of that. But I'm not meek! I wish I were! I don't like meek people. I—"

Lewis caught Nancy's eye. She nodded. He faced Elsa again. His air of almost jocular familiarity was gone. He seemed almost a different person.

"Elsa, I am going to repeat to you a piece of advice that was given, two thousand years ago, by the greatest of all physicians. The particular patient to whom it was given made the necessary effort to understand the advice, and had the courage to follow it. I have repeated the prescription to a great number of patients. Some accepted it, some didn't. 'Take up thy bed, and walk.'"

Every atom of Elsa's bitterness against the Christian texts that mental torturers had used as goads against her in her childhood, boiled to the surface. She parried with the first evasive retort she could think of: "Only a few hours ago you told me not to get well too quickly."

"Yes. I know I did. Take it easy. I didn't invite you to run. I said, walk."

Elsa lost control of her temper: "I'm not a paralytic—and you're not Jesus! Why are you talking in riddles?" Suddenly she fell back on the last resort of the evader of issues—silly, literal fact. "If I were, I would get up and do as you say, just to make you feel clever."

Lewis ignored it. "Meekness," he repeated. "Wrapping talents in a

337

napkin. Daydreams. Luxury of letting the catastrophe convince you that it's no use waking up, and getting up, and doing what you can, instead of being what inertia makes you! Wake up!"

For the moment Elsa couldn't trust herself to answer. She was too indignant. Nancy Strong was leaning back in her armchair, with closed eyes, stroking the purring cat. Elsa made an effort to appeal to Nancy's professed hatred of cruelty:

"Is this a conspiracy? Are you and Nancy teaming up to make me feel sinful? Are you trying to convert me, or convict me, or what? Nancy said I'm asleep. But I understood her to mean—"

Lewis interrupted: "She meant exactly what I mean. She may have put it in different words, but she meant the same thing."

"I don't think she did," Elsa retorted. "Tell me what you do mean."

"You are clairvoyant:"

"I wish you'd cure me of it, instead of talking about it!"

"Clairaudient, too."

Elsa snatched at the chance to defend at least one gap in her defences: "Not so often clairaudient. Only sometimes."

Lewis went on speaking as if she hadn't interrupted: "Nancy Strong will show you, far better than I can, how to develop your clairvoyance."

"I won't develop it! I loathe it!"

Lewis continued: "Otherwise, 'that which you have shall be taken away.' If you leave your talent undeveloped, you will become a victim, just like hundreds of millions of others, of every wave of pitiless ambitious malice that is turned loose on the world by the ignorant fools and godless egotistic devils who create this chaos which we flatter with the name of consciousness."

Nancy opened her eyes: "Gently, Morgan! Gently!"

Elsa started to speak. Lewis checked her with a gesture. He continued: "Only you will be worse than the others. Because you are more sensitive. You might even degenerate so far as to become a medium."

"You mean a spiritualistic medium?"

"Yes. Probably a trance medium. Physical prostitution would be better than that. A prostitute, after all, gives no more than her body to be defiled by strangers. But a medium's soul is at the mercy of every devil and fool who chooses to misuse it. The very least you will become, unless you wake up, and stay awake, will be a sort of radio receiving set employed by mischievous and godless liars. You might become—"

Nancy Strong interrupted: "No, Morgan, no! Not that! Don't frighten her!"

Lewis looked irritated, but he accepted the advice: "Very well, I will add this: Elsa, you are of the same stuff that the saints are made of."

The sudden switch of tactics forced another tart answer that Elsa knew was worthless: "I don't feel like a saint, I assure you. I don't wish to be one! I feel angry and—"

Lewis interrupted: "A cowardly saint is a social menace—much worse even than a venal doctor, or corrupt judge, or political priest. Fear makes saints see wrong visions—report wrong—"

"I said, I'm not a saint! I don't want to be one. I'm—"

"Listen," said Lewis. "I am your physician, telling you truth, for your own good."

"You mean your good, don't you? I didn't invite this. Why are you doing it? Tell your real motive!" Lewis ignored that too. He continued, just as calmly as if he were treating a painful wound: "Saints, devils and credulous fools are made of the same identical stuff. They all have vision. They see the same truth from different aspects. Devils exploit stupidity. They create blinding fear that gives them power over others. It inflates the devils' feeling of importance; and it makes the fools think the devils are the only safe leaders to follow. But the vision of saints acts, by its own nature—to use a feeble illustration—like a prism letting light into the darkness. It diffuses the material fog—the fog that blinds the best of us and makes us victims of want, and disease and crime. The vision of saints lets in affluence and magnanimity and vigor. Naturally, the devils hate it. If they can't pervert saints' vision to their own ends, they try to destroy it."

"Are you trying to tell me that clairvoyance is reliable— dependable—always true? I know better!"

"It's as dangerous as truth," said Lewis. "In the hands of a devil a saint becomes as subtly malignant as poison gas—which, remember, is made from beneficent ingredients."

He was interrupted by the front door bell. The Lepcha servant stopped picking up broken window glass and left the room in a hurry. Lewis continued:

"The whole world is changing under our eyes, and in our ears. Science, sometimes with the best intention, is becoming the slave of the devils, who exploit human ignorance for the sake of the sensation of power. The exploiters of isms! Communism. Nazism. Fascism. Militarism. Anarchism. Socialism. Atheism. Millions of undernourished men and women, stuffed with ersatz dialectics and mad promises, massed into goose-stepping armies and shouting blasphemy against their manhood—! What Kipling called 'all valiant dust that builds on dust'!"

"'And, guarding, calls not Thee to guard.' I wonder whether Kipling understood his own poem."

Lewis threw off the interruption: "Up goes the dust, and we can't see. The roar, and we can't hear. Blind leaders, leading the blind, produced the World War; that was bad enough. Maddened and disillusioned by the World War, its victims are producing worse chaos led by devils and fools and false prophets. Hitlers—Mussolinis—Stalins. Professional liars, to whom truth of any kind is treason. They control or suppress schools, pulpits, press, radio. They even censor conversation. They are hypnotising whole nations with fear of worse horrors to come. Meanwhile, they pitilessly exploit the victims .Victims who don't applaud them as saviors are liquidated or imprisoned for having dangerous thoughts."

Elsa recovered her sense of humour, for just one second: "Dr. Lewis, is it as bad as all that? Aren't there any honest people?"

"It's worse than that," said Lewis. "Because honest people don't know what to think. They're being liquidated."

"Do you believe you know what to think?" Humour deserted her suddenly. She felt now like a cat with its ears laid back. She felt as if she were the accused, on the spot, a sorceress charged with seducing and betraying the human race.

"Think?" said Lewis. "What fools think is thought got us into the mess! Our thought—our mass-materialism created it. Only vision can get us out of it. So wake up! Stay awake! Let some light in! The only hope of the world are the individuals who can, and who dare to be saints!

Religion, science, government, philosophy, economics are all reduced to absurdity. The New Dealers are making bad worse. They're putting synthetic wine into falsely labelled bottles and calling it ideology. Idiotology! Every new ingenious invention, because we're hypnotized by fear, becomes a belly-robber and a new false beacon leading to a materialist's synthetic heaven—a new mechanical Utopia full of bombs and lies and breadlines!"

"Whereas the kingdom of heaven is within us—within reach of us all—here—now—if we would look," said Nancy.

Lewis looked exasperated, Elsa incredulous.

"But Nancy! Can you see the kingdom of heaven?"

"Sometimes. Since I left off helping to create hell. Reality seems nearer—ever so much nearer."

"Reality?" said Elsa.

"If those who can see, won't look," said Lewis, "then—"

He left off speaking because the door opened. Andrew walked in, followed by Bompo Tsering. Andrew, wiping rain off his hair with a handkerchief, strode to the fireplace. He glanced at Elsa, then stared at Lewis:

"Have you been ragging her again?" he demanded. "Can't you let her alone?" He turned his back toward Lewis.

Lewis raised one eyebrow so high that his monocle fell out. He glanced at Nancy Strong. She nodded, smiling. Even Andrew was aware that they were exchanging comments about him, although he had turned and stooped to put wood on the fire, and no word passed between them. Bompo Tsering came and stood in the opening between the bookcases. Lewis studied him:

"So this is Man Friday?"

Andrew straightened himself and turned his back to the fire. "Yes," he said. "I don't want him scared any more than he is. Don't talk metaphysics to him. He's superstitious."

Lewis laughed. Elsa studied Bompo Tsering.

"Why did you bring him in here?" she asked. She sniffed, then laughed too. With the rain on him Bompo Tsering smelt like all Tibet.

Nancy sighed: "It makes me homesick. But someone please open a window!"

"No!" said Andrew. "Not now. No windows. Please. There's a reason."

CHAPTER 17

Bompo Tsering looked shell-shocked. Mistrust of his surroundings numbed him. Tibetans are an intuitive people. He could sense the spiritual strength of Nancy's hospitality. But he was afraid of it. A legion of superstitions crowded his mind. He was afraid of the room. The familiar Tibetan things on the walls didn't lessen the trap-sensation. In his imagination they increased it. Loot. Scalps. The books were overwhelming evidence of occult lore; it might be white, but it was much more likely to be black magic. He had seen Andrew's room at the hotel, and the inside of many a rich man's house in Tibet; but nothing like this room. Andrew ordered him curtly to uncover his head. He obeyed, sheepishly. But curiosity was just a bit stronger than shyness: holding his fur trimmed, filthy hat in both hands, he thrust his tousled head around the corner of the bookcase. First, he recognized Elsa—stuck out his tongue respectfully—grinned self-consciously—then repeated the respectful salutation, to Nancy Strong—to Lewis—with an extra tongue—show thrown in on general principles—perhaps to the gods of the hearth.

"Tongue's furry," said Lewis. "Too much starch. Guzzles rice and *ghee* three times a day.

He'll have an enlarged spleen if he isn't careful."

"He'll work that off soon enough," said Andrew. "Uphill all the way. Pass beyond pass, and the south side always the steeper. Six days a week. That'll cure him."

"You always rest one day a week?" asked Lewis.

"Usually. Rest the animals. Give the gang a chance to repair boots, tents, harness and settle arguments."

The conversation was beyond Bompo Tsering's scope of English. He was unaffected by it. It meant nothing. He stood smiling, flat-faced, stocky, sloe-eyed, bulkily clothed in a wet fleece-lined, padded, long-sleeved leather overcoat; it was made bulkier still by the things in his *bokkus*, which is the space between neck and belt where Tibetans stow all their portable belongings. There was a small splinter from a saint's thigh bone stuck through the lobe of one ear; in the other was a long turquoise earring good enough for a nobleman. Around his neck was a twisted coil of parchment; it resembled a hangman's noose blackened by exposure to storms and human sweat, but it was actually a scroll of beautifully written blessings worth ten times the price of the earring.

"I'd like to talk to him," said Elsa. "May I? Or would you rather I didn't?"

Andrew shook his head: "Later. He has the wind up at the moment. Give him a chance and he'll throw a panic, like a caught animal."

"But why should he be afraid of me?" asked Elsa.

Nancy asked an easier one: "Why bring him in here? Not that he isn't welcome—but why?"

"He was afraid to stay outside," Andrew answered. "Swears there are *dugpas*. Scared stiff of 'em."

"Did he talk?" asked Lewis.

342

"Sure he talked—outside in the dark, because he felt he had to divvy up the funk with someone fifty-fifty. But you try to get him to talk now!" It was quite obvious, Andrew was rather proud of having been confided in. "Watch him try to stop me talking!" he added.

Bompo Tsering's face had become as blank as an old ivory moon—no smile left. His right hand with the thumb between the fingers moved up and down almost imperceptibly, from superstitious habit. His real effort to gag Andrew was mental—a darkly invisible psychic force such as passes between conspirators or in a courtroom when a witness is expected to betray perilous secrets. Elsa spoke up:

"Andrew, can't we help him? I can see his fear, like a fog—yellowy—gray—green—like a London pea-souper. The poor man wasn't as scared as this even when we were cursed by the Black Monks at—"

Lewis took a hand, speaking Tibetan with an accent learned on medical inspection tours in Sikkim. The accent and the monocle together totally masked the sympathy which was all that Lewis intended:

"Tell us what frightened you, Bompo Tsering. Speak. We are friends. We won't laugh at you."

The very use of his name by a stranger aggravated prejudice. Bompo Tsering's eyes changed perceptibly. They transferred dark attention from one dread to another. Beneath his matted black fringe of hair they suggested a yak's eyes, unintelligently ready to stampede—utterly mistrustful. Nancy Strong was watching:

"No use, Morgan!" Her voice had the finality note of experience. "You should have asked his advice. Then he'd have told. I always ask children's advice when they're in trouble."

Lewis smiled wryly: "Mental *jujitsu*, eh? Good tactics. But it isn't a safe plan, always. Try it on some of my patients! Try it, for instance, on Lemon!" He turned to Andrew. "Did he say he saw who fired that shot through the window?"

Andrew nodded: "Said he saw a man with his face half covered by a shawl, who obeyed a *dugpa* who lurked in the shrubbery."

"Did he see the *dugpa?*"

"Yes—so he said. He's always seeing 'em. I guess they're part of his religion."

"He is always very brave about them," said Elsa. "Much braver than I am about the things that I see."

"He's more afraid on our account than for himself," said Andrew.

"That bit of holy shin bone in his ear is all he figures he needs. But we're *pelings*—ignorant foreigners who don't know what we're up against. If the *dugpas* should get, for instance, me, bang goes his meal-ticket. Get the idea?"

Lewis wiped his monocle with a thoughtful, professional air: "*Dug-pas*," he said, "are just as real to a Tibetan as microbes are to me, or to a man with influenza. They're exactly as real as the snakes seen by a man in delirium tremens. They're a symptom. Swat the snakes, and what happens?"

"He saw someone," said Andrew.

"Of course he did. And his frightened senses lied about it."

"Every single one of our physical senses is an incorrigible liar," said Nancy Strong.

"Could he have seen Bulah Singh—" Andrew suggested, "lurking in the bushes—with another of his hypnotized Lemons to do the dirty work?"

Lewis laughed. "No, Gunning, no! If Bulah Singh were as easy as all that, he would have been hanged long ago. Someone in the Lemon category fired the shot through the window. There's nothing much easier than for a devil to find stoolpigeons. You may depend on it: the real culprit was as far from the scene as the real conspirators were who directed the shot at Sarajevo."

Elsa spoke suddenly: "The man in the shrubbery wore a devil-mask! I can see it! I can see it now!"

Nancy Strong frowned: "Nonsense, Elsa! What you are seeing is Bompo Tsering's own mental image of what he wants to persuade us that he saw."

"But, Nancy, how do you know?"

"Because I saw it when you did. That is how panics—even wars get started. It happens to animals and humans. False mental pictures projected from thought to thought by invisible rays of fear."

"But if that's so, how can one ever know the difference between the real thing and a—"

"Child, I told you. Try to remember. If you will insist on believing you are a person with a supposititious soul, or no soul, you will always believe the wrong thing, because your premise is wrong. Change your premise. It is impossible to reason correctly from a wrong premise. If you remember you are a soul, and that you have an unreal but per-suasively realistic person to wear and to manage, as you would man-age an instrument, you will soon learn to see the difference between truth, and lies about the truth. You will find you get increasingly less deceived by tricks of any kind."

Lewis laughed: "That's a very fair example of the odds against the use of clairvoyance for any practical purpose. Who's going to deny his senses? That's what it amounts to."

"It calls for more integrity and courage than most people have nowadays," said Nancy. "It's the hardest work in the world. But it can be done. It has got to be done." There came a knock at the door. Nancy Strong got up, looking grimly patient. "Trumpet call!" she remarked. "Turn out the guard!"

The door opened. A woman teacher, wrapped in an overcoat over a dressing gown, stood in the doorway.

"All right," said Nancy. "I'm coming."

The door closed again. Nancy approached Andrew. He stood up. "The pistol shot," she said, "awakened some of the children in the west building. I must go and ask them to advise me what to do when people break my window." She held out her hand: "Until we meet again, Mr. Gunning, my best wishes! Your secret is safe with me. I hope we have hit on the best way to handle it."

Andrew nodded gravely as he shook hands. "Anything I can do for you in return?"

"No!" She met his eyes, smiling. "If there's one thing I detest it's to be hit with return favours like an actress being pelted with eggs. If I have helped you, help someone else when you see the need. Pass it along Don't dare to think of me as anything but a window that let the light through. Please don't smash me with bricks of hard-boiled gratitude. Goodbye, and good luck to you. Come and see me when you return."

Bompo Tsering stepped away from her. He faced her with his tongue out, staring as if he hesitated between fear and something like reverence. As she passed him she tapped his sleeve with her right hand, as one pats a great friendly dog.

"You smell of Tibet," she said, smiling.

"The blessed, happy, precious land!" he answered. He stood looking at the sleeve as if a *bodhisattva* had bestowed a blessing on it.

"Nancy Strong," said Lewis, as the door closed after her, "is the one person who can make me feel like a ten-year-old. Gunning, my boy, wish I were coming with you to Tibet."

"Come if you want to," said Andrew. "You'll be welcome."

"Sorry to have to say no. But you must get going. I'd like a few

345

words with you in private before you leave."

Andrew glanced at Elsa.

Lewis took the hint: "You will find me in the hall. I want to talk to that Lepcha servant—if he isn't asleep." He walked out. Elsa stood up. "Andrew, then this isn't goodbye? It really isn't goodbye? I know it isn't! But I want to hear you say it! I feel like two people tonight. One of me sings with excitement. The other just doesn't believe."

"No, it's not goodbye. The monks will know where to find me. They'll bring you."

"But, Andrew, you might have to wait—"

"I'll wait."

"It's strangely easy to believe you, Andrew. But you mustn't wait too long. You mustn't let me ruin everything. Delay might prevent you from crossing the border. I mean—"

"I'm betting on Lewis and Bulah Singh."

"Andrew, you're not trusting Bulah Singh, are you?"

"Hell, no. But he wants me in Tibet. If he thinks I'm playing his game, he'll clear the tracks. Pretending to leave you behind will make him cocksure that he has me by the short hair."

"Andrew, I'm trying to see. I can't see any real danger to you at the moment. But—but—Bulah Singh is like a shadow that—"

Andrew laughed gruffly: "That guy's shadow isn't long enough to reach beyond the first pass! We'll climb the mountains and forget him. Nancy Strong will do your shopping. She'll know how to turn you over to Mu-ni Gam-po's party. The minute she says the word, get going. Come after me just as fast as those monks can travel. You'll find me waiting for you."

"Andrew, I won't waste a minute. I promise."

"Okay. But see here." He hesitated. Then suddenly: "Don't let 'em get you buffaloed."

"Who, Andrew? Whom do you mean? I won't even see Bulah Singh. I won't—"

"I mean Lewis and Nancy Strong."

"Hadn't you better speak more plainly? I mean, I want to understand you, so there won't be any mistake. I like both of them. I trust them. Don't you?"

"Sure I do." Andrew reached for a pine knot and set it carefully on the fire. Then, looking straight at Elsa: "Lewis is a good guy. He's a genius: darned close to being a nut. He's on the level, but he's haywire on some subjects, notably psychic phenomena. Yes him. But keep your

346

feet on the ground. Do you understand that?"

"I think so. All right, I promise."

"Don't make easy promises. They're too damned difficult to keep. Don't let Morgan Lewis sell you any superstitious *hokum* about your being someone special who can magic the rest of us out of hell or any tripe like that."

She laughed. "That's easy, Andrew. All right, I won't—"

"Don't promise! Do your own thinking. Keep your common sense hard-boiled and on top while you're talking to Lewis."

"Very well, Andrew, I'll try to. And Nancy Strong? Don't you trust her?"

"You bet. She hasn't a personal axe to grind on other people's problems. But don't forget, she's a hot wire—a government secret agent working for the B.S.I. You can't trust anybody farther than the end of his rope. It isn't reasonable to take a chance on it."

"What do you mean by rope?"

"I mean what ropes 'em to the ground—to the normal, everyday, common-sense view of what's right and wrong. The minute they cut that rope, they all go rainbow chasing. So stay on the ground. Do your own thinking. Watch your step."

"Very well, Andrew."

"You don't seem to like the idea."

"Andrew, it comes like a bit of an anticlimax. It lets out the steam. Nancy has been talking quite a lot this evening. I don't think she said anything that you would object to, but—"

"Go ahead. What?"

"Well—at first I didn't like what she said. But—Andrew, you know how she talks, and—"

"Yes—I know. She's a great talker. Well, it won't be long now. We'll ram you into a brace of blizzards at fifteen or sixteen thousand feet. That'll blow out the illusions. Just try to keep half sensible meanwhile, and don't let Nancy sell you Mt. Everest."

"If you won't let me promise, what shall I say?"

He laughed. "Say so long and good luck. Let's shake on that and I'll be on my way."

"So long, Andrew. I won't even say you're a brick—for fear of making you angry."

He looked as if he were going to kiss her goodbye, but he didn't. He shook hands. The art of going, instead of talking about going, was one of his special accomplishments. He walked away, leaving be-

347

hind him a sensation of finished business—nothing to be added to, or changed, or undone. Elsa gazed at his back as he strode to the door, until Bompo Tsering strode between them and followed him like a big, black, smelly shadow, shutting off the view.

Not even a gesture of goodbye from Bompo Tsering. He ignored her, too intent in his dog-like devotion to Andrew. Andrew didn't pause at the door. He walked through. Bompo Tsering closed it.

Silence. The crack of the new pine knot on the fire. A leaping flame—and suddenly, out of the shadows, on the small table in mid-room emerged the silver-framed likeness of Lobsang Pun—Old Ugly-face—inscrutably, unconquerably smiling—with a bullet hole exactly in the middle of his forehead.

Chapter 18

Andrew almost bumped into Lewis. At the far end of the hallway at the foot of the stairs the Lepcha servant sat on a chair beneath a Tibetan painting of the Buddha. He looked dazed. Obviously Lewis had been talking to him.

"Bad case," said Lewis, glancing at the servant and turning his back. "That poor fellow is a sample of secret vice at war with conscientious love of his employer. He relies on the one to condone the other—hides in the one to forget the other. But it can't be done. One fights the other, almost like a chemical reagent. That leaves him feeling physically weak and morally helpless. He craves relief from self-contempt, so he mentally almost leaps to meet the first hypnotic influence that comes along. Bulah Singh was like a magnet to a bit of scrap iron. Nancy will have a hard time helping that poor fellow to rebuild his self-control."

Lewis was obviously making conversation until Bompo Tsering should move out of earshot. But the Tibetan had to be told to go and wait by the front door. He didn't mind being told, but he hated to wait; he kept trying the lock and fidgeting with the brass check chain. Andrew and Lewis faced each other beneath the ceiling light, between the rows of books and photographs. Lewis screwed in his monocle. That meant business.

"Gunning, I'll ask a favour of you."

Andrew fell on guard—so visibly that Lewis hesitated. Andrew got his own demand in first: "I've a favour to ask, too," he retorted. "An important one. I'm dead set on it."

"Very well, my boy. Yours first. What is it? If it's anything that I

348

can—"

"It's easy," said Andrew. "It'll cost you nothing, and put you to no trouble. Please leave Elsa's mind alone. Don't aggravate what gives her grief enough already."

Lewis nodded, staring, smiling, as if he were diagnosing symptoms of something that Andrew had overlooked.

Andrew continued: "That's a good girl. She's genuine. She'll come out all right if she's given a chance."

"Good?" said Lewis. He thrust his head forward. "Better than you guess, my young friend.—By the way, we are friends, I believe?"

"Suits me," said Andrew. "But I'm the enemy of any man, no matter who, if he gives Elsa less than a square deal. She's in my charge. For the shortest possible time, for the sake of fooling Bulah Singh—which I take it is what you want to do—?"

"Yes," said Lewis.

"—I am leaving Elsa under your protection and Nancy Strong's. I will do what I can for you. But, first, I'd like your promise to—"

Lewis interrupted: "Gunning, let me tell you what I have in mind. Perhaps we can oblige each other. If we arrive at an understanding, I feel sure you will do your part."

"Shoot," said Andrew. "But mind, I've said my say. You know now what I want. It's personal—nothing to do with any government department—you and me, man to man. Let's keep it so."

"Very well." Lewis readjusted his monocle—frowned—raised his right hand and stared at his fingernails. He was about to prescribe. "My thought was this. I would like you to promise to stick to your stonewall mental attitude about clairvoyance."

Andrew looked suspicious. "That's an easy one," he answered. "I'm so by nature."

"Superficially, yes, you are," said Lewis. "It's a sort of mask. Actually, under the surface, you're a poet."

Andrew looked even more suspicious. He laughed gruffly: "You're sure trying to work me for something big! What makes you think I'm a poet ?"

"There's a rhythm in your thought," said Lewis. "You can change the meter without losing the theme. Besides, I glanced at the books you gave to Mu-ni Gam-po. I intend to borrow three of them. It was also my duty to learn what books you've sent forward, to read on the march. We check up on people before we trust them."

Andrew grinned: "You only trust people who read Shakespeare? Is

349

that your yardstick?"

"No." Lewis chuckled. "No, my boy. That was counted against you. Shakespeare, Sir Thomas Browne, Milton, Chaucer, Einstein and the Bible are the world's worst luggage, if you want to be trusted by the world's saviours! We official insiders—we directors of destiny flatter ourselves that we can see through beauty to the worms beneath! It's intelligence that all censors fear. However, you have good sound vices that offset your virtuosity. You're practical."

"You call it practical to throw up a career and take on this game?"

"And you've a rare gift of holding your tongue. I could mention quite a number of highly placed officials whom you haven't consulted."

"Hell, I told you all I know."

"All except just what I needed to know," Lewis answered. "I had to find that out for myself."

"For instance?"

"Oh, lots of things. Some of them important. For instance, you have avoided the mistake of talking to the wrong people. But let's get to the point. Elsa is a very remarkable, very unusual girl."

"I know it."

"She has character."

"You're telling me!"

"There are no available statistics, but it's a conservative guess that there are not more than two or three thousand in her class, in the whole world. And they're widely scattered. She is an instance of emerging evolution. Her spiritual nature—to use a conventional term for an unfamiliar and therefore unclassified state of consciousness—is like a young seedling, of a new species, reaching for the sunlight."

"You're speaking now of her clairvoyance?"

"Yes. That's only another word for the same thing. Kill that, and she's done for."

"Hell, she hates it."

"Yes. Who shall blame her? She's afraid of it. But she must dare to be one of the great explorers—far greater than Columbus. Columbus only discovered a continent, in known dimensions. Elsa's greater task is to abandon known dimensions and explore what Shakespeare called 'airy nothing.'"

Andrew smiled. Whoever quoted Shakespeare intelligently always passed his guard. He almost weakened. "Good stuff, that," he said. "You can't beat him. He's still tops. 'And as imagination bodies forth the forms of things unknown,' we'll 'turn them to shapes.' Hell, that has Columbus backed off the map. But Elsa isn't as tough as Columbus."

"No," Lewis agreed, "she isn't. She must be protected from mockery and from her own mistrust. She needs a line of retreat, so that she can draw back in, so to speak, and recover from—well—let us call it spiritual vertigo. That's a new phrase. I must add that to my list."

"'Such tricks hath strong imagination,'" Andrew quoted. "What's the rest of it? I'm listening."

"Yes, you use your inner ears. That's why I can talk to you. Now then: Elsa's line of retreat must not lead back into her own Cave of Adullam," (David's refuge from Saul in the Old Testament).

"Now I don't get you. That's one of those phrases that might mean anything."

"I mean, she must not draw back into herself—into her own gloom. She must have a different cave—strong, friendly, and, above all, patient. That's a mixed metaphor. However, you will have mixed feelings when I tell you that you are the cave."

"Jesus!" said Andrew.

"I mean it, my boy. That is why I ask you to maintain your stolid, stonewall attitude toward clairvoyance and everything connected with it. Let her lean against your imperturbable calm. Whenever she wants to, let her hide behind it. Let her feel the uncritical comfort of a friendly anchor to windward. That's another mixed one. But the situation's mixed." Then, suddenly: "Is she in love with her husband?"

"Damned if I know."

"Umm. Are you being frank about that? Well, what I mean is: if she should convict herself of treason to her own ideal, there would be no recovery—not in this existence: she would go under."

"She'll get no encouragement from me to cross-examine herself cuckoo," said Andrew. "I don't believe in that stuff. Gets you nowhere."

Lewis agreed: "Worse than nowhere. Hundreds of thousands of people damn themselves by monkeying with the works. They're like amateurs taking radios apart to discover why the program annoys them. Self-examination without experienced guidance is worse than taking patent medicines to cure an undiagnosed ailment. Much worse. A wrong diagnosis is sometimes a sentence to death. Self-conviction of sin is always a sentence to hell. Always. There is no exception to that. Before you see Elsa again, she will receive what your countrymen call a pep-talk from Nancy Strong."

351

"Not from you?"

"No. I'm a duffer at it. I might do more harm than good. I am merely a so-to-speak left-wing medical man. There are more of us than you suspect, but we all know we're treading on dangerous ground. We are hampered by conventional education, conservative theories, public prejudice, our own ignorance and much too much familiarity with evidence that seems to prove the contrary to what our intuition tells us is true. Nancy, on the other hand, is an adept. She has had thorough training. She knows how to encourage spirituality without destroying caution—how to develop caution without destroying courage. That is known, among the adepts, as the Middle Way."

"I've heard of it," said Andrew.

"Yes," remarked Lewis, "you undoubtedly have." He wiped his monocle. He was having a tough time. He was actually sweating.

"Go ahead," said Andrew. "I'm listening."

"So let us exchange promises, you and I. I will not, as you call it, rag Elsa. I won't interfere any further with her mental processes even if she should ask me to do it."

Andrew grinned: "I'll bet a dollar, even money, she won't ask."

"Wait and see," said Lewis. "If she does ask, I will refuse. On the other hand, you promise me you will give her the full benefit of—how shall I say it?—indifference—friendly indifference."

"Hell, you're asking too much," said Andrew. "I'm not indifferent, to anyone, or anything. Can't help the way my mind works—wondering how people and animals feel—whether they're right about what they feel—what it's all about, anyhow. It's the God's truth, I've never enjoyed another creature's grief nor felt unsympathetic when I saw 'em suffer. How does one go about being indifferent?"

"Well," said Lewis, "let's put it this way: you'll be the common-sense man with his feet on the earth. If she chooses to be inconsistent, don't criticize. Don't care. Don't remind her of it. But if she needs a bone to chew on, you provide the matter-of-fact comments for her to tear to pieces. If she blasphemes against her own vision, and accuses you of blindness, and contradicts herself, you never hold it against her."

"I never did," said Andrew.

"Well. Never do. Because she will." Lewis paused. Then, slowly: "Don't let her suspect that you know more than she does about—" He hesitated.

"About what?"

Lewis shut one eye and quizzed him through the monocle: "About the consequences of converting spiritual vision into personal sanctity."

"I don't," said Andrew.

"That's right, my boy, don't admit it. Don't ever confess to Elsa what caused you to leave the United States."

Andrew bridled: "Do you figure you know?"

"Yes."

"I'll bet you don't. If you got your dope from Bulah Singh's file, take it straight from me, you're all wet."

"Wet?" said Lewis. "Wet? Is that American for wrong? Well, I have known Bulah Singh to be wrong about numbers of things. Are we agreed about Elsa? Let us talk now about Bulah Singh."

"Swell," said Andrew.

"This is secret"

"Okay. Shoot."

"Bulah Singh is a mere meddler on the fringe of a wide conspiracy."

"I'd guessed that much," said Andrew. "He's small time. He hasn't the stuff to fill a three-ring circus."

"It's a conspiracy to talk Utopian theory, but to use heartless violence—to throw India into economic and political confusion, and to pull off a Fascist *coup d'etat.*"

"That's easy to believe," said Andrew. "That's the up-to-date style in revolutions. The scornful guys all see 'emselves as duces and commissars. They're too drunk with their own greed to remember that the up-and-coming big boy always kicks 'em in the face when they've hoisted him into the saddle."

"Yes," said Lewis. "They forget that. But it's true. Tyrants can't afford gratitude. They have to kick away the scaffold—shoot the men on whose shoulders they climbed. However, meanwhile, the conspirators are the men to watch. Very few of them guess yet which is actually Number One. Most of 'em are betting on 'emselves. Here in India they're counting, of course, on a world war to produce world revolution—doing their utmost to create it by the subtlest kind of propaganda. A war that tied up the British Navy would be the Indian Hitler's chance."

"Do you know yet who the big buzzard is?" Andrew demanded. "Have you spotted him? Who's to be India's Hitler?"

Lewis avoided that question by asking another: "How many people would have picked Stalin ten days ahead of the time? Napoleon, remember, was a dark horse until he saw his chance and seized it."

"Sure; I get you. If you knew the real buzzard you'd spike him before he could get going."

Lewis drew a forefinger across his own throat. "Right. We have names and past performances on file. But it's too soon to tell who'll be Jack-in-a-box. There are too many possibles. A few are genuine idealists; they wouldn't last a week, but no less dangerous on that account. They serve as stalking horses for the others, who will kill them off when the time comes. Most of 'em are ruthless, contemptuous rogues, who pose as humanitarians and pacifists. Mussolini did that, you remember—even went to prison for urging Italian conscripts to refuse to fight the Turks. Denounced war and nationalism. Denounced the Italian flag. But look at him now! All demagogues are devils—all peas from the same pod. Secretly, with scarcely an exception, they are Nietzschean individualists, who misunderstand Nietzsche. They believe themselves beyond good and evil. They use lies and violence for allegedly Utopian ends.

"No matter what name they assume to camouflage their real motives, you may be sure it's a false name. They despise the fools who listen to them and believe them. Believing themselves to be intellectuals, and aware of their own hypocrisy, they have unqualified contempt for other intellectuals. They don't believe an intellectual exists who isn't a hypocrite. But they know how to flatter the intellectuals, and how to use them, until their time comes. Then they enslave or liquidate them. They know the trick of hypnotising crowds. The crowd's adulation gives them the only genuine thrill they ever get. It's a kind of orgasm. They're good showmen. They let such fools as Bulah Singh run the real risks, until it's time for the big push."

"Jesus! You should write a book!" said Andrew. "Tell me: what does Bulah Singh think he'll get in exchange for the risk he must know he's running? What's his real price? I don't believe what he told me."

"Oh, he told you part of the truth. Bulah Singh is a mere ambitious meddler. Hypnotic skill is no proof of intelligence. In fact, it usually creates such conceit that it blinds and destroys intelligence. But he's studious. He knows his book backwards. He thinks, within his mental limitations. He understands, correctly enough, that any revolutionary government of India would be at the mercy of any Asiatic combination that should choose to invade from the north. That is the perpetual menace that overhangs India—always did—probably always will. That menace would be the Achilles heel of any dictator who could seize power. Bulah Singh believes he foresees the break-up of the British Empire. He thinks it's imminent."

"Maybe he's right," said Andrew.

Lewis ignored the interruption. "Bulah Singh's idea is to make himself indispensable to the coming dictatorship. He proposes to be the man who can diplomatically stave off an invasion from the north—Mongolian, led by Japs or Russians. That's why he wants control of the young Dalai Lama."

"And you know all this? And you don't dump him into the hoosegow?"

"Why catch a minnow and let the pike escape?" Lewis retorted. "We are hoping he'll betray the real conspirators—the real higher-ups—the devils—the brains behind the mere fomenters of discontent. It won't be long now. By about the time you are over the border we rather expect to have found out all that can be learned from watching Bulah Singh. If so, we'll jump him. And—to save himself—we think—we hope—he will betray his associates."

"Swell," said Andrew. "Here's wishing you luck."

"I have told you this in confidence," said Lewis, "for your general guidance. You may share the information with Tom Grayne when you meet him."

"Okay. Tom won't yawp."

"And now this: any help you can give to the Ringding Gelong Lama Lobsang Pun will be all to the good but must be kept off the record."

"Okay."

"We don't even know where Lobsang Pun is at the moment. He is said to be in hiding. But he is the only politically minded Tibetan who can't be bought for love or money. He is as incorruptible as Robespierre was, without Robespierre's bigotry and mad egotism. We believe he is the one man who can save Tibet from anarchy. Find him if you can. Help him in any way you can."

"I'd go out of my way to meet Old Ugly-face," said Andrew. "From what I've heard of him he sounds like a cross between King Alfred of the doughnuts and Marcus Aurelius. Okay. I'll keep an ear to the ground."

"If you can do it, help Lobsang Pun to get control of the infant Dalai Lama."

"That might be a tall order."

"Yes, and dangerous. But don't help Lobsang Pun to bring the child to India. That mustn't happen. Personally I would like to have the child in Darjeeling, under the influence of Nancy Strong. But that's an impractical pipe dream. It would lead to extremely embarrassing complications in addition to destroying the Dalai Lama's political influence. Do your best to prevent it."

"Okay."

"If you come across Ambrose St. Malo, kill him."

"Nothing doing."

"Why not?"

"I've a card in the Live-and-Let-Live Union."

"How about self-defence?"

"He'd have to start it. I don't go around encouraging folks to start things. If that guy has any horse sense—"

"He has a horse face. But he's a louse. I should have brought his photograph from Delhi. Sorry I didn't. He's described as a louse even in the official confidential report that we received from Hongkong."

"Yeah, I've heard that's his reputation. There was talk about him in Shanghai. I know his real name. But don't count on me to bump him off. My long suit isn't being all that scared that I need to shoot lice. But thanks for the tip. I'll watch him."

Bompo Tsering rattled away at the door chain, grunting and shuffling on the mat like a caged bear.

"I'll get going," said Andrew, "before Bompo Tsering blows up." He reached for his overcoat. "It's a bargain about Elsa?"

"Yes. You'll do your part?"

"Okay. Don't make me have to wait too long for her. My Tibetans are restless. They're raring to go."

"She shall follow as soon as we're sure that Bulah Singh is convinced you have left her behind. That is the important point at the moment—to make Bulah Singh believe you're obeying his orders. That may make him overconfident—he'll make his next move, and we'll catch him."

"Swell. Don't let Nancy get shot. She's too good to waste on a murderer's bullet."

"We'll protect her."

"How?"

"By letting Bulah Singh suspect that we suspect him of tonight's attempt. He won't risk it again. By the way, have you a gun with you?"

"Yes. Mauser."

"Where?"

"In my overcoat:"

"Registered?"

"Yes."

"Be careful not to show it. Don't use it."

"You bet."

"There'll be men in the shrubbery. Two of them are my men," said Lewis. "The other is Bulah Singh's, stationed there to watch you and report your movements. Take no notice."

"Okay. Goodbye. And thanks for the help."

"Give my best to Tom Grayne."

"Sure. Any special message for Old Ugly-face, in case I meet him?"

"Give him my love," said Lewis.

"Swell. I'll do that."

"One moment, Gunning. Just one last word of advice! In any emergency, remember that one man—like the fool at Sarajevo with a pistol— can wreck the world as easily as a careless surgeon can kill a patient. So in tight places, don't let yourself get hypnotized by appearances. Listen to the inner voice. Obey that."

Andrew grinned genially. "Same to you! Take good care of Elsa."

They shook hands. "Good luck," said Lewis. "You will find your road to the border littered with intelligently unobservant spotters, who have been told to mind their own business. You won't be questioned if you just say nothing. Don't mention my name."

"I won't mention any man's name," Andrew answered.

He strode to the front door. Bompo Tsering opened it and they leaned together into a blast of rain. Lewis slammed the door shut behind them, like a cannon shot starting the game.

CHAPTER 19

Andrew trudged and splashed beside Bompo Tsering, out through the front gate and along the high stone wall. He took the middle of the road to make sure of being seen by Bulah Singh's spies and to avoid the extra drenching from the overarching trees. A Ford car, badly in need of paint, loaded above window level with the dunnage that Elsa would need, stood parked in an alley.

Curled on the loads was another of Andrew's men—a gaunt, dish-faced countryman from somewhere north of Koko Nor—homesick

357

for the sky-high *steppes* where he was weaned on wild ass meat and barley. He said nothing. Even when Andrew turned a flashlight on him he said never a word. Andrew climbed in and took the wheel. Bompo Tsering scrambled to the front seat beside him. The chilled, damp engine started at the eighth or ninth try.

"So! By-um-by, at last. Our going!" said Bompo Tsering. To use English was the only way to get on even terms with Andrew. It was condescension—a polite hint that Andrew's Tibetan was something less than perfect. "Oh, the happy, blessed country! By-um-by soon there now."

Andrew was unresponsive—busy peering through the storm for wash-outs on the winding road. But Bompo Tsering was in talkative mood, which was a fact well worth making note of, after his recent dumbness.

"Gunnigun." He never could master the pronunciation of Andrew's name—had given up trying—had renamed him.

"Yes."

"Your being *peling*—" He paused for effect. *Peling* means foreigner: a comprehensive word, as packed full of significance as the Greek word *barbaros*—"too much often many times your doing damn-fool thing."

"This time not doing. My much happy."

"Forgotten your *dugpas* already? Left 'em behind, eh? Not scared of 'em now?"

"*Dugpas* being only spirits—can manage. Something else being much worse too bad. My thinking, making sorry. By-um-by now, your not doing, making too glad."

"What were you thinking that made you sorry?"

"Your sending me my buying all this more stuff. My obedient. My buying. But my thinking this more stuff must meaning Ladee Elsa coming also! Uh-uh! No good. My sorry. Too much damn-fool God-damn saying no-no! Also catching maybe 'nother baby—no good—no good! Uh-uh! Too much bad trouble—bad luck."

"She never hurt you, did she?"

"My 'fraid before. Now she not coming, my too much happy."

In proof of his high spirits Bompo Tsering began singing an endless nostalgic wail about the wonders, sacred and profane, of the Home of the Gods, on the Roof of the World, where the blessed snow—and dust-storms hide the holy treasures from the eyes of *pelings*, and the fortunate count their blessings beneath skies of azure. It was a good song, no more mendacious than the latest Broadway and Hollywood smash hit. He made it up himself, and believed every word of it, singing in time to the slap of a broken link against a rear mudguard; singing in the rain, in the dark, with his heartstrings thrumming like a harp within him to the call of his cruel homeland. The gaunt man from Koko Nor joined in the chant, selecting phrases that he liked and repeating them over and over, forcing Bompo Tsering to do the same, so that the song became a weirdly measureless duet.

Andrew preferred that to conversation. He could think through the song without listening to it. Conversation might have made it difficult to hide the tart sub-flavour of the memory that Bompo Tsering had opened a window of Nancy Strong's house, only a few moments before someone else fired a shot through the opposite window, missing Elsa by less that a foot. There was mud on the boots of the man from Koko Nor. There was no imaginable reason why Bompo Tsering should be Nancy Strong's enemy. But by Bompo Tsering's own admission, it was a relief to believe that Elsa was staying behind. The truth, like Bulah Singh's spy in the bushes, was lurking somewhere amid dark facts. It seemed worth discovering.

The smashing of Old Ugly-face's photograph, and Nancy Strong's conviction that the bullet had been meant for herself, were subjects for a kind of speculation that Andrew was in no mood for. Rain, and his job at the wheel, induced no taste for the occult, though he couldn't avoid it. Even less to his taste would be to question Bompo Tsering and be regaled with circumstantial lies or, worse yet, irrelevant lies, like red herrings drawn crosswise on the trail of facts. Steering through the storm suggested the kind of thinking that was needed. As methodically as he had laid all his plans for the journey, he reviewed the facts. The hard ones. The bulky, lumpy ones with sharp outlines. They were like the milestones on the road. The essential, first, number one fact was that he didn't want to get rid of Bompo Tsering. The man was as indispensable as he could afford to let one man be. The shot had fortunately missed, so there was no murder to avenge. It had missed at slightly above stomach level, to the left. Bompo Tsering was a bad shot, who almost always missed high right. Besides, Bompo Tsering had certainly not had time to run from one window to the other and fire the shot.

The rain and the roar of cascading water aided concentration on the problem. Attention to the dark road, the almost automatic alertness at pedals and steering wheel, produced a black-out of all unre-

359

lated thoughts—almost like a blackboard, on which Andrew chalked in white the facts that he selected one by one, of which the first was the mud on the boots of the man from Koko Nor. It was the wrong colour to have come from the place where he loaded the car. It was the colour of the flowerbed earth in Nancy Strong's garden. Perhaps a coincidence. More probably proof of guilt.

But the man from Koko Nor was an ignorant herdsman, secretive by instinct, who would do what he was told. He was tolerably patient, but certainly prone to violence if told the proper story. Bompo Tsering could have told it. Andrew knew more facts about Bompo Tsering than the latter suspected. Originally Tom Grayne's headman and only loaned to Andrew for the journey, Bompo Tsering's loyalty to Tom was indisputable. It held unplumbed depths of selfless devotion, only qualified by Tibetan indifference to Western views of what is important and what isn't. Andrew's own loyalty to Tom, which had a different basis, had been nevertheless a bond of union between himself and Bompo Tsering—a sort of bridge across which gradually some of the Tibetan's loyalty had transferred itself to Andrew. So divided allegiance was a fact to be carried in mind. Bompo Tsering was quite capable of sabotage for what he might believe was for Tom's or Andrew's own good. And there was more than one fork to the divided allegiance; quite a number of forks, all of them likely to confuse and distort the reasoning of an otherwise faithful headman. Andrew's mental blackboard began to be chalked up with the "knowns" of a compound equation that made the "unknown" look insoluble. But order came out of them after a while.

For instance: Bompo Tsering was a devout Tantric Buddhist, happy in his religious convictions, superstitious to the verge of devil worship, and amused—not horrified, but moved to laughter—by the discovery that other people, and especially *pelings* believed in ridiculous other religions or possibly none. Bompo Tsering's actions, especially when he had time to think about them, frequently were guided by a wish to scandalize and mock, as well as to serve and instruct his ignorant employer. Literal obedience, even good smart discipline, wasn't difficult to get from Bompo Tsering up to a point that varied with the occasion; but his subtle reasoning processes could invent and justify extremely tricky means of gaining secret ends without incurring much risk of detection. That fact went up on the board while Bompo Tsering got out to remove a fallen tree from the road and got in again after tying a prayer rag to a bush as a precaution against having to repeat such disagreeable labour. *Pelings* can't be taught that it is invisible devils who make the difficulties, so that all one needs to do is to forestall the devils with fluttering scraps of rag.

He resumed his song when Andrew got the car going again. He sang now about a legendary sorceress who merited death but was blessed by a holy hermit, so that she changed her mind, and became harmless, and so escaped the arrow of ill fortune that her previous misdeeds had launched against her on the bowstring of the Higher Law. The man from Koko Nor grew silent. Andrew noted the fact and the words of the song; he connected the two, and went on thinking about Bompo Tsering.

There was Bompo Tsering's domestic situation to consider. His love life, such as it was. That was another divided allegiance—between local tribal custom and the almost universal Buddhist contempt for women, nowhere recommended in the Ancient Teaching, but invented, like the doctrine of original sin, by sex-obsessed ecclesiastics, who relegate women to the category of dogs and other graceless lingerers on the Path to Bliss. But there are notably extreme exceptions. Bompo Tsering was one of several brothers all married to the same woman; she was priestess, wife and matriarch in one—an almost absolute tyrant, whose husbands took turns at home and spent the intervals wandering, working, earning to support their common proprietress.

So Bompo Tsering had mixed views about women. Probably he believed— although Andrew had never discussed it with him—that Tom and Andrew shared Elsa in some such domestic design as his own. Certainly his mental attitude toward Elsa was mixed of contempt and respect; veiled and made indistinguishable by his Tibetan good humour and by his conviction that it doesn't much matter what *pelings* think or do, as long as they don't steal Tibet. He had even found it amusing to obey Elsa when it wasn't too inconvenient. But he was rather self-conscious about it, rather ashamed. And he had never made any secret of his superstitious prejudice against women on expeditions. As such they were bringers of bad luck. So the fact went on the blackboard with the others, that Bompo Tsering felt no important loyalty to Elsa. There would be room in his consciousness for almost any other emotion that the circumstances, or a prejudice, or someone, might suggest. Who might be the someone? Who could have persuaded him to cooperate in the attempt to shoot Elsa? He undoubtedly had not fired the shot. But he certainly did cause the diversion that brought Elsa into full view from the opposite window.

361

Was that a coincidence?

Several possibilities crowded into Andrew's mind. He rejected at once, as too improbable, the idea that Bulah Singh might have hypnotized Bompo Tsering. And it was a certainty that Bulah Singh did not want Elsa murdered. But it was no secret from Andrew that one of Bulah Singh's spies had been camping all winter on Bompo Tsering's trail, had lost money to him, and had had a thousand opportunities to suggest that secret favours beget favours in return. Tibetans have a passion for intrigue; they always crave what is withheld and overreach themselves to get it, enjoying the bartering more than the actual profit.

That spy might easily have convinced the homesick Bompo Tsering that Bulah Singh could close the passes into Tibet against every member of Andrew's party, unless compensated by a valuable proof of reciprocity, paid in advance. Such talk would have tickled Bompo Tsering's undisciplined loyalty. It would have awakened his delight in mysterious byplay. It would have spurred his eagerness to get started homeward. It would have excited his high opinion of himself as a diplomat. The nicely motivated murder of anyone of whom he disapproved would no more trouble Bompo Tsering's conscience, than it would Bulah Singh's. Tibetans are pious people, but they amazingly indulge in clandestine trickery for which the threatened penalty, in which they thoroughly believe, is millions of years in a merciless, fantastically realistic hell. They behave as if they want to go to hell.

But there was this difference: the Sikh was unsentimental; he hadn't any of the juice of magnanimity. Bompo Tsering, on the other hand, would be unlikely to murder anyone against whom he had no ground for fear, mistrust or hatred. Bompo Tsering wouldn't murder Nancy Strong. But to cause Elsa to be killed because, in his opinion, she might bring bad luck, might seem to him a praiseworthy act, especially if the idea of killing someone—anyone—were suggested to him, in the first instance, by the agent of a man whom he had reason to fear. Scruples have a way of disappearing under pressure—squeezed out.

But fear of Bulah Singh might also—almost certainly would—inspire a delicious, amusing desire to double-cross that gentleman. It would be a typical Tibetan reaction to a blackmailer's effort to make him a cat's-paw. Loyalty to Andrew—certain knowledge that Andrew detested Bulah Singh—would be an added inducement to put a hot one over on the Sikh.

Andrew watched for a chance to discover whether his thought

362

was leading in the right direction. During a pause in the endless song Bompo Tsering spat through the window and then shot a question:

"Gunnigun! Why you not being much happy, same like we making singsong? Blessed happy land soon by–um–by not too far."

"I'm thinking about Bulah Singh" said Andrew. "He might overtake us."

The reaction was instantaneous. Bompo Tsering unbosomed himself of triumph that came like steam from a safety valve. There was pressure behind the words. He selected them, from Andrew's special vocabulary reserved for use in tight places, when yaks and ponies give up and men malinger:

"Hot damn! Son of a bitch! Bastard! Bugger no good! God-damn cockeye! Kick 'um!" Then, profoundly mysterious: "Gunnigun! You by–um–by no more caring about Bulah Singh. My fixing 'um. So. Hot damn!"

Inexperience would have thrust into that opening with sharp questions. But Andrew knew his man. The half-hint, that had steamed off the kettle of truth, was a relief to Bompo Tsering's nerves; but it was also a trick to discover what line Andrew's thought was taking. If Andrew had betrayed even veiled curiosity, the truth would have retired into its hole like a mouse that smells cat. The right strategy was to change the subject.

"Watch for leopards," said Andrew. "The headlights dazzle 'em. If one of 'em should get out from under the wheels in time, he'd likely as not jump in on us."

Bompo Tsering began singing about leopards. Andrew resumed his review of the facts.

Bulah Singh believed Elsa was staying behind. But Elsa would be no use to the Sikh while under Nancy Strong's protection. Nancy Strong was in Bulah Singh's way. She probably knew or guessed too many of his secrets. She had very likely offended him deeply; she was notorious for befriending victims of police brutality. It wasn't in the least improbable that Bulah Singh wanted Nancy Strong murdered, and wanted the job done at exactly the right moment to coincide with other moves on the board. He was evidently a time-table plotter, and pretty good at it. The bullet might have been meant for Nancy— might have been—in the beginning. But artful beginnings often have boomerang ends.

Not to be wholly ignored was Nancy Strong's conviction that the shot had been intended for herself. The photograph business was beyond the pale of Andrew's tolerance; he didn't let his mind go wandering into that metaphysical swamp. But he did trust Nancy's intuition. He had good reason to trust it. Her bare word that she knew the bullet had been meant for herself was at least as good as anyone's who might choose to contradict her. Only so far there was no proof! The bullet missed. Had it been aimed at the wrong target, contrary to someone's orders?

If Bulah Singh, personally or through his agent, had supplied Bompo Tsering with a pistol and had persuaded him, by threats and promises, to shoot Nancy Strong, then it was not unthinkable that Bompo Tsering might have told off the man from Koko Nor to do the job, but to shoot Elsa instead. His oriental mind would calculate that after the event Bulah Singh would be too deeply implicated to dare anything except to smother enquiry and expedite the expedition's departure northward in every way possible. A bit subtle. A bit complicated. But not too improbable.

It would explain Bompo Tsering's almost irrepressible triumph. He might even have been clever enough to contrive that Bulah Singh or his agent was overheard when he made the murderous proposal— or to make the Sikh think he had been overheard. He might believe he had completely outwitted Bulah Singh—by instructing the peasant from Koko Nor to shoot Elsa, not Nancy. Tibetans can't be expected to think of everything. It had probably never occurred to Bompo Tsering that Elsa's death by an assassin's bullet would have blown all secrets galley-west and have made the return to Tibet impossible.

Andrew wondered how much Lewis had guessed, or suspected, or knew about that shot through the window. He rather wished he had questioned Lewis about it. The man was a nut. Any man who can run a bughouse—and study hypnotism and world politics—and be an authority on poisons— and boss a very important branch of the secret intelligence—and believe in Jesus—couldn't be anything else than a nut. But he was a good guy. He liked Lewis—trusted him.

On the whole, things began to look good. Even the rain was an asset, like a curtain at the end of a first act.

CHAPTER 20

Nancy Strong returned from the school building by the back entrance. Near the foot of the stairs she handed her oiled silk raincoat and umbrella to the Lepcha servant.

"Put those away, please, and then go to bed."

He obeyed like an automaton.

"Have you forgotten how to speak?"

"No, *memsahib.*"

"Goodnight, then."

"Goodnight, *memsahib.*"

She watched him hang up the coat and slouch away to his own quarters, turning off the light in the back hallway. He vanished through a swing door. As she faced about she found Lewis beside her. She was startled. Lewis appeared not to notice the nervous reaction; he was putting away a small memorandum book, taking care that it didn't show above the edge of his vest pocket.

"Nothing much left of that poor fellow," he remarked. "You had better turn him out to grass. He's a psychic wreck. He'll be a physical wreck in next to no time."

"Where did you come from so suddenly?"

"I've been using the phone in your office. But about that Lepcha— why not send him home to his village?"

"Leave him to me. Did Andrew Gunning get away safely?"

"Away, yes. Safely, if he has it in him. Good fellow. I like him—intelligent—never tells what he's thinking about unless he expects to be understood. Doesn't expect to be understood too often. By the way, Nancy, you'll get quite a phone bill. Please pay it, and send me a memorandum. I'll settle with you off the record."

"Very well. You will find your bag in the corner guest room."

"Is that a hint?"

"Don't be silly. Your bag is locked, so the servant couldn't unpack it for you, but—"

Lewis held up a warning finger. His voice dropped to a dramatic whisper: "Nancy, I hardly dare to trust even myself with the secrets in that bag!"

"Sherlock Holmes! Where are your pipe and magnifying glass?"

"You mean, where's the needle! Why not say it?"

"I have just come from talking to children. I advised them to go to sleep. Why don't you?"

"Sleep? God and the devil and doctors work at all hours, Nancy. I must wait up for my shadow. Is the back door open?"

"No. If your shadow bangs on it he'll wake the children again. So—"

"Nancy, if my man heard himself make more noise than a cat's ghost, he'd die of shame. However, to save you from anxiety, I will go and wait for him near the back door."

"Take that chair with you and be comfortable."

"Right. By the way, hadn't you better send Elsa to bed? That girl is a bit overwrought. A mild sedative might—"

"Meaning, I suppose, that you want to talk to me alone?"

"Well—time's short. Yes. There's something—"

"Why not say it now?"

"Very well. You know what it is. I've asked a dozen times. However, I'll say it again. Our friend Johnson, of the Ethnographic Survey, was retired because he was beginning to know too much. Some traitor behind the scenes was afraid of him. Who is the traitor? Name him!"

"Morgan, you are too clever, and not wise enough. Have you forgotten about the devil who said his name was Legion? You're a physician. You and St. Luke should understand each other."

"That's an evasive answer, Nancy. You are not being frank. It's out of character—and beneath your dignity."

"Oh? Familiarity has bred contempt? Am I to choose a scapegoat for your baffled vigilance? Whom do you wish me to betray?"

"Nancy, please be serious."

"I can't be when you are in that mood."

"It's black treason. Possibly a member of the council. One of our own race."

"The human race? Well? Did you ever hear of a political, or any other council of human beings that lacked a traitor or two? You, a psychologist?"

"Psychology be damned! We're too late for that stuff. This is hard fact, if we can lay a finger on it. It's a defeatist conspiracy, well hidden, by someone powerful enough to protect such parasites as Bulah Singh, and swine enough to bet on a world war, and a revolution in India, with a front seat for himself at the finish. He might be any of three men."

"Or of a thousand," said Nancy. "I told you. His name is Legion."

"You know who he is. Name him!"

"I know the three men whom you suspect. I think you're wrong. Those are three self-important nobodies with sly minds. Place-holders— Sycophants. They play politics like a game of bridge and quarrel across the table. They can be manipulated by almost any artful man who understands what snobs they are. Cowards. Sail-trimmers. They have no real convictions— no vision—no integrity. In a pinch they will play safe. Mice."

366

"Rats!" said Lewis. "Which is king rat?"

Nancy smiled engagingly: "Fleas are deadlier than rats, and you know it. Fleas spread the plague that rats catch from corruption in the dark. Why not use flea powder?"

Lewis suppressed his irritation. He stuck to his point: "It wasn't those men's parasites who torpedoed Johnson. They did that."

"Don't flatter them," Nancy retorted. "They didn't think of it themselves. They didn't invent spite any more than rats invented bubonic plague. Someone with a poisonous whisper suggested to those three wise mice that pet cat Johnson was intriguing to get them out of office. There was some truth in it, too. Johnson wasn't always innocent of malice, and he loved the sensation of power behind the scenes. They turned on Johnson. It was three to one, with one of Johnson's most tactless mistakes in the scale against him. I know that because he told me about it. I had dinner with him, in Delhi, the night before he left for England."

"Did he say who the poisonous whisperer was?"

"No. He knew no more than you do."

"Couldn't he guess?"

"I don't repeat embittered people's guesses."

"Fair enough. But tell me your guess. Whom do you suspect?"

"I think perhaps Bulah Singh knows."

Lewis's irritation began to break through the crust. "I am asking you!"

"I don't know."

"You do know. You may have no factual knowledge. No legal evidence. That's quite likely. But you've the psychic gift of a human bloodhound."

Nancy laughed outright: "Morgan, that's the most ingenious paraphrase for a vulgar epithet that I ever heard. Go to the head of the class."

"You know very well what I meant, Nancy."

"I guessed it, Morgan. It filtered through."

"Here: I'll be frank with you. Two men's wives have been to see you lately. One was a banker's wife from Calcutta. If the big money is in on this—but of course it is! It always is. Tell me—"

"Morgan, money hasn't any brains. So bankers' wives are less reliable than *ayahs*. Besides I have told you again and again, I will not betray confidences. People come to me with their troubles for private, not public reasons."

"You've a public duty," said Lewis.

"Do yours. I will do mine," she answered. "Take the chair with you. And please don't let your shadow, as you call him, wake the children."

She left him standing. Lewis set his jaw and ground his teeth at her back. She shut the living-room door with a revealing thud that made him grin. It gave him some comfort to know he could make her angry. There weren't many who could. She switched off the light as she entered the room. Elsa stood up, rubbing her eyes. She had been staring at the fire.

"You're tired?" Nancy asked. "Like to go to bed? It's very late."

"I couldn't sleep," said Elsa. "But I don't want to keep you up."

"Very well. Put some wood on the fire. I have to wait for Morgan Lewis. Sit up with me and protect me from him."

"Are you joking?"

"Yes. But the joke is on him. As long as you are in the room he can't ask questions. Tell me about Andrew."

They sat facing each other, in the warm, red, comfortable book-framed glow of firelight. The cat sprang into Nancy's lap.

"There's nothing left to tell. One always knows how Andrew will behave. Unsentimental—"

Nancy's smile interrupted, but she made no spoken comment.

"Nancy, he is! He's the most unsentimental but dependable friend in the world. He just said 'So long' and walked out. Bompo Tsering followed him like a dog."

"No advice? No information?"

"Oh yes. I'm to do whatever you tell me. I will, too. I've promised. And I'm to 'yes' Dr. Lewis: that's American for praise God but keep your powder dry. I'm to overtake Andrew as soon as I possibly can. Nancy, do you think Andrew is in danger?"

Nancy made herself comfortable in the armchair. She closed her eyes for a moment. "What do you think?"

"I told Andrew. I'm not sure he liked my telling him. At the moment, no, no danger. But he hasn't finished with Bulah Singh. There's a link. I saw it. I see it now."

"What does it look like?"

"Like a dull red rope from Bulah Singh to Andrew. When I get a mental picture of them, there the rope is. Only of course, it isn't a rope. It's more like one of those moon rays on rippling water. But it isn't like that either.—Oh, I can't explain it."

368

"Don't try," said Nancy. "I saw it too. If you try to explain too definitely, you will get lost in definitions, like a music critic writing for the penny papers. People will take you literally and make unanswerably stupid comments."

Elsa smiled mischievous agreement: "Good! That's the first easy advice you have given me! I won't try to explain!"

The house was as quiet as a tomb. The fire glow made the silence cordial and comforting and snug. The cat purred. Nancy sat still for several minutes and then suddenly resumed, in a quiet, assured, unemphatic voice:

"If you do try to explain, you will convince no one—not even another clairvoyant unless he is trying to help you—and even then not always. That is why people who know, don't tell, unless they're teaching someone who they know can learn. No two mental pictures are alike, because no two human beings are alike. The point is, what do the clairvoyant pictures mean in terms of common experience?"

"I suppose it's something like translating Tibetan or Sanskrit into English?"

"Only more so. More like calculus into mechanics."

"Well, I think the red rope probably means that Bulah Singh will keep after Andrew, and stick to him like a leech, and make trouble for him, but not on this side of the Tibetan border. Bulah Singh is afraid. He intends to cling to Andrew somehow. When I look at Bulah Singh there seems to be a menace around him, too, coming from every direction except one. He keeps looking in that one direction. Oh, what a beast Bulah Singh is!" She shuddered.

"It's fortunate you said that."

"Why, Nancy? How do you mean?"

"Because it reveals a viewpoint."

"You mean Bulah Singh's?"

"No. Yours. Your attitude. Do you know any mathematics?"

"No. I can't even add. Simple quadratic equations are as far as I got, and I was no good at those."

"It doesn't matter. Shakespeare was no good at them either. Neither were Joan of Arc or Beethoven. They say Einstein can't balance his own bank account. We must think of some other way of illustrating what I want to explain."

"Try plain English," Elsa suggested. "I can think in English—or at least—" she laughed—"you've made me feel that perhaps I can't think."

Nancy stared at the fire. "Let's suppose," she said after a moment, "that what I told you tonight is the truth."

"Very well. I remember most of what you said. I half believe it until you go out of the room. At first I felt angry. But I don't any longer. I rather like it. I would like to believe it."

"Believing," said Nancy, "is no good. None whatever. As I said before, anyone who believes can disbelieve. But one who knows can't not know."

"How in the world can one know?"

"In the same way that you know you are, when you say I am. Try it. You can change what you see in a mirror by changing what the mirror reflects and distorts and reverses. You are not the reflection. You are your soul. Leave off believing you are your reflection. I use motion pictures to explain it to the children. The moving figures on the screen are not the figures on the film. The figures on the film are not the actors. Even the actors are not the author. And even the author is not the idea. You are your soul. You are not what Morgan Lewis calls a sanguinary mechanism. That mechanism isn't you at all. Identify yourself with your soul—I am my soul; I am not its material shadow. You will soon know you are telling the truth, because truth proves itself. One step at a time, you will learn to trust your spiritual vision."

"But, Nancy, surely there was nothing spiritual about that glimpse of Bulah Singh? It was cruel—guilty—afraid, hanging on to Andrew. It was worse than reality."

"It was only spiritual in the sense that it wasn't confined to the normal three dimensions. It was Bulah Singh's own secret thought of himself, hidden behind the false face that he presents to the world. Your eyes didn't see it. But you saw it. What did you do about it?"

"I don't see what you mean. What could I do? I did nothing."

"Your timid consciousness was looking at his predatory thought. Both on the same plane, to use a phrase that doesn't mean much. That is more or less what happens when strangers meet and suddenly become friends or enemies. Without realizing it, they get a glimpse of each other's consciousness. People who are good choosers of subordinates unconsciously possess that faculty. Some of them consciously possess it. It explains most cases of love or enmity at first sight. Being far more clairvoyant than you realise, and almost wholly untrained, you had a glimpse of Bulah Singh's thought. You half interpreted a danger, and recoiled. You were like an ostrich. You stuck your vision back into the nice safe sand of the Desert of Don't Believe and hoped you wouldn't get your tail feathers pulled. What good does it do you to have seen the danger?"

Elsa laughed. "Yes, you're quite right. That's what I did do."

"You recoiled. You refused to look. What good was it?"

"Well, I suppose at least I'm warned against Bulah Singh. What should I have done?"

"Not what you did, my dear. We have to learn to be practical. Unapplied theory is the same as faith without works. It is worse than dead. It is a decomposing spiritual poison. If you were alone in a room with Bulah Singh, could you defend yourself against him from a physical attack?"

"No. He's muscular. I'm sure I couldn't."

"What would you do?"

"Yell for help and try to escape."

"Good. Bear that answer in mind. We will return to it presently. Physically, you admit he is too strong. Your muscles against his muscles would be useless. Do you believe your thought can defend itself against Bulah Singh's thought any better than your person could defend itself against his person?"

"Oh, now you're talking about mind over matter?"

"No. Thought against thought. Thoughts can't run away from each other. Are you naive enough to suppose that your peace-pursuing thought can defeat Bulah Singh's predatory will by merely looking at it and being horrified?"

"Do you mean—I don't quite—say that again."

"No. Try another illustration. Can a Jew in Germany defend himself from outrage by knowing and fearing the greedy mendacious malice of the Nazis' motives?"

"No. I suppose not. No, of course not. It must feel to a Jew something like an inundation to the Chinese when the dikes break on the Yellow River—helpless—nothing they can do about it—nothing. I've been reading about the German Jews in some books Andrew lent me. I've been wondering what the Jews could do about it. I can't imagine. I can only feel sorry for them.—But what did you mean about thoughts can't run away from each other?"

"Well. Can you imagine it? The Jews can't run away from the Nazi persecution. They are trapped. They can't get passports. The Chinese can't escape the inundation. They have no transportation, and nowhere to go. Even more so, twice three can't run away from six times one. Six wins and the other figures lose their independence. It is simply useless to deny it."

"Nancy, what awful pessimism!"

"That is realism, not pessimism. Thought is much more powerful than any other force in nature. But thought can't escape, first from words and symbols, and then from physical expression. It creates them. It builds pictures in the thinker's mind—patterns that guide the person that obeys the impulse. There is nothing covered, that shall not be revealed. Thoughts find expression in deeds, sooner or later, without any exception."

"Aren't any thoughts secret?"

"None—not in the long run."

"I can very seldom read yours, or Andrew's, or Mu-ni Gam-po's. Just now I seem to know what you are going to say before you say it, but—"

"Cover, conceal, delay the transmutation of thought into act, and you merely increase the potential violence. Unless you know how to transmute that violence, then what? Oppose thought against thought and what possibly can happen but collision?"

"I've never thought of it," said Elsa.

"Think of it now. Oppose a pacifist's motorcar to an invading armoured train. What happens?"

"Someone buries the pacifist."

"Very well. Oppose a recitation of the Sermon on the Mount against an air raid on Barcelona. What do you get?"

"Massacre!" said Elsa. "Women and babies blown to bits—airmen getting good salaries—plenty of people remarking that the Sermon on the Mount is a damned lie. Who should blame them? I don't think they're blasphemous. They pray to God for mercy, and the answer is bombs— butchery."

"Aren't you taking it too much for granted that they did pray?" Nancy answered. "They did not pray. That was the trouble. From the beginning of the world until now, no genuine prayer ever went unanswered, instantly! Or was ever answered without humour, beauty and loving-kindness, that blessed and cursed not! Prayer doesn't consist in opposing thought against thought, creed against creed, self-righteousness against self-righteousness—bogey against bogey—fear of defeat against lust for victory. If you oppose your thought against Bulah Singh's, what are you likely to get?"

"Defeat, I suppose," said Elsa. "I never did want to fight anyone. I want to be let alone. I'm sure I haven't enough hatred in my system—

372

at least, I hope I haven't—to be able to out-hate a Sikh hypnotist! It looks as if we're up against that gruesome law of the survival of the fittest—"

"Fittest for what?" Nancy retorted. "What do you wish to be fit for? Pork or poetry? Destruction or creation? Degradation or evolution?"

"I would like to know what good talking about evolution and religion does for the victims of bombs and blackmailers!"

"There is no need to be a victim. Remember the Ninety-first Psalm: 'A thousand shall fall at thy side, and ten thousand at thy right hand, but it shall not come nigh thee.'"

"But, Nancy, that's horribly selfish! I would rather be a victim of almost anything, than be some kind of special person who felt superior and—"

"Gently, child, gently! You are not being asked to be a special person. But don't you want to help? Can the dead stop the massacre?"

"No, of course they can't."

"Can selfishness stop it?"

"Perhaps enlightened selfishness might lead to—"

"To a jack-o'-lantern's quicksand! The way to enlighten selfishness is to realise that only believers in the illusion of personal self can possibly be selfish. They can't avoid it. But the selfish soul doesn't exist. It would be a contradiction in terms."

"Well, suppose that's true. How can one help? By talking? They'd call it propaganda. Talk never stopped people from hating each other. It makes them hate each other all the worse."

Nancy laughed. "Well, I am talking to you! Are we hating each other? My dear, a victim, no matter of what—even a victim of his own generosity or his own greed—is someone who opposed some form of violence, either with lesser violence or with the wrong strategy: One is as useless as the other. Wars are good illustrations of that. The very best that can be said of any war is that it is bravery wasted."

"Then do you teach passive resistance? Non-resistance?"

"No. Far from it. I teach vigorous assault on cause, and let the symptoms take the consequences. I don't look for peace where there is none."

"Nancy, you're too fond of paradox. I wish you'd say what you mean in plain words."

"Very well. Listen."

"I am listening."

"There are three states of consciousness."

Elsa glanced at the shelf beside her. "But Freud says—"

"Forget Freud for the moment. Some of those books are there to remind me to forget what is in them. Freud, Jung, Adler and scores of others have made brilliant discoveries of what happens to people who base their outlook on what appears to them to be the reality of personal material existence. They have discovered some of the mechanics of the illusion. They try to patch up and strengthen the illusion. We propose to weaken it, by letting go of it. Then evolution takes care of us. I will give you the key to the secret of evolution. Lobsang Pun taught it to me."

"You mean this is secret?"

"It is a key to the secret."

"Why is it secret?"

"Because people who are too convinced of the reality of what is known as sensual perception, and who think that intellect and intelligence are the same thing, can't possibly understand it until disaster takes the conceit out of them and they begin to be humble and humourous and a little bit wise."

"Very well. I will try to be humble. What is the secret? Surely whoever knows it should tell it."

"I said it is a key to the secret. There are several other keys, but this is the simplest. The secret reveals itself when you use the key. For all practical purposes there are three states of consciousness."

"I do hope you're not going to use a lot of confusing terms that mean something different to whoever uses them."

"No. Plain words. From, at, and toward.—If you prefer it, call them subconsciousness, consciousness, and superconsciousness."

"That sounds too simple," said Elsa.

"It is. Much too simple for the brain-believers. It amounts to an insult to what pride calls intellect. It doesn't take much intellect to perceive that a bomb kills; a lie hurts; an empty purse can't buy; hunger isn't satisfying; a cold doorstep isn't a warm home. Even demagogues and other lunatics can elaborate that picture and make it worse. But it does require real intelligence to see and to use the beautifully, humorously simple remedy."

"What do you call intelligence?" Elsa asked.

"I call for it," said Nancy. "I don't have to define what it is. I let it define me. I demand it—from superconsciousness. True intelligence is an inseparable dimension of superconsciousness—instantly ready, available to everyone who asks."

"Can you make that clearer?"

"Yes. Wake up and know! Subconsciousness is the storehouse of the mass illusion. Let Freud have it. It is the mist mentioned in the first chapter of Genesis—the common memory pool—the pool of the Narcissus myth. It contains every detail of all the past history of all the people who ever lived in the world. All that they have ever imagined, believed and done. It is continually being added to, every minute. It holds all the false answers to all the false questions. It is a logical, merciless law unto itself, as full of fear as a sea is full of water. Jesus called it the lie and the father of lies. The Hindus call it *maya*. Plunge into it—stay in it—and there you are. Drown in the disgusting ocean of illusion. It's useless to ask mercy of that stuff or to ask it to cure its own corruption. Subconsciousness is the source of instinct, behaviourism, habit. And that includes the habit of death—a very bad habit, but there it is. We must evolve out of it, upward."

"Into superconsciousness?"

"Yes. Superconsciousness is life. The rest is shadow. There is no illusion, and nothing false, in superconsciousness. Intelligence, affluence, humour, spontaneity, beauty and selfless love are inseparable dimensions of superconsciousness. It is the source of genius and perpetual newness. Soul-consciousness—that is to say acceptance of the truth that now, not tomorrow but now, we are our souls—opens the door of superconsciousness. From the moment when we accept the truth that we are living souls, not dying persons, we begin to evolve spiritually. Then, if we demand more, and more, we become masters, not victims. The illusion of selfishness gradually dies. Love replaces it. It's so simple that in the beginning we can't keep it in consciousness for more than seconds at a time. But those are precious seconds. They increase and expand, as we enjoy them and learn to depend on them. We become more and more soul-conscious, less and less stupid. Our consciousness becomes a lens through which reality pours into the world. That is the meaning of Jesus' promise: '*the works that I do shall he do also; and greater works than these.*'"

"Then you really believe what it says in the Bible? We can raise the dead, and—"

Nancy laughed. "Gently, child, gently! Let us raise the living first. Reform ourselves, and then see what happens. There'll be another world war and a relapse into barbarism, unless thinking stops it. So let us think. Remember Shakespeare's line: '*There is nothing either good or bad, but thinking makes it so.'* It all takes place in consciousness. So let's change our own first. We can let our consciousness drift downward, or raise it upward by an effort of will. But it has to be good will."

"You talk of sub- and super-, but what is plain consciousness? You haven't defined that."

"I wish you understood mathematics. But never mind. Remember from, at, and toward. Subconsciousness is from. Superconsciousness is toward. Consciousness is at: the relatively real point at which you are at any given moment, varying as you sink into the subconscious illusion—or rise toward superconscious reality. Is that clear?"

Elsa curled up in the armchair, staring at Nancy, wondering why she had never noticed before that Nancy looked like a *lama*. She had seen more than one *lama* with similar facial expression. True, most Buddhist lamas, excepting Lobsang Pun and Mu-ni Gam-po, had seemed to her no better—perhaps worse, and more self-righteous than the vicar at home, if that were possible. Whereas Nancy—

"It seems clear when you say it," she answered. "But—"

"Think now of your mental picture of Bulah Singh."

"I saw his thought. Yes. What should I have done about it?"

"You yourself gave the correct answer when we spoke of your being alone in a room with him. You should have yelled for help and escaped! That is exactly what I did, when I suddenly knew that shot was coming through the window."

"Nancy, you old prevaricator! You never made a sound! I screamed, when Andrew nearly pushed me into the fire. I'm ashamed of it. But you didn't. You sat still in your chair."

"My dear, I yelled. It was so sudden that I hadn't time to do anything else."

"Nancy, are you dreaming?"

"I was dreaming, at that moment. I was actually thinking of the children, all tucked away in the dormitories, wondering what they were dreaming about. I awoke with a clear picture of the danger—and yelled for help."

"None of us heard you."

"I didn't yell to any of you," Nancy answered. "I cried with all my conscious might for help from superconsciousness. It never fails. It can't fail. Remember Isaiah: 'But it shall come to pass that before they call, I will answer; and while they are yet speaking, I will hear.' I and my soul were one, that moment, and I knew it. And you know what happened. *'Thou shaft not be afraid for the terror by night, nor for the arrow that flieth by day.'* Answer: was anyone hit?"

"Poor Old Ugly-face's photograph—oh, I beg your pardon, Nancy. I mean—"

"I usually call him that," said Nancy.

"To his face?"

"No. Of course not. But he prefers to bethought of as Old Ugly-face. That lets in some humour. It avoids the very human tendency almost to deify one's spiritual teacher. Solemnity is only a humbug substitute for love and reverence."

"Nancy! Tell me! Had that shooting of the photograph anything to do with—"

Nancy laughed. She shook her head. "Elsa, I don't know. I could believe it. The lower consciousness is as full of tricks as a stage magician. But guessing isn't believing, and believing isn't knowing. I haven't told you anything tonight that I don't know of my own experience."

"You seem confident."

"Yes. So confident that—" Nancy almost chanted St. Paul's declaration of faith—"'*neither death, nor life, nor angels, nor principalities, nor powers, nor things present, nor things to come, nor height, nor depth, nor any other creature could persuade me to the contrary.'*"

"Those are grand words," said Elsa, "but they didn't save St. Paul from being shamefully executed by the Romans."

"Do you suppose he suffered for being right, or for having done wrong?" Nancy retorted. "It isn't often wise to argue from the consequences of other people's mistakes. It's more useful to remember the work they did well—spectacularly well! St. Paul's work has survived the Roman Empire. Is it dead yet? Far from it! Perhaps St. Paul hadn't quite learned how to forgive himself for previous mistakes. He may have felt glad to settle his own *karmic* account for having himself been a bigoted and cruel persecutor before he woke up and became a saint. St. Paul himself said: 'there is none righteous, no, not one.' He was a brave little Jew, pressing, as he described it, 'toward the mark for the high calling . . . not as though I had already attained, either were already perfect.'"

"Then what you teach doesn't pretend to change the consequences of—"

"It pretends nothing, Elsa. It is the illusion of materiality that pretends, and makes false promises, and glitters with false causes and their consequences. Truth is the only creator of anything real. Truth never begets ill results, and never lets you down. Never! Truth doesn't rob

377

Peter to pay Paul. It doesn't have to. It couldn't. Acceptance of truth into consciousness is spiritual evolution; it drives out the legion of lies. Falsehood and false consequences vanish, like darkness before daylight, no matter how deeply they are rooted in human thought. But it's a process. It takes time, because we are so full of conceit. However, if we are going forward, we are not going backward. The thing is, to be up, and awake, and on our way."

Elsa leaned forward. "Tell me. Will it—if I try to follow your advice—will it bring some real love into Tom's life?"

"Oh, excellent!" said Nancy. "Full marks!"

"Why? What do you mean? What have I said?"

"Think it over. There's another question at the back of your mind. What is it?"

"Andrew. How can I repay Andrew for all his utterly unselfish kindness?"

"Are you sure it was unselfish?"

"Yes. I'm almost sure he secretly detests the very ground I stand on. Why shouldn't he? I've been nothing but a nuisance. But there isn't one thing that he could possibly have done, to make things easier for me, that he has left undone. Isn't that unselfish?"

"Well then, why try to repay him? How could you? It's only selfishness that accepts repayment. I'm not talking about borrowed money, or the give and take of commerce. But can you repay the sun for its warmth? No! Pass it along. Reflect it. Be kind to others."

"Nancy, wouldn't it be in line with your ideas if I could somehow help Andrew to unburden himself of his secret? I know he has one. It makes him wretched. It is eating his heart out. He keeps it hidden beneath a dark gray cloud that I can't ever see through. Sometimes the cloud is the colour of dry blood. But it's usually dark gray. Do you suppose I could help him?"

"You might mind your own business," Nancy suggested. "That always helps."

"But you said just now—I mean—don't you help people?"

"When they ask for it—with all I have!—to the limit." She laughed. "But there is no limit! The way to help people in the dark when they ask for it is to demand light on one's own darkness—the light of true intelligence. But bad spiritual manners are worse than a common cad's. There is nothing likelier to make people resentful and vindictive than to squirt them with light like a fire hose. You may believe that's light, but it isn't; it's conceited bigotry. It's worse than prodding a tiger.

378

Do you want to deal with a tiger?"

"I wish to God I could help Andrew."

"Has he asked for it?"

"No."

"Then wait. And meanwhile, mind your own business. I have suggested what that is. If you genuinely trust your vision, and distrust your senses, your vision will improve, and your senses will become subordinate instead of enslaving you as they do all of us when we let them. You will discover that your higher vision not only illumines your own consciousness but also acts like a beacon that enables others to find their own way."

"Nancy, I don't like it. It seems to me self-righteous, and top-lofty, and—"

"My dear, can't you be generous enough to accept Andrew's generosity? Must you bask in self-approval? Or is it applause that you can't do without?"

"Indeed I don't want applause. But I would love to help Andrew. I want to reverse things just for once, and be some good to him instead of being beholden to him for almost everything. Nancy, I even owe my life to him."

"You don't like having the conceited meekness pricked like a bubble, and humility put in its place?"

"I said, I'm trying to be humble. Really, I'm trying."

"Humility, my dear, is no respecter of persons, especially of our own persons. Humility doesn't even pretend to know the answer to other people's problems. Humility demands wisdom, from the only source whence wisdom comes. And humility receives it. Always. Conceit never does. Subconsciousness is an incorrigible liar, without humility. But humility imposes self-discipline. That creates self-respect, which reveals the difference between our false, lower habit-nature and our true Being—our soul-consciousness. That in turn creates reliance on soul-consciousness. We begin to have dignity— to know what dignity is. Enjoy that—I said, enjoy it—and then Soul, which is You—will employ your person so wisely that you will betray no one, and harm no one, and no prayer will go unanswered; it will be fully answered, with more and better than you asked, because you will discover how to pray, and how to become unselfish."

Lewis knocked on the door. He came in, startling, preoccupied, carrying something. "May I turn on the light?" he demanded. His voice was on the dead-level professional note. Without waiting for an answer he switched on the light and came forward to the fireside. In his left hand was a muddy Mauser pistol. He began to wipe it with his handkerchief, holding it to the overhead light.

"One, three, two, three, eight, three," he remarked. "Nancy, we'll need to do some thinking. This is one of those hard facts that—but wait a moment while I check it."

He laid the pistol on the mantelshelf and consulted the small memorandum book from his vest pocket.

"Yes," he said, returning the book to his pocket, "that is the number of Andrew Cunning's pistol that was registered last autumn when he crossed the border on his way southward."

There was silence for a moment. Elsa turned deathly white. The cat jumped to the floor and began licking itself, stopped doing it, and crept under Nancy's chair.

"It's a fortunate thing," said Lewis, "that my man found this pistol. One of Bulah Singh's spies is searching for it now in the shrubbery. Bulah Singh planned this. But—"

Nancy and Elsa asked the same question, simultaneously: "Where was the pistol?"

"In the mud under the window. Whoever fired it, dropped it there and ran. No fingerprints; he trod it into the mud to make sure of that."

Elsa spoke in a strained voice. "May I see it?"

Lewis passed it to her.

"Yes," she said, "it is Andrew's. That's his mark on the butt. It must have been stolen from him."

"Unfortunately," Lewis answered, "Gunning told me, in the hall before he left, that this pistol was in his overcoat pocket."

"Then he must have thought it was," said Elsa. She handed the pistol back.

Lewis corrected her sharply: "Pardon me. He must have known it wasn't in the pocket the moment he picked up his overcoat. The pistol is heavy and bulky. He would have missed it at once. He must have known it wasn't there."

Nancy spoke quietly: "Morgan, you are so tired that circumstantial evidence begins to look to you like proof."

"Very well," he answered. "What do you make of it? The deadly circumstance is, that Gunning knew that pistol wasn't in his overcoat. He lied. Why?"

"If he did lie, it would be the first time since I have known him," said Elsa. "Besides, why should he lie to you?"

Lewis stared at her. "Andrew spent an hour alone this evening with Bulah Singh," he answered.

Elsa stood up. She looked very small confronting Lewis, but not afraid, although her face was ghost-white. Her scandalized eyes defied him. She spoke deliberately, like a witness in court:

"Dr. Lewis, if you are suggesting that Andrew has been hypnotized by Bulah Singh, you are mistaken."

"How do you know? Clairvoyance?"

"Yes! I know what happened!"

"Gently, gently!" said Nancy. "Betray no one. Harm no one."

Elsa turned on her: "Am I to be silent when my friend is accused of lying—and I know what happened? I mayn't help him, mayn't I? If that is what your teaching amounts to, then I don't believe in it. Am I to protect a criminal, and let Andrew be—"

Lewis took Elsa's hand. "We are all tired," he said. "You more than any of us. Sit down."

She obeyed, too angry to speak back.

"There is this," said Lewis, after a moment's pause. "Gunning's man Bompo Tsering might have sneaked the pistol from the overcoat pocket. He could have put something else in its place, to make Gunning believe the pistol was still there."

Elsa objected: "He couldn't have! Bompo Tsering couldn't have! He didn't come into the house until Andrew brought him in, after the shot was fired."

"True," said Lewis. "Yes, I forgot that. And then again, why should Bompo Tsering want to shoot you?"

"Oh, I don't know! I don't know!" Elsa buried her face in her hands. "Bompo Tsering didn't fire the shot! I know he didn't."

"Someone did," said Lewis. "If the pistol was used without Gunning's knowledge or connivance, who stole it from him, and how, and when?"

Nancy answered him: "Treason has a way of betraying itself. Quiet, both of you. Listen."

There was silence for a few seconds, then a knock at the door.

Nancy raised her voice: "Come in."

The Lepcha servant entered, quietly closing the door behind him. His eyes were wide open, but he seemed drugged, or asleep, or in a trance. His turban was awry, but he was otherwise presentable.

"Remember," said Nancy, in a low voice. "No one was hurt. We

381

have the pistol. No one can use it to blackmail Andrew or anyone else. There is no need for cruelty."

"No. Nor for credulity," said Lewis. "He isn't sleepwalking."

The Lepcha came slowly forward, looking neither to the right nor the left. He knelt and put the last two pine knots on the fire. Then he turned toward Nancy and sat at her feet, cross-legged. No one spoke for at least a minute, until Nancy asked quietly.

"Why didn't you stay in bed, Tashgyl?"

"Too much bad spirit, *memsahib.*"

"Bad dreams?"

"No, *memsahib.* Not dream. No sleep. Spirit."

"Falling back into your old superstitions, are you? Which spirit was it this time? The thief spirit?"

"Yes, *memsahib.*"

"Have you been obeying the thief spirit?"

He nodded. Nancy signed to Lewis to bring the pistol nearer. "Did you take anything out of Gunning *sahib's* overcoat pocket?"

The Lepcha nodded.

"Did you put something else in its place?"

He nodded again, as if he didn't remember until he was asked.

"Is that what the thief spirit told you to do?"

"Yes, *memsahib.*"

"What did you do with what you took from Gunning *sahib's* overcoat?"

He seemed unable to remember. He looked blank. Nancy signed to Lewis to show him the pistol.

"Is this it?"

He suddenly remembered—nodded—looked relieved.

"Well, you see, the thief spirit has been outwitted. He has gone away now—gone forever. He won't come back. So you needn't worry about it any longer, Tashgyl, need you? No harm was done. The thief spirit will never again give you secret orders. So go back to your room, and this time go to sleep. I will talk to you in the morning. Goodnight."

"Goodnight, *memsahib.*"

He got up and left the room. There was silence again, except for the ticking clock on the mantelpiece.

"Well, I'll be damned," Lewis said suddenly. "Nancy, you're a witch-finder! So that's how Bulah Singh works it! Of course, as a policeman, he knows more than most people do about Lepcha superstition. Thief spirit, eh?"

"This helps," said Nancy, "to explain what we have discussed several times. All thieves, without exception, no matter what their race or education or religion, and no matter what they pretend to believe or disbelieve, subconsciously worship a thief spirit that commands them and sometimes protects them. It creeps into consciousness under all sorts of disguises, but it is always the same old tempter—the old prehistoric tribal bogeyman. Until it is recognized for what it is, there's no cure. Any criminal hypnotist can take advantage of it, although when he does it, the hypnotist is himself obeying the old bogey. However, now I think I can cure Tashgyl."

"Bulah Singh mustn't be left at large any longer," said Lewis. "God knows whether we can make a criminal indictment stick. But it's high time to jump him. I'll have it done, before he—" He hid a yawn behind his hand.

Nancy stood up. "Go to bed, Morgan. You are tired out. Let us all go to bed."

"Good idea. My man is watching the house. Leave the light on in the hall. I'll put the fire out. Good night, both of you. See you in the morning."

Elsa was sitting with her face between her hands, but she got up after a moment and followed Nancy to the door. Outside in the hall she took the older woman's arm.

"Nancy, I was so rude to you that I can't think what came over me. I wasn't even telling the truth when I said I didn't believe. I do believe. I want to know. I will know. I promise—"

"No, no! No promises!" said Nancy. "They are so easy to make. But keeping such promises is the most difficult thing in the world. And breaking them is worse than heartbreak. Much worse. So don't promise. Just do. And when you fail, just try again. We made a good beginning tonight. We were fortunate to have such a simple example. I hope you enjoyed it. I did. And thank you so much for protecting me from Morgan Lewis's questions."

CHAPTER 21

Rain. Rain. Rain. The mechanical miracle that no one gags at nowadays: gas-driven wheels. Thirty miles an hour, where, less than a generation ago, three were unthinkable. Lewis was right: no questions were asked. Andrew was right too: no names were mentioned. In three days, Andrew's car, loaded above window level, traversed the fantastic length of Sikkim without challenge, but with intervals for rain, and rest, and business. Rain is a dimension of Sikkim: length, breadth, scenery and rain: a hundred and forty inches a year against the mountain sides, and much more in the jungle, where Nature is still profligately building and destroying the foundations of a cosmos yet to come.

It would have been easy to misinterpret the appearance of right of way. The more real that seems, the more illusory it usually is. The important thing was to take discreet advantage of the unofficial, unspoken *laissez passer*, that could be withdrawn, as easily as given, for the slightest break of the unwritten law that governs the use of privilege. Exceptions that prove rules must be exceptionally well self-governed; or exception ceases.

There are no absolute secrets. No animal can thread a jungle unsuspected, unseen, unsmelt, unheard. It is always some jungle dweller's business to know. Safety depends on which animal knows, and has he a motive for more than curiosity? It is the same with humans, in the jungle of evolving purposes. No Bhutia, Nepalese mountain farmer or valley Lepcha, and above all no white man could follow the roads of Sikkim and escape detection. Liberty of movement depends on who knows, what he thinks about it, has he a motive for meddlesomeness?—suspicion?—enmity?—or for the silence that is good will's greatest means to aid each other's ends? No car could cross the almost countless Sikkim bridges unreported to the police.

There is a *rajah*, who isn't careless of his throne. He has a government, whose first law is self-preservation. There are telephone wires that stand up well in the war against termites, floods and jungle growth. Obstruction is as easy as twice two. Someone, anyone, shakes his official head, and into the net goes the suspect, to answer questions and to be delayed pending further enquiries.

But someone, in the hush-hush code that baffles censors, had whispered "mind your own business." So Andrew's bulkily loaded, ill-painted car, with its oddly assorted occupants, and its old engine and new tyres in unostentatiously good condition, passed unchallenged to the northwest corner of a land where suspicion is law, and the law looks southward to prevent all trespass into Tibet.

He knew the road, having travelled it from the opposite direction; once is enough, for a man who naturally notices. The switchback miles fell headlong into steaming valleys, where swollen rivers root amid pathless jungle. So many huge butterflies impaled themselves against the radiator that the man from Koko Nor had to get out and scrape them off before the car could begin climbing. Then the labouring engine conquered incredible grades, up past myriads of rhododendrons, pine, oak, up beyond the tree line over wind-swept summits. Then again down—and again upward—endlessly repeated, and yet no mile like another. Andrew avoided the obvious gossip traps, where people gather to mind other people's business. He had *caches* of cans of petrol and oil waiting for him, planted where Bompo Tsering had been told to plant them, now and then in a lonely Bhutia's store, sometimes in the house of a friendly minor official, but always unfailingly ready.

The secret of that, like all good secrets, was simple. It is so easy to learn that complicated people can't be bothered with it. Andrew knew how to leave friends behind him, who would do friendly things without looking so secretive that suspicion invents itself. He had disciplined his quick ability to spot what strangers usually hide—their self-respect. You can't patronise that stuff. It is the opposite of the homage that men have to pay to avarice, malice and fear in its other unsocial shapes. There is always a discoverable virtue, even beneath fawning insincerity. People like being found out, when it doesn't strip them naked to the mockery of neighbours. Genuine self-respect is as shy as a girl, as grateful as a girl for recognition. But coaxing it forth is a trick; and so is its corollary of tactful, inexpensive gifts that can't be duplicated or too soon forgotten. Andrew had even remembered a Bhutia storekeeper's envious glance at his loose-leaf notebook, and had brought him a duplicate—cost fifty cents—worth five hours' talk and fifty dollars more than that much money.

There are no hotels on that route. He avoided *dak* bungalows because of the risk of meeting travellers whose own secrets wouldn't bear investigation. All such people are anonymous informers; they create suspicion as a smokescreen for their own improprieties.

The first night out he made for a monastery perched on a crag of the Singalila Range that hides Nepal from Sikkim. From a distance it looked like a mud-wasp's nest. In the brief twilight, as the car climbed the winding trail toward it, the buildings began to look like a Maxfield Parrish painting. They suggested contemplative calm and holiness. But that was as superficial as the sunset light reflected on the roof. The place was no more deeply peaceful than creation itself. It was a hive of envies sicklied over with insincerity, like a Western office building, only much less candidly barbarous, and much more subtle. And of course, equally as in the West, there was virtue hidden there. However,

Andrew was too occupied, by the rough track and the sharp turns, to give much actual thought to the place and its occupants. They were a remembered dream. The monastery's ruler's face was like a ghost's that awaited him, high on the ledge—grim, gray, like the ghost in Hamlet, loaded with a melancholy anger against sin. Not a genial host. One's heart didn't leap to the meeting again.

The car had to be left at the foot of the cliff. As a precaution against pilfering Andrew parked it close to a ruinous *stupa* that contained ashes of a bygone hermit famous for saintliness.

"Sikkimese thieves are as bad as Tibetans, but I guess they won't steal from this place," he remarked.

Bompo Tsering agreed promptly. "Hot damn, no! They maybe by-um-by too much wanting leaving plunder belonging them where by-um-by come finding it again."

But as an additional precaution Bompo Tsering decorated the car with strips of prayer rag. He had a bagful, expensively blessed by a Bon magician.

It was likely to be cold in the monastery. Andrew's heavy blankets had been sent forward long ago, to await him at the real starting point; so before locking the car door he took out his overcoat—shook it—felt in the pocket. He discovered then that his Mauser was missing. In its place was a piece of pine root. It was shaped enough like a Mauser pistol to leave no doubt about premeditation on the part of someone who had stolen the pistol and left that in its stead. He checked the natural impulse to raise hell about it there and then. Making sure he was unobserved, he put the thing back into the overcoat pocket. Then without turning his head, he studied Bompo Tsering and the man from Koko Nor.

Bompo Tsering looked actually, not studiously, innocent. He was muttering *mantras* to impregnate the blessed rags with more protective magic as he tied them to radiator cap, door handles, and all the other projections. The man from Koko Nor was busying himself with Andrew's bedding roll and a bundle roped in wrapping paper that he had been told to carry; he was trying out various ways of adjusting the loads on his shoulders. There was no exchange of glances between the two Tibetans—no noticeable effort to appear unconscious of the overcoat on Andrew's arm.

Something had to be done. But the dilemma was awkward. If he should let them know he had discovered the theft, they would both be on guard against him. If not guilty, they would resent suspicion. If guilty, they would try to shield themselves with more treachery, there being nothing in the world more faithless than a fool on the defensive. But if he should postpone discovery too long, whether guilty or not they would consider him careless. Leaders of expeditions can't afford to be considered careless by the men on whose obedience success depends. Besides: he must not overlook an opportunity to put an end, once and for all, to any thought in those Tibetans' minds that murder was a profitable, undiscoverable means of changing plans and defeating purposes. In plain words: discipline.

The sickening thought suggested itself, and refused to be mocked down by sceptical logic, that his own pistol might have been used to fire that shot through the window at Elsa. It was a registered pistol: ownership was indisputable. If found near Nancy Strong's house, it would give Bulah Singh an almost perfect leverage for blackmail. He recalled the Sikh's threat: "Do as I tell you, or take the consequences."

In plain words: obey me, or be tipped off to the Tibetan Government by wire to Gyangtse or Lhasa. That would mean being ignominiously turned back, to face interrogation that inevitably would expose Lewis's connivance in an officially forbidden expedition. And that might mean the end of Lewis as Number One on the northeast border. Number Ones can't afford to be found out. They must bury their own mistakes or else be sacked like useless spies. The worst possible mistake is publicity. Bulah Singh could make it a police court case. It might be a particularly cunning move in Bulah Singh's intrigue against Lewis.

So Andrew hesitated. For a second he even considered turning back to confer with Lewis. But he dismissed that thought. The momentum of a well-planned move was safer to depend on than retreat. There was no need to burn bridges behind him, yet. But there would be no sense in not crossing bridges before they could be closed against him. He decided to carry on.

From the ledge, hundreds of feet higher up, a monastery *radong* mooed like a lonely cow. It meant that the monks had seen the car. The long *radong*, resting on one monk's shoulder and blown by another, was serving the twofold purpose of announcing hospitable welcome and preventing devils from accepting the invitation. Delay at the foot of the cliff might be interpreted as devilish dread of the Higher Righteousness. The good impression, studiously built up on the south-bound journey, when he was racing against time to get Elsa

387

into competent medical hands, would be all undone. It wasn't the right moment for a show-down with Bompo Tsering and the man from Koko Nor.

"Let's go!"

The Tibetans liked that phrase. They had grown used to it. It was like the bell to a bus horse.

"Hot damn!" said Bompo Tsering. He grinned. He offered to carry Andrew's overcoat.

That suggested a chance to discover guilt or not-guilt without revealing suspicion. If Bompo Tsering knew about the substitution of the pine root for the pistol, he probably would take the opportunity to grope in the pocket and drop the pine root from the cliff, on the way up. That would destroy the circumstantial evidence. No matter. Knowledge was what Andrew needed. Nothing was further from his thought than to prosecute Bompo Tsering, or even to get rid of him. He needed the man. But he needed him respectfully aware of the importance of being loyal. It was his job to inspire that loyalty. So he let him carry the overcoat.

It turned out to be a missed guess: a minor mistake. Bompo Tsering's manner revealed his motive at once. By swaggering with that good overcoat hung carelessly over his shoulder he hoped to impress the monks. Doubtless, in his winter long activity as Andrew's undercover agent, he had boasted of being almost Andrew's chief, not chief of staff. Now he foresaw humiliation. That overcoat suggested how to save face. He would have led the way, if Andrew had permitted. But Andrew went ahead up the difficult, winding footpath. He gave Bompo Tsering all the opportunity he needed to get rid of the pine root; and at the same time no chance to get first word at the monastery gate, where he might otherwise have developed his self-importance. The man from Koko Nor was too afraid of monastery magic, and too occupied with his loads, to do anything but grunt his way uphill, too far behind to be nagged by Bompo Tsering.

It was pitch dark when they reached the summit. The rain clouds had rolled away; the stars were shining. They stood breathless on the edge of a dark precipice, in front of a featureless doorway in a plastered freestone wall. The two monks who greeted Andrew pointed to the new moon that hung like a flake of silver on purple. They smiled like Chinese ivory statues and said something astrologically wise, but they pretended not to understand Andrew's Tibetan, and they were suspiciously aloof toward Bompo Tsering and the man from Koko Nor.

They led the way in, along dimly lamplit passages, upward from stair to stair, until they reached the great guest chamber. It was the same that Elsa had used on the way southward when she was carried up there, with her baby wrapped in Andrew's spare shirt and his priceless tapestry of the crimson flames beneath a cauldron in which an adulterous lady was being boiled in oil. A very suitable sermon in paint for the edification of guests, profane or otherwise.

The monks said something about food, bestowed their benedictions and backed out, spinning prayer wheels as a precaution against foreign devils that might have entered in Andrew's company. They were monkish monks—a mere couple of mildly pious drones, too timid to sin and too lazy to think.

Andrew sent the man from Koko Nor to clean and refill the brass pitcher with water that hadn't been used a few times already. Bompo Tsering laid Andrew's overcoat on the bed and made experiments with one of the bent-wood chairs; cursing the religion of the man who made it, finally he sat on the floor with his head on the seat, remarking that a *peling's* hams must be different from other people's. Andrew sat on the bed discouraged by the sensation of unfinished business left behind in Darjeeling. The trail ahead seemed as calm as the pale new moon, although he knew it couldn't be. But he felt now, behind him, where he couldn't face it, a menace as dark as the ravines on which the new moon shone. It occurred to him to wonder why it did not occur to him to abandon Elsa to her own devices. It didn't. He saw that thought objectively. It belonged to someone else. It was as remote as the moon.

The monks brought food—the usual tea, in the usual urn; enormous quantities of mountain rice, half boiled, spiced and soaked in *ghee*; three bowls of cooked herbs; bread; goats' milk cheese. Andrew ate sparingly, suspicious of the pungent, anonymous herbs that agree with Tibetans but that sometimes behave like locoweed in a white man's stomach. Bompo Tsering and the man from Koko Nor ate noisily and well, belching satisfaction and remarking that these monks must be wealthy, to provide such provender for passing guests. They licked the platters.

Presently Bompo Tsering offered to return the platters and urn to the monastery kitchen. Andrew ordered the man from Koko Nor to do it; he was likelier to come running back without exchanging gossip. So Bompo Tsering sat still, watching Andrew writing with his forefinger in the smoke on the wall beside the bed. He took the bait

389

before long.

"*Peling's* magic" he suggested, in a fruity sarcastic tone.

"Yes."

Andrew had actually scrawled a brief message to Elsa: Hurry forward. Don't let them delay you. But Bompo Tsering's question gave him an idea. Scowling, he made mysterious passes with his right hand—inscribed his initials in the soot—made a punctuation mark—then turned and studied Bompo Tsering's face until the scrutiny and the silence were too much for the Tibetan. He had to speak:

"My thinking maybe by-um-by our needing too much more magic. This place being too much making my afraid."

"This is hot damn magic," said Andrew. "It makes the truth talk."

Bompo Tsering produced his rosary. He always boasted that its beads were carved from the toe bones of holy hermits from Mt. Kailas, and that they were strung on a saint's sinew. He even knew the name of the blessed saint. Nevertheless, the rosary had been made in Birmingham.

The man from Koko Nor returned breathless, looking scared out of his wits. He sat down by himself in a corner, with his hands on his thighs. He appeared to be praying. Bompo Tsering flicked his beads and muttered *mantras*, shuddering when the night wind howled under the eaves and the draught made the little lamps flicker amid leaping shadows.

Andrew, wondering how long to let that mood ferment, framed the questions he would presently ask. He lighted his pipe. But he thumbed it out almost instantly, when someone knocked on the door.

CHAPTER 22

Bompo Tsering and the man from Koko Nor knelt, suddenly, in a hurry. They laid their foreheads and the palms of their hands on the floor. The Lama Gombaria Rinpoche entered. They remained in that position until he left the room, ten minutes later. The *lama* was accompanied by two black-robed subordinates, who looked like homosexuals—ivory smooth—too lushly conscious of a lechery disguised as *love that passeth understanding*. One was the interpreter. The other carried his master's official chair; he set it against the wall facing the brass bed. They stood thumbing their beads, one on each side of the grim abbot, who was graciously pleased to be seated after Andrew had bowed and received the three-fold-gracious-blessing-bestowing-change-of-heart-toward- righteousness.

He signed to Andrew—an imperious, ungracious, condescending nod. Andrew sat down on the bed, with the soot-smothered painting of hell on the wall behind him. There began to be an otherworld sensation, heightened by the picturesqueness of the black-robed representatives of Secrecy, Serenity and Sacred Law.

Andrew was well aware that the Lama Gombaria knew scholarly English. But he also had reason to know that His Reverence was much too diplomatic to admit it. He kept many another, more esoteric vehicle for thought equally well guarded behind sanctimonious mistrust of plain appearances of any kind whatever. He had a sour, sardonic look that matched his reputation for severity and fasting, and for spending days on end in meditation without perceptibly breathing or moving an eyelid. Many high *lamas* cultivate that habit for the sake of the easy authority it gives them over marvelling monks. But this man had the air of a disciplinarian who needed no such subterfuge to sweeten rule that he could enforce by strength of will.

He was reputed, too, to be a clairvoyant of such astonishing power that he could see through any man's thought to its naked motive; it was said to be useless to tell him lies. And he was famed as a magician who could leave his body at will and travel vast distances, returning with intimate knowledge of things, events and men. Another, less exaggerated rumour, credited and slyly broadcast by the modern-minded newly literate iconoclasts who swarm the world, mocked him for a bigoted old humbug; accused him of being deeply involved in treason against human liberties; classed trim as a black reactionary, a Fascist, a Nazi, a Communist, an anarchist. He was probably all of those things, in some degree, by turns, but nothing longer than his inward humour pleased.

He looked, in his black peaked cap and robe, like a wrinkled old mummy, with bright eyes, unusually long ear lobes, and a long face with a protruding lower lip. But the chiefly remarkable thing about him, that caused Andrew to treat him with watchful politeness, was the sensation of mass. It bore no relation to his weight or his size. He was a small man, lean, emaciated. His underlings, with their backs to the shadowy wall, were taller than he and far heavier; they presented breadth and height; but in the dim, unsteady light they were as flat to the eye as daguerreotypes. The old *lama*, regardless of his frailty, was mass personified, like Memnon's statue on the Nile. He was as motionless. He monopolized attention in the same way, by being—as distinguished from wishing to be. That is great art. A Rodin,

Beethoven, Homer can create it in marble, music, words; but some men use themselves—their own presence—as the stuff they mold into a hint of absolutes. This man did it. Andrew's impulse, so strong that he was conscious of his hands and had to keep them still, was to get out his knife and begin whittling a portrait in wood.

The interpreter broke the silence: "Our Holy Lama Gombaria Rinpoche graciously is pleased to know that you are well."

"Thank him," said Andrew. "Say I'm grateful for his hospitality and glad to see him looking so well himself."

There was no pause for reference. It was like a litany.

"The Holy Lama graciously enquires about the health and happiness of the lady and child who accompanied you at the time of your former visit."

"The child is dead," said Andrew. He knew that the old *lama* already knew that; Bompo Tsering must have told him, during the course of the winter; he undoubtedly had received the news, too, by courier from Mu-ni Gam-po. "But the lady herself," he added, "has benefited from His Holiness's blessing and is now quite well. She sends her respectful greetings and best wishes."

The interpreter whispered. The old *lama* pretended to listen. He murmured an instruction. The interpreter resumed:

"The Holy *lama* orders me to tell you that there is no death of anything but bodies. So the child shall presently receive another incarnation. His Holiness bestows a blessing to ensure a happy rebirth."

"Thank him," said Andrew.

Then came the hot hint. The interpreter had been primed with well premeditated speech. He exchanged glances with his grim superior and then used words precisely, as if choosing them out of a book.

"His Holiness, at this time doing penance of meditation for the world's sins, blesses your journey. But he may not at this time indulge in conversation, because spiritual meditation may not be disturbed by mundane irrelevancies. So His Holiness begs you kindly to be governed by the monastery-rule forbidding—at this time—all unnecessary discussion of matters unrelated to the Higher Law."

"Oh, sure, certainly," said Andrew. "That's quite understood. I won't talk to the monks." The inference he drew was that the Lama Gombaria wanted no official knowledge of the reason for the northbound journey.

But the interpreter wished to be sure that he did understand. He added: "Subject to our Holy *lama's* will, our minds are filled with blessed thinking. Therefore the obligation is silence."

"Thank him for the blessing on my journey," said Andrew. "I will be on my way at daybreak."

"To preserve your will-to-be-silent, and to protect you on your journey, His Holiness caused me to write this *mantra*, which he himself has blessed and bids me give to you."

The interpreter, looking as innocent as a saint in a stained glass window, produced a folded paper from an inside pocket of his robe, came forward with it and gave it to Andrew. Andrew thanked him and made haste with his own gift:

"I took the liberty," he said, "of noticing, when I was here last, that His Holiness showed interest in an old illustrated magazine that I had with me. That one wasn't worthy of his attention. I have brought some good ones. They're in that roped paper package. Shall I order my man to carry it?"

A faint smile flickered on the face of the old *lama*. His beady eyes watched the interpreter pick up the heavy package as if he feared he might drop it and spoil its precious contents. Twelve *Esquires*, twelve Sunday issues of the *New York Times*, twelve *National Geographics*, twelve *Newsweeks*, and twelve *Fortunes* had cost Andrew exactly nothing; they had been given to him by a chance American acquaintance in Darjeeling. But they were worth more than gold to a lonely Lord Abbot, who secretly knew English, secretly delighted in the mad frivolity of Western worldliness, and kept the sources of his information secret to himself. He pretended to be condescendingly astonished, as if a child had surprised him. He dourly accepted the gift, as if manners obliged him to do what virtue forbade. But his eyes were as bright as a bird's. His blessing, as he and his sycophants left the room, was sonorous, and long, and loaded with praise of the blessed dew that brought the giver's thought from heaven. The Lama Gombaria was one more dependable friend to the good, on whom Andrew might count for the little favours that resemble drops of oil upon the bearings of events.

The door closed almost silently. Bompo Tsering and the man from Koko Nor looked up to make sure, then got to their feet and stood gaping at Andrew. He had been allowed to be seated in the Holy Lama's presence, so he had mounted in their estimation. The effect wouldn't last long, but for the moment they were filled with awe as they watched him unfold the sheet of paper the interpreter had handed to him. There was another, smaller sheet inside it. On that was the "*mantra*," printed beautifully with a quill pen, in English capitals:

THE CAT CAME BACK TO ELSA. NO SIG.

It was so startling and different from what he had expected that it took Andrew several seconds to realise that "cat" meant "mouser" and that "mouser" was pun on Mauser pistol. Someone then had found his pistol and it was now in Elsa's possession. Someone—very likely Mu-ni Gam-po at the request of Lewis—must have wired to the nearest telegraph office. The message must have come a long way by runner, probably spatchcocked into a longer telegram to the Lama Gombaria. Andrew put it in his pocket, forcing a smile and looking wise for the Tibetans' benefit. No magic is magic without its showman. He assumed a mysterious air. But he couldn't keep that up. He had to sit down on the bed. He was suddenly seeing things.

Bompo Tsering, bursting with awed curiosity, came nearer: "That must being too much hot damn holy writing."

Andrew made an impatient commanding gesture toward the roll of blankets, but didn't speak. The sceptical part of his mind was wondering how much, or how little, or if at all, the old *lama*, who had just left the room, had to do with the vision that he was seeing with the other part of his mind without in any way changing his view of the room he was in.

It was arresting. There was no shutting it out, although he tried. Nancy Strong's room in Darjeeling. The cat, on the hearth. The fire burning brightly. The electric light full on. Nancy in her armchair. Lewis. Elsa—he saw her last. They were more really present to his imagination than if they had been actually in the dim, shadowy room where he sat. They were vivid-brilliant. It couldn't be altogether a trick of memory. True, Lewis's use (he could bet it was Lewis) of the word "cat" to mean Mauser pistol might have suggested the fireside in Nancy's living room and have brought it vividly to mind. But that couldn't account for their all behaving as they had not behaved while he was there; or for the fact that Andrew himself was not now in the picture. His chair by the hearth was empty. They were all moving. The cat was licking itself. It ran away suddenly and hid under Nancy's chair. Whichever way he turned his head he saw them. He could see they were speaking, but he couldn't hear anything.

It wasn't like a dream, or a motion picture, or a lantern projection on a screen. It was more like something that crystal gazers are supposed to see when they stare and concentrate: something, but not quite, like the reflection in a good viewfinder, except that it wasn't reversed, and it was apparently life-size. Simultaneously he could see the two Tibetans and all the other objects in the room he was in. There was no physical sensation of eyestrain or fatigue. But there was a feeling almost of horror, as if he had lost control of his mind. He could see the vision with his eyes shut. It made no difference whether he kept them closed or open. He tried it several times. He saw the dim room with his eyes, and Nancy's electric-lighted room, two hundred miles away, with some other faculty of perception, as if his mind was in two disconnected parts. By shutting his eyes he could shut out the room he was in, but that made no difference to the vastly brighter and more detailed image. He could even read some of the names on the backs of Nancy Strong's books.

Lewis was standing with his back to the fire, with a muddy Mauser pistol in his right hand. He was showing it to Elsa. He saw Elsa get up and confront Lewis. He couldn't hear what they were saying, but he knew it was his own pistol, and presently he knew what they were talking about because the scene changed. They were still there. Nancy Strong sat quietly in her chair. But there was something added. He could see through the wall to the passage beyond. Tashgyl, the Lepcha servant, was taking the pistol from Andrew's overcoat on the peg in the hall and presently giving the pistol to someone in the dark garden. It wasn't clear how Tashgyl reached the garden. Soon after that, or perhaps simultaneously—there was no clear sensation of time or of sequence—he grew aware that the whole vision was framed by Elsa's face, behind her hands.

He could see her eyes through her hands. They were intelligently, dumbly pleading, like a dog's that wishes it could tell what it knows. He knew that phase of her well. Her face kept fading. The moment he looked hard at it, it faded away. He wondered what that meant. He didn't trust his own wordless interpretation of it, but he felt she was trying to reach him and disliked doing it—feared to do it. She seemed to expect a rebuke, and to flinch from the expectation. Small blame to her. He had been pretty tough, lots of times, repelling confidences, keeping his thoughts to himself and forcing her to do the same. She probably detested him. Quite right, too. He had humiliated her, time and again. He marvelled at the dignity, pluck, patience with which she had endured his reserve. He felt ashamed—but all the same not unreserved—not excusing, nor explaining, even to himself, in secret.

The entire vision, and all the thoughts that accompanied it, lasted less than a minute. He knew that. With the other part of his mind he had been watching Bompo Tsering, who had taken the blanket roll off the bed and begun to unfasten the straps; he hadn't finished undoing them when the vision faded. Less than sixty seconds. Whatever caused that vision, time had no part in it. What he had just now witnessed must have taken place on the previous night. He knew that too, although he didn't know how he knew it. It just was so. Time, then, was only an illusion? God! Even trying to think about that made his head reel. But all the same, time can't limit an idea. Time doesn't alter the fact that a thing did happen. Andrew wasn't an escapist. He wasn't like the Grade B scientists, who stick their heads into realism but expose their fannies to the ridiculing blasts of reality. Miracle? Hell, there's no such thing. Had the Lama Gombaria turned some occult trick with the aid of the folded paper? He experimented—clutched the paper in his pocket—drew it out—opened it—read it again. Nothing doing.

THE CAT CAME BACK TO ELSA. NO SIG.

But the vision did not return. He could remember every detail. But now it was a mere memory-picture, as different as a faded photograph is from the living model. The vision was gone.

He pulled out his pipe and sat reviewing the facts. Bompo Tsering fumbled with the blanket roll. The man from Koko Nor, on the floor in the corner, sat picking his teeth with a sliver of wild swan's thigh bone. It had been specially blessed for that purpose; he kept it in a container made from a Japanese brass cartridge. He had a hollow back tooth that Andrew was going to have to pull before long to keep him from going haywire, but for the time being he was well occupied trying to dig out the devil that caused the pain. Bompo Tsering, on the other hand, needed watching, if for no other reason than because he had turned his back instead of facing Andrew while he undid the blankets.

Elsa. Andrew remembered that, once, on the way southward, in a place where they had found some dead tamarisk and had built a good fire for the first time in nearly a week, he had read to her, to keep her mind off the physical ordeal that was two or three days ahead. He had chanced on a passage in Goethe's *Faust*:

Shall here a thousand volumes teach me only
That man, self-tortured, everywhere must bleed,—
And here and there one happy man sits lonely?

He had continued reading to her far into the night; but they had kept returning to that passage, discussing the evident truth that in the rhythm and tone of poetry there's a mysterious magic that links thought with things unseen. It conjures new views. They pass in a moment but leave their mark on mind, so that nothing, not even a star, is ever again the same as it was. Flowers don't smell the same. Music has higher meanings. Come to think of it, he hadn't always repelled Elsa. He had always welcomed her into the inner mood of poetry that so thrilled him that he sometimes choked when he read it aloud. And while they talked, that night, he remembered how he saw a vision, like this one, of Tom Grayne, seated lonely in his mountain cavern, making a map from memory by guttering candlelight.

He had wondered then, as he wondered now: were he and Elsa the self-tortured, who bled? And was Tom Grayne the happy man who sat lonely? What is happiness? Did anyone know? Had anyone ever found it? Is there an actual difference between happiness and joy? He hadn't asked Elsa whether she saw the same vision or pondered the same thought, because he knew how she hated clairvoyance, and he wanted to keep her thoughts as calm as possible. In fact, he had laid Goethe aside and read from Chaucer's Canterbury Tales. But he hadn't read well, because of wondering, with half of his mind, whether her seeing a vision of Tom had caused him to see it; and whether the flow of poetry might be the agency that, for a moment, had suspended space and time. There might be a connection.

He thought of it again now. He was willing to follow the mood of real poetry wherever that might lead. But there is unreal poetry, to be avoided like poison. Lots of it. Gutless, kiss-mammy, decadent stuff that can't climb, even downhill—written by sirens who pose on rocks but wait for traffic signals from a *führer*. He hated with all his heart and soul the thought of being misled, to a spiritual dead end, by the pipsqueak drum and fife bands that parade as the voices of God. Propagandists! Proletarian apologists! Liars! Treacherous bellwethers leading the sheep up the slope of a mechanical Olympus, where the butchers wait. God's elect, the butchers! He felt anger rising—laughed at the anger, because he knew how useless it was. Anger is exactly what the *führers* can exploit. But if a whole world once gets to laughing again—

Once more, sixty seconds. Time must be an elastic illusion. He had thought of a thousand things in sixty seconds. He had seen Hitler's *Mein Kampf* like a dirty jest scrawled on the universal backhouse by a subhuman misanthrope. He had even reviewed in his mind the true and false poets, setting them on either side of an imagined pale, finding time to loathe Swinburne, to love Robert Burns, and to acknowledge a cagey respect for Walt Whitman.

Bompo Tsering was still leisurely unfolding blankets; he would steal a packet of razor blades presently from the pocket in the canvas carry-all. Strange how some men can't resist trifles. Bompo Tsering could be trusted with any amount of money, barring the small change; he always tried to steal some of that. The man from Koko Nor had both thumbs in his mouth and was busily poking a devil with the swan's thigh bone—very angry with the devil. A bell boomed in the monastery. It sounded far away like a bell buoy on a shoal. Suddenly there were Elsa's eyes again, pleading and yet trying not to intrude. They were gone in a moment. Andrew felt a savage impulse to tell her to let him alone. But he suppressed that—turned the savagery on itself and let it strangle itself in a dark subconscious past, along with some men's poetry, and Sunday School, and certain other things.

He was feeling chilly. He was getting rattled by his thoughts. It was time to do something. With the side of his eye he watched Bompo Tsering secrete a packet of razor blades. Good. That was a cue for the show-down with Bompo Tsering. But first he leaned over the bed and scratched another message on the wall, just to let Elsa know he wasn't so dumb as she thought him:

Got second message. Okay.

Two or three days might pass before Elsa would occupy the room on her way northward, but there was not much risk of the message being noticed and rubbed out by the monks. They never cleaned their own cells. It wasn't likely to occur to them to wash the wall of a room reserved for strangers.

He got off the bed and sat on one of the bent-wood chairs, lighting his pipe, crossing his legs. He ordered Bompo Tsering to dump the blankets on the bed.

"Never mind spreading them now. Bring me the pistol from my overcoat pocket."

"Why, Gunnigun?"

"Because I say so."

There was no noticeable guilty reaction. Bompo Tsering picked up the overcoat, groped in the pocket and pulled out the pine root, stared at it. He appeared genuinely puzzled. He glanced at the man from Koko Nor, who left off prodding his aching tooth and stared back blankly.

"Bring it here," said Andrew.

Bompo Tsering obeyed. "Must being hot damn magic," he said with conviction. Then, looking straight into Andrew's eyes: "Gunnigun, this not my doing."

"Why did you steal razor blades?"

"My not—"

"Give 'em here."

Bompo Tsering, looking sheepish, produced the stolen packet. Andrew took it and slipped it into his pocket.

"Do you want to be sacked?"

"No, Gunnigun!"

"Do you want to be beaten?"

"No, Gunnigun! That not being too much, that little thing,

"Shut up!"

"Gunnigun, your not—?"

"I said, shut up!"

Andrew glanced at what he had scrawled on the wall. Then he pulled out the *lama's* "*mantra*" from his pocket, unfolded it, studied it, returned it and stared grimly at Bompo Tsering.

"How many times have I told you there'll be a last time when you play tricks on me?"

"Too much times. Gunnigun, my not—"

"Shut up!"

"Yes, Gunnigun."

"Open the shutter and throw that pine root through the window."

Bompo Tsering obeyed. The wind blew out the lights.

"Close the shutter. Fasten it."

Now there was total darkness. The man from Koko Nor breathed heavily and began tapping the floor with his blessed cartridge case, to keep devils away.

"My lighting lamp," said Bompo Tsering.

"Stand still!"

"Gunnigun, what your doing?"

"I am making hot damn magic."

"*Peling* magic?"

"Yes."

"That being no good."

"It will be no good for you, if you lie. Answer: whose pistol fired

399

the shot through the window last night?"

"My not knowing."

"I believe you:" Andrew felt fairly sure that Bulah Singh would keep his dupes as ignorant as possible of everything except what they were to do. And it is wise tactics to encourage the first glimmer of truth if you hope to hear more. "Who was told to fire the shot?" he demanded.

"My not firing it."

"I believe you again. You couldn't have fired it. Who was told to do it?"

The man from Koko Nor ceased breathing through his nose. He ceased tapping the floor.

"I know who did it," said Andrew. "Answer this one, Bompo Tsering: shall the fool—who obeyed you—pay a penalty—for having done—what you would have punished him for not doing? Answer!"

Silence.

"You understood me. Speak! Did you not threaten this numskull that unless he obeyed, you would cause the police to arrest him for theft? Did you not say he would be thrown in prison for at least a whole year?"

That was a long shot, but a fairly safe one. The easiest way to persuade a homesick Tibetan to do murder or anything else would be to threaten dreadful confinement within prison walls; the mere suggestion would panic his wild-ass heart. Bompo Tsering didn't answer. So the guess appeared to be good. Andrew followed up:

"Why did you give the order to shoot Lady Elsa?"

"My spirit being too good not wanting shooting other ladee."

"So you did give the order. You admit that. Who told you to shoot Miss Nancy Strong?"

Silence.

"I know who told you."

"Gunnigun, then why your asking?"

"Because I wish you to answer. And by God, if you don't—"

"No, no, Gunnigun! No, no! My answering. Bulah Singh—big top policeman."

"I believe you again. What did he promise you?"

"His saying, if my shooting other ladee, then can get going home. If not, then not get going—getting too much trouble."

"So you changed it and ordered that other fool to shoot Lady Elsa?"

400

Silence.

"If you don't answer, I won't save you from the law."

"Gunnigun—"

"What is the answer?"

"Yes, my doing that."

"Well. Luckily for you there was too much hot damn magic around. So the shot missed. Bulah Singh made a fool of you. It was my pistol that was handed to you in the dark."

"Uh-uh! My not touching it!"

"Liar! Someone gave it to you. You gave it to this other fool. Now then: where is the pistol?"

"My not knowing."

"Ask that other fool what he did with it."

"Gunnigun, why not your asking?"

"Because you are responsible. Ask him!"

There were murmurs in the dark-protests, questions, threats. Then suddenly:

"His lying. His saying—"

Andrew interrupted. "I have been making hot damn magic. I know where the pistol is."

"Then, Gunnigun, why your asking?"

"Because I intend to be answered! Quick! Answer! Where did he put it?"

"Dam fool saying his throwing pistol in mud and then running away."

"Do you realise that if that pistol should be found by the police, you and this other fool would be arrested, and taken back to Darjeeling and tried for your lives?"

"My not having doing nothing."

"You'd get about ten years in prison. The other fool, about three years, for having done what you told him."

"Gunnigun, your not—"

"I am going to punish you."

"Oh."

"Yes."

"Gunnigun, your not—?"

"Light the lamps. All of them."

Bompo Tsering groped for matches and obeyed. The man from Koko Nor, with his back in a corner, blinked wide-eyed like a suspicious owl—a blink, a long stare, a blink, a long stare. Bompo Tsering

401

came back and stood before Andrew.

"I made magic on that wall," said Andrew. "Look at it. The Lady Elsa shall find my pistol. She shall bring it to me, to save your neck and this other fool's. And as a punishment to you, she shall return with us to Tibet."

"But, Gunnigun—"

"She shall have your pony—the good one with the strong legs."

"But, Gunnigun—"

"You yourself shall wait on her. You shall pitch her tent. You shall obey every order she gives you. And unless she gives a good report of you, Tum-Glain shall be told. And what he will do—"

"Oh, Gunnigun!"

"—isn't the half of what I will do to you before he gets second chance. Now spread my blankets on the bed."

"Yes, Gunnigun."

"Spread your own blankets on that stone dais."

"Yes, Gunnigun."

"That other fool may sleep on the floor."

"Yes, Gunnigun."

"Get me that book out of the carryall pocket."

"Here it is, Gunnigun."

"Set two of those lamps in the niche at the head of the bed."

"Yes, Gunnigun."

"Now pull off my boots."

The proud Bompo Tsering knelt and obeyed.

"Gunnigun—!"

"What now?"

"Your not telling Ladee Elsa about that our having—"

"It depends on you."

"My being too much ashamed before her being woman."

"Take care then that she doesn't complain, even once—just only once—about your behaviour on the journey. If I hear no complaints I will bear your request in mind. Give my boots to that other fool. Tell him to clean them. Then turn in."

"Yes, Gunnigun."

Andrew bolted the door, rolled under the blankets, pulled his overcoat over him and lay thinking for a minute or two. He felt damned lonely. He made a deliberate effort to see Elsa's eyes, but he had no success—none whatever. The only mental picture he could summon from the vast deep of consciousness was the mere memory-image of

402

Bulah Singh, facing him in his own room in the hotel in Darjeeling.

For the rest, his thoughts scattered themselves—wondering what Lewis was doing—was the snow really out of the passes—were the ponies too fat—what luck would he have getting extra ponies for Elsa's baggage. There was nothing to be gained by that kind of thinking.

So he opened Sir Thomas Browne's *Religio Medici* at random and read until he fell asleep with the lights burning. He dreamed that the old Lama Gombaria was brewing poison in the monastery cellar, for Bulah Singh to take all the way to Shig-po-ling, to put into Tom Grayne's tea. Elsa was imploring Gombaria not to do it, so the *lama* and Bulah Singh both threw poison at him, Andrew. It made a noise like beaten brass, and he awoke to hear the monastery bells ringing.

Bompo Tsering opened the shutter. It was daybreak; the sun was touching the peaks of the far-off mountains of Nepal. Andrew went and stood half naked at the window relishing for a moment the clean chill of the wind on his skin as he peered down into the gorge, eight hundred feet, sheer. To his right, not fifty feet below, was a ledge that served as passage between a dormitory and another building. There was a group of monks on the ledge; they looked like vultures getting ready for the news of a death, preening themselves. He recognized two of them. They had been all winter long in Mu-ni Gam-po's monastery. He chuckled.

"The obligation is silence!" he said aloud.

"What your saying, Gunnigun?"

"Let not your left hand know what your right hand doeth!"

"My not understanding."

"Let's go—while the going's good."

"Hot damn!—Breakfus'?"

"No. We will cook our own, somewhere beside the road, where there's a stream to wash in. Step lively—pack up the bedding. Hold your tongue on the way out."

CHAPTER 23

A day's drive north of Darjeeling. Darkness. Stillness of dying night. A screen door slammed. Nancy and Elsa came out, still sleepy, from the guest bungalow at the Jesuit Mission. Dawn broke, that moment, on distant mountain peaks.

"There, Nancy! Look! Oh, God! Look! Nancy! There's the Roof of the World! Oh, come too! Say goodbye to all this! Come with us!"

403

"I think I feel the tug as strongly as you do," said Nancy. "But it's the old story. I am too conceited to come. I imagine responsibilities. Oh dear. If only Karl Marx had studied that daybreak instead of the books in the British Museum!"

"Damn him!" said Elsa, with all her heart. Unconsciously, but strongly, she associated Karl Marx with her hosts of the previous night. She was conscious of it as soon as she had damned Marx, and felt vaguely ashamed of herself. Jesuits claim that Karl Marx only imitated, converted and perverted what they knew and practiced before he was born or thought of.

A rain cloud rolled between them and the view. It was dark again, with shafts of warm light streaming through the window behind them.

"False dawn! Another false prophet! Gone!" said Elsa. "Oh, how wonderful it was. How can there be such passion of beauty—and then this gloom?"

"Are you feeling discouraged?"

"No, I don't think so. Deflated is what it feels like. Three days since Andrew left. It seems like three years—longer. Oh, I hope he's all right."

Nancy Strong's white felt hat tilted. She glanced at Elsa. "Why? Have you a premonition?"

"No. Except that I can't even get a mental picture of him."

"I know you can't."

"I tried to send him a message, from Darjeeling, before we sent the telegram."

"I know you did."

"I don't think he got it. I couldn't find him: he was gone. I tried again last night. But I know I didn't reach him last night. He seems to have gone—gone forever. I don't think he even got the telegram."

"I thought of coming into your room last night to stop you from trying. But I thought better of it. It seemed wiser to let you fail. Did you ever hear of radio interference? You can't think here. You would be echoing Jesuit thoughts if we stayed here long enough. Echoing them badly. Jesuits can, so to speak, bend iron. They can wear down adamant. You might as well try to whistle against a thunderstorm as to oppose your thought against theirs."

The mission garden gradually awoke and spread its fragrance to greet the dim daybreak. The birds' hymn began. Elsa found it almost impossible to believe that the recent past was true, it seemed so distant

404

and unreal. The sensation reminded her of an utterly different scene in Southampton, with the gulls around an ocean liner, in a fog, and the siren going, when she was seeing friends off on a long voyage. Utterly different, and yet no difference. Unreal, and yet heartbursting with reality.

The evening's visit had been civilized. The night's seclusion had felt like guarded peace in an armed camp disciplined to silence. The breakfast, brought before daybreak by an earless ex-brigand convert from Bhutan, had seemed and tasted like communion with the invisible presence of Peace. Nevertheless, she had felt uneasy; and now she felt impatient, wondering why the car was so long coming from the barn at the rear of the mssion buildings.

She felt ungrateful for good hospitality. That was a perplexing and contemptible sensation. Unnatural, and not at all like her, but there it was. The scrupulous impersonal politeness of their hosts had rendered almost imperceptible the fact that there was any difference between Nancy's point of view and theirs—her religion and theirs. No arguments. No strained aloofness. Almost familiar courtesy. Bright conversation. Praise of each other's achievements. Mutual exchange of information about children's diet and the frugal use of money. Silence about religion—not even armed neutrality, but silence, and no issue from it that could introduce a hint of the ill-mannered tolerance, that is only insolence in undress. They had agreed on Nancy's treatment of rhododendrons; and on the care of children's lips who are learning to play wind instruments. The Father Superior had shown Nancy a new way to cut down the cost of insulation against termites, and how to keep books free from weevils and mildew. But no peering beneath mental surfaces—no spy work—no leading questions.

The neat, two-roomed guest house had been an oasis of privileged calm, amid hive-like, unhurried energy. Elsa had rather resented the priests' lack of astonishment when she had betrayed, by the merest accident, that she could speak and write Tibetan. They had shown no curiosity. So far as she was able to observe, they didn't even glance at one another. Perhaps they had heard rumours about her, that were none of their business, but nevertheless no recommendation. There had been no hostility, no coolness; but she had felt that her reception as a privileged guest was due entirely to the fact that Nancy Strong had introduced her. It was a compliment to Nancy, not to herself. She wondered why she resented it. She had no right to. She did her half-hearted best to subdue malicious triumph at the thought that she was on her way, in secret, to where even the Soldiers of Loyola might only yearn to go, but could not. She wished they knew where she was going. She would have enjoyed their envy.

The car came—Nancy's old Sunbeam, with the top up—driven by a veteran Mahratta ex-Pioneer *sepoy*, bearded like the *pard*, surlier than Diogenes, but not so interested as that grim philosopher in looking for an honest man. He was quite sure there was none. He regarded Nancy as a beloved lunatic whose will was the higher law, but whose aberrations called for no encouragement from him. A man of few words, and those mainly disrespectful. A man of few miles to the hour because petrol is expensive and Nancy was school-poor; also because his honour was his own and he had no intention to die in a ditch. A man who broke no traffic rules, and could be neither bribed nor bullied. He had been known, when questioned about Nancy's movements, to tell a brashly new inspector of police to ask God, since God made her mad, so perhaps God understood her secrets.

Two Jesuit priests neglected daybreak duty, for two stopwatch minutes, to come and say goodbye. They were polite to Elsa, cordial to Nancy, expert at speeding the parting guests. The rain descended in a squall. The car started. It felt good. They were off.

"So you don't like my friends?" said Nancy, as they headed northwestward, between terraced hills that showed the touch of the Jesuit influence. The peasants' agricultural gods were slowly losing the long war against energy, brains, and a faith that moves men and women, if not their mountains.

Elsa didn't answer until she had rearranged the packed saddlebags that Andrew had left for her. She wanted to think. She took her time about making a comfortable heap for Nancy's feet to rest on. Then:

"I know so little about them. But—well—I mean—how shall I say it?—well, they're Jesuits. I never met any before, but—"

"Why do you suppose I chose that place to spend the night?"

"You said: to throw Bulah Singh's spies off the trail—and to avoid meeting busybodies at a *dak* bungalow—oh, and because we couldn't make the full distance in one day—and—I think that was all."

"Those were only excuses. There was a real reason. Didn't you like the Father Superior?"

"He didn't give me a chance to like him. He didn't like me. I expect he guessed that I was brought up to believe Jesuitry is about the vilest human trait."

"So it is," said Nancy. "But the Jesuits didn't invent it. They have

406

less of it than most people. Haven't you discovered, with all the reading you have done, that politicians, and historians, and priests, and other people with axes to grind, always accuse their betters of the very treacheries that they themselves use and intend to keep on using?— Father Patrick is quite an authority on Tibet."

"Is he? I thought he didn't understand Tibetan. He didn't seem to. He doesn't talk or look like a man who has travelled much."

Nancy chuckled. "He travelled Tibet for three years, in disguise, mostly alone and on foot. Two of his subordinates are there now— secretly, of course; they can't get permits. The first time I saw Father Patrick was in Lhasa. But he didn't see me; or if he did, he didn't know it. That was before the war.—Heavens! If I would only let me, I could be an old woman, couldn't I! Nineteen—never mind—Curzon was Viceroy. Father Patrick was in difficulties—found out—caught— they'd have killed him, I think. He was in a dungeon. But Lobsang Pun was in high standing in those days. As the diplomatic representative of the Tashi Lama, he had the ear of the Dalai Lama. And I was Lobsang Pun's *chela*. So by being very careful I was able to get a plea through edgewise."

"Were you in disguise?"

"Of course. But not the way you probably imagine. I was born without a trace of a gift for wearing false whiskers. I had to hide myself even from me, and it would take a lifetime, almost, to tell how that was done. Letting Father Patrick know who helped him was quite out of the question. But they let him continue his journey. He carried on for two years after that."

Elsa was silent for a moment. But she had to say something to relieve the feeling of deflated malicious triumph:

"But what a strange coincidence. Two *pelings*—total strangers to each other—crossing trails in Tibet, and one helping the other without the other's knowledge."

"No," said Nancy. "There is no such thing as a coincidence, except to the minus-minded intellectuals. To them, of course, everything is a coincidence, including creation itself. Poor things, to believe in a Universal Intelligence would make them feel too unimportant. But, I grant you, it never ceases to be an exciting surprise when things like that do happen, even though one knows they must happen. It's a law of nature."

"I'm afraid I'm awfully stupid," said Elsa. "Perhaps I'm minus-minded. Which law of nature are you talking about?"

"The first law. The very first one that Lobsang Pun compelled me to discover, and recognize, and learn, and practise. The affluence law of supply and demand. That is to say, the opposite of the economic law, which governs greed, which creates poverty, and blinds us to the truth. The real law is that affluence must find work to do. Affluence is positive. Greed and its derivatives are negative. Affluence is an indestructible idea, forever active, perpetually seeking and finding self-consciousness. No matter where we are, nor what our condition may be at any given moment, it is impossible to avoid finding someone who can use what we can give. I don't doubt Father Patrick was praying to the God created by the Jesuits. That is none of my business. The point is: he wasn't pitying himself. So he didn't get between himself and the help that is always ready. I remember what I had been thinking about: I had been studying Jesus's remark about Solomon and the lilies, comparing it with dozens of similar texts in Sanskrit, and with my own experience. I was trying to understand the importance of now, and the absoluteness of the law of affluence. I wasn't arrayed like a lily, and I was equally impotent in any material sense. But I was learning what giving means, and how material need is the room made ready for supply. So I became useful, and no one suffered by it. Of course, there is only one thing really worth giving."

Elsa made a guess at the answer: "I hope you're not going to say love. They all say that. Nobody means it."

"Me? Love a Jesuit! God forbid!"

Elsa leaned back and laughed with relief. "Nancy, you're priceless."

"I deny it! Priceless is an idiotic word. I am a pilgrim on the way toward reality, with a long, long way to go. I refuse to be mislabelled. Machiavelli and Napoleon, and their imitators, sneered quite accurately about that. They were liars in most respects, but they knew enough about themselves to guess that everyone in the world has his price, and it is usually cheap. They were almost quite right about that. But I am not telling my price. It is being notched continually higher. Show me the price, and I'll raise it. The bribe would have to be too subtle for me to recognize it. Even so, I'd never stay bought! I'd wake up and betray the buyer!"

"I didn't mean it that way."

"I know you didn't. But I did."

"What is the only one thing worth giving? Go on, tell me. If you had said it's love I wouldn't even have tried to believe you. People

408

have said they love me, who were so cruel that I would prefer their hatred. I hate them. Surely love must be an individual something that one reserves for one's own lover, husband, children, friends.—What is it that's worth giving? Tell me."

"That is for each one to find out for himself," Nancy answered after a moment's pause. "Definitions usually defeat their own purpose. Perhaps one might almost define the one great gift that we can give to one another as spiritual elbowroom. Mind our own business. Give others a chance to find out for themselves who and what they really are. The only way to do that is to realise who and what we are." Before Elsa could wedge in another question she continued: "But let me tell you about Father Patrick. I have a reason for telling. It isn't just an excuse."

Elsa curled up in her corner of the back seat. "Please. I would rather listen to you than think my own thoughts."

"Aren't you pleasantly excited about Tibet?"

"Yes. But feeling like a parasite, too. I don't want to think, I want to listen."

"Very well. The second time I met Father Patrick was toward the end of the World War, in the year of the influenza epidemic. It spread all around the world. It killed more people than the war did—the best and the worst and the mediocrities, all in one obscene corruption. You remember it? Or weren't you old enough? Great numbers of people called it the hand of God. They did really. The very same people told us that we should love God. But the doctors went to work and fought God with all their might. They were at their wit's end, but they fought back bravely, without a second's respite. If it was God's doing, all the doctors must have been hellions in league with the devil. I was on their side, against God. But there seemed to be no remedy. Thousands died—hundreds of thousands. Eleven children in my school. Of course, what you can always depend on, happened. Helpless people did their best to help one another. Some of the bravest and best work was done by stark materialists, who didn't believe in God or devil. The professionals—the salaried prelates—Hindu—Moslem—Christian—tried to save face by commanding us all to pray. We were to implore, especially our Christian God, in the name of mercy, to undo something, that He had inflicted on us, that was even more devilish than the poison gas we had been using in the war, and that we had no intention of not using in the next one."

"I prayed my last prayer to that God long ago," said Elsa. "What did you do?"

"I made dozens of mistakes. Bad ones. The worst was the first. I went off on the wrong foot, and that led to all the other mistakes. I went fanatical. I tried to prove, at other people's expense, what I hadn't, yet proved at my own cost. It didn't occur to me—not then, in that time of bewildering fear—that I personally had all the faults that I could see in others. I was worse even than those insufferable prigs of prelates, because I might have known better; I hadn't the disadvantage of their tradition and miseducation. I didn't realise that everything vile in my consciousness was being boiled to the surface by the conflict between what I knew and what my senses saw and believed. I was conceited—enough to believe that my little bit of a bud of evolving consciousness, that had been awakened by a great teacher, must already be strong enough to overcome that epidemic, at least for my own school. I hadn't the humility to do what I really could have done. I had to do what I couldn't. That school—so it seemed to me—was the fruit of my own labour. It was mine. It was my vineyard. Hadn't I tilled it? Wasn't I there, where my own soul put me, for the very purpose of protecting those children? Naturally, such nonsense had no effect whatever on the course of the epidemic. It didn't change it one way or the other. But it got worse and worse for me."

"In what way worse?"

"Better, of course, in the long run. But at the time heartbreaking, humiliating, cruel. Because I was cruel."

"How were you cruel?"

"I was as cruel as a politician. Even more cruel than if I had neglected people. I disappointed them. I let them down. I let my ignorance deceive them. I betrayed them with pride, instead of protecting them with humility. I was worse than King Canute defying the sea—much worse. He made himself ridiculous to teach a lesson to fools."

"Then isn't your philosophy any use in a crisis?"

"Philosophy? Have I insulted you?"

"No. Of course you haven't."

"Did you ever read Cardinal Newman?"

"No. Wasn't he the Protestant bishop who switched over and became a Catholic?"

"It makes no difference what he became," said Nancy. "Greater men than he have become beggars, not cardinals. Nevertheless, he was very great. He saved many a poor wretch from hopelessness."

"Wasn't it he who wrote *Lead, Kindly Light*?"

"Yes. He also wrote: *Knowledge is one thing, virtue is another . . . Philosophy, however enlightened, however profound, gives no command over the passions, no influential motives, no vivifying principles.* Memorise that, and have nothing to do with philosophy, it's no good."

"But how does that fit the influenza epidemic? I don't see the connection."

"I knew, what every genuine thinker has known since the dawn of history, that epidemics—and endemics, too, are a product of the subconscious mind of humanity. The only actual substance of that stuff is the fear that builds up the illusion and all its consequences. That is why Jesus called it 'a liar, and the father of it.' The mass mind fears and consequently creates vengeance upon its own secret swinishness. It's a vicious circle. I had challenged the whole ocean of subconsciousness, including my own subconsciousness. Little me! Single-handed! So, of course, the vile stuff came in through my doors and windows. As I told you, eleven children died. Two teachers. Then the overworked government and private doctors asked for one of my buildings for use as a hospital. I lent them two buildings. They became a morgue. Corpses! Corpses!"

Nancy was silent for several minutes. Then she threw a mood aside and suddenly continued: "Spiritual arrogance was the mischief in me. That is a dirtier thing than any pathological disease. Always the most difficult thing is to detect our own falsehoods. I found it finally—tore it out of my consciousness—killed it. But that stuff is a phoenix. It re-appears when you least expect it, out of the ashes of one's own pride. However, I had killed it for the time being. And then I really did go to work."

"What did you do?"

"I used every last human resource available. Money, credit, energy. Then, when there wasn't anything left, I prayed. I had a right to pray then. I had emptied the bin."

"But, Nancy, you don't believe in prayer! You said so!"

"Did I? Don't I! Well, you are right. That's true, I don't believe in it. I know it. So I can't possibly believe or disbelieve. Prayer consists in knowing, and in glorying in what one knows. But what can one expect, if one prays to the very liar and the father of the trouble that one wants to overcome? I hadn't really been praying at all. I had been flattering my personal ego, and what the Hindus call *maya*. But now I really began to pray. First for as much humility as I could possibly endure. Humility until it hurt. I demanded it. Not, meekness, humility."

411

"Nancy, what a weird prayer!"

"And because I wasn't lying this time, and the Lord is my shepherd, I received what I asked for—some humility. Some. Then I remembered the parable of the Prodigal Son. It paraphrased itself: *'Soul, I have sinned against my being, and before thee, and am no more worthy to be called even thy person.'*"

"Nancy, that's very beautiful. But how could you pray to your soul if you are your soul? Isn't that the opposite of what you've been telling me, over and over, for three days?"

"Oh, words!" said Nancy. "Words! What feeble instruments they are. What liars they are! We experience a glimpse of reality. But can we tell it? Not even the poets can tell. Not even Shakespeare could. Even Jesus's words have been twisted to mean the opposite of what he did mean. Elsa, each of us must make our own experience. After that, we know. And though we can still commit treason, we can never again quite unknow. We will always know, after we once have known, that it is treason we commit when we identify ourselves with the illusion and obey that. Then we feel homesick when we do wrong. But upward evolution is a wordless experience. We can't tell it, not in actual words. We can only hint to those we wish to help. Does this help you to understand: I yearned upward toward my superconscious being—my real being— toward beauty and intelligence and light—and prayed for enough intelligence to do the beautifully right thing now—the right little thing—the exactly right thing—not next week—now! The prayer was answered, instantly, although it didn't seem so at the moment."

"Then you didn't really know it had been answered?"

"Indeed I knew. But I hadn't tried to instruct wisdom, so of course I didn't know what form the answer would take. It began to dawn on me that I was only a beginner. I was a recruit, not a commander in chief, in a war against a whole world's ignorance, my own included. I had been trying to do what not even Jesus attempted. Then I saw my teacher."

"Old Ugly-face?"

"Yes. All that time, I hadn't been able even to call up a mental picture of him. But I saw him clearly now. I was clairvoyant again—just a little—not much—but enough. I wasn't clairaudient. He said nothing. But I knew I was on the way again. It restored my faith. Then the phone rang. A total stranger asked whether I could spare a nurse for the Jesuit Mission."

"The Mission where we stayed last night?"

"Yes. Of course, there wasn't a spare nurse. I couldn't even spare myself for more than a few hours. But by getting one of the over-worked teachers to do a double shift to relieve me, and by going without sleep—"

"You mean, you were doing nursing duty all this time?"

"Of course."

"From the way you told it, I supposed you had been meditating."

Nancy raised an eyebrow. "Your 'supposer,' my dear, is just a trifle out of order. It needs adjusting.—I drove to the Jesuit Mission and found them in a terrible way, burying their own dead. Priests using shovels. Converts and servants, some dead, some dying, two or three half dead from overwork, and the rest run away. Luckily I had brought some supplies. Those Jesuits had given away everything. They were living, or rather dying, on native bread and boiled rice. They hadn't missed a mass. Father Patrick had been given up for dead—extreme unction and all the rest of it. He was alone in a room, so I wrapped him in blankets and carried him off in the *tonga*. No car in those days. The other Jesuits were so weak they could hardly help me to lift him. Fortunately he was unconscious, so he couldn't resist. The *tonga* jolted him pretty badly. He almost did die on the way to Darjeeling. But he recovered. He and I have been respectful of each other's claws ever since."

"Claws?"

"Two tigers in a forest. We politely admire each other."

"But wasn't he grateful?"

"My dear! Why in the world should he be grateful to me? He remembered his manners, if that is what you mean. But how could a man, who is convinced that God is the dispenser of all good, possibly be grateful to anyone but God? He was quite consistent. Jesuits are soldiers, remember. Should a soldier on the field of battle be grateful to another soldier from a different regiment, who has merely obeyed the command of the Great Commander in Chief? Acknowledge his quality, yes. Salute him as a fellow soldier, yes. But gratitude?"

"Nancy, you talk almost as if you were a Jesuit!"

Nancy squealed with merry memory. "Elsa, Father Patrick and I both made the mistake of beginning to try to convert each other, for the glory of each other's Lord. We began by delicately hinting at each other's underlying error. He accused me of Jesuitry. I called him a materialist. Honestly we did. We both meant it, and we still think that

413

about each other."

"I can believe anything about a Jesuit," said Elsa, "but I still don't understand why we went there last night. Do they know I am going to Tibet?"

"They do."

"Do you mean that! Who can have told them?"

"There is very little that goes on that the Jesuits don't know!"

"Then it is true that their spies are everywhere?"

"Don't be silly. They don't even bother themselves to ask questions. Jesuits think. They are trained, highly organised, disciplined thinkers. They create a positive—call it that, just to give it a name—a positive thought-force that is immeasurably stronger than any electric current. An electric current is a mere illustration of thought-force. Jesuits are plus-minded, positive, dynamic thinkers. They induce, without even trying to, a secondary thought-force in others. So the minus-minded, negative people keep them plied with information, very often without knowing it."

"But why should Father Patrick accuse you of Jesuitry? You of all people!"

"He considers me a casuist. He believes I can't understand the difference between his way and mine."

"Do you understand it?"

"Perhaps there isn't any. But the signs read that he took a vow of poverty and obedience. I took a vow of affluence and disobedience."

"A vow? Did you? Of disobedience to whom? You obey your spiritual teacher, don't you? I understood you to say that."

"Disobedience, yes, to the death. Rebellion, with every scrap of intuition and common sense and courage I can muster—against the atrocious lie that we are miserable paupers with souls that need saving. My dear, a soul that needed saving wouldn't be worth the trouble."

"I still don't understand why we went to the Jesuit Mission."

"To demonstrate to you the impossibility—at least for anyone of your limited experience—of thinking independently, in opposition to highly organised and well-disciplined thought. I wanted to teach you tactics, as well as strategy."

"Then there's a way of—"

"Three ways. Two are defeatist. One can dive below their influence, and go to the devil. Thousands of people do it; they drown in materialism; deserting, malingering, degenerate Jesuits do it themselves. Another way is, to oppose, be beaten, and surrender: become a meek lamb and wait until you are dead to find out what it is that you bought by surrendering your soul to trustees. Or, you can rise above it. Not even a Jesuit can out-think, or out-pray you, if you refuse to meet him on his own ground. Take higher ground. One only learns by experience how to avoid being caught. If a Jesuit knew there is a higher ground, he would get there first and have a sheepfold all ready to herd you into. They are good shepherds, if you like being a sheep. Their strength consists in thought-propaganda, which is far more powerful than the spoken or printed word. Propaganda, even when true, is a form of violence, which is a product of impatience, which in turn is sacrifice to fear."

"But, Nancy, isn't your conversation propaganda?"

"Yes. Make no mistake about that. But it is aimed at freeing your consciousness now, instead of enslaving you for the sake of a promised land in the hereafter. Yes, mine is propaganda. But if you should let it control your thought instead of waking you up to fight your own battle, I would repudiate you. I would shake you off."

"Tell me this, Nancy. You say you prayed. Then your teacher sent you to save a Jesuit."

"Indeed he did not!"

"But you said you saw Old Ugly-face, and then—"

"My seeing him meant this: that through humility I had reached a state—or let us call it a balance of consciousness—not too remote from his. I was, at least momentarily, on the higher plane of consciousness that he had taught me how to attain. I was catching up with him. A real idea could reach me. It could penetrate the mess of opinions I had been floundering in. A real idea knows no boundaries, no limits; no one can monopolize it. And there is no such thing as a partial, incomplete idea, nor any possibility of an idea not finding work to do. Consequently, because of that law of supply and demand, some total stranger was stirred by the same idea, and he phoned me to ask for the loan of a nurse."

"But you hadn't one!"

"Well? The idea set me moving in the right direction. It employed me. It saved the life of Father Patrick. And among many other things it made it possible for you, all these years later, to return to Tibet."

"Nancy, are you stretching your imagination?"

"No, dear. But I do hope I am awakening yours. It so needs it!"

"What has Father Patrick to do with my returning to Tibet?"

"It would be a breach of confidence to answer that question.

Someone—not Father Patrick—warned me by telephone—and I told Morgan Lewis—that Bulah Singh's meddling had alarmed the Chief of Police of Sikkim. You and Andrew would have been held up if that warning hadn't come through. And it would not have come through unless Father Patrick and I were on excellent terms. But understand me: Father Patrick himself did not send the warning."

"Nancy, do you really feel you can trust him?"

"So implicitly, my dear, that I would tell him anything he might ask, unless it had been told to me in strict confidence."

Elsa laughed. She couldn't help it. "Nancy, you're too bewildering! Just now you said God forbid you should love a Jesuit!"

"Yes." She chuckled. "I hope God heard me! Does this answer your question? I am my soul. I am not this foolish old woman-person who gets disturbed by illusions, and hates Jesuits, and sometimes has a headache. Doesn't that apply equally to Father Patrick? He is a brave, unselfish soul. Integrity is one of his dimensions. He isn't that superstitious masochist who hates talkative females and crosses himself when he sees me coming. He is a soldier in a shabby *soutane*. Father Patrick is one of the few men I know who forces me to remember who I really am, and who he really is. He wouldn't be endurable on any other terms. That is what Jesus meant by saying love your enemies. Don't love their objectionable persons, or expect them to love yours. Love them by remembering who they really are. Then they will love you. Do you see the difference?"

"I am beginning to. Does it always work?"

"You mean for beginners like you and me? No indeed! Not in one lifetime! Not in this world! We have a long way to go before we can finish that part of our education. So we had better get a good start, hadn't we?"

"But if it's really true, why doesn't it always work?"

"Does the Golden Rule work when applied by a conceited egotist? Torquemada thought he was obeying the Golden Rule when he tortured heretics. The rule is really so simple that the complicated illusion of personality blinds us to it. We can only learn gradually, little by little. But each little that we learn is one step on the road of evolution."

"Nancy. Tell me this. If I should try to follow your teaching, do you think it would help me to become Tom's real wife, so that he and I would love each other and be genuinely happy?"

Nancy studied her a moment. "Genuine? Happy? How should I

416

know? Happiness, remember, is a temporary state of mind—a temporary calm, destroyed by the first ripple that comes along. As an end in
itself it is like the pot of gold at the end of the rainbow. As something
to have and to hold, it is as disappointing as money."

"But we can't get along without money. And unless we're happy
now and then, what is life worth living for? We'd be better off dead—
annihilated—nonexistent. I have often wished that might happen to
me. Can't you offer some encouragement about Tom and me?"

Nancy thought a moment. Then: "I was never tempted to become
a fortune teller. What I can tell you is this: happiness is either a fool's
paradise, or else a by-product of continual striving toward spiritual
consciousness. True happiness is a sensation of momentary balance.
When we remember who and what we really are, we do no wrong
and we injure no one. Even our worst mistakes turn out to others'
benefit; and they become profitable lessons for us."

"But how can one learn all this! Oh, how I wish you were coming with us to Tibet! Weeks and weeks on the march, and you to talk
with. One might—"

Nancy's laugh interrupted: "Does it occur to you, my dear, that
selfishness isn't a wish? It is a repudiation of your own higher intelligence."

"Oh. No, I hadn't thought of that. I suppose it was selfish. You have
been utterly kind in coming this far. But—"

"Tonight," said Nancy, "if we are both as unselfish as we can make
ourselves be, I will help you to see why you don't need me. I can prove
it to you."

CHAPTER 24

Elsa and Nancy made themselves more comfortable in the smoke-
smeared monastery guest room than Andrew had done three nights
earlier. Andrew, confusing luxury with comfort, usually dispensed
with both when alone, although he wasn't, like Tom Grayne, a Spartan
about it; for his own purposes, they merely weren't worth worrying
about. Elsa, on the other hand, intuitively knew which little luxuries
make discomfort bearable; and Nancy was an old, old hand at creating
comfort where there was none. So the car had disgorged some incon-
siderable trifles, and the gloomy room became a swept and habitable
refuge.

The bearded old chauffeur, shawled in double blankets, sat on a
mat outside the door, protecting his lunatic charges against only God

could guess what consequences of their madness. He even stood off the monks who brought food—himself carried in the food—himself tasted it first in Nancy's presence to make sure the monks hadn't doped it with magical drugs—himself carried out the dishes and set them at a distance down the corridor where the kitchen crew might recover them without bringing their devilish persons too near. He had eaten his own dry corn and peas porridge. No monkish muck for him. He had brought his old army water bottle, filled in Darjeeling at a hydrant on which no priestly shadow had ever cast its curse. By the light of a Japanese lantern he sat reading a *Life of Lenin*—mistranslated from the French, with footnotes and interpolated comments by a *babu* who had been to Moscow. Revolution snorted through the old man's nostrils as he read.

Nancy and Elsa, in their own folding canvas chairs, sat talking, less at random (though it sounded like it) than for the sake of avoiding a moody silence or any reference to Elsa's baby. This was the first, and next to the last, room that the tent-born baby had lived in. Each woman dreaded the other's reaction to any mention of it. Particularly, Elsa dreaded to be told that her secret sweet-sad longing for the child was morbid self-pity. She knew it wasn't, but she felt sure Nancy would say it was. Nancy, full of her own intention, was afraid of a mood that might make Elsa past-bound and unreceptive. So they talked about the monastery, and about the learned old arch hypocrite who ruled it and was all things by turns but nothing long—excepting always a keeper of secrets.

"Old Gombaria understands," said Nancy, "that secrecy is a secret's only value. That is why he can be trusted. He hoards secrets like a jackdaw."

But memories are irrepressible, one leading to the next. Elsa could hardly keep her eyes away from the smoke-smeared painting on the wall by the bed. The patch where Andrew's handkerchief had rubbed away the soot was still noticeable. On her way southward she had lain with her child in her arms, staring at the picture of the woman being boiled in oil in hell. All the thoughts of those hours returned, now, unbidden, including the questions with which she had tortured Andrew's patience. Especially she had wondered how, when, why religious men had invented such cruel eternities in store for one another. She had thought about the Spanish Inquisition; and about Dante's *Inferno*, and Fox's *Book of Martyrs*; the vicar at home had lent her both books, illustrated in fiendish detail, during his efforts to convict her of the Witch of Endor's sin of seeing with unveiled eyes. She had discussed those books with Andrew—forced him to discuss them.

In her mind's eye she saw him now, seated on one of the bent-wood chairs, imperturbably answering child-like questions while he carved away at a chunk of wood with his clasp knife. He had re-marked, in one of his frowning, analytical moments, that torture, in any circumstances, probably reveals the victim's own latent cruelty. She had disagreed. They had argued about it and she lost her temper because he had refused to lose his. After that, he had read to her from his old, thumbed copy of Browning. Andrew always chanted poetry, maintaining that to read it in an ordinary conversational voice is to neglect the magic that conveys its meaning. She could almost hear him now, as if the walls retained the record:

> . . . I count life just a stuff
> To try the soul's strength on.

The baby had fallen asleep to the sound of his reading. She remem-bered wondering what Andrew's child would be like if he should ever marry. And then she wondered what Andrew would say to a woman he loved, and whether any woman ever would understand him. She didn't. He was as dependable, but as incomprehensible as—Suddenly Elsa left her chair and pulled the bed away from the wall.

"Nancy! Come here! Look! Andrew got my message! Here is his answer! Scrawled on the wall below the picture!"

Nancy's face assumed a mask-like expression. She was not very good at assuming indifference. She was depending on the momentum of events rather than on any skill of her own to get Elsa into the mood for what was coming. "Does he say he received the telegram?" she asked, guarding her voice.

"He says he got both messages! Both! Was there more than one telegram?"

"No. Didn't I tell you? Morgan Lewis asked Mu-ni Gam-po to spatchcock our 'cat' message into his routine telegram to Gombaria. That was all. A telegram addressed direct to Andrew might have made the Sikkim police inquisitive. With no other motive than to do their duty they might easily force the Indian Government to stop you and Andrew from crossing the frontier."

"Then the other message must have been the mental one I sent him! He did get it! Nancy, he got it! It worked!"

"Well? Why not? I suspected it would reach him."

"When? When did you suspect it? You never mentioned it to me."

"Three nights ago—when you sent it, with your hands over your face, at my fireside, while we were talking about the pistol, just before you and I went to bed."

"Nancy!"

"Yes?"

"Are you imagining things? That can't be right. It's impossible. Wasn't Andrew here the night after he left Darjeeling?"

"Yes. Only one night. He left here at daybreak. I enquired when we arrived this evening."

"Then how can he possibly have got my message? If he had got it on the way, at the time when I sent it—"

"Then he would almost certainly have turned back," said Nancy.

"There are two messages on the wall, one above the other. The first reads: Hurry forward. Don't let them delay you. Below that, there's an arrow pointing to the figure 2, and then the second one. It reads: Got second message. Okay.—Nancy, do come and look."

"Why? I can take your word for it."

"But, Nancy, if Andrew did get my mental message, in this room, after he received the telegram, then it must have been almost one whole day after I sent it!"

"Well?"

"How is that possible? It isn't possible. It can't be."

Nancy checked an impulse to explain too much, too soon. Truth can't be taught. But it is learnable. She came back with a question: "Would you describe Andrew as clairvoyant?"

"No, I don't think so. Perhaps just a little bit. Sometimes he seems to know what one is going to say before one says it. But Andrew doesn't invite that kind of intimacy. That was the first time I ever dared to try to send a message to him. I wouldn't have then, if you hadn't been reading the riot act about my meekness. And it did seem so important that he should know about the pistol."

"There are two reasons why I think you reached him," said Nancy. "Andrew loves poetry. I don't mean merely likes—he loves it."

"He never even tries to write it," said Elsa.

Nancy retorted irritably: "Andrew thrills to the spirit that poetry brings into consciousness even more than most music does. It's the old story of the man of action revering spiritual thought but despising its mouthpiece: the man at arms and the non-combatant chaplain.

Andrew is too inherently courteous to admit it, even to himself, but he considers a poet a kind of weakling without the dignity to resist emotional impulse."

Elsa agreed: "Andrew resists all his impulses, except the generous ones. One can almost see him hold them off and look at them as if they were something offered for sale."

"Exactly," said Nancy. "Poetry thrills him. It awakens his consciousness, but simultaneously reveals to him his own shortcomings. So he resists the very force that makes him able to distinguish between good and evil. There is nothing unusual about that. To a greater or lesser extent we all do it. We won't let truth into our consciousness, because it shows us the humiliating meanness of the lies we live by."

"Do you mean by that, that Andrew is a liar, or that he's clairvoyant?"

"Both," said Nancy. "Unwillingly in each instance. If he weren't a liar he wouldn't be human. He has set his strength against clairvoyance. But no lover of poetry ever lived who could shut out clairvoyant visions. If he is vicious, vile visions. If he drinks, drunken visions. If he is honest, true visions. One can tell almost anyone's true character by the kind of poetry he loves."

"Andrew loves strong poetry," said Elsa. "He despises what he calls kiss-mammy stuff, and decadence, and phony realism. He says the test of poetry is that you must hear the wild harps thrumming when you chant it aloud.— But what is your other reason for thinking he really saw my message?"

"Your motive," Nancy answered. "It was almost totally unselfish, as far as I can judge. And Andrew's situation. Being in this room must have brought you into his thought. Mere memory would do that. The monks here do almost- nothing but experimental thinking. It isn't very spiritual, but they create a maelstrom of thought that attracts all sorts of phenomena—good, bad, indifferent—just the opposite of the Jesuits."

"We had a dose of Jesuits," said Elsa. "It was impossible to think there—I mean—well, we talked about it—you explained it."

"It was good for you," Nancy retorted. "Elsa, unless you learn how to guard your thought against intruding influences, even better than the Jesuits guard theirs, you would be far better off among Jesuits than at the mercy of your own craving to be of some use in the world. Better a bigoted disciplinarian than no guide. One's personal opinion, no matter how obstinate, is as porous as a sponge. It absorbs whatever it is

421

soaked in. Squeeze it, and out come its secrets."

"Nancy, there must be lots of exceptions to that. Andrew can keep secrets. So can you. I can read some people's thought without even trying. I can read Tom's almost always. But Andrew's never—not when he covers up."

"Andrew is like anyone else," said Nancy. "The only possible protection—the only one—against mental intrusion, burglary, bullying, blackmail, propaganda, tyranny, dictatorship—is to be a soul and to be conscious of it. Control your person, instead of the other way around. Don't be a tail trying to wag the dog, or an orchestra trying to direct the conductor."

"Nancy, are you sure it wasn't you who sent the mental message to Andrew?"

Nancy smiled. She didn't answer the question directly: "I was minding my own business. Let me tell you what I think happened."

"I wish you would. I feel as scared, inside me, as if I had broken a law. Oh, Nancy, I don't want to be clairvoyant! I don't! I won't! I hate it!"

"Chickens," said Nancy, "can't get back into the egg. They must learn to take care of themselves. Shall I tell you what I think happened?"

"Yes! Please!"

"Andrew must have been thinking of you, or he would not have written the first message on the wall. Later, he received the telegram. Very likely Gombaria brought it to him. It would be just like Gombaria to make a mystery about it. He experiments. Gombaria is a very expert manipulator of mental atmosphere."

"Atmosphere?"

"Yes. That is only a phrase. One has to use words to suggest meanings that words can't convey. Gombaria can, and perhaps did, create a psychic field in which phenomena can easily occur. That is another phrase. It is worthless except as a hint. The reading of the telegram would direct Andrew's attention instantly and very strongly to you. The suddenness, and unexpectedness would shock him enough to make him let go of his own thoughts. He would see your thought. He couldn't possibly keep it out of his consciousness. I believe he would see your mental picture before he would see you. That would be normal."

"But, Nancy! Twenty hours after I sent it?"

"Why not? Time has nothing to do with it. That is one of the many reasons why time—and fact-bound intellectuals can't grasp clairvoyance. It is why professional clairvoyants almost always prove unreliable."

"You mean fortune tellers?"

"Yes. They become confused when they try to translate infinity into time. But there is another reason: the economic one."

"What on earth do you mean?"

"Humanity is gradually, very slowly evolving toward pure super-consciousness, in which there can be no such concept as profit and loss. On the intermediate levels, such as you and I can reach, the profit and loss illusion puts up a fight. It tempts us with suggestions that lead into disastrous mental quicksands, in which we flounder and lose all sense of direction. That is the meaning of the temptation of Jesus by the devil."

"But can the world be run on any other basis than profit and loss?"

"Of course it can't, as long as people are hypnotized by the personal profit and loss illusion. Every materialistic effort to change conditions only provides different opportunities for exploitation. The old exploiters become the new victims, and vice versa."

"Then what is the answer?"

"Gradually, as we struggle upward toward soul consciousness, the illusion loses its hypnotic grip. We begin then to be free to think clearly and to solve problems sanely. We leave off trying to fill holes with shadows. Instead, we fill them with ideas that develop their own substance. But it follows that a clairvoyant—seeing on a spiritual plane but working for material personal profit—and especially for dishonest profit—is committing spiritual treason. That is why gamblers and spies and criminals who use clairvoyance, as many of them consciously do, invariably meet disaster. Clairvoyance perverted to treacherous ends becomes spiritual suicide. Sometimes it leads to the madhouse. It is always, without any exception—without any possible exception—ruinous to the one who misuses it."

"God!" said Elsa. "Nancy—tell me—did I misuse it when I sent that message to Andrew?"

"Don't be silly. Relatively speaking, it was an unselfish message. None of us humans can be quite unselfish as long as we have our personalities to care for. But you were not trying to make a profit or to mislead Andrew. You were trying to give him information, weren't you? Now tell me something."

"What? I'll tell you anything I know."

"Did you know that Bompo Tsering was the go-between who ordered that pistol shot fired at you?"

"Yes. When he opened the window, and Andrew spoke to him, I knew it then. I knew it even before that. That was why I wanted to speak to him. I was quite sure he was up to mischief."

"Did you hope, when you sent the message, that Bompo Tsering would be punished for his treachery?"

"I never even thought of it. My only impulse was to tell Andrew what had happened. To protect him. I mean, so that he could protect himself."

"That is what saved Andrew."

"How do you mean that, Nancy? I don't understand you."

"It is a good example of how clairvoyance works when there is no vindictive, or envious, or profit-seeking motive. Probably—of course I can't be quite sure about this, but probably Andrew would have turned back if he had got your message at once. That might have been disastrous. It would have frightened Bulah Singh, who would almost certainly have tried to save himself by accusing Morgan Lewis of connivance in a plot to cross the frontier. That would have done Bulah Singh no good, but it would have been the end of Andrew's expedition."

"I still can't see why Andrew didn't get my message the moment I sent it."

"Because your impulse to protect him did protect him."

"How?"

"If you had loaded your thought with malice against Bompo Tsering— or with opinions about what Andrew should do—or with some profit motive, you would have robbed the message of its protective element."

"I still don't understand."

"Paradoxically, because time is not an element in clairvoyance, the message could select the right time. And because space is not a limitation of clairvoyance, it could select the line of least resistance and reach him here, at the proper moment, where it is easier than in most other places for a psychic incident to happen. The wrong motive would have spoiled that—might have prevented it altogether."

The old chauffeur opened the door and stood, shawled and breathing Leninism through his loyal nose, awaiting orders. He made a jerky gesture with his head. Nancy nodded. He went out, closing the door with a thud that verged on the edge of the brink of insolence and needed benefit of doubt to save even that verdict.

"I told him to let me know," said Nancy, "before going to find out whether Gombaria is ready to receive us."

"He seems awfully angry."

"Yes. He thinks Gombaria should come humbly. He considers my dignity is being disregarded. And he knows that searchers will visit this room in our absence."

"Had we better lock our bags before we—"

"No. Leave them open. Be generous. Save Gombaria's monks from the indignity of picking locks. They wouldn't dream of taking anything. They will only look. Gombaria likes to know everything—everything—and to tell nothing."

"He sounds a bit unscrupulous," said Elsa.

"Well, he is, and he is not," Nancy answered. "He is like all the rest of us—a human being in search of his soul. Sometimes I suspect him of delaying the search for the sake of intellectual amusement. But not always. And he sends children to my school when he considers them too intelligent to become monks. So I mustn't be too critical."

"Broad-minded enough to send children to your school?"

"Yes, and to pay generously."

"But so stupid that he spies into handbags?"

"We all average out," said Nancy. "Remember: philosophy is not virtue. Gombaria knows one very important thing that you haven't learned yet."

"What is that?"

"Not to expect too much from people. And not to expect too little from life, but to insist on more and more intelligent enjoyment of every moment that he lives.—I hear my old tiger coming back, so wrap yourself in a shawl. It will be cold in the corridors. Are you ready? It is very bad manners to keep the ruler of a monastery waiting."

CHAPTER 25

Elsa began to feel terrified. The fear was inside her, subjective, not due to physical surroundings. It was a wordless sensation, unexplainable, comfortless. It brought up memories of punishment at school—a helpless dread. But she acted brave, like a novice in no-man's land. She and Nancy followed the old turbaned chauffeur along dim, draughty corridors.

She didn't for one second doubt her intuition that Nancy was leading her to an experience that would mean farewell—perhaps to Nancy. Farewell, and a new unknown beginning. It was a sensation of lonely dread. But curiosity was stronger than dread—much stronger. She knew that Nancy was also hard-pressed to subdue emotion.

Nancy said never a word as the old Mahratta's lantern danced in time to his martial stride, making weird shadows leap on the walls. Their footsteps rang with a kind of frosty brittleness. There were echoes. Somewhere ahead in the gloom a monk with spinning prayer wheel was leading the way through hewn tunnels; they saw his back as he turned corners, up and down masonry stairways that followed the pattern of the mountain top to which the buildings clung.

They passed, in almost breathless silence, through a long, dim room where Elsa recognized two monks from Mu-ni Gam-po's monastery. There were dozens of monks in the room, perhaps a hundred of them, all lined against the walls beneath faded banners and shadowy oil paintings. The two whom she knew made no sign of recognition. One of them had carried charcoal and hot water to her cell all winter in Darjeeling. She had talked with him many a time. The other one had been too talkative. He had brought her the ancient books from Mu-ni Gam-po's library, and he had marvelled that a girl should know Tibetan. He loved to watch her turn it into English, and was pleased because she used a brush to write with, on parchment paper, so that each letter and each word was a thing of beauty. He had wanted to stay in the room and singsong the Tibetan text that he knew by heart. He had been hard to get rid of. But now, standing against the wall, with incongruous Jodhpur riding breeches showing under his long travelling coat, he was as blank-faced and immobile as if he had never seen her.

They had to pass through the refectory to reach the room where Gombaria awaited them—long tables, backless benches, a rancid reek of butter, an image of Chenrezi looming in the gloom. Then another narrow tunnel, hewn through a projection on the face of the cliff. It opened into a foursquare chamber, half rock, half masonry, with a door at the farther end, but no window. Stifling, silent, cold. There they were kept waiting. The monk who had led the way stood telling his beads, facing the door with his back toward them.

"This," said Nancy in an almost inaudible voice, "is where Lopsang Pun received initiation from his own great teacher."

"You mean where we stand now?"

"No. In the chamber beyond that door."

Silence. An insufferable tension. Then:

"Who was his teacher?"

Nancy, for once, seemed at a loss for words. Then, suddenly, as if angry at the question: "Who taught Jesus—Pythagoras—St. Paul?"

Silence again, Elsa studying Nancy's face that was lighted from below by the old Mahratta's lantern. It was like a wonderfully cut cameo on soot-black jet.

"Nancy, are you an initiate?"

"Sh-s-sh!"

"But are you?"

"No."

The monosyllable forbade more questions. But Nancy suddenly relented, or perceived an opportunity. She added, slightly louder, so that each word was distinct and the monk might have heard, had he listened:

"By their fruits ye shall know them. And by yours they will know you."

"Who will? You mean the initiates?"

"No initiate would say he is one unless his soul should warn him to remind a younger soul that there is law, authority—a hierarchy higher than ourselves."

"Well then, how should one know he is genuine?"

"His claim would prove itself. There would be no conceit, no power-hunger to prevent that."

A long pause, while the monk's beads clicked and the old *mahratta* fidgeted with the lantern. There was no other sound. Then:

"Nancy, what are we waiting for?"

"For Gombaria's summons."

"Nancy, are you frightened? You look it."

"No."

"I am."

"Sh-s-sh! Not so loud. Try to keep calm."

"It's cold here. Nancy, what happens at an initiation?"

"You will not know that until your own turn comes."

"My turn? Must it? What if I refuse—if I don't wish it?"

"Wishing would delay the day," said Nancy. "Haste is only churning of illusion. You will know when your time is at hand. Be still. Be patient."

Silence again. Elsa could hear her own heartbeat. She stared at the wormy old door, and at the monk's back, and at the stalwart, military

427

shoulders of the old *mahratta*. She tried to imagine the iron, inscrutable Ringding Gelong Lama Old Ugly-face, on his stubborn knees in an embroidered crimson robe like a cardinal's, receiving someone's laying on of hands. But she recognized that as a picture she had seen in the National Gallery. She dismissed it.

"Nancy."

"Yes?"

"Who chooses candidates for initiation?"

"No one. They evolve." Nancy looked straight at her, bright-eyed, excited. "No one can receive, who has not. But unto him that hath—"

"I have nothing. Nothing." Elsa shuddered. "Nancy, I feel cowardly. Inside me, I'm afraid. But I don't know what of."

"Only your nothingness is afraid. You are your soul. Be real! You are not this trembler at the door of experience."

"Nancy, I will go where you lead. But is it right, what we're doing? Please don't get us into any Tantric magic, such as Bulah Singh spoke of."

"Try not to think about Bulah Singh."

"I can't help it. I know he isn't here, but I keep seeing him. Once he spoke of black magic. This place seems—"

"Sh-s-sh! Look straight at him. Order him away! He will go."

Elsa summoned to her aid the so often defeated will that only now and then beat back clairvoyance. She stood off the mental image of Bulah Singh. It was like facing a dog's eyes in the dark.

"You were right. He has gone. I don't see him now. His eyes were staring at me."

"We have nothing to do with black magic."

"You promise?"

"Child, if I should knowingly mislead you, it would be worse than death for me. Worse for me than for you."

"Tell me what is going to happen beyond that door."

"I don't know what will happen."

"Then why go through with it? Why not go back to the guest room?"

"Sh-s-sh! Try reciting the Twenty-third Psalm."

"Very well. If it pleases you."

"Let us say it together. *The Lord is my*—"

The door opened quietly. Two monks came through like dark-robed spirits from a tomb. They stood aside, with their backs to the

428

wall. There was a smell of incense.

"No questions now," said Nancy. She seemed to choke with emotion. "Keep on repeating the Twenty-third Psalm and the Lord's Prayer. Say them alternately, over and over. Try to be conscious of each word as you say it to yourself."

She took Elsa's hand and stood waiting for one of the monks to signal to them to pass through the door. Elsa felt like a frightened child, but she controlled herself, and she knew by the feel of her hand in Nancy's that she was no longer trembling. The monk beckoned. The old Mahratta chauffeur strode immediately forward, like a soldier stepping from the ranks at the word of command. His not to reason why. His to do, and take the consequences. He asserted, square-shouldered, his beloved mad employer's license to do as she pleased. He marched down the short hewn-walled passage, through the door at the far end, and stood lantern in hand, with his back to the Lama Gombaria, until Nancy and Elsa had seated themselves. Mats had been piled for them, a dozen deep, on the floor in the far corner. The Mahratta blew out his lantern to save Nancy's oil, and sat down near them, cross-legged, on one of his own shawls, staring at Gombaria with stony disapproval.

Gombaria was seated on a hewn stone dais, between two looming statues of Bodhisattvas. Those, and a bell and an incense burner, were the only decorations of the chamber. It was hewn from the solid rock—about twenty feet by twenty, with a high, arched ceiling. There was a swimming, underwater sensation, due to incense smoke and the irregular adze-marks on the walls that cast interlacing shadows from the dim light of butter-fed lamps. On the step of Gombaria's dais, at either side of him, his two subordinates stood in attitudes of saintly meditation. They looked incurious, unconscious of the world; but several times Elsa detected them studying Nancy and herself beneath half lowered eyelids. She was beginning to wonder why she had felt frightened.

The doorkeeper monks entered, closed a thick door behind them, and stood motionless. Elsa left off reciting the Lord's Prayer. It was distracting to keep her mind on it and she wasn't afraid any longer. She was fascinated by Gombaria, wondering what he was thinking about. Deliberately, without any success whatever, she tried to get a clairvoyant glimpse of the old *lama's* thought. She couldn't see even its colour. She might as well have tried to guess what a statue was thinking about. She heard Nancy murmuring:

429

Thy kingdom come.
Thy will be done on earth,
As it is in heaven.

So she resumed murmuring the Lord's Prayer, moving her lips to satisfy Nancy that she was obeying orders. Hardly conscious of the words, she caught herself, nevertheless, wondering what good they did. Suppose one did believe in an All-seeing Father—what of it? Sparrows fall—two for a farthing—and Father knows. What of it? Bombs fall, too. And babies die, and—

Something was happening. She couldn't guess what. It was happening. It was mental. It was like the spell that falls on an expectant crowd. A sensation of awe. She glanced at the old Mahratta chauffeur. He was breathing through his nose—shawled—rigid—angry— contemptuous.

Gombaria didn't move. Not even his eyelids moved. His protruding underlip was so massively motionless that it lent an appearance of moulded bronze to all the rest of him. For five minutes there was no sound except the Mahratta's breathing and Nancy's almost inaudible murmur: "'*Yea, though I walk through the valley of the shadow of death*—'"

Then astonishing sound: "*Aum-m-m-m-m-m-m-m-m!*" (Sacred syllable).

It began like the far-away note of a gong, approaching slowly, gradually swelling until it boomed like a chord of organ music. It was Gombaria's voice. He hadn't moved. Even his lips hadn't moved. But it was his voice. His subordinates joined in. Then the doorkeeper monks. Then Nancy, low alto. So Elsa added her own contralto, that some envious forgotten nobody had called a freak voice. After that she had never trained it but had made it a scapegoat for the worse freak, clairvoyance, that she could not get rid of. She could refuse to sing, and she did. Not even Tom Grayne knew what pitch and tone and volume she could produce from her small person. But now, for no reason that she was aware of except that it thrilled her, she gave her rolling *contralto* full rein.

"*Aum-m-m-m-m-m-m-m-m-m-m-m-m!*"

Because she joined in last, she lingered last, alone, on the sacred syllable that, if one knows its secret, links the brain-mind with the soul and lets in floodlight from the higher consciousness. She did not know the secret. But she thrilled, watching Gombaria, hardly aware that her own voice was the last on the lingering note. Then Gombaria's eyes did move. They met hers. In the dim light, from across the room, they looked brilliant black. She couldn't guess what he was thinking. Gombaria moved his right hand and rang one clear mellow note with the small bell. Instantly, silently, the two subordinates thumbed the wicks of the four lamps. There was total darkness. Elsa felt Nancy's hand groping for hers. The old Mahratta chauffeur breathed fiercely.

Nancy's strong, rough hand felt reassuring, like a branch to clung to in a steep place. But Elsa wasn't afraid; she felt excited—tensely curious. She had an unaccountable sensation that instead of Nancy and the old Mahratta chauffeur, Andrew Gunning and Tom Grayne were beside her. Nancy's hand was Andrew's. She knew it wasn't, but it felt like it. Tom Grayne was enormously angry, though she knew that was the Mahratta. For two or three minutes there was no audible sound but the Mahratta's breathing, until Gombaria repeated the chant and they all joined in:

"*Aum-m-m-m-m-m-m-m-m-m-m-m-m-m!*"

As the note died away there began to be dim gray light in mid-room. It was formless, cheerless. It resembled wan moonlight. But it began to be shot through with rays of brilliance, like aurora borealis or the glimmer of the morning on distant peaks—as mysterious and beautiful and as unrelated to any visible source. The light faded, died away and was gone.

Nancy murmured: "He needs help. Oh, if we were less dense—less turgid!"

"Sh-s-sh!" said Elsa. She couldn't imagine why. She just said it. Gombaria's voice, subdued, hummed alone on the sacred syllable, but he stopped suddenly. The wan gray light returned. Then all at once the universal spectrum seemed to pour its colours like a waterfall into a pool of white. It was a blinding bewildering, soundless spasm—gray all around it—murky, miserable, wan and hungry gray—but in the centre pure colour in motion that made the senses reel. There was no reflection on the walls. The room remained pitch dark. When Elsa shut her eyes, she still saw the light. Whichever way she turned her head, she saw the centre of it—increasing—fading—increasing again, as if a will behind it forced it against waves of an unseen ocean. Suddenly it merged its colours into one—flame colour—then God's blood ruby. It turned golden, like the sun on water—and vanished. Where it had been, stood the Ringding Gelong Lama Lobsang Pun—Old Ugly-face. Living, moving, breathing.

It was black dark. He was as clearly visible as if he stood in sunlight, nearer than mid-room. No light exuded from him. But he was visible. He looked natural, in three dimensions, exactly as Elsa had last seen him— hooded and cloaked in the ritual robes of his high order— bulky—ungainly—almost monstrous—peering with his owl's eyes through a mass of wrinkles—homely and human as Falstaff—holy, and as full of irony, and dignity, and inner laughter as if Michelangelo had hewn him out of granite to be breathed on by the breath of Life. He moved. His weird owl's-beak nose twitched. He was talking, making no sound. Elsa knew he and Nancy were talking—knew it, but heard nothing. He changed. He became the younger Lobsang Pun of the smashed photograph. Inaudibly but as overwhelmingly as if the senses heard it, his familiar, jovial belly laugh exploded in Olympian amusement.

So far, to the last, least gesture Elsa recognized him. He was looking at Nancy. That made it all the easier to watch the penetrating attack of his eyes and their equally sudden receptive gleam of understanding— the occasional pout of his lower lip—the habitual, hardly perceptible, slow contraction of his neck, as if he foresaw, and neither feared nor underrated but was ready to meet violence with energy that he held in leash. Old Ugly-face in every incongruous detail, even to the rakish tilt of his cone-shaped hat.

But—as thought lets go its gloom and spirals upward to the surge of music or a remembered poem, until inspiration reaches unknown views that make the heart leap—gradually now he changed into an unknown Lobsang Pun. Nancy's hand on Elsa's gripped with the strength of a vise, and then ceased to be felt. Through the old *lama's* ugliness and robed obesity there shone forth a god, young with eternal youth, as splendid as the calm of everlasting morning, smiling with enjoyment of the fire-born glory of evolving worlds. How did one know what he smiled at? Elsa did know. She remembered the Bible story of the Transfiguration—lost it in views like blind Milton's— glimpsed Andrew—heard him chanting, as she had heard him scores of times:

Sonorous metal blowing martial sounds:
At which the universal host up sent
A shout that tore hell's concave, and beyond
Frightened the reign of Chaos and old Night.

Consciousness surged with wordless experience that knew no

form but beauty. Utterly beyond the shapes of things, and uncommunicable in the terms of time, passion rioted, exulted, gloried in motion that moved of itself, creating realms on realms of spiritual harvest ripening in selfless love, that gave and took not. An eternal moment. Being wholly released from having. Consciously exhaustless power to create new newness, now and forever.

Elsa made no attempt to measure how long the experience lasted. Time was no dimension of it: minutes, hours, ages were incomparable nothing. Words brought her back to self-consciousness and the feel of the pressure of Nancy's hand on numbed fingers.

"'Lo, I am with you always, even unto the end of the world.'"

She didn't know whether Lobsang Pun or Nancy said it. It was a voice. Perhaps her own voice. She didn't know whether she heard it with her ears or with that inner hearing that offended people so that she had almost deafened it by self-inflicted torture of mind and nerves.

It was a voice, no matter whose. She had heard and she had seen Reality. She had seen pure spirit. It had almost shattered her human consciousness. A bursting shell, lightning, death itself could demolish no more totally the deaf-blind unrealities that she had feared, and felt, and cherished.

"Now I know."

Was that her own voice, or some other? "But who am I?"

Nancy let go of her hand. She was alone in the dark. Herself, alone, with Lobsang Pun. The Old Ugly-face whom she knew—clothed now in ragged black, stern, shrunken, apparently suffering—was studying her, looking straight at her. He was seated, cross-legged, it seemed in the snow. He appeared to recognize her—to see through her, to the secret thoughts that fled and tried to hide in the dark womb where she had loved her child toward a destiny that ended almost unbegun. She cowered, flinched, shrunk away—then turned against herself and bared her heart, her very soul, her whole consciousness, to the stare of the terrible eyes. And the eyes changed. Knowledge entered her. She knew, without questioning how she knew it, that Old Ugly-face, hundreds of miles away, had found, clairvoyantly, and with his spaceless, timeless consciousness had reached Nancy, his *chela*. Nancy had presented her for recognition. She was recognized. It was he, yet not he. With her eyes she could not have seen him. But she had seen him—not with her eyes—never again to forget or be forgotten. He was fading—already a measureless distance gone, withdrawn into a

433

murky, dull gray hungry mist of paling light. Then darkness. Silence. And after a breathless, timeless interval Nancy's voice murmuring:

"'Lord, thou knowest all things: thou knowest that I love thee.'"

There were sounds then in the darkness. Someone was moving. The door opened and closed quietly. Then Nancy's voice, hoarse, almost choking:

"Light the lantern."

The old Mahratta fumbled with matches and tugged at the squeaky mechanism of the lantern, lighted it, raised it and showed the room empty. He saw the gleam of tears on Nancy's face, got stiffly to his feet and came and stood in front of her, glaring angrily at Elsa as if she must have offended his beloved mistress. He clucked discourteous sympathy, reproach, and proverbs about women.

"Why?" he demanded. "Why? Why? Isn't it good that nothing happened?"

Nancy stared at him: "Did you see nothing?"

"Nay, there was nothing to see. These monks are an ignorant lot of humbugs. They know nothing. Look, they have fled. They played no tricks, because they knew I watched them. They fled from shame, lest we should ask them: why no magic? Hah! Magic! Dry those honourable eyes that weep because they saw no sin! *Tschut-tschut!* Sin is for men, not for women!"

CHAPTER 26

Andrew Gunning stood with his hands in raincoat pockets, wearing his shabby old felt hat, looking as little as he could like the leader of an expedition. Behind him, fifty yards away, was the Bhutia trading post, where Lan-dor-ling bought hides, sausage skins, wool and whatever else traders might bring from Tibet. It was too soon for the season's trading to begin. His barns yawned empty—a jumble of mud-and-freestone huts, patched with corrugated iron.

Lan-dor-ling was reputedly one of the richest men in Sikkim. He was one part Chinese, one part Bhutia, two parts Tibetan—a slant-eyed, cunning-looking fellow with a broad, flat face, who always smiled and almost always understood what was said to him in English. But sometimes, if a mood was on him, he would refuse to speak English to strangers. In a buttoned cap and padded overcoat up to his ears he was watching Andrew, from a chair on the verandah that ran half the length of the front of the store. Its mud-and-stone windbreak at the north end shut off the best view of the mountains. It prevented the wind from dispersing an all-pervading smell of living pigs and dead hides. But it was a token, like a war debt payment, guardedly acknowledging the theory of civilization. A verandah.

Around three sides of the group of buildings was a mud-and-stone walled enclosure for goats, sheep, pigs, chickens, and occasional ponies. There were sheds in the enclosure; their irregularly shingled roofs were held down with barbed wire and big flat stones. Three of Andrew's ponies, noticeably fat, were near one of the sheds; just inside it, sipping Tibetan tea, Bompo Tsering was watching to prevent them from rolling on their new saddles; but he also had an eye on Andrew; and between gulps of scalding tea he watched the lightning at play in a bank of cloud that rolled like a billion tons of blue-black coal dust down the invisible throat of a pass between two mountain tops.

There were colossal mountains on three sides—north, northwest, and westward. There was no way out of that valley, that the eye could detect, except southeastward, where a rough road curved in a wide arc, away from the mountains. At a point just visible between gigantic boulders it met a better road that curved in search of the highway eastward toward Assam and Bhutan. Andrew was watching the fork where the roads met.

He was in an agony of impatience, trusting no one, not even himself; going over and over in mind the details of his preparations for the dash for the Roof of the World, wondering whether he had forgotten anything that he could not afford to forget. One mile away as an eagle flies—but more than ten miles over almost trackless boulder-hatched ravine and mountain spur—his outfit waited, hidden in a hollow, near the foot of a pass so steep and dangerous that for almost a generation not even the suspicious Gurkhas had troubled to guard it. It crossed a corner of secret, almost unexplored Nepal, so it was doubly outlawed. Three governments in theory barred its use, forbade it, kept it off all but the secret maps; but in fact, it was the only pass that they did not watch and that afforded the slightest chance of undetected trespass into Tibet. According to Bompo Tsering's information, picked up from a smuggler, it was, some seasons, the first pass to be negotiable because rain and wind bullied the snow from its exposed ledges. Smuggled opium, stored day before yesterday in Lan-dor-ling's shed, had vanished—probably over the pass. That was the feather in the wind that Andrew counted on.

Once away, there would be small risk of pursuit, or of being turned back at the farther end. The only dangers would be smuggler-bandits, avalanches, lack of fuel, and the hell's own causeway, where the loads would have to be manhandled, the ponies hauled and lifted, and a miscalculation would mean death on the crags below.

"God, what's keeping her!"

There was a post of Sikkim police less than a mile away. They had a telephone. They weren't very likely to do more than glance at a party of monks, northeastward bound in a contractor's bus toward a monastery near the Bhutan border. But if someone—Bulah Singh, for instance—should have phoned them to be on the lookout for Elsa, not all the ingenuity of Morgan Lewis would be enough to prevent a show-down. Governments can't look the other way when information comes through official channels and is on the record.

"'*He travels the fastest who travels alone.*' A man's a damned fool to stand waiting for trouble!"

But Andrew didn't dream of not waiting. He paced the track, counting his footsteps, turning suddenly for a glimpse of the crossroad beyond the boulders, glancing at the clouds, and at his watch. It was getting late. He would be lucky to reach the bivouac before dark. To attempt to reach it after sundown would be almost madness, even though he had left white phosphorus markers along the trail. He had posted that fool from Koko Nor to lend a hand at the bridgeless torrent, where the ponies would have to be manhandled in, held against the ice-cold water, and hauled out on the far side. But one couldn't count on the man from Koko Nor. He might have run back to the bivouac, afraid of being haunted by the devil that escaped when his tooth was pulled.—Took some pulling, that tooth.

All right, give Elsa one more hour as deadline. Any later, and they would have to spend the night at Lan-dor-ling's. Not so good. Andrew didn't quite trust Lan-dor-ling. He had had to pretend to, but it was risky. Lan-dor-ling was almost certainly a secret spy for the government—perhaps for all three governments—Sikkim, Nepal, Tibet—as well as for people to whom governments are like wealthy women, created to be sponged from, betrayed and laughed at. Lan-dor-ling was too rich to stay bought with a second-hand car: much too avaricious to have refused the gift. On the other hand, asking no embarrassing questions, he had smiled with urbane incredulity at Andrew's hand-out lies, told for Lan-dor-ling's use in case strangers should be inquisitive.

He suspected Lan-dor-ling of being one of Bulah Singh's secret correspondents. There was no evidence of it, beyond a yellowing, creased letter signed by the Sikh, appointing Lan-dor-ling to the honorary post of investigator of local applicants for jobs in Darjeeling. It was framed on the wall of the filthy room where Lan-dor-ling's half-breed clerk kept the accounts. There was absolutely no doubt whatever in Andrew's mind that Bulah Singh had a well-planned grapevine of intelligence that he could use for or against the government, whichever might suit his own ambition. Lan-dor-ling was a probable branch of the vine.

True, Bulah Singh had insisted that the way into Tibet was open. So had Morgan Lewis. Both men, each for a different reason, wanted him safely across the border. Possibly—hardly probably—no man could be quite such a fool—Bulah Singh believed Andrew would obey orders, once in Tibet.

"He can't be such a damned idiot. He can't be! All the same, he may be kidding himself. He thinks he has the goods on me. Perhaps he thinks Elsa is within his reach in Darjeeling. Good God, she may be, at that! He may have held her up! Jesus! And if he knows she's on her way—and if she is—and if he's half awake, he must know—he could have her tracked down and arrested on suspicion of intending to cross the border. Fool! Why didn't I take chances and bring her with me?"

But the worst danger of all was Morgan Lewis.

"He's a good guy. But he's a nut. He plays it like a dime detective. It's a dog-gone cinch he'll bungle the show-down with Bulah Singh. He'll be too tricky about it. Bulah Singh will turn on him and blow the gaff. He'll accuse Lewis of secretly helping me to reach Tibet, contrary to law and orders, international treaties and God knows what else. Spite is Bulah Singh's pet motive. He knows he stands to get broke if he's found out. He'll make it cost 'em something. He'll blow things wide open. He'll involve as many higher-ups as possible in his own ruin—probably all set to do it, in case they spike him.—God, what's keeping that woman! Why doesn't she come!"

Thunder, like a barrage by the clock—drum-fire—all heavy guns. Lightning in blinding spasms. Rain in a seething deluge. Hail. The rocks crackled like glass under machine-gun fire. Andrew ran for Lan-dor-ling's verandah. By the time he reached it Lan-dor-ling had vanished. Andrew sat in the vacated chair watching the forked lightning that rent the storm and made the glimpsed mountains seem to dance to the deafening thunder. He didn't hear hoofbeats—couldn't. The first he knew of a horse was its rider, spurred and swinging a riding crop, striding along the verandah, dragging the door open against the wind and letting it slam behind him. Andrew followed. He couldn't afford not to. Almost any news was likely to be bad news. Better to know it at once than to waste time guessing.

Lan-dor-ling was lighting a kerosene lamp in the low-roofed shop where last year's odds and ends of trading goods were hung, shelved, heaped in indescribable confusion; he set the lamp on a table and went out by a back door. There were no chairs. The man in spurs and a drenched poncho sat on a heap of gunny sacks, in a pool of his own making. He missed a rat with his riding whip, laughed and said something to Andrew. It was impossible to hear for the din of the hail on the low roof. Andrew went nearer.

"I said: I turned over my horse to your man in the yard."

He had removed his rain-soaked hat. He was gray-haired, as handsome as President Harding, but weather-beaten and with no trace of softness—no laziness—only a vaguely luxurious ease, like a healthy animal's, as he relaxed his muscles. His hands were a workman's—scrubbed. A hard, horsy smile. Blue-gray eyes. At first, second and third glance, an intelligent, obstinate, difficult man with a grim sense of humour. But for his hands he would have looked like high finance on vacation. But his hands could do things.

"Surgeon?" Andrew asked him.

"Yes. Presbyterian Mission. Fifteen miles from here. Riding my rounds. I am John Bobbs."

"Sir John Bobbs? Baronet?"

"Yes. You may omit the title."

"Heard of you."

"Are you Andrew Gunning?"

"Yes."

"Heard of you, too. Try that other pile of sacks."

Andrew sat facing him, back to the door.

"We have a mutual acquaintance," said Sir John Bobbs. "Dr. Lambert, Cincinnati, Ohio."

Andrew froze. Sir John Bobbs appeared not to notice it. "Lambert, and I," he remarked, "were together at Johns Hopkins. We correspond—exchange notes on pathology—homicide—suicide—lots of other matters of professional interest. It's a small world. Do you know anyone in Delhi?"

"I have never visited Delhi."

"But you know Darjeeling?"

"Yes, just come from there."

"Pleasant drive?"

"More than enough rain. No accidents."

Sir John Bobbs examined Andrew from head to foot—battered felt hat, raincoat, thin brown shoes and cotton socks, in which no man with any experience would dream of facing the trail to Tibet.

"When you return to Darjeeling," he said, "would you do me a favour? I have a message that I don't care to send through the post."

Andrew thumbed tobacco into his pipe. He felt for matches. Dread was raising goose flesh up and down his spine, but he tried to look calm while he thought like lightning. Sir John Bobbs might be one of Lewis's secret allies. But he also might not be. He mustn't mention Lewis. He knew Sir John Bobbs, by reputation, as a holy terror to transgressors of the law. Not a medical baronet, but a baronet who had specialized in surgery. He represented civilized and scientific Christianity—the spirit of the Ten Commandments, slightly edited in favour of His Majesty the King—iodine—soap and water. He was not a magistrate. But, as a missionary with a tremendous reputation for surgical skill, good sportsmanship and piety, he enjoyed the much more powerful role of confidential adviser, off the record, to the men who appoint and demote magistrates. It was hard to tell what to say to him—what line to take. It was certainly no coincidence that had brought him, in a storm, at the zero hour, to drop hints about Lambert of Cincinnati, Ohio. Lambert might have told professional secrets. Do doctors do that kind of thing? Would Lambert do it?

"Have you no one else who could take the message?" Andrew suggested.

"Oh, yes. I could entrust it to the police. They're not far away. They would attend to it."

A hint? A threat? Or merely an answer to the question? Andrew felt tempted to tell him to go ahead and use the police. But he reminded himself: silence is the best bet when you don't know what you're up against. Sir John Bobbs's eyes betrayed a hint of cruelty, or something like it. He appeared to be enjoying Andrew's dilemma. Andrew kept on trying to dope him out, guessing, rejecting guesses, trying to remember every rumour he had heard about him. But he had to say something. Better a half-truth than a lie. Waiting for a friend should be truth enough for—

"To tell the truth," he began—

Sir John Bobbs whacked at his riding boot. "Truth," he remarked, "is sometimes easier to hide than to discover. Someone told me those

439

are your ponies in the compound. Your man denied it, and I see you're not dressed for a ride. I noticed your car in the godown. The obvious inference is that you are about to return south. Don't deny it. I hate to be treated as if I had no intelligence."

"Your reputation is too well known for me to make that break," said Andrew.

"You will take my message?"

"I'm a stranger to you. Aren't you taking chances?"

"Yes." Sir John Bobbs eyed him with a glint of humour and a hard smile. "You might betray my confidence. I will risk that. The message refers to a phone call I received this morning. The address is on the inner envelope. You may use your own discretion about opening the outer one; it is merely to keep the inner envelope clean."

Andrew accepted the long envelope and stowed it in his overcoat pocket. Lan-dor-ling shuffled into the room and blew out the lantern. The storm was dying. It had grown lighter. The thunder was rolling away in the distance. Sir John Bobbs stood up and shook himself:

"Well—I feel fortunate to have met you. It was a lucky coincidence I must hurry away now. I wish you luck on your journey— ah— southward." He turned to Lan-dor-ling: "You needn't trouble about finding a messenger. I have one. Mr. Gunning will take my letter to Darjeeling."

Lan-dor-ling stared, smiling, looking stupid.

"Any time limit on opening the outer envelope?" Andrew asked.

"Oh no. Whenever you please. Goodbye, and good luck to you. Will tell the police that I understand you are leaving southward to-morrow morning."

Sir John Bobbs stalked out, making his spurs jingle on the rough pine floor, whacking the whip on his riding boot.

"Too much that man many often not minding own business," said Lan-dor- ling. "Sending too much many people into plison too many times."

Andrew drew the envelope out of his pocket—waited—until through the small window he saw Sir John Bobbs ride away, cantering, on a mud-splashed horse.

"His now going police *kana*, making trouble for you," said Lan-dor-ling.

Andrew tore open the envelope. The smaller one inside it was addressed in pencil:

Phone from Darjeeling for Andrew Gunning.

He tore open the inner envelope. It contained a half sheet of plain paper, bearing no date or address. The scrawled, pencilled message seemed to have been written left-handed to conceal the writer's identity:

B.S. disappeared but believed to have phoned Sikkim police to arrest Mrs. G. near border. Have requested medical acquaintance to report your intended movements and to remove one passenger from bus on suspicion of contagious illness. He having no commission, break unauthorized quarantine and get going. Destroy this.

His hunch had been right. Lewis had bungled the breaking of Bulah Singh. The Sikh had vanished. Laid his plans weeks ago—not a doubt of it.

Andrew struck a match, burned the message and powdered the ashes with his heel.

"What that? What your burning?" Lan-dor-ling asked.

Andrew grinned: "I burned a prayer to heaven for the gods to remember me by."

"My playing your player being too good, two being better than one," remarked Lan-dor-ling.

Andrew went out by the back way and found Bompo Tsering. "Take two ponies to the crossroad. When you see a bus stop at the police kana, go and offer your services to the doctor *sahib*. Do what he tells you."

"That man being Mission dokitar is asking too much many question."

"Do as you're told, and hold your tongue. There'll be saddlebags. Bring 'em. And mount her on your pony, remember."

"Oh."

"Yes. Get going."

"Hot damn!"

"Hurry!"

Andrew went back and shook hands with Lan-dor-ling. "Goodbye, old-timer, and thanks for your trouble. I'm on my way now—to Darjeeling."

"Your being too much God-damn good liar, my believing you. So goo' luck—goo'bye, Gunnigun!"

The rain was almost over. Andrew led his pony down the track, hobbled it with the reins and climbed the biggest of the two huge boulders. Even so he couldn't see the police kana. He sat there a long time, fidgeting and glancing at his watch. The sun was almost out of sight beyond the mountains of Nepal when at last he saw Elsa riding Bompo Tsering's pony up the trail. The Tibetan, with her loaded saddlebags, rode behind her. She was wearing a khaki shirt, shorts, and raincoat—looked like a boy in a broad-brimmed felt hat—bare knees—woolen stockings— sneakers.

Andrew glanced at his watch, slid down off the boulder, unhobbled his pony and waited. She almost rode by without seeing him. Then she drew rein, laughing:

"Andrew, I'm accused of bubonic plague!"

With his back to his pony Andrew studied her a moment: "Something's happened to you."

"Happened? It's like a movie! I came in a bus with fifteen monks from Gombaria's monastery. We were stopped by the police at the crossroad just below here. They demanded my name, and I thought it was all up. But I hadn't time even to pretend I didn't understand, before a big man in a poncho on a roan horse cantered up and demanded to feel my pulse."

"Sir John Bobbs," said Andrew.

"Oh, you know him? Well, he told the police I must be quarantined, in one of Lan-dor-ling's sheds, on suspicion of plague. Then Bompo Tsering showed up. Sir John Bobbs ordered him to take me and my luggage up the road."

"How did you shake the police?"

"There were only three policemen. Sir John Bobbs made them stay there and stand guard while he lined up all the monks, to take their temperatures and—"

"Let's go. This way."

Andrew mounted his pony and led, between high rocks, along a track that was the bed of a rock-strewn watercourse. It was a-roar with storm water, but presently it left the stream bed, widened, and there was room for them knee to knee.

"What else happened?" Andrew asked.

"Since you left Darjeeling? Thousands of things. I don't know where to begin."

"Something happened to you. What was it?"

"Andrew, I can't tell you."

"Secret?"

"From you? No. But I don't know how to tell you. Andrew—honestly—I can't. I don't know how."

"Nancy Strong stuff?"

442

"Yes."

"I guessed it. Well, we'll blow that out of you. Draw rein a minute. Do you see that sharp crag with the lammergeier's nest near the top? Tonight's bivouac is just beyond it. You'll be wet to your skin before we get there, but no matter, there'll be a fire to dry at perhaps the last fire but one for a week. Now look upward."

"Andrew, this isn't the way we came from Tibet, is it?"

"No. Look upward, where I'm pointing. Do you see the last rays of the setting sun, on the snow to the left of that big fellow that seems to stick clear through the sky? That's the pass. Seventeen thousand three hundred and eleven feet. That's the way we're going."

"Andrew!"

"Yes?"

"Turn your head a moment. Look straight at me."

"Well?"

"I'm glad it will be difficult. I'm not the least bit afraid."

"Sure, I know you're game. You don't have to persuade me of that"

"You are talking about someone I once was, Andrew. You don't know me. I'm not the same person. But I'm thanking the same Andrew for the—"

He laughed. "You haven't changed much. Let's get going!"

So the journey began, in silence, in single file, toward the Roof of the World, where Tom Grayne, in a cavern—seven hundred miles away as wild swans fly it—expected news and supplies—but not his young wife. The mountains grew dark in the sunset. The ponies neighed at the scent of snow on the wind from their sky-high home.

PART TWO
CHAPTER 27

Clouds rolled up from the Tibetan valley. They smothered mountains that have no names, that are only numbers on the bewildering map.

"Typical Tibetan spring," said Andrew. He sat down opposite Elsa, on a rock in the lee of a ledge that broke the wind. He had a can of salmon in his hand; he was almost too tired to open it. Four of the afternoon. Ten below zero. Five days out from the Sikkim frontier. Ponies all in. But the summit was far aloft and behind. There remained only about three thousand slippery feet to descend into the valley. Even then, they would be twelve thousand feet above sea level; but there would be only two days of hard marching to reach food for the ponies, that were now munching their last ration but one.

"We're in Tibet!" said Elsa. "We've made it! Better than Hannibal! He lost elephants crossing the Alps. We haven't lost a pony, nor even a load!"

Andrew opened the salmon and passed it to her.

"There'll be bad going tomorrow."

Then he hove himself to his feet like a prize fighter coming out of his corner for the last round. He went for another look at the ponies, to make sure the Tibetans weren't stealing the grain: even Bompo Tsering couldn't be trusted not to do that, not though the men had double rations of barley bread, sugar and fat bacon.

Elsa made the bivouac comfortable—blankets in the lee of the rock, on a waterproof sheet, in a sort of cave made by the piled loads. One candle in a windproof lantern. One can of Sterno, in a folding stove that Andrew had invented and got made in Darjeeling. Two narrow air mattresses. Pillows. A couple of books.

Andrew returned along the ledge with some Tibetans to help stretch a tent over the loads, weighting it down with rocks. All the comforts of home. Nothing to do but crawl in and wait for tomorrow. But he went back along the ledge once more to make sure that the Tibetans had enough Sterno to stew their eternal tea. Elsa, in a streaming cloud, near the edge of an invisible cliff between earth and sky, with singing ears and thumping heart, set down the salmon and waited, thinking. Thoughts weren't the same as at sea level, nor even as at Darjeeling. Since Gombaria's monastery they weren't anything like the same. She tried to find a name for the difference. She couldn't. No word was good enough.

The first night out there had been plenty of fuel and a real meal, in a gully beside a roaring waterfall, with two pup tents, privacy and the excitement of a possible pursuit. After that, when the awful ascent began, physical peril had banished all but the essentials, as it always does. Convention went downwind, along with the echoes of falling rocks. Past personal history became a distant dream. The only poignant memory was of a dog, at home in England. Was he being cared for? To save time and the labour of repacking at daybreak, she and Andrew had shared even the same blankets, for the sake of the doubled warmth. They had said nothing about it, they had simply done it, too exhausted when night came to crave anything but sleep. Too breathless, at those sky-high altitudes, to talk. Too tired to dream.

All the same, sleeping with him was an experience. Perhaps it was something to be proud of, meaning that Andrew took her self-respect and common sense for granted. He had done the natural, sensible thing, as he always did. Nevertheless, she had not snuggled in beside him without wondering what he was thinking about, and how would he behave toward a woman he loved. No woman could suspect him of being a passionless man. What sort would she be, whom Andrew would some day love? Elsa had no feeling of friendship toward that supposititious female—so little that she actually laughed at herself. Jealous?

She wouldn't have dared to mention the subject of sex, even now, at a lower altitude, where conversation was possible and nerves were less jumpy. Andrew was under a terrific strain, so concentrated on the almost superhuman task that an ill-chosen phrase might bring down on her, like an avalanche, one of his storms of temper. Those were rare, but terrible. She had witnessed one, months ago, loosed on a grafting Tibetan official, who ran for his life. And she had experienced one, loosed on herself. It had come, like the Himalayan wind, from beneath the cloud that always screened Andrew's inner thought so that she couldn't read it. She couldn't even remember what she had said that angered him; it was a chance remark, without special motive, some-thing about Tom Grayne, not meant unkindly; but it had touched off Andrew's rage against mental cruelty and mean insinuation. He appeared to think physical cruelty—even its worst forms—much less damnable than mental injustice. It had been hours later before he seasoned a manly apology with the remark that it was only from his friends that he expected fairness.

"I don't give a whoop in hell what the rest of 'em think. That's their business. But friends should think well of each other. Say what you like to a friend. But don't speak ill of him behind his back. That's treachery."

So she had known, all these months, that she rated as friend. Very often she hadn't believed; but she had known. Secretly, in her heart of hearts, she had never really even believed, as she had so often said, that Andrew detested her. No human being could do that, and be as kind as he was. If he had been her lover he couldn't have been more con-siderate. He had never once, by so much as a hint, suggested she was the nuisance that she knew she must be. He had never neglected the fundamental decencies, courtesies, dignities due from one to another. He had made her feel like a comrade-in-arms, who shared life's battle.

Who could ask more of a man?

He had probably, she thought, missed his vocation. He should have been a soldier. Soldiers need nobility as much as courage. Only noblemen should lead. Birth has nothing to do with nobility. Was Andrew a reincarnated spiritual aristocrat? That was a strange thought. Some ancient Stoic campaign veteran, reborn to test his spirit on the anvil of events. How else, or where had Andrew learned the self-reliance that had forced that march across a sky-high pass too steep and dangerous for even Tibetans to use unless as fugitives from law? Not one mistake, in a five-day fight against snow, ice, altitude and wind—up a blind trail. It stunned memory. One could only recall fragments of it, disconnected, as from a nightmare.

They had fought their way through snowdrifts, roped their way along storm- swept ledges, off-loaded and lifted the ponies from crag to crag where the ice-ground granite was as smoothly slippery as glass. But no man nor beast had missed a full meal. None had done less than his share of the work. No one was injured. There was not even a lame pony. And as the generous rations were consumed, the loads had been redistributed, pound for pound, so that the nearer they came to the Tibetan end of the pass, and the more exhausted the ponies became, the less the burden each had to struggle with. And not one sore back.

It was all Andrew's doing. Tibetans, who treat wild life as sacred, are incredibly cruel to beasts of burden. They had resented that their riding ponies should be put to pack work along with the others. Even Bompo Tsering had had to be fisted, more than once, from the back of a pony already burdened with all it could carry. Elsa herself had had to climb, where she might have ridden the one unloaded pony, lest the Tibetans should take example, and ride too, when Andrew's back was turned. Bompo Tsering, usually bringing up the rear, had tried to steal rides on her pony. But that would have ruined discipline. Several times she knew she had dared death, forbidding him. It would have been easy to push her off a ledge and claim the wind had done it. She had detected the thought. But when she threatened him with Andrew, he stuck his tongue out humbly, and then grinned and they were friends again. There was something in Andrew that commanded allegiance, but she couldn't name it. It answered to none of the names by which men label those whom they follow.

It wasn't impersonal. It wasn't the ugly, indifferent, cynical spell such as the exploiters cast on their followers, or impose by force. It wasn't egotistical. He did no spellbinding at all. His speech was curt, unsentimental, slow, and usually quiet. It was nothing spectacular, that gift of leadership. But it created goodwill. Perhaps it wasn't a gift. Perhaps it was a studied, deliberate, iron-willed concentration of purpose, that included the utmost use of every faculty he had. That might be it. He flinched at nothing, spared himself nothing, and yet gave the impression of inexhaustible reserves of physical and mental strength. In blizzards, blinding clouds and raging winds, at exhausting heights, on deadly precipices, Elsa herself had felt the same—not impersonal— first person singular—Andrew—force, that appealed to the Tibetans' courage and rallied them over the summit.

What was Andrew? What kind of man? What was his secret? She had known him now, more than a year, more intimately than some women know their lovers. Yet she didn't know him. She didn't understand him. She didn't even know what had possessed him to abandon a career for such unprofitable, Herculean labour.

He wasn't a fanatic. He seemed less bigoted than most people. He wasn't morose. In his own quiet way he was full of humour. He almost never sneered. He laughed with, not at people. But there was something deep beneath his surface that defied search. It was always there, silent, veiled. Elsa was always conscious of it. She felt she had a right to be curious. Curiosity was even stronger than hunger, cold, exhaustion—almost stronger than intuition that warned her not to trespass.

There came a flattering thought that even Andrew might be helpless to conceal his inner consciousness, if subtly tempted. There must be a breaking-down point, where he would need help to retain his self-control. Help from the temptress. The secretly humiliating female thought, that Andrew hadn't found her worth an effort to seduce, suggested means of making him less reserved. That kind of struggle with Andrew was one that she knew she had more than a forlorn hope of winning. But the fact that the thought excited her, set her wondering about herself. How did she feel toward Andrew? Did she love him? How can one love without understanding? Admire, respect, like—yes, but those are cold emotions. Love?

She was thinking about that, and about Tom Grayne hundreds of miles away, getting a glimpse of a clairvoyant vision of Tom in his cavern at Shig-po-ling, when Andrew came and crawled into the shelter. There was just room to sit upright.

"Tea," he said, "before the storm comes. There's a pippin coming. This world's a madhouse."

"Can I help? Has something gone wrong?"

"No. I dumped some stuff we'll never need and repacked a load. That's a few pounds off all the ponies. Every little counts. Our Tibetans have got the wind up. They let me work all alone in the dark. If they dared, they'd run. Listen."

Downwind came the scream of a big bird, then another.

"Lammergeiers," said Andrew. "Nesting. Their aerie's on the crag right above us. The fool birds are cussing us out."

"They can't hurt, can they? Will they attack the ponies?"

"God, no. But our Tibetans think they're summoning devils to give us the works."

"They think we're trespassing on sacred ground?"

"Yes. Some saint died up here. If I should shoot the lammergeiers, they'd call that murder. But they'd murder you and me and call it blessed-happy- release-of-spirit-into-higher-consciousness."

Elsa laughed.

"Why didn't you eat?" he asked.

"I waited for you—felt sociable."

He opened salmon for himself. They ate out of the cans, with spoons, munching dry barley bread to help it down. Then prunes, stewed tea, canned milk, chocolate. Not another word until Andrew tossed the empty cans over the precipice and crawled out once more into the wind for a look at the men. The lammergeiers screamed like furies. Elsa used the last of the warm tea to wash her fingers that were chapped by the cold and cut, through thick gloves, by the rocks she had climbed.

Andrew came crawling in again: "Hell's devils! There's no sense in a scared Tibetan. I'll stay awake, or they may try to murder us both, to pacify the spirits. Move the candle over here. I'll read a while."

"Do you particularly want to read?"

"I'm in a mood for Milton. I want to read about hell."

"Can't it wait?"

Andrew quoted:

What in me is dark
Illumine, what is low raise and support,
That to the height of this great argument
I may assert eternal Providence,
And justify the ways of God to man!

"God's ways need justifying on a night like this," he added. "I dare

448

bet you it's raining at sea; bone-dry and dusty in Oklahoma; lousy, where the climate's bearable; and not a scrap of fuel where it's coldest. It's a mad world."

"It's a wonderful world," she answered.

"I'm in no mood to be Pollyannaed."

"You're overtired, Andrew. You've done three times as much as anyone else. Go to sleep. I'll stay awake. If anything happens I'll—"

"No, no. You sleep. Long, hard day tomorrow. Downhill's worse than uphill—more likely to fall, unless your nerve's in shape. Curl up and sleep."

"I couldn't."

"Why not? What's the matter?"

"I'm not sleepy. I want to talk."

"What about?"

"Anything."

"Okay. Tell what happened that night at Gombaria's, when you and Nancy—"

"No, Andrew. I can't tell."

"Why not?"

"Because it can't be told."

"You're pretty good at telling most things, when you want to. All right, it's your secret. Sorry I asked."

Elsa thought a moment, with her chin on her knees. "Andrew."

"Yes?"

"Could you tell anyone, for instance, what it feels like to be up here in these mountains?"

"Why should I tell it?"

"Can you even tell yourself what it feels like, as compared to cities and sea level? It's an experience, but you can't describe it, can you?"

"Short of oxygen," he answered. "Slows you. Makes your head hum. Felt like being seasick at the summit. That's another of God's funny paradoxes— where you most need oxygen, the less there is."

"Oh, if you're in that mood—"

"Mood? I could play the harmonica, just to annoy myself."

"Don't, please. Andrew, I am not trying to keep a secret—not from you, of all people. I did tell you about seeing Lobsang Pun. It was after that, that's so difficult. I was alone in that room with Nancy."

"Yeah, you said that, the first night out."

"I'm simply bursting to tell. I want to share it with you. But one can't explain what happened."

449

"Why not?"

"There aren't any words to tell it with. It was something beyond music—even beyond thought. One can't even recall it. One only knows it did happen—and was so wonderful that—oh, if I could share it with you! But how can I?"

"Old Gombaria has a reputation," said Andrew. "He's a first-class psychic showman."

"Gombaria didn't do this. It wasn't showmanship. He wasn't even there."

"He fixed me so that I got your Mauser message, and he wasn't there when I got that, either."

"Andrew, that message was just ordinary clairvoyance. But what happened after Nancy and I saw Lobsang Pun was utterly beyond clairvoyance. It was more different from it than these mountains are from London slums."

"It seems to have changed you over. You don't seem scared of your clairvoyance any longer."

"I never will be again. Never."

"Well, that's something. That's a load off."

"Andrew, did you ever know something—I mean really know—and feel you'll almost die if you don't tell, because it's so utterly wonderful that your heart almost bursts with it—and yet you couldn't tell—couldn't?"

"Can't you give me a hint?"

Elsa thought a moment. Then, suddenly: "Andrew, I want you to believe what I'm saying. I'm serious."

"Go ahead."

"If by jumping off this precipice I could give you the experience that I had at Gombaria's, I would jump without hesitating. I want to give, and go on giving forever!"

"Steady!" he said. "Steady! The altitude's got you. It's like ether or being drunk. Lie down. Shut your eyes. Swallow hard. Turn in. Sleep it off."

"There you are. You misunderstood. Words—oh, what use are they?"

Andrew remembered Lewis's advice. He dismissed his own raw nervousness. He grinned. "It's about a thousand-foot jump—maybe more. I'll have to climb down to bury you under a cairn. Maybe I need the exercise. When do you take off?"

"Andrew, please don't blaspheme!"

"I sure will, if you try any circus stunts. I've heard of levitation and flying *lamas*. But I'm agin' 'em."

"I didn't say I will jump off. I wouldn't dream of it. I was trying to hint at the hugeness of the urge to tell you, if I could, how wonderful life is."

"Hello! Hello! Is this the same young woman who was calling herself a calamity, back there in Darjeeling?"

"Yes. No! Yes and no! What I meant was—there couldn't be too high a price to pay—if it were possible—for the joy of giving someone else the experience that was mine, at Gombaria's, after Nancy and I saw Lobsang Pun."

"You say Gombaria didn't provide it?"

"No. No, indeed. Nancy explained that. Old Gombaria is a kind of dweller on a threshold. He likes to open psychic doors for other people, but he never goes in himself. He never talks about it. He knows all about psychic centres, whatever that means."

"It might mean anything," said Andrew. "Psychics spend most of their time thinking up different meanings for words that had just one plain meaning to the Greeks who invented 'em. Forget the Greek words. Try to tell what happened."

Elsa sighed and summoned patience. But instead of it came the storm, in a sudden blast as if the mountains were at war. Hail smote the shelter, seethed, crashed along the ledge. Deafening thunder. Lightning. Wind howled and shrieked like ice-cold devils. Andrew wrapped the blankets around both of them, hugging her close to him, sharing the warmth of his strong body. They sat side by side, not sure whether they or the mountain trembled. Elsa had an almost unbelievable sensation that Andrew was more afraid than she was. Perhaps his was the dread that the last day's march would end in disaster. Her only dread was that she might fail in emergency. Was this an emergency? Did he need reassurance? How could she give it? They couldn't hear each other speak.

But the shelter held. The hail died. Andrew went out again, facing the wind, to make sure that the ponies were snug in the lee of the ledge. He found them all lying down, too weary to be terrified. The Tibetan watchman lay snoring, too tired to fear even devils. Bompo Tsering, tented in the lee of an overhanging ledge, was preaching gloomy Tantrist doctrine to eleven other numbed, awed Tibetans. Their breath steamed; their eyes glowed ghostly in the rays of Andrew's flashlight. He stayed and talked with them, asking questions.

Little by little he eased their superstitious fear, by getting them to tell him about monstrous semihuman entities that guard forbidden heights and whelm the trespasser. They unloaded their fear on himself, teaching him mysteries. Teachers don't kill attentive pupils, even to oblige the devils of a pass into forbidden Tibet. That danger died of its own propaganda, strangled in terrible words.

Elsa sat watching her breath freeze on the heavy blanket, wondering what she should say to Andrew. It was like nostalgia—saddening almost to tears, but she scorned tears as self-indulgence—to know what she knew, and to be unable to tell. No one had forbidden her from trying to tell, although Nancy had warned. She could almost hear Nancy's experienced, humorous voice:

"Tell and be damned! 'See that thou tell no man' was wise advice. You will use words. They will be turned against you. It will hurt. Words mean 'thus far we come, and this we know.' Words are the nails that crucify. It was the literal, accurate word-definers who condemned Jesus out of his own mouth. When your soul—the real soul—conscious you—can speak straight to the soul of another, then you can awaken the other to experience reality. Life has to be lived. It can't be told."

She had a clear clairvoyant glimpse of Nancy, talking to children around her fireside, telling the children truth that grown-ups labour all their days to misinterpret. She kept her promise to send Nancy an "all's well." She saw Nancy again—and Old Ugly-face—and, strangely, Father Patrick of the Jesuit Mission. What could that mean? Why the Jesuit?

Then came Andrew, with his thought full of Bompo Tsering's devils: humourless, monstrous, conscious forces, said to be sometimes visible, whose passion is envy, their motive hate, and their goal the undoing of all things done.

"There'll be glare ice on the lower ledges," he remarked, as he crawled in. "The snow thawed this afternoon. This'll freeze it smooth. We'll have one hell of a day's march. Do you know an antidote for devils?"

"Are the Tibetans badly scared? Andrew, are they—"

"Damn their religion! Damn everyone's religion. The hell with it. It only rots guts."

"Andrew! It isn't long since you reproached me for saying there isn't a God! I've changed my mind. Have you changed yours?"

"God won't get us down tomorrow's glare ice. Gravity'll do it. That's another of God's funny inventions—too much gravity in the

452

wrong place. Well, we'll beat it somehow."

"Andrew."

"Yes."

"Are you still curious?"

"What about?"

"About what happened at Gombaria's."

"Sure. Eaten up with curiosity."

"If I try to tell, will you try to understand?"

"Yep. Use plain words."

"Think some poetry."

"I'm off that stuff, for the moment. Too much grue in the air. They kind o' don't mix."

"Try the first poem that comes to mind. No matter what it is. Try it."

Andrew thought a moment. Grim humour seized him. He began, sonorously, chanting verse so inappropriate that even Milton's music hardly veiled the sarcastic motive:

With thee conversing I forget all time,
All seasons, and their change—all please alike.
Sweet is the breath of morn, her rising sweet,
With charm of earliest birds—

He laughed. "There'll be a dark daybreak. Screaming lammergeiers. Twenty or thirty below zero. Three thousand feet of glare ice. One day's rations for the ponies. Yep. Every prospect pleases."

"Try again," said Elsa. "Try something different. Please, Andrew. Won't you help? I would almost rather die than not tell you. But if you won't get into the right mood, I can't even reach your everyday intelligence. And I must aim much higher than that."

He reached for the candle lantern, held it so that he could see her face, studied her eyes a moment, then set it back in the niche in the rock.

"Sorry," he said. "I didn't get you at first. All right, poetry it is. Here goes."

He plunged into a mood, as she had seen him plunge, numbers of times, into raging cold water and swim for the fun of it. His right fist seemed to strike an invisible gong, commanding silence. Then he chanted:

In this broad earth of ours,
Amid the measureless grossness and the slag,

453

Enclosed and safe within its central heart,
Nestles the seed perfection—

He chanted on, Elsa listening, watching him silhouetted in dim candlelight against the piled-up pony loads—unshaven, free-shouldered, wearing a brown blanket like a toga. He went lost in the poem. Words ceased. Thought went wandering along the overtones toward the universal wonderland whence poems come.

"Andrew."

"Yes?"

"Were you ever in love?"

"Why?"

"If you were, it would help."

"I was. Once. For a short time."

"Do you remember the ecstasy part?"

He didn't answer.

"Did it lead up the same ray of consciousness that creeps upon you when you chant poetry?"

"Maybe. I haven't thought of it."

"And you can't speak of it. Can you?"

"I don't wish to speak of it."

"At Gombaria's, after I saw Lobsang Pun—for a long time—I don't know how long—I was actually soul-conscious. I was me. Not this thing. Me. My soul. You understand?"

"No. Darned if I do."

"I was, what I shall be. What we're all evolving into. What we all really are. There were no limits. Beauty—joy—oh, I can't tell it!—Soul! Make me tell it! Speak!—Andrew, won't you try? There are thousands of ways."

"Tell one way."

"I think one follows poetry, or music, or being in love—all the way inward and up to the heart of the universe—God's heart."

"Leaving the world to go to hell?"

"No, no, no! One loves the world! It's good! It's full of pain and sorrow—"

"You bet it is."

"But one sees it all differently. We are all one vast oneness, working toward—" She hesitated.

"Annihilation?" he suggested. "Do we lose our identity?"

"Never! Awareness of that is what we lack now! Soul is identity!

454

Andrew, does the word 'love' set your teeth on edge?"

"They're on edge already from the wind. An extra twinge won't hurt 'em."

"Does passion offend you?"

"Whose?"

"I don't mean sentimental emotion. Andrew, reality—real being— is an ecstasy of passionate love. That's all I can tell you. It is so far beyond human love and passion that they're darkness in comparison. But they're parts of it. Follow your high thought to wherever it leads. You will find your soul. Say to yourself 'I am my soul!' Your soul will show you what you are!"

"It might show me something I'd rather not know," he retorted. He remembered what Lewis had said. "How about sleep?" he suggested.

"Have I scandalized you?"

"Hell, no. I'm damned interested. But we've a stiff march tomorrow. Get some sleep."

"I wish you would sleep, and let me stay awake."

"No. No more talk now. Turn in."

"Why must you stay awake? Are you afraid the Tibetans might—"

"Hell, no. They'll make no trouble."

"Then what are you watching for? Andrew, you're worried! What is it?"

"No, I'm not worried. Be a good girl now and turn in."

"Why are you thinking about Bulah Singh?"

"Read my thought, eh?"

"Yes. You thought a blood-red picture of him, right then."

"Will you go to sleep if I tell you?"

"Try me."

"Bulah Singh may have been arrested. But I guess not. I think Lewis jiggled the bait too long, and missed him. If so, Bulah Singh's one chance would be to chase us."

"But he couldn't do anything, could he?"

"He could hang on. He could count on my not making a habit of shooting people."

"But could he possibly overtake us?"

"If he's travelling light. We broke a trail for him through all the drifts. There was a light near the summit, just after sunset. It may have been Bulah Singh's lantern."

"But the summit's half a day's march behind! Would he dare to

455

come on in the dark?"

"No such luck. That 'ud be the end of him. He's too wise to take that risk."

"Then why stay awake, Andrew?"

"I want to figure him out. You go to sleep and leave me think about him.

CHAPTER 28

The next day was too dreadful to remember, afterwards, except as flashbacks from a dream, remote in time and space. Fog-veiled precipices—eagles, looming and gone—glimpses of sky amid clouds that wallowed, wave on wave, bursting on mountain peaks, until the world seemed upside down. Ice-slithering ponies, roped, off-loaded, lowered—loads skidded downward—hairbreadth, unbalanced teetering on windy ledges above echoes that boomed in a rolling mist. Standing out in memory like a bell buoy at sea, was a prayer rag on a human thigh bone, protected from storms by a crude shrine to which each passing Tibetan added a stone. Right there the Tibetans mutinied. They declared it was track's end—luck's end. The mountain had been changed into a cloud by magic. Devils. They would turn back. The muffled thunder of an ice-imprisoned waterfall, heard through a hurrying maelstrom of gray mist, was the voice of doom.

"No, Gunnigun. No."

Elsa, too, had premonitions. She said so: she was thinking of Bulah Singh, although she didn't name him. Andrew made no comment. He roped himself and made the end of the rope fast to an upstanding spur of rock. He scouted forward alone, vanishing like a ghost along a foot-wide track that crossed a crumbling rock-strewn slope. To his left, nothing. To his right, a looming, unclimbable glacis. He found the path was practicable. Only a rope's length of it, leading to wide, level rock on the far side. Returning, he kicked loose stones off the narrow track and listened—heard them, after a long pause, crash amid cannonading echoes. No foothold to the left or right. No margin for error. But the stones hadn't started an avalanche. The loose rocks, on the glacis above, were apparently frozen in place. One pony at a time, one man at a time, might make it without vibrating loose the invisible menace.

When he came back he gave his orders quietly, and repeated the command to Bompo Tsering. Then he said six words to Elsa, and himself led the pony that carried the Tibetans' blankets, the precious

456

tea urn and personal odds and ends: a better argument than millions of words. Elsa, obeying the curt command, followed, with her heart in her throat, handing the rope to prevent it from catching under the pony's load, and to prevent the pony from treading on it when it slackened for a moment. They reached the far side safely. Andrew was starting back, to bring the next pony across, when disaster emerged. It came through the fog like the coming of world's end.

Urged by some Tibetan blend of loyalty, obliquity and disobedience; and by the siren tea urn and the life-preserving blankets all gone in the fog; perhaps, too, by shame that he had condoned mutiny, Bompo Tsering went from one mistake to another. He denied it afterwards. He swore a panic took hold of the men and he couldn't prevent. But all the other Tibetans agreed it had been he who gave the order to untie the end of the rope and get going across. It was almost a stampede. They flowed through the fog. They were like scurrying ghosts. Andrew had to turn about and run back to the far end. Prodded by the frightened Tibetans, the ponies trotted. Down came the avalanche—random—sporadic, at first. By the grace of the Unpredictable the rope, with one end made fast to Andrew's shoulders, fell clear of the ponies' feet and down over the precipice. By the time he had hauled it in, most of the ponies and all the Tibetans, except the man from Koko Nor, were safely across, untouched by stones that slid down from the glacis as from a devil's ambush—faster, faster—hundreds of rocks, each loosening another, to miss their marks and plunge into echoing mist.

The man from Koko Nor rode last, on a loaded pony. There being no one to forbid, he had vaulted up over the staggering pony's rump. He was halfway across before he was visible through the haze, perched on the load like a lunatic, waving his arms to balance himself against the wind and the pony's movement. Perhaps he was praying—making yokel-magic to appease mountain devils. The last of the avalanche—one lone clattering rock, struck the pony's hind legs out from under him. Pony and rider disappeared into the fog—like phantoms. If there was sound, none heard it: horror blotted it out. Then, breathless moments later, a cry came up out of the mist. Not a man's cry. It was the heart-breaking scream of a pony. An eagle—so near that Elsa felt the wind of its wings—swooped downward. The pony screamed again. The Tibetans laughed. Andrew cursed them into silence. Then he lay prone on the rock, peering downward, waiting for wind to tear a hole in the driving whiteness. After about two minutes he got up and spoke to Elsa:

"The pony's alive. Perhaps the man is. They're on a ledge about fifty feet below us."

He pulled out his Mauser pistol and examined it. Elsa said nothing.

She thought he intended to try to shoot the injured pony from where he stood. But he returned the pistol to the holster under his armpit, beneath his sheepskin jacket. Then he carefully passed the rope around a smooth rock, tested it, examined the noose around his shoulders, and gave Elsa the loose end.

"Hold that."

She didn't dare to speak to him; she might have said the wrong thing.

He and his anger were one. Anger was the very blood in his veins— the breath that misted from his nostrils. It made him white-lipped. He beckoned Bompo Tsering.

"Give me your Mauser."

Bompo Tsering hesitated, met Andrew's eyes and quickly plunged his hand into his coat. He surrendered his precious pistol, butt first.

"Four men!"

Bompo Tsering beckoned four men. They came slowly, unconfident, wondering, watching the pistol. They followed Andrew's glance and laid hold of the rope.

"I'm going down there." He glanced at Elsa, jerked his head toward her. "Do as she tells you."

Bompo Tsering protested: "Gunnigun! Hot damn! Your not—"

Speech died in time to check the swing of Andrew's fist. "Your saying, Gunnigun—my doing."

Andrew cocked the surrendered Mauser and gave it to Elsa: "Shoot to kill, if they disobey you! Shoot him first. Then the others, one by one until they do obey."

"Very well, Andrew."

"You are not to look over the edge."

"Very well, Andrew."

"Stand back here. When I shout, repeat the order to Bompo Tsering."

With another glance at the rope he was gone, letting himself down hand over hand, until she saw the rope chafe on the rock as he swung in the wind, and heard him shout: "Lower away!"

She repeated the order, pointing the pistol at Bompo Tsering's head, setting her teeth. She would obey. She would kill if she must, and

458

she wouldn't blame Andrew. It should be her own doing. One of the men spoke. He held the rope and leaned outward, staring downward. Presently she saw the rope slacken, heard the scream of the indignant eagle, followed by the crack of Andrew's pistol. He had shot the pony. She wondered what it would feel like, later, if she should have to shoot Bompo Tsering. Then an eternity of waiting, with her fingers freezing on the pistol butt and her imagination fighting against pictures of Andrew losing foothold, falling—falling—ten thousand times she saw him in imagination falling headlong, before she heard him shout:

"Haul away!"

The echoes repeated it. The Tibetans had to be cursed by Bompo Tsering until they feared his curses worse than the voice of the underworld, and set to work hauling, in silence except for their grunts and Bompo Tsering's low-voiced "*Ho-ay-ho! Ho-ay-ho!*" as he set the time. Elsa snagged the rope's end as fast as it came up, with her heart in her teeth, watching the rope chafe—watching for Andrew's head to appear.

And when it came, it wasn't Andrew. It was the pony's load, harness and all. It caught, blown under the overhanging edge of the rock. The harder they pulled, the faster it stuck, until she gave an order to Bompo Tsering, backed up by a gesture with the pistol. He stuck his tongue out, grinned, noosed his belt around the rope, crawled down and hove the load up over the edge. He himself had to be hauled back, scared almost numb. He stood gasping beside the load, smiling at her along the Mauser barrel.

"Hot damn," he said, gasping.

"Lower the rope again!"

He appeared not to have thought of it. She repeated the order. He relayed it. The others obeyed. They looked like fishermen paying a line in a fog at sea.

"Did you see him?" Elsa demanded. "Where is he? What is he doing?"

"My not know seeing nothing. Hot damn."

"Can he catch the rope? How can he catch it? Won't it blow out of reach?"

He grinned—shrugged his shoulders.

"Haul up! Haul it back here!"

She made them bend on a coil of rawhide, to increase the weight and to give Andrew more chance to snatch it as it swayed in the wind. Nearly fifteen minutes after that, and not a sound from Andrew, until at last his shout came up echoing out of the mist:

"All right! Haul away!"

This time it was Andrew, spinning, clutching the rope with one hand, fighting with the other—using his pistol butt to beat off the eagle, not daring to shoot for fear of frightening the crew at the rope. Elsa shot the eagle—the first thing she had ever killed—almost the first time she had ever fired a pistol. The huge bird folded like a blown rag—vanished. Then, when they had hauled Andrew over the edge and he walked toward her, she was afraid—not of him—of his anger. He held out his hand for the pistol. She gave it to him. Andrew's scorn conceded nothing—not a gesture—not the flicker of a sneer as he gave the pistol back to Bompo Tsering. Then he spoke savagely, in a low voice, commanding him to distribute the recovered load among the ponies. He watched him obey, making almost imperceptible gestures to the other Tibetans that sent them hurrying to the headman's aid.

It was several minutes before he faced Elsa again. They hadn't spoken. She hadn't dared to speak. He was gray, grim-lipped. Was he angry with her? Or was it not anger? He wasn't trembling. He was breathing a bit harder than usual. But he seemed to be fighting himself, not thinking of anyone else, except that he kept glancing to make sure the loads were being properly roped. When he did speak his voice was almost normal and he had lost some of the gray look:

"Elsa, I want a sheet of that foolscap paper and a soft pencil from your saddlebag. Do you mind?"

When she brought them, with a pad to write on, he asked her to sit down. He said his own hand was too unsteady. He began dictating as if she were an office stenographer:—

Andrew Gunning to Bulah Singh.
Bad going here. Watch out for sliding rock. Cross carefully, one at a time. If you should overtake me, come day or night.

"—That's all."

He broke the pencil lead and split the wood with his teeth, making a cleft stick, into which he inserted the paper, folding it lengthwise, so that it looked almost like a toy airplane. Then he beckoned Bompo Tsering.

"Go back there and tie this to the holy man's thigh bone in the cairn!"

The headman stared: "Gunnigun, that being too much very holy thigh bone! Long time blessed holy hermit dying that place!"

460

Andrew jerked his head in the direction of the foot-wide track. Not another word. It was Bompo Tsering's chance—to take or leave— to regain lost standing. He understood. It was trial by ordeal. He stuck out his tongue and obeyed. Elsa watched Andrew. Had he gone mad? Was he thinking of some kind of working agreement with Bulah Singh? It seemed incredible. But what else could the note mean? She couldn't read Andrew's thought; he had it veiled more obscurely than ever. She herself couldn't think. She was panicky. But he sat down beside her, and she knew then that he needed her. He wasn't asking for help. He expected it—knew it was there. He was beginning to recover from emotion so terrific that he hadn't dared to relax attention from what needed doing. He was taking for granted that she understood that. She mustn't dare to question him. Let him govern himself, in his own way. Let him feel he was understood.—She felt she was beginning to know Andrew at last.

"The fool from Koko Nor was dead. Poor devil. On his way home. But so was the pony on his way home."

"We heard you shoot the pony."

"Yes. Beat the eagle to it. I gave the pony a swig of water from my flask. That kills the fear for a second. So they die relieved."

"Thank you, Andrew."

"What for?"

"On behalf of the pony. It can't say thank you."

"It doesn't have to. Good pony—did his best, always."

She thought of Tom Grayne, suddenly, without meaning to, comparing him with Andrew. Tom wasn't sensitive, or romantic. What could she say to Andrew that wouldn't jar the sensitive unknown part of him that never quite came to the surface? At that moment it wasn't far from the surface. She had glimpsed it—almost seen it.

"Andrew."

"Yes?"

"I think I know why you don't like gratitude. Deeds produce their own reward, in this life or the next. Isn't that it?"

He scowled—turned his head—stared at her—spoke quietly:

"No. That's lousy stuff."

"Lousy?" she asked. "Didn't you once tell me you believe in reincarnation?"

"Believe nothing. I know it."

"Well then, won't the law of *karma* reward—"

He interrupted, low-voiced: "No. The hell with reward—here or hereafter! That's a rat's motive. The rule is: you are what you do. So if you can, you've got to, or you lose your own self-respect."

He looked away again, listening for Bompo Tsering along the fog-veiled track.

Elsa hesitated. Suddenly she decided she had a right to know. "Andrew, why did you write to Bulah Singh?"

"Because I have to live with my own conscience. Neglect to warn him 'ud be murder. He might have followed that fool from Koko Nor. Warning puts it up to him. I've done my bit."

"But why invite him, day or night! You don't trust him, do you?"

"No. That's why."

"I don't understand."

"An enemy is less dangerous where you can watch him."

"But we might have escaped him."

"Yeah—and might not. As it is, he'll do some hefty guessing, and he'll guess me wrong, I bet you!"

Through the fog came Bompo Tsering balancing his way back cautiously along the foot-wide track, spreading his arms as if he walked a tight rope, treading gingerly not to disturb the devils that loosen rocks. He marked time for a moment, for the pleasure of treading freely at last on firm rock. Then he came and stood in front of Andrew. Sweat had made streams in the dirt on his face.

"Your saying, Gunnigun. My having doing. God-damn! *Peling* paper having writing being too much easy now can being seen. So coming other people—not good."

"March! Get going! You lead for a while."

Bompo Tsering lingered: "Gunnigun."

"Yes? What?"

"Man from Koko Nor, his being dead now—having what—in *bokkus?*" By way of illustration Bompo Tsering thrust his hand into the voluminous swag-bag formed by the lining of his overcoat. "Money?" he suggested.

Seven Tibetans came forward, as alert as vultures, thinking the same thought as the headman, grouping themselves behind him, watched by the other Tibetans, who had to stand by because Tibetan ponies will roll their loads off on the edge of anything—a precipice preferred. Andrew groped in his bulging hip pocket—pulled out a bag—undid the leather thong—drew out money—silver and Indian paper *rupees*. He didn't count it. He thrust it back into the bag and tied the thong. Bompo Tsering held out his hand and the other Tibetans grinned.

462

"Out of the way!" Andrew said sharply. "Stand back."

He tossed the bag over the cliff. There was no sound of its falling, but a long pause, then an awed chorus:

"Gunnigun!"

"March! Get going! Next time man or horse dies due to disobedience, I'll pitch a month's pay of each one of you over the first cliff we come to! On your way! Get going! March!"

CHAPTER 29

It wasn't long before Andrew resumed his normal good temper. He bore no carry-over grudge against Bompo Tsering. So the Tibetans forgot his anger, and their own fear of him. They liked him again. That was part of the secret of Andrew's success with men of an alien race— of his success, too, with animals: he dealt with the passing moment frankly, fairly, as it came, and when it was gone it was finished business. But beneath the surface he was more obscure than ever. Something had hit him. He was less than ever disposed to reveal what he was really thinking about. He avoided Elsa—rode alone—seemed almost suspicious of her, choosing his rare words, certainly on guard. Against what? Did he regret the brief self-revelation? That quick glimpse of his soul, in a fog, on a raw mountain ledge? Did he fear she would take advantage of it? It seemed so. The thought humiliated Elsa; it made her lonely and dejected—made her wonder what the sensation would be when Tom Grayne should see her coming, from far off. But like Andrew, she kept thought to herself. On the surface she was valiant, waxing her lips against the bitter wind, so that she could smile without pain. She kept herself clean, bright, healthy.

"Whom am I trying to please? Me? Two men? One man? Which of them?"

They had to fight every inch of their way down the lower end of the pass. The going should have been comparatively easy, but an unexpected snowdrift blocked them for half a day. The snow was softening—wouldn't bear their weight. They tried to dig their way through it. Nightfall found them less than halfway through, but the snow freezing again. They were too exhausted and it was too dangerous to go ahead in the dark. They bivouacked in the long trench they had dug. Andrew ate what Elsa cooked, hardly speaking to her, then turned in and slept like a dead man. But he was up before daybreak, while the surface of the drift was still frozen hard. Before the Tibetans could cook their eternal tea, he was breaking trail. He almost outraced the morning thaw. Only the last three loaded ponies had to be dug through the end of the drift. But the delays had totalled up to a whole day lost. And now, starving ponies.

The gallant animals struggled through thawing mud toward a distant village, while the mountains behind grew more and more incredible—like a nightmare—a fantastic wall ever in motion that surged like a tumbling sky, between them and India. Andrew rode in mid-column. Elsa came last. That way it was easier to prevent the Tibetans from over-driving and beating the ponies. Andrew had to take away Bompo Tsering's whip, to prevent him from flogging ponies that were bogged so deep they couldn't struggle.

"Where's your head, you fool?"

"Hot damn! My head thinking too much. Coming someone!"

They all knew they were being followed. It was the worse of two dreads. The village they were approaching was bad enough. It looked more like a fort than a village, half hidden amid glacial moraine and tumbled waves of sterile yellow earth. It looked as sinister as its reputation: a mean, inhospitable nest of bandits, amid hungry foothills. No monastery. No sign of cultivation. Andrew had never been there; neither had Bompo Tsering. One of the Tibetans said he had been there, years ago, but nobody believed him, except when he said the place was ruled by a black magician. They all believed that. They were afraid to whisper the magician's name to one another, because devils might overhear, and he was said to control specially evil devils.

But fear from behind is even worse than fear in front. They were running away from a dark unknown. Andrew didn't dare to tell them who was coming. Even though they guessed—though they almost knew—though Andrew did know—it was better to pretend ignorance. Mention of Bulah Singh's name might start another mutiny. Bulah Singh was a chief of police. Police and blackmail are the same thought in a Tibetan's mind. They were still too near the frontier to believe themselves out of reach of the Indian Government. No Tibetan would try to understand, let alone believe that India doesn't crave to conquer Tibet, or that there are limits to an Indian police officer's authority. They might abandon the ponies and run, or abandon the loads and run away with the ponies. Or they might stubbornly halt and fatalistically await the outcome. There was no predicting what they might or might not do, being Tibetans. It was all up to Andrew. One mistake—a hesitation—a suggestion that he didn't know what he was doing— even a hint of a change of plan—and the command would no longer be his.

Elsa understood. She didn't bother him—asked no questions. Even when they halted in a hollow for the noon meal, she merely unpacked the food for herself and Andrew and made it ready on a small canvas sheet in the lee of a rock, wondering what she would say if he should invite her opinion. Should she advise him to wait and face Bulah Singh? That seemed the lesser of two evils. There were six or seven miles to go. The exhausting Tibetan wind that blows from noon, or earlier, until nightfall, had reached full strength; it was hard to advance against—wearying, boring, baffling. That would have made a good camping place. Normally they would have pitched camp. But no one was thinking of that now. The Tibetans were grudging a half-hour's rest for the starving ponies. They were fretting to press forward harder than ever, wondering whether Andrew could drive a bargain for them all at the village. They might be prisoners—slaves—plundered dead men before sunset.

Andrew came and sat on the ground-sheet beside Elsa. He didn't look at her, but he spoke at once, ungrudgingly, as if he were paying a bill.

"You're good. Thanks."

It came from deep within him. Elsa knew that. She knew what he meant. It flowed into her consciousness like comforting physical warmth.

But it suddenly occurred to Andrew that she might think he referred to the food. He wasn't praising her for doing her job right. Any woman could have done that. So he added:

"I didn't want to talk."

"I understood that, Andrew. You had too much to do."

He frowned. He was going to have to explain after all. He hated that.

"I didn't want to be Nancied," he said. "Get what I mean? I couldn't stick it—not now."

"Andrew, you needn't have feared that."

"We're in a tight fix, Elsa. Got to keep my head. Soul talk 'ud get me rattled."

"Andrew, I am sorry I said as much as I did, two nights ago. I promise faithfully, I won't ever again—"

"Easy, now, easy!" He was irritated because she went from one extreme to another. "Why can't women take a man's words at face value?"

465

"I will never broach that subject again, Andrew, unless you ask me to."

"That's different. I'll let you know when."

"I tried to share with you a—a—something that I can't even explain to myself—not in words."

"I know that. Pass it up until later. Listen to what we're up against now."

"I know some of it."

"I will tell it all—if you'll listen."

She accepted the rebuke—sat still, careful to look unresentful in case he should give her one of his quick sculptor's-eye glances. There she made a mistake. He did look. He misinterpreted.

"Why don't you bawl me out?" he demanded. "I know I've been—"

She interrupted: "No, you haven't, Andrew. I understood perfectly. You couldn't help being—"

"What d'you mean, couldn't help it? I did it on purpose."

"Yes. I understood that."

"When I'm up against real trouble, I hate Nancy-ism."

"Don't let's talk about it."

"I'm explaining. Morgan Lewis, last thing before I left Darjeeling, tried to get me to promise to let you fly off the handle whenever you please."

"Yes. He told me he had said something like that."

"The man's a nut."

"But you can't persuade me he isn't a genuine friend."

"He's a genius," said Andrew. "Welsh at that—half druid. All the rest of him is small boy. Darn him, he should have shut the trap on Bulah Singh. He could have. Now we're like an army on the lam. We might as well be brigands. Until early this morning I kidded myself that Lewis sprang the trap for Bulah Singh and missed him. But this morning I woke up. Doped it out. Lewis let him escape."

"Andrew, I could have told you that, if you had asked me."

"You mean, Morgan Lewis told you what he'd do?"

"No."

"Nancy knows some of his secrets. Did she tell you?"

"No. She didn't. I can't explain how I know it."

"Clairvoyance," said Andrew, scowling, thrusting his jaw forward a shade of an inch. "Well—here's the common sense of it. Bulah Singh knew too much. Had the goods on too many hypocrites in high places. So Lewis chased him across the frontier."

"Dr. Lewis hopes he'll be—"

"For God's sake, let me tell it. Bulah Singh had his plans all laid to scram for Tibet if the dice should turn against him. Lewis must have known that. Problem: let him go? catch him? or bump him off? The British do bump 'em off secretly, once in a rare while, when there's someone they can trust to do the job smartly and hold his tongue. But they don't like it. It isn't in Lewis's line. Lewis likes subtlety—force Bulah Singh to beat it and brand himself as a self-convicted fugitive from justice—nowhere to go but Tibet, and take the consequences."

"Andrew, may I say something?"

"Yes. But don't talk to me out of the sky."

"Bulah Singh intended, from the very first, to follow you and to make use of both of us!"

"Oh, say, see here—"

"Andrew, I know. I'm not guessing."

"Are you being clairvoyant?"

"From the moment when he found out that you intended to return to Tibet, he resolved to follow you: and to compel me to come with him. I mean persuade. I don't think he'd have tried to use force."

"You never mentioned it."

"I know I didn't."

"Why?"

"I don't like to be disbelieved by my friends. How could I have persuaded you to believe it?"

"All right. That's the alibi. It gets you nowhere. Now answer the question."

"If I do, you'll be angry."

"If you want to make me angry, don't answer the question. Then I won't ever ask you another."

"Andrew, you can be more cruel than a—"

"Cruel nothing. Tell the plain truth. Why didn't you tell me what you say you knew about Bulah Singh?"

"Andrew, are you trying to make me hate you?"

"I want the truth. Why didn't you—"

"Very well. You shall have your answer. If I had told you what I knew about Bulah Singh you might have thought I was trying to work you."

"Bull's-eye!" he answered. "Yes. I might have thought that. Now and then I am that kind of a—"

467

"No, you're not! Don't say it! I am sorry I spoke."

For a minute he sat scowling with his chin on his fist. Then he suddenly threw off silence like a mask that irritated him:

"I've been a son of a bitch. Sorry."

"Andrew, if you want to be forgiven, I will even put it in writing!"

He laughed. His frown vanished as if the wind had blown it. He plunged into the passing moment: "Here's part of our difficulty. I don't know this village we're headed for. Bulah Singh probably does."

"Andrew, I don't think Bulah Singh has ever been in Tibet."

"Is that out of the sky?"

"Yes."

"Well, maybe you're right. But lots of Tibetans go to India. The magician who runs this village is a first-class stinker who has been to Darjeeling lots of times. So he may know Bulah Singh. His name is Lung-gom-pa."

"That can't be his real name," said Elsa.

"Why not?"

"Lung-gom-pa isn't a name. It's a word."

"What does it mean?"

"Flying *lama*. That's a person who can walk through the air."

"Yeah, I've heard of 'em."

"No one who really can walk through the air would dream of using such a name as that. The real flying *lamas* are secretive. So Tom said. Tom knows; he has seen them."

"Okay. Granted. This man who calls himself Lung-gom-pa is probably a fake of the first order. But he's a hot shot, and he runs this village. I heard all about him in Darjeeling—got the lowdown—figured how to manage him in case I'd have to take this route. He owns a gang of smugglers—bandits—professional thieves. I've got to make a deal with him before Bulah Singh gets at him."

"How far is Bulah Singh behind us now?" Elsa asked.

"Not many miles. We broke a trail for him. He could come at twice our speed. But he and his men and ponies must be darned near exhausted."

"How many men has he, Andrew? Have you any idea?"

"No. I've counted four men through the glasses, and I think eight ponies, one at a time as they crossed a bare ridge. But I may have counted one man twice. Or there may be a dozen I didn't see. I don't know. They'll be well armed; that's a safe bet. It's bad any way you look at it. If Bulah Singh takes our side against Lung-gom-pa and his brigands, we'll be beholden to Bulah Singh. I'd rather be beholden to the devil. And if he takes the other side, we're even worse out of luck. So we've got to use brains, and not let Nancy and Jesus do any backseat driving—not on this detour."

Bompo Tsering peered around the rock. He beckoned. Andrew picked up the binoculars and hove himself off the ground, vigorously because he was tired out but unwilling to admit it.

"We'll know the worst in a minute," he said over his shoulder.

Elsa followed him to the rim of the hollow, bending nearly double so as not to be seen. All the Tibetans followed. Bompo Tsering angrily drove them away, ordering them to stand by the ponies. Andrew lay down and stared through the glasses. Elsa watched Bompo Tsering. He was playing safe, pretending loyalty, ready to play friend or traitor with equal sincerity. He was more mercurial than really treacherous— quite easy to read.

But there was no reading Andrew's thought no guessing what he saw through the glasses. What Elsa did get was a glimpse of her own confusion. It was like a dream. It frightened her. It was a secret fear. It coiled within the coloured spectrum of her thought. Much worse than the fear of precipices. Nameless—nonphysical. She couldn't interpret it. But it seemed to include Andrew, as if she herself were evilly betraying him without knowing how or why. It sickened her. She couldn't speak when Andrew signed to her at last to come and lie beside him. He gave her the glasses, in silence. When he noticed her hand was trembling he thought she was cold. He signed to her to button her fleece-lined coat and to steady the glasses on the rock.

They were wonderful glasses. But when she got them steady at last she didn't believe what she saw. It couldn't be true. One man alone, in a sheepskin hat and long overcoat, walked fifty feet ahead of an unloaded pony that followed, limping painfully. The man strode erect with a long stick in his right hand. Nothing cheap about him. Picturesque. Unpleasant. Stride and gesture were unmistakable.

Andrew's voice was triumphant: "What do you see?"

"Bulah Singh. But he's alone!"

"Yes. Lost his party."

"But perhaps they are—"

"Lost 'em. Gone. Baggage and all."

"What makes you sure of it? Take the glasses again. Look."

Andrew took the glasses, but he didn't need them. "The lame

pony," he answered. "It's the last one left, or he'd have waited for another. Bulah Singh's footsore. He's lost his gang. I'll bet they slipped off that ledge that I warned him against. All right, we needn't hide from one man." Andrew stood up, humming to himself. "Guts! You've got to hand it to him. He looks as proud as Milton's Lucifer. Remember?

> *His spear, to equal which the tallest pine*
> *Hewn on Norwegian hills to be the mast*
> *Of some great admiral were but a wand,*
> *He walk'd with to support uneasy steps*
> *Over the burning marle.*

"Andrew, when you quote your gloomy old Milton, you can sometimes drive away gloom like a bad dream!"

Andrew filled his lungs, as if he breathed new confidence. He laughed: "Let's leave him to it. He has a long walk ahead, and no resources but his own malice. The first trick's ours. Let's go tackle the black magician!"

Chapter 30

Seven miles to go, to the village. Now Andrew and Elsa brought up the rear, riding side by side. The starving baggage ponies could be trusted to find the shortest way and needed no urging. They knew instinctively that food awaited them not far beyond the treeless yellow dunes in the distance. Bompo Tsering and the rest of the Tibetans, by another instinct, knew that danger from the rear had dissolved itself. So they, too, could be trusted. If Andrew had told them in words that Bulah Singh had lost his entire gang and all his provisions, they might not have believed. They would at least have doubted; since how could Andrew know what had happened? But they had read Andrew's thought—or believed they had. That was as convincing as if a skilful political liar had said it. It felt like their own knowledge.

They were even inventing dreams, and telling one another, how the soul of the man from Koko Nor had beckoned through the fog and brought the Sikh's gang crashing down to death to keep him company in hell. Andrew's message, tied by Bompo Tsering to the good saint's thigh bone and re-enforced by Bompo Tsering's prayers, had made that necromancy possible. So Andrew's cap sported another invisible feather and Bompo Tsering, forgetting that Andrew knew at least some Tibetan and unaware that Andrew listened to him downwind, magnified its importance for his own reflected glory:

"I always told you unbelieving, adulterous bastards that Gunnigun knows what he's doing! Wait and see! When we reach this village Gunnigun will know how to deal with the black magician!"

Andrew felt considerably less sure of that than Bompo Tsering did. His head was beginning to feel too much in the sky. His feet weren't on the ground, the way they had been while there were tangible things to be done. Falling back beside Elsa to think over the problem of Lung-gom-pa, he was silent for several minutes. Then, when he began to talk, he suddenly became expansive. He revealed a phase of himself that Elsa had never before seen. It scared her. She didn't know what to make of it. It might be a physical reaction from the exhausting march over the mountains. He sounded almost drunk. He said the exact opposite of things he always had insisted were too true to dispute. He said them aggressively. For instance:

"You can't successfully oppose ideas with facts."

"Andrew, are you feeling the strain of that awful march?"

"Hell, no. You and I have stood it better than the Tibetans. That's because we're not so sure as they are that evil has brains.—But I was talking about—"

"You were talking about a black magician and black magic."

"That stuff's a boomerang."

"Andrew—"

"It's like poison gas. You can't aim it. It flows on the wind. If the wind changes, it blows back on the user. That becomes the problem: is there some way of changing the wind?"

"Andrew, it's not long since you didn't believe in any kind of magic. Are you sure you do now? Is your mind troubled because Bulah Singh's men died on that precipice?"

"Hell, no. They followed their own leader. They were like Germans obeying Hitler. Let 'em take the consequences."

"Andrew, it makes me sick to think of what happened. I believe it upsets you, too. But you're not to blame. Are you blaming yourself? You did your best to prevent it. You sent Bompo Tsering back to post a warning for Bulah Singh."

"Sure. But do you know what happened?"

Elsa did know. That was why she was troubled. But she knew, too, what troubled Andrew; and that troubled her worse. He had been trying to use magic in which he less than half believed. That way lies ruin. She closed her eyes, and saw more clearly than in a mirror what had happened. But what disturbed her much more than the vision of

471

death was Andrew's voice describing it, as if he read it from a book as he rode beside her:

"Bulah Singh was leading. He spotted my message on white paper in the gray fog fluttering in the wind from the saint's thigh bone beside the trail. He dismounted—read it and—" Andrew paused, as if a cloud had covered what he saw. Too well she knew that sensation. She urged him, as others usually urged her:

"What then? What happened then?"

He seemed to see again. He spoke slowly: "Bulah Singh believed my message might be a trick. So he tested it out. He sent one man ahead, lying to him about the ledge being safe. Nothing happened. Then Bulah Singh followed, alone. Again nothing happened. So he used a police whistle to call the rest of his men forward. They came—and an avalanche of rocks and ice swept them all to death on the crags below—every last one of them."

He grew silent again, until Elsa spoke: "That might have happened to us."

"It did happen to them. There was a reason why. It wasn't a mere accident. I want to figure out the reason."

"What happened after that, Andrew?"

"The man who had crossed first turned on Bulah Singh in a kind of panic. Perhaps hysteria. He seemed to go mad. He accused Bulah Singh of being in league with devils. He rode at Bulah Singh. They fought. Bulah Singh shot him. The man's pony went galloping back along the ledge, slipped on a loose stone and fell over to join the rest of them. That's what happened."

"And then?"

"Then Bulah Singh had no course left but to follow us."

"He could have turned back," said Elsa.

"No, he couldn't."

"He thought of doing it."

"He hadn't food, or strength enough. If he'd reached India, he'd have had to face trial for murder."

"Andrew! Do you see that, too!"

"Yes. But if I think about it something gets in the way. If I don't think, it's as clear as daylight. On his way from Darjeeling toward the border, Bulah Singh shot a man he thought was Lewis. He still thinks it was Lewis."

"Yes. But can you see who it really was?"

"No, I can't. But the victim didn't look like Lewis. I believe it was someone who was spying on Lewis. Bulah Singh shot the wrong man by mistake."

"Yes. He did. But where? Can you see where?"

"No. I guess I've never been there—somewhere not far north of Darjeeling."

"Andrew, did you ever see the Jesuit Mission?"

"No. Off my route."

"Did you never meet Father Patrick?"

"No. Friend of Nancy's, isn't he? I never saw him."

"He isn't dead," said Elsa. "Not yet. Bulah Singh shot him, in the dark, near the Jesuit Mission, by mistake, thinking he was Morgan Lewis."

"Are you sure?"

"Yes. Can't you see! You were seeing a moment ago. And now Morgan Lewis and Nancy Strong are both at the Mission, trying to save Father Patrick's life. Dr. Lewis has extracted the bullet from Father Patrick's lung."

Andrew was silent. Suddenly he chuckled. "Well," he said, "we can't prove one word of it. So let's not kid ourselves."

The anticlimax fell like a wet blanket. "That seems to amuse you," said Elsa. "But now, perhaps you can begin to understand what I meant when I said I hated clairvoyance. Sometimes one can see. Sometimes not. But one can never prove anything to the satisfaction of anyone except another clairvoyant; and only then if the clairvoyant can see what you see."

"I'm not clairvoyant," said Andrew. He sounded disgusted. Elsa didn't know how to answer. It was no use arguing. She asked a question instead: "What actually are you—besides being an artist and—and—a sceptic? What else are you?"

"I'm an explorer."

"Exploring what?"

Andrew was becoming irritated. He visibly summoned patience and spoke like a man on the witness stand:

"I believe the world we all live in is different from what it seems to our senses to be. I began with Huxley, who was my father's high priest. I was weaned on Ingersoll, who had more religion in him than a carload of archbishops. And I've tried to follow Einstein into Relativity and all that stuff. I believe we exist in a kind of magnetic field. I'm trying to explore that. I'm convinced there's something phony about time and space. It's possible to get back of them and to know whatever's going on, anywhere, any time. There—is that clear?"

"Perhaps we both mean the same thing," said Elsa, "only we use different words."

"I guess not," he answered. "You're clairvoyant."

That hurt her to silence. He spoke as if clairvoyance was beneath his thought not beyond it: something viciously weak. It hurt all the more because she herself, until Nancy Strong showed otherwise, had thought clairvoyance a curse. She could hardly believe her ears when Andrew continued:

"I imagine Nancy Strong, and perhaps Lewis too, were thinking of us. In some way that I intend to find out, that united their field of thought with ours and we saw what they had experienced. Probably they saw what we've been doing. The same with Bulah Singh. Coming along behind us, hating us—"

Elsa objected: "Nancy and Dr. Lewis don't hate us."

"Probably not. But Bulah Singh does. So love and hate can't have anything to do with it. The point is: Bulah Singh was thinking of you and me, wondering how the devil he could overtake us and outwit us. That coincided with our thought about him. Somehow that united our magnetic fields, to use a phrase for an unknown condition. So we were able to see what he had experienced. And he may have known what we're thinking about. But perhaps not. I've learned one or two tricks about keeping my thought covered."

"So you're not clairvoyant, are you, Andrew?"

"No, thank the Lord!" He spoke with condescension too faint for himself to detect. But she winced at it. "Clairvoyance," he continued, "may be a kind of sensitiveness. Perhaps a form of nervousness. It seems to have made you suffer."

Elsa rode to her own rescue. Even her tired pony felt the spiritual surge that was like a convert's asseveration of new faith in the face of torment

"Andrew, I love clairvoyance! I wouldn't exchange it for anything in this world!"

"Well, I'll be damned!"

"I would rather die than lose it!" She deliberately quoted Nancy Strong: "It's the substance of things hoped for! It's the evidence of things not seen!"

"You'll quote the Pope next!"

"Your talk about magnetic fields is scientific cant—sheer piffle! Did you read it in a magazine off a news stand?"

474

"Say, see here—"

"It's a smoke-screen! You exude it like a cuttlefish to save yourself from thought! Magnetic poppycock! Clairvoyance is evolution! It's the proof of expansion of consciousness—a step forward! The reason why we saw what we did see was the same reason why Bulah Singh didn't see it—couldn't possibly have seen it! We're clairvoyant. So is Nancy Strong. So is Morgan Lewis. Bulah Singh isn't!"

Andrew stared, reappraising, himself feeling normal again but aware of Elsa's new self-confidence. Her eyes glowed with passionate conviction.

"Have I been thoughtless?" he asked. "Have I said something that hurt? If so, I'm sorry. I beg pardon. I wouldn't hurt you for worlds."

"No! But if you thought me your equal, you'd fight! You'd fight to kill!"

"Me? Kill you? Elsa, you're—"

"You're not telling me, Andrew. I'm telling you. It isn't being hit that hurts. You've seen me take it. And I've seen you take it. We've a right to respect each other. It's being treated as an inferior that galls."

"I've never treated you as an inferior."

"You're doing it now! You're talking down to me!"

He laughed. "Have it your own way, Elsa. If this is down, what's up? I was admiring you."

"I know it. The way you'd admire a dog that obeyed orders, or a pony that wouldn't quit, no matter how tired it might be.—Please! I'm sorry I spoke. I won't do it again."

"May I apologize?"

"No."

"Okay. Then you listen to me!"

"Your obedient, humble servant," she answered grimly.

"God!" he retorted. "It's a mystery how a girl can use formal words and make them cut like frost! What have I done now?"

"You? Nothing, Andrew, nothing! '*Blow, blow, thou winter wind! Thou art not so unkind as man's ingratitude.*' Is that what you meant?" She sounded almost more heartbroken than sarcastic. "Dear Andrew, I'm truly grateful to you. Truly I am. I would die to prove it, and be grateful for that too. But I love clairvoyance."

"Very well," he answered. "Let it go at that. You're clairvoyant. You love it. I'm looking for something rational to help to deal with a human devil in this village we're coming to." He urged his pony forward, so that all she saw now was the broad of his back.

475

She felt like crying. She fell farther behind for a moment as the ponies passed between two boulders. When she drew abreast again she was smiling. That gave her away. Even blinded by anger Andrew knew she couldn't smile like that and mean it, after what had just passed. He reined in—dismounted—held her pony's rein:

"See here," he said, looking her in the eyes, "we've got mad at each other for no reason. Let's forgive, and not do it again." He forced a laugh into his voice. "I'm still so angry I can hardly keep from swearing. But I've nothing against you. It can't be your fault. Please!"

"I forgive you, Andrew. Of course I do. Please forgive me."

He nodded, staring. Suddenly they both asked the same question: "What for? What have we done to each other?" They laughed lamely.

"Damned if I know," said Andrew. "What have we done to each other? Something's gone. We were first-class friends until—"

She interrupted: "Andrew, I believe I know what has happened."

"Then I wish you'd tell me."

"You won't get angry again?"

"I'll try not to. Is it something personal? To you? Or to me?"

"Both of us, Andrew! Personal as breathing!"

"Jesus! Now what's coming! Metaphysics? Okay. Go ahead—I'll listen."

"Will you really listen? Will you believe I'm not trying to—not trying to put one over on you, or—"

His voice changed perceptibly: "Sure. I said I'd listen."

"And you begin with Huxley?"

"He'll do. Quote him accurately, that's all."

"Didn't he say there must be beings in the universe whose intelligence is as much beyond ours as ours exceeds that of a black beetle?"

"Yes. Huxley wrote that."

"You believe it?"

"I don't disbelieve it. I'd take Huxley against the field, and lay odds on."

"Andrew! You and I are tuned in with Nancy Strong, Morgan Lewis, and—and they're tuned in with Lobsang Pun—and he's tuned in with even higher intelligences!"

"Maybe. But what are you driving at?"

"Their thought, even when it tells of murder, doesn't make you and me angry."

"No. But something else did. I'm in a bloody temper."

476

"Bulah Singh and the black magician in this village know each other. Didn't you say that?"

"Yes. Lung-gom-pa has been to Darjeeling."

"They're tuned in to each other's thought, and they're thinking about us! We're between them, thinking about them. That's what made us angry. We're between a devil and a would-be devil; and they, too, are tuned into a greater intelligence, such as Huxley spoke of. But theirs is wicked! Ours isn't."

Andrew whistled, softly at first, then louder. He grinned at Elsa, studying her face as if he were going to carve her portrait in wood. "I can't argue it," he said at last. "Your saying it seems to take the strain off."

"Making us angry with each other," said Elsa, "would be the easiest way to make us make mistakes."

"Yes, that's true. It would be. Get a man's goat and you've got his number. Sure that's true. But would they do that deliberately?"

"That's how black magic works," she answered. "White magic works by restoring confidence and cancelling anger and fear. Black magic—"

"But deliberately?"

"They could—if the magician is skilful. But it might work that way anyhow, without their intending it. Nancy told me that crossed mental currents are much more deadly than an electrical short circuit."

Andrew climbed into the saddle, carefully, giving the pony time to get set to the weight. He led the way. Turning in the saddle suddenly, he said:

"See here! If you're right about the anger, then it must be a magnetic field that—what are you laughing at now?"

"Your magnetic field! And your logic! Andrew! Supposing anger should need a magnetic field—does that prove that Nancy and you and I—or anyone else—need one for not being angry in? Does the fact that sharks need water prove that birds can't fly in the wind?—Andrew—didn't Nancy tell you about superconsciousness?"

"Yes."

"Did you believe her?"

"No."

"Are you getting angry again?"

He waited until her pony drew abreast. Then he answered: "I don't understand about superconsciousness. But can you keep me from getting angry until we've dealt with Lung-gom-pa and Bulah Singh?"

"I don't know. I can try. Have I your permission to try?"

"You sure have. Hop right to it. I'm feeling fit to kill the first son of a bitch who—"

"Poetry, Andrew! Poetry! Try Milton!"

He had no use for Milton at that moment. They rode forward to the buoyant *stanzas* of Walt Whitman, chanted, as if harp strings set the time:

Roaming in thought over the universe, I saw the little that is Good steadily hastening toward immortality, And the vast that is evil I saw hastening to merge itself and become lost and dead.

CHAPTER 31

Revolting filth and a breath-snatching stink, which not even the Tibetan wind could deal with, increased the sensation of being close to the village, although they couldn't yet see it. Huge dogs announced its neighbourhood—from over by the cemetery, where the *ragyabas* had carried a recent human corpse and had dismembered it with axes. But no sign of the *ragyaba* carriers-out-of-the-dead: perhaps they had seen, and were scared, and had run for cover. The dogs were quarrelling with vultures for the fragments of human meat, but some of them found time to do their duty and bay downwind, threatening all comers. There was no other threat—no sign of armed men, nor even of a lookout—only smoke, rising over a dune and flattened by the wind into a long smear, like a brush stroke reaching to the sunset on the far horizon.

Bompo Tsering and the baggage train were waiting in a group in a hollow. Beyond that was a gap between yellow dunes. Framed in the gap was the turquoise sky.

"Like the end of the world!" said Elsa.

"Like the jumping-off place!"

"Like one of Dunsany's plays!"

"I never saw one."

"Like you go first—like hot damn being no afraid like me," said Bompo Tsering. He was stuttering—nervous. "Being Lung-gom-pa!" he added.

It was puzzling that no one had come to greet or challenge them. The village was a notorious bandits' stronghold. Its inhabitants had no other known occupation than robbing and smuggling. Bandits, as a rule, don't hide from small numbers. Andrew puckered his eyes, staring:

"If it weren't for that smear of smoke, I'd say the place was deserted. No very recent hoof marks. No new footprints."

Bompo Tsering shook his head. His warning right hand clutched a prayer wheel. "Uh-uh! Plenty peoples catching—what-you-call-um?— ambush—maybe! Uh-uh!"

Andrew questioned Elsa with raised eyebrows.

"No," she answered. "No sensation of immediate danger. It's all strange and new and scary, but not terrifying."

"New?"

"That's how it feels. Changed in a hurry. I can't explain it. It was bad. Now it isn't so bad."

"If we wait too long, they may think we're afraid," said Andrew.

"What are we waiting for?"

"For someone to show up. That's customary. It isn't manners to go forward uninvited." He meant, it isn't wise to be caught, on tired ponies, in a gap between dunes, with no room to turn and run. But he didn't choose to say that to Elsa.

"Why not send one man forward?" she suggested.

He shook his head. He made a signal that re-formed the line behind Bompo Tsering, with the dejected baggage ponies at the rear. Then he spoke slowly, thinking in back of the words:

"This is one of those times when any move may be right or wrong. There's no way to figure it. It's a question of are we in luck? Let's go forward and find out." He gave the command. "Ride behind me," he told Elsa, "just back of me, where I know where you are. Tell me anything you see that you think I don't see."

Eagles—blue sky above the yellow flanks of the notch—an increasing stench—then, suddenly, the village, walled like a secret fortress in the midst of a hundred irregular acres of yellow muck. The surrounding dunes formed a natural rampart that a mere gang could defend indefinitely against anything less than long-range guns. It was a perfect hide-out. Sunset revealed the roofs of long, low buildings, just visible over the village wall. No monastery. Nothing resembling a religious building; and no bells. Only one roof higher than the rest, and even that not visible beyond the outer ramparts. One wooden gate—and in front of the gate, on foot, the reception committee—ten men, clad in long Tibetan overcoats, armed to the teeth.

"Japanese rifles!" said Andrew. "But *Heil Hitler!*—German automatics! I wonder which of 'em is Lung-gom-pa."

"None of those is," said Elsa.

479

"I believe you're right."

"I know I'm right."

One man strode forward, smiling. He didn't stick out his tongue. He wasn't servile. He gave the impression of being something less than friendly, but, if actually hostile, then treacherous; because he certainly offered hospitality. He might have been deaf and dumb for all the response he made to Andrew's greeting. He made a grandiose gesture of invitation, faced about and led toward the gate in the village wall, not glancing backward.

The gate guard stood aside, out of step, but in something vaguely like a military movement. They formed an irregular line and presented arms. No two held their rifles in quite the same way. They certainly weren't soldiers, but they had been drilled recently. Someone who peered through an eyehole opened the gate. Andrew followed the guide and the procession followed Andrew into a very narrow lane that turned sharp left between the wall and a line of one-storied buildings. The gate slammed shut behind the last pony. It sounded like a deadfall. The armed men climbed up rough steps and redistributed themselves along the wall, on watch. Andrew stared both ways along the filthy lane.

"It's a pip of a trap, if it is one," he remarked to Elsa. "That wall's a honey. From beyond the dunes it looks like part of the dunes. It's perfect camouflage. We couldn't see those guys' heads on the wall. But they saw us."

"Someone else can see us now," said Elsa. "We're being watched."

"Yes. It's probably Lung-gom-pa. But where is he?"

"I don't know. But I don't think it's a trap. Not yet, it isn't."

The guide beckoned. At the far end of the narrow lane a man stood with a lantern. Beside him was a boy with a flashlight. It was hardly twilight yet, but the buildings at the turn of the wall cast a deep shadow—almost black darkness. Very strange it felt, under a blue sky. It was freezing hard; the ponies' breath went upward in clouds of steam. From a roof, not more than a couple of feet above Andrew's head, a Tibetan woman leaned over and stuck her tongue out. Realizing suddenly that Elsa was female, she drew in her tongue and spat. She just missed Elsa's eyes. Standing in his stirrups Andrew slapped the woman's face hard with the back of his hand. She fled along the roof, holding her jaw as she ran, pursued by laughter and by a long string of curses from Bompo Tsering.

"Are you angry?" Elsa asked. "Better be more careful. That woman

480

wears gold jewellery. She's someone. She owns a rich man."

Andrew wished he hadn't hit the woman. He had done it on the spur of a moment. However, the guide took no notice; perhaps he actually was deaf, dumb and stupid. With a gesture he turned them over to the lantern man, who appeared to obey the boy with the flashlight. The boy was too well dressed, and too clean to be honest. Andrew disliked him, and the boy disliked Andrew. Making impudent remarks in Tibetan about foreign devils, the boy led around the corner, where it was really dark and as cold as a morgue. Lantern and flashlight revealed a door into a barn-like building that was thatched with straw and floored with flat stones set in clay. The boy led the way in. Someone lighted a torch. In a moment at the far end there was a bright fire of resinous wood; it threw clouds of spark-lit smoke through a square hole in the roof.

"You're right. No trap yet," said Andrew. "This is reckless hospitality. That firewood cost a young fortune. They must have brought it a hundred miles—maybe farther."

The place stank, but it was Tibet, so that was natural. The big room had been roughly swept quite recently. There were only the faint remains of heaps of dung along the side where ponies had been stalled from time immemorial. On the opposite side was a long wooden shelf for humans to sleep on. There was a table—two benches—buckets. At the far end, near the fire, was water in a big iron barrel—frozen on top, but beginning to thaw.

The ponies clattered in and stood in line, rumps to the wall, whinnying a little. Andrew ordered the loads and saddles off first thing, and Bompo Tsering knew better than to hesitate. He prodded and goaded the gang. He even ordered hoofs and backs examined—then the buckets filled. The ponies drank greedily.

Four elderly men entered, with their hands, hidden by long sleeves, crossed on their breasts. They bowed slightly, glancing curiously at the loads that made a big pile, near the table, in mid-room. They were expensively dressed, heavily robed in hand-woven cloth and knee-high cloth boots. They gave an impression of being educated, civilized. One wore spectacles; he went close to the loads. He seemed to be smelling them. The three others approached Andrew. He bowed stiffly, not sure yet just what attitude to take.

"Which of you speaks English?"

None did. Bompo Tsering came forward to interpret. But Andrew didn't choose just then to be at Bompo Tsering's mercy. Neither did he wish to amuse those Tibetans, who were sure to laugh at his effort to pronounce their language. Such laughter isn't always contemptuous. It's sometimes friendly. But dignity is better, to begin with. So he dismissed Bompo Tsering and asked Elsa to interpret.

"Ask 'em first whose guests we are."

They were so surprised by Elsa's fluent Tibetan and perfect sing-song pronunciation that they couldn't find words for a moment. They couldn't make out whether she was man or woman. They glanced at each other; and when they did perceive at last that she was female they were even more puzzled— not embarrassed, but surprised. One of them spoke at last, and Andrew understood him, but he pretended not to. Elsa interpreted:

"He says we are *pelings*, who have no business in Tibet. Consequently we are no one's guests, because the law forbids hospitality to foreign devils. But since we are the keepers of a promise—"

"What does he mean by that?"

"I don't know. Since we are the keepers of a promise we may spend a night here. But tomorrow we must turn back.—You asked me to help you keep your temper!"

"Okay. Anger's gone downwind. I'm feeling swell."

"Shall I ask for the magician?"

"Don't mention names. No. Give 'em nothing to lay hold of. Tell 'em I want food for the ponies."

Elsa interpreted. The Tibetans consulted each other before one of them answered.

"They say they will first send food for us," said Elsa. "It shall be brought now."

"Tell 'em I want food for the ponies first thing."

"They say no."

"I say yes."

"They say 'very well' then, since you are so insistent." But they add that you don't know the danger of giving offense to someone who is better not offended."

"Tell 'em that's fifty-fifty."

"Must I?"

"Yes. Say I'm reasonable if I get fair treatment."

"They say they intend to show you as much kindness as it is permitted to show to a foreign devil."

"Tell 'em my ponies are me, and their empty bellies are my belly. A full meal for the ponies might open my mouth."

Elsa interpreted. One of the Tibetans turned toward the door, where two men lurked who looked like real brigands. They were filthy, bulky, evil-looking fellows, each armed with two automatics in leather holsters. They leaned against the doorposts and listened sullenly while the man who had turned toward them gave an order. Then one of them walked away, and presently he could be heard cursing and giving orders of his own. It sounded as if scores of villagers were out there in the dark, but no one could be seen, although the door was open.

"That man has gone to get food for the ponies," said Elsa. "Barley and hay."

"Good. Ask now why the man in spectacles is poking his nose in among our loads."

Before Elsa could speak, the man in spectacles looked up and spoke suddenly. He seemed excited. He almost shouted a command. The one brigand left in the doorway stood erect at once and strode forward. Evidently the man in spectacles was an important personage. He pointed to one of the loads. The brigand hauled it off the pile and looked around for someone to help him raise it to his shoulder. He had the impudence to tell Bompo Tsering to come and do it.

"Temper, Andrew! Temper!"

"Okay."

Andrew felt strangely at ease, as a matter of fact. He didn't have to pretend to be good-humoured. He suspected Elsa of Nancy Stronging him in some subtle way—perhaps something like Christian Science. Whatever it was, it made him feel good and not the least bit quarrelsome. He grinned quite friendly as he went and stood in front of the brigand—so friendly that the brigand supposed he had come to help lift the load. Elsa followed Andrew, fearful that he might use his fists. But his voice sounded jocular:

"Tell him that load contains my personal belongings."

The man in spectacles ignored Elsa. He betrayed impatience. He spoke rapidly to Andrew. Bompo Tsering came closer, suspecting there might be a fight; at a fight's beginning he was almost always a staunch ally; but his face fell as he listened. There would not only be no fight, but there was a new mystery, of which he knew nothing. He, Bompo Tsering, headman and keeper of Gunnigun's secrets, had been left out of a secret so important that even the man in spectacles spoke humbly of it, using cautious words, avoiding names or any mention of the contents of the load. Furthermore, Bompo Tsering knew that Andrew had told the truth: that load actually did contain his personal private things such as underwear, books, writing paper. It was a canvas bag that fastened with zipper and padlock.

Elsa interpreted: "The man in spectacles says that is 'the load.' I don't know what he means. He says 'look at the mark.'"

Andrew did look at the mark. It was Chinese. It had been painted there by Lan-dor-ling, the storekeeper at the Sikkim border, who had counted all the loads and marked them, as he said, to prevent confusion with other loads that he had in the godown. Andrew tried the padlock, using his pocket flashlight for appearance's sake, not letting on that he had any special information. He seemed just curious.

"Have you a key that fits this padlock?" he demanded. "Or do you plan to break the padlock? Or to cut the bag? Which?"

The man in spectacles pretended not to understand. But Elsa explained. So he had to leave off pretending. He fell back on insolence, signing to the smelly bandit to shoulder the load and be off. Andrew got in the man's way:

"Nothing doing!"

He and the bandit grinned at each other. The man in spectacles spoke rapidly—looked menacing, glaring through thick lenses. He kept opening and shutting his hands and glancing toward the open door. Andrew waited for Elsa to speak:

"He says this load contains some packages intended for the very worshipful ruler of the village."

"Tell him," said Andrew, "that I have the key. If the bag's to be opened at all, it'll be in my presence."

"He says perhaps you may be invited later."

"Okay. If so, if I'm asked politely, I'll bring the bag with me."

"He says the bag is needed now."

"Love my bag, love me!" said Andrew. "Tell 'em nothing else doing!"

Then came sudden interruption. A dozen sturdy peasants, bossed by the bandit, came carrying bags of grain and big bundles of hay. The hungry ponies neighed welcome to the smell; they had to hear and feel the whip to keep them from rushing the corn sacks. Bompo Tsering had to be threatened to keep him from using the whip too fiercely, to relieve his own emotions. There was pandemonium for a moment. Urged by the man in spectacles the bandit took advantage of it and tried to get away with the padlocked load. Andrew got in his way. They were face to face again, grinning. Then another gang brought in food for Bompo Tsering and the Tibetans—a huge urn, big loaves of barley bread, stewed meat in a copper pot—good-smelling food, and plenty. The man in spectacles became angry, or else did a good job of pretending to be:

"You are being well treated! Look! Your servants are being fed! Your ponies have been given plenty! Why do you refuse what is right?"

This time Andrew answered direct: "Tell the ruler of the village he can come here and I'll open the bag. Or if he prefers, I'll take it to his house and we'll open it there."

"But here comes your supper. Eat it while I take away this bag, which is not yours! Look! Excellent food! Rice! Curry! Ummnn! Smell it! Eat the blessed victuals and be grateful!"

Two menials set the food on the table. They grinned and beckoned invitation. The man in spectacles looked impatient. So did the bandit, fingering his two automatics. Andrew glanced at Elsa, wondering whether she felt the same emotion he did, or saw the same weird cloud-like gray-green haze. It made no difference to what else he saw. He saw through it, past it. It wasn't an actual cloud. It was something mental. He couldn't tell from Elsa's expression whether she was scared. She was staring toward the open door. A man with a lantern was standing just outside it, and so was the overdressed boy with the flashlight.

Suddenly the woman appeared—the jewelled, well-dressed hussy with the slapped face. It looked a bit swollen, but that might be the shadow cast by the lantern.

"She has come for revenge!" said Elsa in a low voice. "She has come to watch it happen. Our supper may have been poisoned. Let's be careful."

"I'm sorry I hit her," said Andrew. "But it's too late to—"

Elsa wasn't listening to him. She interrupted: "I believe she's that boy's mother!"

"She's a Tibetan," said Andrew. "The boy isn't."

"But she is the boy's mother!"

There was a strange silence. It overlay the sound of the ponies munching barley spread on sacks in front of them. Even the hungry Tibetans had stopped eating and were watching the door. The man in spectacles, and his three companions, and the bandit who was still holding on to the bag, were all staring at the door. They hardly breathed.

The woman, with her back to the doorpost, glanced once over her shoulder and smiled. The boy came and stood beside her, just inside the door, holding her hand, turning his flashlight on Andrew. The woman spoke to him. He turned the light on Elsa, holding it steady. The woman smiled at Elsa; her lip curled.

Suddenly, quietly, slowly, from the outer darkness—first nothing but a face, then gradually taking form like a ghost in the lantern light—came Bulah Singh. He leaned on a pole. He limped painfully. He showed his teeth. The woman spoke to him. He ignored her. He stared hard at Elsa, then straightened himself and walked in through the door.

CHAPTER 32

Nothing seemed real. The darkness was full of quiet sound, such as the ponies munching corn. The fire at the far end set shadows leaping, that suggested planes of underworld dimensions. There were several lanterns—a flashlight—shining ponies' eyes—smoke— blustery wind through the hole in the roof. And there was a nervous dread of suddenly born peril, awaited by the woman who held the boy's hand. She very definitely thought of magic; it was in her eyes and in her attitude of confident awe.

But the sense that is the least mendacious of the five recognized smoke, sweat, food, and the reek of damp sheepskin. Dreams don't smell. Bulah Singh stank. It was real, not a dream. Swaying on his feet, the Sikh thrust his face close to Andrew's. Though his feet didn't move, there was a sensation of his thrusting himself between Andrew and Elsa. He was so exhausted physically that he couldn't speak yet, but his thought burned like flame. It glowed through his eyes, domineering and less careful than an animal's for anyone or anything on earth except his own will. He had shed his mask, or was it his shield, or both? Andrew spoke to him like a Spartan:

"Where's your lame pony?"

That was comment, not a question. It prodded the lees of exhaustion. Bulah Singh's nostrils expanded. Scorn released fumes of strength that lingered in him somewhere.

"Wolves!" His voice creaked like a rusty hinge. "God damn your stupid soul to hell, you'd pity a rat on the dissecting table, and let people rot! Where's my pony!"

"You'd better rest yourself."

Andrew signed to Bompo Tsering to bring one of the loads for the Sikh to sit on. But Bulah Singh used his pole to prod the bag that the man in spectacles wanted. Suddenly he feigned collapse. His knees gave from under him. He clutched Andrew's arm and sat down on the bag, his weight almost breaking the brigand's fingernails and forcing him to let go.

"Idiot!" he croaked at Andrew. "I'm just in time! No thanks to you! And now, give me a drink! Whiskey! Neat—no water."

He didn't wait for an answer. Grinding his teeth because of the pain in his swollen feet, he looked up at the man in spectacles, and almost screamed at him: "*Aween-aween-ah!*"

For a moment nothing happened. There was astonished silence, except that the ponies went on munching, and the wind blew. Andrew questioned Elsa *sotto voce*: "What does that mean?"

"I don't know. It isn't Tibetan."

Bulah Singh repeated the phrase, twice, louder each time. The third time it sounded like "*Ameen-ameen-ah!*" The man in spectacles threw up his long- sleeved arms and hurried to the door. The others followed, including the men who had brought food. Their stampede almost swept away the woman and boy. She drew a dagger—it had a blade no thicker than a bodkin. A man yelled. He struck at her—missed, and vanished, screaming. The woman laughed. She wiped blood off the blade on the ball of her thumb, and then the thumb on the wall. The boy smiled sweetly, turning his flashlight on the woman's face, making her look like a Rembrandt painting of Mary the Mother of God in a stable waiting for the Three Wise Men.

"Shut that door!" said Andrew.

Unfamiliar impulse caught the boy off guard. He obeyed. He loathed Andrew with a half-breed's instinctive unreasoning malice, as quick as a snake's. Fearful of missing a move, he aimed his flashlight at Bulah Singh, whose fist struck the bag he sat on as he grinned—with pain and beckoned to the boy. It almost looked prearranged. It was the first time Bulah Singh had noticed either the boy or the woman. The boy came forward confidently, with a kind of gloat in his eyes. The woman followed, keeping her eyes on Elsa.

"Andrew, please give me the keys," said Elsa. "I will open a chop-box and get out whiskey for Bulah Singh."

"No. Let's find out what's wrong with him before he gets drunk."

Bulah Singh overheard. "Wrong with me? Drunk? Gunning, you god-damned idiot, take a drink too, to wake your brains! Don't you know what's in this bag I'm sitting on?" Then his expression changed to a confidential leer at Elsa. "Yes," he said. "Take his keys. Be a good girl. Go and get me a drink."

Andrew observed that Elsa showed no symptom of intention to obey. He hadn't expected she would obey, but he was glad she didn't. She was doing her job. By some mysterious means she was avoiding the anger that the woman, and the boy and Bulah Singh were all trying to produce. The little beast of a boy was the worst of the three. He was an obvious homosexual, probably perverted by his elders. He knew by instinct that Andrew loathed that stuff. He deliberately showed off, strutting in front of his mother. She was as proud of him as if he were reciting poems. Bompo Tsering and all Andrew's Tibetans laughed as if it was the funniest thing they had seen.

Bulah Singh sneered, glancing at Elsa: "Like mother, like son!"

Either he thought that would please Elsa, or he wanted to disgust her. It was hard to guess which.

"Is he your son?" she retorted. "He looks like you and this woman."

Bulah Singh ignored the question. He commanded the boy to unfasten his boots and pull them off. The boy knelt to obey; his unctuous relish was worse than servile. He smirked. Bulah Singh harshly ordered the woman to get one of the big copper bowls that Andrew's Tibetans had already emptied of food. She didn't like obedience; she liked it less when Bompo Tsering tried to prevent her from taking the bowl; but he yielded when she drew her dagger. She filled the bowl with water and began to warm it at the fire. By that time Bulah Singh was in agonies as the boy tried to pull off a boot. He kicked the boy in the face—sent him staggering. The boy wasn't hurt badly but he ran to the door, crying.

The woman came on the run, spilling water, clucking, muttering. She went down on her knees, begging Andrew for the loan of his knife to cut the boots with. Andrew beckoned to Bompo Tsering. Bulah Singh called the woman a mother of whores. He ordered her to pull his boots off gently. She didn't dare. He kicked her, hurting his foot. She still didn't dare. Then he turned to Elsa, skilfully changing his voice, forcing himself to smile.

"See what comes of kindness to such bitches! She would let me die of gangrene! Please! Will you kindly help me?"

"No," said Andrew, "she won't!"

Bompo Tsering stood waiting; his expression was as blank as a bun, but his eyes were on Andrew's right fist.

"Your saying, Gunnigun—my doing," he muttered. "Your not—"

"Pick this Sikh up! Carry him over to the fire, where there'll be light and warm water. Take his weapons away and then pull off his boots. Wash his feet. Use lots of soap. Then I'll come."

Bompo Tsering signalled for help. Before Bulah Singh could protest he was picked up by four Tibetans and frogmarched toward the fire, cursing and struggling. The woman and the boy came and screamed at Andrew. He ignored them and went in search of the load that contained the first-aid kit. The boy was crying like a girl. The woman was begging for Bulah Singh's good will, as if Andrew had stolen it. She knelt and clutched the hem of Elsa's overcoat, imploring her to make Andrew listen, blubbering and screaming a long story of how Bulah Singh was the lord of her life, the father of her son; he had seduced her in Delhi, raped, ruined her and then sent her home to Tibet.

Elsa got in a word at last: "Whose woman are you?"

"His woman!"

"Bulah Singh's?"

"No! His!" She spoke proudly, recovering self-control: "I am the ruler's woman!"

"Of this village?"

The woman nodded.

"Well then, what do you want with Bulah Singh?"

"He is mine, is he not? Whom I obey, so he must also!"

Andrew came back with cotton, a roll of bandages and a bottle of iodoform. The woman started to wail and plead again. The boy cried. Andrew ordered both of them to get out or else go to the fireside, where Bulah Singh was cursing like a scalded cat because four Tibetans were holding both his feet in hot water. Standing calmly in firelight so that Andrew could see him, Bompo Tsering was curiously examining Bulah Singh's weapons—an automatic, a '32 revolver and a dagger almost exactly like the woman's. The boy led the woman toward the fire, pulling her by the hand.

Andrew grinned at Elsa: "Do you get the idea?"

"No, I don't—except, of course, that the woman is telling the truth. What can Bulah Singh know, or think he knows about this bag? It's locked. He can't see through canvas!"

"Can you see clairvoyantly?"

"No. Is it something you put in there?"

"Lan-dor-ling did it, down at the border. But I guessed it, so the little trick didn't come off. As chief of police, Bulah Singh must have known that Lan-dor-ling's little game is smuggling opium from India to Tibet. Bulah Singh tipped off Lan-dor-ling to hide opium in my loads. That's why Lan-dor-ling went to such pains to help you and me reach Tibet."

"So we're opium smugglers!"

"It's a cinch we're something. Let's eat before the grub gets too cold."

"I couldn't eat."

"Neither could I. That grub looks disgusting. Let our Tibetans have it. We'll cut a can of something later on."

"That woman loves us like a cobra," said Elsa. "The food may be poisoned."

"Right. I'll warn Bompo Tsering to make her taste the grub before he divides it with the gang. What do you make of the woman?"

"Andrew, she's telling the truth. She belongs to two men. One is the black magician who rules this village. He has sent her to influence Bulah Singh—"

"I can't believe that: Influence him? He must know Bulah Singh's a total loss! Influence him? Why not jump him?"

"I don't know. But I don't think Bulah Singh is as helpless as he seems: Andrew, how would this be! Get that little beast of a boy here and let's question him. You tell me what to ask. I'll talk to him gently."

"No."

"Why not?"

"He'll lie like hell. We've got to shake that brat or he'll be the end of us. His kind of treachery is bred and educated. Our best bet is Bulah Singh. I'll talk to him. Do you want to stay or come with me?"

"I don't like it alone. I'm afraid."

"Come then. But remember: part of Bulah Singh's trick was to get you to take care of his feet, and let the Tibetans see you do it. It was aimed at your mental set-up. That 'ud reduce you to the menial class and give you a claim on him. He could pretty easily reverse that into a claim by him on you. That's old stuff; it's had whiskers since Adam and Eve. All the politicians use it. It works nine times out of ten unless you're wise to it. So watch out. Don't fall for his thanks, or his pain, or his—"

"Andrew, it sounds funny to hear you—"

"Okay! Laugh! But there'll be nothing funny if Bulah Singh gets you hypnotized! Suppose you carry the bandages. Come on."

He strode ahead. The ponies sniffed at Elsa as she passed. She touched their noses, light-fingered. When Andrew reached the zone of firelight he paused for a second and spoke in a half-whisper:

"Remember: don't give him a break. Don't pity him. Leave this to me."

It was like a medieval torture scene in crimson firelight and leaping shadow, With Bompo Tsering acting chief inquisitor, standing aloof with the weapons, waiting for the moment. Nine men watched, fascinated, keeping the woman and boy outside their circle. Bulah Singh was being held down on a saddle by two men who held his arms twisted behind him. Their knees were in his back. There was an arm around his throat. Two men held his feet in the pan of hot soapy water. At a gesture from Andrew they let him lift his knees, so that he leaned backward with his feet in the air.

"Wash 'em some more," said Andrew.

The Sikh set his teeth. They plunged his feet back in the pan. He breathed hard through his nose.

"Andrew, the man's in agony! Be a bit merciful!"

"All right, Elsa, all right! Leave this to me! There's nothing else to be done."

Andrew himself took the soap. His strong hands were far more gentle than the Tibetans' had been. The woman, staring pop-eyed between two of Andrew's men, crooned as she watched the relaxation of relief on Bulah Singh's face.

"Blood poison's the thing to guard against. We'll save your feet," said Andrew.

"You might have saved me this indignity!" Bulah Singh retorted.

"Yeah—I might have." Andrew washed steadily. "But I was wise to your game. I boomeranged you. Know what that means?"

"Gunning, you're mad!"

"No, no, no. I'm easy-minded. Not mad in the least."

"Don't you understand that your safety depends on me?"

Andrew smiled. "Here's a towel. Dry your own feet. After that, I'll dust 'em with iodoform and then bandage 'em. Next time you hit the trail, wear walking boots. Those things you had on weren't even fit to ride in."

The Tibetans relaxed their hold. Tenderly the Sikh dried his own feet, until suddenly he caught sight of the woman's face. He tossed the towel to her. At a gesture from Andrew the Tibetans let her pass. The boy followed her. The woman squatted and took the Sikh's feet in her lap; she and the boy worked gently, each using an end of the one towel.

"You see," said Andrew, "I spotted your plan to have Elsa and me do the Jesus foot-wash act in the presence of all these people. Smart stuff! For a man in a mean fix you've got presence of mind. It was subtle. That would have fixed us, in their minds, as your inferiors."

"My feet are dry," said Bulah Singh.

"You won't walk on 'em for quite a while," said Andrew. He handed the iodoform to the woman—showed her how to dust it on, watched her do it, went on talking: "I suppose you expect to stay here until your feet get well."

"I am coming with you," the Sikh answered. "I and this child, and the woman."

"You don't say."

"You will also say it. You will very gladly say it! You will beg me to come with you—when you have heard my news!"

"Bandages!" said Andrew.

Elsa wanted to do the bandaging, but Andrew wouldn't let her. He did it himself, smiling:

"Elsa, we owe that woman nothing. Get back the towel, soap and iodoform, quick, now, before she hides 'em! If she won't give 'em up, Bompo Tsering shall give her the works."

Bompo Tsering heard. He followed Elsa. The woman surrendered the towel ungraciously, as if to reclaim it were meanness, but she had passed the bottle of iodoform to the boy, who had slunk away with it, and with the soap too. She pretended to know nothing of anything else, until the boy's cries brought her to her senses. Bompo Tsering had caught the boy hiding among the ponies. He was beating him. The woman screamed, jumped up and ran to the rescue. Bompo Tsering slapped her and threw her down among the ponies; then came back with the soap and iodoform. Andrew made mental note of the fact that Bulah Singh's weapons had been stowed away in Bompo Tsering's voluminous *bokkus* but he didn't choose to humiliate his own man at that moment.

Bulah Singh spoke angrily: "Andrew Gunning! Listen well and remember! It is safe to punish the woman. She is only a tart. But beware of the boy!"

"You kicked him!" said Elsa. "I saw you kick him in the face when he was trying to pull your boots off."

Bulah Singh sneered: "But don't you do it! I own him, body and soul! If you injure him—if you insult him—and if I will it, the men of this village will spread your pieces on the burial mound for the dogs

492

and vultures to come and finish. What they will do to you fir—Ah!"

"Damn you, don't—"

Andrew gripped the Sikh's shoulder so hard that he bit a word in halves. "Those bandages," he said, "will do until this time tomorrow. Don't try to stand on 'em. My men shall set a box against the wall and sit you on it. After that, you shall talk."

"And you," the Sikh answered, "you—both of you—had better listen to me—and remember!"

CHAPTER 33

Bulah Singh sat back to the wall, like a war casualty, on a pony load of canned provisions, with his bandaged feet stretched out. Bompo Tsering, wary of Andrew's mood, and shrewdly aware of the safe way to keep on terms, unpacked a canvas chair for Elsa. He arranged it fussily, moving it to and fro, partly to draw attention to his thoughtfulness and partly to show off to the other Tibetans, who felt inferior because of his wonderful manners. Andrew ordered the load dragged up that the man in spectacles had wanted. He sat on it, beside Elsa; they faced Bulah Singh, with a semicircle of Tibetans behind them and the red firelight on their faces. The woman and boy were pushed out in the cold. She tried to force her way to the fireside, but Bulah Singh spoke to her sharply. Then she led the boy away and there was a gust of bitter wind as she opened the door. When the door slammed shut behind them Andrew got up and fastened it. He came back and sat down without saying a word. Bulah Singh broke the silence:

"Andrew—"

"My name's Gunning."

"Oh. On our dignity. You damned snob! See here, Gunning! If I hadn't guaranteed to Lan-dor-ling in Sikkim, and to the magician Lung-gom-pa, who owns this village, that you'd carry this opium safely to its destination—I said, to its destination!—either of two things inevitably must have happened to you. Arrest, in Sikkim—or death, here. Die here if you want to. Sign your warrant tonight." He glanced at Elsa. "And leave her to her fate."

"Not on your word," Andrew answered. He didn't glance at Elsa. He was hardly conscious of her sitting beside him. He was undergoing what was almost a new experience. He went on speaking, staring at Bulah Singh, through him and beyond him: "You were stopped at the village gate by a man you'd never seen before. A man with a beard who wore an Afghan turban. He scared you. But you got past him by

493

boasting you can manage me. That man gave you until nine tonight. It leaves you twenty minutes. I'm calling your bluff."

"I'm not bluffing," the Sikh answered.

Elsa spoke unexpectedly: "What you really mean is that Mr. Gunning is telling the truth and you can't deny it!"

Something—perhaps the falling fire, or it might be a pony's snort—something concrete brought Andrew back to his five senses. Things were suddenly normal. He saw the Sikh as he was, now, with his back to the wall; not as he had been, in the village gate at sunset. But it was a second more before it occurred to him that Elsa had been seeing things. He had seen Elsa's vision. He tried to repeat. He couldn't. He wanted another glimpse of that man at the gate; he was someone much more important than Bulah Singh. He had a face like Lenin of Russia, only that the beard hid his chin.

"Don't!" said Elsa. "Andrew, don't!"

"Don't what?"

"Don't try! You only break the image. It's like reflections on still water! Let it happen!"

Bulah Singh laughed. "Our Gunnigun becomes a god! That's what a woman does to us! Gunning, save your neck and make your fortune! You lucky devil, if I'd died on the mountain these villagers would have simply shot you and divided the loot. This is a stupid village. Fools are dangerous. It's thanks to me you're alive."

Andrew felt only contempt for him. He answered with a curt laugh: "Are they such fools as to fear a fugitive from justice who has lost his followers?"

It was Bulah Singh's turn to be contemptuous: "Justice? You believe in that stuff? Justice, I suppose, slew my men, eh? Divine justice! Oh well, perhaps you're right. Fear and treachery are two ponies that drag one *tonga*. My men were scared. They would have turned on me sooner or later. I'm well rid of them."

"And you've lost your baggage."

"That's nothing either. You can fit me out with what I need. If these villagers kill you, I'll take everything." He looked hard at Elsa again.

Andrew bridled at that. He consulted his watch: "Bulah Singh, you've about fifteen minutes. I've never actually killed a man. Unless you use your fifteen minutes more wisely than I've seen you do anything yet, you'll be Number One."

"Kill me? You?"

494

"Yes."

"Andrew Gunning, you have sentimental morals and grotesque scruples. They won't work. On this side of the border the prevailing sentiment is more natural. It resembles the Christly compassion of German concentration camps, Italian islands, French penal settlements and Russian labour colonies. Good standard stuff with no hypocrisy about it. You may have seen the Japs use some of it near Shanghai—or didn't you? These people, like the Japs, have adopted the little wooden testicle crusher that Mussolini borrowed from the Holy Roman Inquisition and taught the Nazis how to use. It beats anything the Chinese ever thought of—because, you see, the Chinese aren't really religious; they can't understand there's a space-time equation of pain—a limit beyond which the tortured can't feel. These Tibetans are religious; they don't waste torture; like Hitler's and Mussolini's and Franco's specialists, they can keep you alive for a couple of months, if need be, while you tell them all you know! You'll be surprised how much you know that you didn't know you knew."

"You've considerably less than fifteen minutes now," Andrew remarked.

"Bah. I doubt you'd shoot. You're fundamentally sentimental. That means you're cruel, and that at bottom you're a coward. Your indignation is an emotion, caused by fear of reality. Understand this, Andrew Gunning: either you agree to be my partner and we'll play this game together from now on—or else shoot me now and play your own game. Choose! Be quick about it! If you don't I guarantee you shall be tortured to death, and they'll make Elsa look on, just to educate her."

Andrew was seeing again—seeing Elsa's visions. He wished Elsa would let up. It made him angry to feel she could make him see. But anger banished the vision. He craved it back—couldn't see it—had to reach out mentally to her. Then there it was again, and along with it a revolting sensation that Bulah Singh could also see what they saw.

All the Tibetans were silent, almost motionless, except that Bompo Tsering kept steadily spinning a prayer wheel.

"Time's on the wing," said Andrew. "You have until nine sharp, by this watch, to plead your—"

"Huh! You mean to tell what I know! If I talk, do you promise to—"

"I promise nothing."

"Put it this way: if I promise to—"

"No. Your promise would be worthless. I wouldn't depend on it for

495

a second. I will form my own opinion of whatever you say and will treat you accordingly. Now go ahead."

They stared at each other. Bulah Singh looked as if he couldn't believe his own eyes and ears or believe Andrew's eyes and lips. Andrew didn't understand his own reaction. He was disturbed and he wasn't. He felt like two people; one was at a masthead, the other on deck at the wheel. The one on deck didn't quite trust or understand the other, but the other seemed to know, fading away, however, when the one on deck grew angry. So he kept trying to adjust two images, like a range finder laying a gun. The target was not Bulah Singh; it was something, within himself, that he couldn't clearly define through a cloud of anger. He knew Bulah Singh was talking again, but he only partially listened, without deep attention.

"Gunning, you damned idiot, in that bag you're sitting on there's enough opium to paralyse the brains of Tibet—the way the Japs are drugging the Chinese. It comes cheaper than money, because the addicts stay bought. It's better than soldiers. It's more efficient. It can't mutiny or run away. Drug the right man and you need no artillery. If you'd opened your bag you'd have found your own things have been thrown out. Lan-dor-ling did that. I ordered it. He filled your bag with opium. I picked up your stuff when I reached the border. It was on one of my ponies. It's down on the crags now along with all my dead men. That bag you're sitting on holds opium— nothing else. Opium. New. Fresh. Ten times stronger than the adulterated morphine and cocaine and *hashish* that the Japs are forcing on the Chinese."

He paused to make sure whether Andrew was listening, decided that he was, and continued:

"Now I'll tell you about that woman. And by the way, don't give her opium unless you want hell in your lap. That woman was my gift to the charlatan who owns this village. It was a gift with strings to it. She's a whore of hell. I said whore. I don't mean prostitute. Prostitution implies at least a trace of intention to keep a bargain. You can't prostitute whoredom. Below the minus sign there's nothing."

"You should know about that," said Andrew.

"Yes. It has been my business to find out. She is only a brood bitch and no longer any good even for that. I had her sterilized. It's the boy I wish to speak of. He annoyed you because you are prissy. But did you study him?"

Andrew thought about the boy. He didn't answer.

"Did Elsa study him? What did she think?"

496

"Her name is Mrs. Grayne," Andrew said pointedly. "Go on talking about your brat."

The Sikh answered with barbed malice: "The boy is a bastard who happened to live! You are a lawyer, and you'll happen to die unless you use your brains. Do you remember a couple of young murderers—they were rich people's sons—they made the headlines in all the newspapers in the world about twenty years ago? Or are you too young to remember that? One of your famous American lawyers saved them from the electric chair. All the police authorities and psychologists in the world studied those two young criminals. The priests who spoke of devils weren't so blindly stupid as the self-styled scientists who prattled about behaviourism and environment and heredity and glands and God knows what else. There never was worse pile than they've talked and written about those two young perverts. Everyone seemed to miss the point, except me. This boy of mine is younger than they were. You wouldn't believe how young he is. Physically, mentally and biologically super-precocious. Those young Americans were amateurs. My boy Chet is the perfect criminal!"

"You're too long-winded," said Andrew. "Time's almost up."

"I'm telling you, and I'm in no hurry," the Sikh answered. "My accomplishment took years. Be patient. I have used that woman as an instrument, for a specific purpose. I trained her, after she left the woman's jail in Darjeeling, where she was imprisoned for contributing to the delinquency of minors—plural—many minors. She had made a business of it. She was refractory—difficult—wilful. She had to be starved—whipped—disciplined. Finally I made her what she is now. It's her limit. There's no more there. She can go into a trance and reveal all secrets, though she herself can seldom understand what she reveals. As a medium she is *ne plus ultra,* if you know what that means. She is the ideal subject for hypnosis. No inhibitions, no moral restraints—no scruples! She can be made to do anything! Do you understand—anything!"

He paused, stared at Andrew, at Elsa, then spoke with the pride of a street astronomer who owns a homemade telescope that shows the dark deeps of the Milky Way:

"She was made to conceive, and to bring forth, and suckle, and wean, that boy, who—as I told you—is the perfect criminal! He is clairvoyant, clairaudient, hypnotic, a trance medium, a waking medium— a pervert, a homosexual—an intellectual, vicious in all imaginable ways, by all imaginable means. You couldn't possibly imagine

497

how vicious he is; you haven't enough imagination. He has intelligently cynical and incorruptible contempt for anything and everything whatever except his own desires and my will. I control him. He will always obey me. I am his God."

Elsa breathed quietly. Her eyes were closed and her hands were relaxed on the knobs of the chair-arms. Bompo Tsering was pop-eyed. He came forward and put fuel on the fire. The flame leaped and the ponies' eyes shone in the dark. Bulah Singh went on talking, attentively watching Elsa's face as if he doubted those closed eyes.

"You two have probably talked with Nancy Strong about the Virgin Mary giving birth to Jesus. You'd be surprised how many criminals believe that yarn—I mean the immaculate conception part of it. They pretend not to. But they do. Hypnotize 'em and they confess what they believe. It was as a student of criminology that I was interested; you can't possibly understand any criminal without a deep study of comparative superstitions—which is to say religions. Nancy Strong, if I understood her correctly when she tried to convert me, believes that such purity of spiritual love inspired Mary the Mother of Jesus that she conceived and became the mother of the greatest spiritual hero the world has ever known. Is that your understanding of her thought about it?"

"It's near enough," said Andrew. "But what are you driving at? Time's up."

"I don't have to drive at anything," said Bulah Singh. "I'm telling you. All things, and all ideas, have opposites. The opposites are equal, each to each. Black—white. Plus—minus. Above—below. Good—evil. Light—dark. Spirit—matter. God—devil. Jesus—and my bastard son Chet. Chet's mother's thought, at his conception, was as free from what is known as virtue as if it had been surgically sterilized. She was under full hypnosis. She had been commanded to conceive the perfect devil in human form. And she obeyed."

"Time's up," said Andrew, glancing at Elsa. He scowled, but his voice didn't betray emotion.

Bulah Singh began to speak faster: "As I told you in Darjeeling, I and my co-operators mean to capture the infant Dalai Lama—the uncontaminated infant Dalai Lama—who is being raised as a saint, poor little devil! I did not tell you, because I trusted you no more then than now—and you might have betrayed me then, but you can't now—that we will substitute my son Chet, who is a genuine devil, for the infant Dalai Lama, who is only a tin-horn saint. Do you see the significance? Your Christian pope may take a back seat. We will control the world's thought at its source!"

Bompo Tsering whirled his prayer wheel. Elsa spoke as if at that moment waking from a deep sleep:

"Andrew! Did you hear what he said?"

"Sure. I heard him."

"Bulah Singh! What do you mean? What are you thinking of doing—to the other child—to the infant *lama?*"

The Sikh grinned: "Oh—as for that—you may have him— when I'm through. Did you happen to notice that Lepcha servant at Nancy Strong's? He'll be like that, only rather more so. He won't remember much. Yes, yes, you may have him. But of course if you don't care to help, you can't expect us to—"

"You mean—"

"You know what I mean." The Sikh snapped his fingers. "That useless infant means no more to me than Barcelona babies mean to General Franco and his bombers—or than the hungry Ukrainian babies meant to Stalin."

"You said—if we don't care to help?"

"Yes. Take him or leave him. Save him or let him die."

There came a pounding on the door—not very loud—not importunate. It was the pounding of someone who knew he could not be refused, so was in no special hurry.

"Time now, anyway," said Andrew grimly. "We have reached no basis for an understanding, Bulah Singh."

"Oh yes, we have! You are a little stupid, that's all. I will explain it to you. I will make it quite clear."

The pounding on the door resumed, a little louder. Andrew addressed Bompo Tsering:

"Go and open that door. Let them enter, whoever they are."

Bompo Tsering didn't like it. He obeyed slowly—slowly— plucking the arm of another Tibetan to come and keep him company.

"It is this! It is this!" said Bulah Singh. "You, Andrew Gunning, have been chosen to help me because of your special ability. What you believe is your integrity is only frozen habit, but it will serve our purpose. You, Elsa—I beg pardon, of course I mean Mrs. Grayne!—you have been chosen because of your special faculties. I did not say talent. I said faculties. You can be developed, trained, and used. You shall be. You shall be allowed to reach Tom Grayne, since he is also necessary for our purpose."

Andrew interrupted loudly: "Bompo Tsering! Open that door! Let those people in!"

Bulah Singh continued: "As a reward you two may save the precious infant from the kites and ravens. If you wish to, you may have him. That is a promise. And, as a spur to your compliance with the requirements that are about to be brought to your notice—you are guaranteed that Tom Grayne, and you yourselves and the infant *lama* shall die in torment for the least infraction, mistake, or neglect to obey!—And now open that door!"

CHAPTER 34

A dark procession entered, ushered by freezing wind that whirled the smoke and made the ponies restless. It was led by a hooded man with a lantern. He had been instructed. He knew what to do. He hung the lantern from a peg on one of the low roof beams and stood still beneath it with folded arms, about fifteen feet away from Andrew. The wavering shadows made him look like one of Torquemada's men. Two more, who also looked like phantom Dominicans, followed and stood behind him, facing the row of ponies.

Andrew stood up, expecting the magician Lung-gom-pa. But the magician lingered unexplainably among armed brigands in the dark near the door; there was no doubt who he was, but he was only just visible—a looming, lurking, massive presence, furtive and secretive; a bell tinkled faintly when he moved. The man who came forward to meet Andrew was no Tibetan. His beard and the way he carried his head reminded Andrew of the portrait of Sir Richard Burton, in his copy of the famous forbidden pilgrimage to Mecca and Medina. But he also more than vaguely resembled Lenin of Russia. His eyes were larger and darker than Lenin's, but he had similar high cheek bones, some of Lenin's gestures, some of Lenin's rhinoceros-hided arrogance that couldn't imagine itself mistaken. He had Lenin's way of sticking his fist in his right-hand pocket. But on the whole he looked more like Sir Richard Burton, perhaps because of the Afghan turban, which suited him and made him look scholarly. He wore a long, well-fitting fur-lined overcoat. He wasn't nearly as tall as Andrew. He halted some paces away, so as not to have to look up.

Andrew spoke abruptly, just to start something: "How do you do."

Elsa turned to look. Andrew touched her shoulder. She looked away again.

The man in the Afghan turban answered with what might be a

smile, or it might have been the natural wryness of his mouth that twisted when he spoke: "How do you do."

Two Tibetans emerged out of the shadows carrying a short heavy bench—set it down between Andrew and Bulah Singh, spread cushions on it, and withdrew. The door slammed shut. It grew suddenly warmer. The smoke ceased whirling and making the ponies snort. By that time there were not less than thirty people in the room, including Andrew's men, but most of them were in the dark at the far end. They were all silent. The only noticeable noise was when the ponies stamped and snorted. One squealed.

"Are you Andrew Gunning?"

"Yes. Who are you?"

"I came a long way to wait here for you. I am not an oriental, although my turban may have led you to think so. My name is Oliver Blessingwell."

Andrew answered in a low voice: "You wish me to pretend to believe that? Is it your *alias?*"

"Sir?"

"Your real name," said Andrew, "is Major Hugo von Klaus. You were attached to the Turkish command in Jerusalem in 1915 with Djemal Pasha."

"That is a long time ago," said the German.

"You were transferred to the diplomatic service after the Armistice and went to Kabul. From there to China. Later to Japan. One of your occasional correspondents calls himself Ambrose St. Malo."

Major von Klaus managed to disguise his annoyance, but the effort was noticeable. He smiled, but his smile was slow, it had to be forced. "You appear to be curiously well informed. Are you a medium? If so, that stuff, let me warn you, is far from reliable—especially in this land of tricky magicians."

Andrew felt he had the upper hand and was resolved to keep it, masking his thought and not answering what he did not choose to answer. He had never unlearned the American habit of introducing people to each other. It served his purpose now. He half turned toward Elsa.

"Since we know each other's real names, I'll introduce you to Mrs. Grayne."

Major von Klaus looked incredulous: "Grayne? You said Mrs. Grayne? Am I mistaken? Is her name not Elsa Burbage?"

"I told you her right name. Elsa, this is Major von Klaus. He's an orientalist. He should be famous."

Bulah Singh chuckled: "Isn't the right word notorious?"

Major von Klaus ignored Bulah Singh. He bowed stiffly.

"How do you do," said Elsa. "Won't you be seated?" She didn't smile. She was aware of Andrew's tenseness and of the fact that Andrew expected violence at any moment without previous warning.

Von Klaus moved around Andrew, walking as if he wore tight military boots, although his feet were actually encased in comfortable felt. His head hung forward a little when he didn't remember to hold it upright, as if the turban, or else his brain, were too heavy. He sat down on the bench. A Tibetan menial approached from the shadows and wrapped a heavy woolen shawl around his shoulders. Bompo Tsering, feeling that Andrew needed an equivalent attention, came forward and put fuel on the fire. Major von Klaus observed Bompo Tsering, appeared to study him:

"Your man?"

"My foreman," said Andrew.

"And those others?"

"Yes, those are my men."

"Shall we excuse them? I would like a conversation with you."

"Very well. Send your own men away and I'll dismiss mine."

Andrew noticed a heavy ring on the middle finger of the German's right hand as he gestured to command privacy. That is the rarest thing in Tibet, but he was promptly obeyed. The three solemnities under the lantern retired backwards in token of almost religious respect. Andrew ordered Bompo Tsering away into the dark behind the ponies. The others followed Bompo Tsering.

"I believe you've already met Bulah Singh," said Andrew.

The German nodded. He glanced coldly at Bulah Singh but didn't speak. Then he studied Elsa, governing his face, muscle by muscle, until he had it set in a smile that would have passed muster, beyond footlights, as a symbol of the velvet glove on an iron hand. It was as diplomatic as the edge of a knife or the back of an axe.

"I know all about you," he said pleasantly. "Have you enjoyed your journey thus far?"

Elsa surprised them all, herself included. She enraged von Klaus. "If you know so much, why do you ask?"

Bulah Singh laughed. That provided the German with a scapegoat for his anger. He turned on the Sikh:

"As for you," he said savagely, "I warned you that the slightest—"

502

Bulah Singh interrupted. "Yes, and I warned you! Must I say it in German? There's no one but Andrew Gunning who can manage the girl. And there's no one but me who can deal with him. If you insist on acting like one of Hitler's bullies, we'll all have to shoot each other to avoid being tortured to death."

Von Klaus scowled at him: "Silence, you clown!"

"You go to hell," said the Sikh.

"Oh, very well." The German tugged at his beard with his left hand. His right tapped at his overcoat pocket.

"Bulah Singh has been disarmed," Andrew remarked quietly. "Shooting him would be murder. I forbid it."

The German pretended not to have heard the word "forbid." He peered toward the door. "Yes. Murder is unpleasant. We'll let Lung-gom-pa deal with him."

"No," said Andrew. "I protect Bulah Singh. I told him he could come to me, day or night."

"He put it in writing," the Sikh added. His eyes blazed with excitement. "I have it here in my pocket."

The German controlled his anger with an effort. "Are you aware," he asked Andrew, "that this *schweinehund*, Bulah Singh has been betraying you right and left for the last several months?"

"Yes," said Andrew, "I know all about him."

"Did you know he has offered for sale this girl whom you introduced to me just now as Mrs. Grayne? You said Grayne, didn't you? I happen to know her name is Elsa Burbage." He let a sneer into his voice. "Why not call her Mrs. Andrew Gunning?"

"Suppose you try it just once and see what happens," Andrew suggested. "Mrs. Grayne needs no character reference from me. But she gets no gratuitous insults while I'm around. Are those your own teeth?"

"*Tsch-tsch!* We are getting nowhere," said the German. "We are wasting time. Let us send this Sikh policeman away."

"He can't walk."

"He can be carried."

"No. He stays here. I won't have him tortured. I don't trust him. But I don't trust you either."

"Gunning," said Bulah Singh, "tell your man Bompo Tsering to give me back my automatic. Then you and I can control this situation."

"I control it now," Andrew answered. "I don't need your help, or your advice. Sit still and don't interrupt."

The German tried to be tactful: "Come now! Come now! Let us all talk sensibly!"

"About opium?" Andrew asked. He wasn't trying to be tactful, he was just plain belligerent.

"Yes, among other things. Why not? Let us speak of the opium first"

"Okay. Talk," said Andrew. "But let me warn you. Among other reasons, I left America because I didn't choose to defend in court a son of a bitch who'd been peddling drugs. I could have got him off. I wouldn't. Now you've a line on my point of view, so spill the beans."

"Can't we be polite to each other? I wish to speak impersonally," said the German.

"Can't be done," said Andrew. "The hell with that boloney. I'm one person. You're another. I've a personal opinion of you that 'ud file the rough off gray iron."

"But *Gott im Himmel,* what do you know about me?"

Suddenly Andrew knew that he no longer knew in any ordinary meaning of the word. He hadn't been guessing. He had seen. Now he could no longer see. Less than a second ago he had seen clearly that Major von Klaus intended to become Bulah Singh's substitute—to get rid of Bulah Singh, by turning him over to Lung-gom-pa, and to come in his place on the expedition. He still knew it, because he had seen and remembered. But it tongue-tied him for the moment to realise he had no evidence. Von Klaus laughed, letting Andrew know that he understood Andrew's difficulty. Then he tried to smile pleasantly, offering a lie that should serve like oil on troubled water; but a scar twisted his lips so that the smile passed through a sneer and out again—twice—going and coming.

"Andrew Gunning," he said, "don't you think that perhaps the altitude, and exhaustion, and the natural emotion due to a sensation of danger, may have unsteadied your thought?"

Andrew recognized the motive behind the question. "I'm thinking about you and this opium that I'm sitting on," he answered. "My thought's steady enough. It isn't tricky either. I'm not a diplomat."

Bulah Singh thrust straight ahead into that opening. "You fool!" he said to the German. "You conceited ignoramus! Do you think Gunning can't see through such puerile attempts to steal his confidence? I told you at the gate—he resisted all my attempts to hypnotize him. I can't read his thought, except when he's off guard, and that's rarely. So

I'm damned if you can with your stodgy German method. Compared to me, you're a neophyte— a *lehrling!* Stop wasting time!"

"I will speak to the lady," von Klaus answered. A look of disciplined cunning stole over his face. Like many and many a middle-aged diplomat he evidently thought himself a charmer of women when he could give his mind to it. But Elsa surprised him again:

"Please don't!" she exclaimed. "Please don't! I'm busy!"

Her head was resting on the canvas chair-back. Her eyes were shut; the lids looked dark blue in the shadow of leaping firelight. Von Klaus leaned eagerly toward her.

"Can she be conscious on two planes! Elsa! Tell what you see! I command you! Tell what you see!"

Andrew growled at him: "You keep away! Do you hear! Keep your distance!"

Bulah Singh sneered: "She won't tell you! There's only one person she will tell. Von Klaus, you'd better take a back seat and leave this to me."

Von Klaus, showing his aging teeth through scarred lips, stared at Elsa and then at Andrew. Andrew was seeing again—seeing what Elsa saw. First he saw the Lama Gombaria in his sky-high Sikkim monastery. But for a moment he looked like Morgan Lewis—then it wasn't Lewis, it was Nancy Strong, on a chair at someone's bedside. He supposed that was Father Patrick, at the Jesuit Mission; there was a crucifix on the wall. Nancy Strong looked up—straight at Andrew—and grew larger—nearer—changing as she came. She grew hideous. He didn't recognize her, until suddenly he remembered the bullet-broken photograph of the Ringding Gelong Lama Lobsang Pun—Old Ugly-face. It was he. The face became a maze of wrinkles, nodded. The nose like an owl's beak twitched. Pure gold, like the background of a Russian icon only brighter than the sun, began to frame the face, until it changed and for a fragment of a second became splendid. Then it smiled and was gone.

"They are both of them seeing the man whom we want," remarked Bulah Singh in a voice so harsh that it creaked. "The man only sees him. The girl is talking with him!"

The German's voice was as quiet and as earnestly kind as if he were coaxing a child: "Tell what you see! Tell what he said! Elsa! I am your friend! You tell me!"

Elsa sat upright suddenly. She and Andrew looked at each other, questioning. Andrew nodded. Elsa smiled happily.

"Andrew! You saw? You did see?"

Andrew nodded again: "Seemed to me that he gave us the green light."

"You believe it!"

Andrew nodded. "But I never believe what I believe," he added. "I've got to know. How does one find out?"

A bell tinkled, in the dark near the wall at the far end. Something rattled. Bompo Tsering howled on a high note. He and all Andrew's Tibetans knelt and laid their foreheads on the floor. The bell tinkled again, in time to slow footsteps, coming. Gradually, developing like a photographic image on a film, the black magician Lung-gom-pa, the ruler of the village, moved forward toward the firelight. He seemed almost to float on air, effortless.

Chapter 35

Lung-gom-pa the magician approached slowly, with solemn dignity. Thought moved as swiftly as light. The solemnity made no impression on Andrew. The dignity did. The handsome, professional mystery man—his high-cheeked, slant-eyed, dark face reddened by the firelight—stared at Andrew, disguising thought with experienced skill. There was a faint smile on his lips. It was a lie. But it looked good. It suggested scorn so insolent, and secret knowledge so lofty and sure, that there was no need to let lower emotions enter in. He could afford, said the smile, that rare gift, inscrutable patience. But it wasn't patience. It was suspicion, on the horns of a dilemma that the magician did not understand.

Neither did Andrew understand it. But he had studied juries in Ohio, learning to choose and reject by intuition. And he had learned to watch witnesses. He had become very skilful at detecting a lie and its motive. He was no more deceived by the magician's smile than he was awed by the long necklace of miniature skulls carved from human bone, strung on human sinew.

He observed the magician's cunning eyes, that saw cunning where none was. Asceticism, that had made the man lean, couldn't hide the sensuous greed on nose and lips. It couldn't mask his baffled yearning for the luxury of more, and more secret power. Barring toughness of skin, colour, and some pockmarks, Andrew had seen dozens of faces like that one—politicians' faces—white faces of bosses and men of affairs—near enough like it, posing as resolute, patient, farseeing, spiritually informed and very worldly wise—all phonies. He remembered, for instance, an unfrocked priest—

That wouldn't do! Thought was going wandering along tangential planes of memory. He had to bring himself back with a jerk. The wandering was partly Elsa's doing. But he hadn't time to nurse resentment, although he felt it. Elsa sat with the palms of her hands cupped on the knobs of the chair-arms and her head resting on the canvas back. Her eyes weren't quite closed. Her lips, too, were slightly parted. She was conscious and, he felt sure of it, unafraid. She was inviting the state of consciousness that formerly she loathed. It was there. Like a high voltage current of electricity, it set up a kind of induced awareness in Andrew. Assurance overflowed from her and reached him, so that he knew he owed to her at least some of his own self-confidence. He felt no fear of doing the wrong thing—of saying the wrong word. But he knew, without knowing how he knew, that Bulah Singh, with his back to the wall, was making mental experiments to produce a crisis in which to snatch an opportune advantage for himself. The air was loaded with Bulah Singh's anarchic effort. All the Tibetans in the room, including Andrew's own men, were in a state of expectant terror, breathing through their noses. Their bets were on Lung-gom-pa and his magic.

The German von Klaus was less easy to understand. But there were sudden true glimpses of him also. Elsa's mind became a momentary mirror, in which the man himself betrayed himself—not consciously afraid, but pseudo-philosophically justifying boldness by recalling previous success. Heil Hitler! There were memory glimpses of von Klaus in uniform—snatches of visions of clever von Klaus the diplomat, prevailing by treachery over fools who kept faith and perished on the hooks of an ideal. His drilled brain was crowded with instances preserved like pickled specimens in realistic scorn.

So there was a kind of war going on in the realm of thought, all at cross-purposes, in which the black magician was likely to snatch the upper hand. It was his village. He owned it. He was used to obedience, awe, if not respect. Why shouldn't he use violence to regain "face" that he had evidently lost to von Klaus? Somehow the German must have tricked him into submission— promising, no doubt, wonderful things. But where were the things? An unkept or a postponed promise is humiliating, and humiliation stings. He was cunning enough to pretend an indignation that he did not feel. All despots use that expedient. He could work himself up into screaming hysteria. And in that mood he could kill. He was half minded to do it. In his eyes was fear of being understood—fear of being found out. Fear, and cruelty.

"Leave him to me!" von Klaus whispered. "I understand him."

The sensation of time returned then. It was a shock: two simultaneous states of consciousness—of thought and of action—of being and of doing; the one timeless, the other bound and limited by time and space. Thought took no more time than firelight needed leaping from eye to eye. And now Andrew did feel panic. He was afraid of that dual consciousness. One thing or the other! He chose! He struck so swiftly for his self-control that Elsa sat bolt upright, scared, as if something hit her. His spastic plunge back to the concrete realm of things made Bulah Singh breathe sibilantly through his teeth. The magician Lung-gom-pa, whose false name falsely claimed that he could walk without wings on the empty air, stared—stared hard; the magician feared concrete reality more than Andrew dreaded swamps of abstract dreaming. The magician glanced from Andrew—to von Klaus—to Elsa—back to Andrew. Andrew spoke, in English, aiming his words at Elsa. It was an ultimatum to Lung-gom-pa. But to her also, although he didn't look at her.

"Silence! Don't risk speech until you know my will!"

Strange words. Elsa translated them, slowly, accurately. The magician thrust out his lower lip in perplexity. It was like an animal's. He flicked his rosary of skulls. Von Klaus whispered:

"*Sind Sie wahnsinnig? Wenn Sie*—I mean, if you offend him, you undo all that I did! He will—"

Andrew ignored von Klaus. It was deliberate. He was playing a no-trump hand for every point it held, and one point was to snub and irritate the German. So he kept his eyes on Lung-gom-pa. His own were calm, with the assumed indifference that sometimes angers, always arouses weakness to declare itself. Unhurried, speaking without emphasis, he kept the initiative:

"I intend to leave with you some ponies I no longer need. But where are the yaks you promised? Where are the sheep?"

Elsa repeated the words in Tibetan. The magician stared, astonished. Von Klaus whispered:

"*Teufelszeug!* Spoiling my influence? See here, you! Why didn't you warn me you have had communication with him!"

Andrew again ignored von Klaus. Without giving the magician time to answer, subtly he suggested to him how to save face:

"If you should speak to me before all these witnesses, how will you justify your own conduct? How will you explain why you have housed us in a shed with the animals? Why did you send your under-lings to seize my baggage? If I had let them take the bag that I sit on, your people would have mocked you when they saw its contents. But I saved you from that."

He paused to let Elsa translate. She did it low-voiced. Tibetan faces craned forward from the shadows, but none could catch the words. The magician stared at Elsa, then at Bula Singh, then at Andrew.

Von Klaus whispered: "You don't understand these people! There's no use lying about the contents of a bag that he can open when he chooses! He knows what's in it!"

"That's more than you know," Andrew retorted.

The magician was speaking to Elsa. Von Klaus suddenly flew into a rage, grabbed Andrew's arm and ground out words like chopped meat:

"Fool! Ten thousand miles in three months I have come for what that bag contains! Three weeks I have waited in this stinking village! Don't waste lies on me! Don't you know what's in it?"

Andrew shook him off roughly and thrust him aside, timing the insult so that the magician saw. He turned to Elsa:

"What does he say?"

"He invites us to his house. But he says we should bring the bag you're sitting on. He asks, shall his men carry it."

"Tell him no. My man shall bring it."

"Andrew, I think you're—"

Andrew's cold smile interrupted her. She almost bit a word in two, reddening, recognizing the end of Andrew's patience. He wasn't ask-ing advice. He was giving orders.

"Kindly tell him—" the word "kindly" cut. It was the cold ve-neer on anger. "Kindly tell him we'll leave Bulah Singh with my man Bompo Tsering. Say this German may come with us. The magician is to order all his own followers out of the shed. They're to stay out until daylight."

Elsa turned to interpret. Again von Klaus seized Andrew's arm.

"Andrew Gunning, if you think you can treat me like this, I can assure you—"

"Oh, heil Hitler!"

Andrew shoved him away and stood between him and Lung-gom-pa, who was listening to Elsa. The magician was hardly believing his own ears— hardly believing that a white woman could talk such flu-ent Tibetan. Could she be white? Was she a devil in human form?—

He hardly believed that even devils from the unknown world beyond the mountains could dare to order him around as this girl was doing. Was she really translating Andrew's words? Or—

Andrew beckoned Bompo Tsering. He came in a hurry, all eyes and ears, craving gossip, explanations, confidences. What he got was commands:

"Watch Bulah Singh. Give him blankets. Let him sleep if he pleases. But guard him closely. Answer no questions. All but one of you are to wait here until further orders. Do you understand?"

"My understanding. My obeying."

"Select one of our men who knows no English. Pick the stupidest man. Tell him to pick up this bag I've been sitting on and come with me and the German and Lady Elsa."

"That bag being heavy, better my doing it."

"Do as I tell you!"

Von Klaus ceased protesting. It was useless. In an effort to steal a march on Andrew he hurried after Lung-gom-pa, who strode out of the shed without saying a word. Andrew waited with Elsa until all the magician's men had disappeared into the night, following their master. Then he repeated his orders to Bompo Tsering, and tossed one crumb of comfort to Bulah Singh:

"I've no bargain with you! But if you make no trouble for me behind my back, you're likely to regret it less than if you act up! Is that clear?"

"Yes," the Sikh answered. "As one man to another, you may go to hell. If I could ditch you I'd love it. But that German will do you in. If he doesn't the magician will. You'll be eaten by dogs by and by. I wish you joy of it."

Andrew laughed and turned his back, calling over his shoulder to Bompo Tsering to lock the door on the inside. He liked Bulah Singh better in that mood than in any other. It was at least honest. Outside the door, in the dark, he waited until he heard Bompo Tsering shoot the heavy bolt on the inside. Then he glanced upward, once, briefly, at the starlit sky and strode forward through stinking gloom, over frozen filth, to where a lantern glowed in the dim near distance. Elsa kept step with him.

"Andrew."

"Yes?"

"Von Klaus is trying to persuade Lung-gom-pa that we're too treacherous to be let live."

510

"Yes. I know. Plastering us with his own paint. That's the mark of the beast. They all do it. We'll feel his teeth presently."

Elsa detected his irritation. "Oh well—as long as you know."

"Our one chance," he said, "is to be sudden, surprising, unexpected."

He would have liked to ask Elsa to let him alone. He was more than ever uneasy about her clairvoyance. There was something contagious in it. It seemed likely to transmute his own strength of decision into something feminine that had no edges and that merely let things happen. But he could think of no phrase that wouldn't hurt. He had a vaguely grim foreboding that she was going to be hurt soon and badly. He laid his hand on her shoulder, guiding her through the dark.

"Andrew.—Did Lung-gom-pa really promise yaks and—"

"No. I said that to puzzle him—"

"I think it did."

"—and to rattle von Klaus."

"It made von Klaus furious. Now he thinks we are here on purpose to—"

"I may have to break von Klaus, or he'll break us. But it's true we need yaks and sheep, from here on."

"From here on? If!" said Elsa.

"You? Talking about if? Can't you see ahead?"

"Not now. I see nothing now. Only that awful mother of the brat! I see her eyes in the dark—and the boy's eyes!"

Andrew answered calmly: "I will shoot her if she butts in."

"Andrew—don't start things!"

"They're already started. Watch that lantern and walk forward. I won't let you fall. Here—take my arm. There, is that better?"

"Thanks—Andrew! We're in deadly danger—from all around—all sides—everyone."

"I know."

"Even Bompo Tsering."

"Watch your step now. There's a hole here—a bad one."

"Haven't you a flashlight?"

"Yes. But the light might make someone's aim too easy. Hang on to me. We're pretty near now."

"Andrew, I feel certain von Klaus has a trap that he means to spring on us.—Oh! Look! What's that? Who is it?"

"That's our own man, carrying my bag, waiting for us in the shadow."

511

"Andrew, is the bag really full of opium?"

"They all think it is."

"But is it?"

"See here." He had almost lost patience. "What was I doing, that night in the pass, on this side of the summit—that last night, before we knew Bulah Singh was behind us?"

"You said—you redistributed—a load—to save the ponies. Didn't you?"

"I dumped the opium."

"You knew it was in the bag? You knew it then?"

"Sure."

"I didn't. Andrew, how did you find out? You hadn't opened that bag! Could you see? Were you—"

"I used my eyes. I had to look like hell the other way while the Sikkim trader pulled the trick. There had to be some good reason why he—"

"Andrew! What'll these people do when they discover we haven't got their opium?"

"Leave that to me."

"But—"

There was nothing else for it. He halted suddenly, almost within the light-zone of the lantern. He turned, faced, met her eyes. They could just see each other.

"Will you do me a favour?"

"Yes, Andrew. What do you wish me to do? What is it?"

"Pipe down. That's all. Cut that hysterical stuff. Leave this to me."

"But, Andrew—"

"I wonder whether I could say it plainer!—How'll this do: are you and I friends? Then for God's sake act friendly and let me do my own thinking!"

She was silent.

He spoke more gently: "I said we're friends. I mean it. Each do our own thinking. Now then—through that narrow door as if we owned the place—leave the showdown to me!"

Chapter 36

Thought took no time; agony no space. Elsa took four steps forward, toward the lamplit door of the magician's dwelling. Andrew's left hand pressed her shoulder blades. His right hand gripped an automatic inside his overcoat. Within the compass of four strides, a whole world changed—a universe! A state of consciousness, in which all universes lived because there is nowhere else for them, became a dismal wilderness. There is no pain like disillusion. Faith had failed. Cut that hysterical stuff! Andrew's hand on her back was meant to reassure! Whom? Of what? There was nothing left.

Four steps forward—toward a lamplit door, over frozen filth, amid the buttery reek of almost invisible Tibetans who crowded the dark alley. There was a sound of frozen leather rubbing against leather, and of rifle swivels, and of hard breathing. There were glimpses of eyes that craved and expected presently to see victims slowly done to death. Those watchers knew their magician—knew what to expect, what to demand of him. Like life itself, he would amuse himself; but he would presently pass judgment and impose death, for his own importance and their pleasure. Then the watchers would feel for a while like their imagined old deathless gods of Tibet, who await the end of the day of Buddha and the coming of the new cruel night of Bon. Cruel gods. Cruelty—the delicious dreadful stuff that flatters slaves and lends authority to tyrants, who are slaves' high priests. Cruelty! The passion distinguishing man from beast—since only man loves, invents, applies, enjoys cruelty. Man, the creator and image of all the gods!

First they'd see bleached terror in the victims' eyes, artfully increased—the hope encouraged for a moment, teased, falsely fed—contemptuously mocked and killed. Then presently, the horror of humiliation—the lewd stripping—the gloating and laughter. Last, the ingenious, traditional, physical torture. All torture is traditional. Elsa had seen some of it. She had seen a Tibetan woman half beaten to death and then pegged out hand and foot, naked to frost and sun, to die of thirst. She knew what those eyes in the dark expected, gloated for—nakedness, ritual, lechery, blood. She and Andrew were to be sacrificed like bulls in a Spanish ring; like Franco's, Hitler's, Mussolini's, Stalin's prisoners; like martyrs condemned by holy church and given to be burned by creatures of the lower law.

There would be nothing new about it. Sickening. But not new. Bestial, but no worse than the fate of hundreds and thousands of men and women who wage wars for the devils who die in bed. It would be only physical. It couldn't hurt worse than Andrew's snub—than the politeness of Andrew's hand between her shoulder blades. It would be a different pain, that was all.

Four steps forward—alone. Now utterly alone. Andrew had understood her. He had seen her soul, and she his. But Andrew had turned,

513

gone, withdrawn to a polite, cold distance. The stab of a knife in her heart would have felt less cruel. A "great gulf fixed" had revealed itself, wide between her and the only one friend she had ever known. It was like a headlong fall from heaven into hell. Never—never—never—never again would she reach for Andrew's soul to share her own soul's overflow! Hers overflowed no longer! It had died, that instant, and all comfort with it, as the buds die in a chill wind. Dead—dead—dead—dead. Disillusioned. Andrew's hand between her shoulder blades. In the dark. Never, never, never, never! Nancy's stuff was—

Suddenly she saw Nancy!—Nancy's fireside, in Darjeeling! And the cat—why the cat?—Then Lobsang Pun's broken photograph—the Jesuit Mission—Gombaria—the rock-hewn chamber of initiation! Reality! Timeless! Spaceless! Between the fourth step, and the fifth on to the threshold of the black magician's dwelling, she lived an eternity—saw, felt, experienced again the vision of Old Ugly-face, golden, as old as the world, and as young as new morning not yet risen. Blasphemy died before it reached her lips. She heard other words:

The Lord is my shepherd,
I shall not want—

Nancy's voice? Her own? Lobsang Pun's? Andrew's? It couldn't be Andrew's! Hers? Her heart was in her throat. She hadn't spoken. She couldn't have. Her senses failed, reeling in their own sensation. Had she fallen? Had she died? No—Andrew's arm was around her. She was being carried—forward into the dark. She was no longer afraid. But it wasn't fearlessness, it was something positive. It was a warming overwhelming faith. It flowed upon her, until she felt like drowning now in floods of strength, not weakness. Whose strength? Surely not hers!

After an eternity that knew no time, she found herself seated on Andrew's bag, with her back to the wall of a square room. There was reddish light from a charcoal brazier, but there were also two oil lanterns on the floor. Andrew's porter—the big, stupid lad who knew no English— squatted near her, nine parts terrified, one part curious, slobber drooling from his lips, his fingers clutching a charm against magic. Andrew's back was blood-red in the brazier light. He faced von Klaus. The German's back was toward an inner door, that was guarded by two flat-faced Tibetans who loafed on their rifles, the butts resting on their heavy, fur-lined boots. There were two other men in the room, both Tibetans, facing each other, seated on cushions against opposite walls. One was the spectacled man who had first demanded

Andrew's bag; he looked angry and humiliated. The other, too, was an educated-looking person but of much more powerful physique. There were paintings of hell on the walls, very well painted; they looked like plunder from a monastery. On the inner door there was pictured a cross-eyed woman with naked breasts, whose protruding tongue was a forked flame.

Von Klaus scowled at Andrew. It was like an ancient Chinese battle picture, each opponent striving to outface the other with mental power, before condescending to such weapons as mere murderers use. Andrew was smiling; he didn't seem so strained as the German. It suddenly dawned on Elsa that Andrew's thought reached higher than her own. It was more true, less scattered, it had purpose! She watched, listened, spell-bound. The German spoke first:

"Shoot! But if you do, you're done for. I was here first. I dealt the cards."

Andrew answered in a level voice: "If I find you're worth killing, I'll do it. I won't wait for your permission."

The German jerked his head in the direction of a steel bear trap. It hung from a heavy chain on a wall. All the Tibetans smiled.

"I intended," said the German, "to employ you, at good pay. You'd be no good with that thing snapped on to your ankle. Please yourself. This so-called magician Lung-gom-pa will let you continue your journey, in my service, under my direction, if—"

"If what?"

Von Klaus glanced at Elsa. "If I demand it. But I require a hostage for your behavior. That is simple enough. Leave her here."

He paused, expecting a retort. But Andrew waited for him to continue. Elsa suddenly saw Bulah Singh's face as clearly as if he were there in the room. It was the German's lips that moved, but it might almost be Bulah Singh's voice that continued:

"She will be well treated. We won't need her. She would be in the way. We will take with us that other woman and her child."

"You didn't think of that," said Andrew. He glanced slowly around the room.

The German, still watching Elsa's face, retorted: "Never mind who first thought of it. Good plans have many makers. The point is organisation—cooperation. Agree! Then we will talk—"

Andrew interrupted: "You'll talk now. Go and sit down—on that cushion beside the wall—that one—over there—near the man in spectacles."

Beneath his beard the German's face muscles hardened. His nostrils narrowed. "I will stand—here."

"Go and sit on that cushion. I won't warn you again."

The man in spectacles coughed suddenly. Von Klaus turned to appeal to him. But with the side of his eye he noticed Andrew's left fist. He shrugged his shoulders—went and sat down. From then on he had to look up to Andrew. The floor is not an easy position from which to impose one's will. "Sit beside me," he suggested. "There is room." He patted the wide cushion.

"Give me your weapons," Andrew answered, observing that the Tibetans smiled. It was even possible that they understood some English.

Von Klaus moved both hands simultaneously to divide Andrew's attention. He acted the ancient trick rather well, but he underestimated Andrew's quickness. He was too academic. He knew the rules too well. One could see the trick coming. Andrew kicked his wrist. The Luger went off inside his overcoat. The bullet missed Elsa by not much margin—buried itself in the wall, in the dry mud between two lumps of rough-hewn masonry. The German yelped. He was in real pain:

"Blast you! You broke my wrist!"

"Swell. If you move, I'll kick it again."

The man in spectacles seemed to be the senior Tibetan in the room. Andrew beckoned him. But he was either in disgrace, or afraid, or unfriendly; he pretended not to understand. Instead, one of the inner door guards came, smiling. He certainly did understand. He leaned over von Klaus, searched him with quick professional skill, removed a Luger and one reload, stowed them in his *bokkus* and smiled at Andrew. Then he held out his right hand.

Von Klaus sneered through shut teeth: "Now you've done it! This is the end of us all—and it's your fault!"

The Tibetan door guard made a threatening gesture toward the bear trap. He made signs to Andrew to surrender his pistol.

"You blundering idiot!" said the German. "*Schafskopf!*"

Andrew stepped backward, two paces, half turning his head. He raised his voice a trifle but spoke calmly:

"Elsa."

"Yes, Andrew."

"It's getting hot. If it gets too hot, keep quite still, so that I can kill you with the first shot."

Timeless, spaceless, instantaneous experience poured into Elsa's consciousness. She knew, suddenly, once and for all that death was nothing to be feared. But she knew more. She knew terribly more. The swift thought of Andrew's bullet was a physical sensation, sweet and strong, like being kissed between the breasts. She almost fainted of it. No act of will, but Reality, like light in the dark and life in death, forced her to yearn, with her whole being, to be slain by Andrew. So she knew she loved him, and knew there is no death. Her breast thrilled naked to his bullet. Loving-kindness outflowed from her to him. But she governed herself. She answered in a rather hard voice:

"Very well, Andrew."

He turned his back. For a moment she lowered her head, crossing her hands on her breast, steeling herself, to keep her new secret hidden. It was so truly new that it bewildered her. She hadn't known it yet ten seconds. They were ten eternities. She had believed she and Andrew were friends, just good friends. But Andrew had spoken ten words, and her heart had melted. O God. Never, never and forever should Andrew know she loved him. He didn't love her. Why should he? Generosity might make him say he did, if she let him guess her secret. Never, never.

"Thy kingdom come. Thy will be done.

"O God, have I the strength to—"

Andrew spoke suddenly, mispronouncing Tibetan: "Go back to your post at the door!"

The Tibetan door guard hesitated. He glanced again at the bear trap on the wall.

Von Klaus spoke, in German: "For God's sake, man, give him your pistol before he summons help. You can't do anything. If you shoot him, there are fifty worse ones outside! They'll put us both together into that trap. Then they'll turn Bulah Singh's woman loose on us! Can't you guess what—"

Andrew interrupted, not taking his eyes off the Tibetan's: "Elsa!"

"Yes, Andrew."

"In case I have to shoot you, goodbye."

She didn't answer. If there isn't death, there's no goodbye, so why pretend? She watched him. By some almost invisible trick of eye or hand he led the Tibetan's attention to his left fist. It was at about the level of his waist, ready for a pile-driver blow. The Tibetan saw it and smiled and backed away—all the way back to the door, where he stood at ill-drilled attention beside his comrade, beaten for the time being. Andrew took no more notice of him; he turned on von Klaus:

517

"Now your turn. Talk."

The German sat belligerently silent. Elsa tried to be clairvoyant, to be a mirror of the German's thought for Andrew to read. Suddenly she remembered: Andrew had forbidden! She mustn't!—had sworn she wouldn't! Each do our own thinking. Leave this to me! She tried then, loyally, with all her might, to be a numb, dumb witness and let Andrew play his hand uninterfered with. It was too late. She was seeing—seeing. She saw the red-shot bronze of the German's aura, like a beast's at bay, angry and cunning. She saw the desperate steely gray of Andrew's fear to do wrong and the brilliance of his resolution to do right. He was divided against himself. But she remembered his motto, on the book-plate in his copy of *Paradise Lost*: *Facias rem*, Andrew would not do nothing.

Then, suddenly, she knew that the magician Lung-gom-pa was watching. Did Andrew know it? She could see no peephole in the wall, nor in the door behind the Tibetan guards. But there was the magician's evil face, as if the wall were transparent and as if he, too, could see through it. He could see her. She knew he could see her. He could see the wound in her naked breast that was not yet made by Andrew's bullet! Could he see what she saw in the German's consciousness? Could he understand it? It wasn't in German. There were no words. It was thought. Visions vanished as Andrew spoke to the German:

"You'd have told Lung-gom-pa that you'd persuaded me to give my automatic to that guard. There was a chance he'd have resumed his confidence in you."

Von Klaus snarled back to him: "That is a lie! You—you know it's a lie!"

"It's plain English," said Andrew.

"You are a coward, Andrew Gunning. You deal only in insults. If you think to impose your will on me, you are mistaken."

Characteristically Andrew didn't laugh. His slow smile was in recognition of the German's will to win. Elsa herself more than once had mistaken that smile for a mask that hid doubt of himself. It almost looked like it now. She wondered: could Andrew see what she saw?

"You don't know me," said the German.

"I don't need to," Andrew answered. "You're the second-in-command of a Nazi secret commission sent to Tibet by Adolf Hitler's Foreign Office gang to raise hell in Lhasa. You left your gang in Lhasa and came here to enlist me in your outfit. No dice."

518

The German sneered: "You flatter yourself, Mr. Yankeedoodle! But now that we've met—if it is not too late—if you are willing to obey me—I will bargain with you. It will be a hard bargain. But it may save us both from the woman and that bear trap and the red-hot charcoal!"

Charcoal collapsed to ashes in the brazier. The man in spectacles got up and poured on fresh charcoal from a sheepskin bag. There was a sharp smell of fumes. Elsa, with fingers in front of her eyes, prayed, through shut teeth that denied the prayer, that Andrew might see what she saw.

Andrew was standing quite still, staring at the German. He spoke quietly: "What's your idea of a deal?"

Elsa drew in her breath sharply. She couldn't see Andrew's thought— couldn't imagine why he asked that question. The German's intended treachery was as plain as his answering speech—as his arrogant will to win:

"You tool of meddlers! I have been working on this ignorant magician Lung-gom-pa for weeks, using scientific methods to make him afraid of his own magic and of my intelligence. Therefore now he keeps us waiting, giving us time to quarrel with each other and to betray each other. Savage psychology! You, you damned fool, have done exactly what he wanted, trying to force a quarrel instead of trusting me. Now the opium is here he no longer needs you. Nor your woman. Nor Bulah Singh. He needs your ponies, and your plunder to give to his men. He would torture you now, for his men's amusement, if it wasn't for me. But he's afraid. As long as he's afraid, I can control him—unless you—"

Andrew interrupted: "If you've a plan, what is it?"

Elsa bit her lips to crowd back words that tried to break through to warn Andrew to make no bargain. Andrew would be bound by his word. The German wouldn't. It would be a trap. But Andrew listened. She saw his aura again—resolute, but fearful of doing the wrong thing.

"There can not be two commands," said the German. "Either you place yourself and your party at my disposal, or—you may just as well shoot yourself." He grinned—glanced at Elsa. "But why shoot the girl? Why not leave her to enjoy life a bit longer?"

Before Andrew could answer, the door behind the armed guards began to open slowly. The guards stood aside, awkwardly presenting arms. Lung-gom-pa the magician loomed in the door in a dim blue light. He stood staring at Elsa. He ignored everyone else in the room, for about sixty seconds. Then slowly he turned his gaze toward the man in spectacles and pointed toward him with his outstretched left hand. The man in spectacles turned ghastly gray. One of the door guards strode toward him and struck him with the butt of his rifle. The man in spectacles got up and left the room, breathing hard, holding his ribs.

From the dim blue light behind Lung-gom-pa, Bulah Singh's woman emerged. Behind her, clinging to her skirt, came the boy that Bulah Singh had boasted was his bastard. They appeared to be well pleased, but the boy looked sleepy. They were smiling. There was something about both of them that suggested triumph. They smiled at Andrew. The woman's eyes hardened as she stared at Elsa. They walked slowly, following the man in spectacles out of the room. The door closed quietly behind them. Then von Klaus spoke with a dry throat:

"So he dies! Well! For us, that means one *schweinehund* fewer to deal with!"

The magician Lung-gom-pa spoke curtly to the guards. Then he turned his back and disappeared into the dim blue light of the inner room. One of the guards with a jerk of the head commanded Andrew and von Klaus to follow the magician. The other guard crossed the room and took hold of the canvas bag that Elsa was sitting on. But Andrew was quick. He seized the man's neck from behind and sent him crashing to the floor ten feet away.—He ordered his own man to shoulder the bag. The lad obeyed stupidly, too terrified to refuse. The German laughed:

"*Gewiss, Sie bitten dringend, uns auf die Folter zu spannen!*"

Andrew spoke quickly to Elsa: "Thanks for keeping quiet. Sorry I had to talk tough. It may happen yet. I've a plan that may work, or it may not."

"Andrew, Major von Klaus is—"

"Try to leave it to me. There can't be two captains."

"All right, Andrew!"

"Understand, Elsa: I'm playing both our lives on one throw."

"Yes," she answered. "I agree to it. If we lose, I will face you." She tapped her breast, smiling up at him, bright-eyed. "God bless you, Andrew. I know you'll shoot straight."

CHAPTER 37

Andrew's hand again. Between her shoulder blades. But dismalness gone. Strange how a human feels but one experience at a time. Elsa's that moment ranged from spiritual ecstasy to leaden physical exhaustion—even hunger. She was so tired she could hardly keep from swaying. But she felt one experience only. Love overwhelmed all being, drenched all consciousness. Facts hadn't changed, but they meant less. Friendship hadn't changed; it was there, good, variable, relatively unimportant, a derived, phenomenal emotion.

"Love—is this God—or the act of God?"

Memories, doubts, physical and mental fears were far away, perceived through love, dimmed by love that was in itself so absolute, so separate from logic that nothing else mattered. It didn't really matter that she mustn't let Andrew guess her secret. It included him. He couldn't possibly escape it in the end. But could his hand between her shoulders feel—interpret? How could he not know?

Death? Danger? Only drabness dies! Death would be an incident. Everyone dies, sometime. Torture can be endured, until one dies of it. It doesn't matter. Agony dies in the end of its own nothingness, like irrecoverable years. Love lives forever. Now and forever. Pain and the past must be something less than love's chrysalis—its shell—its seed bed, in which necessary nothings rot, to release such real wonders as—as—as the comforting thrill of Andrew's hand between Elsa's shoulder blades!

Consciousness of contrast brought her suddenly to earth—to the guarded door of the stone walled room—walking beside Andrew, into the smelly dim blue spider-chamber of a pagan black magician! Thoughts—thoughts—thoughts—only a few paces—millions of thoughts, all simultaneous—no time—no space—

Had she solved the riddle of the crucifixion? Or, truly to understand it, must one first be crucified? If so, she was willing. But was that really its secret? Was it as simple as that? What is it that gets crucified? Surely not goodness! Surely not kindness—such as Andrew's kindness! Had she herself even a trace of such kindness as governed Andrew? Did she know what kindness is? Did the Lords of Love let Jesus die in agony because it was not really His but the dark world's agony—and He never felt it— only with its eyes the world beheld—Ninety-first Psalm—was that it? Were life—love, joy the real consciousness—the real inseparable wonder? The real Reality? Pain—death—cruelty— were those false consciousness—the unreal lying shadows—dreams of a night that dies at daybreak? Love—is love daybreak? Was she, Elsa herself, all-selfish? Could she be that—and yet feel and experience this? Her baby? Was that experience mere mother love—good of its kind, but not beyond good and evil? Beyond good and evil? Did mad Nietzsche really know?

Andrew's quiet voice interrupted thought: "Walk proudly! Think of something you love! Smile! Don't be afraid. I won't let 'em hurt you."

Was Andrew blind? If he'd look, he'd know how little afraid she was! But it was well that he didn't look! He mustn't know! He mustn't! Thinking sympathetically of each other forms a spiritual mirror. Truth reveals itself in that. He mustn't know! She must speak, to ripple the mirror's surface!

"Think of poetry, Andrew! That always brings you the right idea."

The thrill in her voice surprised her. Andrew mistook it for fear. He laughed curtly, yielding to what he supposed was her mood. Choosing at random, he chanted aloud to help her to be brave. They marched into the dimness of the magician's den together to the rhythm of John Masefield's verse:

O Beauty, I have wandered far;
Peace, I have suffered seeking thee:
Life, I have sought to see thy star
That other men might see . . .

Trust Andrew to set a wild harp thrumming! Oh, Andrew, Andrew! Why did I never know until now!

Lung-gom-pa the magician felt the thought behind the chanted words. He recognized a force, as spiders in their webs perceive a change of a weather. He leaned forward, staring between the two blue glass lanterns that stood on the desk in front of him. On the table between the blue lanterns was a butter-lamp made from a human skull blackened by age and soot. Black-robed, on a black throne like a bishop's, gaunt, emaciated, not without dignity, the magician gazed through sunken red-rimmed eyes that knew evil. They had sought evil, found it and seen. They were like ape's eyes, only larger and more ancient-looking—old by some other measurement than years.

Von Klaus, standing beside a charcoal brazier, warming his fingers, felt tide of thought meet tide. He, too, was sensitive, but he had no magician's genius for silence, nor any patience with what he couldn't understand. Anything beyond his understanding was blind insolence. He would destroy it. Through a dry throat he scolded:

"One would think this *affenschwanz*, (monkey tail), knew Nietzsche's beyond good and evil!"

Elsa shuddered. Was Nietzsche's ghost in the room? Had von Klaus read her thought—or she his?

Andrew's face darkened. He growled at the German: "You've the sun in your eyes. Like you, this old devil confuses means with ends. But the ball's yours. Kick off."

"Sun in my eyes?" Von Klaus shook his head as if he thought Andrew had gone mad; "There is no such phrase in all Nietzsche's writings. I know Nietzsche by heart."

There began to be a rhythmic drumbeat. Very dimly there appeared a dark space where the wall against which the Tibetans leaned didn't reach to the roof. The drumming came through that dark gap, probably from the magician's real holy of holies where his trained assistants waited.

Andrew took the initiative. He signed to the young porter to set the locked canvas bag on the floor at the magician's feet. Furtive, then frantic, like a long-gowned bogey stealing base the porter dumped his load— stuck out his respectful tongue at the magician—ran back to the door—threw himself on his face—covered his head with his coat and lay still. The door guard prodded him with a rifle, just to add to his terror. Andrew didn't show his automatic, he only reached for it. The guard decided further prodding was unnecessary—retired to the door— leaned against it, doing his best to appear unconcerned, but watching Andrew sideways.

So it was safe to be truculent, in spite of that ominous drumbeat and the wordless tension. There was no actual crisis yet. Andrew's face revealed relief. Von Klaus resented that. To help him to steal the upper hand he needed fear, strain, more tension. He tried barbed sarcasm:

"*Kreuzblitzen noch einmal! Ausgezeichnet!* An evil eye! An iron will! An Olympian scowl! You are familiar with Virgil?—*Annuit et totum nutu tremefecit Olympum!*"

The gibe drew no retort. Andrew spotted its purpose to make him feel uncivilized—uneducated—ignorant—out of his class. He felt no impulse to retort in kind. If he had, he would have resisted it. He was aware of a quiet sensation like growing upward—not physically— not mentally—some other way, quite indescribable. He was getting a mental bird's-eye view, beginning to feel he had the German's number. But he had to be careful—cautious. He found that infernal drumbeat irritating. It was irregular. It was a kind of agitator intended to separate thought into its parts to fall, of their own nature, into pockets, there to be manipulated.

The magician sat still, staring at Elsa. A panther was the thought that crossed Elsa's mind. A black panther afraid of the dark devil within himself. His eyes had a similar smouldering fire. But in actual appearance he more resembled an Egyptian statue in black marble, except for that fiery red fear in his eyes that were set too close together. What was he afraid of? In addition to the door guard he had ten men to protect him. So it couldn't be physical fear—unless—unless—could he be one of those mystery priests, whose priesthood only lasts until its magic fails—and then they must die—at the hands of their guardians?

It seemed possible. The ten were armed and booted for outdoors, seated with their backs to the semicircular wall, to right and left of the magician. They were very evidently brigands, self-assured and well armed, wearing the stolen clothes of men of substance. But they also wore strange symbolic jewellery. They were something else besides brigands. Andrew stared at them one by one. Some dropped their eyes. Some didn't. Elsa whispered:

"Poetry! Poetry!"

Andrew resumed his chanting:

> . . . . *Bearing the discipline of earth*
> *That earth, controlled, may bring forth flowers.*
> *O may our labours help the birth*
> *Of nobler souls than ours.*

The magician slowly unfroze, in silence, as if he thawed reluctantly into a less impersonal condition. He became angry, breathing heavily. He appeared to believe Andrew's chant was rival magic—possibly more potent than his own. His nostrils dilated. His movement was subtle, a hardly noticeable menace, like a cobra's. But he didn't dare—yet—or else didn't choose—yet—to join issue—lock ranks—struggle—force against force. He thought of it—his eyes revealed that—but he didn't do it. With loaded silence he appeared to be deliberately tempting Andrew into some kind of magical mental trap. It was like the pull of a magnet. In that dim blue light it suggested an octopus under the sea. But he played safe when Andrew's last syllable died on the air. He droned the sacred monosyllable that is said to join heaven and hell and to release powers that be for purposes to come. White—black—priest—magician—they all use it:

"*Aum-m-m-m-m-m-m-m-m-m-m-m-m-m-m-m-m-m-m!*"

Andrew seized the initiative. "Ask him," he said calmly, "do we meet here as friends to exchange courtesy and to do each other kindness?"

Elsa cooed approval. "Andrew, who told you!"

"Say, would you mind—"

"Oh! I shouldn't! All right, I won't do that again!"

She translated his words into singsong Tibetan. The brigands smiled; the magician knew that without glancing at them; he appeared to resent it as a smear on his dignity. When he answered, after a pause, he spoke more to his own men than to Elsa. Andrew didn't catch the reply, but it might be important, so he asked:

"What did he say?"

Von Klaus answered before Elsa could get a word in: "He speaks like Goethe. He says: *Sie ist im Geisteslande jung geworden!* ("She is rejuvenated in the spirit-realm!") *Donnerwetter, was ist denn los?* ("Dammit, what's going on here?") Is this a *séance?*"

"You know less Tibetan than I do," Andrew retorted. "I don't care a damn what you think he said."

The German stared, stroking his beard: "It was from her I got it. We must use her. *Sie ist eine Geisterseherin,* (She is a medium). I warned you. I was here first. I dealt the cards. I know what will happen unless—"

He paused, expectant. But again he had failed to draw Andrew's fire. Andrew repeated the question:

"What did Lung-gom-pa say?"

Elsa answered: "He said: 'My heart beats like a bird's.'" She almost closed her eyes. "I don't know what he meant by that. But he is afraid—I don't know what of."

Von Klaus nodded and spoke with dark significance: "He fears me! Not without reason!"

All the Tibetans understood there was a mental duel between von Klaus and Andrew. Like their magician they awaited the outcome. Like the watchers of a cockfight they, not the cocks, knew what the fight was about, for whose profit. They smiled at Elsa, like connoisseurs. But something indefinable was lacking. Elsa didn't fear them physically at the moment.

Andrew gave her another sentence to translate: "Tell him it's our custom—yours and mine—to talking sitting down. Ask where are his manners?"

"May I put it less bluntly?"

"No. Say it the way I said it."

She obeyed. Von Klaus clucked priggish disapproval of such a flagrant breach of etiquette. But the effort to embarrass Andrew by encouraging Tibetan resentment failed of its purpose. The magician murmured to the brigand at his right hand. He promptly signalled to the door guard. The door guard laid down his rifle and brought forward the only two chairs in the room. He had to carry them one at a time; they were heavy—not so large, but almost as elaborate as the magician's throne. High-backed, carved, important-looking chairs.

"Stolen," said Andrew, low-voiced; he couldn't resist the silk-smooth feel of old carved wood; he caressed a carving with his thumb. Signing to Elsa to be seated, he took the chair beside her. That left von Klaus standing and staring so hard that Elsa wondered whether she and Andrew looked as ghastly as he did in the wan blue light. Or was the German seeing things? Andrew grinned unfriendly at him:

"Your move. We're waiting."

The German hesitated, vilely angry. He would have liked to shoot, if his eyes told the truth. Elsa whispered:

"*The Lord is my shepherd, I shall not—*"

Irritated, Andrew said grimly: "Cut that! You'll spoil my style. I've got Fritz on the run!"

She looked up at the crooked beams of the stamped mud ceiling: "Very well, Andrew!" But her lips moved: "Give us this day our daily bread, and forgive us our trespasses—"

She felt gay—light-hearted. She was praying for balance— fighting an impulse to laugh—hysterical because she and the magician were the only ones who knew what was going on. She subdued the impulse to laugh, but she couldn't help smiling. She loved Andrew. Loved him. Secretly. Forever and ever. It was irresistibly comical that neither he nor the magician knew that. She and the magician were at opposite ends of a universe, like plus and minus, so near that they could almost touch each other and so distant that they couldn't meet for all eternity. All the magician's brigands smiled when she did. But that wasn't such a good idea; the magician didn't like it. He was growing restless. It might be that he resented the lessening tension. Perhaps it made him feel less supernaturally vile. He loved vileness. But he wasn't beyond good and evil, because he hated good. You can't hate what you have risen beyond. That was another reason why it was difficult not to laugh. But what the magician did have was such strength of silence that Elsa's emotion wavered on the verge of tears. That was another strange thing. She felt sorry for the old man—wondered whether he was hungry, unaware that she herself was famished.

Andrew asked suddenly, aloud, in English: "What are we waiting for?"

Von Klaus answered irritably: "For my interpreter of course! What is your hurry?"

Then something happened as things do in dreams. The brigand farthest from Von Klaus, at the end, on the magician's left, leaned forward. His shoulders were invisible in shadow. His flat face dimly shone in the blue light, smiling as only Tibetan and Chinese faces can, like a mask that signified pure humour, implying no opinion, no relevancy, simply enjoying fact:

"His being dead," he said sweetly. He might have loved the interpreter. He didn't look at the German. He watched Elsa, as if that helped him to recall forgotten English words. Then awkwardly, he added: "Being dying too much soon this afternoon now big bird eating feeneesh."

Elsa suddenly knew how the interpreter had died. She didn't see. She knew. She almost fainted. But Andrew didn't notice that; his eyes had met the German's: "Did you get that?" he asked. "He says your interpreter's dead."

The German straightened himself. He took it well—a mite too well. It crossed Andrew's mind to quote Latin back at him—*summa ars est celare artem*—but it felt better to wait. The German's jaw fell, just a trifle. His eyes narrowed, hardly noticeably. He clenched his fists; the skin turned white under the pressure. He shrugged his shoulders. There was a glint in his hard eyes. It was pretty good acting.

"*Schweinhunde!* Treacherous devils!" He swallowed, seeming to be trying to read Andrew's mind. "Do you believe it?" he asked earnestly. "Or are they—"

Andrew's answer, to the point though it was, revealed nothing of Andrew's thought, belief or disbelief:

"On our way this evening we passed the village burial ground. A fresh corpse had just been thrown to the dogs."

"Did you look at the corpse? Did you go near?"

"No, I sent flowers," said Andrew. He felt glad then that he hadn't quoted a Latin *cliché*.

"Careful!" Elsa whispered. "Careful!" She knew von Klaus asked nothing better than an excuse to fly into a rage. She couldn't sit quiet and let Andrew blunder into a false move. But the warning was too late. Von Klaus began to work himself into a passion:

"Oh! Sarcasm! Eh? Malice! So! The mark of a lying coward! I suspected you from the first, Andrew Gunning! Now I accuse you of having caused the death of my interpreter—in order to—"

Andrew interrupted: "You damned fool!"

"*Wahrhaftig!* I was damned—when I neglected to kill you on sight like the insolent swine that you are! It is due to your treachery that now I have no automatic! It is too late to remedy that. But have you not enough intelligence to perceive this is the end?"

"End of what?" said Andrew.

"The end of us! Do you wish to die of crushed testicles, with red-hot charcoal at your toes and fingers? If it is true that they have killed my Chinese servant, then it is clear they are playing with us. They amuse themselves. This is all prearranged. They intend to torture us presently. Why wait for that? Do me the favour, will you, to shoot first the magician. After that, you may kill your woman. Then me. Or—if you lack the necessary courage, lend me your weapon. I will shoot him, her, you, and then myself, in that order!"

"You promise?"

"Certainly! Yes! Of course! What do you think?"

Andrew smiled. "Not that I give a damn. Because it's no dice. But you wouldn't keep your promise. You might kill the magician, and perhaps me. Then you'd be on top, wouldn't you? Suppose you tell 'em what's in my bag who put it there—why—who the stuff's for—and who paid for it!"

Von Klaus shrugged his shoulders, disgusted: "Die of torture, since you wish it. I don't even know enough Tibetan to ask these devils why they killed my interpreter."

"We'll soon find that out," said Andrew. He glanced at Elsa. She put the question straight to the magician. He murmured to the brigand beside him. The entire proceedings did seem prearranged. The brigand began to speak as if he had it all by heart. Elsa interpreted, phrase by phrase:

"Von Klaus's dead interpreter was Chinese—"

Andrew interrupted: "Not Japanese?"

"He says Chinese. The interpreter, whose name was Fu Ling—"

Andrew interrupted again: "Well, I'll be damned. I might have guessed that. I didn't. Fu Ling—Washington, D.C.—San Francisco—Berlin—London. Good guy. Too bad he's dead. But go on— I'm listening."

"Fu Ling tried to persuade the magician Lung-gom-pa to agree to waylay you and me, and kill us, and steal the contents of this bag. But—he says—Lung-gom-pa used magic and perceived there were seven reasons each containing seven other reasons why not. He means the magician was unconvinced. Therefore, instead, they tortured Fu Ling, to make him tell all he knew about von Klaus and about you and me. But Fu Ling died too quickly, telling nothing."

Von Klaus interrupted: "He must have swallowed slow poison. Damn him, he stole mine!"

Elsa continued: "This man says ravens instead of vultures are pecking Fu Ling's body—and that is proof that Fu Ling's soul is destined for hell. Now Lung-gom-pa wishes to know, and he asks: What can we tell him about von Klaus, who is a *peling* and talks incomprehensibly about religion?"

Andrew didn't exactly stiffen, but something happened to him. Elsa almost physically felt the spark of intuition leap into his mind. He laid his hand on hers, unaware of it, although it made her heart leap like a caught bird. Andrew was like a still hunter—no, he wasn't, he was like a cross-examiner at a court trial spotting a crucial point. She wondered what he had discovered. But he guarded his thought. He waited for Von Klaus to brag and blunder—not many seconds—Von Klaus couldn't resist that impulse:

"*Herr Gott!* All this *umschweif!* Let me tell it. I already said this old *schwarzkünstle,* is afraid of his own magic—and of me!"

"Why were you afraid of Fu Ling?" Andrew asked him.

It was a palpable hit. The German hesitated. He looked startled. "Me? Fear my interpreter?"

"They tortured him—to suit your book. Why?"

Von Klaus hit back: "*Herr Gott!* Have you gone mad from fear of torture? You accuse me of—has the altitude gone to your head? Or—no! I know the answer! Of course yes! Sol! Of course! Why didn't I think of it! Opium! So you are a drug addict? You have been using what you have in that bag!"

But he failed flatly to unmask Andrew's strategy. Andrew touched the canvas bag with his toe, reflectively. "Has that brigand done talking?" he asked.

The brigand had not done talking. When Elsa questioned him he spoke so rapidly that she kept asking him to pause, to let her interpret:

"He says: this *peling* von Klaus came here several weeks ago with his Chinese interpreter, bearing credentials from Lhasa. Good credentials. Here, in this village he imposed himself as an official guest, making many demands. *Peling* though he is, he has received the hospitality due to a nobleman. But this continually happened—"

Von Klaus cut in with a sneer: "Will you listen to muck? Perverted sex is all they think about! I warn you: this won't be fit for any woman's ears unless she is a nymphomaniac. He is going to lie about my relations with Bulah Singh's woman." He went through the motions of wringing ullage through his fingers.

"What we'd like to know," said Andrew, "is why you turned in Fu Ling."

"That man will tell you nothing but lies."

"Well, let's hear 'em anyhow." Andrew tossed an off-hand question for Elsa to ask: "Has Bulah Singh's woman been receiving bribes from von Klaus?"

Elsa had to ask that question twice. There was a whispered conference with the magician. Then the answer: "Yes. Too much money."

"In return for the bribes, what did the woman do?"

"Making too much picture magic-making look-see."

Von Klaus interrupted again: "*Das Weib ist eine*—"

"Thanks, we know about her," said Andrew. "She's a trance medium. Did you make use of her to communicate with Bulah Singh in India?"

"That's what I'm getting at."

"You mean what you would like to get at," von Klaus retorted. "I tell no secrets. But are you an ignoramus? Don't you know as well as anyone that the technique of modern intelligence work—espionage and counter-espionage is—"

Andrew cut in. "Modern? That stuff's older than Jeremiah's school of prophets! The British began organised experiments in thought transmission during the war in 1915. You Fritzies have been trying it ever since. Hitler keeps his private mediums at Berchtesgaden. Your Gestapo has a whole corps of 'em. Do you admit having used that woman?"

"I admit nothing. You speak from ignorance. You imagine imbecilities. But why do you yourself travel with a special woman? Do you burden yourself in that way for fear of syphilis? Or lest your lack of self-sex-discipline should lead to—"

"Ask that brigand to go on talking," said Andrew.

The German believed he had scored. He chested himself. While Elsa listened to the brigand he smiled leanly, nodding. He pretended to have lost all interest when Elsa began to interpret. He warmed his hands at the brazier as if he were washing them in the fumes.

"This *peling*—he means von Klaus—offered to teach and to help Lung-gom-pa by means of a new system of religion—I believe that is what he means—to become Kashgan of all this country."

Andrew raised his eyebrows: "Of all Tibet?"

"So he says. I understood him to say that. Von Klaus undertook to make him Regent-guardian of the infant Dalai Lama, which would give him all power."

Andrew grinned. "I guess the wires crossed that time! Or were they tapped! Bulah Singh's bastard boy-wonder! The bonny pretender!" Suddenly he roared with laughter that made all the brigands and even the door guard laugh too, although they didn't know what he had said nor why he laughed. The magician's ape-eyes widened, but, being beyond mirth and grief where dignity forbade, no smile escaped him. Or perhaps he alone understood that Andrew's smile had been genuine but the laugh was forced. It served its purpose. Von Klaus exploded like a detonated bomb of humourless passion:

"So! A clown, are you? Like an American movie hero! I wash my hands of your Jew-drama!"

He went through the motion of washing his hands in the hot brazier fumes. Andrew kept up the irritation:

"You're too subtle for me. The way you say it, you sound all steamed up for—"

Elsa stirred: "Don't, Andrew, don't!"

But if it was damage it was done. Von Klaus was ready for his supreme effort—his barrage that should break down all resistance. He looked apoplectic. His neck swelled. He screamed, like an enraged parrot, as if rebuking mutineers or Jews in Dachau concentration camp. "You can't bargain with me! Do you think I will tamely submit to your dictation? You came too late! Bah! Phui! You have no right here! You are an interloper! Try on your worst treacheries! Then see how swift—how remorseless will be *die wiedervergeltung*—the reprisal—*die bestrafung*—"

Andrew interrupted: "You're not counting on your little Gestapo gang in Lhasa, are you? Lhasa's a long way from here. How'll they learn you're up against it? Are they using a medium?"

"Bah! You are medium-crazy! You don't guess how near my friends are!"

That shaft almost got home. If the German's friends really were near the game was up. It was more than possible. It could explain why the Tibetans waited with such patience. There was no chance—absolutely none—that a party of Gestapo men would do less than steal all Andrew's loads and ponies. They wouldn't have to do their own murdering. At half a hint the Tibetans would do that for them. Andrew felt the cold premonition of fear like a chill wind. But then suddenly he felt Elsa's influence. He couldn't have explained it. It was warm, and it calmed him. With half-closed eyes, Elsa was leaning back, seeming almost asleep, although her left hand, on the chair-arm, was crushed under his. He realised he must have hurt her terribly. Snatching his hand away, he began framing an apology, but no words came because her lips moved—not speaking to him. He caught the murmur and the rhythm: "Thy kingdom come, Thy will be done—"

He took her hand gently—flexed it to relieve the numbness. "See here," he said to von Klaus, "you've bluffed like hell. But it's no go If you want my help, you'll have to come clean. I won't give you a break if you don't."

Von Klaus stared venomously, smiling with invincible arrogance. "Very well," he retorted. "You have me at disadvantage. Name your Shylock price and I will pay."

Andrew ignored the insult. "All I want is the truth. What was your deal with these Tibetans?"

Then there appeared and explained itself the reason why von Klaus had been selected for a dangerous, deadly mission. The man's genius came forth— his gift for snatching a chance and rising like a Phoenix from the ashes of failure, defeat, humiliation. The truth, too, can be venomous, the way he told it—truth about the lies that he himself believed because they fed his conceit. His movements fascinated the old magician. All the Tibetans watched him, breathless, like spectators at a play. He began to pace to and fro beside the brazier. He appeared to be gathering thought, establishing a rhythm, something like that of a dynamo. There were no words. He didn't mutter to himself. But he was building the mysterious hypnotic force that all spellbinders and all orators use, though none knows what it actually is. They build it until they feel it and then let loose. Andrew heard Elsa's whisper.

"Andrew, can you be gentle? Can you break it and not add to it?"

He didn't know quite what she meant, but he knew the German must be deflated somehow. Quite likely he was working up—besides mental passion—strength for a physical leap at Andrew's throat, to seize Andrew's automatic. Ridicule seemed the best bet. Andrew tried it:

"The words that you're pounding your brain to remember are '*Sieg Heil!*' Shall I spell 'em for you?"

The German stood still—threw an attitude—spoke, gripping his coat with one hand. He held the other clenched fist ready for one of those upward blows at the air that hypnotize because the audience knows they are coming, awaits them in suspense, listens for the magic phrases, that shall make the fist leap upward."

"Lung-gom-pa says that I spoke of religion. *Wahrhaftig!* I did. Day after day I have dinned into his stupid consciousness—as I now tell you—the Christian dispensation, as you call it, is done!—dead!—*kaputt!* It is a burned-out moon! There is nothing more dead than a dead delusion. Jew-Jesus and his ranting hypocrites—his humble parasites—his Peters and Pauls and Popes and other howling dervishes—no longer set the fashion of ideas. There is no law nowadays of offering the other cheek to the smiter. The smitten go down in the dust and the smiter tramples them. The roots of Christianity were in the Sermon on the Mount. Its last fruit was the Treaty of Versailles! And that also is dead! It is a stink in men's nostrils—a putrid corpse, like Christianity. Dead! And with Christianity died Buddhism. Buddha, the more ancient myth-monger, died drowned like a bee in its own honey! Buddhism is dead!—forever dead! And so is Islam dead.

"So are all dreamy religions dead that lure their victims into slavery to priests! *Heil Hitler!* Today's world shakes off Jew-shackles and Jew-ideology! The power of the shameless hymning feminist humbugs of all religions, died with the death of the Lie of Versailles! *Heil Hitler!* A new day has dawned! By virtue of the German race—*Heil Hitler!*—manhood comes at last into its own!—and they shall rule the world who ride the new whirlwind, compared to which Genghis Khan and his hordes—Attila—the Huns and Visigoths—Spain—Alva's infantry—England's imperial greed and all the Jew-bought liars ganged against Germans in 1914—are as nothing! I said 'as nothing'! *Heil Hitler!* I speak of the new conquest of the world—of the rule of Might—of the law that Might shall prevail—and of the truth—the realistic truth that there is neither right nor wrong, but only that which is expedient. Ends justify means."

He paused for breath, sweating, breathing, glaring, estimating Andrew's reaction. He believed he had Andrew half won—or at least shaken—until Andrew spoke:

"But what a hell of an end to aim at!"

Von Klaus gasped as if struck in the face.

Elsa spoke dreamily: "Andrew! Ask what else he said. What did he promise about you and me?"

Her prompting dovetailed so neatly into Andrew's own thought that he hardly noticed it. Somehow he had to avoid the need of using that automatic that he could feel each time he breathed. He must convince von Klaus that his whirlwind of words had not been altogether wasted. He must string him along.

"Okay, Christianity's dead. So you flogged a dead horse and betrayed Fu Ling. What has that to do with me and this bag? What are you driving at?"

The German hadn't time to answer. He was hesitating whether to fling the lie in Andrew's face or to tell a lie of his own, or the truth, when Elsa sat bolt upright. She clutched Andrew's hand with both hers:

"Don't! Don't! Help me! Not him! Please!"

The dim blue chamber began shaking, as if a fluttering arc light struggled against fog. The black magician's features, with monstrous red-rimmed eyes, ten times magnified, loomed—leered—leaped—danced in the shimmer. It was like sheet lightning. The Tibetans moaned. The face grew larger—larger—with fingers beside it that clawed air.

Elsa began chanting: "Though I walk through the valley of the shadow of death—"

Her voice was drowned by the Tibetans' moaning and then, suddenly, by von Klaus's hysterical laughter—shrieks, yells of laughter, like a maniac's. Elsa clutched Andrew's hand. Her nails dug into his wrist. There was a feeling of brain-burst—of terrific tension—and something happened. The black magician extended both arms like long shadows to right and left. Then he failed—faded—and grew small again—natural—lifelike. The blue shimmering ceased. Von Klaus shouted:

"I told you! He fears me and his own magic! Kill him! I tell you, kill him, before he—"

The magician threw up his arms and screamed like a tortured beast. Two of his Tibetans got up and seized von Klaus, twisting his arms behind him until he shouted with pain. They threw him to the floor. One of them kicked him. He lay still. Then they calmly resumed their seats and suddenly Lung-gom-pa stood upright, seeming to grow taller. Pointing long lean fingers at Elsa and at Andrew, glaring at them, he vibrated as if his bones were springs. Then suddenly his

534

voice burst on the silence, worse than the scream of lammergeiers, in a torrent of malediction.

"Pray, Andrew! Pray!—Thy kingdom come, Thy—"

He recited the Lord's Prayer with her—twice through, and again, until the black magician ceased screaming and sank, slowly, like a deflated ghost on to his throne. Then there was silence except that the charcoal fell in the brazier. The German lay still, but his eyes shone in the gloom near the floor like a crouched animal's. Andrew spoke low:

"Did you understand any of that?"

"Yes! The old magician says we're thieves of souls! Von Klaus has told him there's enough opium in this bag to corrupt all Tibet! His men have listened to von Klaus—they want the stuff. Lung-gom-pa won't have it! He says it's too evil: shall he govern wretches whose souls have left their bodies because of this stuff?"

The magician stood up again—screamed again, staggered with the fury of his anger—then sat down, muttering.

"He says: Whose magic are we using? Shall he bring upon us death from which no magic can protect us—"

Andrew interrupted. "Okay. Tell him I'll speak. Will he listen?"

Still clutching Andrew's hand Elsa spoke a few words in Tibetan. There was silence again. The old magician made no sound, no movement.

"Tell him," Andrew began—but then he hesitated. Elsa's fingernails were gouging his wrist. She didn't know it. She was seeing—hearing—gazing at something beyond space and time:

"Andrew! Tell him if he'll work his magic, we'll work ours, and all together we'll save him and his people from this—"

"You tell him. I can't. Tell him in Tibetan!"

"So Elsa said it in Tibetan. The old magician pointed at the bag on the floor. Two of his men—the same two who had manhandled von Klaus—got up and approached the bag. One drew a knife to cut the canvas. The magician screamed. They hesitated. Von Klaus spoke, down on his knees with his chin six inches off the floor:

"Let them have it. They'll be drunk on the stuff by morning. Then we'll—"

Andrew dived into his pocket for his key—found it—held it up.

"Elsa—I want you to translate, word for word." He faced the German. "Get up!" Von Klaus made no move. "I'll come and kick you up if you don't."

Von Klaus staggered to his feet. He went and leaned against the wall, pretending to be worse hurt than he was.

"Answer!" said Andrew. "What's in this bag?"

Elsa translated that into Tibetan. Von Klaus answered in English:

"Opium! Enough to poison Tibet!"

Elsa translated word for word. Andrew retorted."

"How do you know?"

Elsa turned that into Tibetan, and the Tibetans watched von Klaus. He was trying to guess at Andrew's motive. He was like a chess player with less than ten seconds to play. There wasn't a move on the board—not for him. He upset the board. One almost saw the imagined pieces scatter.

"Damn you—I know—because you sent a clairvoyant message about it through Bulah Singh's woman!"

Andrew answered quietly: "I'm not clairvoyant."

Von Klaus pointed at Elsa: "But she is!"

Andrew waited for Elsa to translate. Then he said to the German: "So you know it's opium?"

"Yes. Open the bag. Let the magician see it!"

"Elsa, ask Lung-gom-pa: If this should not be opium—if, instead, it's a present for him, that he needs—then what? Will he help us to travel forward?"

She translated. The magician didn't understand. She asked a second time. He looked suspicious.

"He says: But it is opium."

"I asked: What if it isn't? Does he promise to help us?"

"He insists: 'But the other *peling* says it is opium.'"

"Tell him it's sugar," said Andrew.

Von Klaus laughed like a maniac. "You fool, do you think you can keep up that bluff! That's the bag! There's the mark on the bag! Do you pretend you don't know what's in it? Bah! Give me the key!"

"Sure." Andrew tossed him the key. "Go ahead. Open it."

The drumbeat in the room behind the magician quickened tempo. It swelled, louder and louder, until it sounded like the muffled thunder of approaching doom.

CHAPTER 38

And so, in the black magician's dim blue lantern light, Major von Klaus of the Gestapo, on his hands and knees, believing to the last second that Andrew was bluffing in fear of his life, unlocked and opened the brown canvas bag, with Andrew's key. The truth staggered him. Andrew had told the truth. The exact truth. It was an effrontery. Before he could recover, his chance was gone to invent a string of lies and create a new crisis. Andrew's voice spoiled it, sonorously:

"My gift—to the lord magician—Lung-gom-pa."

Elsa translated the short speech quickly into Tibetan. The ten brigands drew in their breath at the reckless use of the magician's name. But the old man himself ignored the breach of manners. He was like a big dark parrot on a perch. His red-rimmed eyes became a picture of possessiveness qualified by a secret new fear born of knowledge of evil. Not even a vulture ever had such eyes as those. Perhaps the Sphinx did. They were not totally unlike the eyes of a dog with a bone. He had the bone. Now what?

In the next room his assistants thumped skull-drums steadily. The refrain had changed a little. Now it seemed to beat out the words "Brown cane sugar! Brown cane sugar!"

Sugar, in caravan packages—cotton bags, wrapped in blue paper. Not quite priceless. But at a winter's end, in Tibet, costlier than tea. Much harder to come by than minted money. Edible brown gold! Then what was the new doubt in the magician's mind? It was up to Andrew to discover.

Von Klaus had gone berserker or its German equivalent. He had become a Teutonic strafing party on his own, inflicting vengeance for humiliation. In a spasm of wantonness he seized a package of the precious sugar in both hands, raised it above his head and smashed it on the floor. He would have smashed a second one, if they had let him. The magician clucked. Ten brigands howled—rushed—pounced. The scattered contents of the broken package vanished in handfuls—mouthfuls. The drumbeat rhythm quickened, grew louder, faded—and von Klaus lay hurled against the wall, kicked in the groin, groaning. It looked as if he had made his last mistake—ruined his last chance. But he had damaged Andrew's chance, too, by inviting physical violence.

He had started something. No one could predict the end of that.

Elsa struggled against an impulse to go and help von Klaus. She was scared back to earth again, clutching Andrew's hand, no vision left, seeing nothing but what the Tibetans themselves could see and hear. They saw red. They smelt blood. If she or Andrew should move toward von Klaus, that might be a trigger, releasing death. There fell a stillness like the breathless calm before animals pounce on a living prey. One spark of an unseen something and they would seize the German, tie him, drag him outside—turn him over to be bloody entertainment for the villagers. Out in the night the villagers were waiting for that outcome.

After that, no doubt, the ten would turn on Andrew, justifying one crime with another—partly because he had not brought opium and they felt cheated—partly because he was a *peling* who had neither right nor privilege in Tibet—partly because his baggage contained more, perhaps richer loot—and they were brigands—and there was violence awake in the blue gloom. During one immeasurable moment Elsa visioned the furious, sensuous face of Bulah Singh's woman. The fierce eyes turned blood-red, then faded and the face died away in the dark. It meant something. But what did it mean?

The strained silence continued during twenty heartbeats. Andrew was poker-faced, but behind that almost Red Indian calm he was searching frantically for the right thought, idea, word, action. He was tempted, but he didn't trust himself to try, to pronounce the Tibetan sacred syllable. It might act like oil on a raging sea. It might. He had known it to work, once, when Tom Grayne did it. But the least mispronunciation of the complicated vowel would be fatal. Even properly pronounced it might seem like a challenge to the old magician's powers. One doesn't wisely challenge a magician at his own game. Seconds sped like lightning. Thought sped faster than the seconds.

Somehow—before von Klaus could recover his malignant wits—he must change the mood of a dozen Tibetans. The incredible old black magician, whose philosophy was fear—fraud—hatred, was as pleased as a saint by the loss of the opium! But like a lean black leopard he was also hungry to flex his claws again—to feel and to use the power that opium would have undone as surely as death. Opium would have stolen and softened the wills of the thoughtless brigands who were the subjects of his necromantic skill.

He needed his subjects headstrong, healthy, free to be manipulated. No opium to dull their reactions to suggestion! So far, good. It was in his power now to credit his own magic with having changed opium into sugar. If he should so choose. Broadcasted like a bell's vibration, his magic power—so he was telling himself—must have reached Andrew in the mountains—touched him. Being woven of fear, it had made Andrew afraid of the stuff that the magician hated. Andrew must have thrown the opium away the moment the good black magic touched his thought. The cunning pride of the accomplished craftsman was in the old magician's eyes. He believed in his magic. Why shouldn't he?

538

There was also cupidity. Sugar is wealth—in Tibet, before the lower passes open in the spring.

It did not occur to Andrew to wonder how he knew all this. He knew it, without effort, in a moment of time—or rather, in a moment in which there was no time.

But, beneath the surface-satisfaction in the magician's eyes was the leopard-like furtive terror that moves like lightning when it does move. Andrew read that. He intuitively recognised it. It was like a gang leader's hidden fear of his own killers. The same fear and no other that makes generals send unready troops against prepared positions— that makes a Hitler purge his own supporters—that makes financiers kill themselves—makes men on the witness stand swear others' lives away.

Those brigands knew the pricelessness of opium. They cared not one dead egg of a last year's louse for a magician's ethics. If they should believe—as they might, as they were simple enough to believe—that he had changed opium into sugar, they were likelier than not to bid him try some more of his magic, this time against bullets: let him change those into butter. Crude, vulgarly humorous, easily angered men, greedy as dogs. And, as magicians know, bullets obey laws that magic only very rarely can resist. Ten bullets are ten times worse than one.

So it was thought against thought, with Elsa at the moment too tired and scared to help, sickened by glimpsed visions of Bulah Singh's woman—von Klaus, hurt badly, groaning through set teeth, spiteful, rolling over on his belly to watch for a chance to wreck whatever plan Andrew might invent—ten brigands, whose Mongolian smiles could harden just as suddenly as water changes into ice at sunset. Moist-lipped, they were considering Elsa, viewed as loot, not necessarily for her fur coat and her necklace.

For the space of no longer than twenty heartbeats, ten thousand thoughts a second poured through Andrew's mind. Not least was the thought that Elsa's and Nancy Strong's defence would be a passionate Christian outpouring of magic against magic—good against evil. But Andrew was seeking a means of attack. The old black magician—above good and beneath evil— was murmuring spells. His brigands watched his lips-wishing. They wished to be told to do that which they wanted to do. They were breathing in time to the drumbeats. And now Elsa's lips were moving. Andrew could feel her influence. He knew the nature of the loving-kindness that appealed to heart, not brain. But his heart, that beat trip-hammer blows rebelliously out of time to the drumbeat, revolted in that crisis at the too sweet sentimental means that Christians use. He was in no mood for appeasement by humility. Perhaps von Klaus had blasphemed better than he knew. Some shaft of scorn had struck its mark? The thought of lamb-to-the-slaughter Jesus turned Andrew's stomach. He craved not a physical fight, but a fight against powers, against the rulers of the darkness of this world.

He judged he must not stand up—not yet. He must not move his right hand—yet. The automatic, each time he breathed, felt comforting, but he mustn't move his hand toward it—mustn't use it—mustn't appeal unto Caesar. The slightest thoughtless motion might launch a volley of ten bullets. He wished he did dare to stand up. He liked daring to do things. On his feet he always felt better command of himself. He wished, too, that thought wouldn't sweep through his mind like endless comets' tails. He needed to concentrate. He couldn't. He wondered why not. As he stared at the old magician's eyes, his own past came back to him—timeless—layer on layer of memories, interwoven and simultaneous, but as distinct each from the other as the phases of a long dream. The magician's force was like dark lightning, blindly searching and revealing only Andrew's own thoughts, to himself, not to the magician.

"Where have you seen the magician's face?"

No one had spoken. Elsa was staring at space with wide eyes. But he heard words again, within his consciousness—composite voices—many in one—Elsa's—Tom Grayne's—Nancy Strong's— Morgan Lewis's—Bulah Singh's—all asking one question, that he had never answered because it always, whoever asked it, froze him into silence.

"Why did you leave the United States?"

The *tum-tu-to tum-tu-to* drumbeat in the next room insisted on the question—emphasized it—over and over: "where have you seen the ma—"

Memories—memories—millions, like a jackdaw's jumbled hoard of postage stamps, but gradually thinning down to three-two-one:

"Where have you seen the magician's face?"

Cincinnati—Chicago—Cleveland. School—university—law— teachers—professors—judges. Andrew the boy, in his secret heart of hearts a knight in armour—heavy that armour!—but, as Mark Twain made King Arthur say, "*a man stands straight in it*"! Good doctrine, that! Nevertheless, he would never forgive Mark Twain for his gibes at the Quest for the Holy Grail. "*Grailing—the boys went grailing.*" Andrew had done nothing else, all his days, but go grailing—in school, university, courthouse—grailing, setting a course by the farthest stars—and at war—to the death—to the end—against—against what? He had never named it.

Tum-tu-tu-tum-tu-tu . . . "Where have you—seen the ma—"

In the beginning it was a drawing of Satan stalking Jesus, in a book for children, compulsory reading before he rebelled from Sunday School. Later, superimposed on that was Mephistopheles from a library copy of Goethe's Faust. Subsequently added were some heel politicians, a political boss, an evangelist, some judges, pimps, lawyers, bondsmen, political women—homosexuals—a whorehouse madam—two or three authors—a banker—a doctor—a couple of Jews—policemen, taxi drivers, senators—some congressmen—an editor—two reporters—every single lying face that Andrew had ever seen and hated—mixed into one monstrous image of all evil—a living, personal devil.

Tum-tu-tu—"Where have you—*Tum-tu-tu*—seen the ma—"

Von Klaus hoarsely shattered the silence: "Shoot! You God-damned idiot! Shoot!"

Andrew heard him. But the German was out of the picture. He didn't count. Andrew stared at the magician's face, learning something, all on his own. He had always known it. But he hadn't learned it. So he had never known that he knew it. Now, as he stared during twenty heartbeats while time stood still, he knew he could never again forget.

Tum-tu-tu-tum-tu-tu . . . Evil is—organised—living intelligent—The hell with Nancy Strong's stuff! The hell with compromise and false peace! There, gazing at him through the old magician's eyes, was Evil—Evil itself—Satan! As surely as God looks through the eyes of honesty, Satan sees men and women through the eyes of hatred and envy and fear—sees them no otherwise—can see no otherwise!

He was looking straight into the eyes of Evil—giving it power by hating it—lending his brain to its brain and his strength to its strength. He, himself, Andrew, had imagined, created, made real, breathed the breath of life into a mental picture through which, and through the old magician's eyes. Evil could see straight into his soul. Divinity that shapes our ends is good and evil. Evil also is divine. Choose! Choose! The loser is the fool on both sides of the fence!

Tum-tu-tu-tum-tu-tu . . .

"Shoot!" von Klaus repeated. "Kill him!"

Elsa felt the torture of turmoil in Andrew's thought. She began to murmur the Lord's Prayer. But Andrew knew what he needed. The hell with solemnity! He needed laughter—Rabelaisian, irreverent, blasphemous laughter, to break the hold Evil had on him, by mocking, ridiculing, recognizing as a lie the false mask he had made in his mind of the faces of men. Good and evil? Good or evil! Which?

It came to him between two heartbeats. The old magician was between the devil and the deep sea—evil's high priest, trying to do good for the sake of greater evil! His sudden impulse was to whistle, because he always whistled a tune when an idea dawned. But the Tibetans would have called that devil-music. He began to hum—smile—laugh. Then he broke into song. And for the millionth time since 1917 "The Lady from Armentières" did duty as Joan of Arc. The opprobrious, dissolute, bawdy, undignified "Lady from Armèntieres."

He had been beaten—he knew it—until that ribald nonsense flowed into his thought and he perceived that all solemnity is a lying mockery of God. No truth is solemn. It can't be—can't possibly be. Solemnity is a clowning camouflage. To be solemn about evil, and to hate it, is to dignify it and to be and become and remain the bewildered wretch of whom St. Paul spoke: "for the good that I would, I do not; but the evil which I would not, that I do."

So Andrew sang:

The French they are a funny race—
Parlez-vous!
They fight with their feet and—

Lung-gom-pa recognized force up and coming—force on the march! He instantly retorted with a *mantra* to protect himself from that incomprehensible hymn! The brigands joined in, beating the air with their right hands, drowning Andrew's voice—not sure yet whether he was wishing on them poisonous *peling* curses, or blessing them with appetites to enjoy the sugar. They could see he was full of laughter.

But they took no chances. They howled a counter-barrage of invocations to a thousand saints who represented forces of earth and sky.

Through that din, pitched to a harsh yell against Andrew's "*Hinkey-dinkey parlez-vous,*" came von Klaus's voice:

"Kill them! Shoot, you *lümmmel!*, *Jetst ist die Gelegenheit*—the chance—the opportunity! Shoot!"

Elsa suppressed a scream as the nearest Tibetan kicked von Klaus in the face. He lay still after that. He had sense enough to pretend to be worse hurt than he was.

"Easy," said Andrew, "easy." He touched Elsa's hand. The shouting died to a snarling hum like a hornets' evensong. "Now I wish I were a killer."

"Don't, Andrew! Please don't!"

"I won't. Don't worry. I'm afraid to."

"Good!"

"No. Bad. But there's a chance in a million he didn't betray Fu Ling."

"But, Andrew, are we his judges? Even if he did betray him, are we—"

"Each to his own decision. I'll give him one more chance. You sit still."

Andrew stood up. That stopped the Tibetans' humming. Dead silence fell, except for that infernal drumbeat that had died down almost to a mutter. Lung-gom-pa resumed the subtle swaying movement that suggested a cobra. Andrew spoke to von Klaus:

"Did you, or didn't you send Fu Ling to his death?"

After a second's pause the German snarled back: "Is that any of your damned business?"

"Right. Neither are you. The hell with you. That's final."

"Andrew! Andrew! Please!"

Von Klaus struggled into a sitting position, holding both hands to his groin. His beard was bloody. It made his mouth look horrible. It made his words sound bloody.

"The hell with your illusions of importance! So you think you can ignore me? You will do what I tell you or die! If I die, you die. If I live, you live. If we both live, you shall obey me, because I insist on it. If we both die, what becomes of your woman?" In spite of pain he contrived a mock-courteous gesture toward Elsa. His mouth and beard looked unseductive but he did change his voice a little: "*Gnädiges Fräulein, machen Sie schnell! Wenn Sie*—Gracious miss if you can influence this blockhead, do it! Now!"

But the fictional, fanciful "Lady from Armentières" had scattered Andrew's reverence for influence of any kind whatever. Elsa knew it had happened. She couldn't reach him any longer. Even when she touched his hand she couldn't reach his thought. Andrew was someone to follow. He couldn't be led. Mental images of Nancy Strong, Morgan Lewis, and Lobsang Pun's broken photograph, were looming from nowhere and fading again, forced out of Andrew's mind by his own will. He knew Elsa was trying to flood his consciousness with spiritual visions, to produce peace. He preferred war. He would go grailing henceforth in new armour, with a new weapon. He aimed his inner laughter straight at the vision of Nancy Strong. Before she faded he thought she laughed. Mocking him? Swell! The hell with her. He only hesitated whether to try his own crude Tibetan, that might arouse the magician's scorn and remind the brigands to distrust him—or whether to trust Elsa to interpret without talking back. He decided on Elsa:

"Quick! Ask Lung-gom-pa: Does he accept the sugar?"

"He says yes, he accepts it."

"As a gift?"

"As a gift."

"Very well. Now ask those ten men. Do they wish to possess the opium that von Klaus pretended was in this bag?"

She interpreted. They breathed hard. There was a murmur of incredulous but excited assent.

"They do want it?"

"They do. But, Andrew—"

"Please don't interrupt. Tell them—word for word exactly as I say it—"

"Very well. If it's possible. At least I won't change the meaning."

"This man von Klaus has been using the bastard's mother to make look-see magic. They know that, don't they?"

There was time to look around while Elsa translated. Lung-gom-pa leaned forward between the blue lights. The flickering skull-lamp's shadow masked his lower face, but it revealed his tortured eyes that speculated—yes—no—yes—no. It was in his power to kill. At a click of his tongue there'd be ten bullets. But perhaps better not. Better wait. Better listen a while.

Down on his belly, his groin against the floor to relieve the pain, von Klaus, too, watched, listened, speculated. Even though he might not save himself, he would spoil Andrew's game. There was no possible mistake about his intention. Elsa spoke:

"Yes, Andrew. They say they know what the woman has done."

"Tell them to send for the woman!"

"Andrew!—First I want to—"

"Send for the woman!" Von Klaus cut in before she could speak. There was an excited laugh in his voice. It was not pain alone that made his eyes burn. He saw his chance. "*Jawohl!* Yes. Make an end! Tell her to bring in the head of John Baptist!"

"He's off his nut," said Andrew.

"Andrew, he isn't. He's—"

"Tell them to send for the woman."

Elsa interpreted. Von Klaus grinned, listened, waited, watched the old magician teeter on the brink of yes, no—yes, no. Slowly the magician's fear of his men outweighed the craving to be the source of thou shalt—thou shalt not. His men wanted the woman brought in. They wanted to know Andrew's purpose. Above all, they wanted that opium. Evil must be obeyed or perish. All tyrants know that. Pilate knew it. Better the command that will be readily obeyed. He murmured to the man beside him, who got up, swaggered to the door, whispered to the door guard. The door guard looked doubtful, or it might be fearful. But his not to reason why. He nodded—shouldered his rifle. The door slammed shut behind him.

"Now!" Von Klaus gloated. But he waited, in pain, bleeding. He chose not to waste the prodigious effort it cost to raise himself on an elbow and speak distinctly. He was trying to anticipate Andrew's next move. There was almost no sound but that muttering drumbeat.

Elsa whispered to Andrew:

"There's death. I can't see whose. It's—"

Von Klaus spoke, slowly, letting the words linger because he loved them:

"Mister Cunning Gunning! Why did Bulah Singh's Salome leave this room with a knife in her fist? Who plays John Baptist?"

He laid his forehead on his forearm, fighting the pain in his groin, recovering strength to carry on. Elsa whispered again:

"Andrew, this won't be the way you expect. There's something reversed—it's turned backward—I don't understand it. It's—"

Andrew interrupted, low-voiced: "I've a hunch we can't save Fritzyboy. I think I know what's coming. He didn't count on my men being—"

Von Klaus again, hoarse, harsh, gloating: "Blood on her knife! And without that opium, can her bastard become Dalai Lama? So does she love you? Hah! If you'd had the guts to shoot when I told you to shoot—but you hadn't the guts!—Here she comes! Now!"

The door opened. Andrew's right hand didn't move. Two Tibetans entered dragging something between them through the dim gloom.

They weren't self-respecting men. They weren't peasants, brigands, gunmen. Shabbily clad, hangdog-looking, they were *ragyabas*. They stank. Only in time of death were such outcasts admitted across thresholds to do what must be done. They were dragging their burden between them, its heels to the floor. And in the doorway stood Bulah Singh, his dark face faintly outlined by the blue light but also touched with blood-red from the brazier glow. He swayed slightly on bandaged feet. One arm was around the shoulder of Andrew's head man Bompo Tsering. His right hand was out of sight, behind the rifleman who had been sent to bring the woman.

"Andrew Gunning," he said, "here's where I buy your good will!"

Von Klaus gasped. The two stinking *ragyabas* dragged their burden past Andrew into the blue lamplight between von Klaus and the magician. There they raised it, holding it by the shoulders, face upward, so that the head and the wide-open lifeless eyes of Bulah Singh's woman goggled upside down at the magician.

Her own knife had been driven to the hilt into her throat—so powerfully driven that no blood ran.

Elsa gripped Andrew's arm. She didn't mean to. She couldn't help it. Andrew watched von Klaus. Von Klaus stared at the dead woman. The muttering drumbeat, as if it obeyed the magician's will, quickened its tempo, grew louder. Bulah Singh, heavily leaning on Bompo Tsering, limping on bandaged feet came and stood beside Andrew, still hiding his right hand.

"Major von Klaus!" he said. "You sent my woman to kill me. Die, like the dog that you are—you double-crossing, God-damned Hun son of a bitch!"

He fired three shots into the German. He would have fired a fourth but Andrew was too quick for him and too astonishingly strong.

Left-handed, he snatched the repeating pistol. He nearly broke the Sikh's wrist. Then he spoke quietly:

"One shot was plenty. Save your ammunition. Stand by."

CHAPTER 39

It was Bulah Singh's own repeating pistol. That set up a new chain of problems. But it was the wrong moment to ask how he got it from Bompo Tsering, who was on the far side of the Sikh, terrified by the magician's stare, blankly non-committal, looking his stupidest—ready to run for his life and soul and hope of lives to come, if it hadn't been for Bulah Singh's left arm around his shoulder; that and secret curiosity in some way stabilized him. Everyone, even the old magician,

546

waited on Andrew's next move. The ten Tibetans sat fascinated, hands on holsters, leaning forward, ready to draw.

Andrew laid Bulah Singh's automatic in Elsa's lap and she let it lie there. She appeared not even to notice it. That relieved the tension. The ten brigands let go, lolled, relaxed, almost unconscious of their own reaction but tremendously impressed by Andrew's disarming of Bulah Singh. The suddenness and skill, the lack of evident reason why he should have done it, mystified them. They were like spectators at a tragedy, spellbound. Andrew and their old magician were the irreconcilable forces of dramatic conflict, face to face in a setting of blue gloom.

The magician's silence was like a monstrous spider's, loaded with alertness but also with indecision. If he could only guess Andrew's intention, he would know what to do. On the other hand, Andrew felt he knew exactly what to do. He must do it quietly, in the right order, without the slightest suggestion of haste. He knew the magician was trying to read his mind. He was very careful not to underrate his antagonist. Foremost in his thought, for the magician to read, was recognition of the old man's prowess. There was no challenge, no irritation in that. Thought wasn't flowing so fast as it did—not more than two or three thoughts now between muttering drumbeats; but they were concrete thoughts, definite, sharp-edged, having satisfying limits. He could understand them. He felt very pleased with Elsa because she wasn't panicky. She sat still. If she was trying to guide him mentally he couldn't feel it. He felt nothing from her but a warm glow of confidence. He knew he could count on her. She would wait to be told what to do and then do it.

So the first thing was to make sure of Bulah Singh before he could recover self-command. When he did, he would be truculent. Bulah Singh wasn't a maniac like von Klaus; he had no conviction of racial superiority. He was in that sense easier to manage than the German had been. At a higher state of evolution than the victim of his bullets, to a certain extent he could think. He was more open to argument. For the moment he was nursing his hurt wrist, half believing it broken, biting his lip, scowling. He needed a plain presentation of fact. Andrew spoke quietly:

"One word, or one move, and I'll kill you."

The Sikh appeared to believe. He made no comment.

"As dead as von Klaus and your woman."

Again no comment. Reaction was taking care of Bulah Singh. No danger from him for a moment or two. The next two moves were as clear as though they were written on a board in front of Andrew's mind. But they were more difficult—needed more caution. He had to save the magician's face without implying for one moment that the magician had lost it. And he must remove the too suggestive evidence of death, that breeds death as surely as dirt breeds dirt. The sight of slain corpses never—since Cain slew Abel— never induced peace where there was no peace.

There was a dark stream of blood on the floor. It flowed from von Klaus's head, past the magician's feet, between him and Andrew. In that weird gloom it looked snake colour, until it reached the short zone of the brazier light. It moved and it coiled like a snake. Where the light from the brazier touched it, it appeared to have blood-red eyes and a flickering tongue. Its slow flow measured the speed of thought—hundreds of thoughts, but the blood not yet far from where it started.

Solemn stuff, blood—the solemn substance of all necromantic magic. So above all now, no solemnity! Andrew smiled at the magician. He looked down at the blood, at the two dead bodies, and shrugged his shoulders. In smiling pantomime he suggested it might be the master magician's pleasure to command what manifestly needed doing. Corpses dead by violence, in Tibet, are abominations not to be endured in the presence of self-respect. But can a general order his guns away and still give battle? Dead human blood was the stock in trade of the magician's mystery. He sat still—silent. He didn't yet understand Andrew's smile. He wasn't sure yet what Andrew intended. He feared for his dignity.

"Ask him," Andrew said quietly, "doesn't blood bring devils to cause confusion?"

Elsa, with closed eyes, translated. There was a barely noticeable change of tension. The magician's authority had been appealed to. To be obeyed would be a good beginning; all tyrants make use of that entering wedge. His lips moved. He murmured a few words in Tibetan. One of the ragyabas instantly swung the woman's corpse over his shoulder. The other picked up von Klaus. They carried away the bodies. One of them returned after a few moments and cleaned the blood off the floor, using a mop made of sheep's wool that looked like a featureless human head. The other brought water in which the two of them wrung the mop. When they had finished they put their tongues out at the magician and retired backwards—leaving behind them, along with relief from the stench of their persons, a sensation as of a closed book, and of a new page in a new book opened.

"Very clever!" Bulah Singh whispered. "But now what?"

Andrew had waited for that. Instantly he completed the humiliation of Bulah Singh. He pointed to the wall with his left hand. He held his right fist poised suggestively at about the level of the Sikh's liver.

"Go and sit down over there. Don't speak or move until you're spoken to."

The Sikh hardly hesitated. He studied Andrew for one moment and then hobbled away on bandaged feet. He sat down with his back to the wall. The ten Tibetans smiled. Henceforth, in that company, the Sikh would rate as Andrew's subordinate—a mere killer, rebuked—without a chance to regain importance. The Sikh realised it. Cunningly he hung his head, to make Andrew believe he accepted defeat and was henceforth playing Andrew's game.

The old magician studied the board and the pieces on the board. He was beginning to feel ready to answer Andrew's opening gambit. He looked at the packages of sugar and the canvas bag they came in—then at Andrew—then again at the sugar. There was not in his mind one trace, one symptom of the law, which even animals obey, that he who accepts a gift accepts an obligation to the giver. No gratitude. Andrew's sugar, if he could have his way, should be reckoned as tribute. It might be cunningly employed as evidence of Andrew's fear—since who gives valuable gifts unless he thinks he must? Solemn, logical, realistic, untrue argument, older than Machiavelli—as old as sin.

But it had dawned on Andrew that logic and mirth can't coexist. Like death and life, they deny each other. All logic, and all realism leads to tyranny and death. Mirth leads to freedom and life. So tyrants murder mirth as being treason to their logic. Mirth is white magic.

"Quick!" said Andrew. "Say this in Tibetan: The magician so wise that he can make the devils of the mountains fly away with a load of opium, surely can make other devils reveal where the opium is!"

Elsa half opened her eyes—translated. Andrew restrained a smile for the sake of the magician's dignity. He let his eyes laugh, for the magician's private information. Then he turned on Bompo Tsering, giving the magician time to weigh implications. Bompo Tsering almost jumped out of his skin when Andrew spoke to him, low-voiced:

"You! What happened?"

It was like turning on a faucet. Speech poured out. It had been

549

prepared. It was ready. "Gunnigun! My giving Bulah Singh his pistol because that woman coming. Her calling him bad names too much. Her wanting us Tibetans helping her to castrating him, then kill him. But your having ordered us our guarding him. And Gunnigun, his saying that woman your enemy. So our holding her. His using her knife, killing her too much."

The truth. No doubt of it. But not the whole truth.

"What became of the child?"

"His running away."

Also, clearly not the whole truth. But Elsa had finished translating. In another moment the magician might see a flaw in Andrew's strategy. Now, before thought could organise against him, was the right split-second to force the main issue. He spoke fiercely to Bompo Tsering:

"Get out of here! Now. Get the men and ponies ready to march."

"But, Gunnigun! Being too much dark night! Their needing rest! Our needing food to take along—"

"Be ready to march at moonrise! Will you obey? Or—"

"My obeying! My going now! My doing!"

"Take that porter with you."

Scared nearly out of his wits, Bompo Tsering showed his tongue to the magician and was gone. In a moment he was kicking the porter up off the floor. The door guard tried to stop him. Andrew, laughing again with his eyes, said to the magician in English:

"Let both men out!"

Elsa translated. His authority again appealed to, the magician nodded. He slightly raised his right hand. The door opened, admitting a welcome blast of clean cold air. Then it slammed shut. There was a moment's silence. The magician spoke then—one word—in Tibetan.

"He asks 'Why?'" said Elsa. "I believe he means why did you send away Bompo Tsering?"

Andrew knew he had won. His smile now was triumphant.

"Ask him: Does he want my men to hear all about the opium? If so, I'll send for them to come back and listen."

Bulah Singh cackled a curt laugh: " Clever! Krishna! Yes! Who would have thought of it!"

The brigand who knew a few words of English leaned forward, pointing his finger at Andrew:

"You! Your knowing where is—that—that stuff! Your saying—your showing us! Your making us look-see!"

The magician rebuked him, but he looked mutinous. He began

to whisper to the next man. Andrew made his last move but one. The magician's eyes betrayed that he knew himself checkmate even before Elsa had finished saying what Andrew told her to say.

"When we entered the village we saw yak-dung and the hoof-prints of yaks in the mud."

The magician nodded almost imperceptibly.

"Did not those yaks belong to the *peling* von Klaus, who is now dead?"

Another hardly perceptible movement of the old magician's head acknowledged the fear that if he should deny the fact there might be worse to come.

"How many yaks are there?"

Silence. But suddenly Bulah Singh piped up again. "Ten yaks! I asked von Klaus at the village gate. He boasted: ten yaks—two mules—twenty sheep."

The brigand who knew English interrupted loudly:

"Yux belonging us now!" Then he whispered to the brigands near him. They put their heads together. They appeared to agree. But the old magician had understood Andrew. Cautiously, carefully, feeling his way in the hope of seeing an alternative, he surrendered inch by inch to Andrew's terms. He angrily commanded silence, with a bark like an angry leopard's. The whispering ceased. He must have made a secret signal then, because the muttering drumbeat swelled to a low thunder and died down again. Andrew stole that dramatic moment:

"Tell him," he said cheerfully, "I want all ten yaks loaded with bar-ley. I want 'em now. That will be a small thing in return for all this sug-ar. The yaks cost him nothing. I also want the twenty sheep belonging to von Klaus, each sheep loaded with all the butter it can carry."

Elsa translated. Andrew continued:

"He and his men may keep whatever else von Klaus had with him, including firearms, ammunition, and money. But as for the opium—which was in this bag until the lord magician made the devils change it into sugar—I wash my hands of it. It is the lord magician's. Let him command or not command the devils to produce it or not to produce—as he pleases!"

Elsa was heard to the end in silence. But then the storm broke. All ten brigands stood up and shouted. One of them flourished a Mauser. The one who knew English shouted:

"Your will staying here until our having that!"

The drumbeat swelled again. Through the tumult Bulah Singh

called hoarsely to Andrew: "Give me my automatic! This means they'll put hot charcoal to your feet and fingers! They mean to know where the opium is!"

That wasn't such a bad guess. One brigand strode to the brazier. He stirred it with an iron poker and blew on it until it glowed crimson. Then he shook the poker at Andrew.

"Elsa," said Andrew, "go up close to the magician and ask: Shall I tell them—or tell him—where the opium is?"

She obeyed. The brigands stared. The tumult died down, but not quickly enough even for the nearest brigand to overhear what Elsa said. She returned and sat down in the chair.

"You're not scared?" Andrew asked.

"No. Why should I be?"

She loved him too much to be scared of anything at that moment. Andrew patted her hand on the chair-arm. He did it unconsciously, and she knew that. She was glad with all her heart that her love was secret from him. If Andrew knew, it might confuse and make him self-conscious. His whole attention was on the magician, which was where it should be. He didn't even know he had spoken to Elsa. Now he heard Bulah Singh speaking:

"Give me my automatic! We've got to shoot our way out!"

He heard the words—understood—but took no notice. The old magician arose slowly to his feet and there began to be a new unearthly artificial silence, separated into measured spaces by the drumbeat. He had some secret way of controlling the drumbeat. The brigands recognized the changing rhythm. It was an overture to something that they knew too well. It frightened them. There was a chilly sensation like the moment before hail. There came a noise like the rattle of dry bones and a moaning like that of the wind on the hill where they bury the dead. Andrew spoke without knowing it:

"Don't let this scare you. Grab hold of me if you want to."

He laid his hand on the chair-arm. Elsa pushed hers under it. His fingers closed on hers. Her lips moved. Silently, inside himself, where secret laughter was the fuel of a new, unconquerable fire, he began singing ribald nonsense:

The French they are a funny race—
Parlez-vous!
They fight with their feet and—

Even that ceased. The old master hypnotist's mental rhythm over-

552

whelmed mere words. Something was happening. Something like a tidal wave in consciousness. It was impossible to tell how the magician did it, but it felt mechanical—almost electric—as if he knew some way of agitating the glands that govern fear. He pointed at empty space. His brigands began to see what they knew he willed they should see. He chanted, in ancient Tibetan, the language that devils use who sinned so vilely that they may not be reborn but spend eternities in quest of still human souls whose bodies they can seize for a little while and use for a little evil in the dark.

And then—as the Tibetans saw it and lent it material substance, Andrew and Elsa saw too. It was into the dark that the magician pointed—the dark corner where the zone of firelight ceased and there was dim blue gloom. All the Tibetans moaned. The door guard let his rifle fall to the floor with a crash. The magician croaked like a raven—chanting—pausing—chanting. In dim blue darkness a pale disembodied face took form. Bulah Singh spoke hoarsely:

"Give me my automatic!"

It was a face so saturated with the cruel loneliness of death that Andrew's blood ran cold. It was like a death mask. Only it lived. Its eyes opened. They were cold pale green. Its mouth moved, like a murdered mouth that licked dead lips for the lingering taste of hatred that could not die. Then it spoke, in the ancient Tibetan that only the magician understood. Its voice came from nowhere—from everywhere—from all over the room. It seemed to fill the room with a sepulchral sound that had no echo.

"What's he saying?" Bulah Singh demanded. "If you can get this—I mean understand it—you can beat him at his own game! What's he saying?—Give me my automatic!"

Like force compressed beyond compression's limit, Andrew's inner laughter returned suddenly. As it did, the voice died to a harsh, hoarse whisper that rose and fell, continually waning until it ceased. Elsa's hand within Andrew's moved convulsively. Her lips moved. He knew she was saying the Lord's Prayer. He made a sudden decision to pray too, for the sake of unity and friendship and because he vaguely felt he had been unkind and had mistrusted her. Besides, the thought of prayer felt clean. But why in silence? He prayed aloud:

Twinkle, twinkle, little star!
How I wonder what you are,
Up above the—

Bulah Singh interrupted: "What in hell are you talking about! Have you gone mad?"

And then Elsa: "Keep it up, Andrew! It's the thought that counts. The words don't mean a thing!".

That spell was broken. But it re-awoke inward laughter. Consciously he ridiculed himself, and that was a relief like a pulled tooth. It was like waking from a nightmare. And as he watched, that pale face like a death mask began changing. It wasn't only Andrew who observed it. The old magician appeared to lose physical strength. He resumed his seat at the desk between the blue lamps. He looked ghastly. He sweated. Transferred to his face was the tortured lonely murdered look of the apparition. Where the apparition had been, now was the wrinkled, astonishing face of Lobsang Pun. It was alive, alert, in motion. One quick glimpse, and it was gone. Then silence. Not even a drumbeat. All the brigands were down on their hands and knees.

Andrew stole also that moment. He spoke quickly.

"Good girl! Well done! Now! Tell Lung-gom-pa now is the time! Give us yaks, barley, sheep, butter—now—this minute—or I'll tell his brigands where to look for the opium!"

Elsa translated. The frightened brigands, hearing her voice, scrambled to their feet, too late. They didn't hear what Elsa said. The magician turned his head slowly and gazed at Bulah Singh. It was an unspoken question.

"Tell him," said Andrew, "that man doesn't know where the opium is."

The old magician smiled thinly when Elsa told him what Andrew had said. Bulah Singh spoke up, protesting:

"You idiot! Do you think they'll believe I don't know? They'll torture me! Do you think I'll tell them nothing? Jesus Christ! I'll tell them stuff about you that'll—"

He stopped suddenly, because Andrew had picked up the automatic from Elsa's lap. He looked half incredulous, cunning, triumphant and then cautious as he listened:

"Elsa, tell Lung-gom-pa we'll take Bulah Singh with us. And this: We march at moonrise." He reached for his watch. Every brigand in the room reached for his automatic. But Andrew only glanced at the time. He smiled. They all looked clownish and self-conscious. "That means half an hour from now. Repeat: Unless we're on our way at moonrise, I will tell where the opium is."

The magician stared. He opened his mouth wide. His blasphemous

554

lips framed the sacred syllable. He breathed it, murmured it, moaned it. His brigands joined in:

"*Aum-m-m-m-m-m-m-m-m-m-m-m-m-m-m-m-m-m-m-m-m-m!*"

One thing now seemed sure. There would be no killing while that sound lingered on the air. Andrew put his arm through Elsa's and spoke sharply to the Sikh:

"Get a move on, you. Grab my other arm. We'll go now while the going's good."

CHAPTER 40

So the second stage of the journey began, beneath an icy moon, in a moaning wind. The yaks and sheep were not too manageable; they didn't relish a night march. Men and ponies had been well fed, not well rested. Bulah Singh, with his feet bandaged against the cold, rode one of von Klaus's mules, taken from the brigands in trade for his automatic, which Andrew wouldn't have let him have back in any event. He rode darkly alone in mid-column, at the tail of the little flock of loaded sheep. The mule and ponies could be trusted not to override the sheep. The yaks couldn't. So Bompo Tsering led the way with the yaks, singing to keep *dugpas* from misleading him along the shadowy trail.

Andrew brought up the rear, to prevent straggling. Elsa rode with him. For a long time they didn't talk much. As almost always happens after a terrific ordeal there was a feeling of dissociation from events— of unreality—of something not quite like waking from a dream. They listened for random rifle shots—farewell salutes from the magician's village, each whining bullet loaded with resentment, each echoing crack a threat of pursuit. But they were Tibetan brigands, too afraid of ghouls and of the homeless souls of murdered men to be likely to pursue through the darkness. Andrew said:

"They know we'll move slowly because of the sheep. Two miles an hour is our limit. They'll count on overtaking us at their convenience. They'll search for the opium first. The old magician doesn't want us caught. He's too sure we'd fix the blame on him for the loss of the opium. That might cost him his life—his power anyhow. So he'll keep 'em looking for the damned stuff for several days. By that time we'll have crossed the Shigatse. They won't follow us across. It's too danger-ous this time of year. And there'd be too much risk of running into troops from Lhasa."

After that he was silent for a long time. Elsa was glad of it. It was enough to ride beside him. Her love for him seemed to be part of the mystery—part of the night. She must get used to it, now, under the moon and the stars. Secrets are more difficult to keep by daylight. She hugged her secret, as she hugged herself warm inside her overcoat. Andrew didn't suspect it.

She had learned a lot about Andrew. During the last few hours she had thought about him as never before. Her previous blindness seemed incredible. Cursed or blessed, whichever it was, and perhaps it was both, with clairvoyance and sensitivity and pride, how should she account for not having known she was in love? That was the bewildering thing. Why hadn't she known? She could see now that she had been in love with him all along. O God, how glad she was she hadn't known it sooner! If she had known, she could never have come with him on this expedition, even with the wild intention of releasing Tom Grayne from an unbearable yoke. It would have been unthinkable. What had given her the right—the moral right—to travel alone with Andrew had been the fact that they weren't in love. Fact! What skittles facts are! Icicles that melt the moment truth appears!

And now, would she have to confess to Tom that she loved Andrew? Tom would be sure to suspect it. But would it be any of Tom's business? He would be right to suspect herself, yes, because it was true. It was true forever. But not Andrew. Andrew wasn't in love. Had she any right to compromise Andrew—in exchange for his kindness—his generosity—his unwavering respect? As long as she was Tom Grayne's wife, Andrew would treat her as Tom Grayne's wife, no matter what passion might urge him to do. There would be no concessions. Andrew would lean backwards. The worst possible mistake would be to let Andrew even guess she loved him. He would dry up. He would govern himself so grimly that even if he were in love with her, he would deny love rather than intrigue against his friend—even if she were willing. She was unwilling.

Death would be ten times welcome rather than anything shabby or underhanded. In fact, she wasn't at all sure, nor was she disturbed by the thought, that death might not be the acceptable answer. She didn't feel like dying. She was quite sure she wasn't afraid of death. Surely she wouldn't seek it. But she would rather die ten times over than betray Tom Grayne and Andrew—both or either of them. They were men of integrity. To betray them into a quarrel would be a dirty and abominable thing—a whorish thing. It made her shudder to think of it.

Andrew's character had steered them clear of the toils of Lung-gom-pa. Nothing else could have done it. She knew quite well what her own indispensable part had been, but it would have been quite useless without Andrew's spirit—his indomitable integrity. Another man would have trimmed his spiritual sails and have lined up with von Klaus and Bulah Singh, trusting to the future and some trick to clear that entanglement. Or he might have left Bulah Singh to make what terms he could with the magician. But in spite of the certainty that Bulah Singh would be treacherous at the first opportunity, Andrew had snatched him out of danger—brought him along—not trusted him but saved him. The most lovable thing about Andrew was that he didn't suspect himself of being a hero in anyone's eyes— least of all in his own.

As it happened Andrew was still a little afraid he had done the wrong thing. He spoke of it after a while:

"Hell! If I were only a killer. I'm not. I can't persuade myself to take human life. I suppose it's cowardice."

Elsa kept silent. She remembered she mustn't praise him. If she should tell him he wasn't a killer because he wasn't capable of cowardice he would shut up like a clam; his thoughts would be driven back into himself behind that veil that she could never penetrate. Silence was better—silence, the stars, and the magic of frosty moonlight. It wasn't long before he began talking again. He seemed to find comfort in thinking aloud:

"Suppose I'd left Bulah Singh. They might have tortured him to find out what became of the opium. But I think not. He'd have pretended he knows where I dumped it. He'd have bargained with the brigands and trusted to luck. You know of course why he killed that woman?"

He waited for an answer. She had to speak.

"Bompo Tsering said she tried to kill him. Wasn't that the reason?"

"Part of it. I got the whole story from Bompo Tsering while they were loading the yaks and sheep. Bulah Singh was through with the woman. She'd gone her limit for him. She was no more use to him, but she might be dangerous because she knew too much about him.

So his scheme was to take the child and to leave her behind. She'd doped it out. She and the child both screamed the accusation at him when she showed up. Bompo Tsering believes they'd read Bulah Singh's thought— something like tapping his mental telephone. Anyhow, she and Bulah Singh had a battle of words to get control of our Tibetans.

They bid high. Both sides promised anything. But she made the mistake of telling our men that you and I were on the coals already, being tortured by Lung-gom-pa. That gave Bulah Singh his chance to play Sir Galahad. He did such a spellbinding job of it that they held the woman. They gave him her knife and said: 'Kill her!' He did. I guess he wasn't squeamish. After that, Bompo Tsering felt he could trust him, so he gave him back the automatic. We know the rest."

"But, Andrew, what became of the child? Surely they didn't kill the child? Bulah Singh didn't, did he?"

"No. The brat ran away. Bulah Singh tried to get them to catch him, to bring with us. He's like von Klaus, but a bit more subtle, with an obstinate one-plan mind. He still hopes to persuade me to try to substitute that young monster for the Dalai Lama."

"But, Andrew, where is the child? What happened to him?"

"I don't know. I told you: he ran. Perhaps Lung-gom-pa might take him on as an apprentice. He's the type. But Bompo Tsering thinks Bulah Singh may have made a last-minute deal with one of the brigands to bring the little brute along after us. He swears we haven't seen the last of him."

"Do you believe that, Andrew? You don't believe that, do you?"

"I never believe what I believe. I'm one of them there hopers. Bulah Singh did talk with one of the brigands while my back was turned. I'm counting on old man Shigatse. It's one hell of a river. Once across, we'll be rid of pursuit."

"But isn't there a ferry?"

"There won't be, once we're on the far side. I'll see to it."

Silence again. Elsa thought of scores of questions that she didn't dare to ask. She thought of things she was aching to tell. But questioning or telling might make Andrew close his mind. So they rode without speaking for a long time until he unexpectedly broke the silence:

"I suppose you saw what I did—that face in the magician's chamber? I can see it now without trying to. I could carve it in wood. It was one hell of a God-damned face. I guess I'm going to have to carve it, to forget it—to get it out of my system. What did you make of it?"

"Did you see only one face?"

"I saw two. I guess we all did. But I'm speaking of the first one. It burned itself on to the brain like magnesium light. That was plain black magic. Call it hypnotism if you want to play ostrich. Hypnotism is the charlatan highbrow's false name for a lot of boloney. It's an easy word for intellectuals to hide behind."

Elsa forced herself not to answer. She was almost bursting with excitement. For the first time Andrew seemed to be drawing aside, if only ever so little, that veil behind which his purposes lurked— purposes that never appeared except as forthright actions, done, un- explained. Even those few words almost stopped him. He seemed to suspect he had said too much. But she waited in silence. So after a minute or two he continued."

"Barring unimportant details, we had an example tonight of the inside workings of all priestcraft and all politics."

Was he trying to get her to tell what she knew? Was he pumping her? She didn't yet dare to accept the challenge. It was quite possible that he was tempting her into an argument so that he might grind his baffled emotions against her mysticism. Presently, since she said noth- ing, he made another downright statement:

"We're all in the same boat, doing the same damned thing. We either make mental pictures, or else we have 'em made for us. One or the other. We create, or we don't. The cave men did it. Moses forbade it. So did Mohammed. But we all do it. We're either potter's thumb or else the moulded plastic. Get that? Shape or be shaped. Magic—white or black—Christian or pagan—ancient or modern—is the acquired ability to create and project a mental image that suggests to other people what to believe and how to behave."

Elsa listened, too excited to trust herself to speak. Her voice might have betrayed her. Andrew was heading straight into her new holy of holies. Did he know it? Anyhow, silence was the best way to persuade him to continue. Presently he did, looking up at the moon as he rode. His face shone.

"A black magician purposely creates a fear image—fear— vio- lence—need—hunger—sickness—death— all that stuff. That living dead face that we saw was Lung-gom-pa's picture of God. His God's a devil. If you analyse it far enough, it's himself. That was his own inside portrait. But I'll bet you not one of us saw the same face. I doubt we heard the same words. Lung-gom-pa projected his own composite mental picture of himself, his teacher, his black *mahatma,* (a person revered for spirituality and high-mindedness), and his father the Devil all combined in one. But what each of us saw was a symbol of his own fear and his own hate. He made us do it. He used the drumbeat to work up emotion. He's an expert mental technician. But his funda- mental principle's the same as any political priest's or boss-gangster's— it's the same for instance as Hitler's bogey picture of the Jew—or the

Sunday School picture of a devil with horns."

Elsa couldn't keep quiet any longer. "Andrew, don't you think the magician had help?"

"How d'you mean?"

"Is it the wrong time to try to explain what I've—what I've discovered quite recently?"

"All depends. Is it first-hand? Or did someone tell you."

"Both. First I was told. Then I tried—and discovered."

"Ummn. Go ahead. I'll listen."

But was he listening? She was afraid he had retired behind a veil of scepticism into that unexplorable where he kept his passion. It was no use guessing—no use hesitating—no use trying to choose the right words. Elsa plunged in:

"Andrew—suppose you say 'Jesus' to someone. What happens? Instantly that person's concept of Jesus presents itself to him as a mental picture. He can't help it. It happens. It's either the child Jesus, or the Teacher on the Mount, or the crucified or the resurrected Jesus—or perhaps a target Jesus that he doesn't believe in—that he hurls his hatred at. Perhaps it's a dead Jesus—crucified dead, buried and done for. But whoever hears the name Jesus sees an instantaneous mental picture."

"Yes, I guess that's so. I see a picture of Jesus as soon as you mention him."

"You can't help it, Andrew. And you act accordingly. That mental image is an actual structural part of your subconsciousness. So whatever the word Jesus means to you in terms of past experience becomes available to you. To the extent no more, and no less—that the Christ Force and the name Jesus are associated in your consciousness, that Force is yours—your own! It becomes your guide, your immediate standard of values. That is why it's so tremendously important to form strong mental images. Is that clear?"

"Sure. That's another way of saying what I said. Create your mental images or else some charlatan'll do it for you. So Jesus—to me—is pretty much of a fighting cue. Right off the bat I suspect anyone who yawps about Jesus. It's all right as a cuss word."

"You call it a fighting cue? What kind of fight? Can you tell me?"

"Sure. Why not. It makes me want to vomit on the swine who've made Jesus's name a synonym for cruelty—lies—aggression—injustice—rant—cant—damned hypocrisy—and—"

Elsa's gay laugh interrupted: "Andrew, what's wrong with it?

560

Haven't you won any fights?"

He almost drew aside the veil over his thoughts. Almost. She felt it. But she felt it close again.

"I've had some lickings, too," he answered.

He was ready to dry up. She swiftly changed her tactics: "Andrew—didn't you see more than one face in the magician's chamber?"

"Yes. I said so."

"Whose face was the other?"

He didn't answer for nearly a minute. When he did, he had dismissed equivocation. He spoke bluntly: "It looked to me like Lobsang Pun's face." But then he raised his guard: "As far as I'm concerned that was a memory picture—from the photograph of Lobsang Pun in Nancy Strong's room in Darjeeling! There was even a bullet hole in the forehead."

"But you admit you saw it?"

"Yes. And Lung-gom-pa saw something too. It scared him. What I saw was a memory picture of Lobsang Pun. It obliterated the first face. It was like an eclipse. I can't explain it."

"May I try to explain?"

"Sure. Go ahead. But you'll have to more than explain if you want me to more than believe. I'd like to know. I'm fed up with believing."

"Andrew—you'll have to find this out. I had to. We all have to—each for himself. But we can help each other, the way Nancy Strong helped me, by showing which way to look."

He interrupted: "Let's see if I get your thought: '... and I, if I be lifted up, will draw all men unto me'?—Is that the idea? I've tried it. I've been a horrible example of pious rectitude, courageous consistency and all that stuff. People don't copy you. They throw stink bombs. It's no good."

"Andrew, please, I'm trying my very best to tell what I know."

"You mean, what you believe?"

"What I know! Andrew, this is what did happen. My mental image of Lobsang Pun, that I conceived with every scrap of will I could bring to bear, let into the consciousness of everyone in the room, you and me included, a thought force so tremendous that it overwhelmed the magician's. That dreadful living death mask was Lung-gom-pa's own picture of his own soul—of his own black *mahatma*—his own ideal. He projected it to arouse the vilest instincts of every person in the room, because he knows how to manipulate those. But I have

561

been taught what to do. So I shouted for Lobsang Pun. That may be hard for you to believe. I shouted for him—yelled for help—in silence. You saw what happened."

"I admit I saw his face."

Elsa was into her stride. Nothing now could stop her. "You couldn't possibly have seen it if you hadn't concentrated your will on one thing!"

"What do you mean? I swear to God I wasn't thinking of Lobsang Pun."

"Shall I say what you were doing?"

"Yes. If you think you know."

"You were searching—not for the lesser evil, but for the greater good. Isn't it true?"

"Yes. I guess that's true. I've never believed in that fool doctrine of the lesser evil. It's defeatist, degenerate, negative, no good. It's Jesuitical. It leads downhill—all the way to the bottom of rotten politics and rot-gut religion. The hell with it. But say: are you trying to tell me that Lobsang Pun appeared in person and scared Lung-gom-pa and his brigands, just in answer to your—"

"Oh well, if you want to be cruel—"

"I swear I didn't mean to be. Sorry, Elsa. I wouldn't hurt you for worlds. I know you're trying to say something important. But I happen to know that Old Ugly-face is a fugitive. He's running for his life. There's a price on his head. Morgan Lewis asked me to find him and to help him if I possibly can."

"And you will?"

"If I can, yes. Sure I will. I mean to try to find him."

"Then mayn't he help us?"

"How can he? He's on the lam. Down and out. Say, see here: if Lobsang Pun were the magician that you seem to think—who can appear when you summon him—he'd use his magic—wouldn't he?— to get himself out of the mess he's in. If he can't help himself, how can he help you and me?"

"Andrew, did you ever hear of superconsciousness?"

"I've heard Nancy Strong speak of it."

"There are subconsciousness—consciousness—and superconsciousness. Lung-gom-pa used black magic to project that living death mask face from the very depth of subconsciousness. That's where his black magic comes from, out of the infinite dark ocean of all the evil that ever was from the beginning of time until now."

562

"That sounds like Nancy Strong talking."

"Lobsang Pun derives intelligence from superconsciousness. That is to say not from the past, but from the future, which is all new and has nothing to do with the past. Become conscious of him, and his super-consciousness reaches us. Subconsciousness can't touch it."

"That doesn't begin to explain why he's on the lam in danger of his life. Are you feeding me Nancy's pap about evolution?"

"Yes. But with, oh, what a long spoon!"

He laughed, touched. But in another moment he was back at her: "It's like Christian Science. Too much profit and loss."

"Andrew, you don't know any Christian Science. And if you wish to understand what I'm trying to tell, you must open your mind, not think of all the silly second-hand objections that fools have put into your mind."

"Have one more try."

"Very well. This is the law. In superconsciousness, in which the Christ Force is, there is no such idea as profit and loss. Personal prof-it— any kind of profit—can only enter from subconsciousness. Who-ever clings to the idea of profit can't become superconscious. It's im-possible. Does that explain why Lobsang Pun can come to our aid spiritually, but can't help himself materially?"

Andrew turned it over and over in his mind. He didn't answer for so long that Elsa at last sought for some new form of words in which to reach his thought.

"Andrew," she said suddenly, "would you care to tell me, in strict confidence, why you left the United States?"

It was as if the night wind had swept down a house of cards. She could feel him draw back into himself and slam the mental door. After a full minute he said: "I have never told anyone that. It's better dead and buried.— Do you see that low hill? That's where we'll pitch camp until the wind drops tomorrow evening. From there to the river is three days' hard marching. If we've luck we'll make it."

PART THREE
CHAPTER 41

One week's march north of the Shigatse, the roar of the flood-borne ice was still in Elsa's ears whenever she thought backward. She was trying to think forward. Thought wouldn't obey. It flowed back-ward most of the time, marvelling at Andrew—where had he learned such super-human gift of leadership?—in a law office?—loving him, trying to understand him, baffled. The first sight of that river had seemed to set his heart on fire. He became a new-world Hannibal, a Caesar, compelling men and beasts to do what they all knew was impossible until he showed the way, and drove, and led. But he was far from pleased with himself. He had turned morose, almost speechless, kind when spoken to but doling words as if they hurt him: She didn't know why he suffered. She suspected herself of having caused it. She didn't know how.

By night, under the stars, she could see, and even feel the unimportance of herself and of Andrew too, and of the earth and all its ways. Then they were less than microbes in an infinite mystery. It was comforting to feel how small they were. But under the tent they grew larger again. And by day there were no stars by which to measure the absurdity of fear.

There's an irritating magnetism in the Tibetan wind at high levels. The aneroid registered seventeen thousand feet. The Kunlun Range was in sight whenever a buzz-saw wind worried the horizon clouds sufficiently to give a glimpse of the snow-clad peaks. It was typical Tibetan spring. You couldn't hear yourself shout. That increased the irritation. It was further increased by Bulah Singh's hostile calm—his ominous good behaviour—his glowering look of gloating over private information that would presently emerge to everyone's discomfort but his own.

Andrew was having hard work to keep his temper with the men. Bompo Tsering resented his concern for the pack animals.

"Don't you understand we can't reach Tum-Glain with dead ponies?"

"Gunnigun, no beating, going too slow. By-um-by coming soldiers, catching us, then—"

"See here! Next time there's a gall or a sore or a whip mark, you lose a day's pay. That's final."

Less cruelty for a while. More miles covered in consequence. But there was no change in Andrew's mood. He continued to be too polite to Elsa—too considerate of all her possible needs except the only one that mattered. He revealed of his own inner consciousness nothing. Less than nothing. What he did apparently let slip at odd moments was merely some new phase of the veil that concealed tormented thought. The strain was made almost unbearable by their continuing to sleep together, under doubled blankets. She knew he did it to save her feelings, so that she shouldn't feel demoted. She couldn't refuse for fear of hurting his feelings; he might have thought she no longer trusted him. She didn't believe he believed his own excuse that Bulah Singh might play some trick on her if she were left alone at night. Bulah Singh was under constant observation by never less than two Tibetans, who delighted in watching him because it made themselves feel important. He was behaving discreetly. He had kept himself to himself ever since having been thoroughly snubbed at the river crossing, where Andrew had forbidden him to help or to give orders to anyone. He had been made to wait until the last, to be brought over between Andrew and Bompo Tsering—humiliated, relegated to the category of useless baggage. Since then he rode alone, ate alone, pitched his tent alone, and kept his own unsmiling counsel.

But Bulah Singh's dark glance indicated he had drawn his own conclusions about that two-in-one-tent business. As he doubtless intended, it filled Andrew with glowering anger, knowing that Elsa couldn't fail to understand. Keeping herself tidy and good-looking in spite of difficulties, Elsa was desperately careful not to create the impression that her make-up was to please Andrew. But the Sikh's glance dourly inferred the opposite. She had to cold-cream her skin continually against the searing wind. But she removed the smear whenever possible, to escape Andrew's pity—worse, his tolerance. That stuff soon turns to contempt. So she studied her mirror. When each supper-time came she was presentable. By bedtime she was even almost pleased with her own appearance. Andrew would need another excuse than physical distaste for keeping away. But the Sikh could draw his own inferences—or pretend to. He did.

And the strange thing was that Andrew didn't keep away. That was one of the comforting things about him. By candlelight, in the tent, under the blankets, he began to thaw out and become human, giving a little of his confidence, even sometimes speaking first without being questioned, volunteering conversation. When his physical muscles relaxed on the air mattress, his mental strain seemed to let go simultaneously. He never shrank away from her or seemed self-conscious. She got a sensation then that he wasn't so nervously on guard against trap questions. He was trusting her. So she was extra careful, silently rehearsing words before she said them, testing each phrase to be sure it shouldn't sound like an entering wedge.

But except for short moments and trifling details his reserve held, until one night when he sat up suddenly under the candle-lantern listening to the whining yowl of a snow leopard, answered by its mate from not far off. The pair were prowling around the camp, calling to each other, trying to scare loose a sheep or a young yak. But Bompo Tsering was making the rounds. He came and reported the animals all secure, Bulah Singh in his tent, and the watchmen awake. After that the Tibetans kept up a devil's clatter of camel bells and tin cans. Some-one sang to the yaks to keep them from stampeding. Sleep was im-possible. Andrew didn't even lie down again. He sat, elbows on knees, head between his hands, looking dejected. It might be an opportunity. Elsa at last threw caution to the winds and seized it:

"Andrew—would it help to talk? Being listened to is sometimes a great help."

He didn't answer. But during the pause she felt no sharp reaction— no sudden retreat into his inner self. She dared again, carefully:

"Andrew, it's sometimes said that great leaders don't appreciate what they have done. It seems all small to them and disappointing. But I can't believe many of them ever took it as badly as you do."

His reserve broke down a little. But he was captious because she had more than hinted at praise.

"You're not calling me great?" he suggested. He laughed dryly, to take the edge off rudeness. "I ask just to be sure you're in your right mind."

That gave her the idea. She put spunk into it, and came back at him: "Don't flatter yourself. I'm trying to point out what a little-minded man you are, in spite of all your bigness in some ways."

"What d'you mean?"

That was a fair question. He was startled—touched— interested. Elsa cut loose:

"Any man I ever heard of, except you, who was big enough to do what you've done, would have been big enough to chest himself, and thank whatever Gods there be, and even brag a little for the sake of his companions. After all, we all believed in you. That's how and why you got us safely across the Shigatse without losing a man or a load, and only one pony. You're our hero. Haven't we a right to see the leader we trusted look at least a bit proud of himself? Are we nothing? Is it worth nothing that—"

He interrupted with another of his dry laughs. "I get you. There's a lot in what you say. Yes. I know, I've been difficult."

"Difficult? You've been ungracious and contemptible. You haven't had enough grace to thank your own soul for the privilege of playing the man!"

566

He laughed, not sourly this time. She had touched his humour.

"But you don't understand," he retorted lamely.

"I know I don't. I wish I did."

"Did you never feel your own soul mocking you?"

"Andrew! How can you ask that question with a straight face? Have you no memory? Or are you pretending to forget, just to be polite?"

"I guess I know what you mean."

"Yes. Indeed you can't help knowing. How long is it since I was hopeless in Darjeeling? If it hadn't been for you and your strong friendship I don't like to think what might have happened."

"You don't have to think about it," he answered. "It didn't happen."

She had another flash of inspiration. She bit back the retort that almost left her lips. "It didn't happen," she said, "because I had you to talk to."

He thought that over. Suddenly he said: "Is that an invitation?"

"Yes. Let me do for you perhaps a fraction of what you did for me."

"Okay. I accept. If it'll make you feel better, I'll tell you what's burning me up. But it's for your ears only. And it won't bear contradiction."

"I won't contradict. And I promise I'll never tell anyone else in the world."

"You won't want to, if you hear me through to a finish."

"I will listen, Andrew. I won't interrupt."

"You brought this on yourself, remember. I didn't ask you to listen."

"I know you didn't. I asked you. Do you want me to sit upright?"

"No. Lie where you are and keep warm under the blankets. If I bore you, you can fall asleep."

She turned over, away from him, snuggling down so that he couldn't see even the tip of her nose in the candlelight. She felt she couldn't waits for him to begin. But she had to. He sat a long time, listening to the leopards and to the noises the Tibetans made. He seemed unable to force himself to lay bare his thought. But he plunged in suddenly at last:

"I'll tell it all. But please don't talk back. There are two reasons why I'll carry on to the end of this job. One is that I passed my word to Tom Grayne. Maybe you don't know it, but Tom happens to be ranking Number One, in Asia, on the U.S. secret list. Tom isn't the kind of man that one lets down."

"Did you ever let anyone down?"

"Did we agree you'd listen?"

"Sorry."

"Most people think a Number One secret agent's the same as a spy. He isn't. All spies are rats. Every last damned one of them. There isn't a spy in the world, from a cabinet minister or a full-blown general, all the way down to a Wop peepshow guide in Marseilles, who wouldn't sell out his own crowd for his own profit. Never forget that, because it's true. The more a big bug uses spies and believes in 'em the more he himself is corrupt or a stupid fool or both. You can buy anything he knows or thinks he knows from any spy in the world, and you can blackmail it out of any spy-master. Spying and self-respect can't live together under the same scalp. No self-respecting man is a spy. No spy has any self-respect. A spy is a stinker who peeps through keyholes, and pilfers, and betrays, not necessarily for money. Some of 'em do it for excitement and for the feeling of importance it gives 'em.

"But a Number One secret agent is different, and Tom is head and shoulders above all of 'em. Tom does no dirty work. His job is to find out what is really going on beneath the surface, beneath the tides of diplomatic *bushwa*,(baloney) that might start the Continental armies marching—and perhaps drag America in. Tom is out for the truth that's somewhere down underneath the cowardly treachery and lies of the world's so-called statesmen and their toadies. I mean the men who make the headlines. Most of the world's big shots are merely ignorant crooks. Some of 'em know what they're lying about. But they're all unscrupulous. They're criminals in fancy dress. There isn't one so-called statesman or diplomat in the whole world whose word of honour is worth more than Bulah Singh's. Some of 'em can put on a better front, and that's all.

"So why is Tom Grayne in Tibet? Nine-tenths of the world's ruling men don't even know where it is. Tibet cause a world war? Or be a key to world victory? A fine laugh that 'ud give 'em. But it's the truth. Tibet and Jerusalem are two of the three surprises in store for the stinkers who're running us all into hell."

"What is the third one?"

"Russia."

"You mean Communism?"

"No, I don't. Communism is a mental sickness that will hardly outlast Stalin. But I was talking about Tibet. Tom Grayne has been all winter long in that cave in the side of a cliff in the Kunlun Mountains, to get the lowdown on what's moving below the surface. Being the man he is, I bet he knows more now than anyone else guesses. But he must be tightening his belt. If I can keep our overloaded animals on their feet, there's a chance of our reaching him within a week or ten days."

"Andrew, from now on it's nothing compared to that river."

"We'll make it. We'll deliver the goods. But what then? I'll tell you. It'll be purely personal, between me and Tom Grayne. No one else in the whole cockeyed world will owe me as much as thank you."

"Andrew, what do you mean?"

"I'd take thanks as an insult. Tom Grayne's on the level and I've helped him personally, man to man. He'll turn his information in to a man in Washington who's also on the level, although less so than Tom. By 'on the level' I mean he doesn't try to steer other people or other nations into trouble for his own profit. But from him on downward until it reaches the daily papers, every word that Tom turns in will be used and fouled and perverted by every double-crossing political sharp who believes he sees a chance to enrich himself. That's the hell of it. That's why I'm bellyaching."

"Andrew, aren't there any honest politicians?"

"No. Every last one of them, in every country in the world, is a professional liar, thief, hypocrite, charlatan, crook, double-crosser— in plain words, a phony. An honest man couldn't last a week in any important political job. If he were even half honest, he wouldn't accept the job in the first place."

"How about your national hero Abraham Lincoln?"

"He was shot for trying to be honest. Lincoln came mighty close to being an exception. He was honest with himself, which is more than half the fight. I learned my stuff straight from him. It was Lincoln's own statement that you can't be honest and remain a politician, that first set me off thinking about it."

"But, Andrew, you're not in politics."

"You bet I'm not. I'd give my life, right now, this minute, to be done in by any torture anyone can think of, if I could make my blessed idiotic country wake up to what politics are—if I could make 'em look— think—understand that politics has landed all the swine on top and all the decent men and women underneath."

"Andrew, how terrible you make it sound."

"It isn't terrible. It's sickening. It gives me a bellyache. I get no pleasure out of knowing that every lick of work I do on this expedition will be turned to some rotten purpose by a conceited liar in Washington, or Whitehall, or Paris—Berlin—Rome—the Hague."

"Aren't you glad to be blocking the Japanese?"

"They're no worse than we are. If that's a compliment, they're welcome to it. We—I mean the rest of the world—taught 'em all they know about lip-service to ideals along with practical treachery, cruelty, robbery, lechery and every crime there is. I expect you don't get my point. The trouble with me is, that I'm fed up. I have absolutely no respect for anyone, from king or president, pope or labour leader, down to the ten-year-old Wop doing the goosestep like a monkey in one of Mussolini's uniforms—who tries to gain his own ends by lying propaganda and force or threat of force. I've no more use for the rotters who toady to dictators and praise them, than I have for the dictators and political bosses themselves."

He paused for a moment or two, as if reviewing what he had said. Then suddenly:

"My country 'tis of thee! O God! If I could make my beloved country wake up and look at itself! If I could make it only try to be the land it brags of being! But how? God damn it, who can make it wake up—with all those scoundrels drugging it to sleep? If I were a Shakespeare or a Milton, they'd use my words to prove the opposite of what I mean!"

He couldn't stand it any longer. He crawled out of the tent and made a round of inspection with his flashlight. Bompo Tsering begged him not to shoot the snow leopards, saying they were undoubtedly the souls of greedy *lamas* who had charged high fees for blessings:

"Their must living this way too long, then by-um-by, come 'nother life, their being then maybe beginning way up once more."

"Okay. They shall have a life on you. You get the point? If they kill a pony or a sheep, you pay for it!"

"No, no! No, no! That not being—"

"Then watch carefully! Keep your snow-white *lama*-leopards out of camp."

The cold, still night air was making Andrew feel better, or perhaps he had worked something out of his system. He passed by Bulah Singh's tent, making sure that Bulah Singh's mule was properly blanketed and tied so that the leopards couldn't scare him loose. Bulah Singh was awake, seated in the tent opening on a packing case, in Andrew's spare overcoat, smoking a pipe he had borrowed from Bompo

Tsering. Andrew passed him the time of night:

"Have you enough tobacco-matches?"

"Yes, thanks. It's a fine night, isn't it?"

Bulah Singh could make a very ordinary statement sound like treason. Andrew stood sniffing the frosty air, eyeing the moon, feeling the weather.

"Yes," he answered. "Fine now. There'll be a storm tomorrow. We'll start early. Turn in and get some sleep."

He passed along, not even trying to hear what Bulah Singh muttered. But before he crawled back into the tent, where he thought Elsa was asleep, she lay so still, he watched the Sikh for half a minute, still seated facing the moon. He had an idea it would be a good thing to know what the Sikh was thinking about. He hesitated—almost returned to talk to him. It was Elsa who changed his mind:

"Don't, Andrew! Don't! I can read your thought! If the men should see you talking to Bulah Singh they'd think you've forgiven him! It might be fatal! It might give him a chance to win them over to some—"

Andrew's bulk blotted out the moonlight as he crawled into the tent.

"I'm hoping," he said, "rather against hope, that Bulah Singh will escape. I've even thought of putting a supply of food where he can steal it. I know he has money."

CHAPTER 42

The tent flap closed behind him. "So you can read my thought?" He sounded difficult again—on guard—irritated. Elsa wished with all her heart she hadn't spoken. Now she must answer. She was tempted to lie—decided not to—spoke calmly:

"I could. At that moment, I couldn't help it. You see, Andrew, you've been trying to help me to understand you. Then you thought about me in connection with Bulah Singh. And he thought about both of us. It produced a condition."

"Condition, eh? What was he thinking about? Could you tell that?"

Andrew was kneeling, facing the candle-lantern. He tried to see her face. He couldn't. Elsa waited until he had rolled in under the blankets before she answered:

"Bulah Singh hasn't let up on me once, for one single waking moment, since we left the magician's village."

571

"How d'you mean—let up on you?"

"He projects the image of himself, continually, so that he's always in front of my mind, between me and what I wish to think about."

"Oh well, all right, that settles it. I daren't give that buzzard a weapon. He'd use it to kill me. So he shall go without. At daybreak he gets rations for himself and his mule—and marching orders."

"Andrew, must you? It might be a mistake. And it wouldn't affect the mental tricks he could play. A few miles makes no difference."

"No. I suppose not. But—"

"Nor a few hundred miles."

"Can you shake it off? Can't you refuse to see it?"

"I don't have to. If I let it stay, and just think higher, it makes him defeat his own purpose."

"I don't understand."

"May I try to explain?"

"Shoot. I'm listening."

"Bulah Singh's purpose is to compel me to do all my thinking with him in mind. Something like the way a nun in a convent should do all her thinking with her special saint in mind—only that the nun should act voluntarily, whereas I'd be forced. That way he would gradually get control of my thought—altogether qualify it—so that in the end—and it wouldn't be long—I'd be hypnotised, like Du Maurier's Trilby."

Andrew growled disgustedly: "That's how all the propagandist— priest—politicians do their dirty work! You don't feel it's getting you?"

It could get her—it could wear her down, unless Andrew would help. But she was afraid to confess weakness, so she spoke more confidently than she felt: "I was shown at Gombaria's how not to let it. But Bulah Singh believes his will is conquering mine, so that he'll be able to dictate my thought and make me obey his will when the convenient moment comes."

"God damn him and his moments!" Andrew sat up again, elbow on knees. "Sorry," he said. "I didn't mean to interrupt. Go ahead. Talk."

A flurry of night wind blew the tent flap. Andrew reached for the flap, secured it and lay down again. Elsa waited at least another minute before she asked: "Can't you yourself see him now?"

He surprised her by answering without noticeable change in his voice. "I guess I'm beginning to see what you see."

"Is he the way he was when you last saw him, a few minutes

ago?"

"No. He has moved. It's like a glimpse through binoculars—close up."

"Are you sure it's not just memory?"

"Memory, hell! It's one of those damned vision things, like a waking dream, only more vivid. He's moving." Then sharply: "It isn't you doing it?"

"Indeed it isn't."

"It's damned strange," said Andrew. "D'you know—" he laughed apologetically. She had never heard him do that before. He sounded guilty of something: "It's like when you're in love and the beloved's face keeps coming between you and what you're trying to read or write or think about."

For a moment that almost stunned her, not like being hit, like having cold darkness descend suddenly. She had to fight it off. She had to remember Andrew wasn't her lover. She had no right to demand he shouldn't be some other woman's. But for a numbed heartbeat it leadened the whole universe, until suddenly he spoke again and she knew he wasn't thinking of any woman. "God damn his impudence! Is that murdering swine trying to make me like him?"

That gave her a chance to recover and to resume the conversation where it left off: "Andrew, I'm simply praying for the right words. So will you help me by trying hard to understand?"

"Sure. You tell it. I'll try to get you."

"Bulah Singh knows he can't possibly make you like him. The only way he can control you is to make you angry. Ordinary methods fail. So he's sending you homosexual suggestions."

"Well, I'll be damned! Are you serious? You mean he thinks he'll get to first base with that stuff?"

"You see, he knows what will irritate you. You do notice a change in your attitude toward him?"

"I'd like to shoot him."

"You won't—will you?"

"I don't know why not."

"You do feel an urge to act violently?"

Silence.

"Hate him?"

Again silence. Andrew was playing fair, listening with inner ears, checking up as he went along, rejecting nothing, doing his best to understand. "I've noticed this," he conceded after a few moments, "I

573

have been getting curious to know what he's thinking about."

"Andrew, if he can get you curious enough, and make you hate him at the same time, he'll be able to make you make the mistake he's counting on, at the moment that he's waiting for."

"Do you think you know what he's counting on?"

"No. I can't read him that deeply—partly because I'm afraid to look. He has a mind like an octopus. But it's something soon—that's coming. I don't quite know myself what I mean by that, but there's a suggestion of movement toward you and me—something coming."

"God Almighty! I wish this vague stuff didn't go to my fists! It makes me want to get out there and—"

"Andrew, that's just what Bulah Singh wants. He knows you won't kill him. I think he wants you to give him provisions and drive him out of camp."

"But why on earth—"

"I've told you. I don't know why—except that of course he knows he can't escape unless you let him. He wants to get away—in order to turn on you—probably to kill you."

"It beats me how he expects to go about it."

"Andrew, I think he has learned something secret from you and me since we left the magician's village."

"He can't have. I haven't shared a thought with him! I haven't spoken to him more than bare civilities."

"Neither have I. But it's something he learned from us. He doesn't know anything about superconsciousness—or I think he doesn't."

"Neither do I."

"Oh yes you do, Andrew. But he doesn't. Subconsciousness is his field. He is rather expert."

"He's a charlatan."

"But rather expert."

"Have it your own way."

"Andrew, the subconsciousness is like a dark ocean, in which all the knowledge and experience of the entire human race is stored. It can be read by anyone who knows how. It can be made stormy, too, by people who know how. But normally it's like a pool of ink. Then, sometimes, it reflects superconsciousness. That's how secrets get out."

Andrew set his teeth. He retorted irritably: "But for God's sake, if you and I don't know a secret in the first place, how in hell can Bulah Singh learn it from us?"

"Andrew, I want to tell you what I know, so that you can add to it

574

what you know and so keep out of danger."

He checked a retort, remembering his own experience in Gombaria's monastery, when vision after vision appeared before his eyes. Now, again, he could see Bulah Singh, seated in the opening of his tent, facing the moon, smoking, looking pleased with some dark thought.

"Yes, please, let's hear it," he said after a moment. After a longer pause Elsa found she couldn't say it lying down. She sat up beside him:

"Subconsciousness mostly subsists of itself—of and for itself. It's what Jesus called a liar and the father of it. But sometimes it reflects the superconsciousness, the way the surface of an asphalt lake might reflect the moon or lightning. So the dark magicians receive warning that something new is stirring in the higher consciousness of someone else. Andrew, that's how real spying is done. It sounds so utterly absurd to conservative-minded people, that they never even suspect what really happens."

Andrew laughed resignedly: "I don't say I believe. 'Help thou mine unbelief.' Try again."

"Don't try to accept it too literally—I mean about the reflection in the pool and—"

"Okay. Each makes his own picture, I guess—and there are no words."

"But do you feel you're beginning to understand?"

"I'm listening, anyhow. But make it snappy. We've got to get a move on before daybreak, so's to cover as many miles as possible before the weather stops us."

"Andrew, how d'you know there'll be a storm?"

He thought that over a moment. Then he laughed. "Bull's-eye! I read it in the *New York Times*.—I get you. You mean: I read it in the subconscious?"

"Yes. A spark of superconsciousness—a flash of intuition from your own soul—warned you to look. Is there any sign of a storm?"

"No, there isn't. Not even the aneroid—yet. All the same, there'll be one, and the pack animals know it."

"Of course they know. Animals are always watching the subconscious, where all their instinctive knowledge comes from. They read the subconscious quicker than almost any humans can. But the black magicians read it with more skill."

"Easy! You'll be snarled in a minute. Are you trying to kid me that Bulah Singh, and the black magicians, and all the political hypnotists

575

and public liars in the world are at the same stage of evolution with ponies and yaks?"

"Of course not. As long as we're alive, we all exist in the ocean of subconsciousness. But it's consciousness that marks our stage of evolution. Is your consciousness the same as Hitler's or Bulah Singh's or a Chicago gangster's? The consciousness is measurable by its relative receptivity to superconsciousness. The more soul, the higher the evolution. The less soul, the lower. That is the measure of real intelligence. Any person who denies the soul's existence, simply denies his own being, that's all. It has nothing whatever to do with brains or mere cleverness. A person could know everything, and command armies, or be a superscientist and discover wonderful things without having a spark of real intelligence. If real intelligence were a function of the physical brain, or if true genius were related to the subconscious, you'd have to call Judas Iscariot and Pontius Pilate more intelligent than Jesus: Hitler more intelligent than Thomas Mann or Einstein: Mussolini more intelligent than Toscanini. People like Hitler and Bulah Singh and old Lung-gom-pa are stone blind to the direct light of superconsciousness. But they can see it indirectly on the subconscious mirror. And they're alert. They're clever. Not intelligent-clever, like the war lords who convert dye into poison gas."

Andrew snorted: "Like the holy Joes who convert religion, and the shysters who convert the law into a shame and a byword! Like the lick-spit flunky scientists who 'yes' Stalin and Hitler!" He was hardly aware he had spoken. Elsa waited for him to say more, but he didn't.

"Whenever someone receives a gleam of superconsciousness, it is reflected, something like moonlight, on the surface of the universal subconscious pool. There the haters perceive it, indirectly. The receivers of the superconscious light, who don't understand, because it's new, become like the Three *Magi* in the Bible story. They have faith, and they follow the light. But the lovers of subconsciousness become like Herod, in the same story. They hate the light. They start massacres— war—to prevent the coming of superconsciousness that they know instinctively, will utterly destroy their kingdoms.—Have I made that clear?"

"Gosh!" he answered, "if it's true, it would explain why—"

"No, Andrew, it only hints, and suggests. It doesn't explain. It can't be phrased dogmatically. It can't be materialized on a basis of profit and loss. Only the definition-mongers, the splitters of hairs, the materialists— the criminals—and the people who believe that death is the end of everything—can fool themselves into believing they can explain it."

"Well, see here. If you can't explain it to me, what's the use of—"

"Listen, Andrew. You and I have touched superconsciousness. It touched us."

"You mean you did. It touched you. I don't even know what it is."

"The bright light, that will take care of us at the proper moment, lighted our subconsciousness and let the watchers—"

"Who d'you mean—watchers?"

"Bulah Singh, for instance. Also others—lots of others."

"Okay. Let's keep it personal. You say it let Bulah Singh—"

"It let him read something that our subconsciousness reflected from superconsciousness. There, is that clear?"

"I'll be damned if it is. Why couldn't we read it?"

"I believe I can read it," she answered. "But I can't believe it. Or I'd rather put it this way. I know I couldn't possibly make you believe it. You would think me crazy. So I'm afraid to tell you."

"I wish you would tell. I guarantee one thing: even if I don't understand, I'll know you're trying to tell the truth."

"Andrew, you can be wonderfully comforting at unexpected moments!"

"What do you think you can see?"

"Lobsang Pun!"

"You mean—"

"I mean just that, and nothing else. We're near him."

"You mean physically near?"

"Yes."

"You're not talking about his projected image?"

"I am talking about Lobsang Pun, coming toward us—now—near."

"It can't be," he answered. "We've made a wider circuit around Lhasa than we should have, hoping to pick up news of him. But it's no go. I've figured it out. If he's on the lam and they haven't caught him, he must be scores of miles away—perhaps hundreds—perhaps headed toward India."

Elsa insisted: "I can see Lobsang Pun! Andrew! He doesn't want to be seen. You and I mustn't recognize him! Look! Look!"

"I can't see a thing!"

"That was a plain message!"

"What was?"

"He put a finger to his lips. He shook his head. We're not to recognize him!"

"When?"

"When we meet—soon—I think very soon."

"Hell, are you and I going crazy? Well, all right—if we do meet him, that should be simple enough."

"Andrew, there's a big price on Lobsang Pun's head!"

"I know there is."

"Bulah Singh knows it! And Bulah Singh knows we are very soon going to meet Lobsang Pun!"

"Are you really sure he knows?"

"Yes."

"I'll go the rounds again. I'll soon find out."

"Andrew—better not speak to him. Isn't it better to let Bulah Singh believe we don't suspect him?"

"Maybe you're right. I'll go and talk to the men. Just a second while I look at the time. Thought so. We'll be breaking camp by lantern light, in two hours. Do you think you can get two hours' sleep? You're going to need it."

"Andrew, after all those days of grumpiness, you've been so kind again all at once, that I could do anything! I feel like singing! But—yes—I can sleep—I know I can."

"Good. You don't have to worry. I won't talk to Bulah Singh. I'll try not to wake you when I come back. Goodnight."

CHAPTER 43

The storm turned up about an hour late. Soon the snow began drifting like waves on a wild sea. Sheep can't tackle that stuff. The overloaded yaks and ponies couldn't carry the sheep; so Andrew and the Tibetans had to do it, wherever the sheep couldn't follow the ponies through the drifts. They hadn't made more than two miles by noon. Then Bompo Tsering was for calling a halt. But there would be less snow on the wind-swept ledges, and the ledges wouldn't come, one had to go to them; so Andrew had his own way about carrying on for a couple more hours. But then suddenly Bompo Tsering, who was leading, said they were surrounded by *dugpas*. The column halted. Elsa rode her pony in the way of Bulah Singh's to prevent the Sikh from crowding forward. Andrew showed Bompo Tsering his automatic and the head-man agreed, as every Tibetan does, that an automatic pistol is excellent magic. But he said he had never seen a dead *dugpa*. He suggested that a bullet could go straight through a *dugpa's* heart without hurting him. *Dugpas*, he said, could make a lot of trouble by making the animals go lame, even if they didn't do worse things. He said the wise course was to bivouac and say plenty of prayers. He pulled the prayer wheel out of his *bokkus* and spun it furiously.

So Andrew showed him the aneroid in its neat leather case and said it was an infallible protection against all sorts of devils. He even told him the names of the master magicians who made it—showed him their names on the face of the dial—pronounced them for him. Bompo Tsering admitted that Negretti and Zambra sounded wonderful. But he stuck to his prayer wheel. He smiled courteously. And then he demonstrated beyond any doubt in his own mind that Andrew was a silly foreign devil who didn't know what he was talking about.

"Gunnigun," he said, "your talking too much. Now your looking. There being too many *dugpas*. Not going away. Keeping on coming."

He was right. And they did look like ghosts. The whirling snow was black against the sky, shot through and through with lurid gray where the wind tore gaps that let dim light through. The ghosts approached from the moaning gloom of that storm, led by a tall one who rode the ghost of a pony. The others staggered behind him, on foot. Andrew went out to meet them. Bompo Tsering ordered a bivouac the second his back was turned and then ran to help two of the men who were at grips with Bulah Singh. The Sikh had tried to plunge past Elsa through a snowdrift. Elsa cried aloud for help. They seized the Sikh's reins and off-saddled him, so that he lay on his back looking upward, full of anger but—as concerned dignity—lost. Elsa followed Andrew and drew rein beside him.

"I think Bulah Singh knows who is coming," she said. "He tried to snatch my automatic and go over to them. But Bompo Tsering is loyal."

"He's what he calls loyal," said Andrew.

There were thirteen ghosts, twelve of them walking. They all looked like Tibetans. They all looked half dead, famished, including the pony ridden by their leader. Andrew and Elsa waited for them in the lee of a gray rock, where the drift was shallow and it was easier to speak. The leader got off his pony because Bompo Tsering shouted to him to do it or be pulled off. He was dressed like a nobleman, full of assured self-importance. But he had none of the take-it-for-granted authority that clings, even in adversity, like an invisible skin to a man of real breeding. If he had had, Bompo Tsering would never have dared to tell him to mind his manners. In a voice as hoarse as a frog's, he demanded Andrew's name.

Elsa whispered: "Bad accent! Careful!"

So instead of telling his name, Andrew let him see the butt of an automatic and asked what he wanted. He was pretty arrogant about demanding food at once, but that might have been due to hunger; empty stomachs aren't always polite. He ordered his ragged followers to keep their distance as if they were dirt. They obeyed him—one especially—without a trace of enthusiasm. Andrew kept an eye on that one man; he seemed neither to resent the leader's ill manners nor to care about him one way or the other; he looked as ugly as the devil—a big man in peasant's clothing.

Andrew spoke under his breath: "They're a rum-looking lot."

Elsa answered: "They are those we saw coming!"

"You mean, you saw coming! You watch 'em while I do the honours."

It seldom pays to cut the ceremonial in Tibet. Andrew knew the routine phrases. He and the insolent leader expressed the customary happiness at meeting each other. Meanwhile Bompo Tsering and his men made themselves polite to the others and found out all about their weapons. Then they set to pitching a bivouac, making a lean-to of spread-out tents in no time. They had saved plenty of yak-dung fuel; and the conditions are hardly imaginable in which Tibetans can't make tea, salted and greasy with rancid butter. There was a yak's leg, tolerably rotten and therefore easy to eat. One doesn't have to worry about bad meat at that altitude; lucky to get what you get. Bompo Tsering whispered to Elsa, and she told Andrew how many automatics, how many revolvers.

Andrew played host with his back to the lean-to and Elsa beside him. Before long the strangers were all doing their duty by hunks of yak meat and barley bread. They guzzled, as if they hadn't eaten for days. There was one man who kept the lower part of his face covered, except when he thought Andrew wasn't looking. He avoided Andrew. He had very intelligent eyes, but they looked barren, as if even evil would not ripen in the thought behind them. It would windfall, rotten from within. Twice Andrew spotted him reading signals from Bu-lah Singh, who was at pains, when he thought Andrew wasn't looking, to reveal that he had been deprived of his weapons.

Again Andrew whispered to Elsa, if one could call it a whisper that pierces a Tibetan wind:

"That big bozo, who keeps himself to himself at the far end?"

"Andrew, you know! Remember: don't recognize him!"

He thought that over, watching his guests, especially their leader. He disliked the man, despised him. Presently he opened a can of salmon and set it down between himself and Elsa. The leader perked up like an ape at sight of a banana. There were only two who took no notice: the big man at the far end and another who sat next to him. The big ugly man had a long rosary under his coat and kept flicking the beads. The man beside him appeared to be dying. A Tibetan, like a camel, when he decides to die, does it. He chooses almost any old place for the job. The big ugly man appeared to know his friend wanted to die and to be bawling him out. The storm was making too much noise to hear what he said, but it looked as if the other man didn't dare to answer back. The dying man didn't eat, he only sipped tea.

Andrew whispered to Elsa: "If that's your fat friend, can't he recognize you?"

Elsa didn't speak. She didn't know what to answer.

The ape-faced leader, seated near Andrew, gorged himself, said nothing, and kept staring at the opened tin of salmon. He didn't eat like a nobleman, nor behave like one in any other way. He seemed much too conscious of the fine texture of the beautiful black clothing that he wore under his fur-lined coat. He was dressed like a high *lama*. A genuine Tibetan *lama* might have made things rather awkward. But he wasn't genuine. And he was lost. He hadn't the slightest idea where he was. He wanted to be told without having to ask. Andrew didn't tell him. Meanwhile, he kept greedily eyeing that opened can of salmon. Presently Andrew nudged Elsa to follow and went out to look at the storm, taking the salmon with him.

It was a blisterer, growing worse. There was nothing for it but to stay where they were, even at the risk of running short of fodder for the animals. The ponies were on full rations, but now there was an extra pony to feed, and it wasn't strong enough to carry a full load.

"This doesn't look too good," said Andrew. "Several of those men are well armed. They've all got automatics, excepting the two at the far end. One of those two is dying. The other is—"

Elsa interrupted: "Don't name him! Don't breathe his name!"

"All right, all right! But get the hang of this. Their leader's a phony. He's a false front."

"He isn't a real *lama*," said Elsa. "He can't be. But he's wearing the clothes of a very important one."

"The important man," said Andrew, "is the fellow who keeps his face half covered. I know who he is. But I don't want him to know I recognise him."

"Then don't breathe his name, either. Thoughts escape, Andrew. Give them a name and they go leaping from one to another."

"Right. Mum's the word. Our business—yours and mine—is to keep that man and Bulah Singh from joining up to bump me off and grab you and our supplies. I've noticed eyes on you. You're loot." Elsa didn't feel like loot. She felt tremendously excited. But it was no time to argue the point. "We can trust Bompo Tsering," she said.

"Up to his limit, we can. But what is his limit? We need friends. I'll make a bid right now."

Andrew signalled. Bompo Tsering noticed it after the second or third attempt and came out.

"Tell that big ugly old man at the far end I want to talk to him. Ask him to come out here."

Bompo Tsering didn't like doing it. His superstition stiffened. He put up quite an argument, shouting into Andrew's ear against the storm. He said it was very unwise to talk to mysterious strangers, who might turn out to be bandits, or perhaps Chinese soldiers in disguise, which would be even worse. Then, as if to change the subject, or else fishing for a bribe:

"What your soon now doing with that salmon, Gunnigun? Your not wanting, my wanting too much!"

Andrew playfully missed him with a right hook. He obeyed then, sticking out his tongue by way of gratitude, too well knowing how that fist could hurt when Andrew aimed it straight.

"Andrew, what is your idea?"

"I'll give your man a chance to admit who he is. Watch him."

It was worth watching. Ugly-face showed no surprise; he merely shoved his dying friend into a more comfortable position, tucked his rosary under his coat and got up, as self-possessed as a bishop. He had to pass in front of the entire party. The leader made angry gestures and ordered him back to his place. Ugly-face walked past him with the humility of a monarch doing penance with peas in his boots. The leader struck him. He took no more notice of that than he did of the wind. He came and stood in front of Andrew with his back to his own party, ignoring Elsa as if she didn't exist. He waited for Andrew to speak first.

Andrew didn't like to stare at him too hard. Of course, he could be a Tibetan, though he had never seen one who resembled him. He was big and big-bellied. The shape of his head was something like an owl's, and he had a nose not unlike an owl's beak, which is something rare in that part of the world. He looked to be more than sixty years old, but strong and healthy. He was the only one of that party who didn't seem to have suffered much from the privation that had weakened the others.

Instead of speaking Andrew handed him an automatic and some reloads. He made no comment. He simply buttoned the pistol inside his overcoat and stowed the reloads in his *bokkus*. Then Andrew handed him the can of salmon with as much courtesy as could be managed in the lee of a rock in a ninety-mile gale. He understood perfectly. The whorls of wrinkles on his leathery face danced with merriment, although his mouth didn't move. He drank the half-frozen liquid out of the can and saved the salmon for later, glancing sideways at the phony high *lama* and then, at last, blinking at Elsa. He seemed to look right through her to the thought beneath. Then his lips moved.

"Tum-Glain!" he said suddenly. "Elsa!" Then he turned and walked back to his dying friend. There he sat down and ate the salmon, using finger and thumb, reminiscently, as if recalling bygone better days.

"He recognizes you all right," said Andrew.

"Of course he does! Andrew, he isn't a fighting man. Why did you give him that automatic?"

"You saw him accept it, didn't you? D'you know a better way to explain I'm his friend without arguing about it? Do you feel any clairvoyant communication from him?"

"No, Andrew, none. Not any—not even a trace—all flat calm."

"If he's the man you think he is, there's a price on his head. He's a prisoner, for sale, worth more alive than dead. If they can avoid it they won't murder him. So, if he's on our side, and secretly armed, that gives us a double edge. But this isn't going to be as simple as all that. No fighting, I think. Do you see what's happening? Bulah Singh's already in a whispering deal with the real leader—that man who keeps his face half covered. Jesus! If I have to—"

But he didn't have to force a show-down at the moment. Bulah Singh spotted his intention and crawled away to watch two of Andrew's men pitching his tent. So Andrew bided his time. He ordered Bompo Tsering to pull the covers off two yakloads and make a separate shelter for the man who was dying. That made the phony *lama*

583

furious. He faced the storm and came out to pick a quarrel about it, demanding in coarse vernacular:

"Why did you give that good foreign food to my menial, instead of to me? Why do you pitch for him a separate shelter, instead of for me?"

Elsa stood by to interpret. "Tell him," said Andrew, "I supposed he'd prefer whiskey."

Then he knew for a positive fact that the man was a fraud. The phony *lama* shook his head. But his eyes gave him away. He wanted whiskey. He craved it. Now he knew there was some to be had, he intended to get it. He returned to his place, where he listened with very obvious resentment to remarks from the man who kept the lower part of his face covered. Andrew was adding fact to fact, beginning to feel he could command the situation. He said so to Elsa.

"But it's a case of rule or ruin. They believe they've got me belly upward on the half-shell. They think they can take over whenever they please."

After he had got the bivouac to rights, and had fed the animals, he went and helped Bompo Tsering carry the dying man into the tent he had made from two yakload covers. They were very careful to submit the man to no indignities. As Bompo Tsering remarked; a dying man is very near to the spirits of the other world, and who knows what those spirits might do to anyone who is careless? But Andrew did get a look at the man's shirt. It was silk. And he saw the skin of his neck, where the weather hadn't touched it and the Tibetan dirt hadn't stuck. He was as clean as Old Ugly-face, who was as clean as the wind. And he had the same well-bred air of taking privilege for granted. He was too busy dying to pay much attention to Andrew, but he fetched up a smile from somewhere along with a little blood, and he murmured a blessing, moving his right hand. No menial would have dared to do that.

Then what Andrew hoped would happen, did. Old Ugly-face came and crawled under the same shelter with the dying man. For the time being he left them there alone. He went and unpacked a bottle of whiskey and rationed it out in teacups. Divided up, there wasn't enough to make even a chicken drunk, but it was a friendly gesture, and it gave the phony *lama* a grand chance to demonstrate phony virtue. He refused the little metal cup when it was handed to him. He spun his prayer wheel and made a grimace expressing pious horror. But when the others curled up, all close together under the blankets that Andrew had served out, he leaned closer to Andrew and seemed to hesitate. One could almost hear him thinking whiskey. Andrew encouraged him:

"Your Eminence knows best. But is it sinful to take medicine?"

He couldn't fall from grace mannerly. He was too full of fear for his self-importance—too inexperienced in the art of saving face. His was the Teutonic style. He felt the need to insult Andrew before letting down his ill-fitting mask of righteousness.

"You are a mean host," he retorted. "You have saved an extra drink for yourself by offering one to me when those *rhagbyas* were looking and you knew I couldn't accept it."

Andrew told Elsa about it a few minutes later: "No one but a louse would have called his own gang *ragyabas*. You can generally get a good line on a man by noticing the epithets he uses. But I let him go on talking. Presently he said: 'A giver should be generous, or else give nothing. No doubt when those ignorant fellows are asleep you will open another bottle. A little medicine is not much good. There should be plenty': So I asked for his blessing."

"Did he give it?"

"Yes, grudgingly."

"A genuine high *lama's* blessing should sound like echoed organ music from beyond the veil that separates the living and the dead."

"I know it should. I know High Tibetan better than that man does. Believe that or not, as you please. His sounded like mumbling to hide ignorance. I told him I'd look for another bottle, and as soon as he thought my back was turned he grabbed the tot he had refused and swallowed it in one gulp. So we've got his number. We don't have to bother about him."

"Andrew, do you intend you and me to go on sharing this one tent?"

"Yes."

"I was thinking about—"

"I know. But this is no time to change. And don't let's waste time. Let's do some scouting. Come on. I may need you to interpret."

They struggled against the wind to the lee of the makeshift tent where Ugly-face was keeping his dying friend company. For several minutes they couldn't hear because of the storm. But it was springtime; the wind changed with a sudden blast like high explosive, and as suddenly died. Then the snow fell softly in huge flakes that felt warm and comforting. There was a mystic silence, and presently they heard the sonorous voice of Old Ugly-face.

"His friend is already dead," Elsa whispered. "He is reciting from the *Bardo Thodol*."

"What's that?"

"*Oh nobly born, that which is called death being come to thee now, resolve thus: O this now is the hour of death . . .*' It's the *Book of the Dead*. He is instructing the spirit of the dead man how to behave, and what thoughts to cling to, on the plane of existence beyond the Veil on which he is now awakening. Andrew, not ten other men in the world know the Book of the Dead by heart."

"Belly and brains and beauty, he's the real thing, eh?"

"Andrew-please! Until he gives permission, don't let anyone guess that you know who he is!"

"I don't know. I don't believe it yet. Come back to our tent."

It was still snowing heavily. When they reached the tent, someone came out of it on hands and knees. Catching sight of them through the curtain of snow he got up and ran, but he wasn't quite quick enough. Andrew grabbed a steel tent-peg and threw it. When he picked up the peg a moment later there was blood on it—not much, but enough; there'd be no hiding the wound. He stuck the peg into his belt, since it might serve as a weapon and save killing someone.

"This should bring things to a head," he remarked to Elsa. "It's a case of act now or they'll get me before daylight. Look in the tent. See if anything's missing, while I get things going."

He called Bompo Tsering and set a guard around the tent—four men. Then he listened patiently while Bompo Tsering told him that Bulah Singh had been trying to beg a weapon from the man who kept his face covered.

"But their talking English, too fast. My not understanding."

Andrew feigned indifference. "It would be stupid," he said, "to try to learn too much all at once. How much have they learned about us?"

"Nothing, Gunnigun! Nothing! Our telling nothing!"

"But Bulah Singh—?"

"Yes, yes, his surely telling too much."

"What do you make of the man that Bulah Singh's been talking to?"

Bompo Tsering retreated toward his mental funk hole: "Uh—uh! My not knowing. Him not being Tibetan."

"What about their leader—that *lama* who rode the pony?"

586

"Gunnigun, why your asking my such questions? Why not—"

"Never mind. Do you know who the big man is, that we made a special tent for—him with the dying friend?"

Bompo Tsering backed into his funk hole and mentally vanished: "Uh-uh! Uh- uh! Uh-uh! No, no! My not knowing him! No, no!"

Elsa almost thrust herself between them: "Andrew, don't ask! Please don't!"

"Okay." Strangely, he didn't sound irritated. Uppermost was that kind of hunter's patience that appeared when he carved wood or, as now, when he played with his life in his hand. "Anything missing?" he asked.

"Yes. Your little steel lock-box."

She had been almost afraid to tell him, but he didn't seem disturbed by the news. Staring through the snow, thinking, it was nearly a minute before he answered: "It was empty. I expected they'd go for it. I'll get it back. But there's something else needs doing first. While I'm gone, you sit here in the mouth of the tent, and shoot to kill anyone who starts anything. Get me?"

"Yes, Andrew."

"I don't think there'll be any shooting."

"Neither do I."

"But if there is any, it's likely to start soon. If so, shoot first at the phony *lama*, Bulah Singh and—" there was a name on his lips, but he didn't say it "the man who walks on corpses."

She knew instantly what he meant. It exactly described the walk of the man who kept his face half covered and looked over the top of a muffler with vicious eyes.

Andrew continued: "But I guess you'll be safe enough with four men on guard. Just sit here until I come back."

He unpacked a small bottle of rye and stuck it in his pocket. Then he and Bompo Tsering crossed the bivouac to where the phony *lama* sat alone by a scrap of yak-dung fire. His men were cuddled up together, like tired ponies, asleep. Andrew would have sat down beside him, but the fool wouldn't permit it. He screamed like a parrot—tried to overawe Andrew—accused him of being a Russian—told him he had no business in Tibet— threatened to make things very hot for him indeed unless—

He paused, rather artfully building suspense and glancing around for an audience. But his men were asleep or indifferent. Andrew prompted him: "Unless what?"

"Unless you make yourself useful to me."

Having Bompo Tsering to interpret was a great advantage. Andrew always found it difficult to pretend fear where he felt none, whereas Bompo Tsering's quite genuine terror kept the charlatan *lama* well blinded by self-esteem. The rye whiskey helped: Andrew gave him a stiff drink. But even so, it was fifteen minutes, and pitch dark, before Andrew had coaxed him to tell what he really wanted. He whispered it, pulling Andrew's overcoat to make him bend down, and belching in Andrew's ear.

He hardly guessed after that what happened. There was Andrew's knee in his stomach and a grip on his throat that choked his parrot-scream. Force of example was all that Bompo Tsering ever did need. In a second, the *lama* was down on his back beneath two men, being searched; and that was done so thoroughly that he felt even his secrets being torn apart along with his underwear. He wasn't even allowed to lie still; they kept him rolling to keep his mind occupied as treasure after treasure found its way into Bompo Tsering's copious *bokkus*. The phony *lama's* men, exhausted and now full-bellied, didn't know what was happening; or if they did know, they ignored it. Sounds were deadened by the snow. Andrew prolonged the business for the sake of Bompo Tsering's morale. He let his victim sit up. He showed him his Mauser, unloaded it, drew the slide, struck it with the steel tent-peg, broke it, then he handed it back

"No one," he remarked, "will know it's broken unless you tell 'em."

Bompo Tsering translated. And then someone did move in the dark at the back of the lean-to. Bompo Tsering clucked a warning.

Andrew moved away from the dim firelight. He stepped sideways. Suddenly he sprang. He landed fist first on Bulah Singh—knew it by the Sikh's growl of anger, and by his smell. There was a real fight this time. Bulah Singh was no weakling. Even though his feet were still in bandages, he fought like a leopard. But it was less than thirty seconds before Andrew's forearm crushed his throat and he had to lie still and be searched.

Two Mausers. Four clips of cartridges.

"Got to hand it to you," said Andrew. "Come out in the open."

Bulah Singh got up and obeyed, awkwardly, because he was hurt and the snow balled badly on his bandaged feet. But slowness gave him time to think, and he kept on thinking when Andrew stopped and framed him with a flashlight, examining his face in the lee of a big rock.

No bruise—no wound—no blood. "So it wasn't you I hit with a tent-peg."

"Damn you, Gunning, you're in such a blue funk that you would kill your own mother on suspicion! Don't you realise that by taking two Mausers away from those men I have reduced your enemies by two?"

Andrew laughed. "You have now," he answered, "now." Mausers are the easiest to break of all automatics. He unloaded them, drew the slides and smashed them one against the other. Then he gave them back: "You may have 'em." He repeated what he had said to the *lama*. "No one'll know they're broken unless you try to use 'em. No one will know who stole unless you show 'em."

"You are a fool," the Sikh answered, but he accepted the broken Mausers. "You are also a criminal, destroying weapons at a time like this! You need a friend. Have you lost your senses? Why else should you make—an enemy of me? Do you know who these people are?"

Andrew turned the question back on him: "Do you know?"

"I think you don't know," the Sikh retorted. "If you wish, you may come to my tent and find out. I will tell you—on terms—on reasonable terms."

Andrew let him go. He returned to Elsa, carefully arranging the lantern inside the tent so as to spoil anyone's aim, before sitting down to eat the barley bread and canned stuff she had opened. There was tea, too; Bompo Tsering had seen to that. Elsa, aware that men like Andrew and Tom Grayne love to spring their own announcements, said very little and asked no questions until Andrew had eaten and at last broke silence:

"Any spirit message from your fat friend?"

"No, Andrew."

"Does it make you sore when I speak of him that way?"

"Yes."

"I won't do it again."

"Thank you."

Something had happened. Elsa didn't know what. It was something that had changed the relation between them. Something inexpressible in words that, nevertheless, Andrew had tried to express. He didn't look at her. He went on talking, frowning through the open tent mouth at the falling snow that glowed mystically golden in the lamplight.

"This is the lowdown, as far as I can dope it out—yet. Old Ugly-face has had to take it on the lam. His enemies on the Regent's Council ran him out of Lhasa. To make his getaway, he had to change clothes with some low-grade flunky—probably a household steward, who is now masquerading in his master's make-up. I had quite a talk with the flunky and then disarmed him. He wants to reach the Shig-po-ling monastery."

"But that's near where Tom is!"

"Sure. This whole shooting match is Tom's meat. He's like a hungry spider waiting for 'em. The luck's almost too good to be true. A million dollars 'ud be a safe bet, against a hole in a doughnut, that if we can deliver this outfit—as is—to Tom Grayne at Shig-po-ling, Tom will know how to use it to spike the German-Japanese game."

"You mean their game with the young Dalai Lama?"

"Yes. And now I'll tell you the name of the real leader of this outfit. Ambrose St. Malo."

"The man Morgan Lewis spoke of?"

"Yes."

"He knows you?"

"Yes. He recognized me the minute he saw me. It must have been him that I hit with the tent-peg. I guess he's busy now trying to bust open my empty box. He'll keep on trying. He's persistent. Even dead ponies couldn't stop him in that storm. He came ahead. He has that kind of guts. I don't doubt it was his idea for Ugly-face to change places and clothes with the flunky lama. He has that kind of brains. I'm game to bet it was he who encouraged the flunky to humiliate his former master—beggar-on-horseback stuff. He has that kind of humour. And I haven't a doubt he plans to sell Ugly-face at Shig-po-ling for hard cash."

"I believe you're right, Andrew."

"Right or wrong, that's how we'll play it." He paused. Then he added: "Unless you've a better idea."

Something had happened. It was nameless. It didn't make speech easy. But the tent, with its view of lamplit snow, felt cosier than anybody's home that ever was. Elsa almost stammered:

"Andrew, I'm useless. I haven't an idea. The only thing I can think of is that we're so physically near to—I don't want to name him."

"Go ahead. I know."

"We're so physically close to him that he's like a huge dynamo and simply drowns out my clairvoyance! I see nothing. I hear nothing. I'm

590

just normal. It feels actually funny!"

"You've no suggestion to offer?"

"None. Except don't name him! Don't recognise him!"

"Good. Then we'll play it my way. Between now and daybreak, I'm going to boss both gangs or bust."

CHAPTER 44

That was the night on which Andrew, to use his own phrase, "came clean." Sleep was out of the question; too probably someone would make an attempt on his life before daybreak. Someone. It wasn't likely to be Bulah Singh, nor the flunky *lama*. Those two had been sufficiently discouraged.

"Someone," said Andrew. "But who? Bulah Singh hasn't hit it off with St. Malo. Fool, fool, where there is no fool! They're a brace of *weisenheimers*, underrating each other, playing for position. Bulah Singh will have another try to make friends with me. He'll decide, after thinking it over, that I'd be easier to doublecross than St. Malo. That's my guess, anyhow."

"Are you really sure the other man is Ambrose St. Malo?"

"Dead sure. No mistaking him. Met him in Shanghai—guess he thinks I've forgotten. Perhaps he only hopes it. He went by three or four different names. As Louis Lazard he was acting runner for a Japanese-owned joint that had a bad rep. He's a pimp, like Hitler's national German hero Horst Wessel. But that's not unusual; nearly all professional spies live off women. His original name was Franz Schmidt, born in München-Gladbach, Bavaria. He studied music, philosophy, languages, law. Quite a bright lad. Before he was twenty he shook down one of our American heiresses for fifty thousand or so. But he paid most of it out in blackmail. That's how he made the Social Register—I mean, our secret service black book and three stars, meaning dangerous. During the World War he was two years behind the French lines without even being suspected. Smart work, that. Took doing. He is said to have been betrayed at last by Mata Hari. More likely, he betrayed her. There was a secret trial. A French firing squad shot someone. Franz Schmidt turned up later on as Ambrose St. Malo, in Syria, drawing French pay to help spoil England's game in Palestine."

"Can he be working for France now?" Elsa asked.

Andrew laughed. "This is once when the French aren't guilty. I'd put nothing past them. But they've no political interest in Tibet. They can't even claim they've the Catholic Church to protect. No, when the French are once through with a spy it's his cue to clear out. They're killers. So I guess St. Malo shook the French, to save his skin. At any rate, he's being paid just now by Russia and Japan. But look-see! Look-see! What d'you make of it?"

"Andrew, I'm stupid tonight. I've no imagination. You'll have to tell me what you mean."

"Well, no one could accuse von Klaus of being anything but German. So this turns out to be a German plot, to get control of the Dalai Lama. The Germans are double-crossing their friends the Japs, but the Japs and Russians are paying Hitler's bills."

"You think it's one and the same plot?"

"Yes, but it begins to look like a race—with Ambrose St. Malo taking his pick of the runners. There's one sure thing about him. He's never working for the side you think he is."

"Andrew, did you suspect all this when you were talking to Dr. Morgan Lewis?"

"You mean about St. Malo?"

"And his line-up with the Germans."

"Sure. It's my business. I got a clear line on St. Malo in Shanghai."

"Then why didn't you tell Dr. Lewis?"

He laughed again, uncritical, friendly: "Hell, you bawled me out for telling what little I did tell. You were right, too. This is Tom Grayne's party. I'm not paid to blow England's nose."

"Andrew, who does pay you?"

"No one."

"Even your expenses?"

"I'd a great aunt."

"You mean, you're living off an inheritance?"

"Partly. I can earn money."

She looked around the tent, and at Andrew's shadowed face in the yellow lantern light. Shaving had been impossible since they left India, but he had kept his reddish beard close cropped and neatly trimmed. He looked strong, clean, well groomed. He smelt good.

"I believe," she said after a moment, "there's nothing you can't do."

He looked up sharply, stared for a second with puckered eyes and spoke kindly: "You're ahead of time. They haven't got me yet. This isn't my wake."

"Why are you superstitious about being praised?"

"Never mind me. Let's talk of this fix we're in."

"Yes," she said, "yes. There is one thing you can't do."

He evaded the challenge neatly. She knew it was deliberate, although it sounded like the good-humoured flow of conversation:

"Which of a thousand and one? I bet I know what you're thinking about. Have I three guesses?"

"As many as you please."

"I can't figure out why Old Ugly-face is in this mess. He's got his head in a noose."

"But he's here," said Elsa. "You do admit it is he?"

"I take your word for it."

"Very sweet of you, Andrew. Very polite. But somehow unlike you! Don't you know him?"

"From the photograph? I'd have to see it again to be half sure."

"I mean, from your own inside vision—don't you know who he is?"

"You'd make a good cross-examiner. No, I don't know who he is. On the whole, I'd say yes, I suppose he's Old Ugly-face. I'm taking it for granted. I couldn't prove it."

"Don't you suppose he'll prove it, at the right time?"

"Why isn't now the best possible time?"

"He knows best. He's in a very tight place," said Elsa.

"He sure is. So are we—outnumbered—well worth looting—up against at least one, perhaps more, of the coldest blooded devils on earth. St. Malo is as vicious as one of our young coked-up killers in the States. If you could cut his conscience, it wouldn't bleed. I don't know who some of those Tibetans are. But St. Malo picked 'em, so they're no one's woolly baa-lambs. It's a bad stable. Our men are scared stiff of 'em."

"Andrew, he knows all that."

Andrew laughed. "Who's superstitious? What d'you want to call him? Monsieur X or something?"

"Monsieur X would do."

"We'll call him that. So now—what beats me is that Monsieur X is a statesman. He was on the Council of Regents in Lhasa. He knows the ropes."

"So was von Schuschnigg a statesman," said Elsa. "Where is he now? How many of Mussolini's, Stalin's, Franco's statesmen are alive today? Why should Monsieur X be an exception?"

"But according to you, he's also a magician."

"So was Jesus a magician—St. Paul—Joan of Arc— Giordano

593

Bruno—Savonarola. Andrew, are you being serious? Do you honestly claim that just because someone is spiritual he can escape from material hatred? The world hates spiritual people. It only admires material success. It only tolerates shams—until after they're dead."

"But if he's a saint, as you think, why should he be in the soup?"

"Why was Jesus in the soup, as you call it?"

"I wish I knew. Why did Jesus, who knew enough to turn society inside out so it stayed that way for a couple of thousand years, go bumming around Palestine with a crook like Judas? Didn't he know better?"

"Andrew, I'm only a beginner. I don't know all the answers."

"If Monsieur X is as bright as you think—how come that he fell for St. Malo?"

"How d'you know he has fallen for him?"

"That's what's happened. St. Malo is the king-pin of this outfit. I'm gambling St. Malo came overland from Shanghai just to help Monsieur X escape into a worse trap than he was in before. St. Malo proposed to him to change clothes with that flunky. He means to sell him for hard cash."

"Andrew—couldn't it be that Monsieur X knew no other way to reach a definite objective than to agree to St. Malo's plan?"

"Jesuitry, eh? Lining up with crooks and doing wrong that good may come of it maybe, perhaps? That sounds like the church talking."

"Gently, Andrew, gently! What wrong has he done—that you know of? Andrew, you must understand this. Please understand it. Monsieur X is a Ringding Gelong Lama who abandoned the broad road of promotion by meditation, for the perilous and much more difficult pilgrimage, as it is called, of attainment by deeds."

"Attainment! That's what they're all after—attainment— success— every last damned politician I ever met or heard of. They have to do it. They can't do otherwise. Once their snouts are in the swill, they must suck with the rest of the swine. They have to make the front page or go under—feather their nests, or starve when there's a change of government. Rob or be robbed. Lie, steal, chouse, swindle—"

"Andrew—"

"Yes?"

"To take the path that Monsieur X took, he had first to abandon all those things. He had to tear out of his heart the last trace of self-aggrandizement, greed, pride. He had to earn, by almost unimaginable discipline, not only spiritual power but the equally essential spiritual will never to employ that power for his personal use, even in dire need."

"Well. I've heard of that being done. Go ahead."

"You know what *karma* is?"

"I know what the word means."

"Tell me."

"It means the unavoidable accumulated incubus of fate caused by deeds in former lives."

"Near enough. Unavoidable, irresistible, but not unconquerable. Spiritual evolution doesn't wipe out *karma*. It can't. Nothing can. Karma must happen, because every cause is a boomerang that must have its effect, sooner or later, upon the individual who did it. But on the principle which Jesus taught—'*resist not evil*'—spiritual evolution does show how to rise—as it were into a stratosphere—above *karma* and in that way to put it to, good use. Have I made that clear?"

"Get up into an ivory tower and offer the other cheek?"

"Not literally—no. Turning the other cheek suggests the idea of tacking a ship at sea, so as to take advantage of an adverse wind. One can progress against the wind. One can make personal *karma* serve impersonal, spiritual purposes."

"I object to that word 'impersonal,'" said Andrew. "What's more I sustain the objection. It's ruled out. It tries to sidestep the truth that everything happens to persons, through persons. Even an impersonal opinion, so-called, comes through a person. Everything that means anything is personal—from Einstein's relativity all the way down to a five-four Supreme Court decision, or an egg omelet, or a shot in the back.—Just half a jiffy while I move that lantern."

He rearranged the lantern carefully so that the shadow of his head and shoulders fell on sacks of barley that lined the tent wall. There was nothing to aim at from outside. Then he shifted two sacks so that there was one on either side of Elsa and she was well protected against possible bullets.

"So let's keep this personal," he went on. "We're in one personal hell of a jam. I'd like to get your view. I'm doing my best to understand."

"I wish I knew the right words," she answered. "I can feel it, the way one feels music in silence."

"Keep on trying," said Andrew.

She was silent for almost a minute. Then she said: "Listen! Suppose Monsieur X were in Lhasa, hiding from enemies."

"Okay. That's easy. He was."

"While in hiding he heard of a plot to carry off the infant Dalai Lama in order to make use of him deceitfully for cruel purposes."

"Stet! That's what happened."

"What could he do?"

"You're telling it."

"Having no personal ambition none whatever—absolutely none—caring nothing what might happen to his own person—but intensely willing to devote his whole intelligence to the greatest good of all concerned—should he have turned down an opportunity with pious horror because its proposer was Ambrose St. Malo? Or was he right to let St. Malo appear to succeed with his treacherous plan, knowing full well that his own soul will direct him, not only to the right course—but to the only right course? Remember, he doesn't care twopence about his own personal safety."

"Did you make that up?" asked Andrew.

"No. I asked my soul to tell me how to convince you. The words came."

"They make sense," he answered. "Just a jiffy or two. I'll make the rounds."

"Take a guard with you!"

"Sure."

The four whom he had placed on guard were asleep under the fly of the tent, inside two walls of barley bags. He waked up two of them and led the way first to the pony lines, using his flashlight. It wasn't snowing any longer, it was thawing. Someone might have ridden away. He counted the animals. Ponies, yaks and sheep were all there with their harness around them. He thought for a minute, made sure that his automatic was easy to get at, and started toward Bulah Singh's tent. The soft snow smothered his footfall so that he walked like a ghost, but his thoughts were like trip-hammer beats:

"Almighty, if you give a damn, and if you are God, don't fool me this time."

A voice seemed to say, inside his head: "Don't fool yourself."

Who was talking to whom? He wondered about it. He didn't know. His lips didn't move. He wasn't muttering or talking aloud to himself. "I'm going to play this the way it looks right to me," he said. But it was soundless.

The voice inside him answered: "You are the judge. There is no other."

"Nuts!" he said. "I'm damned if I'm the judge! I didn't create this mess!"

"Didn't you? Then who did? This is the test you prayed for. Are you afraid?"

"Hell, I'm not afraid of St. Malo and Bulah Singh."

"Are you afraid not to kill them?"

"I'm going to play it straight. I'll keep 'em both for Tom Grayne."

"Are you afraid of Tom Grayne?"

"Why should I be?"

"Why are you?"

"I'm not."

"You are the judge: Are you afraid of Elsa?"

"God, no."

"Aren't you?"

"Why should I be?"

"Then what do you fear? What is it?"

He hadn't answered himself. He had reached Bulah Singh's tent. There was a lantern burning inside. It cast the shadow of only one man, that looked like the turbaned shape of Bulah Singh. Andrew touched the shoulders of his Tibetan escort to warn them to keep silent, and stood listening. Presently there came the muffled sound of something hollow being hammered beneath a blanket. Suddenly he drew his own knife and cut the lashings of the tent with swift strokes. He bore down on the ridge pole, collapsing the tent, and stood back to watch the result. The lantern went out. Someone inside the billowing tent fired three shots–panic shots at random. Andrew spotted with his flash-light, jumped and landed with both feet on the invisible pistol. Then there were groans. So he moved aside and ordered his two Tibetans to drag the tent free. Bulah Singh sat up in the glare of the flashlight.

"I might have known it was you," he said, readjusting his turban. Both his broken Mausers were beside him on the ground. He had been using one as a hammer to break open Andrew's steel box. "Don't shoot," he said, "unless you specially want to. I'm not armed."

"I will do as I please," said Andrew. "Pull that blanket aside. No, I know what's under that one. The other!"

Bulah Singh sat still. He thought it was a trick. He didn't dare to move. Andrew told one of the Tibetans to pull the blanket away. Beneath it lay Ambrose St. Malo with his head swathed in a torn shirt. It was he who had groaned.

"Next time, I'll aim better," said Andrew.

St. Malo sat up. "What do you mean—next time?" He had a peculiar, sub-acid accent that suggested an immeasurable depth of insolence and self-assurance that relied on treachery and other men's mistakes.

"Next time you burgle my tent," said Andrew.

"You'd be a fool to kill me," St. Malo answered. "Perhaps you are a fool. Who knows? Damn you and your tent-peg! You missed killing me by almost nothing. If I had my gun, you'd—"

Andrew interrupted: "Take your gun back from Bulah Singh! He stole it. Go on, take it from him!"

He didn't have to speak twice. Matter-of-factly St. Malo held out his hand. The Sikh returned his well-oiled Smith and Wesson.

"For your information," said Andrew, "you were bluffed by a couple of broken Mausers. Now uncover my steel box."

Both men were afraid to move, because the flashlight was in Andrew's left hand and his right looked too ready to draw. One of the Tibetans pulled the blanket aside. The steel box was unbroken, though there were deep dents made by the butt of Bulah Singh's Mauser. At a sign from Andrew a Tibetan picked up the box.

"You hadn't brains enough to think of this," said St. Malo. "You're only a strong-arm amateur. I remember you now from Shanghai."

"You are right," said Bulah Singh. "It's that girl. She's clairvoyant. She tells him everything."

St. Malo was beginning to feel a lot less scared, which was what Andrew waited for. One scare is never enough. It needs not less than two.

"If you should shoot me," said St. Malo, "there'd be no one to tell my rescue party you've been hospitable. There's a party from Lhasa close behind us. You'll need friends. You'd better make one now. I'm not vindictive."

Andrew laughed. That might be a half-truth. But it was one sure bet that Ambrose St. Malo had no friends in Lhasa. If he did know, and was known to von Klaus's party of Germans, then he must have double-crossed them and escaped with the man they were after. He had probably snatched Old Ugly-face out from under their noses. It would be a pursuit—not rescue-party.

"If you should shoot me," said Andrew, "you couldn't handle my men. You'd be caught by the pursuing force and strung up. So you may keep your gun. Your five-and-ten-cent *lama* told me you want to go where I'm headed for. So toe the line. From now on you and Bulah Singh share this tent. You'll walk—both of you."

"But my feet!" said Bulah Singh.

"I don't care a damn for your feet. You'll use 'em. I intend to repack the loads to spare the ponies. And get this, both of you. The slightest trouble from either of you, from now on, will be personal— between you and me—settled there and then, on that basis, without further notice."

He didn't wait to watch them repitch the tent. He left the Tibetans to help them and walked alone to the lean-to, where Bompo Tsering and his own gang were huddled all together at the opposite end of the lean-to from the phony lama's men. He awoke Bompo Tsering— whispered to him.

"But, Gunnigun—"

"Do as I say, you fool, or you'll be dead by morning!"

One by one, waking them one at a time, they disarmed St. Malo's men. It was better to wake them before searching them—especially those who pretended to be very fast asleep. They all had Mausers. Andrew smashed them, one against another, then flung them away in the snow. That those were St. Malo's and not the phony *lama's* men was now established beyond doubt, without having to ask questions that might subtly have restored their morale. Being questioned, by someone who needs to know, builds self-importance. If they had been the phony *lama's* men they would have looked to him for explanations, help, advice, orders. They didn't. They never looked at him at all. They didn't care whether he lived or he died. They stared through the dark toward Bulah Singh's tent. And they were all the more discouraged and disenchanted because Andrew told them nothing—said not one solitary word. He simply walked away and left them. Bompo Tsering followed:

"Gunnigun, your being hot-damn fool! Why your breaking all them too good Mausers? Why your throwing away? Why your not giving-um me? My—"

Andrew's impatient gesture stopped him. He blinked in the rays of the flashlight.

"Look in my eyes! Am I afraid?" asked Andrew.

"No, Gunnigun. My being afraid. Your not."

"Good. That's what I thought. Turn in and sleep. I'm standing watch. One hour before daybreak, redistribute loads, dividing up between all the ponies, with a half-load for the new one. From here on, everybody walks except the Lady Elsa."

"Why her not walking also?"

"Because I say it."

"Yes, Gunnigun."

"That's all."

"Yes, Gunnigun."

Bompo Tsering walked off toward the pony lines where the tea-urn and fuel were stowed in a hole in the rock. He hummed a *mantra* guaranteed to ward off devils.

Andrew went to his own tent, rather grim-lipped. His lips didn't move. "Who said I'm afraid?" he demanded. It sounded like his own voice, but he was absolutely sure he hadn't actually spoken. A voice inside him answered:

"I said it. I say it again."

Elsa called to him: "Are you all right, Andrew?"

She opened the tent and held back the flap while he kicked the snow off his boots and went in.

Chapter 45

It cleared suddenly. The low moon broke through the clouds. Andrew sat in the mouth of the tent with Elsa beside him and the pole between them, so that they had a view of the entire bivouac. She wrapped a blanket around her, although it wasn't really cold now the thaw had set in. She hadn't any idea that it made her look wistful and in need of male protection. She wasn't thinking of herself. But Andrew found himself resisting an impulse. It made him lean the other way. Impulses at cross-purposes within him made decision difficult. The thawing snow thudded and tinkled. The ponies neighed, smelling the barley sacks; Bompo Tsering was getting their breakfast ration ready before redistributing the loads. There was a feel of excitement—a sensation of impending crisis, and it was suggested all over again by Andrew's forced calm. The curve of his shoulders resembled a spring under tension. He was ready for anything—eager to employ and relieve his nervous energy. Things seemed real and unreal in undulations, as if thought rose and fell on waves of consciousness.

Elsa spoke first: "Andrew," she said after a long while, "I've meant the opposite—but I've become a perfect infliction on you. If *karma* is what we are told it is, mine piles up—"

"See here," he retorted. "You're always praising me and blaming yourself. Try reversing it."

"I'm finding fault with both of us," she said, resting her chin on her knees.

"What's wrong with either of us?" he retorted. "Aren't you doing your best? I know I am."

"There must be something wrong," she said after a moment.

"Yeah. We're human."

"We have been through so much together. And yet—I have tried to make myself understood—"

"You mean, by me?"

"Yes, Andrew. Just as a matter of fair play."

"Sure it was fair play?"

"What would you call it?"

"Was it fair to yourself?"

"Yes. Of course it was. I shouldn't feel like a stranger to you. And I've tried to understand you, for the same reason. But you've never let me."

"People shouldn't understand each other," he answered. "It isn't decent. To understand is to hate or despise. For instance, I understand St. Malo and Bulah Singh. If you understood me you'd despise me. I don't wish that."

"How could I possibly despise you, after all you've done. And besides, Andrew, you're not a criminal."

It was almost a question. She shrank at the inflection of her own voice. But it was too late to recall it.

"What is a criminal?" he answered. "Where's the dividing line?"

"I meant, Bulah Singh, for instance, is a fugitive from justice. You're not."

"What is justice? I never saw any yet" Something had released the spring. Andrew was coming unwound. "Take an example," he went on. "Do you consider your Monsieur X is receiving justice—from God—humanity—anyone? As far as it's in me to give it, he'll get it from me. But what do I know about him? So how can I give it? All I know is what I've heard about him, what you've told me, and what I infer. That's all. It amounts to damned little justice? I'm a lawyer. There ain't no such animal."

"Andrew, you are difficult tonight."

"Life's difficult."

"Do we know each other well enough for me to say what I really think?"

"About me?"

"Yes."

"You'll have to use your own judgment."

"Is that a challenge? Or a warning? Or—"

"Sometimes things are said that stick like barbs. It isn't wise to tell all you know, or all you think you know. Even when you're in love it isn't wise."

He paused. Elsa held her breath. Had he divined her secret? Did he know she loved him? Was he resenting it? Was that the cause of his moodiness? She breathed again when he continued:

"You should know that. Did you tell Tom Grayne everything you thought you knew about you and him?"

"I tried to."

"But you didn't?"

"Couldn't."

"Women don't understand," he said after a moment. "They don't realise that if a man respects 'em he shows 'em only his best. The mistake they make is in thinking it isn't his best. They can't let well enough alone. So they examine critically. Then they get more than they asked for—and bang goes another friendship, because they discover—or they think they do—what the man is afraid of."

"Andrew, you're afraid of something."

"Maybe you're right. I don't doubt you'd like to be told. You'd take that as a compliment. But believe me, damned few compliments of that kind are worth what they cost."

"Andrew, I wouldn't count costs if I could do you any good. I feel, perhaps I could help, if you'd let me. I know you're not afraid of these Tibetans, nor of Bulah Singh and St. Malo. You're not afraid of tomorrow's march—I know you're not, although everyone else is—except me. But you're afraid of something."

"Meaning, I suppose, 'tell Mamma.'"

"No. I refuse to be Mamma."

"That's good. If she had her own way my Mamma's in heaven. She's in hell if the preacher was right. Anyhow, one was enough."

"You didn't like her?"

"I loved her. But one was enough. When she died, I flew the matriarchal coop. If I hate anything it's one of these synthetic mothers."

Elsa felt she was getting nowhere, slipping backward. She threw caution to the winds: "Well, Andrew, there's no need to tell you I'm burned up with curiosity. I know you're afraid. And yet I know you're not running away. So I think you're afraid of yourself."

Instead of answering, he met her eyes. The moonlight revealed his clearly but it did not tell the meaning of their strange excitement. Was he angry? He got up, strode as far as the pony lines, gave an order, found fault with Bompo Tsering, stood listening for a moment near Bulah Singh's tent on his way back, and came and sat down. This time he didn't look at her.

"See here," he said almost savagely: "I won't even try to tell you all of it. It's too long and too difficult too much about me: But I'll admit this: the arrival of the man we've agreed to call Monsieur X has upset me no end!"

"How, Andrew? In what way? Can't you tell me at least that much?"

"Brought up memories. Conjured 'em—stirred 'em, like mud off a river bottom."

"But you're not an escapist, Andrew. You're not running away from memories. I know you're not."

He looked at her. She marvelled at his blindness that he couldn't read how utterly she loved him. Or was it that her eyes were so dumb with love that they couldn't tell?

"How can you know?" he answered. "You're guessing. Or else you're slapping on the praise to hide what you really think."

"Andrew, do you like being cruel?"

"I hate cruelty."

"Well then, please don't suggest I'm lying when I tell you I know something. I don't believe I do lie very often. I would lie to you last. Do you believe me?"

"Yes, I do believe you. You don't tell lies."

Suddenly she knew the veil that hid his memories was slowly being lifted—like a dark portcullis—by a force beyond his power to control. Her heart thumped so she was afraid he'd hear it.

He said quietly: "You're the first person who has ever given me a square deal about that."

"About what, Andrew?"

"About my not running away. God damn their souls to hell, every son of a bitch friend or enemy who ever heard the name of Freud has called me an escapist. What makes you think otherwise?"

"I suppose it's intuition. Are you forgetting I'm clairvoyant—sometimes?"

He fell silent again, watching the shadows, listening. For the time he was two men. Two separate groups of senses held his attention.

Instinct watched the bivouac, alert for familiar danger. Intuition trembled and leaped toward undanger—unfamiliar—unknown, and very
difficult to trust because instinct said no to it.

Elsa's voice with a smile to it interrupted his thought: "Andrew,
what is it that you're not running away from?"

Heavier humour might have driven thought inward and scattered
it. That light touch took the weight off. He laughed:

"My country 'tis of thee!"

He reached into his huge hip pocket for a hunk of root and his
whittling knife. By the dim light of the lantern he carved guide lines,
blocking off roughly the main planes of a head and shoulders. They
might be anyone's head and shoulders—something unborn yet.

"Andrew, you've always said you love your country. I got the impression that you love America far more than I love England."

"I love America." He whittled one side of the root smooth and
then put it away. "Don't you love England?"

"I suppose I do," she answered. "But not fanatically. What is there
to love? Chamberlain and Lady Astor? Decadence—miles and miles
of awful council houses—dreary monotony—suburbs—keeping up
with the Joneses—snobbery—lip-service to traditions that died in the
war—vulgarity—awful vulgarity—and an empire that means nothing now—always but L.s.d.—pounds, shillings and pence. I love some
people in England. I can think of at least ten people whom I really
love—perhaps a hundred whom I really like. But I think the England
I would like to love died centuries ago. No, I'm not afraid of England,"
she added. "Why are you afraid of America?"

He closed his whittling knife and put it away. It was an unconscious
gesture, signifying nothing to himself. To an observer it was as clear as
the line of his lips in the yellow lamplight that he had dismissed side
issues. He intended to "come clean."

"So you insist on knowing. Well, I'll tell you. But answer this first:
have you any cads in England? Any stinkers? Any lying hypocrites
in high places—*patrioteers*—racketeers—pimps—panders—hogs with
their snouts at the public teat—treacherous labour leaders—nou-
veaux riches, who'd sell their king for a tax rebate—unctuous church-
men drawing dividends from munition factories— double-crossing
lawyers?—Any cowards, thieves, fakers, pompous bureaucrats, place
hunters, sail-trimmers—"

"Andrew!"

"Well—have you any?"

"Yes, of course. All countries have them."

"For every one you have in England, we have half a dozen in the U.S.A. What's worse, ours are more competent. They're bolder. They're just as yellow at heart, but they're tougher skinned and they've ten times the opportunity."

"But, Andrew, surely all Americans aren't grafters. In England we have—"

"Listen!" he interrupted. "You've some good men and women left in Great Britain. Some. No doubt, none better. But for every one you've got left, we've got at least two in the U.S.A. And they're better than yours. There are plenty of reasons why that should be. The United States is the God-damned craziest country on earth. It's a hotbed of all the phony isms, cults, philosophies, diseased religions, chicaneries, iniquities, stupid laws, vices, obscenities and God knows what else. But it's the best country. And it's the last one left that has a chance to lead the world out of the mess it's in. I said lead, not save. It's got the men and women who can do it, given a chance. But do they get the chance? That's what eats me. Let a wise man—or an honest woman—and they're scarce, mind you—make a move toward liberty, sanity, decency, dignity—those are all one, and don't forget it—instantly a thousand greedy liars with tongues in their cheeks—smug, blatant lip-servers—all of 'em drooling for loot, slobbering for a chance to exploit—leap up behind some catch-phrase demagogue or pulpiteer to steal the movement or else kill it."

He let indignation boil a moment, enjoying the emotion. Then he suddenly resumed: "Almighty God! You wouldn't believe what gets by! One of my first important jobs was to help prosecute a political boss. His corruption was so obscene that nine-tenths of the evidence couldn't be printed—even nowadays when people discuss syphilis at dinner. He was hand-in-glove with priests; they took money from him to what they call educate the children of the parents he had looted. He'd stood in with, and taken money from brothels, crooked gambling joints and all the rackets there are. No graft-sow was too rotten for him to milk. A nice, prissy-faced, silver-haired daddy with a smile that 'ud melt your heart. His wife's furs had been bought with a percentage of the earnings of diseased whores, who had to earn it and come across or go to jail. His sons were put through college on the proceeds of the bail bond business. That's another stinking racket that only a son of a bitch would touch. He was proved at the trial to have double-crossed his own gang scores of times, and to have cunningly passed the buck to someone else. He was guilty of almost every crime in the calendar, including incitement to murder. He was a stinking, baby-kissing swine, who had the impudence to call character witnesses to prove he was a faithful Catholic. Even the Catholic Irish judge got sore at that; I guess he added two years to the sentence. But here's where the limit came. This is what staggered me, so that I can't even talk of it now without feeling sick at the stomach. He was brought up for sentence on a Friday. He got twelve years. He should have had life, but he was let off with twelve years, partly because of his age, and partly, no doubt, to encourage him to keep his mouth shut. What d'you suppose he said to the judge? You'd never guess. He said: 'You'll have your conscience to live with! There's a God in Heaven. The Lord Jesus Christ was also sentenced on a Friday.'"

"But, Andrew, why should that man's blasphemy offend you so much?"

"It didn't. It doesn't. This is what burns me. All the newspapers front-paged it. And what did the public do? The criminal himself, the prosecuting attorney, the judge, and all the members of the jury received a total of hundreds of thousands of letters from all over the United States, sympathizing with him and denouncing his prosecutors. Hundreds of thousands of letters. They were turned over to me to deal with. That's how I know."

"How did you deal with them? What did you do?"

"I sorted 'em. Studied 'em. I sort of added 'em to what I knew already from having talked to witnesses and having sat through the trial. At last I got permission to have 'em burned in the courthouse furnace. And by that time I had formed an opinion."

"You mean about America?"

"Yes. And about me and my job."

"Are you still of the same opinion?"

"Yes. I'm going to tell it to you. So get ready to laugh."

Elsa didn't speak. She felt more like crying. The fierce intentness on Andrew's face recalled how he looked when her baby was being born.

"At first," he said, "I thought of throwing up the law and turning politician. But I came across Lincoln's statement, and I thought so much about it that I soon had it by heart. Mind you, Lincoln's my hero. I'm quoting him exactly, word for word:

"'Politicians are a set of men who have interests aside from the interests of the people, and who, to say the most for them, are at least one long step removed from honest men. I say this with greater freedom being a politician myself.'"

"Andrew, is that what you thought I would laugh at?"

"No. Wait. That's coming. It occurred to me that if Lincoln couldn't be honest in politics, probably no one can be. Jesus couldn't. Certainly I couldn't. But I could make a stab at being honest, and I owed that to my country, because I love my country. One thought led to another, beginning with the thought 'my country,' and leading on from that, trying to think honestly and throwing overboard all the pestilential tripe I'd learned in Sunday School about salvation by cruelty-torture on a cross and psalm-singing. Here's where the laugh comes in. Are you ready?"

"Yes," said Elsa.

"Thinking honestly for the first time, I began to see clearly. It was almost a knockout. I discovered that as long as there's a louse-priest, or a pimp-politician—a whore or a racketeer or a mad-dog evangelist crook in the United States; as long as there's a despicable financial buzzard preparing to rule a ruined world, or a hog-swill leader betraying his followers, or a tut-mouthed congressman lying for re-election—I'm it! It's my country."

"Andrew!"

"Laugh all you like. That's what I thought. It's what I still think. It's what I know."

"And you left the United States on that account?"

"No, I didn't. I became a reformer—of me. I took a good long look—and—think about the professional reformers, and at some private ones too. I decided: the hell with them all. There might be one who wasn't doing more harm than good. I couldn't find him. Anti-saloon leaguers, anti-vice crusaders, Watch and Ward keyhole peepers—Ku-Klux-Klansters—every last one of 'em that I could find was parasiting off the public he was supposed to be out to reform. I'd be ashamed to be a professional reformer, simply on the ground of what I actually know about 'em as a class and as individuals, first-hand. God! I'd as soon be a missionary!"

"But you still haven't told why you left the United States."

"I'm coming to it. I could reform me. Couldn't I? I could try, anyhow. So I got busy trying to avoid self-righteousness by bearing in mind that any rottenness I saw was in my own eye—the same way that colour is in the eye of the looker. Started being honest with myself first. I found carving portraits in wood was a great help. Anything you can do with your hands helps train your mind. I tried hard, because I had to do something to keep my belly from turning over at the things I knew about my country—that's to say about me. Then I made a mistake."

He paused for a moment. He had to force the rest out of himself. He hated doing it. Elsa's blood turned cold because she guessed again that he knew she had fallen in love with him and he was trying to cure her of it by revealing the unpalatable truth.

"I fell in love."

He shot the words out like a pronouncement of doom, then got up and walked away, to look over the ponies' rations and check up Bompo Tsering's rearrangement of the loads. Elsa sat still, numbed.

"So it's a mistake to fall in love."

She turned that over in her mind. Or it turned itself over. It repeated, again and again. She smiled wanly. It was hardly a gentle hint. It held none of Andrew's usual kindness. If he knew she loved him, as it seemed he did, it would have been more like him to say something straightforward about it. But she thought that perhaps all honest men hint clumsily and only the treacherous sort do it well. It was just Andrew being honest.

Well, it was getting near daybreak. The moon had gone down. The few visible stars were already paling. The chill that heralds sunrise was like the chill on her heart, but night was nearly over. Was he still in love with that woman? Why was it a mistake? How could one help being in love? Can that which can't be helped be a mistake?

"I'm glad I love him! It isn't a mistake. It can't be, because I didn't ask for it, and I couldn't help it. It's my right! I will love him forever! But I'll tell no one! It's my secret."

She heard Andrew coming, sturdily crunching the snow. The bivouac was stirring; the Tibetans were boiling tea. But it was still dark, and the darkness felt like loneliness—forever.

Andrew sat down beside her and resumed exactly where he had left off. His expression hadn't changed. It had been the other part of him that went the rounds of the bivouac.

"She was the wrong girl," he said abruptly. "Wrong one for me. Sweet, sentimental, much too easy on the eye, if I'd only known it. If they look like the Mother of God, they're not fit to be mothers of men. Too easy on the ear. Voice like an angel's. Eyes like pools of intelligence. I don't see, even now, how I could have known better than to trust her with my whole heart and conscience."

608

"Andrew, it isn't criminal to fall in love. Did she betray you?"

"She did not—in the way you mean. She encouraged me in my determination to be absolutely honest, first with myself, then with her, so that we could both be honest with the world. Sex, for instance: we respected each other. We often talked about sex without ever once crossing the line. It got so that I used to save my thoughts, just to tell to her and to no one else."

"Were you still practicing law?"

"Yes. Trying to drive law and honesty in double harness. Getting hopeful, too—not doing so badly. And then one day I took her boating— on a lake. I'd had a hard week. It was hot. It was nice out there on the lake in the motorboat, so we stayed until after dark. Then I learned we can only be honest one by one. You can't do it in droves. Not even two by two. It's a one-man, one-woman business."

He paused for a full minute, so that Elsa thought he had decided to say no more. But he resumed abruptly:

"I'd got so used to being honest with her—absolutely honest, and no ulterior motives or hidden meanings—that you couldn't have made me believe she'd misinterpret anything I'd say or do. She might not understand. She might ask for an explanation. But misinterpret— no. She'd be sure I was on the level, whatever I'd do."

He paused again. He swallowed a couple of times. Then he looked at Elsa, but she looked away for fear of breaking the train of his thought.

"I belonged at that time to a good, broad-minded gang—young married people mostly—but some unmarried ones—all up and coming and full of fun, without a sour one in the lot. Painters, musicians, a lawyer or two—a young college prof—a fellow who wrote stuff for the magazines—an actress—a couple of rich men's sons who weren't money-conscious. It was a good gang. We used to go bathing by moonlight, and we'd peel like kids at a waterhole, thinking no more of it—and seeing surely no more shame in it than in the couple of drinks we'd have later and the songs we'd sing on the way home."

"Was it against the law to strip naked and swim?" Elsa asked.

"Yes. I reckon maybe it was. There's a fool law against absolutely anything you want to do in the United States. That's what makes black-mail easy."

"I'm sorry, Andrew. I didn't mean to interrupt. I'm listening."

"That evening I felt hot. I craved a swim. It was the place where I was used to swimming with the friends I've just told you about.

There was no one near—no other boat—no chance of scandalizing any mugwumps. I had nothing on but a shirt and a pair of slacks. I pulled 'em off and dived in, feeling grateful to be with a girl who'd see no harm."

"And what happened?"

"She never spoke to me again. Never again. I swam around awhile, and called out to her once or twice to jump in and join me. But she didn't answer. When I climbed into the boat, I couldn't get her to speak. She wouldn't open her lips. I had to return to the car and drive her home to her mother's house without one word from her. She shut the door in my face. That was a Saturday night. Sunday morning I phoned. No answer. Afternoon the same. Evening the same—no answer. Monday I went to work. Sometime Monday she committed suicide."

"Oh!—Andrew!"

"She left a letter addressed to me. It was found by the police. A cop who had reason to hate my guts let some reporters see it. Selections from it made the evening paper in a box on the front page. Next morning I had an eight-column headline to myself, with a portrait and full biography to date."

"Andrew, how awful!"

"It was all that. In her letter she said I had broken her heart. I had destroyed her trust in man. I had captured her love by cunning words about integrity and self-respect—and then I had debauched it—that was the word she used—debauched it for a moment's physical pleasure. Life, she said, for herself was no longer worth living, but she prayed that God would have mercy on me."

"How did she kill herself?"

"Shot. She used my revolver, that I got a permit for at the time of the trial that I told you about, when that political boss's friends were trying to pick off his opponents one by one. I never had to use the damned thing. I left it in her mother's house one night because it was bulky and heavy. I forgot it—never thought of it again until she shot herself and the police identified it. After that they arrested me."

"Andrew—did you have to stand trial?"

"No. The Grand Jury found no true bill—threw it out. But that's why I left the United States. You see—"

He paused a moment, squaring his chest unconsciously, throwing back his head in a gesture that was one hundred *per cent* Andrew.

"—I could have stood it that no one believed my story. In fact, after the Grand jury session I left off telling it. I just shut up. It didn't sicken me too badly to be dropped socially—high-hatted by men and women whose debaucheries I knew plenty about—couldn't help knowing. I could have lived all that down. But what good would it do?"

"Andrew, did your friends desert you—I mean, for instance, those you went bathing naked with?"

"Sure. Some damned rat-reporter got hold of their names. They were as mad at me as if I'd disgraced 'em on purpose. One of 'em did sort of half apologize for passing me up. He said he believed my story, but he couldn't afford to be seen in my company because he had his job and his social position to consider. That wasn't the trouble. I didn't blame 'em. I wasn't even sore at 'em —not at them, I wasn't. What got under my skin was this."

He paused again. He stood up. There was dim light shimmering on gray clouds in the distance—false dawn. He looked down at Elsa:

"How could I reconcile that—I mean what had happened—with my own new theory about me and my native land?" He became angry. He was girding again for the battle. "If it's in my own eye, I'll get it out of my eye—somehow!" His voice, without becoming louder, grew more vehement: "I've learned this much: you can't tell all you know; and you mustn't trust anyone else to understand what may be clearer to you than your name in a printed book."

He looked down again at Elsa. "And now the answer. I don't know the answer. But I will never return to the U.S.A. until I do know it. If, as, and when I go back, it'll be in the full knowledge that I've something to give to my country. That I'll be useful—an asset—not one of the damned reformers—not a politician either—nor a meddler, but a leader of men. Until I know which way to lead, I'll be damned if I'll take a chance on leading wrong: Maybe I'll go home some day."

He strode away from the tent where all eyes could see him:

"Bompo Tsering!" he shouted. "All hands make-ready to march in fifteen minutes!" Then he glanced again at Elsa. "Will you fix something for breakfast for you and me? This is the wrong time to get poisoned. But let's eat. There'll be a long day's march."

CHAPTER 46

The thaw had set in seriously. The going wasn't any too good; it was particularly bad for the remnant of loaded sheep that had to be carried through soft drifts. Andrew pressed forward because at that altitude the wind gets up at about ten o'clock and it's worse than war fighting against it. First, though, the corpse had to be disposed of, although that was no great problem. In Tibet there is no respect for a corpse; it is something that the dead man has no further use for. It belongs now to nature. The wild animals may have it, the sooner the better. The mortal remains of Ugly-face's dead companion were left sitting upright in a snowdrift, naked. Less than five minutes after the start wolves could be heard fighting one another and the vultures.

The three days' march after that was a torment, that left no energy for conversation. The only thought was of the distance made, and of fatigue and how to carry on. But the luck held. They reached the wind-swept ledges before the thaw made the plain impassable, and it was the thaw that saved them from being overtaken by some cavalry from Lhasa. The phony *lama*, who hadn't condescended to tell Andrew his worshipful name, borrowed his binoculars and confirmed his guess they were from Lhasa. They had modern rifles and were well mounted. They were the pursuing party that Ambrose St. Malo had expected, that he had lied about, saying they were his friends. They got stuck in the mud that overlay frozen clay. Not long after that the mud became an ocean of roaring water hurrying down the watershed. So the cavalry turned back, to re-cross the river. Probably their bodies reached the Bay of Bengal.

After that, because there was no more danger of immediate pursuit, Ambrose St. Malo became much less self-effacing, and Bulah Singh ceased to be meek. His feet no longer troubled him. He and St. Malo trudged side by side, exploring each other's minds, letting Andrew carry all the burden of the days and all the worries of the nights.

Andrew made a few attempts to get in conversation with Ugly-face, but without much success. The old man strode along like a mountaineer, in spite of his big belly. He seemed as unconcerned as a drover. Hardship didn't bother him. Andrew favoured him as much as possible, giving Elsa double quantities of soft rations to share with him when the others weren't looking. He hadn't come by that huge belly on a diet of parched barley and rotten yak; deprivation of luxuries would fall harder on him than on others. But he ate what he was given without comment, accepting favours as his natural right, as calmly as he would have ignored their absence. He didn't seem even to notice the phony *lama's* insolence. Humiliated and resentful because Andrew had taken his scarecrow pony to lighten the loads of his own emaciated beasts, the phony *lama* victimized the old man in every possible way, at every opportunity. He even forced him to carry his bundle of belongings, until Andrew spotted it and threw the bundle into a snowdrift. It cost the phony *lama* half an hour's work to get it out again. After that Andrew gave Elsa what amounted to orders:

"Can't you ride beside him all the rest of the journey, so he can hold your stirrup if he needs to, or lay a hand on the pony's neck?"

She was afraid. She protested: "But Andrew, I'm sure he wants me to keep away from him. He doesn't wish to be recognized. He doesn't wish to be asked questions. No intimacies. I'm quite sure."

Andrew turned his back to the wind and stood still, so she drew rein—eagerly, because though they had continued to share a tent together, he had been more than usually reticent since he told her his story. He might be going to open up again—to resume confidences. But he didn't.

"See here," he said, "it's just as easy to be silent when you know, as when you don't know. You haven't had to talk because you knows the lowdown about me. If what he wants is silence, let him have it. I'm asking you to ride beside him and protect him. When I try to help him a bit that phony *lama* turns on both of us and accuses him of trying to tempt me to go in some other direction. It's the same old story of the ex-servant wreaking savagery on the aristocrat when he gets him at his mercy. Your friend Monsieur X is paying for having trusted the wrong man."

"He pays gallantly," Elsa objected. "He never murmurs."

"So you don't want to ride beside him?"

"Andrew, I'd like to do whatever you wish but—"

He interrupted: "Does he know English? I'll ask him."

He strode up to Old Ugly-face, searching memory, recalling as well as he could the intricate, almost fantastic details of rumoured intrigues in Lhasa—wondering at the man's present condition, for he had fallen from high estate like Milton's Lucifer. He looked at Andrew quizzically, reading his thought. His fierce eyes and funny old beak of a nose suggested pained surprise that any man of breeding could be so impertinent. After a moment's stare he said in English, that was at any rate better than Bompo Tsering's:

"Curiosity being a vice of fools and the path to too many hells."

Andrew chose at once to do what he was being blamed for. He asked: did he wish to be taken to the Shig-po-ling monastery? Ugly-face answered simply that he would go wherever wisdom might lead. Then he looked at Andrew again suddenly. His eyes twinkled. His

613

leathery old face broke into wrinkles and rippled with humour. He said two words, making one of them, as they do in Tibet:

"Tum-Glain." Then he added: "Seeing him soon!"

"Damn!" said Andrew. He had believed he had a surprise in store for Tom and for Old Ugly-face, too. But if Ugly-face knew where Tom Grayne was, he had probably also known of Andrew's march and return with supplies, and what route he would take. Had Tom Grayne told him? How? Had Ugly-face used occult, psychic, mental means to guide his party across Andrew's trail, without the phony *lama* or Ambrose St. Malo having guessed they were being steered? No use asking. But Andrew was curious to know whether Ugly-face knew his name. He might have heard it from Bompo Tsering. He tried a few tricks to get Ugly-face to address him by name. The old oriental eyes twinkled again. He remarked:

"What men doing presently revealing what their being. Soon my knowing your being—doing. Name no matter."

Well, at least they were getting on terms. One might say, inside terms. High dignitaries of the most involved religion in the world don't waste epigrams on people who don't interest them. Andrew came to the point. He asked outright whether Elsa might not ride beside him.

The answer was prompt: "My not being leader here. What your being?" He didn't even glance toward Elsa. His bright stare into Andrew's eyes suggested mockery, but along with it tolerance—deep understanding. Understanding of what? Andrew gave it up. He beckoned to Elsa. From then on she and Old Ugly-face were road companions, sharing a measureless silence. The old man accepted the occasional aid of a stirrup. Now and then, in the difficult places, he rested a hand on the pony's neck, or on its rump. But ride he would not, though she dismounted many a time and offered her pony. He simply scowled her into silence, shook his head and trudged forward. Of conversation there was none—not even speech between them.

So Elsa had time and nothing to do but think. Gradually, little by little, she gave up Andrew. Unlove him, she could not. She would not try to. But she could deny herself, for his sake. She surrendered him to his own future, cutting loose one by one the tentacles of thought that seemed to bind them together. It didn't hurt so much as she had believed it would. It seemed clear that Andrew craved to be left alone to build his own destiny from what he could find in the deeps of his own heart. So it was a secret gift to Andrew. Life was working in him, as yeast works. It was kindness to let him alone. Kindness was all she had to give.

So, though they used one tent, and though she cooked his meals, they shared no thoughts, so far as either of them knew. Andrew had plenty to keep his thought occupied, and to guard against, with Bulah Singh and St. Malo evidently trying, like a pair of mutually contemptuous conspirators, to reach an agreement for treachery, murder and loot. He had to watch like a lynx, to prevent his own men from being seduced by the others into some hair-brained plot. His full attention was occupied.

But to Elsa it seemed that his self-revelation that night had closed a door between him and herself. It was as if he truly believed what he had said then, that to understand is to despise. Did he know that she loved him? Did he despise her for having been unfaithful in her heart to Tom Grayne? Or did he believe that she despised him—on account of his tragedy— she who loved him with all her heart of hearts and only craved to help him to forget! There was no guessing. She knew it would be no use asking. Silence was better-silence, courtesy and a show of courage. But God, oh God, how wrong an honest man can be!

What really kept Elsa's courage alive was her road companion's silence. It was like that of a charged storage battery. No throb, no thrum, no sight or sound of power. But power was in him. One knew it. Only a fool wouldn't know it. It was rooted deep in such humility as only the great can attain. It was included, she knew, within his will not to resist his own personal *karma*, caused in former lives by faults that he must purge in this life. The revenge of the past meant nothing to him. Humiliation and fatigue were nothing. There was no profit and loss in his calculation.

She remembered the first and all-important precept, taught that night of nights in the initiation chamber at Gombaria's:

"In superconsciousness, toward which we evolve, all is, and all is free and unconditioned. So, therefore, should the motive and the argument, of profit or of loss, enter into this consciousness, for oneself or for another, by that much we shut the door to superconsciousness and we deny ourselves true vision. Thus we become lost again in the unprofitable wilderness of our illusion."

She knew it by heart. She said it over and over again to herself as she rode beside Monsieur X. She didn't dare to call him by his right name, even in secret thought. He had forbidden. His word was law.

615

Her reverence for him had nothing whatever to do with his present condition or with what she knew of his past. At Gombaria's she had seen him in all his glory, unimprisoned by time and space, transcending by infinities the same man, the mere mortal statesman whom she had seen leading an army, capturing the Thunder Dragon Gate, ordering the whip for monks who needed the corruption beaten out of them. He could be cruel. Or was it cruelty? She remembered his verdict:

"Persons offending personally needing personal rebuke!"

An amazing mixture of a man, three states of consciousness in one. The rebuke, she remembered, was in no case less than fifty lashes with a rawhide whip. She had wondered then, as she wondered now, riding beside him, how anyone who believed in *karma* and reincarnation, could inflict such cruelty on others, knowing well it must return upon himself, sooner or later, somewhere, sometime. But then she remembered his other remark:

"There being duty. Duty—neglect—because—fearing—consequences being greater sin than anger. People-taking-oath-of-holiness, neglecting to be holy, blasphemously mouthing piety like monkeys—perpetrating dirtiness and murder—envying, stealing, lying, setting bad example—huh!—flogging it out of them-huh! Greatest good of greatest number!" He had added, after a moment, staring at her: "Therefore wise ones not hurrying too fast toward beatitude, because as above, so below: the more the blessed knowledge, the greater the cursed sin. Go slow!"

Now, though he made no remarks, she felt her own thoughts, her sorrow, even her loneliness yield and give place to another consciousness. It was not wholly unlike the calm produced by organ music. She perceived, knew, almost captured in thought and framed in words the key of the mystery that her companion pondered as he marched. He was reaching, reaching upward, carrying her thought with his, raised by his spirit. He was opening his consciousness to Idea, his inner eye to Vision, his inner ear to Rhythm whence inspiration comes. So Elsa's heart too was lightened, as by inner sunshine, and for moments on end she understood the meaning of the law that he who will save his life shall lose it. Earth and its agonies—rainbows and their promises, are shadows of things to come. The shadow-lurker, the rainbow-hunter and the jackal are brothers. The glamour of captains and kings is the glitter of Life where it touches the waves of illusion. For moments on end she lived above intellect, beyond reason. Thought was wordless,

616

like the vivid dreams, which waking veils again behind dreary realism.

From that high consciousness, looking downward, as she could look down at the tragic valleys from the trail they climbed, at last she objectively saw her own dilemma—herself, Tom Grayne, Andrew. Tom Grayne and herself. She was Tom's wife. She loved Andrew. God, how she loved him! Andrew did not love her. No doubt he liked her. She liked Tom Grayne, and no doubt Tom Grayne thought well of her, but love her he did not, nor ever would— nor she him. For love of dignity and pride if nothing else, she would not let liking serve as an excuse for clinging like a limpet to a man who craved freedom. Both men were chivalrous. Neither should have excuse or opportunity from her to sacrifice as much as one more hour for her sake. As Andrew had so often insisted, she too had rights. Rights are spiritual, won and kept by spiritual courage. There is no such thing as a material right. She had the spiritual right to take herself out of their lives— to refuse to resist the clash of conflicting forces—to rise above those forces, harming neither man, leaving each to his own destiny, while she attended her own. She saw her way clear—not in detail—only its direction. It looked as lonely and as barren as the man's who strode beside her. But it did have dignity. She would not be the first who had faced Tibet without material resources in reserve. There had, for instance, been Nancy Strong.

The well-remembered trail along the ledges zigzagged toward the ravine where Tom Grayne was supposed to be waiting. Three more days, and at last, on a crag in the distance, the Shig-po-ling monastery glistened into view like a shiny mud-wasps' nest. She could see the roof bells through Andrew's binoculars. The phony *lama's* face became as greedy as a buzzard's. He was already counting the price he would get for betraying Ugly-face. A blind man could have guessed that. Greed and shamelessness are one; he even tried to search his former master for parched barley or some other food that perhaps he had secreted with a view to escape. Elsa signalled and Andrew saw that. He landed a punch on the phony *lama* that nearly knocked him off the ledge. Then crisis came.

Bulah Singh, egged on by St. Malo, seized that moment to take Andrew off guard and kill him. He rushed him suddenly—hurled his weight against him, trying to force him over the cliff backward. No one dared to interfere. Andrew reeled over the edge, clinging to Bulah Singh, who beat at him with both fists, kneeling, bracing his legs against a rock. For nearly a minute they swayed in the balance, until Andrew's strength at last prevailed and he hauled himself back to the ledge. The Sikh shook himself loose and fled out of reach, scrambling between Elsa and the cliff to reach the one pony whose turn it was to carry no load. The pony kicked him and he almost went over the ledge a second time. He recoiled toward St. Malo, limping.

Then St. Malo pulled an ace out of his sleeve and played it with ruthless cunning. Using his left like a trained fighter, he jabbed at the Sikh's face. He caught him off balance. He jabbed again and again. Bulah Singh staggered. He recovered. He staggered again. He tried to throw himself forward on hands and knees. But the fist jabbed him again too quickly. He screamed hoarsely and reeled backward off the ledge to the rocks a hundred feet below.

No one spoke for a moment, except Bompo Tsering. He sent a man down to strip the body and leave it naked for the birds. After that, the first who spoke was Ambrose St. Malo. Chafing his knuckles, he approached Andrew, rather skilfully assuming a casual, well-bred manner, stage Englishman style. It was only very vaguely overdone. His accent was unpleasant, but his manner might have been almost disarming if it hadn't been for the pistol that Andrew had let him keep. Its bulge was visible, inside his overcoat.

"Well. I had an idea, if I waited long enough, I'd have an opportunity to prove whose side I'm on."

He continued chafing his knuckles, where he had cut them a little on Bulah Singh's teeth. No one spoke. He pulled on his fur glove. Then he patted the bulge of the pistol.

"It was good judgment to trust me with this. I didn't draw it, to shoot that dog of a Sikh, for the same reason that you didn't draw yours. The gesture might have been misunderstood."

No answer from anyone. St. Malo's eyes held steady. Their intelligence, expression, colour were almost beautiful; but beneath the surface they were cold, like the eyes of a robot. His lips smiled pleasantly, but his voice gave the lie to the smile:

"Ever since we met, that wash-out has been trying to get me to shoot you. He was self-hypnotised. Obsessed by an idea. He wanted to get possession of your girl friend and to put her to use." At last he favoured Elsa with one of his cold glances: "Yes, young lady! Bulah Singh believed that through you he'd be able to control your husband."

The silence at last told on him. It wore him down. He had to ac-

618

knowledge it.

"Hell," he remarked. "What is this? A *séance*? Can't anyone speak?"

Andrew blew his whistle, one blast, meaning stand by. "Time's up," he said. "Hand over your pistol."

"But surely you understand now that I'm on your side—"

Andrew took one stride forward and plunged his hand into the breast of St. Malo's overcoat. It was a Tibetan coat; it had the usual voluminous *bokkus*. He pulled out the Smith and Wesson, unloaded it and stowed it away in Elsa's saddle-bag:

"Play Number One having failed, Play Two, I expect, would be to take a shot at me. That's stymied. Have you Play Three ready?"

St. Malo smiled. He looked scornful and rather surprised. "I had begun to think you were a sensible man."

"I didn't invite your opinion," Andrew answered.

"Andrew Gunning, I'm a safe man to bet on. I'm a dangerous man to deny! I have dealt myself in on this expedition."

"Tell that to Tom Grayne," Andrew retorted.

He blew his whistle again. The column moved forward. Ambrose St. Malo shrugged insolent shoulders and strode ahead to where the phony *lama* waited, trembling, impatient. They two walked side by side, talking, continually glancing backward to see where Andrew was. Before pressing forward for word with Bompo Tsering, Andrew spoke to Elsa:

"Keep an eye on 'em. Please. Watch 'em carefully. Either they don't wish to be overheard, or they do wish me to think they're plotting something. Either way means trouble. The trail is tough from here on. I'll be busy. So take this whistle. If they quit talking and you spot they're starting anything, blow three long blasts to warn me."

Then he was gone, to overtake Bompo Tsering. He strode past St. Malo and the phony *lama* as if they weren't there.

CHAPTER 47

The trail reached the limit beyond which even the yaks could no longer climb unaided. They and the ponies had to be lifted or else unloaded and then reloaded when their packs had been carried up by hand. In places the ledge was less than three feet wide, with an impending cliff on the right hand. The slippery rock was like a devil's stairway. But it was the last lap; the animals knew it; so they got along without accident, everyone lending a hand. When the phony *lama* made the mistake of refusing to work, Andrew kicked him and made him put his shoulder under a pony's rump to help it scramble while Andrew took the worst of the strain. That was a mistake. He should have known better. Fake dignity can't endure too much humiliation. His life wasn't worth ten cents from that minute, if it should be up to the *lama*.

Tom Grayne's secret hiding-place was away up on the face of a cliff, at least a thousand feet above that terrific trail. It was utterly impossible to reach with the pack animals. There were two ways to it, and Andrew knew the landmarks; but one way would have made a wild goat hesitate, and the other was a cascade, iced over by the frozen vapour from a hot spring. However, there was a more accessible and much larger cavern lower down, where they had *cached* quite a lot of fodder left over from last year's expedition. It wasn't secret, like Tom Grayne's cave; it was too close to the trail, and too near to a weird community of hermits, who are the least talkative but most vigilant spies in the world. It was that lower cavern that Andrew headed for, hoping Tom Grayne had seen them from far off and would save him the trouble of climbing to the hide-out.

He scrambled to the head of the line, to get first word with Tom in case he should have come down from the hide-out. He had a notion it might be wise to break the news about Elsa before Elsa and Tom could confront each other. Elsa's unexpected arrival might embarrass Tom, and his embarrassment might be a shock to her. Andrew's own dread that three good friends might lose their friendship in a collision of wills where each had done his honourable best according to his lights—was something that he kept out of his mind, imprisoned behind the veil that even Elsa's clairvoyance couldn't penetrate. He suspected what Elsa was feeling. He proposed to spare her as much as he could.

And as he led the way around a projecting spur of cliff, there Tom was, striding toward him—the same Tom Grayne, except that his beard was more unkempt. He was clean, but a bit ragged from a winter's hard living. He was wearing the same old windproof hunting suit and laced boots, although he usually wore Tibetan clothing. So Andrew concluded that they were in no danger of being seen by monastery scouts. He stood where he was, to block the trail behind him and swap the first news without being overheard. The wind was blustering along the ledge and what they said to each other couldn't have been heard six feet away.

"How's Elsa?" Tom asked.

"The baby died. She's fine. I have her with me."

Tom froze. It was almost imperceptible, like the effect of a blow in the ring. One couldn't guess what he felt. He recovered instantly.

"You're a day early," he said.

"A day late," Andrew answered.

"I expected you tomorrow," said Tom. "I heard of your getting hung up at the Shigatse River when the ferry broke away. So I counted out two days. Someone else with you, isn't there?"

"You bet. Your spies must have been busy."

"Lobsang Pun?"

"Yes—Old Ugly-face in person."

"Good," Tom answered.

"And—but—also—"

"I know. Ambrose St. Malo."

"How did you know? Were you expecting him?"

"Yes. Who else?"

"Some unarmed Tibetans and a sham-*lama* who can't even pray without making mistakes. You'll have trouble with him too."

"Okay. We'll fix him. Where's the other who was with Old Ugly-face?

"Dead. Ugly-face gave him the proper obsequies."

Tom nodded: "That other fellow was a good guy, but soft—couldn't take it. Now Lobsang Pun hasn't a friend in the world—barring us. Did he say much on the road?"

"Snubbed me a couple of times."

"Oh. Likes you, does he? That's good. Even so, he'll be a handful." Tom grinned at last. "He and I are old enemies. Friends to the last ditch. Enemies at the drop of a hat. There isn't a move on the board that he wouldn't play against me. So watch out."

"Any news at this end?" Andrew didn't dare to use the name of the young Dalai Lama, even with that wind blowing and the curve of a cliff between him and the men.

Tom nodded. "The infant Dalai Lama is in the monastery. He's for sale to the highest bidder. The latest high bid is from Hitler's Gestapo outfit—by secret courier from Lhasa."

"Did the courier get through?"

"He's dead. But we'll have to work fast."

"Any trouble with your Tibetans?"

"Yes. Two died. Three couldn't stick it. I've two left. How's Bompo

Tsering?"

"Getting wise," said Andrew. "Good headman. He's learned how to make the others do most of the work. But he needs watching. He'd bribe himself if no one else 'ud do it."

"Okay. We'll fix him too. Has he spotted the prelate?"

"I don't know."

Tom grinned again. "We'll see. Have you brought some jam?"

"Yes. Plenty of soft tack."

"Good. Where's Elsa?"

Andrew moved his head to indicate that she was somewhere down along the trail beyond the bulge of the cliff. The trail was so narrow just there that Andrew had to hug the cliff to get out of Tom's way and let him pass.

"Look out for the yaks around the bend," he advised.

Yaks are as unpredictable as camels, but the wind was the wrong way. The leading yak was around the corner of the cliff. So it couldn't have been smell, hearing, or eyesight that set the brute going the moment Tom moved. Either the phony *lama* or else St. Malo or one of their men prodded the leading yak in the rump with a sharp goad. It came around the corner like an avalanche. There wasn't room to get out of the way, nor time nor room for either man to shoot. Tom Grayne seized it by the horns, slithered on ice and raw rock and hung three thousand feet sheer above a ravine that howled in the wind as if all the devils in a Tantric Buddhist's hell were clamouring for victims. Somehow or other he clung to the yak's horns. Andrew vaulted the loaded yak. At the risk of being trampled to death he seized Tom's arms and hauled him back to safety, letting the frightened beast go hurrying alone along the trail.

"God, you weigh a ton," he remarked.

There was no time to say more—nothing more to be said. Elsa came, riding alone. Not far behind her, beyond the turn, Bompo Tsering was holding back the column. Elsa got down off her pony.

"Oh, Tom, I'm glad! I was afraid the yak had—"

"Near thing," he answered. "Gunning saved me." He was rubbing his wrists that had taken a gruelling punishment from the yak's horns, but he left off doing it to take Elsa in his arms. They kissed. Then Elsa's face pressed his shoulder:

"Tom, our baby died."

"I know it."

"Tom, I did my uttermost best to be the mother of your son, and

622

to—" She was crying.

"I know. I know." He sounded grieved. He looked grieved. He was. But it was because she was suffering. "You shouldn't have come back," he said, clumsily gentle. "Gunning could have brought the news." His voice was as kind as a lover's, but he didn't say bad news. He patted her back and waited for her to cease crying, but he looked too patient, as if restraining a storm inside himself.

"You agreed to stay in India. Why did you come?" he asked—kindly again, almost too kind.

"Must I tell it here—now?"

"No, of course not. Let's go to the cavern."

But Tom didn't move, for a moment. She looked up at him through tear-dimmed eyes. He glanced from her to Andrew.

"No," said Andrew.

Tom grinned, not exactly incredulous, but alert. "Aren't you quick on the uptake? I asked no question."

Andrew retorted: "I saved you the need."

"Thanks.—Where's Ugly-face?"

"He is near the rear of the column," said Elsa.

"Okay. We'll let him follow. Let's go to the cavern."

Elsa put her arm through the pony's reins and Tom led the way. But Andrew turned back, partly to let Tom and Elsa be alone together—partly to prevent any last-minute treachery. As he took the wall of St. Malo, St. Malo grinned in his face—superior, indulgent, sly:

"Still alive, brother cat? We'll come to terms," he said. "You wait and see."

Andrew ignored him. He walked on.

"Come back!" St. Malo called. "I want to talk to you. It's important."

Andrew slipped into a recess in the cliff and waited there out of bullet range until the rear of the column caught up. Old Ugly-face was walking last, alone, and for once he looked worn out utterly exhausted from the long march. Andrew offered him a shoulder to rest his hand on. The old man accepted:

"Gunnigun," he said, "your being having done your task—your doing well. Now mine beginning."

He hummed a *mantra*. Clinging to Andrew's shoulder with a grip like iron, he hummed all the way along the ledge as they brought up the rear of the column. He only paused once when Andrew interrupted:

"Can you help Elsa? She needs it. She thinks so highly of you that— "

Old Ugly-face turned on him, scowling. His eyes flashed.

"Your being thief? Your robbing her? Your stealing her opportunity to help herself?"

He resumed the *mantra*. It was like the music of the spheres.

CHAPTER 48

It was a grand cavern, as big as a church, well protected from prevailing winds and warmed by a hot spring that you could hear gurgling inside the rock. At the far end there was an easy climb into another, smaller cavern that was ventilated by a long fissure. Fuel had been the worst problem, but Tom had solved that; he had found tons of yak-dung, in a valley, miles away and had had it piled up near the entrance. If the place had been a bit more private, it would have been perfect. It was too near the trail, too easy to find by accident.

Andrew posted a lookout while Bompo Tsering stabled the animals in the lower cavern. Having eaten nothing but barley for days on end they were greedy for the stored hay. Their delight in the warmth and good forage had an effect on the humans. There was a kind of Christmassy feel in the air, suggesting the manger in Bethlehem—a home-coming. Tom and Elsa were sitting together at the foot of the ascending ramp, deep in conversation. No one disturbed them.

The phony *lama* broke the almost mystic spell. The man's stupidity was next to incredible. To call attention to himself he grossly insulted Old Ugly-face, ordered him into the coldest corner of the cavern and commanded two men to watch him. Old Ugly-face made no protest, but St. Malo seemed to be hesitating whether to stand pat or to draw cards. It was his chance, should he choose, to turn on the phony *lama* and repudiate him. He hadn't a good poker face; he evidently despised the man; he let his lip curl and scratched his face with his thumb to hide his mouth. He seemed unable to make up his mind. Andrew was no help to him—gave him no hint.

It was Tom's lead now. The end of the trail had automatically reduced Andrew to chief of staff or second-in-command. He didn't even choose to suggest a line of action or to interrupt Tom, but he did order all the bedding and personal loads carried up the ramp to the upper cavern. He went up after them and had them arranged in a circle. The same old canvas tent-fly was in place at the far end, concealing the pool of warm running water that was as good as a civilized bathroom.

He took a longing glance in there. There was soap, towels—Tom had been using the place. But he resisted temptation, there was too much else to do. Before following the men back to the lower cavern he put his briefcase in plain view beside his bedding roll. Elsa was on her way up, but beyond giving her a hand over the steepest rock and noticing that she was no longer crying he learned nothing from her. She avoided his eyes. All he said to her was:

"My briefcase is a trap. Don't move it."

Below, Tom had taken charge. At the foot of the ramp he was addressing the phony *lama* with the high-falutin phrases due to a man of rank. Tom was an expert at that stuff. He knew all the rituals. He fooled the fellow, urging him to lead the way to the upper cavern, where they might hold a conference without being overheard by underlings. The phony *lama* bestowed a phony blessing on him, whirled his prayer wheel a few dozen times and went up, like a puppet out of *The Mikado*, with all the dignity possible considering he had to pick up his skirts and crawl on hands and knees a good part of the way. He wasn't as active as Elsa. St. Malo went up after him without being invited.

Tom grinned then at Andrew. "Let's see," he said, "whether Bompo Tsering knows.—Want to bet?"

"One U.S. dime," said Andrew. "Betting with you means giving away money. You ask him."

Tom didn't. He merely glanced at Bompo Tsering with raised eyebrows, and from him to Old Ugly-face. Immediately, without a word said, Bompo Tsering approached Old Ugly-face, knelt and laid his forehead on the floor in front of him. Ugly-face leaned forward, touched him with a blessing and stood up. His eyes glittered. His leathery face rippled. His owl's beak of a nose twitched with humour.

Suddenly he opened his mouth and solid laughter roared up from his belly.

"Oo-hah-ha-ha-ha-ha-hah! Tum-Glain!"

Just as suddenly he shut up. But he walked forward.

"Your dime," said Andrew. He produced a mascot coin from an inner pocket. Tom held out his hand, but Old Ugly-face snatched the coin and examined it curiously. At last he stowed it away in his own capacious *bokkus*.

"Now having money," he said, looking quite serious.

Tom smiled slowly and said never a word, but a blind mute could have guessed there was a show-down coming. All the Tibetans laid their foreheads on the floor, including the phony *lama's* men. Tom touched Bompo Tsering with his foot. Bompo Tsering got up. Tom whispered to him. Bompo Tsering went out of the cave to summon the two Tibetans from Tom's hide-out as a precaution in case the phony *lama's* men should get panicky and try to grab the upper hand.

Things were going like clockwork. The phony *lama* was having plenty of time in the upper cavern to confer with St. Malo. Between them they were likely to make lots of mistakes, especially with Elsa watching them. They might even quarrel; most fools do, in a tight spot. Tom seemed to have everything figured out. He and Ugly-face understood each other—no ceremony—man to man—watching points—trusting each other, and as mistrustful as poker players. Tom whispered. Ugly-face nodded. Tom beckoned Andrew and they climbed to the upper cavern, where the phony *lama* was seated on Andrew's roll of bedding. He had undone the cordage and made himself pretty comfortable, arranging it so that his seat was the highest and he sat with his back to the light that poured through the hole in the cavern wall. Elsa had found the hot bath irresistible; she could be heard splashing behind the canvas curtain.

Ambrose St. Malo had just returned from peeping through a small hole in the canvas. The floor near the canvas was moist. He had left wet foot tracks. He was in the act of sitting down opposite the phony lama when Andrew's head appeared above floor level. Elsa's kit-bag had disappeared behind the curtain. She was no doubt using it. But Andrew's briefcase was also missing.

It was two or three seconds before he noticed it, beside St. Malo, in the shadow just beyond the edge of a pool of light on the floor. He had hardly dared to hope that such an old campaigner as St. Malo would fall for that trick. The briefcase was open. St. Malo had sat down in a hurry and had not had time to put it back where Andrew left it.

Of course, after that any fool could have foretold what was going to happen, except for the working details, which were sure to be interesting. Tom and Andrew sat down facing each other, so that they were at four points of a square. After a few seconds' silence, during which Andrew's eyes led Tom's toward the briefcase, Tom said to the phony *lama*:

"Of course, now I know exactly who Tour Eminence is. You must be the worshipful member of the sacred Council of Regents in Lhasa. Your Eminence surely is he who loyally tried to protect the sacred infant Dalai Lama."

Andrew wasn't watching the phony *lama*. That was Tom's job. He watched St. Malo, whose face was a picture. Tom's opening gambit plainly had him puzzled. He didn't realise yet that Tom was wise to him. Tom continued talking to the phony *lama*, using beautiful Tibetan. It was so good that the phony *lama* had to work hard to understand him and not betray his own ignorance of the higher learning:

"Of course, I am an ignorant foreigner," said Tom, "so I speak subject to correction. But as I understand it, the holy Dalai Lama died several years ago in Lhasa. He was the ablest and most enlightened ruler that Tibet ever had. Therefore he was poisoned, to make way for unenlightened, evil politicians."

Tom was using facts like sledge-hammers, preparing the ground. St. Malo realised that. He was growing restless, trying to make sure that the piece of paper he had sat on in a hurry wasn't sticking out where Andrew or Tom Grayne could notice it.

Tom continued: "And as I, in my benighted ignorance, understand it, although the holy Dalai Lama dies like any other mortal, he immediately reincarnates into the body of a newborn child. That child has to be sought for—somewhere, anywhere, in Tibet, and is recognisable by certain marks. Such a child was found, identified and acclaimed. The child was brought to Lhasa and installed in his sacred office to be educated under the supervision of the Council of Regents."

At last the phony *lama* answered him. He might have done better to keep silent but he was too stupid: "As a foreigner your knowing too much. What your doing in Tibet?"

"Learning," Tom answered. "I have learned that many foreigners, from many lands, have designs on Tibet."

The phony *lama* assented: "All foreigners being devils," he remarked. "Having heard of this blessed land, now their wanting it." Then he added sententiously: "But my wishing to reach Shig-po-ling monastery. Thus your acquiring merit."

Tom nodded gravely: "Meaning that if we can serve Your Eminence in some important way, we may depend upon Your Eminence's favour?"

The phony *lama* nodded. Tom went on talking:

"It is rumoured, so that even my ignorant ears have heard it, that one, and only one member of the Council of Regents has been faithful to his sacred trust. Are you that member?"

There was a pause. St. Malo held his breath. He seemed scared stiff that the fool might make a bad break. But the phony *lama* didn't speak. Tom went on:

"I have heard that all the other members of the Council of Regents in Lhasa have been corrupted by the money and by the promises of the secret agents of foreign governments. I have heard they are wicked men. I have heard they quarrel among themselves for the control of the sacred child, each of them perceiving that the sole control would give him autocratic power, which would enable him to grow enormously rich from the bribes of foreign governments, each of whom craves to control the education of the coming ruler of Tibet."

"My having told you," said the phony *lama*, "your knowing too much."

Tom continued: "So there was strife between the Regents. That Regent who is also abbot of the Shig-po-ling monastery over yonder, proved to be the cleverest, if not the most powerful. He poisoned some of the other Regents. Others he slew. He drove the only faithful Regent out of Lhasa, so that he barely escaped with his life. And he carried away the child *lama* to the Shig-po-ling monastery, so as to have the child in his power."

The phony *lama* glanced at St. Malo, paused a moment and then answered:

"All this being not your business."

"But destiny," said Tom, "which is inscrutable, has guided me into the sacred presence of that only faithful Regent. You are he. Are you not?"

The phony *lama* began to be careful, too late. He searched his mind for important-sounding words and bungled them:

"My being nobly born seeing fit to travel wrapped in cloak of anonymity, ignorant foreign devils should not ask improper questions."

Tom persisted patiently: "But I have information for the wise ears of His Holy and Worshipful Eminence, the nobly born Ringding Gelong Lama Lobsang Pun. I must not breathe my information into the wrong ears. It is too important. Are you not Lobsang Pun?"

St. Malo chucked in his hand. He said nothing, but it was as plain as writing on a wall that there and then he abandoned the phony *lama* to his fate. He had seen what Andrew saw.

Old Ugly-Face had timed it perfectly. He must have crept like a cat up that difficult ramp, and he must have been crouching near the top of the entrance into the upper cavern, awaiting his cue. Now he stood up and coughed like a senator about to deliver a speech. But he didn't say anything. He thumbed his beads, flicking them ten to a second. No one could possibly pray that fast. It was a grand moment.

"Are you not His Holy Eminence Lobsang Pun?" Tom repeated. "Member of the Council of Regents and the only loyal servant of the sacred child, the Dalai Lama?"

"Yes, I am," said the phony *lama*. There was nothing else that he could say.

"Then why," Tom asked him, "are you on your way to the Shig-po-ling monastery, where the wicked Regent Ram-pa Yap-shi, who expelled you from Lhasa and did his utmost to get you killed, has wrongfully taken the sacred child and is ready to fight all comers?

"Answer me that."

Everyone but Tom breathed hard through his nose. Barring that, there was silence for about thirty seconds. Then Ugly-face belched like a gun going off. East of, say, Vienna, belching is good manners. A diplomat may politely include the accomplishment in his code of signals. Ugly-face was calling for the show-down.

Tom opened fire: "Since nine days ago, eighteen armed men from Sinkiang have waited in a cave near here. Are they your men?"

The phony *lama* tried to ignore the question, but Tom waited for an answer. Andrew, watching St. Malo, saw a sly, overconfident smile vaguely flicker on his lips and at the corners of his eyes. To him those eighteen men from Sinkiang were evidently good news. He was in a hurry now to see the phony *lama* disposed of and out of the way, so that he might play his own hand. But he knew Andrew was watching him, so he kept still.

The phony *lama* didn't know how to answer Tom's question. Tom did it for him:

"They are not your men. You never heard of them until this moment." Suddenly he turned toward Old Ugly-face. "But who is this, whom you treat harshly?"

Old Ugly-face said nothing.

The phony *lama* answered: "That one being my servant."

Tom smiled. St. Malo almost laughed.

"I am in duty bound," said Tom, "to tell Your Eminence the secret information that has come to my ignorant ears. You will know what it means. This is it: the Regent Ram-pa Yap-shi, who is the abbot of the Shig-po-ling monastery—he who carried off the infant Dalai Lama—has offered an enormous reward for the person of His Holy Eminence Lobsang Pun, to be delivered alive, having been reported dead too many times. This time His Eminence's death is to be witnessed and to be enjoyed by all except His Eminence. Had you heard of it?"

Silence. The phony *lama* had only one chance left now; but the long knife was hardly out of his bosom before Tom had him by the wrist. Tom passed the knife to Andrew and went on talking:

"Someone with more brains than you have, showed you how to make a fortune by betraying your master, His Holy Eminence Lobsang Pun, to be put to the torture and slain. So you pretended to your master you would save his life by changing places with him. He was to seem to be the servant you were to seem to be the master. To which, being in danger of death, he agreed. But who was the man of brains and treachery who bargained with you for a share of the reward for the betrayal of your master? Did he show you an American flag? Did he tell you tales about protection to be had in an American Legation— was it in China? Did he mention China? Were you to escape to China with the money?"

St. Malo sat motionless, except that his eyes moved. They measured the distance to the *lama's* long knife that Tom had passed to Andrew. It lay on the floor. Andrew moved it.

"Such men," Tom continued, "always demand a lion's share. Not a half-share. A lion's share. That same someone sent loads, on fourteen yaks, with eighteen men from Sinkiang, to await him in a cave near here. What, do you think, would have happened to you—at the hands of the men from Sinkiang?"

No answer. St. Malo saw the writing on the wall. He moved his right hand. But Andrew noticed it; so St. Malo let his hand fall and lie limp on his thigh. Andrew leaned toward him, shoved him off balance, plunged his hand into the opening of his overcoat, drew blank and pulled him upright again. He loved Andrew for that. His eyes were like hot flint. Old Ugly-face sat down against the wall and belched again. He wanted action. But Tom was in no hurry. He was having a swell time. He continued:

"What's going to happen to you now, you treacherous scullion? Your real name is Shag-la. You're masquerading as a nobly born, eminent *lama*. There is a penalty of death for that crime. You're found out."

The phony *lama* mumbled something, probably a spell for breaking bad luck. Old Ugly-face walked toward him. He had dignity. Nobody needed to tell him how to behave. He didn't speak. The vigour of his iron will, and the humour of his humility, were enough. Already he seemed almost to have forgotten the cur who had insulted and ill-treated him on that cruel march. He was thumbing his beads like lightning; the eye could hardly follow their flick on the thong.

The phony *lama* knelt to him, put out his tongue and laid his forehead on the floor. Ugly-face ignored him. He sat down on Andrew's bed roll, and the phony *lama* crawled away to the wall where he lay face downward. Ugly-face stared for a moment at Tom and then fetched up another laugh from his stomach:

"Oo-hah-ha-ha-ha-ha-hah!" Then he looked straight at Andrew— saw slap through him to his backbone, the way he did when they first met. He glanced at Tom and said in English: "Tum-Glain, your choosing not bad: Where's Elsa?"

Elsa came out from behind the curtain carrying her kit-bag. She set it down and stood waiting, limned by the light from the crack in the wall. She had made herself look beautiful. But for whose sake? She watched St. Malo, and he stared at her as if he was either afraid or else stunned by a new idea. Tom signed to Elsa and she came and sat down at his right hand, facing Andrew. St. Malo groped in his pocket, found a little silver box, opened it and swallowed two opium pills. Almost at once his smile of self-assurance returned, as if he had resumed the reins of destiny and knew a short way to his goal. Now he looked dangerous.

Chapter 49

The light had changed; the sun had moved across the gap in the cavern wall. They faced one another in a sort of mystic twilight, in which the rough walls were almost invisible. The easiest face to see was St. Malo's because he faced the light. It was a fascinating face—decadent, wilful, incorruptible by any moral considerations. To that extent it had integrity. He hadn't shaved for a long time but his beard was as sparse as a Tibetan's. He had high cheekbones, a dark skin and refined-looking rather Mongoloid features. Now that the opium had begun to work on him even his vicious mouth recovered a kind of charm. His gesture, as if picking up a band of cards and holding them to his breast, looked natural, unconsidered; but it aroused Andrew's interest; he suspected a weapon; his muscles tightened a bit; he was ready.

St. Malo opened, and drew one card—from underneath him. He had been sitting on it. He flourished a sheet of rather crumpled paper that he had taken from Andrew's briefcase, crunched it up and tossed it into Andrew's lap.

"That's the lowdown on you," he remarked. "That's a list of the names of Moscow secret agents between Delhi and Lhasa. You're on the Moscow payroll."

Andrew answered: "You took that bait like a rat. How did you come by your rep? I'd heard you were an ace."

"So I am," said St. Malo. "So is Tom Grayne. So are you said to be. You must be damned well organised to have kept such a check on my movements. You two seem to know nearly as much about me as I know about you. Let's say we're three of a kind and play it that way. Why are we here in Tibet?"

Tom retorted: "One reason is to prevent you from using the United States flag."

St. Malo stared. He had begun to feel out of his depth. Tom made a gesture to Andrew. Andrew put his arm around St. Malo, pulled him off balance and groped again inside his overcoat. This time, since he didn't search for weapons, he found what he was after. He pulled out a silk Stars and Stripes about three feet by two and threw it toward Tom; but it came unrolled, fluttered and fell in Ugly-face's lap. Ugly-face examined it with an expression that might have meant amusement, or curiosity, or guile. He folded it carefully and tucked it away in his bosom. St. Malo grinned at Tom:

"How did you know about that?" He glanced at Elsa, and from her to Lobsang Pun, and back again. "Bulah Singh," he said, "believed that she's clairvoyant." He stared again at Old Ugly-face, who filled the next few seconds with a silence of his own that felt like ponderable force.

Then St. Malo said suddenly: "Take that flag away from him if you value your lives! He doesn't know the meaning of fair play. He'll treat you as he treated me. He'll accept your help and then lead you into a trap. He'll use that flag against you, somehow."

No one made any comment, although he waited for it. So after a considerable pause he said: "Oh well, all right. Let's talk turkey. I've eighteen men. How many have you?"

"All the men I need," Tom answered.

"Mine are well armed."

"What for? What against?" Tom asked him.

St. Malo stared at Ugly-face. "Lobsang Pun," he said, "knows English."

"So do we all," said Tom.

"Oh! So you're one of those mystical buggers, are you! Amateur yogi! Sandwiching a word at a time between two silences to make it sound like wisdom! Here's a fact for you to stick between two noises. My eighteen men are on their way here—eighteen rifles."

"No, they're not," said Tom.

"Guess again! You'd better come to terms with me before they get here," St. Malo retorted. "If we agree, well and good. I'll go you fifty-fifty in that case. But if I dictate the terms, you'll get the lean end. Make no mistake about that."

Tom looked bored. He answered: "Your phony friend Shag-la obeyed your signal. He crawled away just now to bring your men. But he didn't get far." He whistled. Bompo Tsering pitched Shag-la into the cavern. He was an astonishing apparition, as if he had been flung between the darkened flies on to a dimly lighted stage. He rolled into the pool of light and lay still, looking dead, but after a moment or two he recovered and crawled to the wall.

Elsa spoke at last: "Isn't he hurt? Shouldn't someone go and look? Hadn't I better?"

Tom answered: "No. Sit still."

St. Malo sneered: "Too bad he didn't break his bloody neck. We'll have to shoot him soon. Why not now?"

Tom returned to the previous issue: "The point is, your eighteen men aren't coming. Now what?"

St. Malo didn't appear embarrassed. "All right," he retorted. "You win that trick. But what does it get you? I hold all the rest. You've got to come to terms with me. Lobsang Pun, too, since you seem to be dealing him in. This man Gunning is your yes-man, I suppose. Well, all right. I've eighteen armed men, in addition to the men below here who came with us. If you should lay a finger on me, they'd wipe you out. So let's be sensible. The Dalai Lama brat is in the Shig-po-ling monastery. We take your men and mine and go get him. We'll use Lobsang Pun as bait. He'll have to chip in and play with us, because if they catch him they'll torture him. We split the profit three ways—if Lobsang Pun is on the level. If he isn't, we split it two ways, and what happens to him'll be his business."

Old Ugly-face didn't move a muscle or a wrinkle. He didn't blink. Neither did Tom. St. Malo continued:

"After we've bagged the sacred brat will be where the girl friend enters in. She'll be foster-mother, dry nurse—talk to him in Tibetan and keep him from crying his eyes out. They grow sick, those infant prodigies, unless they're babied. After that there'll be three lines of retreat. Three markets. Moscow would pay plenty, but it's a hard trail and we might not get there. Then there's Lhasa—lots of cash in Lhasa, and a gang who'd pay through the nose. But they're treacherous. They'd try to kill us before we could reach the border. India, of course, 'ud be no good. The God-dams 'ud talk morals, and keep us waiting, and finally they'd cheat us and themselves too. The best bet, and the safest, and the easiest route, is China. There, the Germans have a secret anti-Russian nest of experts. They've plenty of money, and they've bought up lots of Chinese. They've a party in Lhasa at this moment gunning for what we're after; but they'd want all the profit for themselves, so we'll beat them to it and leave 'em howling. We'll deal with the head gang in China. They'll see the point of educating the holy child with a view to controlling Tibet later on, when the time comes to break with the Japs. But don't let's talk about Japan."

"No," Tom agreed. "We might get sort of overextended."

St. Malo didn't like sarcasm. He smiled thinly: "Well, there's the set-up. Now we know what we're talking about. Your turn."

Old Ugly-face fetched up another abrupt, thunderous laugh. He left off thumbing his beads, as if prayer had not inspired him and he knew the answer to all riddles:

"Oo-hah-ha-ha-ha-ha-hah! Tum-Glain! Now what? What your saying?"

"I say the hell with him," Tom answered.

"Too many hells," said Ugly-face. "Your knowing all about all of them later on. Sinning too much. Thinking too little. Sun-moon-sun-moon-day-week- month-year—all that time, and what your doing?"

Tom looked straight at St. Malo. "You move first. Get out of here."

Then St. Malo changed tactics. Perhaps the opium had gone to his head. He stood up. He jerked his head at Elsa. He said: "Whose is this woman?"

It was such a shock that he got away with it. Perhaps he had count-ed on that. At any rate, he noticed the astonishment and took advan-tage of it, springing another surprise before anyone answered.

"I'd like to speak to her alone."

Even Old Ugly-face changed expression; his eyes glinted amid the wrinkles. He stared at Elsa. Everyone did—even the discouraged phony *lama*, who was rubbing bruises in the background, and Bompo Tsering, who was lurking in the dimness at the head of the ramp that led to the lower cavern.

"Why alone?" asked Elsa.

"It's that or nothing," St. Malo answered, looking cocksure. "It's something I'll tell you in confidence. I won't tell them on any terms. That's why."

Tom spoke abruptly: "Get the hell out!"

St. Malo stood still. "Is she yours?" he retorted. "You own her?"

"Shall I throw him out?" said Andrew. "Say the word."

"Oh. So she's your woman?"

Andrew seized him by the edge of his overcoat to give him the bum's rush. There came astonishing interruption. Old Ugly-face shouted; he boomed like a clamouring gong: he filled the cavern with protest.

"No violence!" he commanded, in surprisingly good English. "Let go! Stop it!"

Andrew obeyed, stepping back to cut off St. Malo's line of retreat to the lower cavern. Then Tom protested:

"No violence? I saw Your Eminence capture the Thunder Dragon Gate. You ordered monks flogged by the dozens."

"Their being louses!"

"This man St. Malo is a louse!"

"Louses having purposes! Also, not being your duty—your not being responsible *lama*—your being ignorant man."

"Are you telling me—"

"My telling you that even louses having purposes!"

It looked like locked horns and no way out of a quarrel until Elsa spoke up:

"Is there any reason why I shouldn't speak to him alone?"

"We could keep watch from the head of the ramp," said Andrew.

"I am not afraid of him," Elsa objected. "Besides, I have—"

Andrew interrupted: "Yeah, you keep your automatic out of his reach. Here, you'd better give it to me."

She gave it to him. He passed it to Tom.

"That's much safer." Andrew picked the knife off the floor and passed it to Bompo Tsering. "He could have taken it from you as easily as—"

Tom suddenly interrupted: "What the hell now?" He blinked into the light. Old Ugly-face—His Eminence the Most Reverend Ringding Gelong Lama Lobsang Pun—was climbing the wall! He had passed behind the curtain that hid the gurgling water. From there, he was able to reach a fault in the rock that formed a climbable zigzag stair curving upward to the irregular opening fifty feet above, that let in light. He entered the deep opening, glanced once backward over his shoulder like a huge misshapen owl, and vanished.

"Can he get out that way?" Andrew asked.

"No. But there's room up there for ten men."

Tom turned to Elsa: "If you see fit to talk to St. Malo—?" He sounded stiff, as if he resented having to ask the question—perhaps doubted his right to ask it.

"He said he wants to speak to me," Elsa answered. "I think he won't unless you leave us alone."

St. Malo nodded. "You bet I won't."

Tom's eyes met Andrew's. "We could wait on the ramp," Andrew suggested, "just out of earshot."

"Yes. But out of earshot," said St. Malo.

Elsa put a word in: "If they say they will, they will."

"Honey," St. Malo answered, "you're naive. At our trade we would cut each other's throats for a secret. Yours, too!"

"Gunning and I will go halfway down the ramp and wait there," said Tom. "Keep your voices low and you can talk without being overheard. We'll give you five minutes." He met Andrew's eyes again.

"Yes," said Andrew.

So Tom continued: "I'm giving you fair warning, St. Malo. Ten seconds after you start anything, you'll be shot dead. So don't start anything."

"Nuts," St. Malo answered. "Do you know what that means?"

Tom drew his automatic and cocked it. Andrew drove the phony lama and Bompo Tsering down the ramp to the lower cavern. Then he and Tom followed, halfway. In the dark, on the biggest boulder, that almost choked the short steep tunnel, they sat down and waited.

CHAPTER 50

St. Malo came quietly to the head of the ramp and peered downward. His head and shoulders were very easy to see in silhouette against the light.

"Hop to it," said Tom Grayne. "You've five minutes."

Satisfied that Tom and Andrew really were out of earshot, St. Malo returned to Elsa. They heard him talking, but they couldn't hear what he said. Elsa's voice was even less audible. What made it difficult even to try to listen was the tension between Andrew and Tom. They weren't friends the way they had been when Andrew started for India with

Elsa under his protection. Tom said after a moment or two:

"Why didn't you kill that bastard?"

"I'm not a killer. You know it. What's your plan?"

"I had one," said Tom.

"What was wrong with it?"

"Nothing. It's gone fluey. Old Ugly-face won't play. I know the symptoms. He has a plan of his own, and his own use for you and me."

"He hasn't said so."

"No. Why should he? He'll use us now, just as he made use of St. Malo and then you in order to get here."

"How did you know Old Ugly-face was coming—and St. Malo too? Your regular spies can't have told you."

Tom Grayne chuckled. "It 'ud make a story for the archives! But they'd call me bughouse. It 'ud make a book. But who'd print it? All winter long until a week ago, I've had a man here who could turn on mental television to beat Jesus."

"Oh? Who was he?"

"He didn't say. The name he went by was Hut-sum Samdup. He had me call him Sam. He made a sort of stab at teaching me, but he couldn't. Seems I'm unteachable—according to him. He said I'm profit-minded—f not ph. But that was only his excuse. He didn't want to teach. He was using me in some way I couldn't get hep to—using my energy—tapping it. It was almost like a blood-transfusion. It left me weak now and then— kind of light-headed. I'll learn how to do it someday. He could make me see anything he saw—hear whatever he heard. But I can't do it off my own bat—can't begin to do it."

"Did he give any reason for making you see things?"

"No. He was long on meditation—short on talk. I doped out he's a member of the Lodge to which Old Ugly-face belongs. I guess Ugly-face is a kind of younger brother, maybe earning a higher degree. Sam left here the same day we saw you pick up Old Ugly-face's party in the storm and head this way."

"We didn't head this way right off," said Andrew. "We pitched bivouac."

"Yeah, I know all that. I knew Elsa was along. And I knew you and she were sleeping together."

"Hold your horses," said Andrew. "Let's get this straight. I don't want to have to get tough. We were friends, you and I."

"We can be so yet," Tom answered. "Elsa told me just now why you brought her back here."

"She asked to be brought."

"Yes. She said that. She says she came to tell me I'm in the discard—washed up."

"Did she put it that way? I mean—I can't see your eyes in the dark. Are you lying?"

"No. But I guess you're half right. Maybe I'm rattled. I was adding one thing to another. She did say she came to give me my freedom face to face, and she hopes we'll part good friends."

"Since you're telling it," said Andrew, "what did you say to that?"

"What do you take me for? What do you suppose I'd say? I told her I supposed you're the irresistible prince of lovers. Isn't it true?"

"You're telling it," said Andrew. "What did she answer?"

"She denied it. In *toto*. That's what has me beat. She was never a liar. She never had cause to fear telling me the plain truth. She said there's nothing between you and her. She said you've never made love to her."

"That's the plain truth," said Andrew.

"Man, listen, will you! I've sat in this cave, with Hut-sum Samdup up there on that ledge where Old Ugly-face has stowed himself, and I've seen you and Elsa in one bed together."

"Did you tell that to Elsa?"

"No, I didn't. She has feelings. I'm supposed to have none. But is it true or false?"

"It's true."

"Yeah, I know it's true. I saw it as clearly as a movie."

"Did you hear us talking?"

"No. I kind of shut it off. Somehow—I don't know how. I decided I'd shoot you as soon as you'd get here."

"Why didn't you?"

"Changed my mind. Had time to think. The blow-up's my fault, not hers. We never should have married in the first instance. You be good to her, Gunning. She's a good girl."

"Do you think I've been bad to her?"

"She says not. She says you were kindness itself. I guess that part's true."

"Then see here: the man doesn't live who can foist off a woman on me. I haven't as much as kissed her—though I should have done many a time, for the sake of the brave way she faced the journey, and the patience she had with my rough manners. What she has told you is the plain truth."

Tom Grayne was silent a moment. Suddenly he said: "My God, Andrew! Is she cutting herself adrift in this wilderness without a man to turn to? I can't let her go that way."

"It's between you and her," said Andrew.

"Sure you're telling the truth?"

"I've said it twice. I won't say it again."

"Did she tell you, before she left India, that she meant to break with me?"

"More or less."

"What did you say to it?"

"I said it was between you and her. Two or three times since, I've thought she'd changed her mind. But I didn't ask. It wasn't my business."

"Andrew, you fool, you know damn well you shouldn't have brought her here!"

"Says you. That was my business. I didn't offer. She asked. The decision was up to me. I made it. It stands."

"But, God Almighty, man, what's to be done? She says she won't come back to me—won't even think of it! What can I do with her? We'll have to tell off two men that we can't spare to protect her. In the mood she's in now she'll be no use—not even clairvoyant—she never is when she's—"

Andrew interrupted: "Can you see anything now?"

"No."

"Try again. Keep your eyes wide open. Stare."

"Say, what do you know about seeing things? I thought you were a sceptic."

Andrew growled at him: "Look! Listen! Keep your mouth shut! Stare into the dark!"

There was at first a confusion of attention—something that wasn't quite like far-away sheet lightning. It shimmered from plane to plane of consciousness. It was something, but not quite like flashbacks from a partly remembered dream, recognisable as experience but not translatable into symbols of waking thought.

"This is it! This is it!" said Tom Grayne.

"Shut up!" Andrew growled. "Don't break it. Quiet!"

Speech had broken the spell. But it came on again, stronger than ever, steadier, less dream-like. Old Ugly-face appeared, faded, came in again—seen through the rock. Except that nothing was reversed, it was like a reflection in a still pool; but it wasn't fixed in space; it was the same whichever way one looked—Old Ugly-face, seated like an image of Chenrezi, with his legs crossed and his hands on his thighs, palms upward, smiling.

Imperceptibly, and yet quickly, as in a dream, it changed. Old Ugly-face was gone, though one knew he was still there. Now one was seeing through him—through his consciousness. In his place were Elsa and St. Malo, on the cavern floor, standing, she with her back toward the canvas curtain, both of them clearly revealed in rather dim light from the break in the cavern wall. In the background beyond them there was a little vapor rising from the warm flowing water. The vision was more luminous than the light through the gap. The light was subordinate to it. It had its own light. As in certain kinds of dreams, one knew it was real and yet unreal, at one and the same time.

And then voices—soundless when remembered afterwards— inaudible dream voices that reached inner perception and conveyed their meaning without the actual use of words. There was a baffled sensation now—almost a feeling of guilt, as if it were barbarous ignorance not to be able to hear accurately. It was like watching a play in a foreign language, reading meaning from the action and from book memory. The meaning was quite clear.

Elsa, under no temptation, but under the tremendous pressure of St. Malo's trained will, was resisting hypnotic assault. It was like the pressure brought to bear by gangsters upon lonely women to force them to become prostitutes—threats, coaxing, realistic logic, lies, false sympathy:

"Honey, you know you're not so sore at those two big boobs that you'll let 'em be killed when you can prevent it. They were your friends once. One's your husband. The other wasn't so bad while it lasted. Now it's all over and they're both through with you, you needn't take it so hard."

"It is not your business, Mr. St. Malo."

"Oh yes, it is my business. I know how to save those two men. Come now, honey. Won't it give you any satisfaction to have saved their lives? And see here—there's a fortune for all of us. Those two intend to boot me out of here. You come and join me as soon as it's dark."

"No."

"But, honey—"

"Keep your hands off—please! Don't touch me. I won't have it."

640

"Honey, have you ever heard of love at first sight? Have you ever heard of a woman reforming a man by just being what she is—by being sweet and good and—"

There came an astonishing interruption, in a hard voice, that could not possibly be Elsa's. Nor was it Old Ugly-face's voice. It sounded more like Andrew's, or Tom Grayne's—or perhaps both their voices merged in one. Yet neither of them spoke:

"You swine! It's more than eighteen months since you've been with a white woman. Just now you were peeping through a hole in the curtain. You've taken opium. You're sex-crazy! You're—"

St. Malo again: "Come with me, honey. If you do, you'll save your life as well as theirs. If you don't, they're as good as dead now—and you'll be mine then anyway. For then I'll have to protect you. So make the best of it now. I've eighteen men. You heard Tom Grayne say they're not far off. Use your second-sight—I've a bit of my own—we'll work together and dope out their plan. We'll either force them to make terms with us, or beat them to it."

"I'll go kill him," Tom said suddenly. His voice broke the spell. The vision vanished. It was like waking from a bright dream in a dark room. Andrew laid his hand on Tom's arm:

"Take it easy. You're rattled, and who's to blame you. Don't let on what you know. This is Old Ugly-face's doing."

"The damned old bastard," said Tom. "I believe it's he who psychologised Elsa."

"Don't kid yourself," said Andrew. "He hardly spoke to her on the way here."

"Hell. What difference does that make? He's a wizard. He's the only man who can save Tibet, or I'd—"

"Easy," said Andrew, "easy. Let's go back up there and turn St. Malo out before it's too dark for him to find his way."

"I should kill him," Tom answered. "I should. Anyone else would."

"Nuts," said Andrew. "Did you get that line of Old Ugly-face's about 'louses having purposes'? I bet that was a hot tip. If you saw and heard just now what I did, you'll turn St. Malo loose to strut his stuff. Let's see what happens."

"All right. Have it your way. It sounds like horse sense. I was rattled. Let's go do it."

"We're agreed then?"

"Sure."

"Mum's the word about what we've just seen?"

"Yes, mum's the word."

"Okay," said Andrew. "You're the top man around here. You go first. I'll be behind you."

Elsa stood wondering what to say-what to do. There were no signs of peace or the making of peace. Tom came near enough to St. Malo to hit him if necessary. "Time's up," he remarked. "Get moving."

Andrew looked worried. St. Malo smirked at Elsa. He quoted a scrap from his heterogeneous mass of what undoubtedly was culture of a sort—if there can be culture without morals:

"*Manners maketh man.* Did you ever hear that proverb? It's a good one." Then he noticed Tom's fist. "So long, sister. Don't forget now: what we've discussed was for your ears and mine! Don't repeat it!"

He oozed away, like an experienced boxer melting out of range of a slugging adversary; but, in his black overcoat like a *soutane*, he really more resembled an elusive monk avoiding treading on an idol's shadow. When he reached the head of the ramp he turned and smirked again, this time at Tom and Andrew:

"So long, asses! *Auf Wiedersehen! Au revoir!*"

"Take your *lama* with you, and get the hell out!" Tom answered. Then he muttered: "If they are his eighteen men, let's hope they kill him for their back pay."

St. Malo vanished. He made plenty of noise on the way down. Andrew volunteered:

"I'll go down and see he clears out." He started for the ramp. Tom called him back:

"No. Stay here."

"But the phony *lama* and his gang are down there and—"

"They're disarmed—outnumbered. Trust Bompo Tsering."

"St. Malo is making that noise to warn them. It won't take me long to go down there and—"

"No. I want you to listen to this."

Andrew shrugged his shoulders. He came back and stood facing Elsa. They formed a triangle. Elsa didn't flinch from either man's gaze. She didn't seem afraid or unwilling to speak. She looked tragic. She wasn't pitying herself; she was sorry for Tom. Tom spoke, trying to force his voice to sound natural:

"Sit down, Elsa. Let's hear what St. Malo had to say."

She shook her head: "It was nothing—really nothing—not worth repeating. Perhaps he's light-headed. He behaved like one of those French nuisances who nudge you on the street."

"Opium," said Andrew. "Light-headed is right."

Tom agreed: "Let's call it that, anyhow. See here, Elsa. I'm sorry I was mean a while ago. What you said caught me off guard. I guess it hurt, and I squealed. I shouldn't have. I've talked with Andrew, and he confirms what you said."

"Do you believe him?" she asked.

"Yes. I do believe him."

"Tom, you might have believed me."

"I know it."

"It was Andrew—when I consulted him in Darjeeling, but not until then—who pointed out the unfairness to you—I think he said the indecency—"

"No, I didn't," said Andrew. "You must have thought of that word."

Elsa smiled: "—the cowardice, then—"

"I never called you a coward."

"—of sending a letter to claim my freedom and give you yours. I did write such a letter. But I burned it. After that I asked Andrew to take me with him. And he agreed."

"Is that the whole truth?" Tom asked.

"No. But it's the truth about Andrew's kindness to you and me. No one can tell the whole truth to another unless there's true love. You and I don't love each other, Tom—not that way. What happened has been all my fault—not yours—my fault. I came to say so."

"Don't let's argue that now—"

"Tom, there is nothing to argue. It was my fault. I accept full blame. And if it's possible to make amends in any way, I will do it."

"But, Elsa, be reasonable. See here—"

"Tom, is it unreasonable to wish to—"

"Elsa, what about you? What are you going to do with yourself?"

"I am not thinking about me."

"Then begin thinking, right now! You might do that out of fairness to me—to say nothing of Andrew."

"You may forget me," said Andrew. "Leave me out of the picture."

Elsa smiled, not meeting Andrew's eyes. There was a trace of a catch in her voice as she answered: "It is I who should be forgotten, if anyone should be. But we haven't been indifferent to one another or intentionally cruel. Have we? One can forget unkindness—kindness never—not true kindness. No, Andrew, I won't even try to forget you."

Tom ground his teeth. "Oh God! What can you say to a girl when she's in this mood."

"I'm a woman," Elsa answered. "I was a girl when you knew me. Now you don't know me. It isn't your fault. Tom, I am sorry with all my heart for any anguish I have caused you. The very least I owe you is freedom. It's yours. You are no longer responsible for me, or beholden to me, in any way whatever. You may divorce me when it suits you."

"Elsa, listen. Barring Andrew and me, you're a thousand miles from even the vaguest kind of protection or—"

"Tom, I know you believe that or you wouldn't say it. But you're mistaken."

Tom's eyes hardened. "Protection?" he said. "Whose?"

Ten words would have resolved that crisis. Elsa knew it . She hadn't actually meant to say what she did; words had almost said themselves. But she let them stand. She added to them, using truth as a reagent to compel suspicion to reveal its motive. She liked herself no better for being more clever than she had supposed she could be, but the words were said before she could recall them:

"Surely, Tom, you don't think that unless I knew to whom to turn, I would—"

His savage gesture silenced her. Rebellion against even the least binding marriage's restriction of his freedom to go, do, eat, starve, live, die as he pleased—imprisoned within him and dark-dungeoned into silence during lonely months and months by an iron will—now broke loose. It commanded every part of him except his manners. Those, like his will, were of iron; not gracious, but toward a woman incorruptible by anger.

"Very well. Then we're through, you and I. Thank you for my freedom. You have yours, too. You may do as you please. I wouldn't have believed it could happen this way. But here it is."

Andrew almost interrupted, but thought better of it. He had caught a glimpse of Old Ugly-face peering down from the cleft in the wall, through which the light poured dim and watery as the sun sank westward. Elsa said nothing. She couldn't speak. Tom continued:

"Now that's settled—I mean now you know you're free—will you listen?"

"Yes, Tom. Of course I will listen."

Tom gathered self-control. It came hard. He forced back anger within him until its concentration froze all personal sensation. He became governed by one motive, with one objective. First he turned to Andrew:

"Are you going to stand by?" he asked.

"Sure. That was the agreement. As long as you need me I'll see you through."

"Thanks." Tom faced Elsa again. "This man is simply a friend by coincidence. He has nothing to gain from me. He isn't paid for all this. As far as I know, he is spending his own money, taking his own risk. But you heard him. He stands by."

Elsa almost broke down. She felt she must say something. Her voice trembled:

"Andrew could never desert a friend. It isn't in him."

Tom pounced on that. It was the very opening he craved: "I'm asking you to take example from Andrew. My job is to save Tibet from anarchy by restoring the infant Dalai Lama into the hands of his rightful guardian, His Eminence Lobsang Pun. That's a tall order. It means capturing the monastery. It calls for intimate cooperation. One false move by any of us, you included, might ruin everything. Please think that over."

He gave her no chance to answer. He turned away and headed for the ramp. Andrew started after him, then turned back. Tears were streaming down Elsa's face. He didn't know whether she saw him or not. She didn't look at him. Her shoulders trembled with lonely misery. At last she yielded to it—sat down on her own bedding roll, and sobbed into her hands. Andrew stared, swore, hesitated. Old Ugly-face peered down at him like a gnome—a gargoyle; out from the shadowy mass that was his body one hand became visible. It moved with the force of authority, like a policeman's, sideways. It commanded Andrew to be gone.

But he was minded to speak to Elsa. He would have done it, in spite of Old Ugly-face. But Tom shouted from below:

"Hi! Andrew!"

He ran to the head of the ramp. He heard a roughhouse below—crashing—thuds—no shouting—a deadly, grim noise. He went down the ramp like a fireman, heels first. At the bottom it took him a second or two to accustom his eyes to the different light. First he saw Bompo Tsering, coming into the cavern on the run; he must have gone out to change the guard. All the ponies were kicking. One yak had broken its tether and was charging all over the place, with three or four men trying to corner it, making it wilder. At last he saw Tom—down—in a shadow— fighting for life.

He waded in. It did him good. It was what he needed. The phony *lama* had found another knife somewhere. He was stabbing at Tom. Tom held his wrist, but the stabs were getting closer—ferocious— two or three a second. St. Malo, underneath Tom, clung to him, trying to throttle him. Three men of the phony *lama's* party stood by to prevent interference. Andrew tackled them first and they went down like ninepins, one punch to a man, left, right, left, rolling in agony. He didn't know until then that they had knives. Bompo Tsering gathered up the knives. Andrew kicked the phony *lama* unconscious. He hurled him half across the cavern floor, then stooped to grab St. Malo—too late. Tom seized Andrew's arm to pull himself to his feet. He almost pulled Andrew down. St. Malo yelled. Three more Tibetans rushed Tom and Andrew. They were sent staggering back toward the ponies, where Bompo Tsering's men knelt on them. But St. Malo, as quick as a snake on hands and knees, had writhed along the wall-escaped. When Andrew looked for him he was standing with his back to the light in the cavern entrance, steadying himself against the wall.

"Kill him! Quick!" said Tom, out of breath, gasping. "The son of a bitch! He's got my automatic!"

"Easy," said Andrew, "easy. No one's dead yet."

St. Malo smiled. There was nothing even mock-heroic about him. He wasn't posing. He was figuring the odds: a gambler.

"You two—have fools'-luck," he said, breathing hard. "I can kill one of you. So shall we shoot it out, or—"

Tom was whispering to Andrew.

Andrew turned sideways, concealing his right hand. St. Malo aimed at him—squeezed the trigger. He had forgotten the safety catch. He found himself looking straight at the muzzle of Andrew's Luger.

"Drop that automatic!" said Andrew. "Drop it!"

"Hell! You wouldn't shoot," St. Malo answered. But he tossed the automatic. Tom caught it. "Neither would I have shot. I'm no killer. Let's not act like children. Let's make one more try to reach agreement."

He folded his arms, crossed one leg in front of the other and relaxed against the wall, watching with amused eyes the Tibetans' efforts to catch the hysterical yak.

CHAPTER 52

Perhaps St. Malo had seen a signal and knew where to find his eighteen men. Perhaps he didn't. He wasn't saying. Old Ugly-face had come neatly halfway down the ramp and was listening in. Andrew knew that because St. Malo caught sight of him and Andrew turned his head quickly to see what St. Malo was looking at. There was no sign of Elsa. St. Malo's eyes were moving in all directions, watching the Tibetans. Shrewdly he seemed to suspect they would attack him next, in revenge for his having coaxed them into such a fiasco. No one spoke until Bompo Tsering and another man roped the yak at last and threw it to keep it quiet. Then St. Malo spoke:

"Hell. You're mean. You haven't even offered me a drink. I know you've got liquor."

"Stick to opium," Tom answered. "That stuff doesn't mix with liquor."

"I'm hungry. Any soft grub? Jam? Sardines?"

Tom nodded. Andrew went and dug out a can of salmon and a can of marmalade from one of the loads. He tossed them to St. Malo.

"Biscuit?" he asked.

Andrew threw him a small can of ship's biscuit. Now at any rate they possessed two scraps of important information. Tom ticked them off:

"So your eighteen men are on iron rations. But you favour your belly. How come you didn't fit out those men with a few luxuries?"

It might have meant that St. Malo was unfamiliar with the craving for rich food, in Tibet, in spring, at an altitude above twelve thousand feet. But it might not. He stuck a can into each side pocket and one into the bosom of his overcoat.

"I'll let you know when I need more," he said. "I didn't fit 'em out. It was done for me." He sneered. "It's a sure thing, if they started out with fancy stores they've eaten 'em *en route*. I'll have to count on you."

Then he walked out, not looking backward.

"The insolent pimp!" said Tom Grayne. "Damn him!"

Andrew laughed: "But can you shoot a man who turned in his automatic."

"It wasn't his. It was mine, the damned pickpocket."

"Well, all right, you've got it. Will you shoot him?"

Where the long, irregular cleft in the cliff met the ledge that skirted the ravine, St. Malo stopped, outlined against the setting sun, and spoke to the lookout man. Then he turned to the right along the ledge and vanished around the bend. Andrew went and questioned the lookout:

"What did he say to you?"

"His saying, him being my friend—when trouble coming by-um-by, my looking to him."

"What did you answer?"

"Nothing."

That wasn't true. Andrew had seen the man's lips move. Clearly St. Malo was a master of the dubious art which differentiates the spy from the mere informer. He could spot a simpleton a mile off and get his confidence in sixty seconds. Andrew returned to report to Tom, who was already delivering judgment on the men who had attacked him.

"Hard labor," Tom pronounced, "without rations. No tea until to-morrow. Carry rocks and barricade the ledge. Now. Get busy."

For a Tibetan, no tea is punishment. They would rather have been flogged. But they were glad not to be executed. So they stuck out their tongues in token of meek submission and went to work without protest. Tom went out to show them how to fortify the place, and Andrew sent Bompo Tsering with another man to boil tea without fuel. It was simple enough; outside the cavern, well protected from wind and view by the stone barricade that the punishment squad was now enlarging, was a pot-hole full of boiling water from the hot spring. One only had to lower the urn into that. It would boil anything. Baking, against the rock wall near the pot-hole, was just possible. One could warm up meat and make it palatable, or parch barley against it. It almost entirely solved the fuel problem.

When Tom came in, Old Ugly-face had returned to the upper cavern, so Andrew asked for information. He knew how simple it was to get Tom's mind into its own orbit, where nothing except the main objective—not even pain or misery—had much importance.

"Are the monks of the Shig-po-ling monastery armed?"

"You bet. Five hundred new Jap rifles and lots of old ones. No training, of course—or not much. But Abbot Ram-pa Yap-shi has a gangster's brains and he has 'em bulldozed. He's a money buzzard. Buys things. Buys people. Double-crosses. Uses poison. He has never been beaten yet, so he lacks experience. I think he'll take the full count if he gets a sudden upset."

"Yeah. But can we do it?"

"Suddenness 'ud do it. He has the infant Dalai Lama under close

648

guard, in an apartment at the rear of the monastery. The kid's pining for fresh air and exercise. There's an inner guard of picked men, unarmed for fear they might get fancy notions of their own. Only the outer guard have weapons. Ram-pa Yap-shi has been dickering, all winter long, between the Tibetan agents of Japan and Russia. Now he's heard of the Germans. So he shot both sets of agents. He calculates that Moscow'll be pleased because he shot the Jap agents; Tokyo should feel the same way about his having shot the Soviet contingent."

"What's his background?" Andrew wondered. "Is he a *lama?* Educated? Does he know his black book?"

"He's a political priest. He was what's called a lay *chela*. That's to say he took holy orders more or less by proxy. No more education than a Hitler or a Stalin. But good family. His name, Ram-pa Yap-shi, indicates descent from two lines of the ancient nobility. He has no more claim to the title of abbot than Henry the Eighth had a right to be pope. He gets away with it by bribery and force and by poisoning his critics. The monastery monks are scared stiff of him."

Andrew demurred: "If Ram-pa Yap-shi has been in that monastery all winter, how did he boot Old Ugly-face out of Lhasa?"

"Bribery," Tom answered. "Ram-pa Yap-shi has the money. He got away with all the cash in the treasury at Lhasa."

"Then what more does he want? If he has the young Dalai Lama, and money, he owns Tibet."

"He's like all usurpers," said Tom. "He has to keep on going. There's no safety in standing still. He has no genuine dictator's guts, so he intends to sell out to the highest bidder. But the higher they bid, the more he wants. That's another familiar symptom—greedy. And on top of that he's nervous as long as he knows Old Ugly-face still lives. He knows Old Ugly-face would chuck away his own hope of eternity if he could save Tibet. Ram-pa Yap-shi is a crook who'd sell Tibet to save his hide; but he's top dog for the time being."

"And we?"

"We've a tough job. It isn't finished until the kid's in safe hands."

"Meaning Ugly-face's hands."

"Yes."

They sat down side by side at the foot of the ramp and watched two of the Tibetans butcher a sheep for supper. Tom had ordered it for two reasons: the sheep was sick; and the smell of the cooking meat would sharpen the punishment of the men at hard labour. The phony *lama* had been shamming for quite a while. A minute after Andrew kicked him unconscious he had been alert enough to roll out of the way of the mad yak. Now he sat up, sniffed the butchered sheep and stared around him. Tom ordered him out to the labour gang, but he didn't obey until Andrew got up suddenly and started for him. Then he ran.

Andrew turned around and faced Tom. He wanted to glance up the ramp toward the upper cavern without Tom's knowing it. There was no one on the ramp. If he could keep Tom's mind off Elsa for another ten or fifteen minutes, Tom's natural resilience—his power to absorb punishment—his disciplined, stoical courage would come to his aid. Concentration of purpose would exclude even the sense of personal humiliation. That was something that Andrew knew about, having tried it for himself when all else failed. So he invented questions, just to occupy Tom's thought.

"See here. I don't get this. Old Ugly-face is a badly beaten man—"

"Beaten, hell!" Tom interrupted.

"We're all the friends he's got," said Andrew. "He needs us. He'll have to chip in."

Tom raised his head from between his hands and laid a clenched fist on his knee.

"Sit down," he answered. And when Andrew sat beside him, he laid the first on Andrew's knee. "Get this! Old Ugly-face isn't beaten. It can't be done. There's no way of beating him. He's a genuine mystic, and they're the most practical people in the world, because they know what they're doing, and why. Any man can be beaten who has personal ambition, and who believes that death is the end of the road. But Old Ugly-face isn't that kind. He doesn't believe—he's a knower. What he doesn't know, he doesn't bet on. He doesn't care a whoop in hell whether you or I understand him or not. That's our lookout. When he says he has lived thousands of lives in the world, getting a little wiser each time, gradually earning evolution in the sweat of his brow, he isn't guessing. He claims he knows it and can prove it. When he says he'll go on incarnating, life after life, until at last he doesn't have to any longer, because he'll have learned all that the world can teach him, who's going to contradict him? You? The pope? Einstein? The Archbishop of Canterbury? Freud? Bishop Manning? Fosdick? Have you discussed it with him? Death means nothing more to him than passing through a door from one experience to another. Riches are nothing. Even power is nothing, except as a duty. His duty is to

Tibet. How can you beat that man?"

"He must have a soft spot somewhere," Andrew suggested.

"All right, you find it," Tom answered. "By the time Lobsang Pun was twenty-five he had spent seven years, naked, winter and summer, immured in a cave, not far from here, fed once a week on raw barley, through a hole in a wall. That's where he learned how to think and to control himself. By the time he was thirty-five, he was the Dalai Lama's diplomatic representative in China and Japan, and he had tasted every luxury the world can offer. Barring liquor, which he once told me he has never touched, he has sampled everything and watched its effects on other people. He has control of all his appetites. He can take things or leave them. For choice he leaves 'em."

"He has a heart," Andrew suggested.

"You bet he has. For Tibet and the Tibetans. Listen to this: I'm his friend. He knows that, and he knows why. It's because I recognize his integrity. A few years back, when he was in power, he chased me out of Tibet just ahead of the first snowfall. If the snow had caught me, I was done for."

"Sounds friendly."

"Doesn't it? He put a thousand monks to work, praying I'd get through, just to give me the edge. He figured that if I hadn't been too sinful, and if my destiny entitled me to it, I'd get through in spite of the weather."

"On the floodtide of the monks' prayers?"

"Yes. I guess so. He figures prayer can't help the wrong man; and it can't help the right man to do the wrong thing. Anyhow, I got through, no worse off for being prayed for. He'll pray for us now. He'll bless every thought we think, to make us useful to him and Tibet. But the minute he's through using us, he'll want to boot us out of Tibet or I'm a bad guesser."

Andrew demurred for the sake of talking: "You mean, if you and I pull off a miracle, ditch Ram-pa Yap-shi and put Old Ugly-face on top, he'll turn on us?"

"Hell, no. He's not treacherous. But why are we here? To get reliable information. If Old Ugly-face wins out, then we'll have what we came for. He'll owe us nothing. But I don't intend to-be booted out of Tibet. I'll send you back to India with the news. I'm staying on. When the kid's in safe hands, I'm going to get clairvoyant—I'm going to learn to see—hear—think the way Old Ugly-face does—if it kills me.

"I've been told," said Andrew, "that the first few lifetimes are the hardest—the first two or three hundred years."

Tom got up. He looked down at him. Suddenly he used an unexpected phrase. Andrew had never heard him quote the Bible before:

"'*Ask and it shall be given unto you.*' I'll make Old Ugly-face do the teaching. Because of my importunity he shall!"

He walked out then to see how the barricade was coming along. Andrew sat still, pondering, until presently he heard Elsa at the head of the ramp.

"Is that you, Andrew?"

"Yes. I'll bring up some supper."

"Andrew, please—just sardines and tomato juice and biscuit."

"Doesn't Old Ugly-face want a square meal?"

"No. He says not. He has barley. He prefers it. Quick, Andrew. I want to talk to you before Tom gets back."

He wondered how she knew that Tom had left the cavern. Strange that she should know that and yet not have known there was a fight; neither she nor Old Ugly-face had as much as stirred while the fight lasted. He could hear Tom, outside, cussing and showing the Tibetans how to build the barricade; there was no need for haste on Tom's account. He chose Elsa's supper with slow deliberation, adding odds and ends to make it palatable. He knew what she liked. He had a good meal for three by the time he started up the ramp—fruit juice and some honey and tinned cake—all sorts of things.

Elsa had lighted a lantern. It was getting near sunset; almost no light came through the gap in the wall. Elsa looked wan, but tense, excited. She sat down on one of the bedding rolls and spread another as a makeshift table for the food, avoiding Andrew's eyes.

Andrew asked: "Where's Old Ugly-face?"

She glanced up at the gap in the wall.

"Climbed back there, did he?"

"No. He has been there all the time."

"I guess you weren't looking. I saw him just now, part way down the ramp. He was listening in."

"But please, Andrew, I know where he was."

"He was on the ramp. I saw him. He was trying to hear what Tom and I were talking about."

"But, Andrew, I was up there with him. He called me up there as soon as you went away. I have been there all the time. I have only just come down."

"Beats me," said Andrew. "Elsa, I saw him—looked right at him. He saw me."

"Andrew, I think—perhaps you don't understand."

"You bet I don't. Are you telling the truth?"

"You too?" she asked. She bit her lip. She met his eyes for a second. "Oh—oh well, let's not talk about it."

"Sorry," he said. "I'm ashamed. I shouldn't have said that. I guess I'm worked up. Of course you told the truth. But so did I. I saw him."

He opened a can, then another, stabbing them savagely with his knife, slicing off the tops by the sheer strength of sculptor's fingers.

"Oh, Andrew—"

"What? What is it? Shoot!"

She sighed, then pulled herself together and spoke to the cavern at large, as if giving evidence that she didn't expect to be believed:

"When Lobsang Pun wishes to see—or to hear; and when he knows and loves those whom he wishes to hear and see—then—because they also know him—sometimes—the great effort of will projects his image into their imaginations."

"But Tom didn't see him."

"Perhaps Lobsang Pun was thinking more strongly of you. Or you of him."

Andrew laughed grimly: "Loves me, does he! '*Whom the Lord loveth he chasteneth!*' Is that his motto? Tom believes he'll give us the air when he's through with us—boot us all three out of Tibet."

Elsa looked startled—excited. "Did Tom say he will leave Tibet?"

"No, he didn't say that—not to me."

"But do you think he will leave Tibet? Did anything he said give you that impression?"

"Easy," said Andrew, "easy. I don't ever ask that kind of question. So I've the right not to answer 'em."

He was sorry he said it. It sounded priggish. He loathed prigs. So did Elsa. They sat silent a moment or two, listening to Tom returning into the lower cavern, marshaling the punishment gang. They could hear his voice, not his words; it was easy to guess he was ordering the culprits supperless to bed, in the corner beyond the ponies.

"Discipline," said Andrew. "If he went back on his word and gave 'em a bite to eat tonight, they'd think that weakness. He'd have it all to do over again."

They heard Bompo Tsering and two or three men rigging a tent

653

over the entrance to keep out wind and make the place snug for the night.

"Andrew, I have let the time slip by. Now Tom may come up here, and—"

"I don't think he will," said Andrew, "unless you ask him. He's more likely to go to his own hide-out."

"Andrew, will you take a message to him?"

"From you? Can't you tell him yourself?"

"It's from Lobsang Pun."

"Well, all right. Can't Old Ugly-face talk? What's wrong with him all at once? He knows Tom 'ud go the limit for him, now or any time.—Say, eat or you'll be starving. Be a good girl—drink up that tomato juice."

She obeyed, then laughed:"Andrew, I have grown so used to obeying you that I must guard against the habit!"

"Now sardines on biscuit. Wash 'em down with champagne. Go on, that's the last half bottle."

"Andrew, we had six half bottles. What became of the others?"

"Bulah Singh and St. Malo stole 'em."

"You knew it."

"Yes. I pretended not to. The poor devils needed something to keep their hackles rising. You said you've a message for Tom. What is it?"

"Lobsang Pun wants you to deliver it, because Tom will listen to you. He says it was wise to let St. Malo go. But it isn't wise to give him too much time, because he'll waste it."

"So Ugly-face wants action?"

"Yes. He said this:'Devils are not angels. If you buy a devil, he is all the more a devil, having added one more sin to make him worse; and the higher the price you pay, the more certainly he will betray you.'"

"Who'd choose to buy St. Malo?" Andrew wondered. "Governments, yes. They're all crazy. But who else?"

"I don't know. Lobsang Pun told me to say that."

"To me?"

"Yes, to you—to repeat to Tom. Then he said this: 'Devils know how to be devilish, so make them do it quickly. By betraying, they create an opportunity.' And after that he added: 'If a plan has a flaw, turn it inside out, or change it, but don't abandon it unless it's wicked.' He wants you to say that to Tom."

"Well—all right. Tom's the head man. I'll go down and tell him.

654

But I won't say it's my opinion. I'll just make a report."

"Andrew, won't you eat something?"

"Not now. Later. Say: is there nothing that you'd like to say to Tom?"

She paused a second. "No, Andrew." Suddenly she put her hands to her face—spoke through them. "What could I say? Tom doesn't love me— you know he doesn't! You heard him, Andrew. Tom loves his career—his solitude—his—"

Andrew interrupted: "Do you love him?"

"My God! Is that a fair question? Now? No, I won't answer!" Then suddenly: "Andrew! Do you know what Tom believes?"

"Better not say it. I'm Tom's friend."

"He believes I've fallen for St. Malo! He does believe it! I know he does! He thinks I'm so wicked and loose and vile that I'd run off with St. Malo just for—just for—oh, I don't know why he thinks he thinks that!"

"What makes you think he thinks that?"

"Andrew, I read it! I read his thought! Can you love anyone, and think that kind of thought about them?—If he had killed the thought— thrown it out—stamped on it! But he didn't. He didn't try. He let it bore in like a worm into his mind.—Oh, Andrew, Andrew, why was I ever born?"

He tried to comfort her, but he didn't know what to say. He put his arm around her. She buried her face against his breast and cried, struggling to control herself, sobbing, choking. At last:

"Oh Andrew, I can't help it! There—I won't do it again." She sat upright. "I'm all right now: Andrew—"

"Yes."

"Has Tom said anything—about me?"

"Not a word. I don't think he will. He's as proud as hell."

"Do you—do you suppose he'll ask you what I'm going to do?"

"No. I guess not. I wouldn't tell him if he did ask, even if I knew the answer. That's between you and him."

"Shall I—shall I tell you—in confidence?"

"No. Better not. No need just now. You're on the level. If it were my business, I would trust you sight unseen."

"Thank you, Andrew. You couldn't be ungenerous, could you!"

"You mustn't forget. I'm Tom's friend. I've so to speak enlisted for the duration. I'm seeing him through this business."

"Andrew, I must tell you! I will! I'm going to be Lobsang Pun's *chela!* The way Nancy Strong was—and still is! I'm going through with it! I'm—"

"There, there, Elsa! Don't start crying again." He felt his heart grow cold within him. His words grew cold with it. "And don't be rash. Don't do anything just because you feel panicked into it. Think it over. Sleep on it."

"Andrew, there's no other way out—nothing else to do: Please, won't you go and give Tom the message from Lobsang Pun?"

"Yes. I'll go now. All right, I'll—tell him." He got up, hesitating. "Look up," he said. " I want to see your eyes."

"Andrew, I've been crying. I can't—"

"Look at me. Are you sure you've no message for Tom?"

"No, Andrew. None. What could I say? If only I knew what to say that wouldn't make things worse—that wouldn't hurt Tom's feelings and—"

Andrew, too, wished he knew what to say. He felt like swearing a streak. He craved to use his hands on something—to shape a big hunk of wood with long cleaving strokes. What he did say was:

"Well, keep your heart up, Elsa. Be brave; and let's hope for the best. I'll be back later."

He walked away, glancing upward at the great deep, dark gap in the wall. Almost no light came through it now. There was no sign of Old Ugly-face. He shook his fist at the gap.

"You damned old bugger!" He almost startled himself, the unspoken thought was so vehement. "I wish I'd left you to the vultures with your dead friend!"

When he was halfway down the ramp he paused—listened. He heard Elsa sobbing—and then, suddenly, Old Ugly-face's belly laugh:

"Oo-hah-ha-ha-ha-ha-hah! My being damned old bugger! Oo-hah-ha-ha-ha-ha- hah!"

Chapter 53

Tom was ominously taciturn. He and Andrew snatched a hurried meal of canned stuff. Then they went out to the ledge to change the guard. It was still not quite sunset. If the weather should hold there would be a nearly full moon, almost all night long, that should make it easy to guard the ledge against all comers. But Tom looked worried. He and Andrew leaned against the rebuilt barricade, each waiting for the other to speak. At last Andrew repeated Old Ugly-face's message.

"Did you get it from him direct?" Tom asked.

"It's accurate. Those were his words."

"Oh."

"Uh-huh."

Andrew stared into the rising wind across the ravine. Two yards away from his feet there was a sheer drop that the eye couldn't measure, into a ravine that made him dizzy to look at. There were eagles, getting ready to roost for the night, flying and screaming five hundred feet below. In the distance, beyond the ravine, perhaps ten miles away on eagles' wings, but farther on foot, the Shig-po-ling monastery was perched between earth and sky like a painting. It looked theatrical in the sunset. Huge walls. Courtyard within courtyard. An enormous central building with a long roof, studded with belfries and fluttering with prayer banners. Without artillery it would need an army of ten thousand men to capture that place. The only means of approach, at any rate in front, was the ledge on which Andrew and Tom stood; it wound around cliff after cliff and gradually widened until it became a practicable road that looked possible even for carts.

One couldn't see anyone moving in the monastery. There was no one on the walls. The wind-blown blessing bells were inaudible at that distance. Smoke rose from the monastery kitchen. There must be thousands of monks at the evening meal or making ready for it. Andrew returned into the cavern for his binoculars. Through those, on the face of the cliff about two-thirds of the way between him and the monastery, he could see the masonry fronts of the natural caves in which hermits endured privation, alone in the dark. He counted eighteen hermit holes, but there were a lot more than that.

Tom sat on the new barricade, staring at the monastery, saying nothing. Andrew decided to force the issue:

"What beats me," he said, "is why Old Ugly-face couldn't tell you himself. Why use me as intermediary?"

Tom turned his back to the wind, perhaps to see Andrew's face better in the fading light. At first he looked savagely angry, but Andrew's return stare didn't flinch; there was no answering resentment. So Tom's anger withdrew into its own gloom.

"Ugly-face knows me like a book," he answered. "He's right. A man can't think straight when he's feeling sore with himself. I've been figuring out a plan to make it worth St. Malo's while to play with us."

"You're crazy," said Andrew. "St. Malo still hopes to sell Old Ugly-face for cash, and then to steal the kid *lama* and run."

657

"I know that," said Tom. "You can't change his sort. But I was thinking at the moment that there's plenty of gold in the monastery. Those monks own gold mines. They can only work 'em two months in the year, by crude methods, but they dig enough pay dirt, and carry it more than a hundred miles in baskets, to make the monastery rich. I thought of asking Ugly-face to promise St. Malo some of that gold. But it was a lousy idea. Give him gold, and you'd have to kill him to keep him from trying to steal it all."

Andrew grinned: "He would kill you and me for the strawberry jam."

"If we should kill him," said Tom, "Old Ugly-face wouldn't move a finger or pull a string to prevent someone from killing us. You don't know that old wizard. He's consistent. He doesn't kid himself he's a cushion between cause and effect. He lets consequences happen. Then he walks in on top of the consequences."

Andrew scowled: "If he has a plan why can't he tell it to you and me?"

"Don't you get the idea yet?"

"No."

"Then here's the plain lowdown: if Old Ugly-face should take us into his confidence, he'd lose control of the situation. He might even have to obey us."

"You think he controls the situation now?"

"Sure. It's in the bag. What gives him his grip is the fact that he has no personal ambition. You and I 'ud pat ourselves on the back for doing a good job. We like to think well of Tom Grayne and Andrew Gunning. That old wizard doesn't care a damn about himself. He counts his personality as nothing but the shadow of his own soul. He doesn't care what happens to it. You and I do care what happens to our persons. That's the difference. And it's why he'll use us rough and tell us nothing."

"Let's hear the rest of your plan," said Andrew.

"I've ditched it. But we may have to change it around and use part of it yet. You know where the hermits' caves are. They feed 'em by night, once a week. This is the night. A party of monks comes from the monastery to pass food and water through a hole in the wall of each cell. It isn't too difficult to attach yourself to that party in the dark and get into the monastery."

"That sounds easy to say," said Andrew.

"I did it, during the winter, while you were away," Tom retorted.

"It's a bit risky, but not too bad. They count the feeding party going out, but they don't count 'em in when they return. There are so many monks in that monastery that half of 'em don't know the other half. Plenty of places to hide. There were one or two scares, but nothing serious. The first day I was in here I had to punch a holy Joe who asked me what I thought I was doing out of chapel at prayer time. I knocked him so cold that he probably can't remember who hit him. I was in there three days—found out where they keep the young Dalai Lama—how often they change the guard—and all that. It was harder getting out than getting in. Too many big dogs outside. Got out at last with a funeral gang who were taking a corpse to be handed over to the *ragyabas*, who chop up the corpse to be fed to the dogs and vultures. The dogs were hungry, so they went for the corpse and I got away. If I'd had to kill one of those dogs, there'd have been trouble. Cold night, it was. Christmas Eve. Seventy below."

"Don't they suspect you're here?"

"No. I think not. I've been lucky. Got all the breaks so far. Hermits may have seen me through their peepholes. But I think they haven't. They'd have told. There'd have been a party sent to rout me out."

"We'll need more than the breaks," said Andrew. "We've got to capture a fortified city."

Tom grinned at last. "You're telling me. Well—we know the first move."

"Which?"

"Ugly-face said it."

It was dark now. A few stars were shining, but great banks of cloud were rolling up to hide them. Tom peered curiously at Andrew—hesitated, and then said, as if ashamed of himself:

"Do you suppose Elsa's idea was the same as mine—to buy St. Malo?"

"How should I know?" said Andrew.

"Well—anyhow—move number one is to shove St. Malo— goad him—push him—irritate him—make him act up."

"With eighteen armed men," said Andrew. "All he'll need to tell them is that we've got supplies and money. They'll jump us quick."

"St. Malo's no fighting man," Tom retorted.

"Granted. He'd rather clean up after someone else's battle. But he could blockade us in here."

"That's what we've got to prevent," said Tom. "We can't afford a blockade. When the fords are passable, support for Ram-pa Yap-shi might turn up from Lhasa. There's a couple of regiments there that haven't been paid and may come for their money. They'll eat everything they find on their way. Once here, the man with the money controls them. We've got to be it.— Tonight is the night they feed the hermits."

"What of it? What good does that do us?"

"They feed 'em around midnight. We must tell St. Malo. Can you imagine him missing that chance to open negotiations with Ram-pa Yap-shi?"

"You're telling it," said Andrew.

"So we prod St. Malo. And we wise him up about the hermits. It's a rock-bound cinch he'll send word to the monastery, offering to betray Lobsang Pun's whereabouts in exchange for a fat fee. He won't be such a fool as to tell where Lobsang Pun is. He'll fix the price first. He'll want cash on the head of the barrel. That takes time."

"Well then, what's our next move?"

"The next move will be up to Ram-pa Yap-shi. We'll be the problem—the unknown quantity."

At home it had been Andrew's job to spot flaws in cases. He did it as a natural reaction.

"The least it means," he said, "is that we lose the initiative. We'll be cut off, and starved out, if nothing worse happens."

"Nuts," Tom answered. "Where did you learn strategy?—Out of a book? Initiative resides in the ability to take advantage of the other man's mistakes. If he doesn't make 'em, you can't use 'em. He won't make 'em, if you don't tempt him. And until he has made 'em, who knows how good they'll be?"

"So you're betting on Old Ugly-face?"

Tom snapped his jaws: "I laid a bet on Ugly-face," he said, "—to win—on the day I knew he was a fugitive from Lhasa. Let's go irritate St. Malo."

Andrew went back to the cavern for flashlights. He heard Old Ugly-face saying his prayers. All the Tibetans in the lower cavern were down on their knees with their foreheads on the floor. The lanterns, that cast astonishing shadows, shone in the eyes of the stabled animals. It was a weird sight. Old Ugly-face's voice, coming through the gap from the upper cavern, sounded something like a Gregorian chant. It conjured up a mental picture of Old Ugly-face in full canonicals, that were a sort of symbol of daimonic dignity. There was no sign of Elsa. Andrew whispered a few words to Bompo Tsering about changing

660

the guard every hour and then returned to the ledge. Presently he and Tom climbed over the barricade and started along the track, Tom leading. There wasn't room for them side by side. If one should set a foot wrong, or stumble on a loose stone, or slip on the ice there was a long way to fall. There had been a sudden change in the weather; the moon was clouding over and there were signs of one of those spring-time storms that do more to keep foreigners out of Tibet than all the laws and treaties in the world. Tom kicked a loose rock off the ledge, stopped and listened until it struck bottom, sending echoes pinging along the ravine like breaking ice. Then he spoke over his shoulder:

"Keep your hair on and your feet under you. It gets worse from here on."

Andrew answered cynically: "Ugly-face is praying for us. So you should worry. Let's hope he's praying for fine weather."

Tom spoke again over his shoulder: "He'll need to pray like hell. There'll be a humdinger before long—perhaps the last storm of the season. Last ones usually are killers."

They went ahead, leaning against the wind, feeling their way along the cliff on their right. Tom seemed to relish the thought of a storm, although he knew those Tibetan blizzards even better than Andrew did. He strode with vigour that made Andrew hustle to keep up.

It seemed to Andrew that they were taking an idiot's chance. Tom's conviction that Old Ugly-face intended to use them and himself too, for that matter, like pawns in a desperate game, fitted in with Andrew's own conception, now that he had time to think about it. He imagined the old prelate back there in the cavern planning to sacrifice them all, including Elsa, in some subtle move that was beyond their compre-hension because they didn't know the facts. It made his spine crawl.

Tom seemed to be taking no precautions. He led as fast as he could struggle against the wind, along a ledge that zigzagged in and out on the face of a cliff from one natural ambush to the next. At one moment they were outlined by the light of the moon; at the next they were in deep shadow where a dozen men might have been lurking. It would only have needed a sudden shove to send both of them over the edge. That would have left Old Ugly-face and Elsa at St. Malo's mercy. When Tom called a halt for a few moments' rest, Andrew said to him:

"We're asking for it. We'll get it. We're going straight into it."

Tom didn't answer. He walked on. He must have guessed that An-drew had the wind up. The going got worse after a minute or two. The moon disappeared behind hurrying clouds. One could see nothing, nor hear much either, because the wind began blowing a half gale, screaming and moaning among the crags. It was all one sound, worse than the ocean at night. To have used a flashlight would have been an invitation to any rifleman keeping a lookout. St. Malo had eighteen men with rifles. Not good.

Andrew overlooked the fact that, having been there all winter, Tom was familiar with every yard of the ledge. They were more than two miles from their cavern when Tom stopped and grabbed Andrew's arm. It was too dark to see each other. He had to shout against the wind, with his hand to his mouth:

"On our right, two yards from here."

"What?"

"A cave."

They could hear the wind howling through it and thundering the way it does into a tunnel. Tom shouted again:

"Passage at the rear. Into a gorge. Back of that's a cavern. He's there."

Tom had his plan figured out. They entered the cave, using flashlights until at the rear they found the opening into a tunnel. It was three feet off the cavern floor and about half a man's height, the shape of an egg on its side. Someone in the tunnel or at the far end of it noticed their light. They heard noises that were off-key with the wind. At last a Tibetan came crawling along the tunnel on hands and knees. They dazzled his eyes for a second or two, then switched off the light. He called out to them. They couldn't hear what he said. Hoping the moon wouldn't come out suddenly from behind the clouds and give the Tibetan a chance for a pot-shot, Tom answered, in Tibetan. Then at last Andrew got the general drift of Tom's plan, and began to feel better. A good plan does that. It acts like champagne.

Tom began by asking the man whether he had seen the monks from the monastery. The man said no. Tom told him this was the night when the monks came to feed the hermits. The Tibetan hadn't heard about that routine. He asked a couple of questions, and Tom answered them. Then he told the Tibetan to go and fetch St. Malo.

"Tell him," said Tom, "that if he wants to talk to Tum-Glain he must come alone."

The man disappeared, after trying, but failing to discover whether Tom had more than one companion: Tom and Andrew waited one on each side of the mouth of the tunnel. Tom was thinking of Elsa. There was no doubt of that, although he didn't mention her name. He said:

"If St. Malo should shoot both or either of us now, that would tip off Ugly-face. He'd clear out. They'd never catch him."

"Ugly-face wouldn't know," Andrew answered. He, too, was thinking of Elsa. "He's in the cavern, two miles away."

"No he isn't," said Tom.

There would have been no sense in arguing that. Andrew glanced sideways and nearly jumped out of his skin. There stood Ugly-face, in the mouth of the cave, with his back to the faintly luminous hurrying clouds where the moon was fighting its way through for a moment. He was a silhouette; Andrew couldn't see his face; but he was as unmistakable as the Great Pyramid. Shrouded in two of Andrew's blankets, he looked like a big black-hooded ghost. He stepped out of sight, around the corner, along the ledge.

"Damn him, he's gone!" said Andrew.

Tom asked: "No sign of Elsa?"

"No. But I'll go look." Andrew returned after a minute. "No, no sign of her. I bet she's safe in our cavern. Bompo Tsering'll take good care of her. She was pretty well tuckered out. Let's hope she's asleep."

Tom grunted. It might have meant anything; Andrew wished to hell he would say what he did mean. There were sounds again in the tunnel. This time a man came carrying a lantern. Alone. Not St. Malo. He was another Tibetan. He wanted to know how many men there were.

"Tell St. Malo he may count them if he comes alone," Tom answered. "On your way, drag your rifle so we can hear you."

The man turned back, dragging the butt of his rifle along the tunnel floor. Tom crossed to Andrew's side of the opening.

"I guess St. Malo'll come this time. Tell him I've gone to watch the hermit-feeding, so's to give the alarm in case the monks learn where we are. Then tell him we've decided to bolt, and we advise him to. Say we'll let him get the hell out past our cavern, first thing in the morning. Say we'll give him some soft grub for the journey, provided he and his men unload their weapons and pass our cavern one by one at a walk. That ought to fool him."

"Okay," said Andrew.

Tom hesitated, so long that Andrew asked: "What's the matter?"

"Nothing. But see here: don't mention Elsa."

"I won't."

Tom walked out of the cave to follow Old Ugly-face around the corner of the cliff. Andrew, cursing Tom's suspicion, waited, in pitch darkness, and after a long while St. Malo did come. He was carrying a lantern. He had a rifle, too, but he didn't seem to expect to use it. Andrew, taking care not to startle him, told him to lay it down on the tunnel floor. He obeyed. Andrew said:

"You're covered, so no funny business."

St. Malo sneered: "What you need is brains. Why should I start anything? Where's Tom Grayne?"

Andrew delivered Tom's message. He elaborated, remarking off his own bat that Ugly-face feared the hermit feeders might come scouting along the ledge, learn too much and turn out the whole monastery.

"So the tip is to clear out. Beat it for the sky line."

"You're remarkably thoughtful for me all at once," St. Malo answered.

But Andrew had expected that. He was ready for it. "We're afraid you might not get caught by the monks. We don't want a rat like you with eighteen men at our rear. We'll give you until two hours after daylight to go past our cavern—not a minute longer."

St. Malo retorted: "What if I don't choose to do it?"

Andrew didn't hesitate. "We've thought of that too. If you're not in sight by two hours after daybreak, we'll march. Our rearguard will shoot if they see you. Also, in that event, no handouts."

"I believe you're lying," said St. Malo.

"Think it over."

"I will. Meanwhile, you may go to hell, Mr. bloody Andrew Gunning— you and Tom Grayne, both of you."

He retreated into the tunnel, backward, leaving the rifle where it lay. That was too obvious: one of St. Malo's Tibetan riflemen was ambushed at the far end of the tunnel. Andrew ducked about a tenth of a second ahead of a bullet. Then he crept up to the tunnel mouth. Another bullet spat out of the darkness, but it missed him, and he got St. Malo's rifle—a good one; it had a telescopic sight. Someone had another shot at him while he edged along the side of the cave to the ledge and rejoined Tom.

"Where's Old Ugly-face?" he asked.

"I was too late," Tom said. "Missed him. Gone to watch 'em feed the hermits, I guess. Did you talk to St. Malo?—Okay, let's go."

"Where?"

"Follow Ugly-face."

"We'll have St. Malo at our backs," Andrew objected. "If he didn't fall for the bait, I'll eat his rifle. He'll come along behind us."

"Sure. That's the idea. Let's get well ahead of him."

They hurried along the ledge. Ten times Andrew could almost feel a bullet whizz by from behind. But he knew it must be imagination. Even if St. Malo were following, he couldn't possibly have seen them; Tom and he couldn't see each other. When Tom hesitated on the ledge to feel his way around an outleaning rock, Andrew bumped into him. Twice they almost fell together off the ledge. They didn't overtake Ugly-face. He might have fallen into the ravine for all they knew. There was no place where he could possibly have hidden. He couldn't have scaled the cliff, upward; there was no foothold; it was sheer wall, leaning slightly outward, and in places it was covered with ice.

After a while they saw a light moving, far away where the ledge turned leftward in a wide arc toward the monastery. Tom stopped then, in the lee of a rock.

"See 'em? That's the happy-blessed-hermit-feeding-company-of-pilgrims-on-the-path. That's what they call 'emselves."

"Only one lantern," said Andrew.

"Yes, but twenty-five or thirty monks. The number varies."

"Weapons?"

"You bet. Scared, too. They'd shoot at a shadow. They hate this job."

"Any place to hide near where the hermits are?"

"Not that I know of. We've got to find Ugly-face. Quick. Come on."

There wasn't a place where a bird could have hidden, all the way along that ledge until they reached the cliff that was pockmarked by hermits' caves. The moon appeared again for a moment, so they could see the caves clearly. They were irregular, at different levels, some only reachable by footholds cut in the rock. The highest ones were open to the weather and seemed to be unoccupied. All the others, except one, were closed up with mud and stone masonry, leaving a hole, about five feet from the floor, barely large enough for a man to have pushed his head through. But the nearest cave seemed to have been broken into. There was no sign of hermits—no lights—no sounds.

The approaching lantern was out of sight at the moment around a shoulder of the cliff. Tom and Andrew listened for sounds of St. Malo. They heard none. Then, suddenly, through the howling of the wind, they both caught the same sound at the same moment. It appeared to come from the direction of that one cave on the lower level that was only partially blocked up—the nearest one. They turned their flashlights on it. There was a gap in the masonry about three feet wide, extending to about two feet from the bottom. They only used their lights for about a quarter of a second. Both saw the same thing. A big hunk of rock appeared to raise itself and place itself exactly in the middle of the gap. It looked supernatural. Tom laughed:

"I told you there's no way to beat that old hellion! Come on, let's go help him."

His Holy Diplomatic Eminence, the Ringding Gelong Lama Lobsang Pun, alias Old Ugly-face, was inside the hermit's cave, busy immuring himself. First, though, he had pulled out from the cave the weather-mummied frozen carcass of a hermit, who had died since the last visit of the feeding patrol. He had dragged out the corpse through the gap made by brigands, who had searched the dead man's cave for sacred objects such as brigands need to keep away the devils who would otherwise accumulate like flies on the fat of their sinful pursuits. That carcass was good bait now. The oncoming monks would have to pause and say proper prayers, before pitching the remains over the cliff. It was a good enough bet for a prelate, wise in the ways of monks, that there, outside that cave, St. Malo would try to double-cross them all for much fine money.

CHAPTER 54

The moon had vanished. Old Ugly-face blinked at Tom's flashlight, detesting it. He looked like a great grim apparition from another world, too wise in the ways of inferior mortals to feel surprised at anything; but annoyed. He made no secret of his disapproval. If he felt friendly, he dissembled. In his eyes there was, perhaps, no enmity; but he withheld his praise. Having to shout against the howling wind increased the suggestion of irritation.

"Your being much presumptuous!"

"Where's Elsa?" Tom asked.

Ugly-face retorted: "My knowing. Why your not knowing?"

Andrew and Tom got the same hunch at the same moment: there was no time to lose. They barged into the cave and got busy. Andrew held the flashlight between his knees and passed the rocks. Tom laid two rocks in place. Old Ugly-face irritably pulled them down and began to replace them. There is probably an ordained angle at which hunks of diorite should block the opening of a hermit's cave. But Old Ugly-face was petulant, tired, nervous. Tom resumed the work and spoke to him, in Tibetan:

"Blessed-personage-acceptably-praying being more useful than ignorant labouring man." Then in English to Andrew: "Give him the torch to hold."

Andrew gave the torch to Ugly-face and went on playing mason's helper, passing the rocks as fast as Tom could lay them. There wasn't room for both of them to work in the gap. Old Ugly-face held the torch steady but he kept up a continuous growl of objections.

"Being danger in another's duty," he grumbled.

But Tom was well posted in Tibetan proverbs. "Being duty in another's danger," he retorted.

"Done badly. Their observing that wall not being properly build."

"Bless a blindness on them," Tom suggested.

"Devils using your mouth!" said Ugly-face.

He began flicking his beads with his thumb. They clicked like something loose being flicked by the wind. Tom worked like wildfire, but the mud was dry and frozen. There was no means of wetting it. The stones wouldn't stay in place without a lot of manipulating. The wall across the gap was only breast-high by the time they heard the chanting of the oncoming monks. They heard it in snatches because of the wind. Ugly-face switched off the light. They listened.

It was difficult to see, but easy to imagine what was happening. In the face of every one of the hermits' caves there was a hole about breast-high. Through that the hermit could pass out his water bottle to be filled. Then he could hold out one hand to receive his week's supply of parched barley. The feeding patrol, chanting and spinning their prayer wheels as they came, paused in front of each cave just long enough for a *mantra* and for the hermit to stick out his arm to receive the supplies. The monks were in a hurry to get back to their nice draughty cells in the monastery. Besides, they were afraid of brigands, and not notably fond of hermits, whose disdainful austerity might be held to imply a rebuke of monkish luxury and sloth in spiritual exercises.

So the procession came along fairly fast. It wasn't more than fifteen minutes before their enormous, parchment-covered iron lantern cast its rays into the opening. Tom and Andrew had to step back. Someone cried out then and the procession halted while the lantern bearer examined the corpse of the hermit that Old Ugly-face had laid in the way.

It was quite easy now to observe through the chinks in the rebuilt wall. There was an argument going on. The monks crowded one another for a look at the hermit's body. They seemed to be wondering how it got there. The lantern bearer was the important man; he stood gesticulating in a long yakskin overcoat, giving orders that no one obeyed. Ugly-face seemed to understand every one of his gestures. He appeared to decide that he now knew enough. He retreated to the back of the cave and sat down.

The lantern bearer's autocratic gestures became unmistakable at last. He commanded one man to recite the ritual for such occasions. He commanded another monk—a huge fellow armed with a sword, to go and examine the cave from which that hermit's body had been dragged. The monk refused. He was afraid. The lantern bearer struck him. All the other monks upheld the lantern bearer. So the big fellow with the sword came ahead, whirling his prayer wheel, clearly visible in silhouette against the lantern. His padded clothing and hood made him look bigger than he really was, but he was a giant at that. He looked like one of those tribesmen from the plains of northern Tibet, where the only possible survivors of the rigors of the climate are the stalwarts with huge lungs, big bones and iron physique.

"I can count thirteen rifles," Tom whispered.

"Oh, for a baseball bat!" said Andrew.

The big monk stuck his head and shoulders through the opening. His head was within two feet of Andrew's. He had a face like a stone devil's; stupid but more dangerous for that very reason. No predicting what a stupid man would do. But he couldn't see into the dark. Suddenly he turned around and shouted to the lantern bearer that the cave was empty. He said something about brigands. The lantern bearer shouted and gestured, evidently ordering him into the cave, then turned his back to watch four monks roll the dead hermit's body off the ledge. The giant watched that too, leaning against the rebuilt wall. Fearing the wall might collapse with his weight, Andrew leaned against it on the inside. The four monks seemed afraid to touch the hermit's frozen body with their hands. They kicked it, spinning prayer wheels to ward off the devils that hang around corpses, while some of them chanted fragments of the Ritual for the Dead, until the corpse rolled over the edge.

Then at last the giant monk began to climb into the opening, but his long overcoat made it difficult, so he pulled down a couple of rocks. After that, he leaned through for another good look before climbing in, and Tom nudged Andrew. They timed the play perfectly.

Tom's right and Andrew's left landed on the monk's jaw on either side simultaneously like a couple of clubs. He collapsed. They dragged him through.

"Lay him face downward," said Tom. "Then he'll give us warning— he'll try to turn over before he yells."

That fellow didn't stir for several minutes. There was no sound from Ugly face. Neither Tom nor Andrew had heard him come forward, but there he was, standing beside them within thirty seconds of their dragging in the monk. He had seen—sensed something. He knew something. He laid his hand on Andrew's lips. He prodded Tom, for silence. Then he peered through the opening, spreading his arms to prevent Tom and Andrew from doing the same thing. So Tom pulled down a stone, and so did Andrew.

St. Malo had come. He had one man with him, armed with a rifle. St. Malo also had a rifle. He looked like a Tibetan. He stood exactly in front of the opening of the cave, ten feet away, in the lantern light, and waited for the lantern bearer to accost him.

Old Ugly-face laid a hand on Andrew's shoulder. The strength of his grip was astonishing, but that was nothing compared to the daimonic vigour of his mind; it stirred something that responded. The thrill was commanding. It explained the difference between, say, a Napoleon and cannon fodder. The old Invincible was observing the enemy's error, calculating accurately how to turn it to his own use. One knew that.

The lantern bearer took his time about approaching St. Malo. St. Malo might be a leader of brigands. He took care to be covered by the rifles of the monks behind him. Other monks came crowding past and cut off the view from the cave. The wind wasn't quite so gusty now, but the monks were chattering like ravens at a feast, so it was very difficult to hear what was said. Tom and Andrew heard snatches, and had to piece those together.

There was no ceremony—none of those long-winded phrases that should precede any conversation between strangers in Tibet. St. Malo came straight to the point:

"Your Holy Abbot the Lord Regent Ram-pa Yap-shi has offered a reward in gold, for the capture and delivery alive of the deposed and now fugitive *lama* the ex-Lord Regent Lobsang Pun. I claim the reward."

The lantern bearer stepped on glare ice and very nearly fell off the ledge from excitement. All the other monks began to gabble advice.

Some of them wanted to seize St. Malo and drag him away to the monastery to tell his story to the Lord Abbot Ram-pa Yap-shi himself. But St. Malo had arrogant guts in a crisis—insolence beyond measure. He took the high hand, in a loud voice, that reached the cave in wind-blown snatches:

"After daybreak . . . armed men from the monastery . . . come where I direct . . . Bring the reward . . . gold . . . English measure . . . four loads . . . Weighed in my presence."

There was some discussion of that. Then:

"I will show you Lobsang Pun's hiding-place. You shall also capture his accomplices . . foreigners . . . may be lawfully slain . . . ponies, yaks, stores . . . no right to be in Tibet . . . tell Ram-pa Yap-shi . . . no tricks! . . . No gold, no Lobsang Pun. Go tell him."

After that, there was a hot quarrel. The monks surrounded St. Malo. Some of them were packed so tight against the cave that Tom and Andrew had to support the rebuilt wall to keep it from falling inward. They were all shouting, which was why they didn't hear the big prisoner. He had recovered consciousness and had to be jumped on, tied with his own girdle, gagged. That wasn't easy in the dark. He was nearly as strong as both men together. Andrew hammered his jaw with a rock to get his mouth open, shoved a glove in his mouth and tied the gag in with a strip torn from his own clothing. Old Ugly-face offered one of Andrew's blankets and they tied that around the man's head. He didn't smother, for some unfathomable reason.

The monks had their way with St. Malo. He and his man stood them off for a minute or two; they realised that he wouldn't be any use to them dead, so they weren't too violent. They took his rifle away and forced him to go with them to the monastery, to tell his story and make his own terms with Ram-pa Yap-shi. They were so excited—only monks can get as excited as they were—that they forgot all about their missing giant. They didn't even bother about feeding the last few hermits. They marched back toward the monastery, chanting, following the lantern bearer, with St. Malo and his man in their midst. Then the snow began falling—lots of it.

Old Ugly-face turned the flashlight on Tom and spoke English:

"Now my blessing you a hundred million blessings—now your going home—my thanking you too much."

"Home?" said Andrew.

Tom grinned. In the flashlight his face looked easy, almost instantly tolerant. But instead of answering Old Ugly-face he turned to Andrew:

670

"Leave this to me. I'll manage him. Go back to our cavern. Bring Elsa, and all the men, and two days' rations. Quicker the better."

The storm was getting well under way. When Andrew climbed out of the cave he could hardly stand against the wind—could hardly see a foot ahead through the driving snow.

Bring Elsa—along that ledge?—in such a storm as this one? He turned his flashlight on the cave, for a last look, to make sure of his bearings. Old Ugly-face was letting Tom help him through the gap. In an open, unoccupied cave higher up, was a shadow that caught his eye through the driving snow because it seemed to move and he could imagine no reason why it should move. But when he focused the flashlight on it there was only a heap of stones on the ledge. He turned away, facing the storm.

"God damn!" he muttered. "That looked like Elsa."

CHAPTER 55

That night's storm had one redeeming feature-lightning. Hail, rain, snow alternated. The wind blew with hurricane force, sometimes from two directions at once because it roared along converging valleys. Sometimes it blew Andrew against the cliff with such force that he couldn't move. At other times he clung to the cliff to keep from being blown off it—with one hand frozen; he had used his left glove to gag the giant monk. The lightning was like a barrage bursting in no-man's land. It made a swaying, fantastic horror of the thousand-foot drop into the ravine. But it did reveal the ledge.

There's a limit to what a human being can take in the way of punishment and still retain will power. There's a point at which quitting begins to look like common sense. Andrew came closer to quitting, that night, than he cared to confess, except to himself in secret. For one thing, he felt sure St. Malo's men would be keeping a lookout near the mouth of their cave. They weren't likely to trust Tom and Andrew's Tibetans to keep cover. On the other hand, they might even have overcome their own fear of storm devils and have crept out to take the cavern by surprise, grab the booty and run.

Barring human jacks-in-office, there is no worse bully in the world than a storm at high altitudes. A bullied man's brain can suggest a hundred mad reasons for doing the wrong thing. Andrew even thought of entering St. Malo's cave and trying to drive a bargain with his men. He could tell them St. Malo had been captured by Ram-pa Yap-shi's monks and carried off to the monastery. But there would be seventeen men to deal with. And Andrew was numb with cold. He thought better of it—if it was thought.

By the time he had struggled as far as the entrance to St. Malo's cave, he was too exhausted for much else than instinctive action. It was habit that carried him on—the habit of finishing what he had said he would do. He crossed the entrance to St. Malo's cave on hands and knees, waiting for the lightning to reveal the inside of the cave. The wind howled into it, and through the short tunnel beyond. Added to that tumult were terrific peals of thunder—one continuous din that echoed and re-echoed. A man couldn't have fought his way out of the tunnel against the hurricane force of the storm. At one moment a blast of hail swept into the cave so fiercely that it sounded like machine-gun bullets. Some of that hail was sharp enough to rip the leather of Andrew's overcoat.

Two more miles of ledge—a waking nightmare. The last half-mile was something like the last round of a fight, in which the bell may save the loser from a knockout if he can only hang on. Andrew hung on. He made it. And Bompo Tsering was keeping a lookout, in spite of storm and devils. Lightning lighted, in the whirling sleet, Andrew must have looked like a devil. Bompo Tsering fired at him. He fell, unhit but exhausted. Bompo Tsering and two others dragged him into the cavern, where they chafed his numbed legs and arms.

It was warm in there. The barricade across the ledge served as a windbreak. The tent, stretched across the entrance, howled and thundered like a topsail at sea, but it made the place habitable.

Andrew couldn't speak for a while. His first words were: "Where's the Lady Elsa?"

They all shook their heads. Bompo Tsering suspected Andrew's motive. The question must be a trick:

"Your not knowing?" he demanded.

"Damn your eyes! If I did know, would I ask? Come on now! Answer! What happened?"

Then, cleaning his Mauser carefully, pausing every few words for confirmation from the other men, Bompo Tsering told how Elsa had gone with His Holiness Lobsang Pun.

"Did she say nothing?"

"No, Gunnigun."

"Didn't she write a message?"

"No, Gunnigun."

Andrew believed and refused to believe it. He grabbed a lantern and climbed the ramp. It was all dark in the upper cavern. All was in order. He opened the brief-case—examined the straps of the bedding rolls—every place he could think of where Elsa might have left a scrap of writing to explain her movements. There were the remains of the food he had carried up for her. He sat down where she had sat, and ate what she had left—thinking—thinking—while the flickering lantern cast ghoulish shadows on the walls and the wind in the opening where Ugly-face had sat howled like lost souls in torment.

Presently he felt the not yet familiar glide of consciousness into other dimensions. He saw Elsa. Very distinctly. Looking straight at him. It was one of those dream-like visions, much more intensely vivid than the sight called real. Like other visions that he had seen since he knew Elsa, it was composite, timeless, spaceless. In one and the same moment, she was as he had first seen her in this same cavern, with Tom; simultaneously he saw again all that long journey to Darjeeling. He saw himself, objectively as through a camera lens, delivering her child, in a storm, by the light of a burning packing case. Darjeeling. The monastery. Nancy Strong's house and Morgan Lewis. The incident at Gombaria's, and then the trail again—the return to the cavern—the completed circle—all that had been said and done until now—this moment. And this moment looked like farewell. It looked like a glimpse of another life. Was Elsa dead?

Or was she doing what she had said Old Ugly-face habitually did— thinking with such power that her image entered the imagination of the one she thought of? It might be. He had been thinking of her. And he remembered she had said something else. He had joked about it at the time. Elsa's face began to recede into nowhere, until only melancholy eyes remained. Then they, too, vanished.

He felt nervously disturbed, all the more so because there was no one with whom he could share the experience. Even to himself he couldn't describe it in words. Had it been a signal? If Elsa were dead, could she possibly project a vision of herself into his consciousness? He had heard of it being done. He had even read of it. But he didn't believe it. No. No. No. In Shanghai he had seen a Chinese necromancer produce one after another accurate visions of men and women dead numbers of years. But Andrew had proved that was a trick, by substituting, in his own mind, one memory for another. He had found he could control the necromancer.

But he couldn't control this vision of Elsa. He couldn't restrain, or reduce, or suppress the pain it gave him—the heart stab—the nostalgic yearning.

Was that her yearning? Or his? Was it farewell?

Was that Elsa whom he had seen through the whirling snow, above the dead hermit's cave, when he left Old Ugly-face and Tom?

Snatching up the lantern he looked around once more for a written message. He found none. Then he shook himself—flexed his muscles—threw off a mood, and started for the lower cavern. He felt better. He supposed he had been so exhausted that emotion got the better of him. Elsa was Tom's wife. Hell damn it, he could go Tom Grayne one better if it came to a tug of Stoicism. Self-control, discipline, self-respect-dignity, decency— those are the substance of things hoped for. The hell with theft. The hell with ends unjustified by means.

He laughed at his own sententiousness as he descended the ramp. He was feeling much better. He had thrown off a perilous mood that came near losing him his will to do Tom Grayne no treachery in thought, or word, or deed. He had not even let treachery enter his mind, although he had felt its pressure.

He helped himself to tea from the Tibetans' urn—swallowed two cupfuls of the nauseating bilge, spat out half of a third cupful, and then tackled the problem of getting the Tibetans out of the cavern. It had to be done quickly. At the first mention of what he intended, Bompo Tsering refused point-blank. He mutinied. He quoted Tibetan sacred scripture, to confound Andrew and to strengthen his own obstinacy:

"Nobly born, the lesser of two evils always being the greater good. Sin and folly being sister harlots. Having commerce with them causing too much evil. Nay, my not going."

Bompo Tsering's smile suggested that Andrew was one against many. He placed a roll of bedding for him with his own hands, offered more tea, and remarked:

"Tum-Glain being boss now. Your not being boss no longer."

He couldn't have done Andrew a more signal favour; all he needed was opposition. It aroused his fighting humour, and there are more ways than one of fighting. He used genius, if leadership is that. If it isn't, he used some other intangible quality that has never failed him who counts on it, by land or sea.

"You Tibetans aren't murderous people," he said. "Your religion forbids. You poison your friends and rob your enemies. But you've a conscience. When you get hysterical you're like any other mob, with fifty thousand superstitious impulses added. But on the whole you're swell people. You can laugh at yourselves."

"My not understanding," said Bompo Tsering.

"You will. You'll catch on in a minute."

"Our not going out in storm," said Bompo Tsering, buttering his obstinacy with a smile. He had changed from "my" to "our." He felt the need of support. Andrew noticed that.

"You've come a long march with me," said Andrew, "in winter and spring. A long, hard march, at great risk. We were hunted by brigands and soldiers. We worked like the devil. We didn't always have enough to eat; and frequently we nearly died of cold. You and I were almost drowned three times—once when a ferry upset; twice in ice-bound rivers, when the ice broke. We escaped from pursuit. We rescued His Holy Eminence the Ringding Gelong Lama Lobsang Pun, and—"

"Thus acquiring too much merit," Bompo Tsering interrupted. "Nobly born Gunnigan, your needing much merit in lives to come. Such excellent merit as this perhaps saving you from many hells that your otherwise enduring after this death soon."

Andrew took up where he left off: "You've come all this way, and endured all that hardship, and acquired all that merit, only to chuck it away tonight—merit and money and—"

Bompo Tsering glanced around the cavern. Trade goods. Provisions. Clothing. Blankets. Yaks. Ponies. Sheep. And no doubt money in one of the loads. His thought was quite clear. Andrew didn't wait for him to voice it.

"Unless you obey me," he said, "I'm going to shoot all these animals. You and the men couldn't carry the loads very far. You'd soon be overtaken by the monastery monks. You know what they'd do to you: they'd turn you loose naked to cherish your sins in the snow. That 'ud be a fine reward for months of hardship such as you have borne so bravely. Don't you think you're a fool?"

Bompo Tsering answered smiling: "Gunnigun, we blessed Tibetans obeying higher law." But his grin, in the quivering lantern light, looked vaguely less confident. He spun his prayer wheel.

"I'm going now," said Andrew, "to help Tum-Glain and His Reverend Eminence Lobsang Pun. First, I will shoot the animals and take your money. You may do as you please and take the consequences. Your wife won't miss you; she has six other husbands, you adulterous dog. As for those hells you speak of, I shall mention your conduct to Lobsang Pun. He can bless—"

Bompo Tsering interrupted: "His Holiness having blessed us all, especially me!"

675

"And he can curse! How many of the curses of Lobsang Pun are needed to obliterate his blessings that a fool sees fit to throw away?"

"Nobly born, this is terrible talk," said Bompo Tsering.

"I have been told," said Andrew, "there are seven hells, and the worst is reserved for fools, who sold their store of merit for the sake of momentary comfort."

He made that up, that moment, on the spur of necessity. There are volumes of books about Tibetan hells, written by men who believe they remember them. But Andrew had never read those books. Bompo Tsering hadn't either, so the breaks were even.

"Maybe there being something in what your saying," Bompo Tsering admitted. "Life short time. Hell long time. Yes." He began hunting for justification. "Those men—" he pointed to the phony *lama* and the other culprits—"being hungry, no can do. Tum-Glain for punishment saying no tea, no food."

"Feed 'em," Andrew retorted.

But that gave another excuse. Bompo Tsering pounced on it: "Your not being Tum-Glain. Tum-Glain saying no, not feeding them."

"Very well. Shall we leave them behind us to plunder the loads?"

"That being too sinful. No, no!"

"And the sin," Andrew observed profoundly, "would be on your head. You would be the hell-bound fool who let them do it! Aren't you ashamed of yourself?"

Bompo Tsering smiled. There was no shame in him; only guts, superstition, good humour, liking for Andrew, and natural dislike of danger.

"Nobly born, your knowing too much," he answered. "My choosing lesser of two evils. My obeying you, then what happening being your fault." He chuckled. Then he added: "But let us take the animals. Being better letting beasts struggle against storm, leaving us strong at end of journey."

Only a Tibetan could have suggested that, with that storm raging. He knew what the ledge was like. The ponies were utterly out of the question; the poor scarecrow brutes couldn't have kept their foothold for a minute. The sheep could have balanced themselves, but what use would they be, except as food later on? In a bad storm, a sheep lies down and quits; they would have had to be carried. A Tibetan will carry a tired sheep until he has to lie down and die beside it. But Andrew had no use that night for dead sheep or dead Tibetans. The yaks might have carried them. But you have to blindfold a yak and mount him by vaulting on over his rump. After that, when you remove the blindfold he goes where he pleases. If they could have got the yaks past the barricade and started along the ledge, they could have kept their foothold. But a yak, especially when in single file, has a neat little trick of going crazy in a storm. And Tibetans have strange ideas about animals. They will jump on top of the loads and ride an already over-burdened beast up a steep hill. If anything goes wrong they will call it the animal's karma. At the top of the hill they will get off, to "double the easiness going down hill." No, the yaks, too, were out of the question. It broke Bompo Tsering's honest heart to leave those animals in comfort in the cavern with plenty of food and water, where, as he objected, brigands or St. Malo's men might come and steal them. Every Tibetan is almost as superstitious about brigands as he is about *dugpas* and devils. But Andrew couldn't be persuaded.

He won the argument finally by telling Bompo Tsering to choose his yak and try to drive it outside into the storm. The yak chased him all over the cavern. That put everyone into a good temper and after that there was not much trouble. They loaded themselves with two days' rations of canned food, in addition to a small bag of dry barley for each man, and the inevitable tea urn. They were full of virtue—eager to acquire more merit, now that Bompo Tsering had made up their minds for them. They roughhoused the phony *lama* and his fellow culprits out into the open. Bompo Tsering flatly refused to disobey Tom's order not to feed them. He declared they had been let off too lightly: they should have been shot or thrown over the cliff. However, he compromised by bringing them along some extra barley, so that if Tom should choose to let them off part of their punishment they could feed them without depriving themselves. Then the real battle began. Bompo Tsering warned Andrew not to lead the way along the ledge.

"Nobly born, come last! Bring up the rear!"

He said it wasn't safe to trust some of the men—not safe to have them behind him. They might turn back. They might make other kinds of trouble.

"True. Then that's your job," said Andrew. "You bring up the rear."

He gave Bompo Tsering a full load for his Mauser, not for use, but for his spiritual comfort. All Tibetans believe Mauser pistols are the one infallible weapon. Even when the darned things jam, they still believe it. Mauser pistols are white man's magic.

Then Andrew led stubbornly, not too fast, although it was a race between life and death—against time and the elements. The storm increased in violence. Hail, rain and snow in alternate blasts iced up the ledge. It sloped out in places. The force of the wind doubled. One man was blown into the ravine, but Andrew didn't know about that until afterwards. He couldn't see a yard. He couldn't hear the man next behind him, though he shouted the news at the top of his lungs. Anyhow, it was one of the phony *lama's* men, so he didn't much matter. He wasn't carrying a load. His loss made the phony *lama* easier to manage later on.

Although he had covered the distance twice before during the night, Andrew couldn't recall landmarks. He couldn't judge time by distance, or distance by time, because he had to slow down wherever the ice was bad. He had to lead blindly, trusting faculties that all men have but only few can use. He was raging within, damning the guts of Old Ugly-face for having dared to mislead Elsa.

"God Almighty, he's as good as a murderer! She'd have obeyed him, whatever he said! Couldn't he forbid her to follow him?"

Anger was the fuel that kept him going, until intuition warned him he was near the mouth of St. Malo's cave. The wind confirmed it by the change in its tumult as it howled into the cave and through the short tunnel beyond.

He craved no fight with St. Malo's men. He approached, groping his way as alertly as numbed muscles and ice-covered rock would permit. Judging by the change in the sound, he had just reached the edge of the opening of the cave, where the ledge was a little wider, when a hand reached out from total darkness, seized him by the shoulder and dragged him into the mouth of the pitch-black cave. He struck out with all the strength he had left—hit nothing. A hand seized his wrist. He heard a voice close to his ear:

"This is Tom Grayne. Keep your hair on!"

Andrew cursed him. "Damn your soul to hell! Do you know where Elsa is? Do you know what's happened to her?"

They couldn't see each other. They couldn't hear without shouting. Tom thrust his face close to Andrew's:

"Wasn't she in the cavern?"

"No!"

"Then she's here!" Tom shouted. "Must be! Unless she's fallen off the ledge, there's nowhere else she can be! I believe she made a trade with St. Malo!"

"You do?"

"Yes. Martyr complex!"

"Nuts!" Andrew yelled at him. "Nuts! Do you hear me—nuts!" He wanted to crash his fist into Tom's mouth. He backed away for fear he might do it. Tom followed him, shouting against the wind:

"She's lost! It's your fault! Why in hell did you bring her?"

Andrew suddenly grew calm. He had to shout, but the anger was gone:

"You mean, you've lost her! She has broken her heart—turned *chela*! But come on—what's your game here? Let's get busy!"

Chapter 56

One by one Andrew's column filed like ghosts into the cave. Tom counted them as they passed into total darkness where a curve of the wall afforded protection from the wind.

"One missing," he shouted.

Bompo Tsering reported the man dead. Then Andrew asked:

"Where's Old Ugly-face?"

Tom cupped his hands to Andrew's ear and shouted angrily: "Disarm St. Malo's men and we'll go find out."

There was no sign of St. Malo's men, but Tom expected them. In a moment or two there came a light along the tunnel. The wind blew it out. Tom switched on a flashlight but directed it away from the tunnel, outward, toward the ledge, leaving everyone in darkness. After that they heard men in the tunnel, fighting against the wind. Tom cupped his hands again:

"I've told St. Malo's men that he's a prisoner and they'll be scuppered by the monastery monks unless they join us. That scared 'em. They're bringing out their loads. That'll make 'em clumsy. Take 'em one at a time. Bring Bompo Tsering here."

Andrew crossed the cave, ordered the men to be quiet, gave Bompo Tsering his flashlight and led him to where Tom was standing. Then he stood facing Tom, one on each side of the tunnel. He knew what Tom was expecting, and he hated him for it. He wondered what Tom would do if Elsa should show up with St. Malo's men. He knew she wouldn't, but he couldn't help wondering. It gave him a hunch. He cupped his hands and shouted to Bompo Tsering:

"No kill! Fool 'em with the light! No kill!"

The pitch-dark tunnel was filled with tumult; the men in it could neither see nor hear. They came out one by one, too heavily burdened to use their rifles, and believing they had only Tom to deal with.

Bompo Tsering did a swell job. He flashed the light on his own men, letting the first man in the tunnel see them for a second, confusing him. He tried to back, but bumped into the man behind him. Andrew jerked the rifle out of his hands. Tom's fist knocked him spinning on the cave floor, where he was pounced on by Bompo Tsering's men. Andrew flung the rifle out into the night.

The second man was more alert than the first. Tom had to hit him hard. He stumbled into Andrew and fought for his rifle, but Andrew twisted it out of his hands and hurled it after the first one. The third man was easier; Tom tackled him single-handed. Then it was Andrew's turn, and by that time Bompo Tsering's gang had caught on and were waiting like wolves to pounce. The floor was becoming littered up with, men and loads. It was almost like a shambles, where the steers come one by one along a passage. Only the last of the seventeen gave any real trouble. He was suspicious. He had come last on purpose. He went down on his hands and knees in the tunnel and tried to peer into the cave. He didn't move until Bompo Tsering used the flashlight again. Then he shot at the flashlight, missed, and Andrew went in after him. He dived under Andrew, to grab his legs, but Andrew kicked free and got behind him to block his retreat. Tom was in the tunnel by that time. So the last man went out, rifle and all, head first into the glare of Bompo Tsering's flashlight, where he fought pluckily and had to be beaten half unconscious.

"You stay here," Tom shouted. "I'm going on in." He had to shout three times before there was a lull in the wind and Andrew understood what he said.

Then Andrew got out of the tunnel and took charge. St. Malo's men were professional brigands. They couldn't be given a break or they'd take quick advantage of it. It was all to St. Malo's credit as a conman that they had made the toilsome march from Sinkiang to meet him, probably on his bare promise of loot. Even if they were escaped felons, with only pursuit at their rear and no future but what St. Malo offered, nevertheless he must have made them believe in him. But now St. Malo was a prisoner. They were puzzled, bewildered, disposed to preserve their lives on any terms, and in no hurry to make matters worse for themselves.

For the moment, Andrew's own men were the more dangerous. Too many loads of loot. Too many loaded rifles had not yet been thrown over the cliff. Even Bompo Tsering, who could be sensible about some things, wanted to pack three rifles for himself as well as his own bag of rations and one of the plundered loads. He and his men mutinied when Andrew began chucking rifles into the ravine. They threatened to make common cause with St. Malo's men. Andrew had a tough two minutes. It was dark. A couple of flashlights weren't much help. He didn't want to kill anyone. Certainly he wouldn't start the shooting—there'd have been a shambles in ten seconds. But it would have been madness to leave those captured rifles within reach of the punishment squad.

In the glare of the flashlight he grabbed that last man to come through the tunnel, who had fought so hard and had given the most trouble. He was rubbing his ear and still unsteady on his feet, but beginning to think.

"What's your name?"

"Ga-pa-dug. My being headman."

Andrew had him by the throat, but he grinned into Andrew's face, cheerfully impudent. He shouted in the teeth of the wind:

"Your giving back our rifles-our making your men obey."

He shouted so loud that Bompo Tsering heard it and relayed it to his men. No Tibetan craves to be bossed by brigands. Andrew snatched a rifle from the nearest man, threatened to break skulls with it, and within sixty seconds rifles were being pitched over the ledge as if they weren't worth a dollar a piece.

Then Bompo Tsering rose to the occasion. It was a heartbreaker to have lost those precious rifles, but it was wonderful to be on the winning side. He approved of Andrew—gave him credit for having tricked Ga-pa-dug to say exactly what he wanted him to say. That amused, inspired, encouraged him. He turned to and helped to line up all St. Malo's men against the wall, with his own men staggered between them at proper intervals to prevent ganging up. He saw the point, too, of compelling St. Malo's men to carry their own burdens:

"Their carrying now! Our taking later on. Good."

Then Tom came out of the tunnel, cursing when Bompo Tsering turned the flashlight on him. He looked humiliated—mortified—ashamed—consequently furious. He snatched the flashlight from Bompo Tsering and used his own, too.

"Where are the rifles?" he demanded.

Andrew answered him: "Over the cliff."

He nodded—made no other comment. He was in no mood to praise Andrew. He inspected the prisoners one by one, going up close

681

to each man, looking him straight in the eyes. Andrew understood very well that Tom was recovering some kind of peace with himself; so he waited patiently. He allowed him all the time he needed. He was seeing Elsa again—eyes, then her whole face, quite apart from the darkness and in no way affected by it. He couldn't understand what it meant, although he felt sure it was a message. Warning? Summons?

He wondered that Tom couldn't see it. But Tom was seeing only his own necessities. He came and asked Andrew to lead the way along the ledge.

"Get going. I'll bring up the rear."

So Andrew led. The storm was worse than ever. At intervals he waited, in the lee of dykes and broken rocks, to let the straggling column catch up; but he could never be sure how many had caught up. All the way he was out of touch with Tom. Along the worst parts of the ledge he had to wait for the lightning to show the way. They were inside a snow cloud. It felt solid. They could hardly breathe. It wasn't so cold as it had been and the wind wasn't quite so strong, but it piled up all the more snow for that reason. They had to shove snow off the ledge before they could crawl forward. It came so fast that it was all piled up again before the next man crossed the cleared space. But the Tibetans couldn't have turned back without having to face Tom's Mauser. The third or fourth or fifth man might have got to him and hurled him over the ledge. But there was no one to lead the mutiny. One by one St. Malo's men dropped their loads over the cliff, unable to struggle with them any farther. The column followed its leader.

The night was far spent when Andrew crawled on to the widening end of the ledge where the hermits' caves were, and staggered to his feet. Then he stood aside, waiting for Tom, counting the men as they hurried to the dead hermit's cave for shelter. Bompo Tsering waited beside Andrew, after crashing into him in a chaos of snow that was snatched up from the ledge and wind-whipped into their faces. He seemed cheerful enough. He shouted, spinning his prayer wheel:

"This happy blessed country being too many devils their wanting it too much! No can get it!"

Andrew ordered him into the hermit's cave, to keep the men from coming out until wanted. In passing he struck Andrew with his prayer wheel, on purpose, as a precaution, to prevent devils from getting him. Andrew called him back:

"Try to make friends with Ga-pa-dug."

He struck again, and then hurried away before Andrew's special private devils could invent a crazier task.

At last Tom came. He and Andrew walked together to where the ledge widened and turned a corner and there was less wind. Intuition—instinct—something guided them. They pointed their flashlights suddenly in the same direction. At the end, of the zone of light, someone, whose back was toward them, stood talking to Old Ugly-face—two black phantoms nearly smothered in snow, gesticulating, shouting to each other against the wind. Then lightning—and incredible scores of phantoms—naked. Like a Doré illustration of Dante's *Inferno*.

Forked lightning. A huge cliff, pockmarked with dark holes. Tumbled stone and broken masonry near the mouths of the holes. A ledge that ribboned into darkness. To the left, beneath the ledge, a sheer drop into swirling chaos. Phantoms along the ledge—so many they were uncountable. Naked. Stark naked. Scrawny and bearded and some of them old. They squatted along the rim of the ledge staring downward into that horrible abyss as if it were a hearth toward which they yearned. They didn't move much. Even when forked lightning shattered the darkness and they were as clearly outlined as by a photographer's magnesium flash, they didn't seem to move. Except that their hair blew in the wind, they might have been gargoyles carved of rock.

One thing was clear. Old Ugly-face had broken open the cells and turned out the hermits. They hadn't clothing, food or weapons. Some of them looked too old and feeble to march half a mile; those were the fanatical ascetics, whose only ambition was to starve their bodies slowly into useless clay, that their souls might grow and they need not return to earth after death and be encumbered by new bodies and endure more austerities. But those were a small minority. Most of them were sinewy stalwarts, all the stronger for their ordeal—theological students—the everlasting miracle of Tibet strength of will and body achieved by abstinence and conquest of desire—authority attained through passionate humility. Old Ugly-face had gone through that ordeal in years gone by. He had lived stark naked. So he understood hermits.

Between peals of thunder Tom yelled in Andrew's ear: "The old man's crazy! He's counting on hermits to force the monastery gates!"

Andrew hardly heard him. He stared, waiting for the lightning flashes. At last he gripped Tom's arm:

"Do you know who that is talking to him?"

Tom didn't speak. When Andrew turned the flashlight on him he merely nodded.

"Won't you go speak to her?"

"No."

"Then I will."

"Suit yourself."

"Come with me."

"No. I'm through."

"What d'you mean?"

"She has wiped my eye! She knew damned well I'd planned to be Old Ugly-face's *chela!*"

"Says you! How should she know? Did you tell her?"

"She knew all right. Go ahead—you talk to her. Don't mention me. I'll wait here."

Andrew strode forward alone.

CHAPTER 57

Old Ugly-face saw Andrew coming. A crackling flash of lightning revealed the old prelate's glittering eyes and every grained wrinkle on his face. He made no sign of recognition. He turned his back and walked away toward the hermits, saluted by a cannonade of thunder that sounded like bursting mountains. Then Elsa turned and faced Andrew. He couldn't tell whether she welcomed him or not—whether she was surprised or not. There wasn't much of her visible under the peaked hood as she braced herself against the wind.

The storm had reached its crisis. It began to exhaust itself in spastic squalls that tore rocks loose and sent them rolling over the abyss. A broken ice dam loosed a torrent across the ledge; poured out fifty feet into the wind before it curved downward and was lost in the dark whirling uproar. It was impossible to speak. Andrew threw an arm, around Elsa. He almost lifted her off her feet. She made no protest. She let him half carry, half drag her across the ledge to an empty hermit's cave, where the hollow roar within was silence compared to the tumult outside. There she braced herself, back to the wall. He used his flash-light. She shook her head. After that they spoke when they could see each other by the flash of forked lightning, and when they could hear between peals of thunder.

"Take your glove, Andrew." She was breathless. "This is yours, isn't it?"

It felt like a gift glove. He pulled it on. "Where did you get it?"

"From the big monk—you gagged with it—in the dead hermit's cave. He recognized Lobsang Pun—loves him—would die for him. Lobsang Pun has sent him—to the monastery, to confirm St. Malo's story."

Andrew had no suspicion how stern he looked and sounded: "Where were you when St. Malo came?"

"In the cave above. You saw me when you went away. Didn't you?"

"Yes," he answered. "Saw. But I didn't believe. I went and looked for you, back in our cavern."

She had recovered her breath now—spoke as measuredly as he: "Did you see me there?"

"Yes."

"I meant—I hoped you would."

"I saw you, very clearly. But I didn't understand. I got no message.— When did you get here?"

"Before you did. I came with Lobsang Pun. When he looked in on you, in the entrance of St. Malo's cave, along there on the ledge, I was close behind him—almost touching him, ready to cling if the wind should—"

Andrew swore with concentrated vigour: "Lobsang Pun shall answer for it! Damn him!"

"Answer for what, Andrew?"

"For bringing you here. Why did you give us the slip? Why didn't you stay in our cavern?"

He couldn't hear her laugh because thunder out-crashed all other sound. Perhaps she only smiled. The lightning revealed her pale face, bright-eyed, merry with unexpected humour. When the thunder rolled its echoes away after it and ceased, she asked him:

"Andrew, if I had asked you, would you have brought me here? Would you have let me come?"

He laid his hands on her shoulder. She put her hands on his.

"No," he answered, unsmiling.

She nodded. Then he surprised her:

"I've no right to let or not let."

Her eyes widened. Her hands fell. She clasped them in front of her. "Your life is yours," said Andrew. "What are you planning to do with it?"

"Must I tell?"

"No. You don't have to."

"I've already told. I told you in the cavern."

"I didn't listen."

She looked puzzled. "But now, if I tell, you will listen?"

"Yes."

"Why?"

"I've been talking to Tom Grayne."

Her eyes tried to read his while the zigzag lightning tore the storm apart; but all that she saw resembled anger, and beneath it the veil she could almost never penetrate. When thunder ceased again she asked:

"Andrew, how is Tom taking it?"

"Badly."

"Did he speak of me?"

"Yes."

"He knows I'm here. He saw me. Does he understand now that I didn't even think of joining St. Malo?"

"Yes. He knows that."

Thunder silenced them again. Lightning showed them to each other, in shimmering flashes that brought the cave walls leaping out of darkness. A furious squall battered the ledge with hail. Then, relatively, there was quiet.

"Andrew—is there something I should do to help Tom—to make it easier?"

"There's always something," he answered, "but second-hand stuff's no good."

"You mean I should go and speak to him?"

"No. You should do what you choose, off your own bat."

She nodded. "I don't feel vindictive. But I don't choose to speak first. I haven't told you what he said, ten minutes after we met."

"Don't tell me."

"Andrew, what is there I can do?"

"I know what I'll do," he answered. "I'll stand by Tom until he needs me no longer."

"He doesn't need me," Elsa objected. "He said so."

"After that I'm off home to America. I guess that'll be soon. I know Tom's intention."

"What? What is it? Tell me!"

"He told me in confidence."

The storm was fighting a rear-guard action now, bringing up new batteries of thunder to mask the main retreat that rolled away along the valley southward. Frenzied blasts of wind shrieked like charging devils, reached their objective and died. Then speech was possible again.

"One night you told me about what you will do in America."

"I'll take the first job that offers. One thing leads to another. I won't forget what I've learned. I guess I'll do what I know."

He laughed. The humour of it suddenly occurred to him: a little personal equation was lifting its head amid almost cosmic grandeur. And why "almost"? Reality was there—then—eternally—now—that minute—microcosm within macrocosm. It was his to command—part of his consciousness—his to mould as he pleased.

He didn't hesitate. He took Elsa into his arms—hugged her to him—kissed her storm-wet face until she sobbed for breath— struggling. He didn't know his own strength.

"Andrew, please—please!"

Tom Grayne came in then, using his flashlight. He had the generosity to switch it off. He had the self-control to wait for one of them to speak.

Andrew said quietly: "Elsa will come with me to America, as soon as this show's over."

Tom used his flashlight again. He was about to speak. Elsa burst in ahead of him:

"No, Andrew, no! Tom, it isn't true!"

"I wouldn't share a wife with my best friend," Tom answered.

Andrew cautioned him: "Easy!"

Elsa thrust herself between them. "Tom! Andrew! Please! Listen to me! I'm not worth fighting for! This is all my fault—all of it! Andrew, I will no more be a load on you—ruin your life—than I'll consent to spoil Tom's any longer!"

"Your life's your own," Andrew answered. "I have asked you to share it with me."

"I know, I know! Oh, Andrew, you're too generous to live! You think I'm helpless, so you offer—"

"I asked," said Andrew.

"Andrew, I couldn't accept that, even if—even if—"

"I do," he interrupted. "I have loved you since before Darjeeling."

"Andrew, please don't blaspheme! You know that isn't true! It couldn't be. You're being generous and—"

He interrupted again: "Tom—turn your light on both of us.— Now, Elsa—in the presence of Tom Grayne—chin up—I love you. Do you love me?"

She couldn't answer. She stared, wide-eyed. He repeated:

"I love you with all my heart. Do you love me?"

She spoke suddenly, in gasps because her heart was thumping:

"Andrew, it's too late! I have asked Lobsang Pun to take me as his *chela*—"

She stopped—stared. Tom followed her gaze. He moved the flashlight, turning half around to face the entrance.

The light framed Old Ugly-face.

The wind had died. Like a back drop behind him, snow fell in big silent flakes that looked like shredded gold in the rays of the electric torch.

CHAPTER 58

There was no wind now, but a hushed silence, in which the soft snowfall was almost audible. Except that his eyes glittered in the light of Tom Grayne's torch, Old Ugly-face looked like a statue wonderfully carved from grained wood—an image of the daemon of the storm—who had compelled the storm to cease—hooded—dripping with thawing snow—contemptuously angry. At last he spoke:

"Faggot! Three fools in one! Tied in one bundle by knots of fear!"

"Fear of what?" Andrew demanded.

Elsa shuddered. Andrew was too calm. He was an explosion—conceived—on the brink of becoming. She reached for his hand—held it. He crushed her fingers until she could hardly endure the pressure. But she did endure it, in silence—until Old Ugly-face said sternly:

"Fearing means being end, and end being means!"

Elsa's right hand disengaged Andrew's fingers. She chafed her own, then took his hand again, knowing a scapegoat is an almost irresistible temptation. She herself—how often!—had been whipping girl for the relief of prejudices that had power to be cruel. Ministers, teachers, parents had habitually vented hatred on her that was really hatred of their own grossness. More than once Tom had forgotten dignity; reason, justice. She could forgive Tom's outbreaks; him she no longer loved, nor did she wish him to love her. But the dread that Andrew might behave unmanly made her heart sick. She prayed for him, almost in words aloud.

Old Ugly-face continued to answer Andrew: "Seeking spirit! Three hungry jackals sniffing blood from far-off!" He paused. "Seeking vision! Ravens pecking eyes of corpses!" A longer pause. Then, with rising scorn: "Hunting happiness! Pigs rooting for fallen fruit to glut their bellies!" He thrust out his lower lip. His eyes glittered indignation: "Your begging favours—of me!"

Silence. He had such power that waiting seconds became aeons of humiliation—eternities, in which to fall from self-esteem into the stagnant deeps of self-contempt. It was beyond Elsa's endurance that Andrew should be so cast down. She pleaded:

"Father Mahatma—"

Old Ugly-face rebuked her savagely: "Your calling me by that blessed name, your lying tongue soon bearing false witness against you also! My being less than dirt at my Master's feet!"

Silence again. He glared at Andrew, his lips moving amid the wrinkles as if he chewed on words to moisten them. He selected a phrase—hurled it:

"Life!—Liberty!—P'soot of happiness!" His gesture was like the down-turned thumb of a Vestal. "Life too small, too short for your stupidity—if your thinking liberty and do-as-damn-please being same thing!"

Andrew showed interest. The far-away lightning stabbed the dying night. Thunder rolled sullenly. Old Ugly-face raised a huge prayer wheel that he had taken from some hermit; it looked like a mace from a house of parliament. In its bronze bulb, that revolved when shaken, were a thousand incantations written on scraps of parchment. Each turn of the shaken wheel was a thousand blessings on the footsteps of the pilgrims on the Path from mortal matter—nothingness to spiritual being. He shook the thing at Andrew again and again:

"My telling you! Your listening! P'soot of happiness being same as running away from happiness! Idiot! How can your p'sooing what is beautifully p'sooing you? Running away round—around! Circle! Time your waking up! Snoring deep-sleeper! Happiness being cause, not effect! Grief becoming yours because your p'sooing happiness! Burrowing vole! Why your not letting happiness overtaking you, employing and bringing wisdom? Your being fearful of being—doing what your knowing! Man not being means toward end! All ends being means toward man!—Damned old bugger, am I!"

Almost imperceptibly Andrew bowed acknowledgment that the Force behind the scourging words had aimed straight, blow upon blow. Old Ugly-face glared, scowled, turned on Tom Grayne, reading him now. Anger waned. The Asiatic eyes lost no fire, but they burned with another flame, less merciless. After a long pause he said slowly:

"My also being too much sinful—liquidating *karma*—must not

refuse!" Silence for ten heartbeats. Then: "But can your being hum-ble?"

"I don't know," Tom answered. "I wish to find out." His voice sounded so screwy and his words so flat that he himself balked; he coughed— pretended to clear his throat. But he stole a triumphant glance sideways at Elsa, his thought leaping like a spark from pole to pole:

"Steal my track, would you! I win!"

Andrew caught the thought as clearly as if it were directed at him. He squeezed Elsa's hand. Old Ugly-face said to Tom:

"Time now for being-doing! Now our soon seeing what *karma* bringing forth!"

The old man rounded his lips and boomed the sacred syllable that holds within itself all ends and all beginnings, leaving only the Path to appear:

"*Aum-m-m-m-m-m-m-m-m-m-m-m-m-m-m-m-m-m-m-m-m-m!*"

Then he turned his back. Shaking the big prayer wheel, he trudged away into the snow and vanished.

Tom looked like the shadow of anticlimax. He had boasted not secretly enough and too soon. After a moment, forcing his voice to be calm, he said to Andrew: "Shall we keep together?"

Andrew switched on his flashlight. He answered stiffly: "It's up to you. You're head man."

Tom's voice changed again. He sounded shameless, because shame tortured him: "The worst is ahead. Old Ugly-face thinks he fooled me, but I know him. He believes he can finish without our help. If he can, he will. Foreigners are outlaws. He's the anti-foreigner. It 'ud look bad to succeed with foreign help. So, if we can't hang on, he'll shake us and say it was our *karma*."

"We must finish what we started," said Andrew.

"That's the point. This is the last move. Let's stick together."

"We'd better feed our men," Andrew suggested.

Tom agreed: "You attend to it. I'll watch Old Ugly-face. I'll have to go close or maybe lose him in the snow. When he gets going I'll—" He hesitated.

"Fire three shots," said Andrew. "We'll be able to hear that."

"Right. I'll do it. You look after the men."

Andrew framed Elsa in torchlight against the cave wall. Tom didn't look at her. He switched off his own light and vanished. Andrew took her in his arms.

"Kiss me," he said, "and say I'm wonderful! I need a pep-talk."

"Andrew, you're—"

"That's enough. Hold it. Probably we'll all be dead by sunrise, but let's give it a whirl. We won't die lonely, you and I. Oh, Jesus Christ, I hate to see Tom Grayne crack like a politician!"

"Andrew, Tom has been a long time all alone—almost like Peary and the North Pole—sacrificing, enduring, striving to win a secret. He has worked and worked. Now he feels we're stealing his—"

"I know. I know. Christ give him the guts to finish clean! Elsa! If I should lose sight of the end for the sake of the means, just shoot me, will you!"

"Andrew, I won't ever be there—Turn of the light. It's a symbol. It hurts. Let us talk in the dark, it's truer."

He did as she asked.

"Andrew, you're being nobly generous. I know that of you. But as for loving me, I simply can't believe it."

"But who wants to believe? What do you know? What does your heart say?"

"Andrew, it trembles."

"You're tired, that's all that's the matter. You need sleep. You've been on the go since daybreak."

"Andrew, I'm only bewildered. I don't feel too tired. I think you don't understand that I asked Lobsang Pun to take me as his *chela*. That's irrevocable. Don't you understand it's a solemn act of submission? It commits me until—"

"Did he say yes?"

"No."

"What did he say?"

"He said a strange thing."

"What?"

"He said 'Patience! Love doesn't come between man and woman!' I think he meant me and Tom."

Andrew laughed grimly: "You listen to me. If that old mystic knows a tenth of what I credit him with, he knows how long I've loved you, and how hard I've had to fight to keep you from finding it out."

"Andrew! You mean—"

He rearranged the hood of her overcoat—re-tied her muffler. He switched on the light, tucked her arm through his and set out through the snow for the cave where the Tibetans waited, talking as they went.

691

"I've played square with Tom—gave him the last chance he's entitled to, and one more for good measure. So now you're mine. If Uglyface believes the contrary, he'll have to be taught."

She stopped him after a moment, clinging to him, pulling, so that they faced each other.

"Andrew! Look at me! You must! You must understand! This temptation! It is what they say always happens—"

"Who said it?"

"Nancy Strong said it."

"Damn Nancy Strong. Let her mind her own business."

"It always happens, to everyone who makes a vow of—"

"You haven't made your vow yet. I've made mine. I made it to me and to you."

"Andrew, always the temptation comes. It's always wonderful—so luring—so tender! It looks like heaven. But oh, Andrew, dear, I love you too much to ruin your life. I won't! So this is hail and farewell! It's goodbye. Kiss me again, once more—this one last—"

He switched off the light . . . When he could speak he said:

"Swell. That settles it. It's goodbye to the old life—on with the new!—You'll like America," he added.

"Andrew, I'd love anywhere where you are, but—"

"Love me, love my U.S.A.!" he answered. "Come on, let's turn out the men!"

The crowded cave where the Tibetans waited hummed with argument. They had boiled tea long ago, using yak-dung they had carried with them. Bompo Tsering had doled out cupfuls to the phony *lama's* men—"to keeping them alive for Tum-Glain's killing," as he explained to Andrew. Bompo Tsering and St. Malo's headman Ga-pa-dug seemed to have struck up a friendship; but the phony *lama* had been telling wild tales about *dugpas* and the spirits of dead hermits. He had more than half of the men verging on mutiny. Even some of Andrew's men were hesitating. A breech-bolt clicked. Andrew thrust Elsa out of the way. The phony *lama* picked up a lump of diorite and hurled—missed Andrew's head by an inch.

That saved the situation. It was the catalyst. It crystallized emotions into plus and minus. Men knew their minds. Bompo Tsering and Ga-pa-dug jumped on the phony *lama*—kicked, beat, cursed him—tore away his rosary and relics—ran him out into the snow and left him sprawling more dead than alive.

"Barley!" said Andrew. "Give the rest of 'em barley."

"But, Gunnigun—"

"Feed them! Did you hear me?"

The spare barley bag was tossed to the punishment squad. They pounced on it filled their mouths, then pockets.

"Now then! Who marches with me? Who gets thrown over the cliff?"

No answer, though Andrew waited while a man could chew on hard barley five or six times. Ga-pa-dug nudged Bompo Tsering, who spoke to Andrew:

"Gunnigun—what now?"

"I have wasted food! Throw them over the cliff. Begin with that man."

The only difficulty then was to prevent the execution. The malingerers begged mercy, crying, struggling, protesting willingness, flinging themselves on the ground—kicked, beaten. Andrew's shouts were unheard in the tumult; he had loosed savagery that he couldn't stop.

Luck interfered—chance—the signal chosen at random and the stark coincidence of time. Tom Grayne's three pistol shots, deadened by the snowfall, announced that Old Ugly-face was on the move. They sounded like torpedoes on a fog-bound railroad track. Andrew answered instantly. He fired three shots at the sky. The fighting ceased.

Andrew roared: "Fall in!" Then after a moment the familiar command: "Bompo Tsering leading—column two by two—march!"

They obeyed. They left their phony *lama* sprawling in the snow and trudged forward, not knowing whither or why. The phony *lama* slunk back to the cave.

"Jesus!" said Andrew, tucking Elsa's arm through his. He shortened his stride, so that she could keep step. "You and I have seen death close up lots of times. But that was the nearest. We've got to watch out. They're as touchy as fulminate."

CHAPTER 59

The storm, veering around in a wide arc, began to return, like a dog to its vomit. Thunder and lightning again, but not much wind yet. From a black sky lightning stabbed the whirling snow and revealed the procession, in shimmering glimpses—Old Ugly-face leading. The grand old mystic had seized his moment, and doubt was not in him. He was destiny's agent, self-identified—a swimmer on the rising tide of spirit—beyond praise. In his right fist he shook the prayer wheel. Andrew and Elsa couldn't hear him, but he appeared to be chanting. Behind him, in groups of twos, threes, dozens, the naked hermits trouped like ghosts arisen from their graves.

"Lord love and look at us!" said Andrew. "It's almost too crazy to fail! Almost! It's like the Angels at Mons. Did Old Ugly-face tell you his plan?"

"No. I saw him rout out the hermits and harangue them. I heard some of it—a little. It was like the end of the world and people rising from the dead. Lobsang Pun pulled and kicked down the wall of the first cave and dragged the hermit out."

"How near were you?"

"As close as I could get without Tom seeing me. I didn't want Tom to see me, because I knew—well, you know what he did think. Lobsang Pun shook that first hermit—pulled his beard—told him it was time to translate merit into action. The hermit resisted. He pleaded sanctuary. Lobsang Pun accused him of having guzzled virtue in his cave like a pig in a pen—said he'd need ten million years in hell to purge his vanity unless he stirred himself. He said the Shig-po-ling monastery has become a cesspool in which the monks wallow in lust. He blamed that on the hermits—especially that first one. 'If you're a saint,' he shouted at him, 'you should know better. If you're not a saint, now is your opportunity to be one!' It was from him that he took the prayer wheel. He beat the hermit with it. After that they prayed together, and presently the hermit was helping him to break into the other caves."

"What was Tom doing?"

"Watching, at first. But pretty soon he was helping to pull down rocks and rout our hermits. I kept away. I didn't want Tom to see me."

"Do you suppose he told Tom what his plan is?"

"I don't know. I saw Tom talking to him. Soon after that Tom went away—I suppose to overtake you."

"No," said Andrew.

"Why do you say no? Tom came back with you later."

The thought in Andrew's mind was: "Tom went looking for you in St. Malo's cave." He had almost said it. It was true. But he thought of a truth that tasted less sour:

"Tom helped me to bring St. Malo's men."

Even so, they fell silent for a minute or two. There began to be glimpses of Tom Grayne. Through the snow, by lightning glare, his windproof overcoat was distinguishable amid the hermits' naked skins.

694

At moments he looked like a shadow. At other moments he bulked big and husky, striding from group to group, working his way forward, gradually overtaking the seven naked scarecrows who seemed to have elected themselves Old Ugly-face's bodyguard.

"I suspect Tom knows part of the plan." said Andrew. "I think he doubts it'll work. So do I. This is too simple—crazy, yes—but not crazy enough. It looks to me he's going to march up to the monastery gate and count on the superstition of the monks. He figures they'll open and let him in for fear of offending holy hermits. But then what? Three or five thousand fanatics, obeying Ram-pa Yap-shi! We've a fat chance!"

Silence again for a while, rhythmed by the snow-deadened tramp of the Tibetans close behind them. Andrew wondered at Elsa's physical endurance. He didn't speak of it, for fear it might remind her of fatigue. She was striding along beside him, keeping step, with her arm through his, not leaning heavily. Even Old Ugly-face's vitality was hardly more remarkable than hers.

But the wind was rising again, whining amid dark crags. Talking had become too difficult. He wanted to ask questions, but Elsa would have had to shout. The physical strain on her would be too great. The questions phrased themselves in his mind as vehemently as if he were examining a witness. All they lacked was voice:

"Old Ugly-face can't be all that crazy! But what does he know? What can he know?"

The answer phrased itself as if Elsa replied: "'*Ask and it shall be given*.' Can't he ask? You heard him speak of his own Master."

But Elsa hadn't spoken. A flash of lightning revealed her gazing ahead as she trudged beside him, leaning a little more heavily now because the snow was deep. There was a dark cave on the right; he even thought of taking her in there to shelter a while. Then he could question her while she rested. But wordless, imperious impulse urged him forward; and a question kept time to his stride:

"Then were Homer, Virgil, and the ancients literally right? And the Bhagavad-Gita? Are there beings who guide and protect us Guardian angels? Did Joan of Arc really hear voices? What is a Master? Who ever saw one, and told, and got himself believed by anyone but yokels and nuts?"

"Haven't you seen Lobsang Pun? With the physical eye—and with the inner eye—?"

"But he denied he's a Master!"

695

"Jesus also denied it!—'*Why callest thou me good?'*—"

"But dammit, this isn't Jesus—"

"Who said he is?—How about you? In all your life have you ever originated one idea?"

"How do you mean—originated?" Question and answer came and went like a tussle between counsel and witness—only that he knew the answer instantly when he asked each question; and, though the witness in his mind was Elsa, it wasn't she who spoke. That made sense, at the moment, unless he thought about it: then thought rebelled, and he saw only the nightmare procession of naked hermits, storm-lit, more incredible than—

"But why incredible?" That wasn't Andrew's question. It was the witness turning on him. "Don't you believe your senses? Which part of it is true?—which untrue? Which is the dream? Which is Reality?"

"Oh, I know all that argument. Descartes put it: '*Cogito, ergo sum.*' Because I think, therefore I am. I must be."

"But you haven't answered the other question. You think. But does the thought originate with you?"

He was on the defensive now. Why? Who put him there? He wanted to think about Elsa as a physical girl whom he loved. Thought wouldn't obey. What is physical? What is love? Were the two ideas compatible?

"Can they cohabit, like man and woman?"

Who asked that question? He was getting confused. Thoughts, ideas, can't cohabit. Ridiculous.

"Don't they? Is thought never raped by propagandists? And what comes of that? What is conceived of it—gestates—gets born to suck the public teat and call itself survival of the fittest?"

"Who's gloomy now! That isn't even pessimism. It's fear—lack of faith! How can you change that? How do you always change it?"

"Poetry."

"Try."

"'*There is nothing either good or bad but thinking makes it so.*'"

"Where did that thought come from?"

"Shakespeare."

"Not from you."

"No."

"You didn't originate it?"

"No."

"Didn't Shakespeare say a poet's function is to reach to heaven for ideas and bring them down to earth?"

"Yes. He said that. '*The poet's eye is a fine frenzy rolling*—'"

"So, did Shakespeare originate the ideas that his poems convey? Did Jesus originate the Sermon on the Mount—or did he, like Shakespeare, take an ancient theme and hold it up to be drenched with Idea, like dew from heaven? Where did Beethoven go to find his Fifth Symphony? When great poetry and great music inspire you, what is conceived, gestates and gets born of that?—The wrong thing or the right thing?—Do you act nobly, or contemptibly, when you have let Shakespeare's or Milton's vision illumine thought and—"

He interrupted, growing irritable: "Then am I a ventriloquist's dummy—parroting what's put into my mouth?—A mere marionette—one of the lumpen-proletariat who—"

"Some people are. God pity those who misuse them. But you can choose, can't you, between noble and ignoble? You understand poetry and music love them—you can let them flow into your consciousness. What else stirred you to such undreamed of effort that you're here, in the wilds of Tibet—instead of where?"

"Are you trying to link me with some kind of metaphysical chain to Old Ugly-face?"

"Aren't we all linked to the sun, moon, stars? Isn't Lobsang Pun a poet? Like you—more so—more intelligently—doesn't he raise his consciousness to higher planes—and see—"

"See what?"

"As from a masthead—past, present, future, all in one moment, seen from above, through the eyes of—"

"Whose eyes?"

"You answer it! Through whose eyes did you see at Gombaria's, and at Lung- gom-pa's, and in the cavern tonight?"

"Damned if I know."

"But you do know. Only you won't admit it. It's the denial that hurts. Obey prejudice, stay in the dark and drown in the subconscious ocean— all pain, frustration, hatred, forever and ever—nature red in tooth and claw—survival of the damned! But whoever becomes superconscious, sees as a shepherd who guards his flock—sees through the shepherd's eyes. If Lobsang Pun sees through his Master's eyes—"

"Who is his Master?"

"Who is your Soul? Who are you? Who is it who sees dimensions that an artist's hand imprisons in the thing he carves? If someone—

perhaps many—in the monastery also perceive the idea which Lob-sang Pun—"

Thunder, wind, hail reopened the battle. For a minute Andrew and Elsa clung to each other. Then the squall ceased as it began, suddenly. In the ensuing calm, without pausing to think, but conscious of un-finished thought that had verged on vision, Andrew said:

"All right now. Go on talking."

"But we haven't been talking."

He pondered that a moment. "True. I guess we weren't. What were you thinking of?"

"Andrew, I was praying I might love you so that love should be a mirror in which you'd see yourself reflected—you, as you really are—your Soul!"

"Hell," he retorted, "I've seen me too often—Mind your step—here's a bad place—That squall cut a sluice—"

He held his flashlight for the Tibetans. The snow fell heavier than ever. It was near daybreak, but one couldn't have guessed it. The long column of hermits shimmered in and out of sight. Old Ugly-face, leading along the fanged edge of a ravine that snaked amid crashing landslides, used some abnormal faculty, like a deep-sea captain's in thick weather. He led unhesitating. There was one glimpse of Tom Grayne, away forward—then, by another lightning flash, Old Ugly-face turning to the hermits, waving his arms—and a glimpse of Tom returning as fast as he could run through the whirling snow. He was shouting, uselessly. He had to come close before Andrew could hear what he said:

"Get 'em off the track! Hide! Monks are coming!"

Then he ran back toward the head of the column, vanishing in darkness. Andrew didn't dare to use the flashlight. He looked for Bompo Tsering— couldn't find him—couldn't wait for him—got hold of the new man, Ga-pa-dug, shook him to put life in him, told him to help get the men out of sight. The man seemed to know he'd be killed if he hesitated. He got busy. A brigand by trade, he was an expert at quick getaways. The lightning flashed along a broken ledge that paralleled the trail a few feet lower. Andrew explored that, waiting for the lightning to photograph the handholds and the footholds in his mind's eye. Then he lay on the brink of the pitch-dark cauldron. Bompo Tsering came and helped, and they handed the men down one by one. In less than five minutes the last man reached the lower ledge and clung there with his head and hands below the level of the track. Elsa next. Andrew last, lingering, waiting for lightning, to watch the snow obliterate their tracks. They had to hang on or the wind would have whipped them away and blown them into the ravine. Andrew had to crouch. At his end of the ledge the narrow foothold was less than four feet below the track.

Now and again the naked hermits were visible, flashed into view by forked lightning but screened from the trail by fantastic boulders split and tumbled in confusion from the cliff face. Old Ugly-face and Tom had guided the hermits to a crag. It resembled a storm-bound island. There, amid whirling snow, they perched—and many of them died for the lack of their draughty caves.

Death came too close for anyone's comfort. A slip by anyone, and Andrew with Elsa and all his men, would have crashed to the rocks a thousand feet below. An outcry from one of the men, and there'd be five hundred armed monks to deal with—self-styled pacifists—killers, deadlier than brigands, because they had no humour—armed with Japanese repeating rifles, turned out into a Tibetan storm near daybreak to hunt not only foreign devils but an outlawed prelate of their own race with a huge cash reward on his head. Pacifists! Grim, determined, drilled believers in hell for heretics—trudging in close formation, two by two, depending on the storm to give them the advantage of surprise. They weren't even alert, there were no scouts in advance they were so sure of their quarry. *Tramp—tramp—tramp—tramp—*

The right feet of the outside files passed so close to Andrew's head that in spite of the wind he could hear the crunch of the soft snow—the sound of their long coats against their naked legs—an occasional low voice. He had a good foothold; he wasn't in much danger of falling off; but he was afraid Elsa's hold might weaken. Cramp from the strained position might make him useless for a sudden emergency. The marching monks hadn't seen the hermits or they'd have turned to investigate. Andrew could see them by lightning flash. But he didn't dare to raise his head to get a glimpse of the monks—didn't dare, either, to try to pass the word along to the men to keep silent. One of them—he was one of the phony *lama's* men—slipped—fell—screamed—vanished. But the monks didn't hear him; or if they did, they thought it was the wind. But someone else did hear—guessed right—came trudging along by himself at the rear.

Cramp, impatience, anxiety had almost exhausted Andrew's self-control. He was nearly positive that the last of the monks had gone by. He had tried to count them by their trudging; his estimate was more than four hundred and fifty men. He was about ready to raise his head cautiously above the level of the ledge when a man stopped within three feet of him and peered over. Andrew was too stiff to leap up at him. If the man should jump down, nothing could save both of them from death in the ravine below. Andrew couldn't shoot; he needed both hands to cling to the rock. The man couldn't see to shoot. He was waiting for the lightning. Andrew figured him out-guessed him—became quite sure he wasn't a monk; if he were he'd have cried the alarm. He couldn't be anyone else than St. Malo.

But why didn't St. Malo give the alarm? He must have guessed what he had stumbled on. If he had agreed to sell Old Ugly-face to Ram-pa Yap-shi, here was his chance to deliver! His chance for revenge—for a fortune! Why didn't he shout? There could be only one reason: something must have gone wrong with St. Malo's plan.

"Give me a hand up," said Andrew, suddenly.

St. Malo jumped as if he were shot. Quick thinker though he normally was, it took him ten seconds to make up his mind. Then he knelt, stuck his toes in the snow and gave Andrew one hand. Andrew demanded the other, too, to make sure there was no weapon in it. As he scrambled up he clutched both hands in a grip that made St. Malo curse through clenched teeth—foul stuff. Andrew shoved him back against the cliff, to have the inside track in case more monks were coming.

"Now! What's your game?"

"I've important information."

"Tell it!"

"Where are Tom Grayne and Lobsang Pun? Where's Elsa? Where are your men? We've got to act quickly before those monks turn back. If they catch us—"

Andrew seized his wrist and kicked his heel from under him, throwing him on his back

"Now talk, quick!"

"Deal me in then! Promise! If we can build a scaling ladder and climb the monastery wall—man, I've been in there—I can lead you straight to where they're keeping the young Dalai Lama! Once we've got him, we can threaten to kill him if they touch us! It's the only chance we've got for our lives!"

"You're something less than a man," said Andrew. "I don't mind killing you.—Where have you been?"

"I've been scouting!"

"You've betrayed Lobsang Pun, and us, too! I'm going to kick you over the cliff, now, unless you tell what's happened! Last chance!"

One kick landed on St. Malo's ribs. He yielded: "Well, all right, I'll tell! That's enough! Don't kick! I admit it—I did try to get the reward for delivering Lobsang Pun. But I was double-crossed. That dirty swine Ram-pa Yap-shi guessed where Lobsang Pun must be hidden. So he turned out all his fighting monks to go look for him. He turned me out after them—to be shot if I'd brought false information."

"How did you escape from the monks?"

"I didn't have to. They knew there was nothing for me but to follow them. Where else—"

Andrew didn't believe him. But why argue it? He went and reached down for Elsa—lifted her. One by one the Tibetans followed, stretching themselves, stamping and beating their hands. Then Tom came, running:

"Get moving!" he shouted, breathless. "Lead the way! Old Ugly-face is saying prayers for dead hermits! He'll be too late if we don't force his hand!"

Tom was gone again, into the dark. Andrew put Bompo Tsering and another in charge of St. Malo, and led, with Elsa's arm through his again. They didn't go far. At a bend where the ledge was fifty feet wide Old Ugly-face was marshalling all the hermits who hadn't died of cold. They were crowded between two huge dykes that projected from the face of the cliff like flying buttresses. It was safe to use flashlights there; a light couldn't be seen from up the trail or from the monastery, either, though they were now within four or five hundred yards of the monastery gate.

Tom was in trouble. Old Ugly-face, with his back to the naked hermits, was unloading on him the vials of his reverend anger:

"Your not having faith, not having nothing! Wanting everything, too soon, not knowing how!" There was plenty more of it, that was snatched away by the quarrelling wind.

He caught sight of Andrew—Elsa—St. Malo—the Tibetans. He shook the prayer wheel at them. Angrily he ordered lights out. Then, booming a Buddhist hymn, he set himself at the head of the hermits and resumed the march. Tom came up beside Andrew. Andrew asked:

"What's the old bugger up to? Do you know now what his plan is?"

"I'm not even sure he knows," Tom answered. "But if he can, he'll shake us. He'll leave us outside the gate. Tell Elsa to go forward and talk to him."

Elsa didn't hear the suggestion. Andrew made no comment. Tom fell back for a moment's conference with Bompo Tsering. A moment later he was questioning St. Malo.

Chapter 60

It must have been two hours after daybreak, but the great monastery gate was invisible until it loomed through a murk of snow and they could touch it. A faint luminescence suggested the sun was somewhere on the right, but the monastery walls couldn't be seen. Tom and Andrew turned their flashlights on Old Ugly-face. With Elsa between them they forced their way through the hermits until they were within three or four paces of him. They had to shove hard; the hermits were stubborn and resented getting out of the way.

That was how they lost sight of St. Malo; Andrew was counting on Bompo Tsering to attend to that job. Tom spoke without turning his head. He didn't want to meet Elsa's eyes; he was trying to be impersonal.

"Our job is to beat the old man to it and be first to find the young Dalai Lama. We'll be out of luck if we don't. Once Old Ugly-face is on top, we'll be a liability."

"He doesn't overlook his liabilities," said Elsa.

Tom ignored that, although it stopped him for a moment. He spoke to Andrew again: "No shooting! No killing! Follow me, and keep close."

Old Ugly-face was busy talking to someone through a hole about four inches square in a narrow postern that was part of the big gate. The top of the gate was almost invisible; through the whirling murk there was a gray bulky something up there that was probably a fortified arch. Something belched flame and there was a deadened roar—not lightning—not thunder. An old-fashioned big-bored rifle had gone off like a cannon. The naked hermit next but one to Andrew fell dead; blood pumped and then flowed through a hole in his neck. Tom was all nerves; he exploded:

"God! Now we're for it!"

"This is how we get in!" said Andrew with grim confidence. "The Tibetan closed season for naked hermit shooting runs twelve months solid!"

Old Ugly-face pounced on the chance as if he had planned, or at least foreseen it. His passionate roar was like a lion's. He used the prayer

702

wheel like a two-handed battle-axe and smashed it on the monastery gate. Some of the fluttering scraps of parchment fell into the hermit's blood. Bompo Tsering and the others scrambled for them. A great bell boomed behind the monastery wall, and set a hundred bells going—more than a hundred. Old Ugly-face turned to Tom and Andrew and ordered them to burn down the gate. "How does he think we'll do it?" Tom demanded.

Old Ugly-face was telling what to do, not how. His own wrath could have done it better than any implements they had. Andrew was about to break open a cartridge for its smokeless powder when the gate opened, to the squeal and clatter of winch and chain. They poured through, Old Ugly-face leading. He was in his element, a pilgrim on the path of glory, as iron-willed as the angel of Judgment Day—followed by nine and thirty naked hermits—a novelty, even in Tibet. He never hesitated—not once, though there was nothing to be seen but falling snow. It was darker in there than outside.

Andrew turned back to bring in the body of the dead hermit.

"Why—why—why?" Elsa demanded.

"Follow Old Ugly-face! Keep close to him!" he answered.

Elsa obeyed. Tom hesitated, just inside the gate, shouting: "Come on, you idiot! This way!" Then Tom followed the procession.

Andrew was keeping his head. He knew that corpses cut no ice in Tibet; but sacrilege does. The evidence of sacrilege might swing the balance between success and failure. He made four men carry the corpse and lay it inside the gate, in a drain, where he could find it later if needed.

Tom came looking for him—furious. "God dammit, what are you waiting for! We've Ram-pa Yap-shi and twenty-five hundred monks to beat."

"Where's Elsa?"

"Gone with Old Ugly-face—I lost sight of 'em waiting for you!"

Bells, bells, bells—booming and clanging like fire alarms. Shouts—hundreds of voices shouting to and fro from roofs and galleries. There was a weird suggestion of a fog-bound railroad junction. The watery sun burst through for a moment. It revealed shadowy figures ghosting through the snow across courtyards, running in all directions like ants in a broken hill. Lamplight shone through slits in stone walls, some being extinguished as fast as others were lighted. Panic. Never before in Tibet's history had one hermit, let alone nine and thirty, marched naked through a snowstorm behind a Ringding Gelong Lama to demand a monastery's purging of the sin of spiritual sloth. Old Ugly-face's broken prayer wheel was a symbol that stabbed the air with meanings that the monks understood; they knew their ritual; they were schooled in ceremonial and Tantric magic. Their souls shook within them. Hundreds of them bunched up their skirts and ran, bare-legged—ran anywhere—nowhere—from one building to another. Ancient guns went off at random, each one starting a new panic.

It was like the fall of Babylon, only there was no royal banquet to interrupt. Old Ugly-face, guided by his own daemon, turned to the right. Tom recovered command of himself, shouted at Andrew, and led straight forward, guided by memory. Old Ugly-face was *de facto* Lord Regent of Tibet within fifteen minutes after that.

The monastery could have lent itself, like a medieval city, to the worst kind of street fighting, but there was no one willing to fight. It was perched on the side of a mountain—all up and downhill on different levels. Courtyard led into courtyard through unlighted arches. Huge barrack-like buildings faced inward. At the rear, with its back to the mountain, was an enormous building like a keep, apron-fronted like the Potala at Lhasa. Cannon that once belonged to the Chinese Army peered through gaps in the wall. The sun was beginning to fight its way through. The storm was failing. Everything could be seen now, dimly, like a negative that is beginning to develop. Someone fired one of those old cannons. It burst—knocked down a ton of masonry—scared some monks so badly that they fled into the courtyard through a door that Tom might otherwise have missed. The main door was barred. Tom wrenched at it, but Andrew grabbed him and shoved him in the right direction. In a second they were using their fists on monks' ears to force their way past a stream of them that poured through that other door. It was like a theatre panic. None knew what he was afraid of, but they ran—ran like rats.

Tom remembered the way now. He led as if he had the ball on the twenty-yard line. Andrew and the Tibetans bucked the hurrying stream of monks and followed him up a huge stone stairway to an upper corridor. It was lighted by parchment covered lanterns.

Then they remembered St. Malo, because they saw him. He was at the end of the corridor, standing beside the young Dalai Lama and the Lord Regent Ram-pa Yap-shi—their backs to a door—caught in the act of flight. Andrew gasped:

"God, for a camera!"

St. Malo heard that. "What you need is brains!" he retorted. "Did you bring 'em with you?" He had an automatic, stolen somewhere, somehow. He placed its muzzle against the Dalai Lama's neck—a young lad with a face like a porcelain doll's, clothed in embroidered red silk. The boy looked bleached by being too long indoors—placid, amused, contemplative, curious. Large, long-lashed Mongolian eyes. He seemed to like St. Malo. Surely he didn't suspect that his life trembled on St. Malo's trigger finger.

The Lord Regent Ram-pa Yap-shi had been hit hard by someone. There was blood on his face. Punch-drunk, he stood six feet away from St. Malo, with a dozen monks behind him. The monks weren't eager to protect him; it might be one of them who had hit him; they were hesitating, telling each other what to do, and doing nothing. Ram-pa Yap-shi wasn't Chinese, but with his thin beard and horn-rimmed spectacles he looked it. He was wearing the gorgeous embroidered robes of a High Abbot. Barring the spectacles, he very closely resembled the painted figure on the wall beside him—a portrait of an ancient notoriously cruel king of Tibet, represented as a suppliant at the Seat of Judgment of the dead.

There was tense silence for about two seconds. Then St. Malo delivered his ultimatum:

"Now you two geniuses-quick! I've got the kid. I'll bring him. You shoot these monks! Grab the abbot and run. I'll show you where to run to. We'll make our own terms!"

It was no use doubting St. Malo. He meant business. As long as he had his hands on the holiest child on earth, no Tibetan would dare to touch him. He would shoot the child dead rather than surrender his advantage. But there was a chance yet.

He interrupted a glance between Andrew and Tom. "I've warned you!" he said sharply.

Andrew moved, sideways, toward a niche in the wall in which rested all kinds of religious objects, including a bronze *dorje*, (religious sceptre), like an ornamental two-pound dumb-bell. Tom watched for an opening, not daring to draw his own weapon, but holding St. Malo's attention while Andrew lifted the bronze *dorje* from the shelf. He hurled it—hit St. Malo on the jaw—staggered him. St. Malo fired at Andrew—missed. Before he could fire again Tom's fist sent him staggering to the floor in a corner. Then Bompo Tsering shot him dead.

The boy *lama* laughed.

It was a strange laugh—so unexpected that it almost stopped Andrew from searching St. Malo's pockets; but that was public duty number one that he didn't dare to leave entirely to Bompo Tsering. He found a thin wallet, containing what looked like the key to a code. It sounded as if the boy *lama* was laughing at that—merrily. Or was he laughing because he had never before seen a dead man? Or because Andrew let Bompo Tsering pocket St. Malo's money? Drawing blank in St. Malo's remaining pockets, Andrew looked up—saw delight in the boy's eyes—followed their gaze toward the end of the long corridor. Old Ugly-face's head and shoulders appeared, at floor level, like a bronze bust.

He was ascending a curving stairway at the far end. The boy had recognized him; the laugh was spontaneous greeting; he hadn't turned his head even to glance at the shooting; he appeared unconscious of it—bright-eyed, pleased and relieved beyond words. Old Ugly-face as he mounted the stairs looked like a great hobgoblin with a hundred ghosts behind him. He had left all except one of the hermits somewhere; that one, wrapped now in a curtain snatched from a wall, strode beside Elsa—a bearded skeleton in a *toga*. The rest were monastery monks. Counter-revolution brooded on their stern faces. Reaction. Grim, unforgiving piety. As Old Ugly-face paused midway along the corridor, four monks overtook him, genuflected and then robed him is the vestments of high office, shaking incense on him. He was no longer a ragged pilgrim. His Holy Diplomatic Eminence the Ringding Gelong Lama Lobsang Pun no longer wore Andrew's blanket over a peasant's rags. He gave the blanket to the hermit. He stood arrayed in the embroidered yellow and crimson to which high rank entitled him. Then he went down on his knees and touched his forehead to the floor, doing reverence to the child who had laughed with delight when he first appeared. Elsa, close behind him, knelt beside the hermit.

"You've lost her!" Tom murmured. "We've both lost her." He sounded ashamed.

There wasn't one weapon in sight among the monks who followed Old Ugly-face. As they reached the corridor they, too, laid their foreheads on the floor. Rifles clattered as Bompo Tsering, Ga-pa-dug and the others followed suit. There was almost no other sound as Old Ugly-face moved slowly forward, giving the monks time to make their obeisance. The child *lama* blessed Old Ugly-face with a gesture of his right hand and a movement of his lips. Then he blessed Elsa, the hermit, the monks, Tom, Andrew. He beamed, exuded blessings. Andrew watched Ram-pa Yap-shi-gaunt, tall, high cheeked— something less than inscrutable. Tibetan—in-bred—autocrat—caught un-aware—dazed. No Tibetan fears death. But pride fears humiliation, and the prouder the rogue, the worse he fears it. The paralysis of fear resembled dignity—almost—until one noticed his eyes.

Breath steamed in the chill air. Outside, on roofs and in courtyards, there was a prodigious clamouring of bells. In the corridor, silence—almost like the silence of the painted Bodhisattvas on the wall. At last, Old Ugly-face made an imperious gesture. He made it with his left hand. Four monks advanced from behind. Ram-pa Yap-shi didn't move; nor did his attendants. The four monks unceremoniously dis-robed Ram-pa Yap-shi. They took his rosary and jewels, and the rings from his fingers, but offered him no other indignity. They left him standing in a long black cassock, with bowed head, shivering a little because it was very cold in the corridor. Then Old Ugly-face moved both hands and the monks behind him opened a lane through their midst.

Without a word being spoken, Ram-pa Yap-shi strode forward with folded arms. His attendants followed. Old Ugly-face did not get out of Ram-pa Yap-shi's way. He almost appeared not to see him; but as Ram-pa Yap-shi approached he made a very slight gesture with the fingers of his left hand. Ram-pa Yap-shi obeyed the gesture—passed left to left, instead of right to right. It signified condemnation, commi-nation, excommunication and acceptance of defeat. Only an outcast, stripped of hope in this world and condemned to unimaginable ig-nominy in the next, would pass to the left of anyone or anything that symbolized a religious idea. Even Tom Grayne shuddered.

The astonishing thing was the boy *lama's* behaviour. He took it all unemotionally, as if it were part of a ritual. The impression was that he had been expecting this—knew it would happen—had foreseen it. Since that one peal of delighted recognition of Old Ugly-face he hadn't made a sound. He gazed chiefly at Elsa. She puzzled him. Since he was weaned he had been denied any association with women, even of his own race. But his gaze was as unselfconscious as a statue's—it suggested intelligent interest. Andrew stared at him without a thou-sandth of his manners, memorizing his features, for a portrait, to be carved before memory should have time to grow dim.

Old Ugly-face said something in Tibetan to a monk behind him. Two monks, one on either hand, strode forward and struck the double door, both together, with the palms of their right hands. One panel opened. The boy *lama* smiled, turned and led the way into his apartment. Old Ugly-face followed.

There was a glimpse of a long carpet in a stone walled passage lined with paintings of saints on silk. Then the door closed behind them and a murmur went up, of monks whispering to one another, that filled the corridor. It suggested a waterfall in an echoing cavern.

Elsa, Tom Grayne and Andrew stood facing one another for a moment, each waiting for the other to speak—until Andrew noticed blood flowing from St. Malo's body and began looking for something to cover it with. Front-rank monks guessed what he was looking for—whispered. Other monks came from the rear with a piece of carpet and covered the corpse contemptuously, as the attendants at a bull fight cover the gored dead horses.

Andrew and Tom waited for Elsa to tell what had happened and was happening outside. Surely she must be bursting with news. But when she broke the strained silence she said:

"Tom, only one of us may remain here with Lobsang Pun."

"Yes, I know it," he answered glumly. "You win."

"He takes only one *chela* at a time. Never more. And only one who needs his help and whom he knows he can enlighten."

"Yes. I've heard that of him."

"I had asked him to accept me as his *chela* before I knew you intended to ask.—Tom—please believe me: if I had known you wanted it, I would never have—"

Tom interrupted her: "If so, why did you return from India?"

"Tom, to give you your freedom, face to face—no other reason! When I left Tibet for Darjeeling you never expected to see me again, did you?"

"I don't know," Tom answered. "I didn't suppose the baby would have a chance to live. I was surprised when you did come back. I thought we had parted good friends, and you'd see the—"

He hesitated. The monks were staring at them. Andrew was listening. Elsa's eyes looked straight at his. She seemed to be expecting something— almost praying for it. He yielded.

"I'm ashamed," he said abruptly. "I tried, as you know, to learn your gift from you. The effort only exasperated both of us. All winter long I tried to learn it from the Tibetan who shared my hideout. He said I'm unteachable. So I set my heart on Lobsang Pun. It made me jealous— envious— suspicious. I behaved like a cad."

"Tom, then do we part good friends?"

Andrew was about to speak, but the door opened and all the monks

708

stopped whispering. The door closed again quietly behind Old Ugly-face. The monks genuflected. Old Ugly-face stared at Tom as if he hadn't seen him before—scowled—his eyes flashed with anger:

"Your believing Jesus saying—asking being same as getting! Yes. But who asking? And who getting? My telling you, it is more blessed to give! His saying that also!"

He took no notice of anyone else. The monks opened up and he passed down their midst as Ram-pa Yap-shi had done, but his head was unbowed and his hands weren't folded on his breast. The monks faced about and followed, so that the hermit came last. Tom shrugged his shoulders and followed the hermit. Andrew touched Elsa's arm. She met his eyes. He looked more troubled than she had ever seen him.

"Andrew," she said, "Andrew, I have trusted you—through thick and thin. We are all on the verge of death. Will you trust me—this once—now?"

"I must," he answered. "I have said: I love you."

She nodded. "Then for my sake, please keep your promise and stand by Tom Grayne, to the end.—Follow him now! No—this isn't the end—not yet."

She slipped away from him, struck the door with the palm of her hand and vanished into the boy *lama's* apartment. The door closed behind her. A bolt clicked.

CHAPTER 61

The snowfall had ceased when Andrew overtook Tom in the courtyard. The sun was fighting its way through breaking clouds. Wind, whirling the snow off roofs and walls and piling up deep drifts under archways and cloisters, saved both their lives; monks, as ferocious as hornets, couldn't gee at them in sufficient numbers or quickly enough. They were able to dodge from cloister to cloister; they had to keep hiding, pausing, ducking behind columns and into doorways.

Lusty-lunged bull-bellowers, instructed by Old Ugly-face's hermits, were hard at work proclaiming that Ram-pa Yap-shi's fall was due to sinful intrigue with foreigners. Lo and behold, the foreigners! Who should distinguish, in a crisis, between good and bad ones? Old Ugly-face had pitched on Tibet's xenophobia as the basis for his *coup d'etat*. He was playing it up. In the name of religion, the law, the prophets, and the higher spiritual beings to whom Tibet yearns for guidance, he denounced all foreign influences—at the top of his lungs—to the booming of gongs and the blare of the big *radongs* that sound like foghorns in a fog-bound sea.

Part of a tile from a broken coping-stone missed Andrew by six inches; he reached for his automatic, but Tom restrained him. Old Ugly-face had seen it—he noticed everything—he snapped out a command. The nearest monk went running, jumping through snowdrifts with his skirts tucked into his girdle, to stop that foolishness. Presently a monk fell like a sprawling vulture from a roof—likely to throw no more tiles in this world.

Scores of monks lay dead in the crimsoning snow. Grudges and private spites were being worked off—bitter monastic hatreds that had secretly boiled for the day of revenge. The arrogant bullies of Rampa Yap-shi's reign were pursued by the bullied, who were in haste to repay cruelty before the tide could turn.

The tide was turning. Tom nudged Andrew, speechless, pointing southward. Retreat was cut off. Vengeance was on its way. Descending from level to level they had reached a platform where there was a clear view over the top of the outer wall. Already, the five hundred who had marched in darkness to plunder the cavern were on their way back; their advance guard was nearing the main gate. The commander and his *aide* were riding Tom's and Andrew's ponies and the yaks were loaded with the plunder from the cavern. The five hundred armed monks tramped behind the plunder in fours, in good marching order, nearly knee-deep in snow though the front ranks were. Tom snatched Andrew's binoculars—stared through them.

"The leader's *aide's* a Jap! Now we are done for! He'll take charge and give us the works! Where's Elsa?"

Instead of answering, Andrew asked: "Who timed these moves? Look! Who's that over the gate?"

Tom focused the glasses carefully: "Looks like a Russian. His back's this way—but—he has a thick beard—might be German— good boots—fur hat—yes—looks like a Russian rifle. Might be either— Russian or German."

Andrew reached for the glasses. "Let me look." After a moment: "He might be anything except Tibetan. Tibetans can't grow that kind of whiskers.—I bet you something—I bet he's St. Malo's Number One! I bet he's laying for the Jap! I bet he thinks he'll save his own stake now by killing the Jap! Watch!"

Tom took the glasses again. The man on the footwalk above the main gate thrust his rifle through one of the embrasures in the arch, took aim and fired. The Jap fell from the saddle. He struggled a moment and lay still. The Tibetan leader of the column glanced up once at the gate, wheeled his pony and went galloping back past the loaded animals, throwing them into confusion. The man who had shot the Jap withdrew his rifle—by a heartbeat, by a breath too late.

From the gate towers at either end of the footwalk Tibetans approached him—two men, who crouched like skilled hunters and moved with the agility of cats. Tom exploded:

"By God, that's—"

Andrew took the words from his lips: "It's Bompo Tsering and St. Malo's headman Ga-pa-dug!"

Both Tibetans had firearms, but they couldn't use them for fear of shooting each other. They laid them down. They drew knives and closed on the man who had shot the Jap. He hadn't time to use his rifle. He screamed as the long blades plunged into him. His rifle fell to the ground, where a monk pounced on it. The Tibetans' knives had struck their victim so hard and deep under the ribs that he almost dragged them with him when at last he toppled backwards and fell in a shapeless heap near the postern door. He almost fell on the monk who had taken the rifle. The monk ran.

Tom nudged Andrew, who resented being nudged:

"Quick! Search him before the monks do it!"

Andrew followed him down from level to level—past Old Ugly-face, who was haranguing and giving orders to crowds of monks—past naked and half naked hermits who were putting the fear of the lives to come into every monk they could get to listen. The hermits howled imprecations after them:

"Foreigners! Devils!"

But two monks detached themselves from Old Ugly-face's inner-guard and checked that foolishness. They screamed at the hermits. They followed Andrew and Tom to the gate, protecting them. They stood there whirling prayer wheels, watching for a signal from Old Ugly-face to tell them what to do next.

There were more than twenty corpses near the main gate. The snow was blood-red and trodden to slush. Tom was stooping over the knifed mystery man to search his clothing and Andrew was standing guard, when Bompo Tsering burst out through the door at the foot of the gate tower:

"Gunnigun!" he gasped. There was blood on his coat. He was panic stricken. "Gunnigun!"

711

Andrew shook him. "Steady now. What's up? Say it slowly, one word at a time!"

"Nobly born, my having killed Ga-pa-dug!"

"Where?"

"In gate tower!"

"Why?"

"His telling me, my should killing you."

"What for?"

"Hot damn—then his and my being too rich. But my not shooting you! My dying sooner!"

Andrew changed the subject. "What's through that door?"

"Gatehouse. Stair. Machine—open-gate."

"What else?"

"'Nother door. Shut tight."

"Leading which way?"

"Leading belong passage inside big wall—that way—wall all hollow." Tom came up, washing his hands with snow.

"Nothing doing," he said. "Might be Russian or German. No documents—no identity mark.—We'd better find Elsa."

"Elsa's all right. She has her orders from Old Ugly-face."

"How do you know she's all right? Where is she?"

"She asked me to trust her," said Andrew. "You do as you please."

"When did she ask?"

"Just now. Say—d'you notice how few firearms these monks have—"

"Five hundred outside—on their way!" Tom answered.

"But almost none inside!"

Tom nodded, impatiently. "Ram-pa Yap-shi," he said, "disarmed all except the five hundred he thought he could count on. At one time, not long ago, there were three or four thousand rifles in—"

Andrew interrupted: "Where are they now?" he pointed. "Are they in that big building where the six hermits are posted at the door?"

Tom agreed. "Right! That's the main storehouse."

Old Ugly-face had posted six naked hermits at the only entrance to the storehouse, to prevent looting. No monks, no matter how they longed for firearms, dared to try to pass those hermits to force the door. Hermits are very holy. Eternities in hell are too much to pay for a rifle and ammunition.

"God! If they do get at those rifles," said Tom, "there'll be a slaughter to beat Jesus. Listen to that, will you!"

712

Rifle butts were thundering on the main gate. The five hundred outside were demanding admission. They were shouting. Some were firing their rifles. But that was a good sign; it meant lack of discipline. If their officers couldn't control them—

"If Old Ugly-face hasn't a trick in reserve now, he's a goner," said Tom. "That means us too. So—"

Old Ugly-face did have a trick in reserve. He came chanting, followed by chanting monks, and stood facing the main gate, fifty feet back from it, on the pediment of an urn-shaped *stupa* that contained the ashes of a saint. Two hermits, each wrapped in a blanket, approached the postern, and stood one at each side of it. It was a narrow postern, almost in the middle of the gate—not room for more than one person to pass through at a time.

Andrew and Tom stood back against the gatehouse wall. There was no shadow there, but they were less noticeable. Andrew whispered to Bompo Tsering to get his gang together and hold them ready for sudden orders. He had to threaten him to make him obey. A vulture landed above the gate and perched there, moving restlessly. Another dozen vultures soared out of the sky and perched on a roof ridge. The first vulture joined the others and they sat all in a row.

Tom's nerves were ragged. Inaction fretted him. "God, what's the old man waiting for?"

"You need food," said Andrew. "Here, eat this." He gave him chocolate. Tom munched it.

Then they saw why Old Ugly-face was waiting. The number one hermit had reached the top of the wall, by the stairs in the righthand gatehouse. He was wearing Andrew's blanket, but not for warmth, he let it flutter in the wind. He was already talking to the monks outside and they had left off shouting. His voice had a weird carrying power, but Andrew couldn't understand him, and if Tom could distinguish the words he was too attentive to repeat them; he shook his head when Andrew asked what the hermit was saying. All the monks in the wide courtyard were spellbound, many of them open-mouthed—expectant—afraid. A door opened suddenly.

"Christ! Who's timing this!" said Andrew.

It was a door at the end of a lean—to shed that was evidently a covered passage for use in winter. It made a circuit around two sides of the courtyard, turning at right angles along an inner wall, toward a monastery building.

Ram-pa Yap-shi came through the door, all alone. The door closed behind him and someone inside shot the bolt noisily. His hands were not tied, but he held them behind him as if they were. He walked with dignity toward the main gate but, while still ten feet away from it, turned and stood still. There was no sign of recognition between him and Old Ugly-face. Not a word was spoken. Less than an hour ago Ram-pa Yap-shi had gloated over the tortures prepared for Old Ugly-face. Now he awaited his own fate.

"As calm as Christ!" said Tom. "God! What's going to happen now?"

The hermit on the wall kept talking to the monks outside. Andrew and Tom both watched Old Ugly-face. A monk was whispering to Bompo Tsering. The two hermits at the postern waited for a signal from the one on the wall. Bompo Tsering shouted suddenly to Andrew and came running.

"Hot damn! Gunnigun! Our letting only one man come in!"

Andrew strode toward the postern and Tom followed. The hermit signalled from the wall. The hermits below opened the postern. Instantly a big monk with a *bandolier* over his chest barged through as if there were pressure behind him. He thrust his rifle muzzle at the hermit who stood in the way. Another monk followed; he, too, was being shoved from the rear. Tom spoke:

"Now! Both together!"

It was Andrew's fist that socked the third man who tried to get through. The man staggered back. Tom slammed and bolted the postern. He and Andrew stood with their backs to it. Old Ugly-face's lips moved, giving orders to a monk who stood beside him.

The two armed monks who had forced their way in were bewildered. They had prodded a holy hermit and felt afraid. They couldn't make head or tail of things. They couldn't retreat. They had their rifles; but Tom and Andrew made no secret of having automatics, and, besides that, had the drop on them. So they didn't know what to do. They stood looking from Ram-pa Yap-shi to Old Ugly-face, and back again. Old Ugly-face spoke to a monk, and the monk came and said they might take Ram-pa Yap-shi away. He said more than that, but Andrew and Tom couldn't hear it. Ram-pa Yap-shi made no comment, but he turned his back toward Old Ugly-face. He was shivering a little—doing his best not to.

The hermit on the wall began talking again to someone outside. The wind blew a sudden squall, clanging the roof bells and raising clouds of snow. The hermits opened the postern and Ram-pa Yap-shi

714

walked out, followed by the two armed monks. Almost before the postern bolt slid home there was a ragged volley of rifle fire.

Tom glanced at Andrew: "Well, he's got his. Quick! Merciful! We'll be lucky if nothing worse happens to us.—Where in God's name is Elsa?"

Andrew snapped at him: "It's none of our God-damned business where she is! Her life's her own."

He felt a sudden hunch that was like the pull of a magnet. He obeyed it.

"Where are you going?" Tom demanded.

"There are stairs in the gatehouse. When I've seen what's doing, I'll come back and let you know!"

He opened the door of the gatehouse and closed it quietly behind him—bolted it. He intended to find Elsa. But he couldn't have told why he should look for her in the gate tower, nor why he bolted the door behind him. He just did it, feeling that he did right—feeling confident.

CHAPTER 62

It was almost dark inside the gate tower. The machinery for opening the gate took up most of the space. Beside a bench for the use of the gate guard was the door of which Bompo Tsering had spoken. It was locked; Andrew tried to force it—kicked it—couldn't shake it.

The narrow stairway followed the curve of the wall. There was no guardrail. The stairs were worn and loose. He went up them two at a time. At the top, a narrow door gave access to the footwalk above the main gate. The door was held open by the body of Ga-pa-dug that lay across the threshold in a pool of blood. Bompo Tsering hadn't taken the man's rifle. That was a mystery all its own. Andrew took it, unloaded it, tested the breech mechanism, reloaded it, and went out to the footwalk. Looking for Elsa? He couldn't have answered the question. He asked it of himself, but with no special emphasis. He had a more than vague feeling that he was doing the right thing.

In the corner between tower and footwalk was an irregular masonry platform roughly eight feet square, protected from everything but wind by a pierced *barbette*. By standing well into the corner he could look down into the courtyard without being seen—and on the other hand, through the opening in the *barbette*, he could see the armed men outside. Inside, he could even see Tom Grayne, although Tom had his back to the gatehouse and was almost hidden by the

715

bulge in the wall.

First, he directed his attention outside. Ram-pa Yap-shi was not dead. Very much not dead. The ragged volley that had greeted him when he went out through the postern must have been a salute, or perhaps a display of emotion on the part of the armed monks. They didn't look much like soldiers— more like brigands. They had abandoned formation and were milling around him, most of them shouting; but the gusty wind carried away the uproar so that it only reached Andrew like the noise of surf on a distant beach. Ram-pa Yap-shi, in his long black robe, with his hands behind him, looked like a Catholic martyr about to be burned at the stake.

Because of the wind it was impossible to tell what was going on. But Old Ugly-face knew; he was being kept posted. The hermit on the wall near the opposite gate tower—quite naked now—Andrew's blanket had blown away—was shouting at the top of his lungs, first to the monks outside, then relaying their answer, again at the top of his lungs, to another hermit below, who relayed it to Old Ugly-face at his post of authority on the broad pediment of the *stupa*.

Old Ugly-face was no longer standing. They had brought him a high-backed chair like a bishop's throne. Some of the monks who clustered around him had sent for their own official robes, so that it looked something like a court. There was dignity, colour, organisation. There was even a table, at which a secretary sat taking dictation from Old Ugly-face. It looked like a proscription list. If it was, it was good tactics. Numbers of monks were presenting themselves for registration on the "good" list before it was too late; they were kneeling in the snow, calling out their names and begging a benediction.

Many more than a thousand monks had lined up in hollow square with their backs to the courtyard wall—perhaps obedient—perhaps not daring to come nearer. Andrew studied them. He thought they looked dangerous. All crowds are alike in that they all reveal their mood more distinctly than individuals do. Remembering crowds of strikers in Ohio, and Chinese dock labourers in Amoy and Shanghai, Andrew decided those monks were waiting to be swayed one way or the other by the turn of events. He wondered why Old Ugly- face didn't pay more attention to them—flatter them a little—win them over with some demagogic fireworks.

But a strangely subtle mental change began to take place. He found he couldn't think of Old Ugly-face and failure in one and the same thought. There was a calm, unhurried feeling of exhilaration that existed entirely apart from events and things; and yet it controlled them, in a way not easy to define, but that filled experience, so that it was. There was no arguing it. The things—people—movements, that one saw, heard, felt, were the same and yet otherwise. There was a sensation of new reality. They were part of a pattern—not pawns, but intelligent agents, each fulfilling a destiny—moving intricately toward a predetermined future that could not possibly be avoided except in one way.

He remembered Elsa's "subconsciousness, consciousness, super-consciousness" —"From—at—toward." A change of consciousness, and all things, events, beings, change their meaning, lose confusion and stand simplified in new perspective. Old Ugly-face, as Andrew then perceived it, was the conscious outlet through whom superconsciousness flowed, to which anyone might tune in within the limits of his spiritual stage of evolution.

"I guess I'm a one-tube outfit," he reflected.

He didn't wonder any longer that Elsa should have asked to be accepted as Old Ugly-face's *chela*. He could understand the relief to her of being recognized as an evolving spirit rather than being condemned, and self-condemned, as a freak unfit for confidence.

God, how he loved her!—or was that selfishness? Was it his own craving to perceive with an inner eye—to see the ravishing beauty of new dimensions—as he did sometimes perceive, when Elsa, with her mystic companionship, lifted his thought upward?

He felt Elsa's hand in his. It seemed part of the mystic moment. He didn't turn to look. He went on watching Ram-pa Yap-shi, realizing that he hadn't once ceased watching him. Timeless and measureless thought had filled his mind while Ram-pa Yap-shi spoke perhaps ten words—inaudible from where Andrew watched. The words were bitterness made visible—as scornful and cold as the wind. Ram-pa Yap-shi had refused something. But what?

The hermit shouted from the wall. The message was relayed to Old Ugly-face. He spoke. Monks ran to do his bidding. Tom beckoned Bompo Tsering and the two of them were almost swept off their feet as they tried to line up their men in front of the main gate. Andrew decided to go down and lend a hand. He didn't want to; it meant losing a spiritual vision that he might never regain. He lingered one more moment, thinking of Elsa—until she tugged at his hand, and he turned. She was beside him, sheltered from the wind, between him and the gatehouse wall.

717

"How long have you been here?" he asked.

"I don't know. Two minutes—hours—days! Was it good? I was away up—from the moment when I took your hand until you turned."

"So was I. But I must go down there now, and—"

"No. Don't. Watch from here. I know what will happen."

"How do you know?"

"I will tell later."

He hugged her close to him and leaned, between her and the wind, against the barbette where they could see both sides of the wall.

"Andrew," she said, "can you help Ram-pa Yap-shi? Can you reach him with a thought that may make him feel less lonely?"

"I can fix him so he'd quit feeling at all," Andrew answered. "I've a rifle."

"Aren't you ashamed?"

"No. That's how I feel. He looks like Satan to me. If such a thing's possible, he's Old Ugly-face's opposite. Have you talked to the kid *lama?* What does he think of him?"

"He pities him."

"That child? Kids of his age are pitiless."

"Can a Dalai Lama—even only seven years old—return evil for evil?"

"If he's such a prodigy of virtue, can't he use his virtue to prevent—"

"No. Watch."

There was talk going on at the gate, through the hole in the postern. Outside, five hundred monks, noisily bullied by platoon commanders, were piling their rifles in fairly orderly stacks. Hermits opened the postern. It seemed a protocol had been arranged. The plundered baggage animals were led away to another gate. Tom and his Tibetans marched off to see the ponies safely stabled and the loads put under lock and key. Then, one by one, led by their commander, the disarmed monks filed in through the postern. One hermit took them in charge, striding like a mountaineer as he led them past Old Ugly-face to the door through which Ram-pa Yap-shi had walked alone. They saluted as they passed Old Ugly-face. He took no notice. Someone called out their names as they passed. The secretary's writing brush moved on the page—nemesis, writing. Andrew speculated: "To the dungeons"?

"No. What has happened in this—"

"Are you psyching it?"

"No. The Dalai Lama's personal attendant told me. First; Ram-pa

718

Yap-shi was offered to those monks whom he armed and misled—to be their leader. They might take him and go wherever they pleased."

"He got his answer," said Andrew.

"After that, since his own would have none of him—and even Ram-pa Yap-shi knew that would happen—he knew that terrorists are always turned on by their favourites when failure sets in—he was offered two alternatives. They were both in accord with the Tibetan code of justice. He might claim hospitality—of the dungeons, in which he has tortured and starved his enemies. Or he may, of his own free will, earn merit."

"What does that mean?"

"Watch. Think kindly if you can!"

"Damn him, I can't. He's a son of a bitch."

"Andrew, we are going to see tragedy. He's as lonely as Judas. He needs pity!"

"Well, okay then, God pity him! Now what?"

Ram-pa Yap-shi had stood motionless until the last of his men had stacked their rifles and passed in through the postern. But now he moved, slowly, with bowed head, his back to the wind—like a man in a trance, except that he clearly knew where he was going, and deliberately forced himself to go. He walked between the piles of rifles and along the trampled track between banks of snow, until he reached the bend where the ledge began that skirted the thousand-foot deep ravine. He never paused once—never hesitated.

"Bless him!" said Elsa. "Be kind to him, Andrew! There's nothing else we can do!" She didn't know it, but she was driving her fingernails into Andrew's wrist. "Try to love him, just one little bit! Love him! He's human! He's doing his best, at his world's end!"

Ram-pa Yap-shi walked straight forward, knee-deep in the snow, instead of turning where the track curved eastward. Two vultures followed him. He reached a wind-blown crag that leaned out over the precipice, kept walking forward with his hands clasped behind him, trod on air—vanished. The vultures followed.

"Good God!"

Andrew didn't speak again for a moment. He hugged Elsa close to make sure she wasn't shaking from cold. From a roof, where the bells were ringing in the wind a *radong* like a foghorn, blared Ram-pa Yap-shi's requiem.

"He took it standing," Andrew said then. "He didn't squeal."

Elsa faced about. She met his eyes and put her hands on his shoulders. "Andrew! Do you realise what happened?"

"No. I'm thinking. You tell it. It feels somehow loaded. I can't explain what I mean."

"Andrew, it means this. Ram-pa Yap-shi acknowledged—to himself, and to his own soul, and to the world—that his sins misled thousands, who obeyed him through fear and ignorance. Disaster showed him the end of that road. So he chose death as the death of his own sin and theirs too—"

"Steady!" said Andrew. "Steady! If there's a hell, that's where he's gone! Sins like his, nor mine either, can't be wiped out in a moment."

"No?" she said. "Do you remember the repentant Thief on the Cross? '*Today shalt thou be—*'"

"You mean—? Lord God! You don't mean—?"

"'*For if ye forgive men their trespasses, your heavenly Father will also forgive you*'—Andrew, the Dalai Lama has asked for 'the big man they call Gunnigun.' He is waiting below. Will you come?"

CHAPTER 63

At the foot of the gatehouse stairs both doors were open, although Andrew had bolted one and the other was locked when he entered. There was a commotion outside. Old Ugly-face was coming—looking, Andrew thought, so physically tired that he was almost out on his feet; but so spiritually vigorous that no fatigue could conquer him. Andrew and Elsa stood back to let him pass, but at the threshold he waited for someone while the monks swarmed around him and had to be driven back by main force. It was only when he turned and faced them, raising his right hand, that they retreated to a decently respectful distance.

Through the other door there appeared a long, dim passage, lighted with little brass butter lamps set in niches in the wall. Somewhere about fifty feet along the passage there appeared to be a chamber corresponding to a buttress that supported the main wall on the inside and formed the base for an enormous *stupa*. Several Tibetans dressed in silk robes stood facing the entrance to the chamber.

"Where's the boy *lama?*" Andrew whispered.

Elsa nodded in the direction of the chamber: "Those are his attendants."

One of the attendants, smiling at Elsa as he passed, came and spoke to Old Ugly-face, murmuring to him from behind. Old Ugly-face bowed his head in token of assent. The attendant returned, and presently the young Dalai Lama came walking alone, preceded by the attendant walking backwards and followed by four other servants, two by two, ten feet behind him.

The boy was wearing the same gorgeously embroidered silk as when Andrew first saw him. He smiled wonderfully when he saw Elsa. With a gesture as spontaneous as the flash of delight in his eyes he clasped his hands, then spread his arms wide. In a moment, to the horror of his attendants, he was standing between Andrew and Elsa with his hands in theirs.

"Gunnigun!" he laughed. "Gunnigun!"

"Hello, feller!" said Andrew. "What's your name?"

There was no time to answer. The clucking attendants tried to separate them. Old Ugly-face turned and reproved the attendants so savagely that they slunk back into the passage and tried to get out of his sight. Then Old Ugly-face went down on his weary knees and made obeisance to the child, whose guardian he had again become. The child blessed him with the unselfconscious gesture of an ancient of days. Then he took Elsa's and Andrew's hands again. Old Ugly-face stood up, unsmiling, unoffended, his gaze fixed on Andrew. He spoke in Tibetan, Elsa translating:

"Because ye are three, who of your best have given—"

"God's sake, where's Tom?" Andrew wondered.

"And because your best has been acceptable to Destiny that serves His Holiness who clasps your hands in peace and good will—"

The boy *lama* chuckled and squeezed hands. He seemed to know what was coming. Old Ugly-face spared him a reproving frown and continued:

"Ask! What will you?"

"Nothing," said Andrew. "It has been my great privilege to contribute my services. I would do it again. Your Eminence owes me nothing."

Old Ugly-face smiled. He thrust his hand into his bosom and produced the silk flag taken from St. Malo. He unfolded it and showed it to Andrew. But he gave it to Elsa. Then he spoke what he considered to be English:

"Your country needing you. Your needing her. Damned old bugger, am I?"

"Your servant," said Andrew. "My respects to you, sir."

Old Ugly-face took Elsa's hand and put it into Andrew's. His lips moved for many seconds before he spoke aloud:

"Her being my *chela*. My sending her forth. Your being her fellow pilgrim helping her give—My blessing you. Many, many million never failing blessings—finding wherever your being, always, always. Tum-Glain my keeping here—his needing too much." Then he spoke again, at length, in Tibetan to Elsa. She interpreted:

"Andrew. Tom is waiting near the *stupa*. We are all to be blessed in public by the infant *lama*, so that the monks may understand that we're protected as long as we're in Tibet. When we've rested a couple of days we're to say goodbye. Tom will stay here; he begged it, and I begged it for him."

"And you're coming with me?"

The boy *lama* took their hands again. Old Ugly-face turned and led, booming the mystic syllable that leads, like all true music, upward, universe by universe, to an infinity beyond eternity, whence pours all newness—

"*Aum-m-m-m-m-m-m-m-m-m-m-m-m-m-m-m-m-m-m-m-m-m-m-m-m-m!*"